Praise for *Ad Astra*

"[A] World War II-era love story set against the B-17 bombing raids in the South Pacific...[E]xceptional writing...I find it difficult to believe that a major publisher wouldn't have found this worth releasing. It's quite a good book, all the way through to its touching ending."

~ *Writer's Digest* 20th Annual Self-Published Book Awards

"This is a story of heroism as a byproduct of a love and determination to fly... Del Hayes has written a richly detailed book, which gives the reader the vicarious sense of being with Gene behind the wheel of his beloved B-17. Hayes also brings that skill to bear in dealing with the human element in the story. We become closely involved with Gene and Mattie, and share an anxiety for their future that can only come from knowing them both so well. This is a wonderful novel."

~ Douglas P. Walker
Son of Brig. Gen. Kenneth Walker, commander, V Bomber Command, SWPA

"[A]n excellent representation of the sadly under-reported Air War that the US Army Air Forces fought in the Southwest Pacific Area in World War II ... [A] beautiful love story... This fact-based book touched me deeply ... I HIGHLY recommend it."

~ David Armstrong

"...a real pleasure to read. It has about everything you could want in a good read...Nostalgia, pathos, history, adventure, romance are all brought into the story...Our service men and women and those who supplied the planes and the means to fight the war are truly honored "

~ Ron Bartlett

Ad Astra

A Novel

Del Hayes Press

Princeton, TX

Published in 2011 by Homestead Press

Reprinted in 2020 by Del Hayes Press

Copyright © Del Hayes 2011
All rights reserved.

Back cover photo courtesy of Del Hayes

Cover and interior design and layout
by Clint Hayes, Del Hayes Press

Visit our website at www.delhayespress.com
for information on bulk orders.

ISBN-10: 0-9822706-5-8
ISBN-13: 978-0-9822706-5-3

Printed in the United States of America.

Ad Astra

A Novel

Del Hayes Press
Princeton, TX

Published in 2011 by Homestead Press

Reprinted in 2020 by Del Hayes Press

Copyright © Del Hayes 2011
All rights reserved.

Back cover photo courtesy of Del Hayes

Cover and interior design and layout
by Clint Hayes, Del Hayes Press

Visit our website at www.delhayespress.com
for information on bulk orders.

ISBN-10: 0-9822706-5-8
ISBN-13: 978-0-9822706-5-3

Printed in the United States of America.

Also by Del Hayes

The Old Man

"[A] very sweet love story... Hayes expertly weaves historical facts into a novel that follows one couple's search for love against all odds ... [making] it hard to put the book down."

~ *Writer's Digest* 2006 Self-Published Book Awards

Grace Will Lead Me Home: The Albert Cheng Story

"[This] is riveting testimony of the transforming love of God. Albert Cheng's story will inspire all who feel they have been taken captive by forces beyond their control."

~ The Rev. Bruce Reyes-Chow

Happily Ever After:
A Tribute to Marriage from a Fifty-Year Veteran

"[A] rare peek into the nooks and crannies of an honest, real, ordinary fifty-year marriage with extraordinary candor and insight....These fifty-year veterans have much to teach to anyone willing to listen."

~ Dr. Stacy Ikaard

Coming Soon
Final Approach: A Memoir

Acknowledgements

Many thanks are due to my son, Clint Hayes, for his important contributions to making this book a reality. His countless hours of research on missions and aircrews of the Fifth Air Force in the South Pacific aided materially to the development of the story, and added credibility that would have otherwise been lacking.

His relentless determination to root out all my various mistakes and oversights while editing the manuscript greatly reduced the likelihood of embarrassment on my part. Any such errors that may remain are my responsibility, and not due to lack of effort on his part. His design skills, applied both inside and outside the book, are also greatly appreciated.

Also, I wish to thank my wife, Colleen, who read much of the manuscript, or listened to me read it, and kept me from going so far off into the weed patch, as I would have done on my own. Her patience and understanding during the many moons that I have spent on this were above and beyond the call of duty.

Preface

Once upon a time…a boy was born on an isolated farm in rural Kansas. The year the boy turned six, "Lucky Lindy" climbed into his Ryan monoplane and cranked up his Wright Whirlwind. Minutes later, his *Spirit of Saint Louis* sucked its wheels out of the mud of Roosevelt Field in New York and disappeared eastward into the mist and murk, to reappear thirty-three hours later on the pages of history. As that farm boy grew, he came to admire Lucky Lindy, and the pilots of those planes that began to appear in the sky over his farm. And as he grew, a dream grew with him—he wanted to be a pilot.

Years passed. The boy was becoming a man. The year of his twentieth birthday, a pilot of the Imperial Navy of Japan radioed "Tora, Tora, Tora" to the Commander of aircraft carriers that had sailed unseen in Pacific storms to within three hundred miles of Pearl Harbor—and America was awakened from an isolationist slumber to find itself at war, in a battle to the death.

Two years later that farm boy found himself stationed in England, a member of the United States Army Air Forces, and flying in America's greatest air weapon, the B-17 *Flying Fortress*. But his dream had not come true. He was not a pilot. He was the tail-gunner, bearing the responsibility of keeping his plane, his fellow crewmen and himself from being blasted out of the sky by deadly Messerschmitt fighters.

One July morning in 1944, a month to the day after the historic invasion of Normandy, somewhere in France a German crew rammed yet another 88-millimeter shell into the breech of their Flak36 anti-aircraft cannon and fired it nearly straight into the sky. It screamed upward, toward the formation of B-17 bombers darkening the sky overhead. At its appointed altitude the shell exploded, with pieces of its lethal shrapnel arcing outward from its ugly black burst. One of those pieces penetrated the fuselage of one of those bombers, close by the side of the tail-gunner position. My cousin Eugene did not live to finish his first combat mission.

I was but five years old on December 7, 1941, when the attack on Pearl Harbor plunged America into World War II—just old enough to remember my older brother having to brave a frigid December morning to deliver a special edition of my hometown newspaper detailing the shocking story.

War was half a world away from our small town in Kansas, but in a very real way it was very much among us, in every living room. It affected everybody, and everything we did. *Movietone* newsreels at the local theater showed us in stark black and white images what we were involved in, where and how those whom we loved were fighting and dying.

I have only random and disconnected memories of the war years. I remember the "Gold Star Mothers" flags hanging in windows, indicating that a son, or perhaps husband or father, had been lost in the war. Dad always had a garden, but we were all proud to start calling it a "Victory Garden," when asked by our government to aid in the production of food for the war effort.

It was a fun game to wrap the tin foil from sticks of chewing gum into silvery balls, to be added to the old pots and pans donated to the scrap metal drives. I saved my pennies and nickels, and eventually became the proud owner of a Victory Bond book. I remember the colorful little coupons in the rationing books, but had no awareness of the difficulties Mom must have faced in feeding a family of five from what remained of those coupons at the end of each month.

But I especially remember the day my parents and relatives gathered at the home of one of my uncles. We were there to support my Aunt May and Uncle Ray, who had just that day received the telegram from the War Department informing them that their son, my cousin Eugene, had been killed on his first mission during a B-17 raid over France.

I had just turned eight years old, and didn't understand very well what was happening. But the pall of gloom that seeped through the family that day clung to us like the musty odor of an old house. It still seems so real, nearly seven decades later, that I can almost smell it—just as I can almost taste the bitterness voiced by Uncle Ray, decades after his son had been killed, when I once asked him about it.

One August day in 1945 I was sitting on the roof of our porch, watching a repairman work on some shingles, when all the sirens in town began to wail. Normally, that occurred only at the noon hour as a daily test, but this was mid-morning. It took a moment for the repairman to comprehend what was happening—the war was over!

Those four years of my early youth don't comprise much of my total of more than eighty now, but they influenced my life in ways that overshadowed much of who I became as a person. Perhaps it was because I was at such an impressionable age. Or perhaps it is because of my lifelong love affair with airplanes, and World War II made aviation come of age. It gave birth to classics such as the B-17 bomber and the P-51 fighter, and ended with

German jet fighters flashing past those P-51s, leaving them behind in the scrapbooks of history. I can't say for certain why World War II has been so much a part of who I have been, for virtually all of my life. But it has. I have read countless books about it, seen countless movies about it.

I was, and am, an avid lover of airplanes, and became a private pilot. Airplanes have been a part of my lifeblood since my days in kindergarten. The B-17 bomber, perhaps because of its association with the loss of my cousin, has remained my favorite airplane, at least in a sentimental sense. I cannot see, or hear, that aircraft flying over without choking up. Its mystique transcends its war record, which will never again be equaled in terms of either quantity of planes involved in a war or the effect it had globally on the outcome of its war.

A number of years ago, my son wanted to try his hand at writing a movie script, and was looking for ideas. He asked me, one evening, if I had any suggestions. I had read most of the classics on the air war in World War II, such as *A Wing and a Prayer* and *Twelve O'clock High*, and had recently finished reading *Flying Forts: The B-17 in World War II*, by Martin Caidin. Those classic stories had already been made into movies, but Caidin's book related numerous missions that I believed to be worthy of a movie, but that had not been told.

I suggested to my son that he consider basing a script on one of those stories. As we talked about it, we came to the realization that virtually all the movies that had been made about America's air war had featured the massive bomber raids in Europe. Little was known of the war of desperation that had been fought almost single-handedly by air crews in the South Pacific, so he decided to concentrate on one of those untold stories. He spent endless hours doing research, interviewing surviving members of the crew, as well as their family and friends, and poring over every available record and story about the air war in the South Pacific.

During that time, I became interested in writing a novel based on those same stories. As I developed ideas, two considerations emerged. First, I developed a deep respect for the members of those crews. It was tempting to pick one and develop my book as being based on a true story. But I also found that I kept thinking of my cousin. I wondered what it must have felt like to be snatched from the isolation of a small farm and find yourself, virtually overnight, in a strange land far from home, in the thick of war. I wondered how he must have felt as antiaircraft fire burst around him, and enemy fighters swarmed over them. I wondered how I would have felt, how I might have reacted, had I been the necessary few years older so that I, too, would have been drawn into that maelstrom.

And thus *Ad Astra* was born. It is inspired by, and in many respects is based on, the real experiences of the men of the 5th Air Force, which was heavily involved in the air battles of the South Pacific. I wanted to bring attention to a group of guys who actually had to do what my fictional protagonist, Gene Stoddard, does in this story. While *Ad Astra* is fiction, throughout the story I have made every effort to keep any reference to actual events as factual as possible. Every mission described herein is inspired by real missions experienced by people we came to know, or to learn about, during our research. I have included a bibliography listing a few of the sources which I drew upon for *Ad Astra*. I highly recommend any and all of them for the interested reader.

I have taken some liberties with details of operations in the South Pacific. For example, the concept of skip bombing was very real, and used with deadly effectiveness by aircraft of the 5th Air Force. However, as best I can determine, no B-26 bombers were involved in the Battle of the Bismarck Sea. B-25, A-20, B-24 and B-17 bombers carried that battle to the enemy. However, the 22nd Bomb Group, flying the B-26, was heavily involved in the battles for New Guinea and in early raids on Rabaul and New Britain, and was also highly effective. I wanted to bring attention to this early battle that played such a pivotal role in the defense of New Guinea—and hence, Australia—and to get my protagonist involved in that fighting. My apologies to any who were involved, if this editorial license creates a problem for them.

I made no particular effort to maintain the exact periods during which the bomb groups and squadrons mentioned moved to various locations in Australia and New Guinea. My intent was to portray what those young guys had to contend with in order to turn the tide against overwhelmingly superior forces, and to eventually defeat them.

On the other hand, I made every effort to ensure that technical details of any aircraft and battles mentioned were accurate. If errors are found, they were unintentional, or the result of faulty information.

I didn't get to—or, depending on your perspective, didn't have to—fly a B-17 bomber during the war. But I do have a deep, abiding respect for those who did, whether it was the young men of the Fifth Air Force in the South Pacific, my cousin, or any of the tens of thousands of others who took to the air in defense of our country. I only hope that I could have passed the test with the same degree of courage and selflessness as they demonstrated.

Ad Astra is a love story, both the love a young couple discovers during adverse times and the love many pilots feel for flying, and the aircraft they fly. I love airplanes, and have loved flying them for forty years as a private pilot. So if this is a tribute to the young men who flew during World War II, it is also a tribute to the planes they flew. I hope that I have done at least some small measure of justice to both the men and to their magnificent flying machines.

Del Hayes
Saint Albans, ME

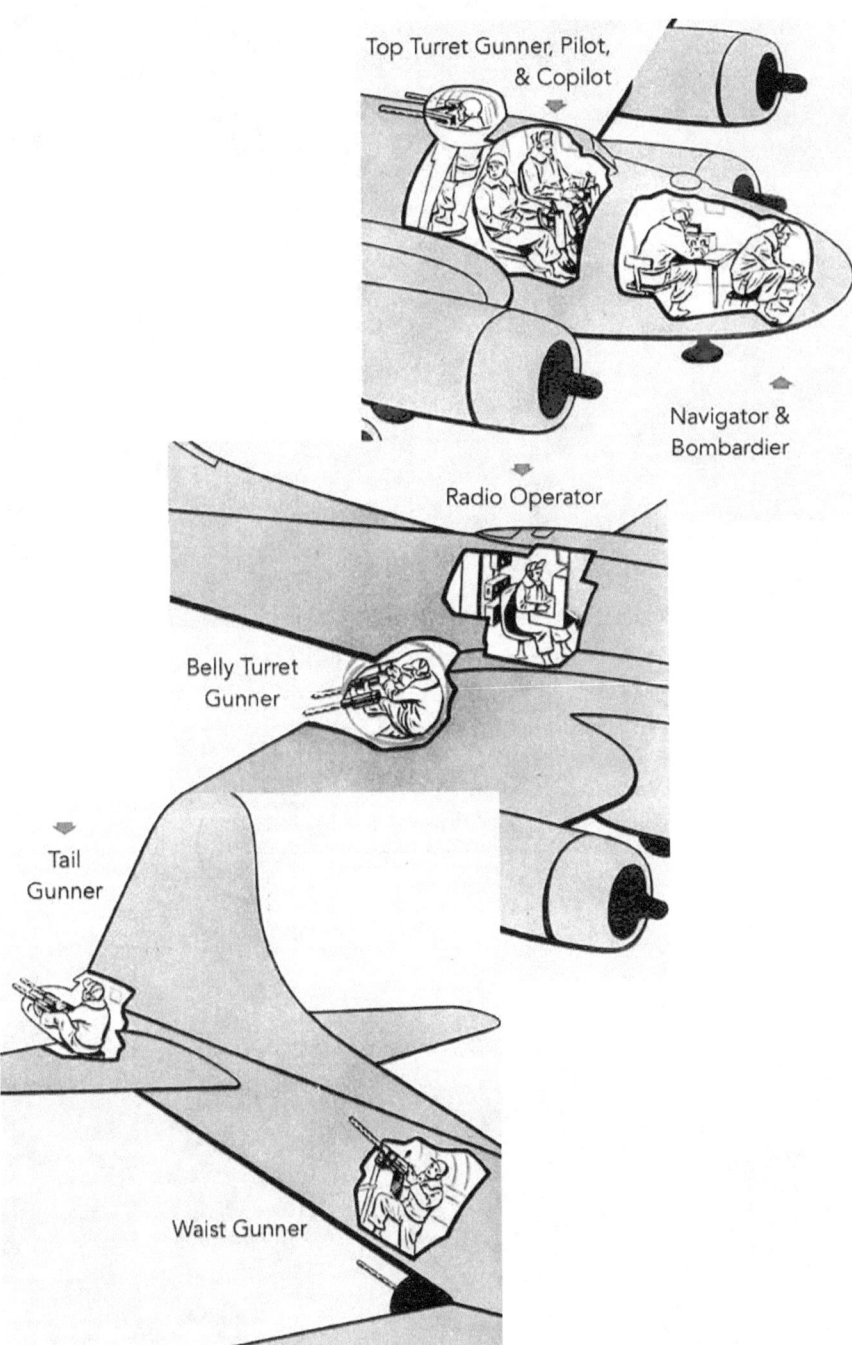

Crew positions in the B-17 *Flying Fortress*

USAAF via B-17 Pilot Manual

Duty board outside operations hut, 64th Bomb Squadron,
43rd Bomb Group, Mareeba, Australia, 11/14/42

USAAF via Fold3

Ground crew service B-17E #41-9023 "Yankee Doodle"

USAAF via National Museum of the United States Air Force

B-17E #41-2633 "Sally," personal transport for 5th AF commander
Gen. George Kenney, at Seven-Mile Airstrip, Port Moresby, May 1943

USAAF via https://ww2db.com, Bob Rocker collection

B-17s in revetments at Jackson Airdrome (Seven-Mile) in 1943

USAAF via Wikimedia Commons

Personnel tents, likely at Seven-Mile, 1943

Bud Thues collection

Sydney Harbor Bridge

engage.haveyoursay.nsw.gov.au via The Holiday and Travel Magazine blog

Crew of the 64h BS, 43rd BG, next to its B-17E, Mareeba, Australia,
November 17, 1942

USAAF

B-17F 41-24457 "Aztec's Curse" of the 26th BS, 11th BG, 13th AF,
over Gizo on Ghizo Island, Solomon Islands, October 5, 1942

USAAF,, courtesy Steve Birdsall

The natural function of the wing is to soar upwards and carry that which is heavy up to the place where dwells the race of gods. More than any other thing that pertains to the body, it partakes of the nature of the divine.

Attributed to Plato

Ad astra, per aspera ("to the stars, through difficulties")

Kansas State Motto

Awakening

Hesitantly, reluctantly, black nonexistence gave way to a vague awareness. Faint music, reminiscent of hymns sung long ago, floated in the blackness like singing heard from an open window of a distant church on a summer's night. A light began to form, growing, brightening, like a door being opened to a brightly lit room. Silhouetted within the light was a figure, blurred and indistinct, robed in dazzling white. Red-tinged light radiated from around its head like a halo. Within the halo was a featureless mask, shadowed by the glow of the surrounding light.

What's happening? Am I dead? Is this an angel? His mind was a vaporous mist, evaporating, condensing, struggling to form some reality, something he could hold on to. But the image in the light held no meaning for him.

He felt chilled, detached, troubled by this figure in the light that now seemed to be reaching out to him. A pleasant, cooling sensation passed over him. He struggled to open his eyes. A hand reached out from the figure, and again passed the damp washcloth over his face, gently wiping his matted eyes.

"Hi, Yank," the apparition said, with a soft, quiet voice filled with concern. "You ready to join the land of the living again? You've been out for quite a spell, now."

At the sound of her voice, he forced his eyes farther apart, blinking to clear the blurred image. Standing at his side, wiping his face with a damp cloth, was the prettiest angel God could have sent to escort home a fallen pilot. Sunlight from the window behind her silhouetted her slender figure, brightening the white of her nurse's uniform and highlighting the red tint in the auburn hair framing her face. Large dark eyes smiled at him from her finely shaped face. There were hints of Ireland in her eyes and mouth. She tilted her head and arched her eyebrows. The corners of her mouth turned upward in a quizzical, irresistible smile, awaiting his response. He could only stare as he tried to force his mind to once again assume its former role in his life, and assimilate where he was and why he was here—and why this beautiful girl was standing next to him.

"What's the matter, Yank? Cat got your tongue?"

She spoke with an unmistakable Australian accent, sounding as though she were teasing him back to consciousness, and yet concerned about him. He attempted to pull himself upright on the bed, but could not. He felt paralyzed, unable to persuade his body to respond, and tried to speak but his mouth was a desert wasteland.

"Water," he rasped.

"In a moment," she replied, "as soon as you're a little more awake. We wouldn't want you to choke on it."

She placed her hand behind his neck, lifting his head, and moistened his parched lips with the damp cloth. The delicate touch of her hand made his neck tingle. He looked at her dark Irish eyes, smiling back at him. His mind seemed mired, bogged down, unable to move. Nothing made any sense.

"Where am I? What happened?"

Struggling to form the words, his voice cracking and hoarse, he asked again for water. She held his head and helped him use a straw to draw a small trickle of water from a glass, watching to make sure that he could swallow, before she answered.

"You're in the hospital, in Sydney. You've been in surgery for several hours. I'm Mattie. I'm here to watch over you while you recover from the anesthesia."

"Hospital?"

A window behind her looked out on what appeared to be a large park, with the distant waters of Sydney Harbor sparkling in the sunlight. The room was painted bright white and cluttered with various kinds of hospital carts and equipment placed willy-nilly around his bed. A metal rack, looking like a chrome hat rack with bottles of fluid hanging upside down from its hooks, stood near his head. That the clear tubes dangling from the bottles were attached to him didn't register.

He looked at the two legs at the end of his bed as though they belonged to somebody else. The right one was entombed in bulky bandages from just below his knee, the left encased in a large white plaster cast from mid-thigh to his foot, and elevated above the bed by pulleys and cables dangling from the ceiling. His left arm was in a cast of lesser enormity, but folded across his chest, giving him the appearance of posing for a Napoleon portrait. His right arm was not in a cast, but swathed in bandages from below his shoulder to over his wrist. It all reminded him of a car-wreck scene from an Abbott and Costello comedy.

"What happened to me?" he asked, looking up at her. "How bad is it?" His eyes searched hers for the telltale signs of kindness masquerading as truth.

"I'm sorry," she apologized, "but they don't tell me much. I'm just a volunteer nurse's aide here at the hospital. All I know is what the nurses tell me, or what I overhear the doctors telling them. They said you were wounded on a mission somewhere over the Pacific. Don't you remember it? And don't worry, there's nothing missing. You were hit in both arms and legs. Your left leg was injured the worst, but they were able to save it. The corpsmen at the field where you landed up in New Guinea got you patched up enough that they were able to fly you down here. You'll probably be here quite awhile for recovery and therapy. Is there anything I can get you?"

She leaned over him to straighten the sheets and to fluff his pillow, her hair lightly brushing his face. Her perfume made him catch his breath. It was the first breath of femininity he had inhaled since—when? He couldn't remember the last time he had even seen a female.

The shock of the operation and lingering anesthesia, her perfume, the feel of her hair brushing his face, the touch of her hand, her very presence were all too much and he felt himself floating, spinning back into the void. He closed his eyes, slumping back into his pillow. She brushed his hair back off his forehead. Her hand was cool, and soothing. He felt himself drifting farther away.

"I'm fading," he told her, his voice sounding hollow, distant, to him, as though coming from someone down a long hallway.

"Looks like you need some shut-eye, Yankee boy," she agreed, patting him on the shoulder. "I'll pull the blinds and let you sleep awhile. I was listening to some church music on the radio while I was waiting for you to come back to us. Do you want me to turn it off?"

"No, leave it on. Be seeing you," he replied, his voice trailing off.

She nodded, and smiled at him, but he was gone. She pulled the covers back over him, straightened them, and stood looking at him for a moment. He looked so young—no more than twenty-one, she imagined, if that—and yet, so old. Still pale from loss of blood, his face was gaunt and haggard, with several days growth of stubble aging him. He had not yet been cleaned after being wounded. She ran her fingers over his face, touched his eyes. Dark splotches of blood smeared across his face, caked and dried in his whiskers, made chills run down her as she tried to avoid imagining what those eyes had seen.

There was something in his face that drew her to him. Most of the wounded she helped care for in her role as nurse's aide seemed so immature. Although he appeared to be as young as the others, he seemed to have a seriousness, a maturity, in his face that she did not sense in most of them. As she looked at him she became aware of feelings stirring within her that were new to her nineteen years. She started to leave, then turned, looking at him another moment.

"Yes, you'll be seeing me, Yankee boy. Quite often, I think," she said quietly, and left the room.

It was nighttime when Captain Eugene Stoddard, United States Army Air Forces, again became aware of being alive. He forced his eyes open, blinking to clear them, and looked around the room. It was a different room than before.

The lights were out, but the door was ajar. Dim light from the hallway was just sufficient that he could see that he was alone in the small room—there were no other beds. His left leg was still held elevated with cables and pulleys. The shades of the window beside his bed were drawn. He wondered why, but then remembered that it was wartime and a blackout would be in effect.

After months of growing accustomed to nights filled with the raucous noises of the jungle that surrounded his airbase, the quiet of the hospital night was unnerving. He heard hard-heeled shoes clunking along the hallway, and the sounds of the wheels of a cart rattling along on stone-hard floors. Then it was quiet again, with only occasional faint voices coming from down the hallway.

He stared into the dimness of the room, but she wasn't there. *She was probably just a dream*, he thought. A strange sense of disappointment, depression even, settled over him. *She said I was wounded on a mission over the Pacific... seems like I should be able to remember that.* He closed his eyes, and vague images of enemy fighters flashing by, of guns blazing, of explosions and fire and chaos in the cockpit teased at the edges of his consciousness, but nothing felt real about them. Maybe they were dreams—or maybe not. His mind still felt dull, leaden. It was hard making sense of what had happened to him. He wondered if it might all be a dream and he would wake up soon on his cot at Seven-Mile Strip, his airbase up at Port Moresby in New Guinea.

As uncounted minutes crept by and his senses gained a degree of alertness, he began to be aware of pain developing in his arms and legs, like the first flashes of lightning from a distant thunderstorm. And like the approaching storm, the pain grew more intense, the lightning flashes more frequent and severe, forcing the pain to the front of his mind, excluding all else. Flames began to shoot throughout his body. He cried out, even as he struggled to stifle it. Straining against restraints he hadn't known were strapping him to his bed, twisting, sweat breaking out on his face, he was vaguely aware of people rushing into the room, of a needle being jammed into his thigh. Then the blackness came again.

Meeting Mattie

Pain and drug-induced sleep were Captain Eugene Stoddard's reality for a period of time that held no meaning for him. As sedatives that rendered him unconscious wore off, pain that had been pushed into the blackness would return, slowly at first, toying with him, then flooding over him. He would try to endure, but inevitably could not, crying out, and sometimes passing out, before a nurse could administer more drugs and he would disappear into nothingness again.

As days passed, for brief periods he could endure the pain without being rendered unconscious and thus he began to be aware of the activity around him that defined life in a hospital. Each morning a nurse—usually a big, no-nonsense middle-aged woman who appeared better suited for work on the farm than in a hospital—would come to check on him, and inspect his bandages. The nurses talked at him as though they were in it together—"Looks like we need fresh bandages on our arm"—though they seldom talked to him. But they did their jobs professionally, and with surprising compassion.

On occasions he came to dread it was necessary to have his bandages changed, be sponge-bathed and have his physical needs attended to. This should have been embarrassing to a healthy young male, but most of the time he was too deep in a stupor to be much aware of it. He was fed with intravenous fluids and given medicine to control infection and to help control the pain without the heavy sedatives that had been required at first.

As periods of consciousness lengthened, he was able to start eating real food. Of course, because both arms were immobilized and useless to him, he had to be fed. A nurse's aide would bring a cup of soup, or sometimes some Aussie stuff that he didn't recognize but that tasted okay. She would offer him a spoon full of soup, or a bite of something, and wipe his chin for him when he spilled some, which he often did as he was not accustomed to being fed. It was harder to drink, even with a straw, when someone else was holding the glass and he often dribbled down his chin. It would have been embarrassing, except for the fact that the nurse's aide who came to feed him was named Mattie.

She had come into his room one afternoon when he was awake and the pain was relatively tolerable. Bright sunshine filled the room and reflected off her pink and white uniform. She looked even prettier than he remembered from when he first saw her.

"G'day, Yankee boy. Glad to see you awake, for a change," she said, as she breezed into the room. Her voice was warm and pleasant—not the perfunctory, artificially friendly tones the nurses affected. Hers felt more personal, like she was talking to him, and not at him. She came to his bedside, wiped his face with a damp cloth and brushed his hair back. Her hand felt soft and smooth. He enjoyed the attention she paid him, but did not say so.

She was wearing a sharply pressed pink and white-striped blouse under a crisp white pinafore sort of dress, and had on a perky white cap that resembled a nurse's, but was smaller, less official looking. It reminded him of the pictures of the Candy Stripers who volunteered in hospitals back in the States. The pink stripes seemed to accent her auburn hair.

Her smile was delightful, and she looked very starched and bright. He had never seen anyone quite so pretty. He wanted to tell her that, and to tell her that her hair was the soft red of a Kansas sunset after a summer thunderstorm had passed through and that she smelled nicer than the lilac blooms on his parents' farm, that he loved her Aussie accent and the delicate touch of her hand and the way her eyes sparkled when she spoke to him.

He smiled at her, but didn't say any of that, of course. In the first place, Stoddard men didn't say those sorts of things to women. In the second place, he made the mistake of trying to turn to better see her smiling face, putting a twisting strain on his left leg—the one elevated by the cables and pulleys—and passed out from the resulting bolt of pain which seemed to electrocute him. He was unaware of Mattie calling for the nurses, and the rush to get the needle in.

When he regained consciousness it was dark, and raining. His room lights were off, but no one had remembered to pull his shades for the blackout. It was the first he had been able to see out after dark. A large thunderstorm was moving across Sydney Harbor, and flashes of brilliant lightning brightened the room with pale, ghostly light. It made him feel like he was back in his B-17 bomber, fighting his way through yet another thunderstorm over the Pacific on a bombing mission. The constant crack and rumble of thunder sounded like the bombs that sometimes fell on his airbase at Port Moresby. His heart began to pound and he felt clammy. Closing his eyes, he took a deep breath and tried instead to picture Mattie's face. In a little while he was asleep.

When he awoke, the sun was once again shining, but not so brightly as before. It appeared to be early evening, but he had no idea of which day. He had not been awake long before the door opened and Mattie came in, carrying a tray.

"I peeked in a bit ago, and saw you were awake. I thought I'd see if you would be up to trying some fine Australian chicken noodle soup."

She set the tray on the bedside table, pulled a chair beside him, and placed a napkin over him before he could respond. When he did attempt a reply, his voice broke and she reached for a glass of water. She held his head and helped him drink, then wiped his mouth.

"Soup sounds good," he agreed, his voice now clear. "Thanks."

"Getting some appetite, are you? That's a very good sign," she replied, as she took a small spoonful of the soup broth, held his head in her hand, and eased it to his lips. He swallowed, and nodded his approval.

"That's pretty good."

She smiled, and helped him with another spoonful. They were silent for a while, as she helped him with each spoonful, and wiped the drips from his chin when necessary. After he had managed about half the cup of soup, he laid his head back on his pillow, her hand still under his head. Her hand felt cool, and he liked her to touch him. After she wiped his face with the napkin, she pulled her hand away, but stayed in the chair beside him. He turned and looked at her.

"Thank you, Mattie. Your name is Mattie, isn't it?"

"Why yes, it is. Had I told you that?" She appeared surprised—and pleased—that he knew.

"You were the first thing I remember seeing when I came to after the surgery," he answered, nodding. "I was really groggy, and the sunlight from the window behind you made it hard to make out anything. You were all in white and your hair was glistening red in the sun. I couldn't even see your face, it was so shadowed…and there was church music in the background. For a minute, there, I thought I'd died and you were an angel coming to take me to Heaven." He paused a moment, then a smile tugged at the corners of his mouth. "Then you told me your name was Mattie, and I didn't remember any Mattie from the Bible, so I figured I must still be alive."

Mattie sensed mischievousness in his eyes that she had not noticed before.

"Well!" she said. "I don't know whether to be complimented that you thought I was an angel…or insulted that you concluded I'm not." Her voice had an edge that he hadn't expected. He hoped she was teasing him, but feared that he had offended her.

"Well, you've certainly treated me like you're one," he countered, hoping to offset any damage. She appeared to take it in good humor.

He had a tendency to make comments that he intended to be good-natured kidding, but which could often be misconstrued or even barbed at times, causing him to spend a lot of his time in high school trying to remove his foot from his mouth. But she smiled at him, and laughed with a soft, pleasant lilt that somehow made him think of the Irish tenor who sang on the radio back home. He wondered if she really were Irish, or if maybe it was just the Australian accent affecting her laugh. In either case, he liked it. She stood, picking up the tray to leave. He looked up at her.

"You leaving me?" he accused, a most pained expression on his face.

"I'm afraid duty calls," she answered, ignoring his pained look, but thrilled that he would want her to stay. She started toward the door.

"Mattie?"

"Yes?" She stopped, looking back at him.

"Could you, uh...well, maybe stay a little while? Maybe just talk a little?"

The tone of his voice had changed, she realized, no longer teasing her. He sounded pensive, or troubled, and Mattie came back to him, setting the tray on the bedside table.

She reached out and brushed his hair back from his forehead. If she were honest with herself, she would have had to admit that the gesture would seem terribly personal to him. It was her normal practice to have very little physical contact with the wounded guys she assisted. They were all young, and she was well aware of how long they had been isolated from any females while they were on active duty, especially after they were shipped to the advanced combat bases. She knew how they would react and didn't want them to misinterpret any gestures. During physical therapy it was often unavoidable, and they would sometimes try to take advantage of it. She would have to playfully—or sometimes not so playfully—slap their hands. So she normally limited herself to smiles and cheerful talk, and perhaps an occasional comforting pat on the shoulder. But with this particular Yank, she ignored her self-imposed rule.

Even though she knew nothing about him, except his name as it appeared on his charts, and though there had yet been little opportunity to talk to him, she realized once again how different he seemed from the others. She liked the sensitive, serious look on his face, his dark eyes with their long lashes. She liked the way his face looked with his hair up out of his eyes.

"Tell you what, matey," she said, straightening the covers a bit and giving him a comforting pat on the shoulder, "I'm off duty in a little bit. Let me take this tray back and finish up. Then I'll clock out and come back and stay a while. Okay?"

He nodded, and she left with the tray. After what to Gene seemed so long that he began to wonder if she had forgotten him, but in reality was no more than fifteen minutes, she returned. Twilight was approaching and the light in the room was softening. Mattie sat down on the chair next to his bed, crossed her legs and smoothed her skirt over her lap. The warm sunlight highlighted her auburn hair and made her face even more radiant. The white in her uniform seemed to turn to gold. He stared, in spite of himself.

"Okay, I'm all yours. What would you like to talk about?"

"Oh, I don't know. It just gets kind of quiet in here, sometimes," he confessed, sounding a little embarrassed while wondering how she could always sound so cheerful in such depressing circumstances. "It's sorta nice to have someone here."

She nodded, and sat looking at him. He was still as trussed up and encapsulated in casts and bandages as on his first day there. She had no idea how long his left leg would have to stay elevated with the uncomfortable pulley arrangement. Even though the nurses saw to it that he was clean-shaven most days, he still looked drawn and pale, and had lost quite a bit of weight. She felt he looked more like a sick little boy than a grievously wounded combat pilot. Intravenous fluids were still being fed through needles in his arms. *Lord in Heaven, what these young men have to endure because some arrogant old men want to rule the world*, she thought as she studied his face.

"How bad am I, Mattie?"

The question, though innocent sounding, caught her by surprise. His eyes looked troubled, maybe even frightened. She started to give him the usual "You're going to be just fine in no time, soldier," pep talk but sensed that this was not a person who would be easily fooled. She took his fingers, as most of his hand was covered by bandages, and looked at him.

"The chart tells me your name is Eugene Stoddard. Do you go by Gene?" He nodded. "Well, Gene, first of all, please understand that the doctors don't speak to us lowly aides, so officially I know virtually nothing. I shouldn't tell you anything, because it could be wrong. But I do talk to the nurses, and I can read the charts. Besides, I see far too many like you in here and I know what they have to endure…so I won't try to mislead you."

She looked at him a moment, trying to read his face. He nodded, and waited for her to answer.

"Gene, I'm sure you must realize, you were very seriously wounded. They don't believe you will lose your leg, as long as they can keep any infection down. But you lost an enormous amount of blood. They're giving you IVs to get your cell count back up and to fight infection. Your right leg and right arm were hit in several places, but not as seriously as your left side, and they should heal properly—probably with not much to show but scars. Your left bicep was hit pretty bad, they said. But the doctor seemed to think that you can regain most of the use of your arm, over a period of time."

She hesitated, unsure of how much to tell him.

"Best I can count, that's only three out of four. What about my left leg?"

"I'm sorry," she apologized, smiling, but obviously embarrassed. "I didn't mean to upset you. Your left leg was…well, it was quite badly shattered, I'm afraid. I heard one of the surgeons tell Nurse Adcock—she's the head nurse, for this floor—that they were unable to completely repair it. It's shorter than before. And, your knee was damaged…it won't have much flexibility. But the good news, if there is such a thing, is that I heard him say he thinks you will be able to walk without a cane or crutches. Of course, it will require a lot of therapy. I'm afraid you're going to have to tolerate us Aussies for quite a while."

Gene nodded, but was silent. She couldn't tell how he was taking the news, and wanted to get his mind off himself so changed the subject.

"Where's your home, Gene Stoddard?"

He looked at her a moment, his mind coming back from its inner thoughts.

"Kansas," he answered, somewhat unenthusiastically. "I grew up on a small farm there."

Mattie waited for some possible elaboration, but none was forthcoming.

"And do you have family?" she prompted.

"Yeah. One each brother and sister—they're both younger. And Mom and Dad, of course," Gene replied, nodding slightly. She waited, wondering if there might be more to his life's story, but he remained silent.

"I see." She paused, for dramatic effect. "And do you offer any information about yourself without being interrogated?" she asked, feigning indignation.

For the first time since she had started talking to him, Gene smiled, and seemed to laugh at himself a little.

"Well, talking was never considered to be a Stoddard strong point—at least not for the men in the family," he admitted.

It went on, for a while, with Mattie asking more questions about his family and where he was from, and Gene giving his usual taciturn answers. As he began to relax, he began to be a bit more expansive. After a while, Mattie stood.

"Gene, speaking of parents, mine will be starting to worry about me. I think I'd better be going. Do you mind?"

"Well, yes. I do," he objected, sounding rather emphatic, and catching Mattie by surprise. "I'd like for you to stay and visit some more. But I understand. Could you maybe stay again, sometime?"

"It would be my pleasure, Mr. Stoddard," she assured him. "Perhaps tomorrow evening. We'll see." She started toward the door.

"Mattie?" She turned and looked at him, then came back and stood next to him.

"Yes?"

"I can't remember things very clearly yet from my last mission. I don't know what I'm remembering and what I'm just dreaming. I know it got pretty rough. Do you know anything about my crew? Did any of them…?" He fell silent, not wanting to finish a question that he feared to have answered.

Without thinking, she reached out and brushed the hair back from his face. She couldn't seem to resist.

"Gene, I'm sorry. I really don't know a thing. Is there someone I could ask for you?"

"I don't know how to tell you to get in touch with any of them," he answered, staring at the ceiling. "Maybe some of them will be able to make it down here, one of these days," he added, without much conviction.

She nodded, paused a moment, and then, unsure of what else to say, said goodnight and left the room.

He watched her as she left, feeling stirrings of emotions that he had never experienced in his superficial dating in high school. He wondered about the feelings for a moment then dismissed them, turning to stare out the window. Talking about his family with Mattie had made him realize he had no idea if they were even aware that he had been wounded. He knew from when other guys on the base had been seriously wounded, or killed, that the squadron commanding officer would write a letter to the parents, and assumed that his C.O. had done so for him.

He could only imagine how upset they would be, wondering and worrying about him, and wondered how he would be able to let them know anything since he would be unable to write for weeks.

Write what? he wondered. *Dear Dad. Sure enough, you were right. I went and got myself shot up. I'm going to be a gimpy cripple the rest of my life. Wouldn't have happened if I had listened to you. But, oh no. I had to insist on flying them infernal airplanes.* The lingering resentment toward his dad on the topic of flying was never far from the surface of his feelings, but the intensity of those feelings surprised him as he lay thinking about the carnage that had come from his trying to turn his dream into a life.

Flying had indeed been his childhood dream—obsession, really. As he lay in the dark, staring at an unseen ceiling, his mind wandered back over the improbable series of events that had brought him to this hospital bed. It had all been literally his dream come true, from first learning of a government program that would teach him to fly while he attended college, to the shock of the attack on Pearl Harbor that had thrust him into war. But even that tragedy had served to nurture his dream, for he had soon found himself at the controls of America's most advanced bombers as the country began to strike back against its enemies.

Each mission he flew, each time his wheels left the ground, he was gaining the experience and skills that would lead with virtual certainty—if he survived—to the fulfillment of the rest of his dream. For as long as he could remember, he could not imagine himself being anything other than an airline pilot. All through his flight training it seemed his boyhood dream was coming true. Once the war was over, and he was back home, he would be flying sleek new airliners across America.

But now, not yet having seen his twenty-first birthday, that dream was as shattered as his leg. Instead of flying, here he was in a hospital in a country he had known while growing up only as a big pink island on the wall map that he kept in his bedroom at his home in Kansas. He looked like a figure from a Frankenstein movie, and apparently was now a cripple for life. If so, it would be impossible for him to fly. And a future without flying was a future too bleak, too unacceptable, for him to even contemplate. He felt a cold blanket of fear and bitterness, resentment that was edging into anger, being pulled over him— feelings he had never before experienced in his twenty years.

The western sky was now a soft shade of purple blending into black. Soon, his curtains would be pulled and his only connection to the outside world cut off. His spirits seemed to darken with the fading light, as night settled over his room. As he stared into the gloom out the window, his mind began to drift back over the short span of months that had brought him from an isolated farm in Kansas to flying a huge B-17 bomber from a God-forsaken island half way around the world.

For a moment, his spirits lifted as he thought back over all the fun he and his close friend, Mike Kingston, had experienced as they had gone through flight training together, then darkened again as he reflected on their many dangerous missions over enemy bases.

They had talked often, between those missions, of the day when the war would be over and they could begin to fly airliners together. He knew that others had died on those missions, and knew that he could, too. But he had never considered this possibility, trapped in a foreign hospital bed, wondering if he would be able to walk—and knowing he would never be able to fly.

He had felt that in a very real way his life had started the morning he took his first flying lesson. Now he was staring at a future as black as the ceiling above, feeling that his life had ended with his last mission. For young Captain Stoddard, a life without flying would hardly be a life worth living.

The "Seepy Teepee"

It was August, in Kansas. By mid-day, the sun was burning a hole in the sky like a ball of molten brass, searing the countryside without mercy. On the far southern horizon a single wisp of cloud let farmers cling to the hope that on some distant day, others would arrive and together they would bring rain to the parched fields. Fine dust stirred earlier by a passing car hung like gossamer, suspended in lifeless air over the gravel road nearby, slowly adding to the layers already coating withered grass and wilted sunflowers in the ditches alongside. Cicadas—most folks in the area called them locusts, but they were cicadas—in nearby trees droned their monotonous two-note opus to boredom, trailing off and falling silent occasionally as though they had lost their place on the page, until stirred by some unseen conductor to once again take up the effort.

Summer of 1940 was slowly dying. Wheat fields had been harvested, golden straw and stubble turning dull and brittle as it baked in the heat, waiting to be plowed once the rains finally returned. Alfalfa hay was stored in the barn, ready to feed the dairy herd through the winter months. Fields of corn were turning brown, leaves curled tightly in the arid heat, the soil a gray, crumbling pewter.

Eugene Stoddard was in a foul mood. Stagnant, dead air pulled sweat out of every pore on his body. Relentless heat grated on his nerves as he brushed futilely at a fly that persisted in settling on his sweaty face. He wiped his shirtsleeve across his forehead, sweat forming behind it as water closes behind a passing boat.

In two weeks, he would start his senior year in high school, but was no closer to deciding what to do with his last year of school than he was to deciding what to do with his life. He knew that time was running out. Decisions on career, college, the direction of the rest of his life would have to be made in the coming weeks. But what those decisions, those life choices, should be remained as elusive as ever.

On this Sunday afternoon, Gene had made a vain attempt to get his mind off the oppressive heat by climbing up to his favorite reading spot. Years before, the upper portion of a trunk of an elm tree in the back yard of their farmhouse had broken during a thunderstorm. Gene's dad had climbed up and cut it off, leaving a flush base. Over the years the trunk had grown and expanded until the base was more than a foot in diameter. Smaller limbs had grown out of its base on one side and branched upward. It made a perfect chair, shaded by the leaves overhead.

The tree was easy to climb. Gene would take a book and climb up to spend a peaceful Sunday afternoon in the shade and quiet, lost in his reading. There would often be a gentle breeze. It would be cool, and the trunk would sway gently. Sunlight and shadows would play across the pages of his book as the high upper branches moved with the breeze. It was his favorite spot, a hide-away, of sorts.

But this day there was no breeze, the air stagnant and lifeless. The heat was becoming intolerable, even in the shade, and the flies persistent and annoying. He decided to give up and go back in the house. It would be just as unbearable, but at least it would be away from the flies.

As he started down, the distant droning of an airplane engine caught his attention. A moment later he spotted it, a biplane slowly circling around to enter the airport pattern from the south. *Looks like a Stearman*, he observed, and climbed more quickly to the ground. There were still a couple of hours before the milking would have to be started, and his parents were most likely taking their Sunday afternoon nap. How they could sleep in such heat was beyond Gene, but they appeared to do so without difficulty.

He jumped on his bike and pedaled hard. The rushing air as he sped along the dusty gravel road refreshed him, and in minutes he arrived at the airport and leaned his bike against the fuel pump. The plane was parked nearby. Its pilot was checking something on the engine and hadn't started refueling yet. Gene recognized him as one who had stopped for fuel a couple of times earlier.

The pilot was not as coarse and taciturn as most of the others, and would answer politely when Gene asked questions about the plane, or about flying. He would thank Gene for his help with the fuel hose, and offer the possibility that one of these times he would take Gene for a plane ride, if his parents didn't disapprove. But it hadn't happened. Gene knew his parents would disapprove, and he also knew he would lie about it if need be to get a ride. But the opportunity for either transgression hadn't yet presented itself.

The pilot greeted him cordially as Gene dragged the fuel hose to him. Gene stood close by as the pilot began to fill the tank.

"Lord-a-mighty, it's hot down here," the pilot complained, wiping an arm across his forehead in a vain attempt to remove the sweat running down into his eyes. "I came up from Oklahoma at five thousand. It's always cooler, up there. But this'll fry your brain."

"It gets pretty hot around here this time of year, that's for sure," Gene replied, not knowing what else to say. It was always hot in Kansas, in August. "It was about a hundred and ten when I looked at the porch thermometer, but it looks right into the sun. It might not be that hot."

The pilot didn't respond, but kept looking into the tank. Gene began to tell him that he had been thinking about a career as an airline pilot. The pilot at least acted interested as Gene described his belief that there would be a future in piloting for the airlines, and appeared to nod in agreement on occasion. He didn't comment as Gene expressed his frustration at not being able to learn from anyone what he would have to do to become a pilot, or how to get hired by one of the airlines.

Gene waited in silence as the pilot pulled the nozzle from the tank, and put the cap back on. The pilot walked along side as Gene dragged the hose back to the pump. He looked at the pump, counted out some bills from his wallet, and put them in a metal box on the pump with "Pay Here" in faded hand-painted letters on its lid.

"Damn, boy, let's find some shade before this flying suit renders me down to nothin' but a puddle of lard," he complained, walking back to his plane.

The pilot was tall, lean, almost lanky, his shock of brown hair matted with sweat after he had removed his flight helmet. He was good looking, in a coarse sort of way, with a face wind-beaten to leather by years of flying in an open cockpit. His eyes had the distant, withdrawn look of a person who had hardened himself against further loss of friendship—friendly, but not a friend. He took off his leather flight jacket as they sat down in the shade of the large fabric-covered wing. The pilot rolled up his shirtsleeves a couple of turns, then pushed them above his elbows. He leaned back against the large tire, wiggling his long frame on the grass to try to get more comfortable. Gene sat facing him, knees drawn up, hands clasped around his legs. The pilot removed a sandwich from its wax-paper wrapper, glanced at it as if to remind himself of its contents, and took a bite.

"What'd you say your name is? Gene, right?" He didn't wait for affirmation. "Well, Gene, if you'll pardon my prying, why do you want to fly?" he asked, taking another bite while waiting for Gene to answer.

"Why?" Gene asked, looking at him, unsure of what the pilot was asking."You mean because it'd be dangerous? I know that, but—"

"Oh, hell no," the pilot scoffed. "You're as likely to get killed on one of them tractors of yours as in a plane. Besides, you can get killed at pretty much anything. What I asked was, why do you want to fly?"

"I don't know if I can answer that," Gene replied, after a rather long hesitation, realizing he had never been asked that question. He straightened his legs and leaned back on his elbows, staring at the side of the plane as though the answer was hidden somewhere there inside its steel tubing frame, behind its fabric skin. "Heck, I've never even been up in a plane. I just know that flying, and planes, are about all I ever think about. I'm crazier about airplanes than I am about girls, it seems like," Gene confessed, glancing at the ground to hide the blush that flashed across his face. The pilot grinned at his embarrassment.

"I try to imagine what it would be like to be up there, to be able to just float among the clouds," Gene continued. "I sometimes just stand and watch a hawk circling around up there, drifting free in the wind, not even moving its wings. I feel like they're the luckiest things that God ever created. I'd like to be like that hawk, I guess."

The pilot nodded, took another bite of his sandwich. He chewed for a moment, swallowed, and wiped his mouth on his shirt sleeve.

"You're pretty much like me—except maybe for the girls part," he said, laughing. "When I was growing up, on a farm in Georgia, I'd do that. I swore that someday, I'd be up there with that hawk. When we got into the war, I joined up. Had to lie about my age a little bit. Before I knew it, I was up there. I got sent to France, part of Eddie Rickenbacker's Ninety Fourth Squadron. We called it the 'Hat-In-The-Ring' squadron."

"Wow! You were in that? I've read about it quite a bit. You all were pretty famous," Gene exclaimed, before realizing how childish it must have sounded.

The pilot ignored him, staring across the fields.

"There were some really great pilots in that outfit," the pilot finally replied, sounding a bit subdued. "Lufberry…Campbell…and Eddie, of course. They were all swell guys, too." He paused, drew his legs up, resting his arms across his knees. He sort of half-chuckled, a sardonic grin appearing and as quickly disappearing. "Of course, you don't really spend much time thinking about being famous, when you're fighting for your life. I gotta tell you, Gene—them dogfights sometimes scared the holy shit out of me. I lost a lot of good friends. I don't know if any of us really believed we would live to see the end of it. But, mostly, we just figured we had a job to do, so we did it. We figured if it was our time, it was our time. No one said much."

He paused, looked down at the dirt between his legs, then at distant fields shimmering in the heat.

"We were all afraid of burning. Those planes were all wood and fabric and dope—and gasoline. And with all the wind rushing by, they'd usually just explode into flames when you got hit. They were beginning to use parachutes for the balloon observers, but we didn't have any. Wouldn't have mattered, though. You'd be burning so fast you couldn't get out, even if you had one." He hesitated a moment, his mind's eye seeing things Gene couldn't imagine. "Most of us were so scared of burning to death," he confessed, speaking so quietly that Gene felt he was embarrassed by the admission, "that we carried a pistol with us so we could shoot ourselves."

Gene felt a little awkward, not knowing for sure what to say, almost as though he had eavesdropped on a conversation that was too personal, and none of his business. After a few seconds, the pilot continued, gazing past Gene, seeing another world.

"You know, Gene," the pilot said, a slight smile working the corners of his mouth, "sometimes when I'd be coming back from a mission, the sun would just be setting. The sky would be all washed in gold and fiery red, like a big campfire when it's burned down to coals. There would be rays from the sun shining down through the clouds, looking like golden airways from heaven down to earth…"

The pilot paused, still looking at the distant horizon. Gene sat silently, entranced. He had never heard a grownup say anything like this, unless perhaps when his English teacher would read poetry to the class. The pilot stretched his long legs and shifted down further against the airplane tire, squirming his frame in the dirt to find a more comfortable position.

"It's funny how your mind, your feelings, work," he continued. "A few minutes earlier I could have been fighting for my life. I might have just killed someone. But then, somehow, my mind would just shut all that out. I don't know how your mind works, how it does it. But everything would sort of smooth out, and seem to slow down…just get real quiet—almost as though none of that was real. I'd feel like I could just fly up one of those sunbeams and right on through the sunset…and when I did I'd come out on the other side in a place where the fields were all green and there was no mud, and they wouldn't be torn with craters and trenches. The trees would be full of leaves, and not just splintered stubs shattered by artillery. It would be quiet and peaceful, and nobody would be trying to kill you. I could fly lazy-eights over the tops of willows along clear blue rivers, and not have to be scared of snipers shooting at me from the trees…and float around through the clouds like those hawks, without having to look for someone waiting behind one of them to jump me."

He glanced at Gene, appearing embarrassed at letting himself ramble in such a personal manner with a total stranger, and a kid to boot. He shook his head as if in disbelief at himself, grinning self-consciously.

"But then," he sighed, "I'd see a flash of gunfire from the ground and know that some trigger-happy soldiers were taking pot shots at me, and the real world would come crashing back down on me. It didn't pay to play the part of the romantic pilot for very long—unless you wanted to be a dead romantic," he added, chuckling at himself.

"Funny thing was," he continued, picking up a small chunk of dirt and tossing it aimlessly across the grass, watching it break into pieces and scatter, "I felt, at times like that, almost like I was already dead and flyin' around with the angels. Tell you the truth, Gene, I don't see why God gave the birds wings, instead of us. Flyin' is about as close to being able to consort with the angels as we can get."

A faint smile replaced the faraway stare. Gene returned the smile, wondering if he would ever get his chance to "consort with the angels." But before he could react the pilot shifted himself upright against the tire and began brushing dirt off his pants legs. It was clear that the reverie was broken.

"You're right, though," the pilot said, returning to Gene's original concern. "If you want a flying career, it's going to be with the airlines, not the mail service. Most of us airmail pilots are a bunch of independent misfits. We'd never fit into some big fancy-pants corporation like the airlines. But that's where the real jobs will be. And the best way to get into the airlines, with no flying experience, would be to enlist in the Army Air Corps and get into bombers. Let dear old Uncle Sam teach you to fly."

Gene smiled, feeling a sense of excitement growing inside, as this was the first time a real possibility had been opened to him.

"How old are you, Gene?" the pilot asked, looking carefully at Gene, as if seeing him for the first time. "Junior, maybe senior, in high school?"

"Senior," Gene answered, nodding. "I'll graduate next May. Why?"

"Well, I won't try to talk you out of flyin'—if you're like me, I'd be wastin' my breath—but you need to go into this with your eyes wide open."

"What do you mean?" Gene asked.

The pilot stood, stretched, and dusted the dirt off his pants seat. Gene stood, facing him, waiting for his answer.

"I'd bet this Stearman, here, that we'll be in a war within a year, or so— hell, probably in a few months, the way things are going. Hitler's already taken half of Europe. Just a couple of months ago he drove the Tars and the Frogs onto the beaches of Dunkirk. They had to be rescued by every Brit that could float a boat across the channel. He went into Paris like the French army was down sunbathing on the Riviera. Most of us pilots think it won't be long before he tries to cross the channel and take on the Brits. You watch any of those Movietone newsreels? You see those planes of his—those Stuka dive bombers, and Messerschmit fighters?"

He wadded the sandwich wrapper into a ball and tossed it into the open cockpit. Gene looked at him, waiting to see where this all was headed.

"Those planes are so far ahead of anything we're flyin' right now, it's scary. While we were flying mail in worn out Jennies, he's been off developing a real air force, and it's plenty clear he ain't afraid of using it. And the Japs are flying stuff in China that's just as good. Their new Zero will fly rings around most of our fighters. Sooner or later, somebody's gonna decide to try out all that stuff on us—and anybody that believes that we can hide behind our oceans hasn't taken a good look at an aircraft carrier."

The pilot began to walk around his plane, wiggling a control surface, feeling a tensioning wire, checking it over in preparation for continuing his flight. Gene walked along with him, wondering simultaneously about the message the pilot seemed to be trying to get across to him, and what the pilot was looking for as he carefully inspected his plane.

"When we pulled out of France after the war," he continued, "people thought there would never be another world war. Uncle Sam let the air corps pretty much go to pot. Hell, we couldn't whip a bunch of Girl Scouts with the junk we've got to fly today."

The pilot finished walking around the plane, appearing to be casual, but his experienced eye noting every detail of his plane. When he reached the side of the cockpit he paused, an arm resting over its side.

"Gene, if there's a bright side to all this, it's that the bigwigs in D.C. are beginnin' to wake up to the fact that if we're forced into war anytime soon we'll get our red, white and blue butts kicked. There's starting to be a lot of talk in Washington about it, and before long the Air Corps is going to have money it can't count. There's going to be more new planes put into service than you can shake a stick at, and they're gonna be hotter'n a night in a San Antonio bar. Thousand, two thousand horsepower engines, and they'll fly faster than we can even dream of."

He paused a moment, shaking his head, a look of near incredulity on his face.

"Lordy, I envy you, or anyone else that'll get to fly some of the planes this country's beginning to design, now. I can't even imagine what that'll be like. But, here's the kicker," he added, punching Gene on the shoulder with a finger for emphasis. "There's no one to fly them. There'll be a big push for getting new pilots."

Pulling his flight jacket and helmet on, the pilot climbed into the cockpit and fastened his seat belt, ready to start the engine. He turned to Gene, who was now standing beside the cockpit.

"I might be wrong. Maybe they'll all come to Jesus and see the light. Maybe there won't be a war. Lord only knows, I'd welcome that. That being the case, then the airlines will really get going and they'll need pilots, just like you said." He set his fuel valve handle, and looked again at Gene. "I assume you can crank up my starter for me, can't you?"

Gene nodded. He had done so any number of times.

"Good." He glanced at his panel, adjusted his altimeter, and handed Gene the starter crank.

"Gene, I want you to listen carefully to this. It could mean a lot to you. Last year, Roosevelt realized that if war starts anytime soon we're going to need lots of pilots in a hurry, and the military can't possibly train them fast enough. So, he got Congress to approve what they're calling the Civilian Pilot Training Program—the CPTP. We call it the 'seepy teepee,'" he added, laughing at his little insider's joke. "Basically, they're using civilian flight schools to train pilots, and the government is paying for it. Several universities are doin' it— Kansas University, up in Lawrence, has its own airport, and they've started the program. You go to college and learn to fly, and Uncle Sugar pays for the flying. You have to agree to go into the service if we go to war. You'll be required to join the Air Corps. But, if there's no war, you'll at least have a pilot license. It might be your chance to get on with the airlines."

The pilot pulled his goggles down, adjusted his helmet, then turned one last time to Gene.

"Here's the thing. If there is a war—at your age, you're going to be in it, like it or not. And believe me, being in the air is the only place to be in a war. I used to look down at those poor bastards in the trenches—nothin' but mud, and artillery and gas. Frankly, I'd rather take my chances on bein' flamed. So if we go to war, you want to be in a plane."

He made a last cursory scan of his instrument panel. "It's too blasted hot to just sit here—crank this thing up for me, and I'll be on my way."

"Thanks." Gene said, smiling. "This is the first time anyone's ever given me the time of day on the subject. I really appreciate it. By the way, I don't even know your name."

"Doesn't matter. You likely wouldn't remember it, anyway. Good talkin' to you."

With that, Gene began the arduous task of cranking up the starter on the aircraft engine. It was a heavy flywheel that was spun up to high speed with a hand crank. Its spinning momentum was then used to crank the engine. Gene was sweating heavily by the time he had the wheel spinning at full speed. He pulled the handle to engage the starter, then handed the crank back to the pilot. The starter whined down like a dying siren as its inertial wheel was quickly slowed by the torque of cranking the engine.

The engine sputtered, belched clouds of blue smoke as oil that had drained into the bottom cylinders burned out, then smoothed into a deep, satisfying rumbling. The big propeller spun lazily, glinting in the sunlight. Gene stepped back, and watched until the plane had taken off and was becoming a flyspeck on the horizon.

Gene pedaled home, slower this time, his mind replaying the conversation. He had seen the Movietone News reels at the movies, and had been fascinated by the planes. He knew that there was fighting going on, but it had seemed foreign and very far away. He had no idea that the world might be headed for a war that would drag the United States into it—and him along with it. His parents led rather isolated lives, and paid little heed to what was happening on the world scene. They felt they had problems enough of their own, without borrowing more from abroad.

He had never heard of the CPTP, and grinned as he remembered the name the pilot had given the program—the "seepy teepee." He would still go to college—it just wouldn't matter much, now, what he got his degree in. With a pilot license he could go into a flying career, and not have to be cooped up in some engineering office doing who knows what. He would just do so with thanks to the Army Air Corps. And, as the pilot had said, if there was to be a war he would without doubt be in it, regardless. Might as well be on his terms, more or less.

Gene had taken it for granted that he would go to college at Kansas State, in Manhattan. It had the reputation of being more practical than the liberal arts schools, and was less expensive than the private schools. It was where most of the farm families sent their kids, if in fact any of the family went to college. Gene knew about Kansas University, in Lawrence, but had never considered it. KU was considered to be too elitist, too upscale for country kids. K-State had a renowned veterinary school, and the joke was that the farmers sent their daughters to KU, and their cows to K-State.

He wondered if all that might really be true—and whether he would be able to afford KU. His parents had expressed a willingness to help with college, but Gene knew they couldn't afford anything. He would have to work his way through, and wasn't sure he could make it.

Somehow, as he started his bike down the backside of a steep hill that stood between the airport and his house, all those concerns faded into the background, replaced with a growing excitement that suddenly burst over him. Racing down the hill, he thrust both hands high in excitement and yelled so loudly that the neighbor's cows grazing next to the fence looked up, startled.

"I'm going to be a pilot! Hear that, you bony bovines? Gene Stoddard's going to be a pilot!"

He reached the bottom of the hill, still breathless with excitement, but began to slow down, letting it all sink in. He wanted to share his news with someone, wanted to share his excitement. Talking with his folks was out of the question, so he decided to call Christy. He and Christy Beckstrom had grown up together in their parents' church, although Gene was a year older. She lived in town, and he went to a country school, so they only saw each other at church. But once in high school, they had become "good buddies," as they put it. She had become a virtual member of the Stoddard family, and the one person with whom Gene felt he could share his thoughts and problems.

Somehow, the oppressive heat seemed less stifling as he rode on home. It was still hours before the sun would set, and the temperature hadn't retreated, but his mind was now full of bigger and grander things. In his mind, he was cruising at 10,000 feet, and it is always much cooler at altitude, the pilots had told him.

Gene Stoddard stepped out of the glaring sunlight into the drug store, pausing a moment to let his eyes adjust to the darkened interior. In spite of the relentless August heat, the store's high ceiling helped keep it comfortably cool. Ceiling fans rotating lazily overhead added to the perception, whether or not they were actually moving any air. A lady Gene knew from their church was thumbing through the latest issue of *Good Housekeeping* magazine at the racks at the entrance. Gene visited briefly with her, then went on to the back of the store.

Midway back was the focal point of the store, the marble-topped soda fountain with its chrome-plated drink and phosphate dispensers, backed up by large cylinders of various flavors of ice cream. Padded, rotating bar stools stood like sentinels along the front of the fountain, tempting one to sit and overindulge. Because of that fountain, and its many treats, the store was a favorite gathering place for the high school crowd. With classes still two weeks from starting the fall term, however, the only customer was the lady at the front.

A boy Gene knew only slightly—he was two classes behind Gene in school—busied himself behind the soda fountain, looking quite bored. Gene interrupted his boredom by ordering a cherry Coke. While waiting for it, he saw his friend, Christy, waiting for him at a back booth. He paid for his Coke and joined her.

"Hi. Good to see you, again," Gene said, smiling at her as he set his Coke on the table and sat down opposite her in the booth. "Seems like I've hardly seen you this summer. Haven't seen you much at church. You gone heathen on me?"

"Hi, yourself," she replied. "Seems like it, doesn't it? We spent Dad's two weeks of vacation over on the Lake of the Ozarks with Aunt Mabel and Uncle Ralph. That was really swell. We swam a lot, and they have a motor boat to play around in. And you know Dad. He likes to take weekend jaunts here and there. We went up to Kansas City one weekend, and over to Wichita a couple of times. I don't really know where the rest of the summer's gone." She paused, waiting until he finished a drink of Coke and had set his glass back on the table. "So—what sort of trouble you got yourself into, this time?" she asked, in her typically blunt manner, getting to the point of their meeting. "I assume it can't be girl trouble, yet. Classes don't start for a couple more weeks, and you've been stuck on the farm all summer."

"You're right about that," Gene agreed. "Hard to do much dating when you work until dark every night. No, it's not girl trouble. In fact, it's good news. Or at least I think it is."

"Oh? Now you do have my curiosity piqued." She leaned forward, resting her chin on her hands, elbows on the table, and arched her eyebrows in an overly dramatic look of anticipation. "I'm all ears. What's the big news?"

"Well, I was down at the airport yesterday afternoon, talking to a Stearman pilot, and—"

"Ooh, boy," Christy interrupted. "Now I do smell trouble coming. Anyway, so what did the Stearman pilot have to say that was such good news?"

"Well, what he told me was a way I can get to be an airline pilot. That's always been my dream, but I had no idea how to do it. There was no way in creation I could pay for flying lessons. Besides, Dad had a conniption fit every time I ever tried to talk about planes. So I had sort of given up on it…until yesterday." He paused, sipped at his Coke and looked at his friend, who was waiting for the other shoe to drop. "But now, I know how I can do it. I've made up my mind. I'm going to be an airline pilot."

She leaned back, arms folded across her chest, with a look that Gene had long since learned did not reflect wild enthusiasm about whatever he might have just said. That look, and the long hesitation before she responded, was as unexpected as it was deflating to his sense of excitement.

"I take it you're not wild about the idea," he said, breaking her silence. "I thought you'd be excited for me."

"I'll be excited for you when I'm sure you've thought it through, and are making the right decision for your life," she responded. "What about your engineering career? You know that's what everyone thinks you're going to do."

"Think it through?" Gene reacted, shaking his head in frustration. "Good grief, Christy. It seems like all I ever do is quote, think it through, unquote. In a couple of weeks I start my senior year in high school, and until yesterday I had no more idea what to do with my senior year than what I'd do with my life. I'd be out baling hay, and watch a dust devil going across the field, churning up dust and hay and swirling it all around, and I'd realize that's the way my mind feels all the time. I'm tired of thinking it through. I've made up my mind."

"I'm sorry, Gene," Christy replied. It wasn't like Gene to get this testy with her, and she realized she had pushed him a little hard. "I don't want to be a wet blanket. I just thought you'd pretty well decided to go to K-State, and go into some kind of engineering. Have I misunderstood you that much, all this time?"

He slumped down into the booth, stretching his legs out into the aisle, momentarily distracted by two younger girls giggling over a banana split they were sharing at the soda fountain. In a few seconds, he turned back to Christy.

"No, you didn't misunderstand," he replied, straightening himself in the booth and resting both arms on the table. "I'm sorry. I didn't mean to turn grouchy." He picked up the Coke glass, emptied it, studied it a moment, then set it back down. "At least you didn't misunderstand any more than I have, most all my life. I don't know, Christy. It's just been hard to figure it all out.

"When I was a kid, I figured I'd be a farmer, like all the other Stoddards. I like living on a farm, and I enjoy the fieldwork. But you know me. All through school I've got straight A's in math and science. The teachers constantly badger me, as they so delicately put it, to use my talents to make something of myself." He paused a moment, thinking about it. "That kind of chaps me, sometimes. Sounds like they don't think much of being a farmer—either that, or they think I'll just be a bum if they don't prod me along."

Christy was accustomed to such comments, and ignored it, waiting for him to get on with what he really wanted to say.

"I just sort of assumed I'd go to K-State, and get into engineering of some sort. I didn't know what else to do. By the way, are you aware its official name is Kansas State Agricultural College? It was founded in 1863, and was the first college formed under the Land-Grant Act, just a year after President Lincoln signed the act into law."

"You know me too well to believe I would actually know anything like that, Mr. Encyclopedia," Christy rebutted. "So that's why you were going to go to K-State, because it has cows?"

"Yeah, I guess so," Gene replied, grinning at her teasing. "I liked the fact that it was an agricultural college. I guess I believed I would feel more at home at a college that supports farming, even if I didn't plan to take any ag courses. My problem has always been that I didn't know what to take. I sort of presumed I would enroll in mechanical engineering. Of course, I've never understood exactly what a mechanical engineer does. I had trouble enough getting Mom and Dad to finally accept that it has nothing to do with trains. Some of my teachers told me I would design cars and tractors, or machinery of all sorts. I've always liked engines, and machinery, and stuff like that. That all sounded interesting, I guess…in a hypothetical sort of way."

"You don't seem to be putting a very happy face on it," Christy observed, rather dryly.

"Very perceptive, Sherlock. Designing a new John Deere might be fun, but I'll guarantee you that sitting at a drafting table all day, cooped up in some office, most decidedly would not."

"Doesn't sound all that bad, to me," Christy countered. "It would probably even have air conditioning. But for a farm boy used to being outside all the time, I guess you have a point. Isn't there anything else, something that might have more appeal?"

Gene shrugged a noncommittal response and sat watching the two girls at the fountain for a moment, before turning his attention back to her question.

"I don't know. Mr. Caldwell is always talking to me after physics class, and conducting his own guerrilla warfare campaign trying to talk me into a career in physics. He's shown me articles on new theories about the atom, and stuff about some scientist named Einstein who came up with some new theory called Relativity. He says scientists just last year split the atom—whatever the heck that means. He's certain that all kinds of exciting new knowledge in physics will come from all that stuff, and constantly bugs me to look at colleges with strong physics programs. He also keeps telling me that with a physics background, I could have a career in astronomy." Gene paused a moment, then laughed a bit. "I guess that's his attempt at a *coup de grace*. He knows how nuts I am about astronomy."

"I assume there's a 'but' coming along, about now," Christy interjected. "Sounds to me like they've been giving you some pretty good advice. You sure you want to just…ignore it?"

"Well, of course it's good advice," Gene said, barely masking the frustration he was feeling. "Lord only knows I've given it all a lot of thought. I appreciate their being concerned about me. Problem is—and here's the 'but'—none of it really matters."

"What do you mean, it doesn't matter? Why wouldn't it matter?" Christy challenged him.

"It doesn't matter," Gene replied, attempting to keep the impatience out of his voice, "because all I've ever really been interested in is airplanes. I've still got pictures I drew in kindergarten of planes. While all the other kids were drawing pictures of stick people and kitty cats, I was drawing airplanes. I've never even been in a flyable airplane, much less ever flown in one. But that's never stopped me from dreaming that somehow, someday, I would get to be a pilot. Of course, how you get to be a pilot, or pay for flying lessons, and what I would do after becoming a pilot, were questions that were as unanswered for me as what I would do as a mechanical engineer or physicist—until yesterday. Now, I have my answers."

"Well, it's always been pretty obvious that you liked airplanes, but I had no idea you felt so strongly about it," Christy replied. Sensing Gene's rising frustration, she attempted to defuse the conversation a bit. "So tell me. How do you do that? What great insight did the Stearman pilot reveal to you?"

"Well, at first I just sort of blabbered," Gene replied, responding quickly to her opening. "I started telling him all my theories, based on all the stuff I've been reading. It seems like commercial flying—that is, flying passengers—is steadily gaining in acceptance. And there are newer, safer and more comfortable aircraft coming into service.

"There's getting to be a lot of competition between the new airlines, especially Transcontinental and Western Airlines, and American Airlines. They're trying to get planes that have more appeal to passengers, and that's resulted in rapid advances in airliner design. I've seen pictures of the new Douglas DC-3 that has interiors the equal of a Pullman railway car. Can you believe some of them even have sleeper berths? Of course, with those new planes, speed records for coast-to-coast passenger flights are being set almost daily it seems. Anyway, I was telling him that I'm convinced those airlines will be growing rapidly and would need new pilots. But, I didn't have any real idea of how I could get my pilot's license, or get into the airlines if I had one."

"Okay. You've convinced me," Christy interrupted. "You want to be an airline pilot. So what did he tell you? Is he going to pay for your flying lessons?"

"He doesn't need to. Uncle Sam is going to do it," Gene countered, ignoring her little jibe.

"Gene Stoddard, are you telling me you're joining the Army?" Christy reacted, her eyes wide in disbelief. "If so, you're a bona fide idiot."

"No, put your guns away. I'm not joining the Army. Apparently, the big shots up in Washington, D.C., don't think the country has enough pilots if we have to go to war sometime, so they're paying colleges to give flying lessons while you go to college. It's called the Civilian Pilot Training Program. He says KU has the program, so I'm going to apply for it. I'll work on some engineering degree, I suppose. I guess I could fall back on that if my dream goes poof."

"Saints preserve us," Christy exhaled. "You're going to snobby KU instead of K-State, and you're going to be taking flying lessons? I assume you've talked this over with your folks, and they're giddy with excitement about it?"

"Yeah, right," Gene reacted, making no attempt to mask his feelings. "There's no way on God's green earth I would try to talk to Mom and Dad about this. They barely managed to survive and not lose their farm during the Dust Bowl and the Depression. I know that in their minds having a secure job and paycheck is the most important thing there is in life. Risking my life in such an impractical contraption as an airplane, as Dad calls them, and risking my financial security in such a risky career, is as incomprehensible to them as if I wanted to join the circus as a trapeze artist. I understand that. So no, I haven't talked to the folks about it. Frankly, I don't know when I will.

"I used to try to talk to some of the other pilots that came by to refuel, but anytime I'd say anything to one of them they'd just laugh, and tell me I'd be better off being a bull fighter in Mexico. They'd bust a gut laughing at their own joke, and tell me that bull fighting would be safer and the pay would be better. But then, they'd start telling me stories of dogfights, and of nights alone in a cockpit carrying mail all over everywhere. It was obvious that flying was as much a part of them as breathing. It was the same way with this Stearman pilot, but at least he took me seriously and talked a lot about all of it. Then he told me about the program up at KU, and said that would be my best bet. Christy—I'm sorry, but I want that. I want to be a pilot more than anything else in life. So whatever it takes, I'm willing to do—even if it means going to snobby KU, as you so graciously put it."

Christy was silent for so long that Gene wasn't sure if she was going to respond. Then she looked at him, and smiled.

"Gene, I won't even pretend that I understand it. I don't. I'm afraid I agree too much with your folks. But it's obvious you've given it a lot of thought. So go be a pilot, if that's your dream. But sooner or later, you're still going to have to tell your parents."

Gene nodded, but didn't respond, staring out the front windows of the store. Finally, he looked back at Christy.

"Thanks, Christy. I appreciate you letting me spill my guts on the subject. But I think I'll vote for later, when it comes to telling the folks. And for gosh sakes, keep this under your hat. You know how stuff spreads, around here."

As Gene's senior year was winding down, he learned that Kansas University had excellent engineering and physics departments. At Gene's request, Mr. Caldwell, his Physics teacher, composed a letter of recommendation to the head of the College of Engineering—on the pretense that if he changed his mind about engineering, he could switch to physics. His letter made special note of the fact that Mr. Stoddard was in a strong position to be Valedictorian of his graduating class, a fact that surprised Gene as he had no idea that his grades were that much better than the others—even though he rarely saw anything less than an A on his grade card.

Mr. Caldwell received a response in short order, thanking him for considering Kansas University for such a promising student. The letter indicated that a scholarship was still available in the Electrical Engineering Department, if Mr. Stoddard should wish to consider such a choice. To Gene, it made little difference, now. He knew as much—or as little—about electrical engineering as he did mechanical engineering, and it was a virtual free ticket to get to enter the CPTP.

His applications for acceptance to the Electrical Engineering Department and for the scholarship were quickly approved, and a part time job was arranged for him. It would be mostly janitorial work, but Gene wasn't afraid of dirty work. It couldn't be as hard, or as unpleasant, as many of his duties on the farm. Plus, he would be working in the engineering labs and would eventually be allowed to assist with the lab work.

All these developments were perplexing to Gene's parents. They trusted him to be making good decisions for himself, but could only shake their heads when friends or neighbors would inquire about Gene going to that fancy school, and just to learn about "electricity," of all things. They had even less of a concept of what an "electricity engineer" would do for a living than they did that of a mechanical engineer.

A neighbor informed them with a certitude unencumbered by actual knowledge—an annoying habit typical of some people of the area—that Gene would be helping put in electrical power lines for the REA, the new Rural Electrification Administration program started by the Roosevelt Administration to bring electricity to the farmers of the country. Another insisted, with equal freedom from doubt, that he would wind up repairing radios and toasters.

Of course, Gene failed to tell them that if his plans worked out, his career would have nothing to do with his obtaining an engineering degree and everything to do with the trips to the university airport that he would be making every day.

Friday, May 2, 1941, dawned bright and clear, a good omen for Gene Stoddard. Today was the day that he was to pre-enroll at Kansas University and—secretly—sign up for the Civilian Pilot Training Program. He was to meet with the head of the Electrical Engineering Department at 1:00PM, and the trip to Lawrence would require over two hours. After finishing the milking and other chores, and a hurried breakfast, Gene and his parents got in the family Chevy and headed north.

Lawrence, Kansas, home of the University of Kansas, sat astride the Kansas River about halfway between the state capital of Topeka to the west, and Kansas City to the east. During the Civil War it had been the site of the infamous Quantrill raid and massacre, in which over one hundred and forty men of the city were slaughtered because of the free-state partisanship of the town.

Lawrence had maintained a certain mystique in Kansas history because of the raid and boasted a population of over twenty five thousand, five times larger than Gene's hometown. As the Stoddards drove through the bustling town to the university campus, Gene's parents felt out of place and ill at ease. Although Gene was driving, the "big city" traffic made them visibly nervous. They sat stiff and silent, looking at the stores and people walking the sidewalks, feeling as alien as if visiting New York City, or some other foreign country.

The campus, sitting atop Mount Oread—a 250-foot limestone mound that dominated the terrain around Lawrence and that had served as a natural site for a university—was breathtaking to the three of them, with limestone buildings topped with red-tiled roofs dotting a tree-covered campus. The site had first been referred to by this name in 1854 by Ferdinand Fuller of Worcester, Massachusetts. He was part of a group of settlers from the New England Emigrant Aid Company that had camped for a short time on the hill. Mr. Fuller had named the site after Oread Seminary in Worcester, which sponsored the expedition. The name survived, and the prominent hill was known as Mount Oread from that time on.

Neither Gene nor his parents had ever been to Lawrence, or had seen a campus quite so much like the calendar pictures of the big universities back east. Of course, none of them had ever been to a college campus of any sort and except for the brochures that Gene's teachers would occasionally give him, they had no perception of what to expect. His parents didn't say much as Gene drove around the campus, silently looking at the sights and feeling even more out of place. After eating dinner at a small diner at the edge of the campus they parked in front of an imposing stone building identified as the home of the Engineering Department.

A few minutes before 1:00 PM, Gene walked up stone steps worn crescent-mooned from years of use and into the cool, dark hallway. He hesitated, looking around for a moment, taking in the quiet, musty smell of tradition and old buildings. Twinges of intimidation rose to the surface, and he began wondering just what, for sure, he was getting himself into. He had never before been in a hallowed hall, and felt decidedly out of place.

Two guys about his age walked past him, talking in muted tones as one might in a cathedral, paying him only scant attention. He noticed the slide rules in leather cases hanging from their belts, like holsters hanging low from the belts of gunslingers. Mr. Caldwell had given his physics class a few brief lessons on the use of a slide rule, but Gene had no real understanding of how to use one. Engineering was beginning to seem more daunting than before. But he soon shook off the feeling and started down the hallway toward the administrative offices.

There he was welcomed to the university and introduced to his curriculum advisor, and to the department head for whom he would be working. They were stereotypical university professors, quiet, somewhat stiffly formal, courteously friendly, and given to using proper English. After a few moments of polite inquiry into Gene's family and background, and pleasantries about his coming grand adventure into college life and an engineering career, he was taken in tow by the curriculum advisor who was to assist Gene in selecting his course of study.

Gene listened attentively, answered as best he could the questions about what field of specialization might interest him most—given that he had not the vaguest idea what any of them entailed—and a plan for his degree was agreed upon. He signed the enrollment papers, and inquired as to where he might be able to apply for the pilot training program. They expressed their surprise, mixed with awe, at this request, and the office secretary located the administration building on a campus map for him. Gene thanked them politely, gathered up his folder of materials, and left the office. He knew, to the core of his being, that he would do anything required to get to be a pilot. But the thought crossed his mind that his coming plunge into electrical engineering might challenge that conviction.

Through all this, his parents stayed in the car, watching people come and go and marveling quietly over how their son could seem so confident in such a foreign and overwhelming atmosphere. They wondered aloud which side of the family it could have come from. About forty-five minutes after he had disappeared into the imposing stone building, Gene reappeared, a folder of papers in hand, and informed them that he was now a bona fide member of the student body of Kansas University. He then told them that he had to walk to the administration building to "sign some papers." It would only take a few minutes, he said, so they could wait in the car if they wanted to. And, of course, they preferred to do so.

And thus it was that he was able to meet the administrator for the "seepy-teepee" program and apply for admittance to pilot training, without his parents' knowledge. He signed the papers acknowledging that in the event of dire national need he would accept assignment to the Army Air Forces for duties to be assigned at the time. The administrator introduced him to the chief pilot, who happened to be in the office. The pilot asked Gene if he would like to go out to the strip to see the planes. Of course, Gene ached to do so, but thanked him politely and declined. His parents needed to get back home before chore time, he explained. His acceptance was made on the spot, based on his grades and good standing with the Engineering Department.

He stepped out into the sunlight and stood looking across the campus, but not really seeing. His mind was working too hard trying to assimilate what had just happened. After years of dreaming, of wondering, of imagining, with one signature it all became real. Eugene Stoddard was going to be a pilot. He shook his head in disbelief, and started walking back to the car.

During the previous fall of 1940, just as the Stearman pilot had predicted that August afternoon when talking to Gene, Hitler's Luftwaffe had nearly brought England to its knees. Hitler had ordered his generals to plan an invasion of England. More than 160,000 German troops were to be ferried across the English Channel for the invasion, to be called Operation Sea Lion. But without air superiority, he could not take the risk of losing his troops while crossing the channel. The British Royal Air Force had to be neutralized at all cost, or Operation Sea Lion could not proceed. In a three-month Battle of Britain, a small group of dedicated fighter pilots fought the vastly superior German air arm to a draw, but the cities of England had been bombed extensively, and many citizens killed.

This gallant, dramatic struggle was followed closely by Gene, as well as by all those who perceived that the U.S. was being drawn inexorably into war. The brave and epic air battles had been shown on newsreels in the movie theaters, as was the carnage wrought by the bombing of the cities. Exhausted pilots would be shown waiting for the next—and perhaps their last—combat in the clouds. After England had survived, Winston Churchill, the Prime Minister, had paid elegant tribute to the pilots with the claim that, "Never in the course of human endeavor have so many owed so much to so few."

From the movie newsreels, and the local newspaper, Gene knew that the pilots of the Royal Air Force had held on against the mighty Luftwaffe. What Gene did not know was the role that his engineering and physicist counterparts in England had played in that historic battle.

The invention of a device which would later come to be known as "radar" had permitted the British military leaders to know in advance when the enemy planes were coming, and from which direction. They had been able to have their dwindling numbers of fighters lying in wait, greatly enhancing their odds of success. It was the first of a long series of examples in which scientists and engineers brought new tools and weapons to the scene of the battle. Without them the final outcome would have been much different.

As in all wars, however, the fallibility of man played as great a role in success and failure, victory and defeat, as did the bravery of the airmen and the great technological triumphs. Britain was at its limit. The ability of the gritty islanders to endure and fight on had been stretched perhaps past a breaking point. Prime Minister Churchill had found it necessary to buck up their resolve with a stirring speech, in which he assured them, "…we shall fight on the beaches, we shall fight on the landing grounds, we shall fight in the fields and in the streets, we shall fight in the hills; we shall never surrender…"

Over the following months, Europe spiraled into chaos and war as countries chose sides, aligning themselves either with Hitler, or with Britain and those attempting to battle against him. Troops moved into Africa, and the Soviet Union became more aggressive, capturing some of the Baltic states. Through it all, Hitler and his Blitzkrieg forces appeared unstoppable. The countries of

Europe still trying to oppose him appeared doomed to fall under his jack-booted heel, and Britain along with them. But just at that time, Hitler initiated Operation Barbarossa, the insane plan to invade Russia. Millions of German troops and military resources were shunted away from a pending invasion of Britain and sent to the Eastern front. Britain had survived to fight again.

But Gene had only superficial knowledge of all this. What was uppermost on his mind was that in the last week of May he would walk across the stage at the Memorial Hall in Colborn and accept his diploma. And on Monday, September 8, 1941, he would start classes at Kansas University. A week later he would start ground school for flight training, and take his first flight sometime thereafter.

What Gene did not know, nor did any of his fellow countrymen, was that on the other side of the globe, in Japan, the Commander of the Japanese Combined Fleet, Admiral Isoroku Yamamoto, was honing final plans for a daring carrier-based strike on American naval forces at a United States base in the Pacific— called Pearl Harbor.

College

The two-hour drive to Lawrence to move Gene to Kansas University was made largely in silence. No member of the William Stoddard family had ever lived away from home and no one was quite sure how to deal with the fact that, starting that day, Gene would no longer be a member of the Stoddard household. Gene was, of course, driving, with his dad in the front seat and his mother sitting quietly in the back, each appearing to be fascinated by the countryside passing by but silently absorbed in thought. His dad would occasionally comment about this farm, or that herd of cattle, and Gene would nod, or answer perfunctorily.

They had skipped church—a rarity for the Stoddards, but Gene was to be checked in by 2:00 PM that Sunday, and Stoddards were never late. They departed immediately after chores and breakfast to avoid the heat. It was early September, but Kansas was still very hot. Both the front windows were half way down, and the blast of air made conversation difficult. No one was motivated to do so anyway, so little was said.

Once there, Gene checked in with the dormitory office and was given a key to his room. He and his dad carried his two suitcases and a box of personal items in from the car. Gene unlocked the door, and the three of them stepped inside.

"My goodness, Gene," his mother exclaimed as she entered, "it seems awfully small for two people. Why, there's hardly room for the beds. And with those chests-of-drawers and desks on the wall, there's scarcely room to take a breath."

"Oh, don't worry about it, Mom. It's not that bad," Gene said, smiling at her. He tossed his suitcases on the bed and began to unpack. "Don't forget, I won't be spending much time in here. All I'll do is sleep or study—so it really doesn't matter that much."

"Well, maybe so," she answered, still dubious as to how well her son was going to be housed. "But it still doesn't seem like much of a room, for such a fancy school. We're poor as church mice, and your room's bigger'n this."

"Looks like my roommate got here first," Gene said, smiling at her and changing the subject. "Whoever he is, he's apparently neat—and considerate.

He's got all his clothes hung on one side, and he looks well organized. We'll probably get along fine."

After his clothes were hung in the closet, his few books placed on the shelf above his desk and freshly laundered underwear and socks put away in his dresser, there was little left to do but figure out how to say goodbye. They gathered up the empty box and suitcases, and walked to the car. There they stood, stiff and uncomfortable, looking around to avoid looking at each other.

"I've never seen ivy grow up on buildings like that. And all those red roofs. It is a lovely place, isn't it, Bill?" Gene's mother exclaimed, standing with both hands clasping her purse, unsure of what should happen next. She looked first at her husband and then to her son, each appearing to be seeing the ivy for the first time.

"It sure is, Mary," Bill agreed, continuing to inspect the ivy-covered buildings. "Maybe we could do that to the barn, so I wouldn't have to paint it." They all smiled, and nodded, then fell silent. Gene decided the time had come.

"Well, Dad, I guess I'm about as moved in as I'm going to get, and you've got the drive back. You'll want to get back before chores. Think you'll have any problem finding your way home?"

"No, I think I'll be alright. We just stay on 59 down to Garnett, right?"

"Yeah. You'll catch 169 south of Garnett, and take it on into town. You shouldn't have a problem, once you get out of here. The street we came in on is highway 59—just keep going south on it."

Gene's dad looked at his shoes, then reached out and took Gene's hand, gripping it tightly. One sure measure of a man in Kansas was the firmness of his handshake, and Gene was always surprised at the strength in his dad's grip. He did not appear to be an overly strong person, but years of farm work, and of milking cows by hand, had given him surprisingly strong arms. They looked at each other, briefly, then released their grip. Nothing was spoken. Gene's dad removed his hat, ran his hard, calloused hand through graying hair, and replaced his hat. He knew he needed to say something.

"Well, I guess I don't have any fatherly words of wisdom to offer you. You're already a lot smarter'n I'll ever be. Just remember your upbringing, and stay away from those hussy college girls." They both grinned. His dad's face flushed beneath its weathered brown.

"Come on, Dad," Gene teased. "Why do you think I came to KU instead of going to K-State?" His dad grinned a little, not understanding the joke.

"Well, goodbye son...and good luck."

"Thanks, Dad," Gene replied quietly. "I'm sure I'll need all I can get."

His dad hesitated, then walked around the car and got in.

Gene turned and wrapped both arms around his mom, squeezing her until she laughed self-consciously.

"My goodness, Gene," she exclaimed, smiling affectionately. "You'll break every bone in this old body."

"Bye, Mom. And don't worry about me. I'll get along fine," Gene assured her, as he opened the front door of the car. She paused before getting in.

"You be sure and write us when you can, and call us once in a while. Call collect. It'll be all right, and I'm sure you won't have much extra money. I'll send you some cookies. I doubt that cafeteria knows how to make a real oatmeal cookie."

She gave him a brief hug, patting him on the back, and quickly got into the car. His dad waved a last time to him, and started the engine.

Bill Stoddard knew that his world had just changed, but couldn't be sure in just what way. He knew that his son was becoming a man, responsible for himself, and sensed that he had now become a spectator to the rest of his son's life. No longer would he be looked to for advice, nor deferred to in decisions. He also believed that he and Gene's mother had done a good job, that their son was going to be a good man.

But in a dark corner of his mind, where he didn't want to look, something told him there was going to be another war, even worse than the last one. If so, their son would be in it. That thought was so repugnant, so incomprehensible, that it was rarely allowed to see the light of day and was soon pushed back from whence it had come. He put the car in gear, and moments later they were headed down the campus drive toward the exit.

Gene stood at the curb and waved, watching the aged Chevy disappear down the street. Surprised at how alone he suddenly felt, Gene was also aware that his life had just changed and was just as unsure of how that would manifest itself. He did have a vague awareness that the next time he saw those two good and caring people, now barely visible as they left the campus, the next time he returned to his home, it would be as a visitor and not as a member of the household. Going home, and being home, would never again be the same as it had been for his first eighteen years.

"Well, here I am. I wonder what I do now?" he asked aloud.

He looked around, trying to fully comprehend that this was suddenly his new home, his new life. Other students were coming and going, some still moving into the dormitory and appearing as bereft as he felt. Small clusters would hurry by, talking animatedly, too engaged in their own conversations to notice him. Others would smile and nod to him as they passed, and Gene would smile in return.

After several minutes of aimless gawking, and being unable to decide what, if anything, he should do, he went inside to his room. He rearranged some of his books and personal items to pass some time, and tried to imagine what his roommate would be like. Gene was used to sharing a bedroom with his younger brother, but had never had to share a room with a total stranger.

Later that afternoon Gene was lying on his bed, hands behind his head, staring at the ceiling and trying to imagine what the coming days would hold. He was aware that several of the kids who had left his high school and gone to KU had experienced early problems with the classes, and some had even flunked out. But Gene also knew that many, if not most, of them had not been very conscientious students in high school. With his work and study habits well established, he wasn't especially worried about being able to maintain a good grade point average.

If not worried, he was at least curious about the pilot training program that had brought him to this place. He tried to imagine what it would feel like to be soaring among the clouds, looking down on the fields that had been his home and his life. *What if I get airsick—or worse, scared?* he wondered, but the worrisome thoughts were quickly pushed aside by a growing sense of anticipation and excitement that he could not recall ever feeling before. As his mind wandered, meandering across the hills and dales of his life, a voice from the doorway startled him back to the present.

"Hi—I'm Mike Kingston. You my new roomie?"

The owner of the voice stepped into the room, hand extended, as Gene quickly spun off the bed and rose to greet him. He was good-looking and about Gene's height and build, though slightly shorter, well tanned but with darker hair, closer to black than Gene's brown. In most respects, they could have been twins.

"Well, if you're the owner of those clothes in the closet, then I guess you got the black bean. I'm Gene Stoddard. Pleased to meet you, Mike." They shook hands briefly. "You been here long?"

"No," Mike replied, shaking his head. "I came in on the train yesterday afternoon. You from around here?"

"Not really. My parents own a farm about eighty miles south of here," Gene answered. "It's just outside a little town called Colburn. You know where that is?"

"Good Lord, no. I'm from California—the northern part, almost to the Oregon border. I had trouble enough finding Kansas," Mike reacted, laughing.

"California? Wow." Gene was openly surprised, and impressed. "I've never been to California. Heck, I've never been anywhere. This is as far from home as I've ever been."

Mike grinned, but didn't respond. After a moment of awkward silence, he turned toward the door.

"I thought I'd check in, and see if my new roomie had made it. Want to join me for a Coke? Maybe we can get acquainted, a little bit. The Student Union is clear across campus, but it'll give us a chance to start finding our way around."

"Sure. Sounds swell," Gene agreed. "And I need that. I don't know where anything is."

They left the dormitory and started walking across the shaded campus, checking names of buildings as they passed them against their campus maps. They said little in the way of getting acquainted, talking mostly about the campus and its buildings, until Gene could no longer resist asking the one question that most puzzled him.

"Mike, my dad always taught me not to pry into other people's business, but I can't resist," Gene said. "How did you wind up coming here, from clear out in California?"

"You mean, why did I leave sunny California, land of Hollywood and sandy beaches and beautiful women, and come to a hick place like Kansas?" Mike replied, laughing good-naturedly.

"Well, since you put it that way—yes," Gene answered, wondering if he appeared to be as much a hick-from-the-sticks as he felt he was, at the moment.

"I suppose it does seem a little strange," Mike agreed. "I had planned on going into engineering—civil, maybe electrical—didn't really matter a whole lot. Of course, I could have gone to one of our engineering schools out there. But I've always been a nut about airplanes and frankly, I'm really here for something that KU offers that the California schools I could afford don't offer."

"Really?" Gene reacted. "What on earth could KU have that you couldn't get at the California colleges?"

"Ever hear of the Civilian Pilot Training Program?" Mike asked. "It's a program where the government pays for you to get a pilot's license—"

"You've got to be kidding," Gene interrupted. "Man, talk about coincidence. That's the only reason I'm here. I figured I'd go to K-State, but a pilot I met last summer told me about the program here at KU so I applied for it, and got accepted. I was able to get a scholarship in the electrical engineering department, or I couldn't have afforded it."

"You serious?" Mike asked, looking at Gene with obvious surprise. "You're in the CPTP, and double-e, too? What are the odds? Some of the colleges out there offer it, but the schools I could afford don't. I have an uncle who lives in Kansas City, and he told me that KU had started one here, so I applied and was accepted. I wound up enrolling in electrical engineering, but I'm primarily here to get my pilot's license."

"That's unbelievable," Gene exclaimed. "Looks like we really lucked out."

"That's for sure," Mike agreed.

They walked on in silence for several seconds, trying to let the enormity of the good fortune fate had paid them sink in.

"Well, here's the Student Union," Mike said, breaking the silence, nodding toward the large building they were approaching. They entered, and found the cafeteria. It was rather crowded, not surprising in light of the fact that classes started the next day. They got their drinks and managed to find an empty table near windows that looked out on the campus.

"Man, I can't believe the coincidences—and my good luck," Mike exclaimed, shaking his head in disbelief. "Tell you the truth, I was afraid I was going to get stuck being roommates with some Caspar Milquetoast education major. Instead, we're both going to be double-e's—and we're both going to be flyboys. Looks like we ought to get along just fine."

"You're right about that," Gene agreed. "I hadn't given much thought to what my roommate would be like. I'm still trying to get used to the fact that I don't have to milk any cows tonight."

Mike smiled, but didn't respond. They were silent a few moments, neither one too sure of how to proceed with the ritual of Getting To Know Your Roommate. After a couple of swallows of Coke, Gene turned the conversation to the topic that would come to consume them both.

"Have you done any flying, before?"

"Not really," Mike answered, shaking his head. "They were selling rides for a penny a pound at the county fair one fall when I was around twelve, and my dad paid to let me go up. We got to take about a twenty-minute flight over the local area. I've always been nuts about planes, and that pretty well hooked me."

"Well, you're one flight ahead of me," Gene replied. "I've spent more hours at our local airport than I can shake a stick at, but no one ever took me up. I can't even imagine what it'll be like." He finished his drink and set the empty bottle on the table. "We live close to the airport and I'd ride my bike down to visit with the pilots when a plane would come in. Last year, a Stearman pilot got to visiting with me—first time one of them ever talked to me like I was more than just a dumb farm kid—and told me about the program up here. I had to sign up in secret. My folks don't have any idea I'm in it, yet."

"Really? Why? They afraid of them?" Mike seemed genuinely surprised at Gene's revelation.

"Oh, Mom is—she's pretty reserved, and protective," Gene agreed. "But I don't think it's that, really. The Depression has been awfully hard on people out here. Mom and Dad barely hung on, and several of the farmers they knew lost their farms to the banks. They had to just pile everything they could on their old cars and head west. My folks want me to get a good education so I can get on with some big company and have a secure paycheck the rest of my life, so I won't have to go through what they did. To risk all that on something that seems as impractical as flying? Well, to them that's beyond crazy. I suppose I can't blame them."

"Yeah, I know," Mike said. "I didn't mean to make light of them. Most of those people you talk about heading west came to California, you know. Guess they thought it would be the land of milk and honey, but things were tough out there, too. Most of them went to southern California, down around Los Angeles, or maybe San Francisco. They'd get on at the canneries, and get jobs cleaning fish, and stuff like that, but the others..."

Mike shook his head, and took a long drink from his Coke, then leaned back on his chair.

"You know, Gene, sometimes a car would pull into our place. It'd be piled high with whatever they were able to tie on when they headed west.

Mom and dad in front, and usually two or three kids in the back. They'd say they needed water for the radiator, or something, but they really wanted some food and just couldn't bring themselves to ask. Mom would come out with a pile of sandwiches and stuff. They'd eat like they hadn't had food for a week. I just couldn't get over the look on their faces, in their eyes… the men would look just whipped, totally beat down—and so ashamed and embarrassed they could hardly look you in the eye. And the women…they looked like they wouldn't have felt it if you stuck a pin in them. I've never seen people who looked so totally defeated. The kids never seemed to really understand what was happening—how bad off they were. They would just hang back, with this look of disbelief at the food, like they'd never seen such a feast before."

Mike looked out the large windows at the green expanse of the campus, with its tailored lawns and graceful trees. The contradiction of scenes was overpowering.

"Damn, Gene. How did this country ever let itself get into such a mess, that it could do that to people? I'll never get the look of those people's faces out of my mind."

"I don't know. I've never understood what caused such a financial collapse of the whole country," Gene acknowledged. "And Dad says things aren't a whole lot better now, even with all of Roosevelt's programs. He believes Roosevelt is secretly trying to get us into the war in Europe just so there will be more jobs—he's not a big Roosevelt fan."

"Neither is Dad," Mike agreed, grinning at the comment. "But, roomie— Roosevelt got the CPTP approved, so for now, he's my guy."

"You got that right." Gene laughed and raised his empty Coke bottle. "Here's to our hero, founder of the CPTP, our esteemed leader, President Roosevelt."

"To FDR. Long may he keep us flying," Mike agreed, clinking his empty bottle against Gene's. "Now, what say we head back and start getting ready to face this bold new venture. My first class is at eight o'clock—and I assume you've got the same schedule."

Gene adapted quickly, and rather easily, to his college courses. He had always been a dedicated student, and although the material was more advanced his study habits kept him from having too much difficulty. While Mike was a generally good student, he was not as academically inclined and struggled somewhat. Gene was more than willing to assist, and together they kept Mike at a solid B grade level.

In truth, the classes were primarily a necessary evil for both of them. Their mutual preoccupation was the flying program, scheduled to start a week after classes had begun to allow new students time to acclimate themselves to the campus and the rigors of university-level coursework. But the time had come, and Gene and Mike were sitting in a makeshift classroom created from a converted storeroom in the hangar that served the campus airport.

There were about three-dozen students enrolled in the program. They had arrived in a retired school bus that had been resurrected to serve as a shuttle between the airport and the campus, taking seats on metal folding chairs at long tables that had been set up to create the classroom. A large slate blackboard was attached to the front wall. Windows on the back wall looked out on the landing strip and flight line, where the trainer airplanes were tied down. The smell of fabric dope, hydraulic oil and aviation fuel permeated the classroom from the adjacent hangar.

A low hum of conversation, spiked with an occasional burst of nervous laughter, hovered over the room, and a sense of anticipation grew with each passing minute. Promptly at the scheduled starting time, a tall, angular man entered the classroom. He appeared to be in his forties, graying slightly at the temples. His demeanor suggested he was not too thrilled at being there, as he glanced around the room, waiting for the students to quiet down.

"Good morning, gentlemen. My name is Fred Matthews. We're pretty informal here: you may all call me 'Sir.'" The students chuckled slightly, uncertain if he was joking. He was not, which soon became apparent to all.

"As you know, or at least you should, the Civilian Pilot Training Program is funded by the United States government but is administered locally by Kansas University. It is administered by civilians, and all instructors are civilians. You will receive approximately sixty hours of flight training, along with relevant ground school courses. This program is the equivalent of Primary training in the Army Air Corps, where the program normally takes three months. Ground school includes basic aerodynamics, map reading, dead-reckoning navigation, basic meteorology, and many other topics related to flight. You will take your flight training in the Fairchild PT-19, which you see parked on the flight line."

The instructor knew he was throwing a lot of information at them, and looked the class over to see if it appeared to be registering. Too much of the time, the students were so convinced that they were simply going to jump into the nearest cockpit and take off that little of what was told them was comprehended. But the group seemed to be paying attention, so he moved on.

"As I said, this program should take about three months. However, because we adhere to the university schedule, and it spans the Thanksgiving and Christmas holiday breaks, we should complete it sometime in January. Of course, Kansas winters don't always cooperate, so that will depend on how the weather affects flying time. There will be two progress check rides during your training, with a final check ride to determine if you get approved."

He paused again, looking over the group of eager young faces, the excitement of the coming weeks clearly evident in the smiles showing on them. Then he changed course.

"Gentlemen, you are well aware—that is, you are if you read the papers you each signed—that in the event of national need you will be required to join the Army Air Corps. All of us here are veterans from the last war in Europe. We've all flown in combat, and have been shot at, shot up and shot down. We are thus well familiar with the signs of when countries are about to go to war. To a man, we believe that this country will soon be at war...most likely in a matter of months."

He again paused. The room was silent, all faces fixed on him.

"The obvious conclusion is that, at least in our humble opinion, every one of you who successfully completes this program will soon be in the Army Air Corps—and eventually in combat. We therefore consider it our duty to conduct this program on a military basis, with all the associated rigors and disciplines. Quite frankly, we believe we will be doing you a favor to do so."

Mike glanced at Gene, eyebrows raised in a "Where'd this come from?" look. Gene could only shrug, and shake his head. Other students shifted in their chairs, under-the-breath comments muted by the rustling. The instructor ignored them, waiting for them to get quiet.

"If we are correct in our assumptions," he continued, "by the time you complete this program, or not long thereafter, we will be at war. If so, you will be inducted into the Army Air Corps—excuse me; the Army Air Forces. They changed the name, this past summer, and old habits are hard to break— pursuant to your signed agreement. You will have a pilot license, and have completed the equivalent of Primary training. You will be ordered to a flight school to start Basic training, competing with students who will have had several months of military life. You will be at a definite disadvantage unless you have comparable indoctrination in military conduct. We plan to eliminate that disadvantage for you. You will probably hate us now, and thank us later."

The instructor glanced toward the back of the room, where a not-so-silent "You got the 'hate' part right" comment seemed to have originated. For a second, it appeared the stone-faced instructor was about to break into a grin, but the attempt failed and he continued his speech.

"You will, therefore, treat all instructors and classroom teachers as officers. You will address them as Sir, and salute them. Since we are not active officers in the Army, and have no actual rank, you will refer to all of us as Colonel. None of us ever made colonel, so we promoted ourselves." At this, a sliver of a smile broke through, just as quickly evaporated, and he proceeded onward. "We will have at least an hour a week of marching and close-order drill to acquaint you with that idiotic practice, and give you training in various military procedures and protocols. All ground school subjects will be taught just as you would experience in Primary flight school. Any questions, so far?"

The room was silent.

"Good. I assume from your silence that you are in full agreement. If any of you find these requirements not to your liking, meet me after class and we can discuss your options. The ground school schedule is posted on the bulletin board in the hallway. Tardiness is unacceptable. Be here ready to study at the assigned hour. There will be one, and only one, closed book test at the end of each curriculum section. A grade of seventy is passing. You must pass each section to progress. Fail any one section and you will be dropped from the program."

He looked around the class once more.

"If there are no questions, class is dismissed. See you in the morning."

With that he turned and left a room full of stunned students. For a few seconds no one spoke or stirred, then the silence was broken by an emphatic response from the back of the room that spoke for them all:

"Well, shit!"

Metal chairs scraped across the floor as they stood and began walking out of the room, groups of two and three talking animatedly, reacting to this unexpected development as they boarded the shuttle bus for the trip back to the campus.

"So, we're in the Army now," Mike exclaimed. "Not exactly what I had in mind. Maybe I should have stayed in California."

"And maybe I should have joined you," Gene said, as he watched the scenery passing by. The comments of the instructor and those of the pilot who first told him of the CPTP tumbled around in his head. "Do you really suppose we're that close to going to war?"

"I guess we must be," Mike replied. "Certainly Mr. Friendly Freddie must think so. I wonder if that guy's face would crack if he ever laughed?"

Gene smiled, but was silent as he watched the Kansas River bounce past the bus as they crossed over the bridge into Lawrence.

"You know, Mike," Gene said, finally breaking the silence, "this sort of throws me for a loop."

"What, having to play soldier?" Mike asked, obviously puzzled. "That shouldn't be all that big a deal—just huff out a few 'Sir's, snap a salute here and there. What's the problem?"

"No, I can deal with that," Gene objected, shaking his head. "I mean...I just didn't really think much about actually having to go into the service when I signed up with the CPTP—and I certainly didn't give a thought to having to go into combat. That all seemed pretty hypothetical. All I could think about was wanting to be an airline pilot."

"Yeah, me too," Mike agreed. "My dad's sort of a pessimist in his old age, and seems to think the world is going to hell in a hand basket pretty much all the time—or at least that's the way I took it. I never paid much attention to all his ranting. 'Roosevelt's going to get us into another war, the Japs are going to attack.' It just seemed like crap to me. Now I have to wonder. Maybe he knows more than I gave him credit for."

"Yeah, I don't tend to pay enough attention to my dad, either," Gene agreed, staring at the back of the seat in front of him. "I get pretty annoyed with all the grown-ups in my family. Seems like they waste a lot of energy worrying about stuff all the time. Of course, several guys from my hometown got killed in the last war. I wasn't even born then, but Mom and Dad knew some of them, or knew their folks. I imagine it seems a lot more real to them. I've just been too naïve, I guess—and probably too immature—to take it seriously. Looks like maybe it's our turn, now."

"Well, look at it this way, Gene," Mike philosophized. "If we don't go to war, we'll get a pilot license and a head start at getting into an airline job. If there is a war, we'll be in it anyway—and what better way to fight a war than in a plane. Either way, we get to fly and Uncle Sam is paying for it. Can't beat a deal like that with a stick."

"Yeah," Gene laughed, appreciative of Mike's lightening his mood. "The pilot that told me about the CPTP flew with Rickenbacker. He said he got pretty scared at times, but when he would be flying over the trenches he really felt lucky to be up in a plane, compared to what those guys had to go through. I guess it would be the same for us. And he said sometimes when he would be coming back from a mission and see the sun setting, or would be flying around through the clouds, he felt like the luckiest guy on earth. A lot to be said for that."

"You got that right," Mike agreed.

First Flight

Aerodynamics, meteorology, navigation, Morse code, all subjects that Gene and Mike would be required to master to become pilots, seemed at times hopelessly complicated. In addition to their college classes—and those were rapidly becoming increasingly difficult and demanding—it was becoming clear that the CPTP ground school was going to subject them to a continuous onslaught of arcane new subjects.

During the first three weeks of college, setting the pace for the semester to come, Gene and Mike found their days consumed from daybreak until after midnight with class work and homework. But, more than anything else, they were unprepared for the endless lists of items that had to be memorized as part of becoming a pilot. While Gene was growing up, and dreaming of becoming a pilot, he had naively assumed that he would show up at an airport some day, get in a plane with an instructor, and begin to learn to fly. That those lessons would be accompanied by college-level coursework, he had never imagined.

But they were now being made painfully aware that every facet of flying, from pre-engine start to final shutdown, had its own list of gobbledygook terminology that had to be committed to memory and spilled back to the classroom inquisitor at a moment's notice. During a class, while discussing some topic, the instructor would suddenly, and without warning, interrupt his lecture and demand of some unfortunate student the recital of a checklist.

"—Airman Benson! What is the loss-of-engine-below-500-feet procedure for the PT-19?"

Airman Benson, usually preoccupied with the lecture or, more likely, daydreaming about the girl he met in Psychology I class the day before, would look up with a blank, startled face and immediately jump up and stand at rigid attention—not infrequently propelling his metal chair clanging to the floor in the process—as his mind raced trying to fetch the correct list from some dusty file drawer of his mind where it had last been stored.

"Colonel, Sir! The loss-of-engine-below-500-feet procedure for the PT-19 is…" Airman Benson would parrot, trying to buy time for recall.

For the student, it was an adrenaline-pumping experience that often left him feeling defeated and shaken, after stumbling and having to pause, retreat, and repeat himself as he struggled through the list. The other students would watch in much the same way as gazelles would watch as a lion took down a member of the herd to have for lunch—feeling sorry for the victim, but relief at one more escape from a similar fate.

The instructors recognized that emergencies in an airplane, unlike class-room tests, were not posted on the blackboard seventy-two hours in advance. They were life-threatening events that occurred without warning, requiring instantaneous and correct response if they were to be survived. One moment the pilot could be flying a perfectly normal aircraft, and a second later be confronted with his impending doom—no time to think, no time to look up the answer in the back of the book. As the complexity and sophistication of the aircraft increased, as was rapidly occurring in the new planes being developed and manufactured, that fact would become overwhelmingly true. Reflexive response had to become ingrained.

As days blurred into weeks, and the lists became second nature, the students began to perceive that they were being transformed—they were beginning to think like pilots. However, during all this preparation for becoming a pilot, as necessary as they recognized it to be, Gene and the other students had yet to even sit in an airplane. It had, in fact, been just over three weeks since the start of college classes. But it felt as though months had passed, and they were beginning to wonder if they ever would get to actually fly.

After what felt like endless days of study and marching and close-order drills and tests, of more study and recitation of countless lists, the day finally arrived when they were to start actual flying lessons. The students began filing into the classroom, to expectantly await the arrival of the instructors so they could start.

Gene had arrived on the early shuttle and was sitting alone in the empty room, forearms resting on the edge of the long wooden table, absentmindedly twirling a well-chewed pencil. He glanced up as a chair was noisily pulled back and Mike sat down beside him.

"Hey, Stoddard. I was a little worried, when you weren't on the bus. A bit on the eager beaver side today, aren't we?"

Tilting back on the metal chair, Gene stretched, yawned briefly, and smiled in response as he glanced briefly at the other students entering the room.

"Morning, Mike. Yeah, I guess so. But, man, today's the day! I could hardly get to sleep, and woke up before sun up. It's wild blue yonder time."

"You betch'um, Red Ryder. You scared?"

"Scared? Of what?" Gene asked, a bit taken aback by the abruptness of the question.

"Well," Mike replied, "scared you'll screw up and be washed out before you get to your first solo. Scared of the instructor. Scared of the plane. Me? I'm scared shitless. Of course, I guess that's a good thing, since I wouldn't want to do it in my pants, up there."

Gene smiled at the crude bluntness of his friend, and realized that the only difference between them was that Mike wasn't afraid to say what Gene was feeling. He had been so nervous as the fateful day approached that he couldn't eat breakfast, which for a Stoddard was a sure sign of a fatal illness, or worse. He lowered his chair back down and leaned both arms on the table, doodling with his pencil.

"Yeah, I've been so nervous the last couple of days I could hardly eat—although that cafeteria food can do that to you anyway," Gene agreed, laughing. "I've dreamed all my life of nothing but flying, and now that I'm about to get a chance, I'm scared I'll blow it before I even get started. I hear the instructors are really tough on new cadets. They try to wash you out so only the best ones get through. I don't know if I've got it."

Before Mike could respond, a commotion at the back of the room announced that an officer had entered.

"Ten-HUT!"

Chairs scraped and clattered across the floor, as thirty-five would-be air cadets snapped to attention. The Squadron Commanding Officer, Colonel Riley, came to the front to address the students.

"At ease, gentlemen. Be seated." He looked the group over as they took their seats and faced him, excited and expectant.

"Well, gentlemen, this is the day you've all been looking forward to: you start actual flight training. I'm sure you've heard the rumors about how tough military instructors are. I want to assure you that whatever you may have heard, you shouldn't believe a word of it." He paused for effect. "They're actually much worse."

The class laughed nervously, falling silent as he continued.

"The rumors are right. We want you to wash out. That is, if you don't have what it takes to be a pilot in the United States Army Air Forces, then it is our duty to wash you out. Air combat is a kill, or be killed, situation. Only the best survive. If, however, you have the innate talent, and the guts and determination to be a combat pilot, we will start you on the road to being the best there is. Listen to your flight instructor, do what he tells you, do it until it becomes basic instinct, and you can become a pilot in the Army Air Forces. Fail to heed him, and you will soon be learning the fine art of trench warfare, or worse yet, be at the bottom of a smoking hole in the ground. Now—with this bit of cheery optimism, I wish you good luck. The Chief Flight Instructor will fill in the details. That is all."

The class again snapped to attention as the Squadron C.O. walked briskly out of the room, to be replaced by the Chief Flight Instructor.

"Okay, men. You have been divided into four flight groups. Group assignments have been posted on the bulletin board in the hallway, with the first week's flight schedule. Those not flying will be in class, as posted. The first flight group will report to the flight line at 0830, the others to their respective classes. Dismissed."

Gene elbowed his way toward the wall to find his name on the postings. Before he could get close enough to see, Mike called out.

"Way to go, Stoddard. You're in the first group."

Gene broke into a smile, and headed out the door to get his flight suit and other gear. He wanted to be the first at the flight line.

A row of Fairchild Aircraft Company PT-19 primary trainers sat parked with military precision along the edge of the ramp in front of the hangar. Painted in military colors, with a dark blue fuselage and bright yellow wing, the planes had two tandem open cockpits, a front one for the student pilot and a rear one for the instructor. Red and white stripes attached to a vertical blue stripe at the rear of the vertical tail made it obvious that these were airplanes of the Army Air Forces, and not civilian trainers. Flare spots from the sun reflected here and there from the windscreens that provided some small protection for the student and instructor from the propeller blast and wind stream while flying. A low-wing monoplane, it stood proudly on slender, non-retractable main landing gear. Its small tail wheel let the tail sit low, elevating the 175 horsepower engine into the air and giving the plane an appearance of eagerness to be flying.

Inside, in the tandem cockpits, all was tubing and gauges and switches and handles. Nothing was covered, giving the impression that in the haste to fill the needs of a nation going to war the machine was simply snatched from the production line before the interior crew could finish their job. It was all utility and function. The plane was not burdened with an electrical system. Its instrument panel contained only the most basic, and requisite, flight instruments. The instructor talked to the student through a voice tube, called a Gosport Tube. The pilots' parachutes formed the seat cushion for the bare metal bucket seat in which each would sit.

Every airplane has a personality, determined by the appearance as well as the performance designed into it by its creator. The PT-19 looked like what it was—a simple, straightforward aircraft whose purpose was to allow a trainee pilot to learn to become its master with neither guile nor treachery. Most military pilots had been trained in the PT-17, the ubiquitous Boeing Stearman "Kaydet" biplane trainer, a slow, forgiving plane that was simple to fly. But military aircraft were rapidly becoming more sophisticated, more complex, faster and more difficult to fly. The benign Stearman was not adequately preparing pilots for these new aircraft.

To meet this need, the Army had requested airplane manufacturers in 1939 to submit designs for a low-wing monoplane primary trainer that would have higher landing speeds and perform more like the advanced aircraft that the pilots would later have to master. The Fairchild design had won the competition, and flight schools had readily taken to it.

Its job was to roll and pitch and yaw and takeoff and land in accordance with the aerodynamic laws presented in the classroom, and to do so in obedience to the commands of tentative hands on the stick and hesitant feet on the rudder pedals. It knew it was not to be a front-line fighter.

But, like a dutiful mother, it would teach a needed lesson and ground loop when inadequate attention was paid to the use of rudder on a crosswind landing. It would not snap roll into an inverted flat spin during a high-G turn, but it could easily make a new recruit airsick during spin training, so that the fatal mistakes could perhaps be later avoided. But neither would it be ashamed of the role it had to play. It would be reliable and responsive, forgiving of the many indecencies that its students would visit on it over the course of a training period.

Still, it would not fly itself. If it could have spoken to its putative pilots, its message would have been this: If you are to learn to be a pilot, then you must first learn to master me. I will not do your job for you. You must fly me, in cruise or on final approach, on take-off or touching down in a crosswind. Leave your job to me, and I will embarrass you—and you may harm us both.

This was the plane that awaited Gene Stoddard to climb in and begin his odyssey into the realm of flight, and end his years of flying only in his dreams.

Gene had put on his flight suit, checked out his parachute, and arrived early at his assigned aircraft. A mechanic attending to some minor detail glanced at Gene, then ignored him. Gene walked slowly around the craft, taking in every facet as he walked. He knew the basic design of aircraft from his years of building models, and his many days at the hometown airport, yet he now began to comprehend how little he actually knew about them. What would it feel like? How did the controls feel? He knew instinctively what to do when driving the truck, or a tractor. But what does one do to turn, to climb, to dive or land in an airplane? All the instructions and knowledge presented by the classroom instructors now seemed remote and theoretical. He was about to confront reality.

A surge of nervousness clutched at him. It began to sink in—he was intimidated by this simple-looking, but inscrutable piece of machinery awaiting him. *Great heavens, what have I got myself into? I have no idea what one of these things does, or how to do it.*

He began to breathe deeply, trying to shake off the feelings, and walked to the edge of the asphalt apron and out onto the grass. The familiar feel of the dirt and grass under his flight boots, the smells of back home on the farm, began to quiet his nerves.

"Stoddard—get up here!" The sudden command startled him.

Gene spun around. The flight instructor was standing at the cowling of the plane, looking at him.

"Yes, sir!" he called, already at a trot to the nose of the plane.

"You ready to fling yourself at the sky, Stoddard?"

"Yes, sir," Gene snapped, trying to sound his most confident, while his mind was praying *Please, God, don't let him see me sweating. If he knows how nervous I am right now, he'll wash me out and never look back.*

"Good. Now, first of all, don't let this thing scare you. Most kids never been in a plane before. Don't know shit from Shinola about one, so screw everything up, at first. Just relax, remember what you've been taught so far, listen to what I tell you, and we'll get along just fine. Don't listen to me, and I'll bust your ass outta here. Got it?"

"Yes, sir." Gene was beginning to breathe again.

"OK, Stoddard, what's the start-engine procedure for the PT-19?"

Gene reflexively snapped to attention.

"Uh, Sir…the start-engine procedure for the PT-19 is…uh…mixture rich, throttle cracked one quarter inch…"

Gene continued on with the list, hesitating a couple of times in his nervousness, but correctly completing it. He stared straight ahead, hoping that his nervousness wasn't too obvious.

"Correct, Airman Stoddard—except for the 'uh' parts. You can stand at-ease. Now, what's the engine-out procedure for loss of engine within 500 feet of the ground on take-off?"

For endless minutes, Gene was immersed in deep concentration, trying to remember the answers to the questions being fired at him by the instructor as they reviewed every procedure for every maneuver, every emergency—take-off procedures, rotate speeds, best rate of climb speed, best angle of climb speed, cruise speed, pattern speed, approach speed, landing checklist. They had walked around the craft inspecting it for safe operation, just as Gene had seen the pilots at his hometown airport do so many times on his trips down there. At least he now had some idea what to look for.

Finally, he was settled in the front seat, safety harness securely fastened, and the propeller spinning in front of him at approximately the same RPM as his head seemed to be spinning from the previous inquisition. Gene's t-shirt was damp under his flight suit, and he had to wipe sweat out of his eyes with his sleeve, until the steady blast from the propeller began to dry him off and settle him down.

"Ready to go?" The disembodied voice of the instructor came from the rear cockpit, through the Gosport tube to the earpieces in his flight helmet.

Gene signaled with a "thumbs up" above his head. The instructor could speak to him using the voice tube, but Gene could not respond. He was to signal that he understood his instructor by raising his hand above his head, with a thumbs-up signal.

"OK, I'll get it out on the ramp, then you can taxi to the active from there. Don't chase the rudders or you'll be all over the place. Here we go."

The engine came alive as the instructor advanced the throttle, and the plane began to inch forward out of its parking spot. It was only then that Gene looked up from his concentration on start-up of the engine, to watch as they taxied out on to the taxiway—only to see nothing but engine cowling.

Good grief, I can't see over this thing. How can he see where we're going? Gene leaned left and right, and struggled to raise himself in the seat enough to see over the aircraft nose, still elevated above the horizon as the tail rolled along on the short tail wheel. The narrow cowling let him see to either side, but nothing of the runway ahead.

"That won't help, Stoddard. That's why we have to S-turn. It's your airplane. Taxi us to runway one seven. "

As Gene settled back in his seat, embarrassed at being caught, he pushed gently on the right rudder and looked down the left side at the long taxiway as the nose gently swung away. Suddenly his left rudder pedal went forward and the nose swung quickly back as the instructor used his duplicate set of controls in the rear to regain control.

"I said S-turns, dammit, not taxi across the pasture. Keep your mind on it."

Got to pay attention. Legs too tense. Gotta relax. Use just the balls of my feet. Just a little lag after I press the pedal. Got to anticipate that, press in a little early. Only have to press about an inch, then relax it. Seems strange steering with my feet. A little like using the brakes to turn the tractor. Gene willed himself to relax and leaned back, starting to get in the rhythm of looking down the opposite side each time the nose swung through in gentle turns as they progressed down the taxiway toward the awaiting runway.

Lesson number one. Gene smiled to himself.

After the standard engine run-up, both magnetos checked, and all gauges and flight controls had been checked, they taxied to the center of the runway, nose pointed expectantly down the center stripe.

"OK, Stoddard. I'll handle the rudders on this first takeoff, and talk you through the lift off. You ready?"

Gene straightened himself, sitting stiffly upright in the seat, right hand firmly gripping the stick. He could feel his heart beginning to pound as he signaled a quick "thumbs up." His throttle handle at his left side moved forward as the instructor advanced his in the rear cockpit, and the engine roared to full power.

"Don't forget, Stoddard, we have to add right rudder on takeoff. Feel how much I've got in?" Gene felt his right foot move forward, as the instructor pressed the pedal in the rear. He nodded, forgetting that the instructor could barely see him.

They were rolling, slowly at first, then rapidly gaining speed, the pavement on each side blurring.

"Airspeed's forty, get some forward stick in, get your tail up...easy, not too much...fifty...keep your nose level...that's better...sixty...back pressure, pull your nose up a little...good...now, just let it fly itself off."

With the tail up, Gene had his first unobstructed view ahead. Onrushing asphalt blurred to either side in his peripheral vision, as wind whipped in his face around the windscreen. He could feel himself becoming increasingly tense in anticipation of the lift-off, as he unconsciously gripped the stick harder. He had driven faster than this in a car, but everything seemed to be happening at breathtaking speed.

Suddenly, the earth was snatched away from under him, and he was airborne, climbing straight ahead into a clear blue sky showing signs of scattered cumulus starting to form in the morning heat.

This is it. I'm flying! Thank you, God. I'm flying!

No matter how he tried to ignore the feeling, he could not deny a sense of child-like awe from overwhelming him as he stared at the new world he now saw stretching from horizon to horizon, in every direction. It was that delectable feeling of pure fantasy he experienced as a child on Christmas morning, staring at Christmas tree lights shining in their dark living room and at packages that had mysteriously appeared overnight.

Farm pastures and fields, some already plowed and others with cornfields awaiting harvest, created an irregular patchwork quilt of green and yellow, black and brown. They soon were passing over the Kansas River, that separated the airport from the main part of Lawrence. Much larger than the Neosho River that cut through the bottom lands west of his parents' farm, the Kansas had seemed almost daunting to Gene the first time he had driven over the bridge spanning it. Now, to his amazement, it seemed nearly inconsequential—flat and featureless, a muddy-brown swatch painted on the earth's surface.

Red-roofed buildings of the campus were already surprisingly tiny. They reminded Gene of the little wooden block buildings they used during the many Monopoly games his family played to pass long, dark winter nights. He attempted, for a moment, to see his engineering building, but they somehow all appeared the same.

Mt. Oread, so dominant above the surrounding town, was scarcely discernible from the lower elevations it overlooked. The land around his home had rolling hills, but had none of the rugged beauty and sense of character of the hills and valleys along the Kansas River that Gene had admired from the first time he had come to Lawrence. Now those hills and valleys were nearly indistinguishable, almost two-dimensional.

Muddy creeks bordered by cottonwoods and willows, mere scratch marks through the farmlands, meandered their way toward the Kansas. Small dots that he recognized as herds of Guernsey and Holstein cows grazed in pastures that, from this lofty new perspective, appeared as neat as a golf course.

Countless small farm ponds sparkled in the morning sun, marked by smooth, flat patches on the lee side of the shoreline and by rippled surfaces where grazed by the breeze that was now beginning to stir as the sun heated the morning air. A truck crept along a country gravel road, pulling a plume of dust behind it that drifted slowly across the fields in the light breeze.

It was his former world seen from on high. He was now an observer rather than a participant—an impartial outsider who looked on the scenery and activities below with silent detachment. He was looking down on people who had no idea they were being observed, feeling a strange sense of embarrassment, as though he were some celestial Peeping Tom. Gene felt as if he were viewing his own life much as if he were God, gazing down on His creation and His creatures.

"Okay, Stoddard, that's your sightseeing tour for the duration." Gene was startled back to reality by the voice coming from the hearing pads under the ears of his flight helmet. "You ready to learn to fly this thing?"

"Yes, sir!" Gene immediately exclaimed. Just as quickly, he remembered that the instructor could not hear him, and raised his right hand with a thumbs-up.

"We're going to start with some basic turns," the voice told him. "I want you to start with a gentle turn to the left—just keep it going until I tell you."

Gene gingerly pushed the stick to the left, not sure how much he should let the wings bank. He watched as the horizon slowly rotated in his windscreen, concentrating on keeping the bank shallow.

"You've got to get more rudder in as you start the turn. Remember adverse yaw. Now, roll back into a turn to the right, about the same amount of bank—but use more rudder," the instructor called, after they had turned about ninety degrees.

Gene complied, pulling the wings back level and then banking into a right turn. He realized he had been unconsciously gripping the stick so hard that his hand was starting to ache, and tried to relax his grip. But he was finding the little plane far easier to control than he expected, and was struggling to keep from over controlling. He frequently let the plane bank too steeply, only to overreact and jerk it back to a more shallow bank.

"Look at your altimeter." The hollow-sounding voice interrupted his struggles to maintain his bank angle.

Gene glanced at the altimeter in his panel and was stunned to see that during the turns they had descended over five hundred feet. Involuntarily jerking backward on the stick, he ballooned upward and let his bank angle increase, clumsily jerking and pushing on the stick while trying to get the plane leveled out and somewhat back under control. He felt totally incompetent, and could feel himself getting more tense and frustrated by the second.

"Don't forget, Stoddard, you have to apply back pressure in the turn to maintain altitude. Now, try a ninety degree turn each way, and try to maintain altitude," the instructor called to him.

Each time Gene attempted a turn, he would apply too much backpressure and zoom upward, only to shove the stick forward and zoom back down—all the while struggling to maintain some semblance of a constant bank angle. He was growing increasingly annoyed with himself, and fearful of what the instructor must be thinking. Sweat began to build on his forehead and run into his eyes. He tried to wipe it off with his left arm, while engaged in hand-to-hand combat with the stick in his right hand. His legs were aching as he unconsciously pushed with both feet against the rudder pedals.

Gene's first flight, his moment of consorting with angels and soaring with eagles, was turning into a nightmare of fumbling frustration. After letting him struggle through several attempts at a smooth turn, the instructor reached his limit.

"Stoddard, you're not riding some damn mule! You don't have to jerk it around like it's too stubborn to mind! I've got the plane."

Gene raised both hands over his head to signal that he had relinquished control of the plane, assuming that he had flunked the flight and that the instructor was taking them back to the airport. Instead, the instructor, who had experienced this overreaction many times with new students, took a new tack. He leveled the wings and let it fly straight and level for several seconds, then called again to his student pilot.

"Now, Stoddard, take the stick between your forefinger and thumb." Gene did as instructed, grasping the stick as best he could with just his thumb and finger. "Fly this thing with just those two fingers and see how easy it is. You don't have to jerk it around—just tell it what you want it to do, and it'll fly itself."

Gene took a deep breath, trying to settle himself, reassured by this second chance. Holding the stick tentatively between his finger and thumb, he began a gentle bank—uncertain of whether he could, in fact, maintain control of the plane with so little grip on the stick—while easing the stick back as he banked. To his amazement, the plane docilely responded and he began to turn with little change in altitude. After a few seconds he gently rolled back level and into a turn in the opposite direction, the nose deviating little from level flight. He felt a smile beginning to well up within him as his confidence began to return. Driving anything—tractor, truck, car, motorcycle—had always come instinctively to him. Maybe flying could, too.

"That's more like it, Stoddard. Just keep making some turns, like that."

Gene continued making turns left and right, amazed at how simple it was becoming when he was gentle on the controls. The instructor let him practice without comment for several minutes, pleased that his suggested technique was yielding fruit. As Gene rolled out of a ninety-degree turn to the right, ready to roll smoothly back into one to the left, the instructor broke his concentration.

"Much better, Airman Stoddard. Now take us to the barn. It's time to go home."

Gene glanced quickly at his watch, unable to believe that the hour was nearly over. After his first struggles with constantly gripping the stick as if choking a mortal enemy, and unconsciously pressing so hard with both feet against the rudder pedals that his legs were aching, he had begun to relax and enjoy the experience. Now, all too suddenly, it was time to go back. Gene looked to either side of the plane, expecting to see the city of Lawrence, and the airport, nearby, and was introduced to his next shock.

From this altitude, all the world within his view looked alike. One field looked like another. Each direction looked like any other direction. Roads and railroads wandered across the plains, coming from where they appeared to be going. A small town, nothing more than a drab collection of featureless buildings and trees collected along black lines that were its streets, intercepted the roads here and there but offered no means of identity. Each looked virtually identical to the others. It was as though he was looking at a map with no names, no labels.

But most disconcerting was the fact that the airport, with its hangars and long landing strip, and the city of Lawrence and its university campus—all of which had seemed so huge to him compared to his modest home town—were nowhere to be seen. The instructor saw him looking around in futile attempts to orient himself.

"You got us lost, Airman Stoddard? Look at your three o'clock—on the horizon. That cluster of trees and buildings is Lawrence. Head for it, and you'll see the field north of it."

Gene was flabbergasted. The city of Lawrence, Mt. Oread, and the beautiful red-tiled roofs of the campus, were all just one small collection of indistinguishable objects embedded in a mottled patch of trees on the horizon several miles distant. He couldn't believe that a town so large could shrink to such insignificance, so easily. It gave him a whole new perception of relative size and distance—and of how challenging navigation was going to be in practice, when it had seemed no more than simple mathematics in the classroom.

As he came closer to the dark patch that had been Lawrence, Kansas, he began to make out individual buildings, and could identify the campus. At some distance north of the town, across the river, he saw a small building that he began to realize was the airport hangar, but he could not yet make out the runway that he knew was there.

Gene was beginning to realize that flying, unlike anything else he had ever done, was going to be as much a mental activity as a physical one. He had to visualize himself moving over a map, and see that map in his mind when he looked at the earth below.

"Get us down to pattern altitude, and see if you can get us into a standard pattern entry," the instructor called, interrupting Gene's concentration on orienting himself. Gene quickly acknowledged him.

It was all beginning to be fun, just as Gene had always imagined it would be. At some point, he realized that he had stopped using his thumb and finger, and was casually holding the stick like he used to rest his hand on the gearshift lever of the pickup. It was already starting to feel natural, second-nature, almost.

They were in the landing pattern now, with Gene concentrating on adjusting his descent and airspeed to set up for a proper final approach, coached along by instructions coming through the voice tube. As they approached the end of the runway the earth, which only minutes earlier had seemed so distant and detached, crawling lazily below him like a stagnant creek, now rushed at him like a charging bull. Green carpets were becoming blurred patches of weeds and grass reaching up to snatch at his wheels, to jerk him out of his sky.

He tried to judge his height above the runway, but couldn't tell if he was five feet or fifty feet above it. Too low, and he would bounce terrifyingly off the unforgiving pavement—too high, and he would stall out and crash to the pavement below. The end of the runway rushed at him at breathtaking speed and blurred under him as the plane flashed over it. He had to steel himself to keep from jerking the stick back to avoid crashing into it.

"Ease your nose up. Steady, now." The calm voice from the rear cockpit settled Gene's nerves, as he concentrated on the landing. "That's good, hold it…chop the throttle…keep the nose coming up…up some more…hold it there. Now, just let it settle on."

A chirp of rubber on asphalt, a slight jolt, and his virgin flight was over. Gene could feel the rudder pedals moving under his feet as the instructor worked to keep the plane rolling straight down the runway. The nose rose again to block his view as the tail settled to the ground, and the instructor helped guide it off the runway.

Gene taxied back, trying to make his S-turns look smooth and himself confident as he passed along in front of other fledgling pilots waiting for the first group to return so they could take their first flight. The instructor nosed into the parking spot, clamped hard on one rudder and gunned the engine, deftly spinning the plane around into the parking position.

"Okay, Stoddard, shut her down."

Gene pulled the mixture to cut-off, and as the engine coughed to a stop, switched off the magnetos. He pulled off his leather flight helmet, letting his matted, sweaty hair catch the light breeze. His ears were still ringing from the noise as the instructor stepped up the wing walk beside him.

"Well, Stoddard, not too bad for a first time. Still think you want to be a flyboy?"

"Thanks, sir. It was incredible—after you got me to stop being so ham-handed on the stick. That really helped. I always knew I wanted to fly, and now I know why."

"Well, it loses some of the glamour when you're getting bullet holes through the wings…but it does have its fine points," the instructor acknowledged, grinning briefly at Gene. "Do your post-flight check and I'll see you in the debriefing room in a few minutes to talk it over."

September 30, 1941

Dear Mom and Dad:

Sorry it's taken me so long to write. Hard to realize three weeks have passed since I got here. As you can imagine, it's been pretty busy getting started in all my new classes. The classes are quite a bit harder than high school, but I'm getting used to it and doing OK, so far at least. The professor that I work for is really nice, and is teaching me stuff that we don't learn in the classroom. Mike, my roommate, and I are getting pretty well acquainted by now. He's from clear out in California. He's a really swell guy and we get along fine. We're both in electrical engineering, and have most of our classes together so we study together a lot. That helps us both.

How are you all doing? Is Sis behaving herself? I bet Jerry likes having the room—and bed—all to himself. We're supposed to get an extra week off after Thanksgiving break this year. I don't remember why, but I get off November 23 and don't have to go back until December 8 or 9, I think. Anyway, I'll probably be able to catch a ride with someone headed that way. They have a ride-sharing bulletin board where you can sign up.

Not much else to say, I guess, and it's getting late. Mike and I have a big exam in a couple of days and we're staying up late to study, so better get back to it. I'll try to write more, if I can, but we study until well after midnight most nights—doesn't leave much time for anything else.

See you at Thanksgiving,
Gene

September 30, 1941

Dear Christy:

I figure I better drop you a line, or you'll probably skin me when I get home. Sorry I haven't written, yet, but they're keeping me awfully busy. College is going well, but I am getting worked pretty hard. My roommate is a really swell guy named Mike, from California, up above San Francisco. He's in electrical engineering, so we have most of our classes together and study together a lot. He's pretty good-looking, too. Maybe I should introduce you two.

Well, Christy, I've done it. I took my first flying lesson today. Seemed like we were never going to get to fly, with all the ground school we had to go through, first. But finally, today, I got to take my first flight.

Christy, I just can't describe what flying is like. I've always tried to imagine it, but couldn't. Flying the plane is more complicated than I thought it would be, at least at first. It's nothing like driving a car. I got so scrambled I felt like a total idiot, but the instructor was pretty patient and I began to catch on to it.

But the actual flying—being up there—is nearly impossible to describe. There is a sense of freedom, like you can go anywhere you want and not be stuck on some old dusty road. But it's a lot more than that, too.

For one thing, the world seems so huge, like you can see and go forever with no limits or boundaries. And everything on the ground seems so small that it's almost like make-believe. I was surprised at all the farm ponds. You can see dozens in any direction you look. They reflect like pieces of a broken mirror scattered all over the country.

I think the most unexpected feeling was how detached from the world you feel. I don't see how God can stay interested in us when we seem so irrelevant when viewed from on high.

When it was time to go back to the airport, I was shocked to realize I couldn't find Lawrence. It was so small from 3,000 feet and several miles away that it was just a dark clump on the horizon. I couldn't make out the campus buildings or anything. It makes me realize how limited my life has been. I want to get out and see more of this vast world I see from up there.

It's hard to believe. All my life I've dreamed of being a pilot. But it was always just that—a dream. Now, it feels like I'm waking up to discover that it's real. Yes, I know. I've only had one lesson. But now it feels real, and not just imaginary.

This letter writing is for the birds. I've taken far more time from studying than I can afford, but had to share it. Tell all the kids at school hi for me.

Your friend,
Gene

P.S. PLEASE don't tell the folks, or anyone else, about this. You know how everybody gossips down there. I know I've got to tell the folks, but I dread it. I know they won't get mad. They'll just be puzzled and hurt, and disappointed in me.

Pearl Harbor

A crystalline blue December sky, scrubbed clean by an earlier blizzard, gilded to amber then briefly reddened as the winter sun settled into its nest beyond the Neosho River, meandering its way through the hills of southeastern Kansas. Tall clumps of prairie grass, poking brown and lifeless from snowdrifts heaped in random sculptures along barbed wire fences, brightened to gold then blushed red in the setting sun. Gnarled wood fence posts and isolated trees, standing starkly naked in the icy cold, cast long, oblique shadows on red-tinted snow as the departing disk hesitated—much as a friend might linger on the porch step to say a last goodbye—then disappeared.

There was no sunset. All moisture had been wrung from the atmosphere to blanket fields frozen hard as the limestone rock which lay close below. Scarlet faded to purple and then to black, as the curtain was lowered to bring to a close this seventh day of December, just as December was drawing a close to the troubled year of 1941.

Winter darkness had settled quickly. By all appearances the frigid blackness, moderated only by faint starlight reflecting off snow-covered fields, had frozen the country into an alien world devoid of life. A silence so absolute as to be unnerving lay over the land. No dogs barked in the distance. No tractors droned lazily in the fields, no cars roared down dusty gravel roads.

Yet even as the stark blackness and frigid cold gripped the land, signs of life began to appear. On far horizons, dim yellow lights from isolated farms bravely refused to yield to the dark, lighthouses beckoning warmly from distant shores. Across shallow valleys, clusters of lights huddling mutely in the cold marked the presence of tiny rural towns. Faint lights, some white, some red, stretched like fake diamonds and rubies on a cheap necklace as a scattering of cars and trucks silently inched their way along snow-packed highway U.S. 54, cutting its way westward toward the great wheat plains.

At the crest of one of the small hills overlooking the Neosho valley, tucked into the intersection of two of the countless gravel roads that scribed the land into a checkerboard of one-mile squares, was the small farmstead that was home to the Stoddards. One road connected the farm to the town of

Colborn—the county seat, with a population of just over five thousand—two miles to the north. The intersecting road formed the northern boundary of the farmstead, and of the Stoddard farm.

A smallish wood-frame house and collection of outbuildings comprised the modest farmstead. Dominating the group, and isolated from the rest by a barbed wire fence that formed the cow lot, was a large milk barn with steeply gabled haymow filled to capacity during the summer with lush alfalfa hay. Opposite the barn, with roof sagging like the back of an aging mare, was the granary. Its grain, and the alfalfa hay stored in the barn, provided the necessary feed for the dairy herd during these winter months when pasture grass was dormant and covered with snow. Between the house and barn, and off to one side as though somehow offended and unwilling to associate with the others, was a small henhouse.

While not impressively built, the buildings were sufficient for their purpose. Made of locally milled rough-sawn lumber, they had been painted white some years ago and though now faded, still possessed a certain neatness of appearance. The buildings seemed lonely and isolated in the cold and darkness that now engulfed them.

At the front of the farmstead sat the small, white clapboard house that was home to the Stoddard family. During the spring and summer, peony bushes surrounded the house with bursts of color, but now they were shapeless brown clumps piled against the foundation. Spirea and lilac bushes had been planted in no particular order along the east-west road, and two sprawling cedar spreaders bracketed the entrance to a gravel drive that led past the house to a two-car garage at its rear. Three Dutch elm trees, two walnut trees, and a twenty-foot pole for the yard light completed the landscaping.

Light shining through frost-covered window panes beckoned from the warmth of the house to the barn, which returned the greeting through three small windows in the milk parlor. These, and a wispy column of white smoke drifting listlessly from a brick chimney into the black void overhead, lent the only signs of life to the scene.

Inside the closed-in back porch, Gene Stoddard finished buttoning a heavy, faded mackinaw over his flannel shirt and sweater, pulled the earflaps of his chore cap snugly over his ears, and donned wool gloves. Taking a stainless steel milk pail from the wash counter, he stepped out into the frigid blackness, shuddering involuntarily against the sudden shock of the cold. A waning gibbous moon would rise later in the evening and turn the landscape into a Courier & Ives painting, but at the moment, although not yet 6:00 PM, it might as well have been midnight.

Two days earlier a polar storm had plummeted down across the Canadian border, leaving the Dakotas and much of Nebraska paralyzed by five- and ten-foot snowdrifts and temperatures as low as thirty degrees below zero. Some of its fury had abated by the time it stabbed as far south as the Stoddard farm, but they had been buffeted by piercing winds and several inches of snow, piled mostly in drifts along fence lines and road ditches. The thermometer read five degrees below zero and was slowly falling in the darkness. Frozen snow squeaked gratingly beneath Gene's boots, sending goose bumps down his back as he trudged the path to the milk barn.

It had been a typical Sunday for the Stoddards. After the mandatory church attendance, several of Gene's aunts, uncles, and cousins had gathered at the Stoddard farm for Sunday dinner, followed by an afternoon of the uncles sitting around the parlor talking "men talk," while the ladies finished clearing the dishes and "gossiped." The youngsters were part of none of this, of course, as both they and the adults preferred their own worlds.

After a futile attempt at a snowball fight, with snow much too cold to make a decent snowball, Gene had entertained the kids by pulling a large, homemade sled around the pasture behind the tractor, occasionally whip-lashing it to send its riders flying into the snow. Having arrived home from college for the Thanksgiving break, Gene felt he had now graduated into the world of adulthood and would have preferred to stay and visit with the men. He wanted to hear them talk about the war in Europe, and whether they thought that America was soon be involved in it. He had protested, but the younger ones begged him to join them outside, and had won him over.

The other families, also being farmers, took their leave about four o'clock to get home and attend to their respective herds. Gene enjoyed farm life—indeed, as he had grown, he couldn't imagine having to be a "city kid."

But he hated, after having come inside and grown warm and sleepy by the large wood-burning stove in the living room, to have to bundle up again and face the cold and darkness to help feed and milk the dozen head of dairy cattle. He had quickly grown fond of not having to help with the milking, morning and night, once he left for college. But he would not have considered staying inside and leaving it to his brother and dad while he was home.

In spite of the bitter cold, Gene stopped midway to the barn to stare at the India ink bowl that was the sky overhead, gazing at stars that crackled with the brilliance of a distant arc-welder in the blackness. He had studied astronomy as a hobby while in high school, and was irresistibly drawn to the sky above. Standing rapt in frozen silence, clouds of vapor forming around him from his breath, he stared intently at the tiny pinpricks of whitish-blue that seemed so mystical. Tilting his head far backward, he watched as his slowly exhaled breath drifted upward, still finding it nearly impossible to believe that he could now be a part of that mysterious realm.

Gene had made attempts while growing up to share his sense of excitement about flying, but to little avail. Kansas farmers weren't much interested in impractical things such as airplanes, that didn't directly contribute to getting in crops or caring for the cattle.

"Dumb fool things just get you killed. No sir, if God meant for man to fly, he'd have given him wings."

Gene had detested that idiot cliché with all the passion of idealistic youth.

"I suppose," he would retort indignantly, "that also means if God meant for us to ride, He would have given us wheels instead of legs."

His antagonist usually would choose to miss the point, laugh at "such nonsense," and be on his way.

But Gene had been determined to not let such provincial thinking deter him. Someday, somehow, he would share the sky with Charles Lindberg and Wiley Post and Amelia Earhart—a fellow Kansan, from up in Atchison, he would proudly point out—and the other pioneering aviators who had explored the realm above, just as others had explored the land which had held him captive.

As he stood in the frigid Kansas darkness, staring into that beckoning universe above him, he could hardly believe that he had now broken free and joined his heroes in their sky—even if he was only a couple of weeks past his first solo flight.

Bitter cold soon broke the hypnotic spell cast on Gene by the scene above, and reminded him that his present duty lay at the barn. His dad, Bill, and younger brother, Jerry, were already there, each seated beside a cow, quietly relieving her of her lactose burden in steady, rhythmic motions. His dad looked up as Gene entered the barn.

"Decided to honor us with your presence, I see. Glad to have you," Gene's dad called over his shoulder, smiling as he greeted Gene in typical farmer fashion, masking anything so personal as a greeting behind a teasing insult.

"Yeah, you don't deserve it," Gene rejoined in kind, grinning at his dad, "but I decided I'd give you a hand out of the bountiful goodness of my heart."

Gene picked up a T-shaped milk stool made of two-by-four scraps, and parked himself beside one of the dozen Guernsey cows, milk pail clutched tightly between his legs. Though he had been absent for nearly three months, the art of milking, once learned, was never lost.

The barn was unheated, but body heat from the twelve cows, especially when seated next to one, made it seem quite comfortable compared to the cold outside. When it got this cold, the cows were kept in the barn overnight, and a thick layer of wheat straw had been placed on the concrete floor, providing a layer of insulation. The rhythmic "whoosh-whoosh" of warm milk being squirted into foamy pails, and the soft chewing of the cows as they consumed the piles of grain which had been fed them, combined to create a state of bucolic peacefulness. They all three soon fell silent as their minds drifted off to distant ports of call, the task of milking being a purely mechanical skill that demanded little of the intellect.

Minutes passed, the silence broken only by the background music of the Edmond Denny show from "WIBW, Topeka, Kansas, capital of the breadbasket of America," spilling forth from the little Sears & Roebuck four-tube Superheterodyne Silvertone radio. It was Gene's pride and joy, which he had purchased several years earlier from his share of milk money. He liked to say "superheterodyne silvertone." He had no idea what it meant, but liked the alliteration, the way it rolled off the tongue. He, more than any of the rest of the family, loved music and enjoyed the sense of being connected to the world outside, and his little white plastic-cased radio let him feel that.

During the Depression years there was no spare cash for frivolous indulgences such as gasoline to take vacation trips, and the farm and cattle could not be left unattended for even a full day. Thus, until he had moved to attend Kansas University up at Lawrence, Gene's world had been confined to a few square miles of rural Kansas. He knew little of what the rest of anywhere was like. But he read voraciously and had a vivid imagination. Geography was one of his favorite subjects in school, and he and his brother and sister would often make a game of calling out a strange city or country, and see which of the other two could find it first on the large world map he had hung on his bedroom wall.

While growing up he usually kept the little radio next to his bed. Late at night, he frequently listened to music from the station in Del Rio ("That's D-E-L-R-I-O, Del Rio, Tek-sus, broadcasting with 500,000 red-hot watts"). Its radio transmitter and huge antennas were just across the border in Mexico, where they were not controlled by U.S. government regulations, and probably exceeded a megawatt of transmitter power at times. It was a clear channel station that could be heard all the way to Canada.

There was little of interest to Gene on Sunday evenings so he had put forth no argument when his dad wanted to listen to the popular Irish tenor, paying little attention to the music. His mind returned to his first flight lessons and progressed to thoughts of being master of one of the amazing new airliners now being flown by the expanding airline companies. Of course, the Stearman pilot was also right—new, advanced fighters and bombers were being put into service as quickly as they could come off the drawing board and poured out of burgeoning production lines. Gene tried to imagine what flying one of those powerful aircraft would be like. The docile little PT-19 was still about all he could handle.

As his thoughts wandered, he began to be aware that the radio announcer was talking about something that sounded very serious. "…Surprise attack… Japanese bombers…Pearl Harbor…Oahu…thousands of soldiers and sailors killed and wounded…many ships sunk…"

"Dad, are you listening to the radio?"

Gene stopped milking, and moved closer to the small plastic set.

"Yeah. What's he talking about? What surprise attack?"

Bill and Jerry set down their pails, and joined Gene at the tiny radio that linked this small farm in rural Kansas to the smoldering ruins of what had, until that morning, been the pride of the United States Navy.

The announcer continued: "To summarize what we have thus far been able to learn from the various wire services, today, December 7, at approximately one PM Kansas time, the United States naval base at Pearl Harbor, on the island of Oahu in Hawaii, was attacked without warning or provocation by aircraft of the Japanese Imperial Navy. Enormous damage was inflicted on the base facilities, and many ships damaged or sunk. Total casualties are not known, but it is certain to be in the hundreds, if not thousands, of dead and wounded. No word was given on where the attacking aircraft came from, or how they got to a location so far from their home country. Stay tuned to WIBW. Additional details will be announced as soon as they are available. We now continue with the Edmund Denny program."

The older man, and his two sons, looked at each other in puzzlement as they tried to assimilate the meaning of what they had just heard.

"What are they talking about, Dad?" Jerry asked. "Where's Pearl Harbor? Gene, do you know?"

"Said it was in Wahoo," Bill responded, applying a farmer's take on the pronunciation of this strange-sounding place. "The radio said it's in Hawaii." Like all people in their circle, he called it "Hy-wah-yuh"—a fantasyland everyone said they were going to visit some day, but no one ever did. "Why would the Japs want to bomb a nice place like that? What did we ever do to them?"

Gene thought a moment, then asked, "If the attack started about one o'clock, I wonder why we didn't hear about it before now?"

"Well, we were all talkin' all afternoon. Didn't turn the radio on, as I recall," Bill answered.

"Yeah, but you would think someone would have called us," Gene countered, feeling somewhat annoyed and insulted that no one would have thought to alert them to such a momentous announcement.

"Could be the phone line's down from the storm," Bill replied, after considering it for a moment. "Haven't tried to use it for several days."

"Yeah, I suppose so," Gene agreed, still feeling a bit out of sorts about it all.

They stood there for a moment, staring at the little white radio as though it could somehow explain to them what to make of this news, or what it might mean. Bill shook his head, picked up his milk pail and stool, and went back to finish the cow he had been milking.

"Don't make no sense. Why would they want to go and do a thing like that?" he muttered, as he sat down beside the cow.

Gene and Jerry returned to their milking, without comment. After a couple of minutes, Jerry paused.

"Dad?"

"Yeah?"

"Does this mean that we'll be going to war?"

There was no answer but the sound of Mr. Denny singing the ever-popular "Danny Boy."

Gene had his head pressed into the cow's flank, watching without interest the foamy mound about to overflow the rim of his pail. He reflected on the words of the instructor at the flight school, and of the Stearman pilot he had talked to over a year ago. Airman Stoddard suspected that his college days were numbered.

"Gene! Gene, did you hear?"

Gene's attention was drawn immediately by the sound of the familiar female voice as he climbed the worn concrete stairs inside the main entrance of Colborn High School. He had decided to go in to his old alma mater to let some of his favorite teachers know how his first semester at KU was going. The news of the surprise attack at Pearl Harbor had also shaken him more than he wanted to admit, and he wanted to ask them about it.

Looking up the stairs to the main floor, Gene saw his friend, Christy, standing at the head of the stairs, waiting on him. Gene could normally count on her quick smile and friendly banter to cheer him up, but this morning she looked nervous and tense. Her arms were wrapped tightly around her textbooks, and she had not yet removed her heavy coat or the scarf from her coal black hair. Gene was not accustomed to this look. For a moment, he forgot about the ominous announcement of the day before and wondered if there had been an accident, or maybe trouble in the family.

Christy was of typical stock for that area, with a strong sense of independence and self-reliance. While seldom suffering fools gladly—or in any other fashion, for that matter—she was by nature friendly and extroverted, and a pleasant counterpoint to Gene's more introverted and private nature. Her parents belonged to the small church that Gene's parents had attended since their marriage. Gene attended a small country school while growing up, so they saw each other mostly at church. But they grew up feeling much like brother and sister. During high school, Gene had come to depend on her commonsense advice to help him sort out his various "socialization" issues. She was a year younger, and now a graduating senior.

"Gene! Did you hear about the attack?" Christy repeated, her voice rising as Gene's momentary hesitation prompted a more insistent demand, directly to the point. "We're going to war, Dad says."

"Hi, Christy," Gene greeted her. "Yeah, we heard it on the radio while we were milking, last night."

They began walking down the hallway to Christy's first class, making their way through knots of schoolmates. An unusual seriousness dampened the buzz of conversation among the various clusters of students, made even more evident by the absence of horseplay and loud banter normally present.

"Hey, Stoddard!"

Allen Murphy, who had played halfback on the football team with Gene, grabbed him from behind. "What brings you back to these hallowed halls? Thought you were at KU?"

"Hi, Allen," Gene greeted him, shaking hands with him. "Good to see you, again. Yeah, we got an extra week off for Thanksgiving break. I've got to go back Wednesday morning."

"You hear we're all goin' to war?" Allen nudged Gene playfully in the ribs. "You've shoveled enough cow manure you should feel right at home diggin' trenches. Me? Soon as I graduate, I'm headed straight for the Navy, just like my old man."

"Oh, get lost, Allen. I've got to talk to Gene." Christy shoved him away, not at all playfully, and turned again to Gene. Allen smiled, waving good-naturedly over his shoulder as he departed, and headed down the hall. Taking Gene's arm, Christy turned him toward her.

"Gene, what's happening? Can we really be going to war?" The look on her face left no doubt as to the concern, maybe even fear, that lay behind the question as she looked up at her friend. "What will you do? What about that pilot program you're in? Will you have to go?"

"Christy, I don't really know, for sure," Gene answered, sensing that this was not the time to be flippant, as he was often disposed to do with his feisty friend. "Like I told you, the agreement said we have to join the Army Air Forces in the event of a national crisis. But I don't know if that means they will immediately transfer us, or if we'll finish getting our license first. I don't know if we're actually at war. Our phone line was knocked down in the blizzard, so we haven't been able to call anyone. Dad won't say much, and Mom's mostly trying to keep from looking worried in front of us kids. What have you heard?"

Before she could reply, the class bell intruded noisily on their conversation. Christy turned to enter her classroom.

"I have study hall after second period. Can you meet me at the library?"

"I'm going to see if Mr. Caldwell is free, and visit a bit—and President Roosevelt is supposed to address the nation on the radio later this morning. I'm going back to the house to listen. Can you meet me at the drugstore after school?"

She nodded, and entered her classroom. Gene went up the stairs to Mr. Caldwell's physics class on the third floor, but he wasn't there. After wandering the halls a few minutes, feeling strangely out of place considering that he had spent most of his last three years in this building, he went back to his car and headed home.

Shortly before the announced time, Gene and his family gathered around the big Zenith in the living room. Gene tuned it to WIBW and carefully adjusted its green iridescent "Bull's Eye" tuning indicator to get the best signal. They listened in stunned silence as President Roosevelt declared that December 7, 1941, was a day that would live in infamy, and asked that the Congress declare that from that day forward the United States of America and the nation of Japan were in a state of war. When the broadcast ended, Gene's dad, looking somber and ashen, walked silently out of the house, jaw muscles clenching and unclenching, while his mom tried unsuccessfully to hide the sobbing behind her apron.

That afternoon, Gene drove into town to the drugstore to meet Christy. He was at a booth at the back of the drugstore when she came in, arms full of books. Gene glanced up as she unloaded the stack of books on the booth table, and plopped into the seat opposite him.

"Hi. Quite a load you have there," Gene greeted her, nodding toward the stack of books.

"Don't I know it," she agreed, sounding rather overwhelmed. "I've got several tests next week and, as usual, I'm way behind. As you well know, I tend to put off studying 'til the last minute."

She glanced around the drugstore, looking to see who all might be there. It was surprisingly empty.

"Seems strange to be here without Larry. I haven't seen him. Was he in town? Did you get to see him?" Christy asked, still looking around.

Larry Hoskins was a close friend of the two of them, and they had spent many hours together at the drugstore cutting up and telling jokes. He had graduated with Gene, but had gone to an out-of-state university back east.

"No," Gene replied, "I called his folks last week. They said he couldn't make it back—it was just too far, for the time he had. I'd like to see him, again. I don't know, now, what may become of us all."

Gene's comment brought Christy back to the present.

"How are your folks taking it? Mine are still sort of in shock."

"Mom's pretty rattled," Gene agreed. "You know Dad. Wouldn't say anything. Just went outside after the president's speech. Hasn't said a word to me, directly, about it."

She reached over and began to pick at imaginary lint on the sleeve of his sweater. Gene was well familiar with the signs of when something was especially troubling her.

"Okay. What is it?"

Christy smiled, recognizing how well her friend understood her, then turned serious again.

"I'm really worried, Gene," she admitted. "What's going to happen to you? Surely there's some way you can stay in college until you graduate. Do you think you'll be drafted? Some of the guys are talking about dropping out of school and enlisting. They're such idiots."

"Well, it's like I said this morning. I won't know anything official until I get back up to KU. But that's not my biggest problem, right now at least."

Warning bells went off in Christy's mind. She knew that embarrassed look too well.

"Okay, Gene. What's going on?"

He glanced around the drugstore, as if to see if any one might be eavesdropping. He wasn't sure why—force of habit, probably. The Stoddard family was not disposed toward airing its laundry—dirty or otherwise—in public. But there was only one other couple in a booth nearby, and they were obviously too interested in each other to notice anyone else. The clerk behind the counter was busy, and paying no attention to anyone. Still, Gene dropped his voice.

"Well, the problem is, I still haven't said anything to the folks, and—"

"Gene Stoddard," Christy cut him off, with an explosion of indignation. "You are such a coward! When did you plan to do it—or were you going to make me do it after you left?"

"I don't know, Christy," Gene replied, his frustration not quite masking his chagrin. "They're just so hard for me to talk to."

"Oh, Gene, everybody's hard for you to talk to," Christy rebutted. "What are you going to tell them? You surely have some idea of what will happen to you, don't you?"

"I don't know what to tell them," Gene replied, rather defensively. "That's the problem. It doesn't matter what I tell them—they're not going to like it. Besides, none of this had happened before I left. Our instructors told us at the start they thought we could be at war before we finished the program. Looks like they were right. They've been training us just like we're already in the Air Force. They said this program was the same as the Air Force primary training. I'm about half way through, so I'm guessing that they'll have us finish the course—we'd have to some place. Technically, I'm still a civilian. I assume after I finish, they'll transfer me into the Air Force and ship me off for basic and advanced training. After I get my wings, who knows? Looks like we're going to be at war with both Germany and Japan. I could go to either side of the globe."

"Good God!" Christy exhaled quietly, blanching as this possibility flooded over her. "What is this country getting into?" she asked no one in particular. "What have you got yourself into?" she asked Gene, a strong hint of accusation in her voice.

"Oh, I'll be all right," Gene said, attempting to reassure her. "You know me, I'm no daredevil. I'll be careful. And I know I should have told the folks sooner, but I didn't want to upset them."

"Well, you blew that one, big boy," Christy retorted. "I suppose you think they'll feel great about it, now?"

"I know. But Christy, great heavens, be realistic." Gene was becoming more fervent than Christy had seen before. He was typically rather quiet, relying more on logic and understatement than animation when he was talking. "America's been attacked! You heard the news. They killed two or three thousand of our soldiers and sailors in a dirty sneak attack. They sank practically every battleship we had out there. It makes your blood boil. No one I know is willing to stand for it. Our fathers, our grandfathers, every man of every generation has fought for our country when they had to. Now it's my turn. Guys my age have a patriotic duty—and moral duty, I might add—to serve our country when it's been attacked." Gene paused, realizing he was probably starting to sound overly zealous.

"I suppose you're right…but it still doesn't make it any easier to accept," Christy said, shaking her head in resignation.

"Besides," Gene continued, "I'll turn nineteen in six months. You think the military is going to let a healthy nineteen-year-old lolly-gag around in college while the rest of them are being shipped off to fight?"

Christy nodded silently, looking out the drugstore windows at the large elm trees in the courthouse lawn across the street, wondering what the coming months would hold. It was clear that her last year in high school would not end the way she had always imagined. Gene waited for a response, but it became obvious there would be none. He leaned forward, arms crossed on the booth table.

"Look at this from my perspective. Those battleships weren't sunk by other ships—they were sunk by planes from aircraft carriers. There are more new types of planes being designed and built right now than even I could have dreamed of a few years ago. There are fighters like the new P-51 that are more powerful and faster than anything that's ever existed, and the B-17 bomber looks bigger than Colborn. This war may be fought on the ground and on the sea, but it's going to be won in the air."

Christy looked at him, seeing a person she had never seen before. His eyes sparkled with an excitement she rarely saw him exhibit, and knew the inevitability of what he was saying.

"Christy, look…I've always wanted to fly. You know that. I've told you enough times. I've got to be honest with you. Forget duty. Forget patriotism. Even if I didn't feel those things, there is nothing—and I mean nothing—that can keep me from getting to be a part of the greatest aviation and flying opportunities in history. I know Mom and Dad will be disappointed and upset with me, and I'm sorry about that. But I'm not going to miss out on being a part of the most exciting flying to ever be possible…come hell or high water. And, assuming I survive it all, it'll virtually guarantee that I can get into the airlines when I get back."

He slid out of the booth and stood, a little taken aback and embarrassed by his emotional outburst. Christy offered no comment, no recognition of his intense desire to be a part of the exciting new world of combat aviation. He waited a moment longer for her to respond, then changed the subject.

"I have to get back up to KU Wednesday morning. I presume they'll tell us more when we get there. I'm going to have to tell Dad—tomorrow, I guess. Unless you want to tell him for me." He grinned at her, nodding hopefully.

"Fat chance," Christy retorted. "Do your own dirty work. You got yourself into this fix."

"Yeah, I know. Worth a try, though," Gene teased, laughing awkwardly, unsure how he should end the conversation. "Well, I'd best be going. I probably won't get to see you again before I leave."

She nodded. He started to leave, but she reached out and took his hand, holding him back. Her face, usually crackling with orneriness and radiating enthusiasm, was surprisingly blank.

"Gene, be careful. I mean…well, you moron, you know what I mean. Just be careful."

"I will, Christy. You know me that well," he assured her. "I dread it, but I guess it's time to face confession with Dad. I'll let you know when I know something. Behave yourself."

The blizzard of a few days earlier had drifted snow over a portion of the pasture fence, straining and loosening some of the barbed wires. When the snow melted, the cows could probably get over the wires and into the adjoining fields. With Gene available for one more afternoon to help, his dad had decided to try to repair the damage. They put snow chains on the pickup, tossed in the necessary tools and started on the task as soon as the noon meal was finished. It was now mid-afternoon and the job nearly done.

"Pull 'em a little tighter. It's still too loose," Gene said to his dad, while leaning against a fence post cut years ago from a nearby line of Osage Orange trees. The farmers called them hedge trees, because they had been planted in rows around fields to serve as fences. The wood was supple and exceedingly strong when green, but turned iron-hard and virtually impermeable when dry. Farmers used them as an unending supply of rot-free fence posts. Gene's left arm was draped loosely around the post, hammer at the ready in his right hand. He was waiting for one last tug on the block and tackle wire stretchers. When satisfied, he pounded the fencing staple in, then tested each of the three wires with a gloved hand.

"That should keep 'em…at least for a little while," Gene concluded.

His dad removed the stretchers, tossed them into the pickup bed, and leaned against it, looking across the rolling fields. He was like many of the farmers in that area, standing just under six feet tall, strong but not muscularly built, thickened from years of eating more fried meat, mashed potatoes, and numerous desserts than his constant hard work could burn off. Of mostly German heritage, he was firm—"bull-headed" was the usual term applied to it—but not overbearing, cordial but not affable, and given to strongly held convictions he was largely incapable of expressing in any manner other than through time-worn clichés and Bible verses.

He cared deeply for his family, but was pathologically incapable of allowing those feelings to be expressed or to be seen in public—or private. His parents had seen little value in an education beyond the eighth grade, as there was little use for it on a farm in those generations. This lack of education left him feeling vaguely embarrassed and inferior, even though he was an intrinsically intelligent person.

If at home on the farm, it was a rare day for him to be seen in anything but faded bib overalls, with the top side-button undone, summer or winter, whereas his standard blue cotton work shirt was buttoned at both the wrists and collar—summer or winter.

His forehead rarely saw the light of day, always protected by an ever-present cap or hat, and was white as a baby's bottom. It stood in stark contrast to the remainder of his face which was permanently tanned and weathered by constant exposure to the sun and wind, and looked more like leather horse harness than skin. He removed his hammer from its loop on the side of his overalls, and tossed it in the pickup. Then, forearms resting on the pickup bed, he addressed his son without turning to face him.

"Gene, you have any idea where you stand on the list?" he asked, his face not quite masking his concern over what the answer to this unexpected question would be.

"List? What list?" Gene asked, obviously puzzled.

"You know, the draft board list," Bill answered, awkwardly shuffling his feet. "Are you going to be able to stay in college, at least for awhile?"

"Actually, I have no idea," Gene responded, not yet willing to admit that for him, at least, the "list" was irrelevant. "I had to register when I turned eighteen, of course, but I haven't asked about it since. I have no idea where I am on it."

Gene tossed his tools into the pickup bed and crawled into the driver's seat, evading the second part of the question. He had started driving the truck and tractor when he was so short that he had to sit on the edge of the seat in order to push in the clutch pedal. Bill was now quite willing to concede his right to the driver's seat, and slid into the passenger side. They began to slowly grind their way across the snow-covered pasture. Bill was not of the opinion that Gene's answer, or lack of answer, offered either information or reassurance.

As the pick-up crept through the snow toward the barn lot, Gene looked out the side window at their dairy herd staring disinterestedly back at them as they passed. He wondered if he would ever again assist in helping with calving, or any of the many other farm duties. He then turned back, staring straight ahead. The time had come. He could put it off no longer.

"Dad, you know I've always been crazy about planes."

There was no real need for that preliminary. Gene's bedroom ceiling was covered with model airplanes he had made since he was in grade school. His dad was well aware that at every opportunity Gene would ride his bike down to the county airport, but had no idea what Gene did when he went to the airport and never asked. Gene's parents could never understand his interest, and mostly ignored it on the assumption that it would all go away when he grew up.

Bill glanced briefly at Gene's tanned face, his brown hair rumpled from his cap, which Gene had removed when he got in the pickup. He realized there was beginning to be a lot more man in that face than the boy he always enjoyed seeing. Gene looked at him, waiting for a reaction to his unexpected comment.

"Yeah, that's for sure," Bill finally replied. "Never did understand what you see in the tomfool things, but couldn't much miss the fact you liked 'em. Why?"

Gene stared intently ahead, mustering his courage.

"Well, I know how much you and Mom are counting on me getting a job with some big company. And I know you're proud that I'm getting an engineering degree. But, Dad, all I've ever really wanted was to fly, and to be an airline pilot. I had no way of knowing how, I just knew I wanted to do it—more than anything else there is."

Gene glanced sidelong to see if his dad was registering any reaction, but he was as inscrutable as he had been to Gene all his life, so he forged ahead.

"Well, last summer, a pilot I met at the airport told me about a program where the government would pay for flight lessons while you go to college. It's called the Civilian Pilot Training Program. The government pays for your flying lessons while you go to college. That's the real reason I switched and went to KU—they've got the program, and K-State doesn't. I joined it when I went up to enroll. I had planned on getting my pilot license while getting my engineering degree, then trying to get on with an airline. If I couldn't, then I would go ahead and go into an engineering job. I'm already about half way through to my pilot's license."

During this confessional, Gene's father made no comment, registered no expression, staring straight ahead as though he had never seen the outbuildings of his farm before. Gene glanced at him again, waiting for some sort of response. Bill shook his head slightly, his brows furrowed, his face making the shock of Gene's announcement obvious. He removed his cap, ran his fingers through brown hair that was now largely gray. It was a nervous habit that Gene knew well.

"I don't understand, Gene. Why on earth would you want to throw away a college education on something as impractical and dangerous as flying one of those airplanes?"

"Dangerous? Did you give up farming when Claude Toland got killed when his tractor flipped over on him? Or when Mr. Tucker got his head kicked in by one of his horses? Farming is one of the most dangerous things you can do. Haven't seen you quit because of it," Gene challenged, his voice rising in anger.

"Well, I gotta admit, this pretty much comes from out of the wild blue yonder."

If Gene's father recognized, or accepted, the validity of Gene's accusation it wasn't apparent, and Gene was in no mood to point out the unintended pun.

"Your mother and me just took you at your word. We didn't understand why you decided to go up to KU, but figured you knew what you were doing. Course, that scholarship helped a lot. I don't reckon we could have done much for you. It's going to be pretty hard on your mother. She's always counted on you getting a college education, and getting a good job."

Gene struggled to control the anger welling up from deep within him, knuckles turning white on the pickup steering wheel, born of years of frustration and disappointment at the love of his life being ignored, or worse yet, ridiculed. It required several deep breaths to calm himself enough to respond.

"Dad, I know I should have told you and Mom earlier." The words came out clipped and flat. "But blast it! I knew this would be your reaction. Instead of ever trying to understand me—or, God forbid, even support me—I knew you'd just be upset and disappointed. So I did what Stoddards always do, and kept my mouth shut. I don't know if you've always been a farmer because you wanted to, or because you felt you didn't have a choice. But I have a choice, and what I choose is to be an airline pilot. And dadgummit! It would help if you'd actually listen to what I'm saying. I didn't say I was dropping out of college. I said I would still get my engineering degree. So if my lifetime dream falls through, I'll go be an engineer until I die, if that'll make you both happy. But what I would really like is for you and Mom to at least try to understand how much flying has always meant to me, and try to support me a little instead of constantly belittling it."

Were it not for the muffled sound of the truck engine, and the whining of transmission gears, it would likely have been possible to hear the heavy breathing as Gene attempted to get his temper back under control. Talking to his father on this subject—or much of any subject, for that matter—had always felt to Gene much the same as when he had to use their heavy, iron crowbar to pile-drive his way through thick layers of limestone rock when setting fence posts. Except that in the case of setting fence posts, Gene at least was able to make some discernible progress.

William Stoddard was a man of few words in the best of circumstances, and these were not the best of circumstances. He had no perspective from which to know how to respond to his son. He had never heard his son react so emotionally, and especially not to him. It had never occurred to either him or Gene's mother how much flying had actually meant to Gene. They had always assumed it would be no different than a boy having a dream of playing baseball for the New York Yankees—a childhood fantasy that would evaporate when he grew up and had to face the real world. But Gene had never been the type to confront his father, and Bill was totally unprepared for Gene's outburst.

Bill realized that the person sitting next to him may have still been his son, but he was no longer his little boy. Indeed, he was now a grown man who was going to be making his own decisions, whether his parents approved or not. As hard as the shock of Gene's announcement was to accept, somewhere beneath it all Bill felt a sense of pride in the young-boy-turning-man that was his son. He had been a good boy, and Bill knew he would be a good man. And good men knew their minds and made their own decisions. But turning loose of a son was not an easy thing for a father to do. Somehow, Bill knew that it was now time to turn loose, and to support Gene in what he wanted for his life. But how he was to respond to Gene, and how he was to tell Mary, were still unsolvable mysteries to him.

In the remaining few minutes required for them to reach the granary where the pickup was kept, Bill had not yet been able to respond. He got out and pulled the sliding door open. Gene drove in, switched off the engine and got out, slamming the pickup door behind him. He stepped out of the shed, and Bill pulled the shed door shut. They started walking toward the house in grim silence. Gene glanced at his dad, at a face still as indecipherable to Gene as the hieroglyphs of a Pharaoh's tomb.

"Dad, look. When I enrolled at KU all I could think about was that I was finally going to have a chance to get to fly. I have to admit, I didn't give much thought to anything other than the fact that the government would pay for flying lessons—and I certainly didn't count on us going to war. As part of that program you have to agree to join the Army Air Forces in time of national emergency. I guess that's pretty much now."

His father, stone-faced, remained silent, walking alongside as Gene struggled to throw enough words together to break through the mental and emotional brick wall that seemed to him to be his father's mindset.

"Dad, whether we like it or not, we're at war. You know as well as I do that all us guys are going to get called up. I want to fly. I've always wanted to fly. If you'd been paying any attention all these years you would have known that. And I for darn sure don't want to get stuck being cannon fodder in the army, or buried in the engine room of some ship. If I have to be in a war—and you and I both know that I will—I want it to be in a plane. You know good and well that if I wasn't already in, I'd be drafted before my next birthday."

They were at the back porch door. Bill stopped and looked at Gene, started to speak, then hesitated. He reached for the handle of the screen door, then dropped his hand to his side. Gene looked at him, searching the passive, weathered face for some sign of understanding, then continued.

"I'm not sure what will happen now. I imagine they will have me finish my training at KU—that'll probably take another month, six weeks at most, depending on the weather—then send me on for further flight training after that. I promise you that I'll finish getting my engineering degree when it's over. But you might as well get used to the fact that I plan to be an airline pilot, if there is any way possible."

Gene stopped talking, realizing that he had said all that could be said. He stood at the back steps, waiting.

When the silence had become almost more than Gene could bear, Bill turned to him, took a deep breath and let out a sigh of acceptance—or perhaps resignation.

"Well, Gene, you know what the Good Book says."

"What's that?" Gene asked, baffled. That his dad would refer to the Bible was not unexpected, but that the Bible might have something to say about his flying career, was.

"Well, Isaiah said it," Bill continued. "'They shall mount up with wings like eagles...'"

Gene, surprised, smiled and completed the verse.

"'They shall run and not be weary, they shall walk and not faint.' Yeah, Dad, I'm going to mount up with wings like an eagle—already have, as a matter of fact. Maybe you and Mom will let me take you up, some day." His dad smiled weakly at the teasing, but didn't reply.

Gene had no idea whether this suggested acceptance and support, or simply resignation, from his inarticulate father—but he did know it was all he could reasonably hope for.

"Should I tell Mom, or do you want to?"

"She'll probably take it better coming from you," Bill replied, carefully studying his boots. "But I'll tell her, if you want me to." He dreaded having to break the news to his wife, and the effect it would have on her, whoever might tell her.

"No, I'll do it," Gene volunteered. "Not much looking forward to it, though," he added, pulling the screen door open and pausing to let his dad enter first. As Bill opened the porch door and started to enter, Gene laid a hand on his shoulder. Surprised, Bill turned to look at him.

"Dad...sorry I blew up at you."

Bill nodded silently, and continued on into the house.

As Gene pulled off his winter coat and boots, he tried to figure when and how to break the news to his mother. By living on a farm during the Depression, there was usually not much concern over having sufficient food, but cash was another problem. Though his mother had perennially "put on a happy face" for the sake of the kids, she had grown weary of "never having two dimes to rub together," as folks complained frequently, and of always having to scrimp to find money to buy shoes, clothes, and all the other needs of a growing family. It had exhausted her physically and drained her emotionally—she couldn't imagine her own children having to live such a life.

She had been ecstatic when Gene started to college. It was her constant dream come true—even if she was uncomfortable with him going to that "citified" school at KU. At least he wouldn't have to spend his life the same way she had. And although she had no idea what an engineering person did to earn a living, at least he would be able to get a well-paying, secure job with a big company—and he had given up talk of airplanes. Throwing a secure future away in one of those dangerous machines would fall somewhere between insanity and suicide, in her assessment. And Gene...in a war? The thought was incomprehensible.

To Gene's surprise, she had not yet washed the dishes after the noon meal so he volunteered to help her, while Bill took a nap on the living room sofa.

Gene tried to approach the subject by mentioning that a lot of the guys he knew were already starting to enlist to beat the draft, then tried to explain how he had got into the CPTP and was going to be a pilot, and how much better that would be than being in the Army. She listened in silence as he stumbled along, trying to finds words that would make some sense to her. None of them did.

But she loved her son, and he had hugged her and promised that he would not take unnecessary risks, and that after the war he would finish his degree and if the flying didn't work out he could still get a job with a big company. She had put on her happy face, hugged him back and wished him well. He thanked her for listening and understanding him, and went in to the living room and turned on the radio to see if there might be more news about the war. She went into her bedroom, closed the door, and cried her heart out.

Gene returned to KU the next day. The flight school administrators were now under pressure from the government to accelerate his group through to graduation, and had them flying every minute the weather was even remotely acceptable. The open cockpit of the PT-19 was frigid in the winter air, even with the heavy wool flight suits issued by the school, but the flying continued as long as visibility and cloud conditions were above minimum acceptable.

They were not permitted the full Christmas break of the KU schedule. Gene came back home the day before Christmas, and returned two days later. He was gaining confidence as a pilot, and was beginning to look forward to moving on to the more sophisticated Vultee BT-13, which would be used when he advanced to Basic training.

On Friday, January 16, 1942, Gene was congratulated by his CPTP Squadron Commander, and handed the simple government document that declared that Mr. Eugene Stoddard was approved to exercise the privileges of a civilian pilot. Because of the pressing need for new pilots, he was given orders to proceed to Kansas City, Missouri, on January 21, 1942, where he would be inducted into the United States Army Air Forces. From there he was to report for duty at Randolph Air Base, San Antonio, Texas, on or before January 26, 1942, to begin basic flight training. His friend, Mike Kingston, received an identical certificate and set of orders.

There was no chance that Mike could have gone to his home in California for the brief Christmas break, so he had accepted Gene's invitation to enjoy Christmas with the Stoddard family. Mike enjoyed meeting them all, and quickly became a willing foil for Christy's repartee. After the graduation from CPTP, it was obvious once again that he would be unable to go home in the brief time available, so spent the few days visiting Colborn, and the Stoddards, with Gene. On January 24, they said their goodbyes, and boarded the train for San Antonio, Texas, and a future that none of them could even attempt to imagine.

As winter turned to spring, news from the foreign fields around the globe where war was raging continued to be dismal. Hitler's forces had long since occupied France and the Netherlands, and were moving into most of the remainder of Europe and North Africa. Britain was holding on, but had avoided invasion only because Hitler had made the most critical mistake in judgment possible, and had invaded Russia.

In the Pacific, General MacArthur's forces had been driven out of the Philippines, to take refuge in Australia. Bataan and Corregidor in the Philippines had fallen, as the apparently invincible Japanese juggernaut occupied ever-expanding portions of the Pacific, virtually at will. United States military forces showed no more capability to stop the armed forces of the Rising Sun in the Southwest Pacific than could the farmers stop the rising sun in Kansas.

The days following the news of the Pearl Harbor attack passed in a blurred juxtaposition. Christmas was approaching and people made a show of attempting to retain a normal life, preparing food for Christmas dinners, wrapping gifts and decorating trees, smiling as children dressed in bathrobes kept watch o'er their flocks by night and angels with wings held on by bands of elastic tape watched over the doll in the manger wrapped in swaddling clothes.

Yet while all smiled and offered a "Merry Christmas," few added the traditional "and a Happy New Year." Every facet of normal life was being knocked akimbo by events and battles occurring at locales that even Gene's high school geography teacher had trouble locating on the classroom wall maps. People whose lives were predicated on the predictability of the seasons, whose sense of time was set by breakfast, dinner and supper, and the rising and setting of the sun, were left to wonder if the next season would see their sons working in the cornfields, or dying on the battlefields.

In April, there was exciting news of a daring bombing raid by General Doolittle and some of his pilots. Doolittle had trained sixteen crews to fly fully loaded B-25 bombers from the deck of an aircraft carrier. The planes had been loaded onto the U.S.S. *Hornet,* and secretly set sail for Japan. They were inadvertently discovered by a Japanese surveillance ship before the fleet could reach its intended launching point. The enemy ship was quickly sunk, but Doolittle had to assume that a radio message of warning had been sent out. He and his B-25s were therefore forced to launch several hundred miles prematurely for their targets in Japan.

All the planes arrived and bombed several Japanese cities. The planes had insufficient fuel to return, and were incapable of landing on an aircraft carrier anyway, so the crews continued on to try to find pre-selected friendly fields in China. Although some of the planes crash-landed, most of the crews survived and eventually returned to the United States to rejoin their units.

The raid was an enormous psychological boost to the citizenry of the United States, and although little actual damage was done by the handful of bombs, it was an equally large shock to the Japanese. Their military leaders had assured the Japanese citizens that the Kamikaze, the "Divine Wind" that had spared Japan from attack by Kublai Khan nearly seven centuries earlier would now protect them from attack by the Americans. Japanese cities could never be bombed, they had arrogantly claimed, and the blow to their credibility was palpable and worth the price in men and planes. But little else in the news was of any encouragement as the Japanese continued to wreak havoc in the Pacific.

Basic Training

Randolph Field
San Antonio, Texas

Dear Christy:

Hard to believe it's been over two weeks since Mike and I headed for Texas. Sorry I haven't written, but we finally got some free time so figured I'd better get some letters off.

Basic training is going pretty well. We'll be here for ten to twelve weeks, and then we go on to Advanced Training. We're flying the Vultee BT-13. It's bigger than the one we flew at KU, and has a much more powerful engine. The cockpit is enclosed, which is a blessing. Everybody calls it the "Vultee Vibrator." It does seem to be well named.

Mike and I both had a little trouble getting used to sleeping in a barn (they call it a barracks, but barn is more accurate) with about sixty other guys. At first, I had an overwhelming feeling of having lost all identity as an individual. I suppose that is really the point—to make you feel a part of your squadron. Every bed is precisely the same as every other bed, with identical footlockers, towels, clothes, etc. Every bed has to be made exactly as ordered, and everything folded just so.

I couldn't sleep very well at first because there are so many strange noises from guys snoring, snuffing, talking in their sleep, coughing, etc. But I'm getting used to it. I found out that the guy that snores in the bunk next to me is from Alabama and is allergic to something here that keeps him real stuffy. And the guy across from my bed that seemed real stuck up is from Wichita, and had gone to KU. When he found out I was from Kansas and went to KU he really loosened up. Turns out he's just real shy and doesn't make friends very well—sort of like me, right? Mike met a guy from close to his hometown in California. So, day by day, it becomes home, and the noises turn into people who turn into friends.

Randolph Field is one of the most impressive, and beautiful, places I've ever seen (I know, I've never been anywhere, but it's still amazing). The main administration building is so elegant that it's referred to as the Taj Mahal. It is all built of white stone, or brick of some sort, with graceful covered walkways and arched entries, giving it a cool, peaceful appearance. A center tower, in the shape of a hexagon, rises up out of the main building at least six stories, with a domed top sort of like a state capitol building. It's very ornate, with sections of red tile roofing. Some of the guys here say Randolph is called the "West Point of the air," because it is so classy looking

We get our first passes next weekend, and a bunch of us are going into San Antonio. Did you know this is where the famous Alamo is located? I remember the expression "Remember the Alamo," but none of its story. I'll see what I can find out. I'm going to try to find some picture post cards while we're in town. I'll try to get some of the base and the Alamo and anything else that looks interesting.

I've written a short letter to the folks, but please share this letter with them. I don't have time to write another one like this. Take care of everyone up home for me—I do miss all of you.

Gene

March 15, 1942
Colborn, Kansas

Dear Gene,

Thanks for the newsy letter. Sounds like Randolph is quite the place. I'm glad training is going well for you. Not too much to report, from here. The war is beginning to seem more real and closer to home. Had you heard that Tommy Roberts was killed during the Pearl Harbor attack? He was on the battleship Arizona, and was trapped inside when it got hit. Their whole family is taking it pretty hard. The church has been taking food to them. I saw the pictures of the attack on the Movietone news, and cried through the whole thing. It was horrible—just makes you sick. Don't know if I told you—I've been dating his brother, John, but he just got his notice to report to Ft. Riley in two weeks.

They have already begun rationing gasoline and tires. The guys that run the milk routes are really upset because they can't get tires for their trucks. We had a practice air raid drill last night. Dad is one of the air raid wardens that have to walk the streets to make sure no lights can be seen during the black-out. I feel much safer now from any Japanese air raids on our little burg here in Kansas. Sorry—it just seems a bit silly. A couple of the guys dropped out of high school to enlist. Can't see why they couldn't have waited a few more months and graduated first. Seems rather stupid to me. You remember the dress factory down on West Street?

They're going to be making uniforms. I've applied for a job after school and on Saturdays. Sounds like they are going to pay fairly well.

I've got to cut this short. I'm writing in the library. Mrs. Miller says to tell you hi. I talked to Liz awhile this morning. She said they got a letter from you a couple of days ago, but I gave her mine, like you asked. She says your folks are doing okay. Jerry's able to take on a lot more of the work, now that he's growing up. He's getting to be quite the good-looking guy—takes after his big brother. You take care of yourself, and remember what you promised me about being careful up there. I forgot to tell you, before. You created quite the stir at church when the word got out that you had started flying. Really had the grapevine buzzing.

Will write more later.
Christy

March 29, 1942
Randolph

Dear Christy:

Thanks for the letter. Sorry to hear about Tommy. He was two or three classes ahead of me so I didn't know him very well, but he seemed like a swell guy. I was surprised to hear about the rationing—I didn't know they had started that already. You're right. The blackouts do sound pretty silly. Glad to hear the folks are doing OK. Do you get to see them much? Mom writes me once or twice a week, but it's all just how the cows are calving, and what have you. She would never tell me if there were any problems because they wouldn't want me to worry about them. Liz adds some to Mom's letters, and writes me some of her own, but she's busy in school and doesn't get to write much. I did get a letter from Jerry, last week. Glad to hear he is able to help Dad, now. I'm worried that Dad won't be able to handle all the work, especially as Jerry gets busier in high school. Sounds like he might be getting into the dating game, too, from what you say.

I know they worry about me. Please tell them that I really am doing fine. I wish they could understand how exciting the flying is to me, so maybe they wouldn't be so afraid for me. I'd like to be able to share how much I love it. I'm a little embarrassed to say it, but I have to be honest—I'm having the time of my life.

Flying the plane has really become second nature, just like driving the truck or tractor. Most of our practice now is in operational problems— cross-country navigation, night flying, and stuff like that. We've begun formation flying, and aerobatics. I'll tell you more about flying upside down, later.

We've begun doing quite a bit of night flying. It was really intimidating (all right, it sort of scared me) the first few times, but I'm getting used to it. It's so dark over the desert that you can't see the ground— there's just black above and black below. Your altimeter tells you that the earth is one mile below you, but you look out and there is nothing there.

It took a while to get used to the night landings. All you can see is the double row of tiny lights that outline the runway. The runway itself is so dark you can't see it. The lights appear to just be hanging in space, and their shape is your only real perspective—but your mind and senses don't want to believe it because the lights just float out there. I'm getting used to it now, and it doesn't bother me so much.

I found some pretty good picture post cards of San Antonio and the Alamo, as well as Randolph Air Field. I mailed a set to the folks, so you can keep these. Mike says to tell you Hi.

Gene

April 20, 1942

Dear Christy,

Well, we are now well into aerobatic training to make us capable of flying right side up or upside down, and to teach us all the air combat maneuvers. It is also supposed to make us so familiar with every trick of our aircraft that there's no situation we couldn't cope with. At least that's what they tell us.

We started with spins. They sort of scared me, at first. In order to spin an aircraft, you must do several things wrong in just the right way. The airplane rewards this mistreatment by plunging nose first towards the ground and spinning rapidly as it descends. I've done enough of them now that I'm getting used to them—actually, they're beginning to be fun.

The other aerobatics, I really enjoy—especially loops. We dive to pick up speed, then haul back on the stick. You sink into the seat, since you pull more than three times your weight as you start up, seeing nothing but sky. Your stomach falls and your cheeks sag. As you come over the top you're upside down—the sky is where the ground is supposed to be, and you have to look far back over your head to see the ground beginning to come over into view. As you come over the top you are diving at the ground, but pull out level at the bottom. Sounds a little weird, but still a lot of fun.

We've also been spending a lot of time practicing flying on instruments. Missions have to go regardless of weather, so we have to learn to fly in anything. A plane simply cannot be flown in clouds, or with no visual reference, except with the aid of instruments. Enter a cloud, and think you are flying straight and level, and within thirty seconds you will be in a "graveyard spiral" as they call it, plunging toward the ground in a rapidly tightening spin and not even know it. So, we have to learn to fly with only our instruments to keep us safe.

You have to train yourself to ignore your senses and believe what the instruments are telling you. It's strange, but I'm finding that in many ways I enjoy the instrument flying the most. I suppose it's just my personality. I like the mental and technical challenges of it all.

Christy, if someone had told me last year that by the time I turned nineteen I would be flying all over the country, day or night, in the clear or in the clouds, doing aerobatics, flying formation with other planes only a few feet from my wing, I would have thought they were crazy—or that I was dreaming. I still have to pinch myself sometimes to believe it's all real. I know that what the guys that are in the fighting are going through is nothing to look forward to, but it is a job that must be done and I'm proud to be a part of it. Until then, I'm going to enjoy every minute that I'm allowed to fly.

Take care,
Gene

April 24, 1942

Dear Gene,

So—your idea of being careful is to fly upside down, spinning into the ground, with another airplane just a few feet off your wing tip!!

Sorry, had to rib you just a little. Sounds like you're having the time of your life. I'm thrilled for you. The hardware store on the square burned down last night. No one knows what started it, but lots of people turned out to watch, even at 4:00 AM (I wasn't one of them—I try never to get out of bed in the dark). I got the job at the dress factory. We're making army field jackets. Makes me feel good to be doing something to help win this atrocious war. I volunteered to head up the War Bond sales committee for our part of town. We're supposed to have our first meeting next Tuesday, and will find out what our sales quota is to be. Maybe I can help buy you a new airplane, for when you get your Wings.

I talked with Liz a while this morning. She said it hit your mom pretty hard when they found out about Tommy Roberts. She knows his folks pretty well, but I think it mostly makes her think about you. But you know your mom—she never lets it show. She just smiles, and goes on with cooking and cleaning.

I've got to head for work. Keep the letters coming. I really miss you. School just seems so empty, and pointless, now. And it's certainly no fun, without my buddy here to talk to. I know it's fun, but be careful up there.

Christy

April 27, 1942

Dear Christy:

Sorry to hear about Mom. I know they think I would somehow be safer if I wasn't flying, but look what happened to Tommy. Mom and Dad just don't seem to be able to accept that there's really no safe place in a war. It would be nice to get to visit with you again, but I have to say that I don't miss high school one little bit. I'm exactly where I want to be, doing what I most want to do—don't take that too personally.

Well, basic training is rapidly coming to a close. Next week we have to make a choice as to whether we want to stay in single engine planes and go into fighters, or go into the multi-engine bombers. Everybody thinks that to be a real pilot you have to fly fighters. And I'll admit that they are pretty tempting. The new P-51 and the twin-engine P-38 are beyond description. It would be something to get to be in one of those, doing loops and Cuban eights and all that.

We're not being trained to put on an air show—we're going to be in combat. And I'm frankly not sure my personality is suited to being a fighter pilot. You know me—I never was a daredevil. I think Mike wants to go for the fighters, and it will be hard to not get to stay with him. We have become really good friends through all this. I'm not sure what I'll do.

Tell the family hi for me. I try to write them at least once a week, but I can't think of much to say—just the usual "I'm fine, how are you" sort of stuff. Makes me a little embarrassed at myself, but we Stoddards were never much for family chit-chat, as you know. If you would like, you can share these letters with Sis, and she can decide how much to tell the folks.

Take care,
Gene

Gene and Mike both enjoyed flying the Vultee Valiant, the BT-13 basic trainer, although it had gained the unflattering nickname of "Vultee Vibrator" because of vibrations that were common in it during flights. It was larger than the PT-19 they had flown in the CPTP training, with a 450 horsepower radial engine, but the two looked similar and handled much the same. Gene and Mike easily mastered the more challenging flight maneuvers and grew to enjoy the aerobatic training. Gene was growing more confident in his cross-country navigation and night flying skills.

An aircraft simulator, developed by Link Corporation, allowed the pilots to train for instrument flying without actually getting in an airplane. Sitting atop a pedestal, the small toy-like airplane in which the pilots sat simulated the motion of a real airplane, moved by air bellows adapted from pipe organs. A hatch-like cover was closed over the pilot to shut him off from outside visual references. Real aircraft instruments in the toy plane let the pilot learn the fundamentals of instrument flying as it pitched and turned in response to the pilot inside moving his stick and rudders. Gene and Mike spent hours sweating in the blue boxes, developing their skills until they were second nature.

With each actual flight, they became more precise, more in total command of their craft. They began flying in formation, in groups of four to six, learning to move as one, connected to the lead aircraft through the combined skill and finesse of each of the pilots. After each flight, they would talk about it, feeling themselves turning into skilled pilots and developing a bond of comradeship. As the end of the ten week basic training period approached, they realized that a decision would soon be required that would determine how they were to experience their personal version of war.

Gene and Mike had both finished grueling sessions on the Link instrument trainer earlier in the afternoon, and were sitting in the enlisted men's club trying to unwind. Mike was enjoying a cold beer, but Gene had not yet overcome his teetotaler upbringing and was having a Coke. They had picked up on an on-going conversation which had occupied much of their spare time, but which seemed no nearer now to a resolution than when it had begun.

"How can you call yourself a real pilot, and not want to get into fighters?" Mike again challenged. "Have you seen pictures of the new Mustang? I have wet-dreams over flying a plane like that."

Gene grinned at his friend's crudeness. He had grown up in an environment in which the strongest expletives ever heard were "dadgummit," or "heck" and "golly." He was most uncomfortable with swearing of any form. But, he had long since grown numb to the non-stop profanity and talk of sex that dominated the conversation of all the guys around him.

"If you think you'd be such a hot-shot flying around behind one engine, imagine what it would be like with double that," Gene countered. "You do realize that the new B-26 has a total of nearly four thousand horsepower, and a top speed of three hundred?"

"Well, hell, Stoddard. If all you want to do is to get to your target real fast, drop a bomb, and get home real fast, I guess that would be a pretty good deal. Man, that's not flying, that's just high-speed delivery service. Sort of like dropping a firecracker under the milk wagon horses," Mike teased.

"Yeah, you're right. I admit it. I get weak-kneed just thinking about what it would be like to fly a fighter like the P-51. But, confound it, Mike, I have to be honest with myself—I'm just not fighter pilot material."

Mike's raised eyebrows made his reaction to Gene's confession obvious. It was not one he had heard from his friend before.

"What do you mean?" Mike asked. "You can fly as well as anybody I've seen around here." Mike emptied the glass of beer, walked to the bar for a refill, and came back to the table. As he sat down, Gene answered his question.

"I'm not talking about flying skill, I'm talking about me—my personality. Look at some of these guys around here. They're crazies—certified lunatics. I think they'd fly into a whole swarm of enemy fighters single-handed before bothering to think about what they'd do when they got there. They're the idiots that start bar fights, then look around and wonder where all their friends have gone."

"No doubt about it," Mike agreed, laughing at the image. "And you're not like that, I assume is your point."

"You kidding?" Gene scoffed. "Look at me. I drive tractors. I do my homework. I think too much. I analyze and evaluate. While those guys would be ripping into anything they could find and have half of them shot down, some Kraut would be on my tail and blow me to Kingdom Come while I was still trying to analyze the optimum attack strategy. I have to face it. I'm a bomber pilot. I would never survive as a fighter pilot. And, don't forget—my dream has always been to get a job with the airlines. Bombers will give me the experience I need. Flying fighters won't do that. Bombers would be best for me, any way you slice it."

Mike took a long drink from his newly filled glass, wiped the foam off his mouth, and began to chuckle at his friend.

"Gene, you're probably the most perceptive person I've ever known. I can't think of anybody I know who would analyze himself like that. But, truth be told, you're also the most honest person I've ever known. And you're right. You're not fighter pilot material, but you'll make a hell of a bomber pilot."

"I'll take that as a compliment, I guess," Gene replied. "I had hoped we would be able to stick together after we get our wings, but I'd hate to see you lose out on fighters." Gene finished his Coke and set the empty bottle back on the table. Mike took another drink from his beer, set the glass on the table and looked seriously at his friend.

"Well, buddy," Mike said, leaning back on his chair, "I don't know how much attention you've paid to your old roomie, but in case you hadn't noticed I'm not much different from you. I've never been able to see myself as a fighter pilot. And, in case you forgot, I'm also planning on a career with the airlines." He paused a moment, letting his comments register, grinning at the surprised look on his friend's face. "I've just been stringing you along, wondering when you were ever going to come to your senses and recognize that we're a lot alike."

Advanced Training

Lubbock Army Air Field
Lubbock, TX

Dear Christy:

Well, a lot has happened since I was last able to write. Mike really surprised me by letting me know that he's just like me, and couldn't see going into fighters. We both want to fly for an airline when we get out, and bombers will give us experience with multi-engine planes like the airlines will fly. We were accepted for multi-engine training and have both been assigned to Lubbock Army Air Field for Advanced Training. We got here late last week.

Lubbock, and the airfield here, are the complete opposites of everything at San Antonio and Randolph. Lubbock is way out in the so-called High Plains of West Texas, nearly up into the panhandle part of the state. It's easy to see why it's called the High Plains. Surprisingly, the elevation out here is over three thousand feet above sea level. And "Plains" doesn't do it justice, as the land is flat, barren, treeless and desolate—except for the lush farms! I couldn't believe it when we first began to fly around here. The land is basically just scrubby wasteland. But, scattered all over that wasteland, like big throw rugs tossed around the countryside, are cotton fields and sorghum fields everywhere you look. And they are unbelievably lush and green. Apparently, there is an underground water table, and lots of irrigation is done using engine-driven pumps to pull water up to water the fields. They have far better crops out here in this desert than we ever grow at home.

Much to my surprise, Lubbock is a lot bigger than Lawrence, with a population of over fifty thousand. It seems to be a booming town, from what little of it we've seen. The airfield itself doesn't amount to much— it's only been open about a year. There's just a paved runway, with a bunch of wood frame administration buildings, barracks, etc., built nearby. I'm glad we will be busy flying all the time, because ten weeks would otherwise seem like ten years, out here.

We are flying a twin-engine trainer plane built by Cessna in Wichita, would you believe. It is officially the AT-17 Bobcat, but we all call it the Bamboo Bomber because quite a bit of it is made from wood to save aluminum for the real bombers. It's easy to fly, and we are spending a lot of time learning how to drop bombs (makes the war begin to seem more real, somehow), fly bombing formations, and so on. I met a bombardier, a farm kid from Illinois by the name of Ollie Olsen, who's been helping in our bombing training. He's a really swell guy. It's been fun comparing stories with him about the differences between growing up on a farm in Illinois, and in Kansas.

There's always a lot to learn, and as always yet another test to pass. But, in a few more weeks we graduate and get our wings. I'm really beginning to have to pinch myself to see if it is actually happening to this farm boy from Kansas.

Love to all
Gene

                                                    Lubbock Army Air Field
                                                         Lubbock, Texas

Dear Christy:

My dream has officially come true! I'm a pilot in the Army Air Forces, with wings proudly clipped to my uniform!! I am also an officer in the United States Army Air Forces. I wish you and all the family could have been here to see our graduation exercise. For once, we were able to march like we were proud to do so. All the guys looked so straight and proud and "military-ish." I wish I could say something more profound, but I'm still getting used to the fact that something I've dreamed of since I was a kid has come true. I hope Mom and Dad are as proud of me, and as thrilled for me, as I am. Somehow, I still feel like I'm letting them down.

Mike and I had a friend take several pictures of us, and the ceremony. I'll send them along when he gets them developed. There is a studio in town, where I had an official portrait taken in my uniform, with Wings attached. I've sent a framed 8X10 to the folks. They should get it soon. Got to admit—the kid looks pretty handsome, all decked out in his uniform.

Mike and I have both been assigned to B-26 Transition School at MacDill Air Base in Tampa, Florida. I have no idea what to expect that *area to be like. Certainly it will not be like Lubbock, Texas. All I know about Florida is that they grow a lot of oranges.*

I'm relieved that Mike and I are getting to stick together. We are both excited about getting the B-26. It is one of the hottest new twin-engine bombers to come out. I can't imagine what it will be like to fly something so powerful and fast. But we're growing more confident of our skills as pilots every day, and look forward to finally being able to put all this training to use against our enemies, wherever that turns out to be.

We get some leave before we have to report to MacDill, but I don't see how I can work in a trip home. Mike and I wondered about getting up to see all of you again, but we're afraid we'll barely have enough time to make the trip clear down to Florida.

Love to all,

Your PILOT friend
2nd Lieutenant Gene Stoddard

Colborn, Kansas

Dear 2nd Lt. Stoddard!!

I can hardly believe it's true, that you are officially a pilot already. I'm so thrilled for you. Your folks got your picture a couple of days ago. They worry about you, but are so proud of you!! Your mom just beamed when she looked at your picture. She put it on the china cabinet, in front of everyone else. Jerry wanted to take it to school, but she wouldn't let him. She was afraid it would get damaged. They took one of the snapshots you included and had it put in the paper. I'll send a copy along, if they don't beat me to it.

So you're going to sunny Florida? I can hardly believe all that you're getting to see. Makes me wish I could join up, too. Maybe I need to volunteer in that new women's pilot group, the WASPs, that I've been reading about.

Don't suppose you'll get this until you are in Florida. Let us know your new address as soon as you can. And I repeat myself: be careful up there.

We miss you,
Christy

In 1939, within the United States military it was becoming clear that America could not indefinitely avoid involvement as the threat of war spread across the globe. These military men, who would be responsible for taking America to war when it came, recognized that in its present unprepared military state the results would be appalling. This circumstance was nowhere more true than in its deplorable lack of modern air power.

Congress was also beginning to acknowledge this weakness, and began to make funds available to develop truly modern aircraft. In March 1940 the Army Air Corps solicited proposals from aircraft manufacturers for development of a new medium bomber. The specifications called for a twin-engine bomber far advanced beyond any that existed at that time.

Among the aircraft manufacturers that responded to this request was Martin Aircraft Company, of Baltimore, Maryland. Their design called for a radically different aircraft that would incorporate many design and fabrication features never before tried in an operational aircraft. Its two engines would be the most powerful then available, the new Pratt and Whitney Double Wasp, each capable of nearly two thousand horsepower. These engines would be the first to use four-bladed propellers, nearly fourteen feet in diameter.

But the single most dramatic departure from conventional design, the feature that gave the plane its ultimate edge and the one that nearly doomed it, was the use of a significantly shorter wing than was typical of conventional designs. The shorter wing would permit the plane to fly faster, but also resulted in a plane more demanding to fly.

This innovative new aircraft design was rated highest of all designs submitted to the Air Force, and an order was placed for nearly two hundred, sight unseen. The new bomber was to be designated the B-26, and known as the Martin Marauder. Orders for more followed close behind, before the first model even flew. In preparation for the introduction of the B-26 into operational status, two training bases were established. One of these was at MacDill Airbase, at Tampa Bay in Florida.

In 1941, very few military pilots had any significant multi-engine training, and none whatsoever in a plane as advanced and demanding as the B-26. By the end of 1941 and continuing through 1942 a series of fatal training accidents nearly doomed the plane.

As crashes mounted, unflattering nicknames such as "The Baltimore Whore" (because of its place of manufacture, and the fact that the radical short wing gave it "no visible means of support"), the "Martin Murderer," the "Flying Coffin" and the "Widow Maker" soon came to be used for the aircraft, making it obvious what most pilots thought of the plane.

At the heart of the problem was its fundamental design. When the two powerful engines with their huge propellers were performing together as a team, the plane was a speeding gazelle. But if one engine were to fail, the pilot was instantly presented with the problem of having two thousand horsepower on one wing charging forward, and on the other a massive, powerless propeller acting as a huge airbrake, dragging that wing backward. The speeding gazelle rapidly metamorphosed into a thrashing, bucking bull.

If the pilot immediately recognized which engine had failed and dealt with it properly, the plane would fly quite manageably and safely. Conversely, any failure on the part of the pilot to quickly, and properly, respond would result in the plane rapidly rolling inverted. Upside down and out of control, usually at low altitude when taking off or landing, a fatal crash was a virtual certainty.

Adding to this problem was the higher than normal landing speed dictated by the short wing. Pilots were simply not accustomed to landing a plane at such high speed, and would frequently let the airspeed drop to an unsafe level. With little warning, the plane would stall, with too little altitude to recover. Also, if an engine failed at such low speed there would be insufficient capability from the controls to counteract the forces trying to roll the plane upside down. Let the plane stall, or an engine fail, at such low speed and low altitude, and the pilot was writing his own death certificate.

As crashes and fatalities mounted, Congress held hearings and production was nearly brought to a halt. Accusations were hurled and defenses mounted. In the face of this conflict two factors emerged to save the plane. First, trained factory and military pilots demonstrated that proper flight techniques could easily manage any engine emergency. Second, by late 1942 the B-26 was in constant use in the Southwest Pacific. Its crews had very low accident rates and praised it highly as a combat aircraft. The crews out there, woefully short of modern aircraft, were begging for all of them they could get. And to a nation at war, success in combat was the ultimate criteria. Production of the plane continued without interruption throughout the war.

It was into this cauldron of conflict and distrust—even irrational fear—of the aircraft that Second Lieutenants Gene Stoddard and Mike Kingston found themselves being thrust as they arrived their first day at MacDill Airbase, Tampa Bay, Florida, to report for transition training in the B-26 Marauder.

B-26 Training

MacDill Air Base
Tampa, Florida

On their second day at MacDill Airbase, after they had reported for duty and found their bunks in the barracks, Gene Stoddard and Mike Kingston walked out to the flight line to see, for their first time, the B-26 Marauder—the twin-engine medium bomber that was to take them to their version of global war. They walked slowly around one of the planes, pausing, looking, touching, wondering about this inanimate object that was the source of so many fearful rumors and nicknames, founded and unfounded.

"Mike, this thing's huge. I knew it would be big, but good grief—I just never imagined it would be this big," Gene exclaimed quietly, almost as though he was afraid of waking the sleeping giant. "This propeller's nearly as tall as our house."

Mike nodded in silence, looking up at one of the engines. He walked under it, past the main gear wheel that came to his waist, inspected the open wheel well, and walked back to stand beside the propeller.

"You know, Gene, this engine alone seems bigger than the Bamboo Bomber. And these Pratt and Whitneys are rated at two thousand horsepower each. You realize, that's nearly ten times the power of those Jacobs we've been flying behind? Lord-a-mighty, would you look at that thing!"

He ran a hand up the knife-edge of one of the propeller blades, glancing upward at the massive engine attached to it. They stood staring with open-mouthed awe up into the mechanical wizardry that was the engine installation.

The hatch to the pilot compartment was open, so they climbed inside and installed themselves in the pilot and copilot seats. A utilitarian control wheel projected outward from the instrument panel in front of each seat. Gene and Mike, somewhat reflexively, each placed a tentative hand on their control wheel.

They scanned the instrument panel, the myriad knobs and handles and switches scattered around and about, looking for those items they had become familiar with in their prior training. All the usual instruments were about where they expected them to be—flight instruments, engine instruments, those things essential to flight and engine operation. But on a console between the two seats, and scattered elsewhere in the cockpit, were knobs and levers and wheels and buttons of every type and description; red knobs, black knobs, white ones, serrated ones for gripping, all giving an overall impression of overwhelming complexity, far beyond anything they had thus far experienced in any of the planes they had flown.

Gene and Mike were mostly silent, each placing their feet on rudder pedals, touching a control knob here and there, gripping it, moving it slightly, as though somehow trying on a new piece of clothing, testing the fit and function, wondering all the while about the persistent rumors of crashes and of an aircraft too difficult to fly to be safe—and wondering how much of it all might be true.

Gene glanced out the side window at the huge engine and propeller, whose blades seemed to come right into the cockpit.

"Man, those props look even bigger from in here. Think we're men enough to handle this 'Martin Murderer'?"

Mike was still testing the controls, as though trying to get acquainted, trying to imagine the effect of each, once the aircraft had come to life. He ignored Gene's joking—if it was a joke.

"I think I'm falling in love. God-a-mighty, Gene, I can hardly wait to fly this thing."

Gene was silent for a moment. "It should be interesting, that's for sure."

Their training was intense. In sixty days, they were expected to transition from being greenhorn graduates, still somewhat in awe of the pilot's wings pinned on their uniforms, to combat-ready B-26 pilots capable of handling this challenging aircraft, heavily loaded with bombs and fuel, on any mission assigned to them.

It was assumed by their instructors that when they arrived at MacDill Airbase the new pilots knew how to fly a twin-engine airplane. What they now had to master was flying a highly complex, challenging aircraft under the most difficult weather conditions, while being attacked by enemy ground fire and fighter planes, and do so with one engine shot out, a wounded crew member, and barely enough fuel to make the return flight to their base. There would be no "routine" training flights. Every departure from the airbase was an exercise in emergency conditions, a challenge to stretch and test the skills of the would-be B-26 combat pilots.

Gene and Mike were nearing the end of the transition training. As Mike had suggested the first time they saw the plane, he had fallen in love with it and was progressing rapidly. Gene, somewhat to his surprise, seemed more challenged by the plane. He generally flew it well, and was also making adequate progress, but was not as comfortable with it as Mike obviously was becoming.

The flight this particular day had involved low-level bombing-run practice. Gene believed he had handled it well enough, and was generally pleased with how it had gone. He was emotionally drained from the non-stop challenges presented by his instructor, who seemed to stay in a perennially sour mood. But they were now in the landing pattern, about to land—the flight would soon be over, and Gene was looking forward to getting a cold Coke and relaxing.

As he rolled the B-26 level on a short final, Gene had just completed the pre-landing checklist. His attention was focused on the approaching runway, judging if his altitude was correct for a safe approach to landing. Without warning, his attention was snatched back to his aircraft as an engine suddenly shut down, yawing the nose hard to the left as the right wing started up.

Engine out! Gene knew he had to respond quickly, and not let the aircraft get further out of control. But he was drained from the stress of the day's flight. His mind was too tired to respond properly. Before he could think about what he was doing, he over-reacted and shoved on the left rudder pedal. Instantly, the horizon spun toward the vertical. They were quickly rolling inverted.

"DAMMIT, STODDARD!" The instructor screamed at Gene in disbelief, as he jerked back on the right throttle, shutting down the right engine to eliminate the unbalanced power on the wings. "YOU TRYING TO KILL US?"

Gene's mind had recognized, even as his left foot was moving downward, that he was making a critical mistake. But when confronted with danger the body often instinctively reacts before the mind can assimilate what is confronting it—reflex action takes control. At some subconscious level, probably seeded into the genetic structure by millennia of fighting for survival, the mind tells the body "right or wrong, don't just stand there—do something."

His foot had continued downward even as his rational mind was screaming *"No, stop! That's the wrong rudder,"* and was sending out corrective signals. Belatedly, reason gained dominance over reflex.

Gene slammed his right foot on the other rudder pedal, correcting his mistake, as he twisted hard on the control wheel in an attempt to recover. As the plane came back to level flight, the instructor shoved full throttle on both engines and Gene pulled back on the control wheel to regain the lost altitude. The entire episode was over in seconds. The red-faced instructor glared at him in open-mouthed disbelief and anger.

Gene remained silent, his heart pounding, as he got the airspeed and altitude back under control and crossed over the runway threshold to an uneventful touchdown. As he rolled off the runway, he shook his head. Nothing more was said as Gene parked the aircraft and started shutting down the engines. The instructor climbed out before the propellers had stopped spinning, leaving Gene to complete the shutdown. When Gene exited the aircraft, the instructor was standing near the nose, waiting for him, tightly-fisted hands on both hips. If his face was less red, it wasn't obvious.

"WHAT THE SHIT WAS THAT ALL ABOUT?" the instructor exploded, in a bellow that drew the attention of every member of every crew of the other bombers parked nearby.

"I don't know what happened. I just shoved the wrong rudder pedal before I realized what I was doing. It'll never happen again, sir."

His instructor was still fuming mad.

"You're damned right it'll never happen again," he vented, "because the next time you'll kill yourself and everybody else on board! In the first place, do you know why I chopped the power on you?"

Gene was puzzled. "I assumed it was a loss-of-engine-on-final exercise, sir."

The instructor shoved his face, still red with fury, within inches of Gene's, his tightly clenched fists still on his hips.

"Damn it, Stoddard, it was a keep-making-this-same-dumb-ass-mistake-and-you'll-be-a-smoking-hole-in-the-ground-exercise, was what it was," he blasted. "Do you know what your airspeed was when I pulled the power?"

"Uh, not for sure, sir. It was 135 to 140 when I looked as I turned final," Gene said, hesitantly.

"What's minimum single-engine control speed for this aircraft?"

"One thirty, sir."

"And why do we maintain 130 on final?"

"So we can maintain control if an engine fails. That's why I was trying to maintain about 135, to have a little margin." Gene still looked puzzled.

"Well, disregarding the fact that you pushed the wrong damned rudder pedal and would have killed yourself anyway, your airspeed when I pulled the power was 125 and falling. Are you not aware that it's government policy that you're supposed to die in this war because of hostile action—not suicide? You let your airspeed fall off like that in this aircraft and you're a dead man flying to his grave. You copy, lieutenant?" The instructor glared, his red face still inches from Gene's pale one. Gene nodded, avoiding eye contact.

"YOU COPY, LIEUTENANT?"

Gene visibly jumped.

"SIR! YES, SIR!"

Gene wiped his sweating hands on his pants legs, trying to keep them from shaking. The instructor turned on a heel and stalked away, leaving Gene standing there, humiliated and wishing for a hole large enough to crawl into. The other crews watched for a moment, then assumed the show was over and turned to their own affairs. Gene finished the checklist, then walked in silence back to the debriefing room, staring at the pavement.

He assumed the instructor would be waiting for him, ready to take a few more pounds out of what remained of his confidence—and his rear-end. He also fully expected that he had just flown his last flight for the U.S. Army Air Forces.

Fortunately, for Gene, no one was present when he went in to change out of his flight suit. He doubted he would have been able to face any of the other pilots after the embarrassing dressing down he had just received. He quickly showered, dressed and headed for the Officers Club, where he expected he would find his friend, Mike.

Indeed, as Gene entered the darkened room and let his eyes adjust from the brightness of the sun, he saw Mike at a table near the bar. Mike was drinking a beer. A cold bottle of Coke, already opened, was awaiting him. Gene took a long drink, pulled out the chair, and sat down.

"Looks like you were expecting me."

"I thought you might be in the mood for a little friendly chit-chat," Mike agreed.

"My reputation precedes me, I take it. The jungle drums must have been busy. What were they saying?" Gene took another long drink from his Coke, set the bottle down and looked at his friend for a response.

"Oh, I just heard that your instructor seems to think you are a mite hard of hearing, so had to speak up a bit on the flight line. What happened?" Mike leaned back on his chair, waiting.

"Which part do you want to hear about?" Gene asked, obviously agitated. "The part where I let my airspeed bleed off to where we were being passed by tractors? Or the part where I rammed in the wrong rudder when he jerked an engine to make an ass of me, and nearly flipped us inverted?" Gene shook his head in obvious disbelief at himself.

"Wow! All that on one flight?" Mike teased, trying to lighten his friend's mood.

Gene leaned back in his chair, twirling his Coke bottle, the day's experience playing and replaying in his mind.

"Mike, I damn near killed us up there today," Gene admitted, still staring at the bottle, unable to look his friend in the eye. "You know as well as I do how screw-ups like that usually end up on the Twenty-Six. By all rights, I should be feedin' the fish at the bottom of Tampa Bay, now. What the hell happened to me?"

MacDill Airbase was constructed on a small peninsula jutting into Tampa Bay. The primary runway extended close to water's edge and any unfortunate incident often resulted in the plane plunging into the bay—hence, the unkind criticism of "One a day in Tampa Bay" that soon came to be applied to the B-26.

Gene stared at his friend, wondering what it must have felt like to those unfortunate pilots who failed to recover from their mistakes as they plunged into the bay. Did the crash kill them? Were they trapped in the plane, and drowned? However it occurred, what had seconds earlier been a young, vibrant life eager to live to a ripe old age now lay at the bottom of the bay. Mike was silent for a moment, studying the face of his friend.

"Well, I can't say, for sure," Mike intoned, rubbing his chin thoughtfully, "but it's obvious that it's a lot more serious than I realized."

Gene was blank. "What do you mean? How much more serious can it be?"

"Because that's the first time I've ever heard you cuss. Twice! It must be bad," Mike replied, grinning impishly.

Gene rolled his eyes, knowing that he'd been had by his friend.

"Well, never mind that. How can I avoid it with all the swearing heathens I have to live around? Anyway, am I to assume you are making light of my great fiasco?"

"Well, not really," Mike countered. "Look, Gene. I know it was serious— and I know that a bunch of guys didn't live to be kidded about it. But I do think you have to keep some perspective. So this all started when you let your airspeed drop, and your diabolical instructor decides to teach you a lesson, right?"

Gene nodded affirmatively. "The reason he pulled the engine on me, he said, was because I had let my speed drop nearly to one twenty. I could hardly believe him. I would have sworn I was keeping it above one thirty all the time. I know it was over 135 when I turned final."

"You can lose airspeed awfully fast in that thing, once you get gear and flaps down, that's for sure. You really have to watch it. Anyway, after he pulled the engine, you started to do what we're trained to do and put in opposite rudder to stop the roll. But in your haste you over reacted and shoved in the wrong rudder. What did you do, after that?"

Gene shook his head, still somewhat in disbelief himself, at what had transpired.

"I knew before I had the rudder all the way in that I'd screwed up, but couldn't seem to stop myself in time. So, I immediately slammed the other rudder in and cranked the ailerons into the locks to roll us back level—he had already pulled the power off the other engine. I knew we'd lost a lot of airspeed so I kept the nose down. Then when we rolled out level, he shoved the throttles in, and I got the nose back up to regain the altitude I lost. I came on in and landed. Why? What would you have done?"

"So—if I understand you correctly," Mike said, ignoring his question, "you made a mistake, immediately recognized it, then did exactly the right things to correct for it, with no serious consequences. Correct?"

"Well, yeah, I suppose you could look at it that way," Gene replied, looking a bit taken aback. "Didn't seem to impress the instructor much, though. I doubt his face is back to normal color yet, after that ass-chewing he gave me."

"Aw, Gene, don't let it rattle you," Mike countered, attempting to prop up his friend's ego. "Look. We all make mistakes. I almost did the same thing the other day. Only difference was I caught myself just as I was starting to push the wrong rudder, so nobody noticed. The important thing is that you didn't panic, recovered, and kept control of your plane. The ones that crash don't do that."

Gene finished his Coke and set the bottle on the table. "I suppose you're right. But it sure rattled me. Not sure I'm over it, to tell the truth." Gene held both hands out in front of him, palms down. "Look at that—I'm still shaking."

Mike nodded, looking at Gene's trembling hands.

"Gene, listen. The Twenty-Six is a hell of a lot of airplane—and we're still green pilots. We're going to screw up, sometimes. I will say, though, that you just can't let it get ahead of you—and it'll do that damn fast. You could make about any kind of mistake possible in that tugboat Bamboo Bomber we flew, and it was no big deal. The Twenty-Six is totally unforgiving. Anyway, just try to learn from it, and don't make the same mistake twice. You'll be okay."

Gene nodded. "Yeah, I guess. Just hope the instructor sees it that way. I'm not sure he'll sign off on my transition, after today."

"Oh, you'll make it. Don't sweat it. The Army needs combat pilots, and you're a good one. They're not going to wash out a promising bomber pilot over one mistake that you handled correctly." Mike decided it was time to change the subject. "You know, we only have about two more weeks of this fun and games. Heard any scuttlebutt on where we might be assigned?"

Gene was relieved to have the conversation ended, and was happy to jump to answer Mike's question.

"Not really. But from what I'm reading, the Twenty-Second Bomb Group seems to be doing most of the B-26 operations. Ever hear of a place called New Guinea? That's where they're operating."

"New Guinea? Where the hell's that? Or maybe I should ask, what the hell's that?"

"Actually, they're both pretty good questions. As you're well aware, by now, geography was one of my favorite subjects. I went to the PX a few days ago and got a map—which I just happen to have with me in my flight bag." Gene opened his bag, pulled out a map of the Southwest Pacific and spread it on the table.

"Good Lord. Leave it to Joe College to have a map," Mike kidded, starting to try to find something he recognized on the map. Gene pointed to a large land mass shown in the blue of the southern Pacific Ocean.

"Here's Australia. New Guinea is this humongous island above it. According to the encyclopedia, it's the second biggest island in the world—it's close to fifteen hundred miles long. Right now, the Twenty-Second is based at a spot called Iron Range, up here on the far northern tip of Australia. Problem is, they can't reach their targets from there so they have to refuel in New Guinea, at a base called Port Moresby. It's here, on the southern side of New Guinea."

Gene pointed to the location on the map. Mike looked it over, trying unsuccessfully to find anything that he remembered from high school geography. Unlike Gene, it was not his favorite subject. Gene spread his thumb and finger to span the distance between the two locations, then compared it to the mileage scale on the side of the map.

"It looks like it's three or four hundred miles from Iron Range. They fly to Moresby, refuel, then fly several hundred miles to their target, and back, then refuel again at Port Moresby, and finally back to Iron Range. Each mission takes about three days—the guys are really pooped when they get back."

Mike looked dubious. "What sorts of missions do you fly from some God-forsaken island? Bombing head hunters? I thought we would be fighting the Japs. Where the hell's Japan?"

Gene pointed to a group of small islands at the top of the map.

"Japan's clear up here, several thousand miles north."

"You mean that little dab of islands is Japan? That's who's kicking our butts all over the Pacific?" Mike asked in astonishment.

"Good grief, Mike. Did you sleep through every geography class you took? Yes, that's Japan. And yes, the Twenty-Second is fighting Japs. The Japanese army and naval forces control all these islands between their homeland and New Guinea. See all these areas here, the Philippines, Indonesia, Sumatra, Leyte, New Britain—the Solomon Island chain, down here?"

Mike nodded as Gene pointed out the various landmasses and islands scattered across the map from Asia to Australia.

"Judas Priest, Gene. You mean they own all that stuff?" Mike asked.

"Well, they don't own it, but they now occupy most of it. Japanese forces have invaded pretty much all of this part of the Pacific, as well as the northern part of Papua and New Guinea. They have air and naval bases established all over all those places," Gene informed his disbelieving friend.

"See this big mountain range, here, that runs down the middle of New Guinea," Gene continued, pointing to a range shown on the map that bisected the island. "It's the Owen-Stanley range. They're nearly as big as the Rockies—around twelve to fourteen thousand feet, I believe. The Japanese are trying to push their army across those mountains to get to Port Moresby. If Moresby falls, they'll have a port and air base they can use to attack Australia, so it's pretty strategic. The Twenty-Second is supporting the defense against that attack."

Mike looked at the map more closely. "Call me crazy, but it looks like if they had any sense they would just borrow a few of those carriers that wiped us out at Pearl and come driving up to the port and take it. What's to stop them? We don't have anything out there to stop them, do we?"

"Good thinking. Maybe you will make general," Gene said, smiling at him. "But they've already tried that. You remember when we were in Basic we heard about a big carrier battle, called the Battle of the Coral Sea? We sank one of their carriers, and they got the *Lexington*?"

Mike nodded in recognition. "So that's what that battle was all about? Port Moresby?"

"Right. The Coral Sea is this part between Australia and New Guinea. The Japs were bringing a convoy around to attack Port Moresby. They knew if they could get the base at Moresby, they could attack Australia, and maybe make them leave the war. And without Australia for a base, we couldn't operate in the Southwest Pacific. The Japanese would own it all. The war would essentially be over, at least in the Pacific. But the Coral Sea battle stopped them in their tracks. They retreated and haven't tried a naval assault since."

"Damn, Stoddard, where do you come up with all this stuff? You eavesdrop on the C.O.'s phone lines?"

"Don't need to," Gene replied, laughing. "He has me over for cocktails a couple of evenings a week to brief me and ask my opinion on strategy."

"Well, there are just two things wrong with that statement," Mike countered.

"Other than the obvious, what's the other one?"

"Well, get real. No tee-totaller like you would ever be invited to a general's cocktail party," Mike replied.

"Touché. But, to answer your question, I spend as much time as I can in the base library reading the major newspapers. They seem to have a lot of information. And Stars and Stripes gives some background."

"Well, thanks for the geography lesson. But back to my question—what sort of missions is the Twenty-Second involved in?"

"There's not too much information. Most of that's classified, and censored out. They are apparently bombing the Jap airbases on New Guinea, and convoys trying to re-supply their bases. They also apparently fly missions clear over to Rabaul."

"Rabaul? What's that? Where's that?" Mike studied the map, looking for the strange name among dozens of even stranger names.

"It's a huge Japanese naval and air base—over here on New Britain, about five hundred miles northeast of New Guinea."

Mike studied the map for several seconds, something about it obviously bothering him.

"Gene, are you telling me that to do a bombing raid those guys have to fly five hundred miles over open ocean to get there? Do you remember being taught anything in our navigation training about flying five hundred miles with no landmarks? And what happens if you get shot up during the raid? You've still got five hundred miles of ocean to face to get back."

"That's what they're doing, all right," Gene agreed. "Maybe we should have asked for fighters, instead of bombers."

"Maybe you're right," Mike replied. "So, who else is fighting over there, besides the Twenty-Second?"

"I'm not sure. Sort of sounds like not too many of any outfit. The Nineteenth, a B-17 group, got run out of the Philippines, along with General Macarthur—that's up here between New Guinea and Japan. I think they're in Australia. Truthfully, it sounds to me like it's pretty one-sided over there. If we get sent to the Twenty-Second, I get the feeling we won't have any trouble finding trouble."

On October 25, 1942, Gene Stoddard and Mike Kingston were graduated from the B-26 transitioning course at MacDill Airbase, Tampa, Florida. As

Gene had anticipated, they were then assigned to the 22nd Bomb Group, currently based at Iron Range, Australia. They were given a two-week leave, and were to ship out of San Francisco, bound for Australia, on November 15, 1942. It was expected that they would arrive at the base at Iron Range shortly before Christmas—just over a year after Gene had stood in the barn and listened to the reports of the attacks on Pearl Harbor.

Mike had assumed that he would head directly to California, to be able to spend time with his parents. Gene was going home first, and then to the base in California. However, the train routes made it easy for Mike to accompany Gene to Kansas, where he got to visit again with Gene's family, and Christy. Liz and Christy joined them to go see the new John Wayne movie, *Flying Tigers*.

This story of a small group of fighter pilots fighting against overwhelming odds to assist the Chinese in their struggle against the Japanese invaders, and the Movietone News reel showing the latest struggles against both Japan and Germany, made the war seem a little too real and imminent to them. Little was said as they left the theater. Gene and Mike half-heartedly teased each other again about how they should have gone into fighters, instead of bombers. It was not until they were visiting at the small restaurant on the town square, having hamburgers and a Coke, that the mood lightened somewhat.

Their visit was quite enjoyable, and Mike appreciated getting to see Gene's family, and Christy, again. He liked her spunky spirit and sense of humor. But after the intensity and total immersion of their year of training for combat, and its looming reality, small-town Kansas no longer held any appeal for either of them. After a couple of days, Mike headed on to California, leaving Gene to follow later.

It took only a couple more days for Gene to realize how completely out of place he now felt in his home, and his hometown. He had matured beyond his years, and could find nobody that he could feel comfortable with, except Christy, and she was at work most of the time. He soon made the excuse that Mike wanted him to get to visit his home in California and to meet his parents. So, only five days after arriving in Colborn, his family was seeing him off at the Santa Fe depot. He couldn't help but wonder when—and they wondered if—he would see them again. His departure was not a happy occasion.

On December 18, 1942, Gene and Mike walked down the gangplank from the troopship that had been their home for over a month, and onto the shores of Australia, at Brisbane. Two days later they arrived at the base of the 22nd Bomb Group in Iron Range. They felt trained, and were ready to finally start putting their training to some use for the Uncle Sam that had been paying for them to fly for the past year. They felt ready for combat, ready to start doing their part.

Iron Range, Australia

Dear Christy:

Merry belated Christmas!! Well, after a year of training and a month at sea on a beat up rust bucket of a boat, I'm finally over here, rarin' to start doing my part. The trip over was uneventful. Just boring, and incredibly hot, on the ship. It's summertime "down under." Christmas in the summer—that's going to take some getting used to. The ship was really cramped, with no place for anything. I used to think the barracks didn't have any privacy, but those were five-star hotels compared to life on a troop ship. You have to put up with it, but I'll never get used to it. Glad it's over.

Mike and I arrived at our base on the 20th of Dec. It's clear up on the northern tip, or peninsula, of Australia, called Iron Range—see if Jerry can find it on our map at home. It's a temporary base literally cut out of the jungle. The trees and underbrush are almost too dense to walk through, and very tall. Our engineers cut a landing strip, as well as taxiways and parking areas for the planes, by blowing up the biggest trees, and taking bulldozers to the rest. It's so dusty that it's hard on the engines—until it rains, and then it's a quagmire. They plan to hard surface it when they can get the machinery and material shipped in, but that will be a while. They've put down temporary steel matting, in the meantime.

There are snakes (some are unbelievably huge; a couple of the guys shot a python nearly fifteen feet long) and every imaginable form of insect—especially mosquitoes. There are no buildings, of any sort. We live and operate in tents, with nets over our cots to keep the bugs and mosquitoes off while we sleep. Mom would be horrified to see the place—and the food we get. It's barely edible, but enough to keep body and soul together.

We had a pretty good Christmas, considering. The Brass somehow made some liquor available for the troops, and most of them got pretty lit up—guess that takes the place of Christmas lights, right? Mike and I have just been trying to get acquainted. We haven't been assigned to crews, so I don't know when we'll begin to do some flying. The other guys tell us we'll probably just be put on as substitutes, and go on several training flights before we get to go on the real thing.

The "real thing" seems more real, now. Last night—the day after Christmas—some B-24s (4-engine bombers, quite a lot bigger than our B-26) from one of the heavy bomb groups also based here were supposed to go on a mission to some Jap base up north. The second one off had a problem and crashed just after lift-off, and blew up. It nearly knocked me off my cot. All ten guys were lost, of course. Nobody says anything. They just seem to accept it and go on about their business.

Christy, I don't know how the guys over here do it. They've been living in hellholes (pardon my French, but there's no other description for this place) like this for months, and fly really tough missions. But most of them are still the scrappiest guys I've known. They know that the next plane to be lost could be theirs, but they're still cocky and spoiling for a fight. The crews complain about not having any leadership on the flights—everybody's just sort of on their own. I don't know if it's a real problem, or just the usual bellyaching about the Brass. Of course, they haven't been over here very long, and it probably takes a while to get such a complex effort organized.

I don't really have much I can tell you. They don't let us say anything about the missions, or too much of anything else, or it gets censored out. I wrote to the folks, but you can tell them Hi for me again. Haven't got any letters from home since we left California. Hope they catch up with me in not too long. Sure seems like a long way from Kansas, over here.

Your old Kansas buddy,
Gene

Combat

Dear Christy:

Looks like I may finally get to go on my first real mission in the morning. One of the copilots has come down with dengue fever, and I've been put on as his replacement. I'm not allowed to say anything about it, even if I knew anything, which I don't. I wasn't invited to the briefing. We take off before sun-up.

I'm really ready to get to do something that I've spent the last year training to do. Guess I'm a little nervous, but mostly excited to finally be getting my chance. They've had me go as copilot on several training flights, and on a couple of supply runs down to Sydney, but I'm ready to do something useful. Sydney's a really pretty city, from the air. Has a huge harbor with a really impressive bridge across it. I'd like to get to go on leave down there and look it over, some time.

There's not much to say, right now, and I need to get some shut-eye, so guess I'll sign off. I finally got a batch of letters from you all. Took all afternoon to read them, and re-read them—it beats anything else there is to do. It gets pretty boring here, when we aren't flying. The guys play catch, or cards, or whatever they can find to pass the time. The married ones spend a lot of time writing letters. Can't say I'm getting homesick, but I do miss everybody. Seems like I miss home more over here than when I was in training—I guess just because it's so far away, and it's such a totally different kind of world.

Take care of yourselves over there.
Gene

Port Moresby, New Guinea

The flight from Iron Range to Port Moresby had been routine. Gene had been assigned to fly as copilot on this, his first combat mission, as an introduction to the techniques and procedures that were being used by the squadron for their missions. It would also expose him to combat for the first time, giving his airplane commander a chance to see how this new arrival would react under fire, and the stress of combat.

As Gene had learned while still in training at MacDill, the absence of protective fighter aircraft made it impossible to base the B-26 bombers at Port Moresby. The field—actually, little more than a temporary landing strip bulldozed out of the hills surrounding the harbor—was bombed at will by the Japanese. The bombers, safely based at Iron Range, in Australia, were over a thousand miles from their targets at Rabaul and could not fly such long distances without refueling.

Before departing Iron Range the pilot, Roger Schell, had been terse, but direct. "Stoddard, since this is your first combat flight, you'll be strictly an observer. Until a pilot's been exposed to combat, you never know how he'll react. I've seen guys completely freeze up, really panic, so I can't take chances. Consider this a training flight. Watch, and learn. But I'll do all the flying—unless I'm too wounded, or I'm dead." A quick grin flashed over his face. "Then it'll be up to you to get us back."

Gene recognized that he was an unknown quantity, and could only imagine how a person might be affected under the stress of combat. For that matter, he had no idea how he would react, and didn't blame the pilot for not taking chances until he was sure how Gene would handle it. He could only hope he would stand up to the test, and could eventually be trusted to do the flying.

As the plane was being refueled for the departure from Port Moresby for the mission, Gene sat down under the bomber wing, and began visiting with the bombardier of the crew, Jeff Hanson, a fellow Kansan from the western part of the state.

"Jeff, do you have any idea what we're going to be doing?" Gene asked. "Schell hasn't said anything to me. Are we going to be bombing an airbase, or what?"

"Don't take it personally," Jeff replied, smiling at him. "It's been kept pretty hush-hush, but it's probably a skip-bombing mission. I suppose they've spotted a convoy, somewhere. Whatever it is, it must be big. We had a full-scale dry run about a week ago. The B-17s and twenty-fours from the heavy bomber groups, and all us B-25s and B-26s joined up in a hit 'em high, hit 'em low practice mission. It was the biggest thing I've seen since I got over here."

Gene just nodded, thinking about it, but looked puzzled. "What's skip bombing? I've never heard of it."

"It's what's going to win this war for us, at least out here," he answered. "It didn't take long, after Pearl Harbor, for "Hap" Arnold—I assume you've heard of him. He's the Commanding General of the Army Air Forces—to recognize that we had piss-poor leadership down here. He kicked them all out, and put General George Kenney in charge of the 5th Air Force—which includes about everything with wings in Australia. He's a sawed-off little guy, but a tough son-of-a-bitch, and he's really making things happen. The guys all love him, because we feel like we're finally being able to kick some ass."

"Yeah, I read in *Stars and Stripes* about General Arnold assigning General Kenney to take over down here, but I didn't know much about any of it," Gene replied.

"Anyway, to answer your question," Hanson continued, "it didn't take General Kenney long to recognize that one of our biggest challenges was hitting a moving ship with a bomb. We were doing what we'd been trained to do. To avoid anti-aircraft fire, we'd bomb from a relatively high altitude. Hell, by the time the bombs got there, the ships could be halfway back to Tokyo. Somebody did an analysis that found that barely one per cent of all the bombs we were dropping did anything more than kill a bunch of fish. That's when General Kenney started experimenting with low-level attacks, using skip bombing."

"How does it work? Do the bombs literally skip?" Gene asked, intrigued by the concept, and curious as to why he had never been told about it, or trained to use it.

"Yeah, it's just like throwing rocks across a pond. We approach the ship from broadside, a couple hundred feet off the deck. We drop 'em about a hundred yards from the ship and they literally skip across and hit the side of the ship. There's a five-second delay on the fuse, to let us get the hell out of the road, but it also allows the bomb time to sink below the water line before exploding. It does a lot more damage that way."

"Wow. That's fascinating. I never imagined such a thing," Gene exclaimed. "So, does it work?"

"Well, it didn't at first. Nobody could hit squat. Bombs would bounce over the ship, or fall short. We had to do a lot of experimenting, and practice a lot to perfect the technique. And there were all kinds of problems with the delayed fuses. But it's working great, now. I've heard that over seventy five percent of all bombs dropped using the technique are hitting their targets."

"I'm really anxious to see it," Gene said. "How many have you guys hit?"

"Well, we're as green as you are, on the real thing," Jeff confessed, laughing. "We've never had a chance to use it on anything that shoots back. We've been practicing with dummy bombs on a derelict old freighter in the Port Moresby harbor. Looks like we finally get to find out just how good we really are."

Gene thought about it all, trying to imagine how it would look and feel. One aspect of the concept raised some concerns.

"Jeff, if you guys come in only a couple hundred feet off the deck, doesn't that…well, I don't want to sound like a scaredy-cat, but seems like you're a little close for comfort."

Jeff laughed out loud at this confession, momentarily embarrassing Gene.

"You noticed that, did you?" Jeff replied, still laughing. "Hell yes. We're sitting ducks. That's why we'll be taking off so early. The captain plans to hit them just before sunrise so they won't be able to see us very well. That's another thing General Kenney's done. He got some gunnery sergeant—called Pappy Gunn, can you believe—to figure out how to replace the bombardiers on the B-25s with eight fifty calibers stuck in the nose, so they can hose them down while they're on the bomb run. They're calling them 'commerce busters.' I shudder to think what it would be like to be on the receiving end of eight fifty calibers, but it lets them stand a chance going in during daylight. We'd never survive it."

Gene and Jeff continued talking about the mission, and the new bombing technique, for several minutes. Then the pilot called the group together to brief them on the upcoming mission.

"Well, guys, the big show is on. That humongous combined dry run with the heavies of the Forty-Third, and us mediums, that we participated in a few days ago is now the real thing. Looks like we've got a chance to have some really happy hunting. I wasn't permitted to tell you much of any of this, until now. Our G-2 had suspected that the Japs were going to try to reinforce the troops here on New Guinea, with a huge convoy out of Rabaul. They were pretty sure it had launched, but couldn't spot it because of all the rain squalls in the area. Finally, a B-17 spotted them, but they were out of range for us medium bombers. The Forty-Third B-17s have been working them over, and have sunk several of them—but there's plenty left for us."

He could see his crewmen's faces lighting up at this opportunity, and they expressed their excitement rather loudly—and profanely. After waiting for their babble to quiet down, he continued the briefing.

"They're now in the Vitiaz Strait, northeast of Finchhaven. They're loaded with troops to reinforce the ones already here. There are at least eight freighters, and several light cruiser, or destroyers, for escort. And, there will be plenty of fighters for protection. So—it'll probably get pretty hot."

As Gene listened to the briefing, his mind was bouncing from trying to remember all that he had been taught during his training, to wondering what it was going to be like—and how he would react under fire. The other crew members had become noticeably quieter, as the pilot continued..

"As you know, every Jap that doesn't get off those ships is one that can't kill our guys. General Kenney himself said that it is imperative that none of those troops make it. We're going to sink as many of the bastards as possible. This will be our first chance to try out skip bombing for real. We'll take off at 04:30. I want to be able to be on target just at early daylight, so as to silhouette the targets, and so they won't be able to see us. We'll be joined by B-17s from the Forty-Third. They can't risk skip bombing in daylight, just like us. The commerce busters, and higher altitude heavies, will keep up the fight the rest of the day."

As planned, they took off in pitch black at 04:30. After making the long climb to clear the Owen-Stanley Mountains, they descended to cross the ocean at 2500 feet. They headed for the position where they expected to find the convoy, based on estimates of its speed and heading from its last reported position. The pilot planned to fly to a point somewhat west of the expected position, to keep the convoy between him and the eastern horizon, and then establish a north-south search pattern until it was located. Lady Luck was with them, and the convoy was spotted, just discernible against the light of the early dawn, less than twenty minutes after they had arrived.

"Hot damn, we got us a convoy! Pilot to bombardier: I'm dropping down to two hundred feet. The destroyers are usually on each side. I'm going to keep power off until we're past the destroyers so they won't hear us. Then I'll head for the biggest transport we can pick out. Be ready on my command to drop all four. Here we go."

The convoy was on Gene's side of the plane and he was pleased that he had been the first to spot it—a flotilla of toy ships, black and indistinct, silhouetted against the pale light of a pre-dawn sky. The pilot leaned forward for a better view, nodded briefly and winged over to head toward it, before calling to the bombardier. He eased the throttles back, adjusting the engines to start a descent. The engines became noticeably quieter. It would be difficult for the crews on the destroyers to hear the approaching aircraft over the sound of their own ship's engines, until the plane literally flew over their heads. In the near dark, the plane would be difficult to see, even if the ship's guns could be put into action.

Gene quickly realized all the tactical implications of what the pilot was doing, and was impressed with the skill with which the plane was maneuvered. There would be little chance for the destroyer to put up any significant defense. Nevertheless, he could feel a cold sense of fear in the pit of his stomach, and realized his pulse was pounding, as a silhouetted destroyer loomed larger ahead of them. Beyond it, he could see the outline of a much larger ship, presumably a large transport carrying supplies and troops for the Japanese forces on New Guinea. It was obviously the one that the pilot was headed for.

As they flashed over the destroyer, Gene could see its crewmen rushing to man their weapons, and within moments he could see streaks of red arcing past the plane as incendiary tracers helped the gunners find their target. For a brief moment, he thought of Fourth of July fireworks shows—until he remembered that these fireworks were intended to kill him. In truth, he wondered how there could be so many of them filling the air around their plane without their being hit. He marveled at the concentration of the pilot, who appeared unaffected by it all.

"Pilot to bombardier—about ten seconds. Be ready."

"Roger, ready when you are. Damnation that mother's big. Looks like at least eight thousand tons."

Gene was reminded of his first landing, when the earth, which had seemed so distant from several thousand feet of altitude, had suddenly come rushing up at him at breakneck speed as they had approached the runway. The targeted freighter had at first appeared no larger than a bathtub toy ahead of them, then quickly began to loom larger until it seemed it would fill the windshield. At only two hundred feet above the water they appeared to be barely higher than its stacks and antennas. As it came charging at them, the pilot suddenly called to the bombardier.

"Target on the nose…bomb, bomb, bomb, bomb."

Gene felt the plane lurch upward as a ton of explosives fell away from its bomb bay as they flashed over the transport.

For what seemed an inordinately long time, nothing happened. He had expected immediate huge explosions from the bombs, and assumed for the moment that they had missed, or that something had gone wrong—forgetting that there was a five second delay in their fuses. Just as unexpectedly, there was a sudden shout in his intercom headphones.

"Yee haw! There's one…two…three hits." He paused a moment, then let out an excited burst. "Gawd-a-mighty…that mother just blew all to hell! We must've hit a tanker!"

It was the top turret gunner, who had an unobstructed view back at the ship. Three of the four bombs had hit the ship, exploding against its hull below the water line, nearly lifting it out of the water as they exploded. Seconds later, the ship erupted in a massive explosion. They had been fortunate in their choice of target, hitting the fleet oiler and supply ship, usually listed at nearly nine thousand tons. The force of the explosion bounced the plane around rather severely, as the shock wave caught up to it.

"There's another one going up—must be Tex. Damn, there's a third one. Looks like we got a hat trick." The excited top gunner was calling out the other explosions, as other planes in their group found targets.

Gene had assumed that since they had dropped all their bombs on the one ship that they would "high-tail it for the barn," as the expression went, and head back to Moresby. To his surprise, and puzzlement, the pilot banked around and headed back toward the burning ships that had just been bombed. The sun was starting to show above the horizon, and it was by now becoming noticeably lighter. Chaos was breaking loose in the convoy.

The dry run exercise that the pilot had referred to in his briefing was paying off. It had been a carefully orchestrated plan to have B-17s bombing from higher altitude, as soon as sufficiently daylight, to draw fire away from the B-17s and twin-engine medium bombers attacking at low level to skip bomb. To be successful, and reduce their own losses, all aspects of the attack had to occur with precision timing. General Kenney had insisted on a "dress rehearsal" to maximize the probability of success. The old saying of "practice makes perfect" was paying off in spades.

But the Japanese warships were just as determined that the Americans would pay, and the attack would fail. The enemy destroyers were firing in virtually every direction as their gunners attempted to hit anything that might be an enemy plane. The sky was, indeed, lighting up like a Fourth of July fireworks show from the tracers of every gun on every ship in the convoy. In addition, two of the three bombed ships were burning fiercely, lighting up the area and pouring black smoke into the sky. The third was dead in the water.

High-altitude bombers had arrived and were joining in the battle. Geyser's erupted where bombs missed frantically maneuvering targets, and explosions could be seen as others made contact. Bright flashes in the sky from the ships' heavier guns looked like the Roman candles Gene fired as a kid. For a moment, Gene was puzzled, as it appeared that tracers were coming from above, downward toward the surface. His puzzlement was quickly answered by a frantic call from the top turret gunner.

"Holy shit! Captain, break left! There's bogies firing at us, but I can't see them." Just as he called, a stream of tracers raked across them. Gene instinctively ducked, as he heard, and felt, the plane thunking as some of the rounds hit their plane. The top turret opened fire, firing blindly at where the tracers seemed to be coming from. Moments later, Gene saw the dark form of a fighter, which he assumed was the one that had fired at them, zoom low in front of them and pull up sharply, climbing back to altitude. He could see tracers criss-crossing the sky as the higher altitude bombers came under attack and were defending themselves.

Gene had often tried to imagine what a battle scene would look like, but his imagination had never come close to the real thing. He watched it almost in awe.

"Thanks," the pilot responded to the turret gunner's call. "Keep an eye out for more of them. I'm going to make a pass down the port side of that burning troop carrier. Look for survivors."

The call from the pilot puzzled Gene. *What can we do about survivors?* he wondered, as they approached the sinking ship. As they came close, Gene could see that the explosions from one of the other planes had ripped the ship into two sections. The bow section was barely showing above the surface, and the stern was pointed high, its propellers and rudder nearly vertical. Large areas of the sea around the sinking sections were burning fiercely from the spilled oil that had gushed out of the ruptured ship. Gene noticed hundreds of small figures jumping, or falling, off its decks into the water, joining the others that were floating nearby, trying to swim away from the ship and flames.

Gene jumped involuntarily again, startled as every machine gun on the plane that could be brought to bear opened fire, and the water around the figures floating near the burning ship was churned into a froth by hundreds of machine gun rounds. Just as quickly, the guns fell silent as the plane left the ship behind.

It was all beginning to be more than he had bargained for. Gene felt his stomach clutching. He swallowed hard, trying to get his stomach, and his nerves, back under control. The pilot banked hard to pass down the other side of the burning ship, where once again the machine guns erupted. As the pilot completed a second pass, a concerned voice came over the intercom.

"Captain, there's two destroyers closing fast. Let's get outta here."

It was the top turret gunner calling. He knew his captain would keep after the convoy with whatever weapons he had available, but he also knew the odds against them were rapidly increasing. The passes over the sinking ship had given the destroyers time to close on the ship, and it was by now sufficiently daylight that the planes were rather easy to spot by the destroyer's gunners. Gene could see tracers from the enemy destroyers passing disconcertingly close to their plane. Just as the turret gunner called, a bright flash erupted not far off Gene's wing tip, as a shell from the closing destroying exploded near them. Gene instinctively ducked, and heard pieces of shrapnel hit the plane.

"Roger that," the pilot reacted to the turret gunner's call. "Any damage? Anybody hurt?"

No one reported injuries or damage, and the pilot zigged and zagged to throw off the aim of the anti-aircraft gunners as he turned to a southwesterly heading, skimming along close to the surface to prevent fighters from attacking from underneath the plane. When well out of range, he began a slow climb to altitude.

As they departed the area, Gene glanced at his wristwatch—the entire episode had lasted less than thirty minutes. The long flight back to Moresby was flown largely in silence. There had been a few excited calls between crewmen on the intercom exclaiming over the explosions, but in a few minutes the adrenaline began to wear off and they all fell silent.

As they droned along, Gene tried to make some sense of what he had just witnessed. It was obvious that he had not even remotely anticipated what war was going to be like. As time passed, Gene could feel his emotions, and adrenalin, crashing down. He had to struggle to keep from visibly shaking, swallowing hard and staring out the side cockpit windows at the glassy sea passing along below to try to quell his stomach.

He wondered if every new crewman went through the same thing, and hoped the pilot hadn't noticed him looking a little pale. After what seemed an interminably long time, the Owen-Stanley mountain range passed below them and they started their descent into Port Moresby. By then, Gene's emotions had settled down.

The crew inspected the plane for damage after landing. To Gene's surprise, there were several bullet holes from where the fighter had raked them, and jagged holes in the fuselage and right wing, outboard of the engine, from the flak blast. It occurred to him that had the airplane not been equipped with self-sealing fuel tanks, they would in all probability be dead now. Combat was beginning to seem less hypothetical. While the plane was being refueled, the pilot joined Gene in the shade beneath the wing.

"Well, Stoddard, I guess you're no longer a virgin. What do you think of air combat, now that you've been shot at?"

Gene was surprised by the question, since the pilot had seemed somewhat aloof prior to the mission.

"Well, I had no real idea what to expect. There's a lot going on, and it all happens awfully fast. It must be kinda hard to keep your wits about you. That's going to take some getting used to," Gene offered, not wanting to admit that it sort of rattled him, for a few minutes.

"Yeah, it does at first," the pilot agreed. "Sort of scares the crap out of you, the first time or two. But after you get used to it, everything actually seems to slow down, in some strange way,"

"I was impressed with the skip bombing, and the way you approached it," Gene added, hoping he could get the pilot to elaborate a little on his tactics. "That seems pretty impressive."

"Yeah, it's made a hell of a difference, that's for sure. We couldn't hit a bull in the butt with a bass fiddle when we were bombing from high altitude. Photo recon shots showed we weren't putting more than one or two bombs out of a hundred on a target. Our missions against shipping on the open sea were mostly just exercises in navigation. Strike assessment photos are showing now that at least three out of four are hits—makes all this shit seem a little more worthwhile. Skip bombing looks simple, but takes a lot of practice to get very good at it. I imagine someone will begin to show you the ropes, one of these days."

Gene nodded. The pilot didn't seem inclined to elaborate, and a reply didn't seem to be called for. They sat in silence for a few minutes, but Gene finally had to broach the subject that had most shocked him.

"I didn't expect the strafing. I have to admit—that hit me a little hard."

Gene glanced sideways at the pilot, not sure what to expect in response. The pilot didn't reply for a moment, as he watched the crewmen pumping gas to the plane. He glanced at Gene, then looked away.

"Stoddard, there's one thing you're going to have to get used to down here," the pilot finally replied, his voice flat. "This is a brutal war—barbaric in many ways. When I came over, I knew we would be killing people when we dropped bombs on targets, but that didn't bother me much. I recognized that's what war is. You kill the enemy, or they kill you. I was rather zealous about getting back at them. The damned Japs started this, after all. I could be home getting cozy with my wife instead of being over here in this hellhole, if they hadn't attacked us first. I actually looked forward to the bombing missions, at least at first. It was sort of a 'let's get this over with and get home' mentality, I suppose."

He paused, staring off into the brush that surrounded the field, and glanced up again to see how the refueling was progressing, before continuing.

"A few days ago, one of the Forty-Third's B-17s got hit. All the guys bailed out through the bomb bay. The other planes saw their chutes open. Then, those bastards started strafing them—killed them in their chutes. We always believed you never shot a pilot in his chute. Some of the P-38s tried to come down and protect them, but they were outnumbered. Three of them got shot down."

The pilot's voice trailed off. Gene could see his jaw muscles clenching and unclenching. He stared into the distance a moment, then continued talking to Gene, but without looking at him.

"That's really got us all royally pissed off," the pilot admitted. "And as if that wasn't enough, we've been hearing stories of captured crewmen being beheaded by the slant-eyed sons of bitches…I mean, what in hell kind of people are we fighting over here? I can't imagine a person doing that to anyone. To tell the truth, the war's taking on a whole different nature. It's becoming very personal. My best buddy's plane didn't come back from a mission a couple of weeks ago. When I think that he may have been captured by those…"

He had to pause. Gene didn't know what to say, and didn't know if the pilot would continue. So, he waited. After several seconds, the pilot picked up where he had left off.

"There's no question that we want revenge, want to get even. But mostly, we've just accepted the fact that every dead Jap is a Jap that can't kill one of us, and it doesn't much matter how we kill them…bomb them, strafe them…I don't much give a shit, as long as they're dead. And the sooner they're all dead—or at least enough of them are—the sooner this damned war will be over. When you get right down to it, if it comes to a choice between killing them, however I have to do it, and being able to be back home with my wife and little girl—well, like I said, it's become a very personal war."

Gene nodded, not expecting anything so personal from a pilot who until then had not displayed any emotion of any sort.

"I guess you're right," Gene replied. "I just wasn't expecting it—wasn't prepared for it, I guess."

The pilot stood. "It's best if you just think of them as targets," he said quietly, and walked off to check on the refueling of his plane.

Over four days, every available aircraft—both American and Australian, medium and heavy bomber alike—was thrown against the convoy. It was an unmitigated disaster for the Japanese. By the time it was over, the official tally listed fourteen enemy transports—every single one in the convoy—sunk, six of the escorting destroyers sunk and two others damaged, and as many as eighty enemy fighters definitely, or probably, shot down.

Of the enemy troops that had embarked on the convoy when it left Simpson Harbor in Rabaul, it was estimated that as many as fifteen thousand had been lost, and only approximately eight hundred that had been rescued by the surviving destroyers made it to New Guinea. The press had reporters interviewing crews as they returned from the battle. It was headline news in the States, bolstering the spirits of the country that had thus far found few reasons for optimism.

General Macarthur used the battle, which became known as the Battle of the Bismarck Sea, as a basis for requesting troops and air support to begin his invasion of New Guinea, a first step in driving the Japanese invaders back up the Pacific.

Iron Range

Dear Christy,

Well, I'm a veteran now. At least, I guess I qualify, in the sense that I got to ride along on a mission. The pilot told me they normally have a new pilot ride along on several missions, both for training and to see how he reacts to the stress of the combat. It was good to see how the pilot handled the attack. I learned a lot from him, just by watching.

We got back late yesterday. I can't say anything about it, but I've heard it's really getting played up, back home. So if you read anything, or see any Movietone News reels, about a really big battle over here involving a Japanese convoy, keep me in mind. I guess I have to admit I was a little scared, once the action started. But it goes so fast there's not much time to think about any of it—you do all your thinking once it's over.

The pilot talked with me about the flight, after we got back—sort of surprised me. He hadn't said anything before we took off. I guess he just had a lot on his mind. It kind of helped me put some of what happened in better perspective.

I don't know what I really expected it to be like, over here—or if I even gave it much thought. But, I realize now, nothing can prepare you for it. No matter what I might have thought, it wouldn't have done justice to what it is all really like. The living conditions, the violence of the combat, the isolation, all are difficult to explain in any way that comes close to telling what it really is. When I would see the Movietone News reels, in black and white like it was in a dream, it all seemed so imaginary. Now, when it's happening live and in color in front of you, it's just as hard to accept as real. But, the guys are all really swell joes, and just do their job and keep on going.

I seem to be rambling, so might as well knock it off. I hope all is going well at home—I don't get much real news from Mom. Let me know if Mom or Dad seem to be having any problems. I know they wouldn't tell me. Take care, and tell all the folks at church Hi for me.

Take care,
Gene

Dear Gene,

Was so good to hear from you. Glad to hear that your first mission was a success. We hadn't received any letters for quite a while. I wondered how it was all going for you. I went to a movie the other night, and the Movietone News was about a big sea battle over there. They called it the Battle of the Bismarck Sea. I have to assume you were one of the "stars" in the movie. I sort of hoped you weren't.

Gene, I don't know how to respond to your letters. I'm sitting here in my cozy bedroom. There's frost on the window panes from a late winter storm, and we have several inches of snow. It's evening, and the street is quiet. Looks like a Christmas card. My biggest problem is trying to meet my bond sale quota by next Tuesday. You, on the other hand, are in some horrible jungle camp half way around the world—or you may at this very moment be in the middle of a combat flight, getting shot at. I can't even pretend to imagine what you are going through, nor do I want to know. We can't know for weeks at a time whether you are OK, or not. I don't know how to keep it in perspective. We all get awfully worried about you, sometimes.

I know I shouldn't write this sort of thing, but I can't seem to help it. I hope you don't let it get you down. We're all really doing fine. Your folks seem to be OK. Jerry is getting to be quite popular at school—he's such a nice guy, and good-looking, too, just like his big brother. Of course, Liz is hounded by all the guys for dates. You won't believe how she's growing up since you left.

I feel like I should write a lot more, but it would just all be small town stuff that seems so trivial when I write it. I'm sure you will find it hard to believe that I can be "speechless." We all miss you, and pray that you are safe.

Be careful over there, and tell Mike "Hi" for me when you see him.

We all miss you,
Christy

Conflict

Based on the number of enemy fighters destroyed by their bombing mission to a Japanese airbase on the northern coast of New Guinea, pilot and aircraft commander Lieutenant Sutherland should have been pleased as he revved up an engine, spinning his B-26 around in its revetment to ready it for departure on the next mission. Blistering mad, perhaps, but pleased he was not.

After a terse, angry outburst from the pilot directed at his copilot as they had approached the target, the bomb run and return flight were completed in silence. The flight leader of the mission, Lieutenant Mike Kingston, and the other two B-26 bombers in the group had inflicted enormous damage on enemy fighters that had been parked ridiculously close together on the enemy airfield.

In spite of that, and in spite of Sutherland's B-26 lagging behind the others—due to his copilot screwing up the mission, in Sutherland's assessment—his bombardier had managed to drop their bomb load directly in the middle of a group of fighters that had escaped Kingston's attack unscathed. Whoops from his top turret gunner confirmed their success, and Sutherland should have been elated. Instead, he fumed in silence.

A cursory scan of the engine instruments assured that all was fine, and he shut down both engines. Sutherland glowered briefly at his copilot, Lieutenant Gene Stoddard, who stared blankly straight ahead, ignoring the pilot.

"Switches off," Sutherland called out his side window to the sweaty, shirtless teenage ground crewman, who moved in to chock the wheels.

He normally left the mundane task of completing the shut-down checklist to his copilot but was still too irate to deal with him, so angrily completed it himself. Assured that his aircraft was properly secured, he turned out of his seat to climb down the lower hatch, ignoring the copilot as he brushed against him in the narrow cockpit. Gene sat silently in his seat, staring out his side cockpit window, oblivious to the tantrum of his pilot and the activity around the plane as the ground crew began to prepare the aircraft for its next mission.

Gene sat morosely in the abandoned plane, his thoughts drifting aimlessly over this unpleasant circumstance and his dubious future. The metallic tick-ticking of the engine exhausts cooling down, and the monotonous buzzing of flies gathering in the cockpit, seemed almost hypnotic and Gene retreated into his thoughts. He waved a hand across his face mechanically, unconsciously, at the persistent flies, oblivious to the layer of sweat forming on his brow and unaware of the dark stains spreading across his shirt as the cockpit temperature climbed rapidly under the Pacific sun.

His mind drifted back to that August afternoon in Kansas, now seeming to have existed in another life, when he tried to read in the heat and dust, and maddening flies, the day the Stearman pilot had first told him of the Civilian Pilot Training Program. Little did he imagine then that the suggestion made by the pilot passing through his hometown that day would lead to his sitting here in this hellhole in the Southwest Pacific. Little did he realize what good training the heat, humidity and flies would provide for his future combat assignment.

He thought, too, of his days of training to become a pilot—of his first flight at Kansas University, the excitement of moving up to the Vultee Vibrator and moving into twin engines with the Bamboo Bomber. Those times had seemed so heady, and full of promise. He felt nothing could stop him from assuming his rightful place in the left seat of a hot new bomber, to do his duty and help defeat the enemy that threatened his country—and, of course, prepare himself for a future back home as an airline pilot.

He had always believed that he belonged in a plane. While he was aloft, he didn't think of himself as someone simply following procedures learned from hours of training. No, in his mind he and his aircraft were melded into one being, each an extension of the other. He was, as his friend Mike Kingston had once told him, a natural. Or, so he had thought.

His first mission, the skip-bombing mission against the convoy, had shaken him at first because of the intensity of the combat, and the stark brutality of warfare in the Pacific. It disappointed him, on a personal pride basis, that he had not been allowed to do any of the flying, but he recognized it was the result of the exacting demands of air combat and his lack of combat training and experience. But those, he reasoned, would come soon enough. As soon as they had landed, he found himself looking forward to another mission.

His next mission had been over the harbor of Rabaul, in New Britain. Rabaul had one of the best natural harbors in the Southwest Pacific, and the Japanese had captured it quickly in their march across the Pacific. Heavily fortified, and ringed with airfields to base fighters and bombers, it was not a target which generated overwhelming enthusiasm on the part of the aircrews.

It was, however, a target too valuable to avoid. The harbor was usually packed with shipping, both transports and war ships, and the wharves laden with materiel. Before the U.S. could hope to be successful at reclaiming any of the Solomon chain of islands, Rabaul would have to be, if not destroyed, at least neutralized. It was to provide many exciting moments for numerous aircrews over the ensuing two years.

Gene had flown copilot on that mission. They departed Port Moresby about midnight, after landing to refuel, and arrived over Rabaul approximately three hours later. Although night attacks kept the fighter planes on the ground, the antiaircraft gunners were wide awake. Scores of searchlights scanned the sky for the attacking planes, and one so luckless as to be spotted was soon illuminated by several others. Every gun emplacement on the ground quickly came to bear on the formerly invisible aircraft.

Starkly visible and feeling quite alone and naked, if the pilot didn't take evasive action quickly and violently their fate was soon sealed. In spite of the fact that the anti-aircraft fire was especially heavy that night, their planes had done a masterful job of getting their bombs on the targets and they left several impressive fires burning behind them. Gene was pleased to have been a part of another important mission, and especially pleased to have arrived back at the base unscathed.

He hadn't thought too much, at first, about the fact that he had not been able to get signed off to ascend to the coveted left seat of aircraft commander before they shipped out from the States. He assumed that as soon as they were settled in overseas, and he began flying combat missions, he would quickly move up to left seat.

Missions came and went, but he remained copilot. His friend, Mike Kingston, had been checked out as aircraft commander after a few training and indoctrination flights, and had flown a number of missions as lead pilot. He had asked Gene to fly copilot on a Rabaul mission with him—his regular copilot had come down sick, he had told Gene—and had let Gene fly the entire mission. It had been pretty "hot," but Gene believed he had handled it well

Now, here he sat, just shy of his twentieth birthday—he would no longer be a teen-ager, he realized—at some ungodly hellhole that no one could conceivably actually want, apparently a washout. Although given several opportunities, he had as yet been unable to get signed off. The check pilot would just mutter something to the effect of "I don't think you're ready yet," and walk away. Gene was never sure of what his deficiencies might be, as he was never told. No one had said anything about it, at least to him. But he imagined that he was rapidly sliding into a position of near contempt on the part of the other pilots.

He couldn't believe the C.O. would take him off flight status. Crew members were constantly coming down with dengue fever, or malaria—or being wounded, or killed. Experienced combat pilots were in short supply. *But Lord in Heaven help me*, he thought, *I can't just keep riding along as a spectator. I've got to be able to fly.*

His thoughts trailed off, his mind weary of asking questions that seemed to have no answers. He wiped sweat out of his eyes, on the back of his shirtsleeve.

Taking a deep breath, he let out a sigh of resignation, oblivious to the activity of the crew around the plane.

Sutherland had stormed out of his plane, headed for Mike Kingston's plane—but Mike was already headed for him. Mike had landed first, and was waiting for him.

"Sutherland, what the hell happened up there? It's pure luck you didn't get your ass shot out of the sky, coming in behind us, like that. You were a sitting duck." It was obvious to Mike from the look on Sutherland's face that the problem had not been a mechanical one.

"What happened?" Sutherland glared at Kingston, wagging a finger in his face. "I'll tell you what happened," he growled. "They gave me a son-of-a-bitch copilot who won't keep his head in the game during the bomb run. Am I supposed to fly these damn missions solo?"

He continued venting before Kingston could respond.

"When I got your signal to climb for the bomb run, I called to Stoddard to give me climb power, but nothing happened. He was sitting there, gawking out the side window like a damned tourist. You were already starting to climb and pull away, and I hollered at him again. I thought I was going to have to belt him to get his attention. I finally did it myself. By then there was no way I could catch up. You want me to fly formation with you, then get me a damn copilot who has enough interest in this war to pay attention during some of it." That said, Sutherland turned and stormed off towards the debriefing tent.

Still sitting in the plane, deep in his black thoughts, Gene was unaware of the unflattering appraisal of him that had just taken place.

"Stoddard! Dammit, wake up! What's with you?"

Gene jumped, startled back to the present by the loud, accusing yell from the lower hatch.

"What?" Gene turned and looked down the hatchway, to see who was yelling at him.

"Get your butt out here. Lieutenant Kingston wants to see you." It was Bob Gunther, the turret gunner, who obviously had a very low opinion of this washout of a pilot.

Gene made no comment to the gunner as he exited the bomber. He walked mechanically, resignedly, toward his long-time friend and the leader of this flight, who was standing near the entry of the revetment. Mike stood waiting for Gene, looking at him as he approached.

"Let's go to my tent. We need to talk."

Mike started up the dirt path to the personnel tents, with Gene following silently along side.

As they entered the tent, Mike pushed the mosquito netting aside, sat down on his cot, and looked questioningly at Gene, who had stopped just inside the tent. Mike nodded towards a cot, and Gene sat down. Neither spoke for a few moments.

"What happened up there, today? Sutherland's madder'n hell at you—says that you weren't paying attention during the bomb run and jeopardized the mission."

Mike studied his friend, looking for clues, waiting for answers. Gene leaned forward, elbows on his knees, and stared blankly at the opposite side of the tent. *So what do I tell him?* he wondered. *That I love flying more than life itself, that if I'm not at the controls my mind wanders? That I'm bored silly? That I wasn't paying attention to Sutherland because he's a chrome-plated jerk?*

"So what happened?" Mike pressed Gene.

"Mike, what am I doing wrong?" Gene finally responded, so quietly that Mike had to strain to understand him over the roar of a distant engine being run up to full power for testing.

"What do you mean?" Mike asked, shaking his head, puzzled by Gene's question. Mike hadn't seen his friend look like this, or sound like this, since the day at MacDill Air Base when Gene had been royally chewed out for nearly inverting his plane.

"Look. I'm going to level with you. I've got two big problems. First, call me whatever you want, but if I've got to be over here, I want to do something that makes it worth it. Watching Sutherland fly doesn't do much for me. And second, I'm staking my future on flying for the airlines when we get out of this crapper, and I'm not going to be able to compete with guys who have a bunch of missions as pilot-in-command. I simply cannot deal with being stuck as a copilot."

He rolled over and stretched out on the cot, hands behind his head, staring at the tent top. Neither spoke for several seconds, Gene lost in his own thoughts, while Mike attempted to form a response.

"Besides," Gene continued, "you try flying with Sutherland. The SOB is too arrogant to let me touch anything important. Of course I wasn't paying attention. I was bored out of my mind. Why should I pay attention to the jerk? Sure it was wrong, but do you think you could be treated like a Spam can all the time on these missions, and just take it? Try flying a few of 'em from the right seat for a while, and see how long it takes you to lose interest. Mike, I've got to get in the left seat, or I'm going to get myself court martialed. Why can't I get signed off?" It was more of a demand, than a question.

Mike got up off his cot. Pulling up an ammo case for a chair, he sat down next to Gene's cot and faced his buddy.

"Yeah. I figured it was something like that. Sutherland's an arrogant ass. But that doesn't change the reality of anything—or the perceptions, either. Something's got to change," Mike replied, failing to respond Gene's demand.

"Roger that," Gene agreed, anger and resentment edging into his voice. "I've got to get signed off, and start flying. What's stopping that?"

Mike hesitated, knowing what had to be said, but not wanting to say it. He got up, walked to the tent entry, looking across the camp for a moment, then went back over to his cot and sat down, looking at his friend.

"Gene, in many ways, you're the most natural pilot I know," Mike assured him. "The problem is, you're just not suited to the B-26. It's the wrong airplane for you."

"What in God's name is that supposed to mean?" Gene reacted, sounding as offended as he was defensive—barely avoiding being insulted by the comment. Mike recognized he was skating on thin ice with his friend, but knew the issue had to be confronted.

"Gene, you remember the mission to Rabaul with me, a couple of weeks ago? I told you that my copilot was sick, and I needed a substitute, so I asked you to fly with me. I let you do all the flying. Did that seem at all unusual to you?"

"Well, of course it did. None of the other pilots ever let me touch anything. I assumed you were just being kind to an old friend. Are you saying you weren't?" Gene's suspicions were immediately aroused, and his voice hardened perceptibly. He wasn't sure he liked the direction things were going.

"Well, truth be told, I wanted to see how you handled it," Mike replied. "Clancy and Abbott have both tried to get you checked out. We all want to see you make it. But neither one of them felt they could sign you off. I know you're a good pilot—I wanted to see for myself what the problem might be, so I asked you to fly with me."

"Well thanks a boatload for taking pity on me," Gene said, his face taking on a decidedly hard edge. This admission from Mike struck him as disingenuous, if not downright deceitful. It didn't seem like something a friend would do. "It makes me feel like some kind of problem child. Everybody's trying to figure out why poor little Gene can't fly the mean old airplane."

Gene knew he sounded petulant, and should be pleased that his friend was taking a personal interest in his "problem." But, in fact, he was struggling to not be offended that he was, in fact, considered to be such a "problem," and failure as a pilot. He realized Mike hadn't answered him.

"So? What is my 'big problem'?" Gene repeated, trying to not sound sarcastic, but without much success.

Mike eyebrows raised briefly. Testiness was not one of Gene's usual character traits. He knew he was touching on raw nerves.

"Well, the good news is that you're the coolest cucumber I've ever seen in a plane," Mike began, choosing his words as carefully as he could. "We took some pretty heavy-duty flak, and you did exactly what I had suggested was the best way to handle it. Then, when those Zeros jumped us, you handled them like it was a walk in the park. You used every trick I had told you about, and a couple that I hadn't thought of. You just never lost your cool, and handled the mission as well as anybody over here."

Mike paused, letting this information sink in. Gene looked at him, knowing he hadn't heard all that he was going to hear.

"I assume there's a 'but' coming along, after blowing all that smoke up my skirt," Gene reacted, rather sarcastically.

Mike smiled. He knew that Gene was not so naive that he didn't recognize that the story hadn't ended.

"Well, the 'but,' as you call it, is this. I don't suppose you even noticed me doing it—but Gene, I had to be on the throttles just all the damn time. You were letting your airspeed bleed off, when you were in those steep turns and climbs, to the point where we could have spun out if I hadn't been adding power. You just never seemed to be aware of your airspeed, and in the B-26 that will kill you, sooner or later."

Gene looked completely taken aback. He had, in fact, been totally unaware that Mike had been changing the power while he was maneuvering. He had been looking so intently out the cockpit windows at the action, as he maneuvered to avoid the flak concentrations and the enemy fighters, that he had paid no attention to what Mike was doing.

"I don't know what to say, Mike." Gene raised up, and sat on the edge of the cot, facing Mike. He shook his head in disbelief. "I didn't feel like I was letting the airspeed get away from me. The controls felt okay. I don't see why—"

Mike knew he had Gene's attention, now, and interrupted him.

"Well, think about it. The controls felt okay because I kept our power up. Maybe I should have let you spin it out. It would have been a more dramatic reminder. But I didn't feel like it was the right time, or place, to do that. Come on, Gene. You know the Twenty-Six's reputation."

"Yeah, yeah, I know," Gene interjected. "The 'Baltimore Whore.' No visible means of support."

They both grinned fleetingly at this tired nickname with which the bomber had been anointed.

"Right. Lots of guys couldn't handle it. You know how many of them washed out of flight school—or augured in. Why? Because of its high wing loading."

Gene, surprised by this unexpected turn, looked puzzled, but didn't respond. He wasn't sure what any of this had to do with his problems with the plane. Mike hastened to explain.

"It's like they told us in ground school. The designers of the Twenty-Six wanted it to perform basically like an overgrown fighter, so that it could perform well at low levels and have the speed to fight an even battle with fighters."

"I know that," Gene protested, "but what's the point? I still don't see what it has to do with—"

"It has everything to do with it," Mike cut in. "To do that, they had to use the smallest possible wing to minimize drag, and make up for the lack of wing area with airspeed. You let the speed bleed off, and it'll fall out of the sky on you. Or, if you lose an engine, you'll not have enough rudder control, and go inverted. You saw it happen to guys. They let their speed bleed off, and went swimming in Tampa Bay. You do remember your episode at MacDill?"

"Well, of course," Gene interjected, rolling his eyes. "I won't likely forget the ass-chewing I got on the flight line. I haven't pulled that stunt since, so what's your point?"

"Let me ask you," Mike replied, ignoring Gene's question. "Do you remember when we were talking about whether to go into fighters, or bombers? You remember what you told me about yourself?"

"Yeah. I said I wasn't cut out to fly fighters." Gene didn't know whether to be curious, or offended, at this puzzling and personal inquisition. "Now, it appears I'm not cut out to fly bombers. I say again…what's your point?"

"That is the point," Mike rejoined, "You said you think too much, you analyze too much. Frankly, you fly like an engineer."

"Oh, Judas Priest, Mike," Gene complained, beginning to be rather exasperated. "What kind of crap is that? And what's any of it got to do with—"

"It's got everything to do with it," Mike interrupted. "You plan every detail, and fly your plan. And you're absolute ice water under fire. But, in a B-26, you can't plan—you have to anticipate. And you damned sure can't ignore your airspeed. You have to sense what it's going to do, and react before it does it. Personally, I love the Marauder. I'd rather fly it than anything else in the air. But, frankly, you're just too relaxed with it. The plane gets ahead of you, and you don't realize it's happening."

Mike paused, looking at Gene for a reaction. Gene rolled back onto the cot and resumed his examination of the tent top.

"Well, something's wrong, that's for sure. But supposing you're right. What do I do now? I know Sutherland wouldn't trust me to hold his maps for him. I doubt that any of the other check pilots would sign me off now, if it'd get them a one way ticket home."

Mike got up off the ammo case, and went to stare out the tent flaps towards the flight line.

"Yeah, you're probably right. Personally, I think you should try to get transferred to a B-17 squadron. I'd hate to lose you out of the Twenty-Second—we've been together from the git-go. But I think you'd be a natural in a B-17."

"A B-17?"

"Sure. They're just like you. Solid as a corner post. Predictable. No tricks."

Gene sat up, resting on his elbows, and grinned a little. "I guess I'll take that as a compliment—sort of smacks of damning with faint praise. Fat chance of getting a transfer, though. You know they don't turn loose of pilots here, even misfits like me. I'm stuck in this crapper."

"Well, it's worth a thought. In the meantime, I'll talk to Ops and see if anything can be worked out for a different crew. Come on, I'll buy you a Coke."

"Naw, you go on. I'm going to my tent to write home," Gene replied, not wanting to admit that he didn't want to face the other pilots.

At 0900 hours, the tropical sun had been up long enough that the ever-present heat was already lying on the base like a blanket. Gene walked along the dirt path from the personnel tent area towards the base headquarters tent. *This is probably an exercise in spitting in the wind*, he thought, as he approached the tent, *but it can't be any worse than the mess I'm already in*. With that bit of uplifting self-motivation, Gene entered and announced himself to the private playing the role of priest to the sanctum sanctorum.

"Lieutenant Stoddard to see the major." Gene stared straight ahead, ignoring the bored private at the desk, whose devotion to his job appeared to derive entirely from his awareness of the alternative duties open to a private in a combat zone. The private briefly entered the C.O.'s office, mumbled something and came back to his desk, giving a disinterested nod toward the office door.

Gene entered and saluted.

"Well, Stoddard, what can I do for you today?"

He was looking at a manila folder filled with papers, and nonchalantly saluted without looking up.

"Sir, with all due respect, I wish to request a transfer."

The major continued looking at the papers in the folder for a few more moments, then closed it and looked at Gene, his face an impassive mask that Gene could not even pretend to interpret.

"It won't do any good to run from your problems, Stoddard. A B-26 flies the same in anybody else's squadron. Besides, I don't have pilots, or copilots, running out my ears, here. What brought you to this action?"

He moved from behind his desk and sat on the front edge of it, arms folded across his chest, looking hard at Gene. It was obvious that he was aware of Gene's "problems." But, somehow, his reaction didn't seem quite as harshly negative as Gene had anticipated. In fact, Gene felt that he discerned a hint of actual concern.

"No sir, I'm not trying to run from any problems. I just don't believe that I'll…that I will be able to get checked out in the Twenty Six—and frankly, Sir, I don't want to spend the war being a spectator, flying right seat. Kingston tells me he thinks I would do better in B-17s. I've given it a lot of thought, and I believe he's right. I was hoping to get transferred to a B-17 squadron."

Turning around, the major picked up the folder which he had been holding when Gene entered, opened it and flipped casually through a few of the papers, then looked at Gene.

"Stoddard, I've studied everything there is on you—your fitness reports, instructor evaluations…your check ride reports. College student—electrical engineering, no less—high marks in all classes. According to all these reports, you're one of the best pilots to come along since Icarus. But out here, where lesser guys are putting their asses on the line and doing a damn fine job of blasting Japs, you not only aren't a pilot, you can't even copilot! Damnation, Stoddard, what happened up there yesterday? Sutherland claims you refused to follow his orders, and jeopardized the plane and the mission. If that's true, I should have you court martialed!"

The C.O. looked at Gene, trying with some inner sense of fairness to mask his impatience and frustration, waiting for a response. Gene hesitated, trying to collect his thoughts, trying to make something sound rational which, in this war environment, could only sound unforgivable. What was he supposed to tell the C.O., that if he couldn't be the pilot-in-command that he simply had no interest in the flight? That he was daydreaming? That he was bored silly?

"Well, what happened?"

"Sir, I don't really know how to explain myself. I want to get checked out more than anyone else can want me to, and I've been as puzzled as anyone about why it hasn't happened. I want to do my duty and what I was trained for."

He paused, collecting his thoughts, and then continued.

"It's just that…well, sir, when we're on a mission, there's usually not much the copilot's allowed to do. I guess I just begin to fly the mission myself…in my mind, I mean. I start thinking about how I would approach the target, what I'd do about ground fire, where the fighters are…all the stuff that the skipper of a flight has to think about…I just sort of tune out everything else. I simply didn't hear Sutherland call for the power increase. He thought I wasn't paying attention, or refused to do what he said, but I was just engrossed. I admit I wasn't paying attention like I should have been, but I wasn't being insubordinate. I would never do that."

Gene paused, not knowing if anything he had said made any sense, because he wasn't sure that it did to him. He continued, before the C.O. could respond.

"Sir, I don't know if this makes any sense. I just know that I want to do my part. I don't mean to cause problems. But I didn't come over here just to be ballast. I want to be a pilot, an aircraft commander. And if I can't do that in a B-26, then maybe I can in a B-17."

Gene started to say more, then stopped, realizing he had no further defense or explanation.

Moments ticked by. The C.O. returned to his desk, picked up Gene's folder, started to open it, then tossed it back down. He looked out the open tent at the ground crews attempting to patch the hand full of worn-out aircraft, to be ready for yet another mission. Finally, he looked back at Gene and spoke, quietly now, his face revealing no clues to his thoughts.

"Strange as it may seem, I think I do understand. In better times, I felt the same way about flying." The C.O. spoke quietly, pausing to watch a B-26 take off for a test run. Gene's hopes lifted ever so slightly at the unexpected response, but he waited for the C.O. to continue.

"B-17s, huh? Interesting thought." He walked back around behind his desk, looked out across the camp for a moment, then turned back to Gene.

"Stoddard, I'm going to level with you. I'm trying to fight a war here, with practically no men or planes. I need every crew member that can climb into a plane unassisted. Now here you are, supposedly one of the best, and not only can't you get checked out, your pilot thinks you refuse to follow orders. True or not, it creates a big problem for me, and an even bigger one for you. Maybe you're right about the B-17. Maybe you are more suited for it."

He glanced down at his desk, then back at Gene.

"My problem—and therefore, your problem—is that I need pilots. You're supposed to be one. Sorry, Lieutenant. I need you here. You're just going to have to do whatever it takes to do your job here, like it or not, left seat or right. But—I can't send a bomber crew out to risk their lives with a daydreaming copilot. I'm going to do some inquiring to see what it's going to take to make a command pilot out of you. But in the meantime, you'd better be the most responsive copilot on the base. Request denied. Dismissed."

Gene blinked at the sudden turn. He had felt a fleeting moment of optimism, but now could only react from military discipline.

"Yes, Sir." He saluted, turned, and started to leave the office.

"Oh, Stoddard, one more thing."

Gene turned back to face the C.O.

"Sir?"

"Just to help tempers cool off, I've got a flight down to Townsville scheduled to pick up some priority supplies. Go to Ops and tell them that I assigned you to fly copilot with Jacobs in his B-26. He's scheduled to depart around 1400, and be gone a couple of days. Maybe by the time you get back, you and Sutherland can figure out a way to coexist."

"Yes, sir."

Gene was glad for the opportunity to get away from the base. Maybe he could sort things out a little better. He left the headquarters tent and headed for operations.

Port Moresby

Dear Christy,

Well, as Laurel always says to Hardy, "It's another fine mess you've got us into." Except this time I've got myself into the mess. It seems my dream of consorting with angels and soaring with eagles is turning into a nightmare. I just can't seem to get the knack of handling the B-26 we fly well enough to suit the check pilots so that they're willing to sign me off as pilot. And I'm going to go stark raving mad if I have to keep flying as a copilot.

Mike can seem to make the thing do anything but roller skate. He had me fly a mission with him, to see what the problem might be. Didn't tell me that was why he had me fly with him, until a couple of days ago. Frankly, it sort of ticked me off, when he told me. That's not really like Mike. It was a pretty hot mission—lots of flak, and several Zeros jumped us. I had thought I handled it pretty well. He says I did everything right, like I had ice water in my veins. Except—he had to keep adjusting the power to keep the thing from stalling! I had no idea he was doing it. He says I'm just too "relaxed," and let it get ahead of me. I suppose that's the problem—you know me well enough to be able to believe it.

Mike suggested that I try to get transferred to a B-17. It's a four engine plane, and much larger than the B-26. But, from what he says, it flies like I do. He says I'd be a natural, in it. I requested a transfer, but got turned down. Seems I'm too important to lose.

Pardon my French, but I've got myself in a hell of a mess, and don't know what to do. Dad always says to "just put your faith in the Lord." I suppose that's worth a try—nothing else has worked.

Sorry to unload on you, but you're used to it, by now, right? No one else I can do it to, so I appreciate it. Don't mention it to the folks. They think I shouldn't have started flying, anyway. Looks like maybe they were right. Maybe I should have stuck to digging trenches.

Thanks for "listening."

Your messed up friend,
Gene

Transfer

Townsville, Australia

Tiny beams of sunlight pierced the many cracks and knotholes in the rough siding and wood shutters closed over the windows of the base canteen, brightening the dark interior and giving the room a quiet, mysterious sense. Dust particles stirred by a ceiling fan turning lazily overhead sparkled as they floated through the sunbeams, creating enough of an illusion of air movement for it to seem cool, even though the room temperature was already passing ninety degrees in the afternoon heat.

Lieutenant "Ollie" Olsen relaxed at one of the tables, slowly nursing a Coke. He was alone in the canteen, sitting tilted back on the chair with his feet on the table. The scene reminded him of old murder mystery movies he used to watch in the States, usually starring someone like Humphrey Bogart, and set in Africa, or some other mysterious foreign locale.

Ollie was feeling bored, probably with a bit of homesickness thrown in. He missed his wife the most when he had nothing to distract him. He had mailed his latest letters when they first landed at Townsville, and although he always felt a little closer when he got a letter off, there hadn't been many chances to write. Now, however, there had been little to do since his flight had landed, yesterday. Time was weighing heavily while he waited for his pilot, Major Carlson, to finish with the staff meetings that had brought them here. *Something big must be in the works,* he surmised. Commanders from all the other squadrons in the 43rd Bomb Group—their group—were there, as were the staff from Group headquarters.

As Ollie sat staring at his nearly-empty Coke bottle, he was vaguely aware of someone entering the canteen, but didn't turn to look as the sound of heels clunking on the planks of the wooden floor approached his table.

"Hey, Olsen. Fancy meeting you here."

Somewhat startled by this unexpected familiarity, Ollie looked up to see who was addressing him. It took a moment to place the tall, lean figure, then his mind clicked with recognition.

"Hey, Stoddard. How you doing?"

Gene smiled, and reached out to shake hands.

"Didn't expect to see anyone I'd know, down here. Haven't seen you since Lubbock. You were teaching us all how to hold a steady enough course that you could drop 'em down the proverbial pickle barrel."

"Yeah, I guess that's right." Ollie agreed, smiling his quiet smile. "Seems like a long time ago."

"That's for sure," Gene agreed. "And a long way away, I might add. This place definitely ain't Texas." He started towards the counter. "That Coke looks good. Can I get you another one?"

"No thanks. And you're certainly right about this not being Texas. I'm not sure what it is, but Texas it is not. Nor Illinois, for that matter."

Gene got his Coke, and returned to a chair across the table from Ollie.

"So, tell me, what they got you doing down here."

"I'm squadron bombardier with Major Carlson, in the 403rd squadron of the 43rd Bomb Group. He's the squadron C.O. The Forty-Third didn't really exist, except on paper, until a few months ago. We're getting pretty busy now."

"What do you mean?" Gene took another swallow of his Coke, looking slightly puzzled. "How could it be here and not exist?"

"Well, they could only get their hands on a few broken-down bombers when they got here, and all those got shot up so badly they couldn't be repaired. So, the guys were just assigned to painting flagpoles and peeling potatoes. But we got reactivated, or rejuvenated, or something, several months ago."

"Really? Seems like a strange way to win a war. Anyway, what have they got you doing now?" Gene asked.

"Oh, we're beginning to get pretty busy. Several of the crews in the Sixty-Fourth and Sixty-Fifth squadrons are getting pretty good with skip bombing. They've had a number of missions over Rabaul."

"Really? They're skip bombing with Seventeens?" Gene exclaimed. "I'd like to see that. We've been using it since the Bismarck Sea battle, but I never imagined they used the heavies for it—well, now that I think of it, our pilot said that B-17s would be skip bombing when we were during the Bismarck Sea battle, but I didn't see any. Have you done any?"

"No, not yet," Ollie said. "Don't know if we will. What have they got you doing?"

"Oh, I'm in the Twenty-Second Bomb Group. We've had quite a few missions since we got here just before Christmas. My first mission was the Bismarck Sea battle. We've been to Rabaul several times, and hit an airbase up at Lae, a couple of days ago." Gene set his empty bottle on the table. "That Coke hits the spot. Think I'll have another one. Sure you don't want another one?" Gene got up to go back to the cooler.

"Sure, why not. So what are you doing down here in beautiful downtown Townsville, if you're all so busy kicking Nip fanny?"

"Long story. I'm copilot on a B-26 that came down for some sort of priority supplies that couldn't wait for the ferryboats. We're supposed to head back tomorrow. Where are you based?" Gene asked, anxious to change the subject.

"Torrens Creek," Ollie answered, "about a hundred miles southwest of here, out in the desert. Town has more goats than people, and more flies than sand."

"We're at Iron Range. Sounds like we both got it pretty cushy, right?" Gene said, leaning back on his chair and putting one foot up on the crude table. It was good to get to talk to someone without wondering what they were thinking about him. His usual relaxed nature was beginning to return, and he was feeling better.

"I've heard the Twenty-Six is a handful. Killed a bunch of guys, didn't it?" Ollie asked, suddenly changing the mood.

Gene dropped his foot back down, and stirred rather restlessly in his chair. He didn't particularly want to get back on this subject.

"Yeah, it can be tricky. You're in a B-17, then?" Gene asked.

"Yeah—an 'E' model. It's the best bombing platform I've ever flown in."

Gene's interest was immediately aroused. "I see them around Moresby, sometimes, but never got to see one close up. I hear they're a great plane."

"Well, come on out to the flight line with me, and I'll introduce you to ours, such as it is, if you're interested."

"Sure, I'd love to." Gene got up, and followed Ollie out the door, squinting against the sudden glare.

As they approached the graceful, four-engine bomber parked nearby, Gene stopped suddenly, staring at it.

"Man-kind, Ollie. It's beautiful. I didn't realize how big it is, or how elegant it looks."

"Elegant?" Ollie repeated. "I hadn't heard it called that before, but I guess you're right. It is a magnificent bird."

Ollie followed Gene as he slowly walked around the aircraft, taking in its lines and features. Its wing, with a span of nearly one hundred and five feet, was nearly forty feet longer than that of his B-26, and considerably wider and thicker at the root where it joined the fuselage. The wing looked massive, compared to what he was used to seeing. Coupled with having four engines, rather than two, it created an impression of being much larger, of ruggedness, indestructibility.

Its designers had carried the raised flight deck back past a top gun turret, past the radio compartment, and then tapered it into the fuselage at the point where the curving dorsal fin swept down from the huge vertical stabilizer. The curving, sweeping, tapering lines all blended in a way as to appear to have been designed more by an artist than by an aeronautical engineer.

The plane rested on two large main gear, each located in the inboard engine well, and on a small tail wheel at the rear of the fuselage, just forward of the tail gunner station. This design resulted in the plane sloping dramatically upward when parked, poised to fly. Machine guns projected out from top, bottom, side and tail positions located strategically about the plane.

Without doubt, it was a war machine. It's official name was the "Flying Fortress." But its pleasant lines seemed to suggest that it served its purpose much in the same way as its crew: it would have preferred to be somewhere else, doing anything else, than fighting a war. But it had a job to do, and it was well prepared to do it.

"I'm not used to a tail-dragger, since they put me on the Twenty-Six. It looks more natural, somehow. And look at that wing. I could land a Stearman on it. Of course, everything's bigger. It's quite a lot larger than my plane. Mind if I crawl inside?"

"Sure, go ahead."

Entering the plane just aft of the motor driven top turret, which was located immediately behind the flight deck, he turned sideways to move around the turret and stepped up into the left pilot seat. Placing his feet on the rudder pedals, he took the control wheel in his left hand, and grasped the four throttle levers, located in the center console, in his right. The console looked neatly arranged, and organized. The engineers at the Boeing plant had realized that the pilot of their new bomber would have to contend with the demands of flying a complex aircraft under combat conditions, probably while in close formation flight. To make his job easier, they had designed an ingenious throttle control arrangement to make it simple for the pilot to control all four engines with one hand.

He looked out his side window at the huge expanse of the graceful wing, two big Wright Cyclones where he was accustomed to only one engine. He turned and took in the top turret assembly, and looked back down the fuselage into the bomb bay area. Turning back, he adjusted himself into the seat, and looked out the window at the distant sky. Gene Stoddard had found his home.

"Well, what do you think of her?" Gene's reverie was broken by Ollie's query. "Quite a bird, isn't she?"

Gene didn't respond, but just continued to inspect the cockpit, randomly touching the various control levers and switches. It was clear he saw himself flying this magnificent machine.

"Of course, my home's down there in the nose," Ollie continued. "Well, it's pretty blasted hot in here, with no air blowing. Want to see more, or you want to get back where it's only ninety degrees?"

Gene smiled. He liked Ollie's easy sense of humor and infectious smile. They hadn't had a chance to get to know each other very well when they were in training together, but Gene remembered that he had liked him. They seemed a lot alike.

"It's a great bird, but you're right," Gene agreed. "It is a bit warm in here. Let's head on back."

As they were walking back to the canteen, Gene decided that it wouldn't hurt to do a little judicious campaigning on his own behalf.

"You know, as coincidental as it may seem, I requested a transfer yesterday—to try to get into B-17s."

"Really?" Ollie looked at him, not expecting this revelation. Usually, a B-26 driver wore it as a badge of courage and superiority that he was able to fly the plane that had a reputation of being more than the average bus driver could handle. "What brought that on? I thought all you B-26 hot shots looked down your nose at mere truck drivers." Ollie was smiling, but obviously curious.

"Well, I've always been intrigued by the B-17, wondered what it would be like to fly it. But just between you and me, I hope to get on with the airlines when this fun and games is over. I'd like to have the four-engine experience." Gene hoped his rationale didn't sound too self-serving, but didn't want to get into the real reasons.

"Makes sense," Ollie agreed. "So what happened?"

"What do you mean, what happened?"

"What happened to your transfer request? Did you get it?"

"Oh. No, it was denied. Seems I'm considered too valuable to lose. Except when it's time to fly down for supplies."

Ollie sensed an edge of defensiveness in Gene's response. It appeared there might be more to Gene's story than he was telling, but he didn't feel it was appropriate to pursue it further.

As they approached the canteen, Major Carlson came walking toward them. They saluted, and Ollie introduced him to Gene.

"Major, this is Lieutenant Gene Stoddard. We flew together a bit when I was teaching bombing school at Lubbock. He's with Major Robinson's squadron."

The major shook Gene's hand, and looked him up and down. "So, you're flying Twenty-Sixes then, right? Quite a bird, I hear tell. Never flew one, myself. Always been partial to the Seventeen."

Ollie laughed, and put a hand on Gene's shoulder.

"Funny you should say that, sir. I've just been giving him a tour of ours. He says he's always wanted to fly one. In fact, he tells me that he tried to get transferred into a B-17 squadron, but couldn't swing it."

Gene glanced at Ollie, then at Major Carlson, a little taken aback at this airing of his private linen in front of the Major, but Ollie's grin indicated that he must know his pilot well enough to feel it was acceptable. Major Carlson looked at him with a degree of curiosity at this unexpected bit of information.

"Oh, really? Think you'd like our old Fort, do you? Any luck? I hear transfers are a little hard to come by."

"You're right, sir. Or at least this one was."

Major Carlson looked thoughtful for a moment. It wasn't good military protocol, or politics, to mess around in some other squadron's business.

"Well, war's hell, as they say. But after the 19th was sent home, and the 43rd was reactivated, business has been really picking up for us. I can't go into details, but you might want to know that some decisions were made today that will get us even busier. We'll probably be trying to pull some new crews together."

Gene looked at Major Carlson rather intently for a moment. *Is he trying to tell me something?* he wondered.

"That's really interesting news, sir. I'll certainly keep it in mind. Thanks for telling me."

"Well, scuttlebutt travels faster than the speed of heat, it seems, so I'm not telling you anything that you won't hear soon, anyway. At least this way, you'll know there's something to it, for a change."

They laughed at this, and walked into the canteen together for another thirst quencher.

Iron Range, Australia

"Sir, there's a Major Carlson on the line for you."

The clerk for Major Robinson stood with the C.O.'s office door partially ajar, his head stuck in to see if the major was "in."

"Fine. Put him through."

"Morning, Major. What can I do for you, this bright, cheery day?"

"Well, don't know if the scuttlebutt has reached you yet," Major Carlson replied, laughing at his friend's attempt at humor, "but we're expanding the operations of the Forty-Third. Don't suppose you could help me find about fifty new B-17s, now, could you?"

"Yeah, I heard that—didn't know whether to believe it, or not. Good luck on the planes." They both chuckled at such fantasies, and Carlson continued.

"Oh, by the way, I ran into one of your B-26 drivers yesterday, down at Townsville—Stoddard, I believe was his name. Seems he knew my bombardier from the States. I told him to tell you hi, for me. I thought you guys were busy kicking Nip fanny up there. Didn't suppose you had spare hands enough to send 'em lollygagging down to drink Cokes at Townsville."

What're you up to, you SOB? Robinson wondered, getting more curious.

"Well, you know how it is. Sometimes the inmates get time off for good behavior. What can I do for you, old buddy?"

"Oh, not much, probably. Looks like we are, in fact, getting some Seventeens in not too long. I'm not sure when we'll get new crews from the States, so we'll probably try to pull some together over here. I just wondered if you knew anybody that might have some pilots that they could spare?"

"Carlson, you gold-plated SOB!" Robinson didn't know whether to laugh, or to hang up on him. "You know that I can count on one hand my really experienced pilots as it is, and you go behind my back and try to shanghai them. Thanks a lot, buddy."

"Calm down, Dan. I wasn't talking about you. Unless, of course, you have someone who doesn't seem to fit into your organization, or something. Maybe someone you'd be happy to get rid of. You know I'm desperate. I'll take anybody. Even copilots. Well, anyway, just wanted to visit. Good talking to you."

Major Robinson slammed the telephone down, and leaned back in his swivel chair. *Damn him, he always could snooker me.* He pressed his intercom button to summon his clerk, who quickly appeared at his door.

"Sir?"

"Get a transfer form. I'm transferring Lieutenant Stoddard to the 43rd Bomb Group, effective immediately. Major Carlson's squadron—I believe it's the 403rd, but check it out. When Stoddard gets back from Townsville, tell him to come see me.*" Well, crap. It's probably better for both of us,* he mused.

Iron Range

Dear Christy,

Well, what can I say? Looks like maybe Dad is right—just put your faith in the Lord. At least something worked, as I am now officially a B-17 pilot!! I got transferred into the 403rd Squadron of the 43rd Bomb Group. I'm still not sure how it happened. I met Ollie Olsen when I was on a supply run to Townsville. I knew him from when I was in Advanced, at Lubbock. He's a bombardier, and flies with a Major Carlson, who is the 403rd squadron C.O. While we were having a Coke, he took me out and showed me their B-17. It was love at first sight! I told Ollie about wanting to get into a B-17, but that my request for transfer had been denied. Kind of embarrassed me, but he told Major Carlson about it. I guess he pulled some strings, because when I got back to my base I got called in to my C.O.'s office—made me wonder what else I had screwed up. But, he just casually informed me that I was being transferred— just like that. This is the same guy that denied my request just three days earlier because "he was desperate for pilots." One day the entire war effort depends on me being a copilot in a B-26. The next day, I'm transferred before I can blink. The military is a strange beast.

I made several supply runs as copilot, but got to do all the flying. Mike was right. It felt like putting on an old shoe. Lordy, I love that airplane. I was beginning to wonder if I really had what it takes to be a pilot. Major Carlson gave me a check ride—sure didn't pull any punches. Cut engines on me at low altitude, did about everything he could think of to make me screw up. But I just feel so at home in that plane. He signed me off as pilot—said I certainly passed. I'm still pinching myself—can hardly believe it's actually happened.

We got four new planes the other day, but don't have enough to go around, so I just have to beg for missions wherever I can get them. I need a plane of my own, and a crew. Guess I should just "trust in the Lord," right? I wouldn't object if someone threw in a couple of "requests" on my behalf.

Well, I'm obviously in a better frame of mind than in the last letter. Now, if I can just get a plane and crew, maybe I can do something to help win this war so I can leave this island paradise and come home—and start flying for the airlines.

I got several letters from all of you at last mail call. They sure are a welcome sight. Keep 'em coming. Tell everyone hi for me.

Your B-17 Pilot friend
Gene

Rabaul Photo Mission

Iron Range, Australia

By the end of the month, his first with the squadron, they had seen their fleet grow from only four B-17 bombers to eleven. Missions were growing steadily, but always with Gene left behind, or "riding shotgun" as copilot. Major Carlson had been understanding enough when Gene bugged him again about being assigned some missions, but offered only the suggestion that he continue to be patient. Gene decided the time had come to take matters into his own hands and paid a visit to the Ops (Operations) tent, where "Bronx" Riley—so nicknamed because of his accent, though he insisted he had grown up in Brooklyn—posted mission assignments.

"Bronx, I'm desperate. You've got to get me on some missions as pilot, before I go nuts."

Somewhat startled by the voice from the entrance of the tent, he turned to see who was interrupting his concentration. Bronx was navigator for the squadron C.O., Major Carlson, but also served as the squadron Operations Officer. That meant that he assigned missions to the various crews, and had been penning in missions and crews for the coming days. To Gene, that meant that Bronx Riley could be his salvation.

"What's the problem, Lieutenant? You rob the locals and gotta get outta Dodge?" he joked.

"Nah, nothing so nefarious," Gene replied, smiling, as he reviewed the chart on which Bronx was posting mission assignments. "I just can't take much more of this playing second fiddle. I want you to put me down as a volunteer for any and every mission, I don't care what, as long as I'm pilot and it goes north instead of south. I've flown as many trips to the scenic highlights of Australia as I care to for the rest of my natural born days."

"You must be desperate," Bronx reacted, eyebrows raised in surprise. Shuffling through his papers, he scanned down the lists, pursed his lips in apparent consideration of some as-yet unannounced mission, then looked back at Gene.

"Okay, here's what I can do for you. There's a photo recon mission over Rabaul harbor scheduled for day after tomorrow. Schell and his crew was scheduled, but he's come down with malaria and can't make the flight. I was going to assign it to a different crew, but I'll put you on in his place," he replied, and began jotting in the information on the schedule board.

"Thanks, Bronx. But I meant what I said. I want to be at the top of the list for anything that comes up." Gene's serious look made it obvious that he wasn't kidding.

"You got it, Lieutenant. But if you haven't flown over Rabaul in the daylight by yourself before, you may want to reconsider after you get back from this one."

"I've been there before, daytime and nighttime. You put me on the board, and I'll make the flights. Where can I find the crew, to get introduced and get them briefed?" Gene began walking towards the tent entrance, as he waited for an answer.

"They're over in the 65th area. Someone will point them out. Good luck."

"Navigator to pilot. Sir, it doesn't look like we're going to find any breaks in this cloud cover. Do you want a heading back to Moresby?"

The navigator was well aware that his substitute pilot would not need a heading back to their base—it was simply the reciprocal of the one they had flown to get there. His question was a not-so-subtle suggestion that they give up the mission, and return to base.

The lone B-17, with Gene at the controls, had been circling over the area where Rabaul, and its strategically important Simpson Harbor, lay nearly two miles below, totally obscured by clouds piled up against the volcano that served as a prominent landmark for the adjacent harbor. Their mission was to photograph the enemy shipping in the harbor, but this was obviously impossible from their present altitude because of the cloud cover. They had been circling for nearly thirty minutes, hoping that the cover would break, but to no avail. The crew assumed that they would scratch the mission and head for home before fuel could become an issue.

"Negative. There's usually enough warm air sliding down off that volcano to keep the clouds at a pretty good altitude above the surface. I'm going down and see if we can get under the overcast and get our pictures."

"Sir, are you serious? There's enough flak and fighters down there for twenty of us. One plane doesn't stand a chance."

It was not the usual protocol for a crew member to question the pilot, but the navigator felt free to voice to this substitute pilot what he knew they were all thinking.

Gene had already reduced power on the engines and started his spiraling descent. It was quite clear that he had every intention of making good on his statement.

"We'll be alright. Maybe we can take them by surprise." The crew couldn't tell if their pilot was joking or not, but no one laughed.

And maybe they can blow our asses to Kingdom Come, thought the navigator, rather bitterly, as he watched the view out the Plexiglas nose turn gray as the bomber entered the clouds. Gene switched his view from out the cockpit window to his panel gauges, and continued the descent on instruments. Minutes ticked by as the altimeter continued unwinding.

At about six thousand feet breaks began to show in the clouds, revealing glimpses of the harbor below. Even with such cursory views, Gene could see that the harbor appeared to be filled with shipping.

"Pilot to camera. We're about to break out. I'm going to stay in the clouds and head back out over open water, then make a diving run to pick up speed for a fast pass over the harbor. I'm going to stay on the open side of the harbor, so you'll have to take them out the right waist hatch. Be on your toes and ready to go. We'll only have one chance."

"Camera to pilot, I'm ready anytime." *Ready to be out of here,* he thought, sarcastically. *Who the hell would have figured on busting in under these clouds? We should have stayed on top and headed back.* Picking up his heavy camera, he braced himself at the waist gunner hatch, ready to start taking pictures as soon as they cleared the clouds.

Gene banked the bomber around in a tight turn, leveled off, then pitched the nose down as he shoved the throttles forward.

"Got this place confused with the Indy 500?" the copilot demanded, his frowning gaze fixed on the airspeed indicator which was climbing steadily toward its redline maximum limit. Gene didn't have time to look to see if the copilot was joking, as the plane broke into the clear. Ahead and below lay more shipping than he had ever seen, even in this normally busy harbor.

"Pilot to camera. Looks like something big may be in the works—this place is jammed. We've got to get it all, so get on it." Gene was looking carefully at the black puffs of antiaircraft fire that were already starting to erupt in front of them. The camera operator was concentrating too hard on his task to reply.

"Turret to pilot. I've got fifteen, maybe twenty fighters at two or three o'clock, bird-dogging us. Looks like they're staying outside the flak area, just under the cloud layer." *Just waiting to wax our asses! What's this maniac doing down here?*

"Roger, keep an eye on them."

"Damn!" The expletive erupted on the interphone from an unidentified crew member as a flak burst rattled the plane, jarring it as though hit by a gigantic fist.

"Captain, that stuff's thick enough to walk on. Let's get outta here." The navigator's whining was quickly wearing on Gene's nerves, but he was too busy to reply—and it wasn't his crew, so he kept his thoughts to himself.

The navigator was feeling naked and vulnerable in the Plexiglas nose. It was obvious that the Japanese had heard the sound of the engines circling above the clouds, growing louder as it had descended, and had been waiting for the plane to emerge. Every antiaircraft site in the harbor area, and most of the war ships rapidly zigzagging to escape an attack by the bomber, had opened fire as the lone bomber streaked across the harbor. The sky ahead was rapidly turning black from the exploding bursts, and red tracers were lacing the sky but most of it seemed to be falling below them.

Every few seconds, the plane would jolt from the concussion of flak bursts close by. Gene heard a few pieces hitting the plane, but most of the bursts appeared to be above them, and no one reported any damage or injuries. Without warning, he stood hard on the left rudder, slipping the plane sideways, all the while keeping the column shoved forward to continue his screaming dive. The engines surged as the propeller controllers strained to maintain their preset speed, and the airframe groaned and creaked under the strain.

In the rear, the camera operator bounced against the fuselage, nearly losing his balance, as he attempted to keep the camera pointed at the ships below under the evasive maneuvering. *Damned idiot must have escaped from the loony bin. He's more likely to kill us than the Japs are. How am I supposed to get these damned pictures when he's throwing me all over the plane?*

"Watch your airspeed!" the copilot yelled, as the airspeed needle continued its journey around the dial to regions he had never seen explored.

Ignoring the copilot's warning, Gene suddenly slammed in the opposite rudder, slipping in the opposite direction to throw off the gunners below. Engines and airframe groaned together under the forces. Flak bursts continued increasing in intensity, but seemed erratically random, as the gunners were unable to establish a track on the erratic flight path of the diving aircraft. The opposite edge of the harbor was now racing rapidly towards them. Tracers continued arcing upwards from several ships in the harbor, but the gunners were apparently misjudging the aircraft's speed and altitude, and none of the tracers seemed to be getting too close.

"Turret, where are those fighters?"

"About four o'clock, five miles, or so. Looks like they've got sense enough to stay outside the flak."

Gene ignored the barb. Even in the intensity of the moment, he was aware of how undisciplined this crew had been allowed to become. He swore to himself that no crew of his would ever exhibit such unprofessional compo-sure under attack. They were rapidly approaching the far side of the harbor, and their job was essentially done. All that remained was to fight off the swarm of enemy fighters keeping pace with them, awaiting an opportunity to attack.

"Camera, you done back there?"

"Roger. Let's get the hell outta here."

Without comment, Gene rolled sharply left as he shoved the throttles to maximum power and pulled back firmly on the control column, taking the plane into a steep, climbing turn toward the cloud cover and away from the waiting fighters.

Once the fighter pilots saw where the bomber was headed, though, they split into two groups and charged forward on arcing intercept paths, hoping to circle ahead and attack it from both sides before it could reach the sanctuary of cloud cover. Within minutes, they were ahead, circling in on the bomber as its airspeed bled off rapidly in the climb.

"Pilot, turret. Bandits one, two o'clock, closing."

"Waist to pilot—they've split into two groups. There's more over at nine o'clock, trying to get ahead of us."

The top turret gunner was already starting to fire at the first of the circling Zeros, and the waist gunner was swinging his fifty-caliber to join the fight. As incendiary tracers from the first fighter arced toward the bomber, Gene began a circling turn inside the path of the lethal fire. The maneuver kept his plane from being hit, but also forced the enemy fighter to continually steepen his turn in an attempt to bring his guns to bear on the bomber.

"Son of a bitch!" The top turret gunner reflexively let out the burst, as he ducked down out of his turret. The enemy fighter had exploded, so close overhead that several pieces of debris banged off their bomber. "That bastard was nearly inverted going over me—I could have knocked him down with my pistol."

He quickly recovered his equanimity, and stood back up in his turret, frantically searching the sky ahead. "Where'd that second one go? Anybody see that guy?"

"Turret, waist—he peeled off, trying to miss the pieces—you blew that bastard all over the sky."

"Pilot, nav—we've got two, maybe three more lined up coming in from one o'clock"

"Roger, I've got 'em—turret, you see those guys? I'm turning into them."

Three enemy fighters were lined up in trail, circling around to make their passes. As the first one approached, guns blazing, Gene began a turn inside it, again forcing it into an ever-steeper bank as it flew past, close overhead.

"Good going, turret, he's trailing flame—you got him."

"Pilot to crew—those other two are breaking off, they're coming down our right side. Waist, you see them?"

"Roger. Turret, you're goin' to have to give me some help, I can't take both those guys—"

"Forget it, they're already out of range."

"Watch those two at ten o'clock. Are they coming back in? Waist, you see them?"

"I've got 'em…"

"Pilot, waist—they don't seem to be coming in. They're just hangin' around out there."

The evasive maneuvers of the bomber, and the fact that the first two at-
tackers had been sent down in flames, had taken the fighters by surprise. As
they attempted to regroup, the bomber slipped into the cloud layer and disappeared. The attack was over.

The guns on the enemy fighters were fixed in the wings and nose of the
plane. The pilot had to adjust his flight path so that the trajectory of the rounds
from his guns would intercept the flight path of the bomber. It was easiest to
do this by attacking the plane in a circling arc from the nose. But Gene's turns
into the fighter's path, a trick he had learned while flying with the Twenty-
Second crews, threw off the aim of the fixed guns of the Zero, forcing it to
constantly increase its bank to attempt to turn into the bomber. The maneuver
could force the fighter to be nearly inverted by the time it passed over the
bomber, presenting a target to the flexible guns of the top-turret that could
hardly be missed. The fighters had not expected such an effective defense
from the lone B-17.

Although several hits were taken, there was no serious damage to the
B-17, and none of the crew injured. The unexpected tactic had kept the fighters
at bay until the bomber disappeared into the clouds. Surrounded now by the
cumulus security blanket, the adrenaline began to subside in the crew, and
heart rates began to slow towards normal.

"Damn! What was that all about?"

Phil Williams, the nineteen-year-old navigator, slumped against the curving nose, looking at the grayness of the cloud layer that was protecting their
escape from the enemy aircraft searching below them.

"They didn't tell me in nav school that we'd have to take on the Japs
single-handed with a certified lunatic for a pilot."

Jackson, the bombardier, sat against the opposite side of the nose, smiling
at his emotionally exhausted navigator.

"Well, he may be crazy, but he's crazy like a fox. That was some piece of
airmanship. I've never seen anything like that."

Not much was said as the plane droned its way back to the base. After
they had shut down and the rest of the crew was headed back to their tents, the
copilot, Jeffrey Scott, fell in alongside Gene as he walked toward the Ops tent
for his mission debriefing.

"I don't know whether to compliment you on your determination to complete the mission, or recommend you for court martial for reckless endanger-
ment. What was that all about, anyway?"

"What was what all about?" Gene asked, obviously puzzled.

"That little exercise over Simpson Harbor, that's what. What's your deal?"

"Deal? What are you talking about?" Gene glanced at him, confused over
what the copilot was getting at, and barely able to conceal his annoyance.

"You know damned well what I'm talking about," the copilot challenged.
"Most pilots I know would have headed for the barn when they saw that the

harbor was overcast. I don't know anyone, on the other hand, who would have run the gauntlet of that harbor alone, in daylight. Like I said, what's your deal, anyway?"

"There isn't any 'deal,'" Gene rebutted, emphasizing the word. "Good grief. What'd you expect me to do? We flew for eight hours to get photos of the harbor. Our guys can't plan any missions, or know about any convoys, without good intelligence. Going back without pictures shouldn't even be an option, if there's any way possible to get them. I knew from when I flew up there with the Twenty-Second that there's usually several thousand feet clear under the overcast over that harbor because of the warm air off the volcano. I figured with our speed they'd just be scatter-shooting with their heavy stuff, and we were fairly high for the small caliber stuff—I didn't think it was too likely we'd get hit. I just hoped that by firewalling it, our speed would keep us away from the fighters. I have to admit, though, they got to us a little quicker than I expected. They usually attack from the front, like they did today. I thought I could outrun them and be in the clouds before they could get ahead of us."

"You want me to believe all that was…premeditated?" the copilot responded, sounding a bit dubious, not sure if his leg was being pulled, or not.

"Well, what did you think it was?" Gene reacted, his growing frustration with this undisciplined crew becoming apparent. "Good Lord, every flight can't be a milk run. Do you guys always just turn around and high-tail it home at the first sign of trouble? Seems to me, if you have a good plan, and take into account both your capabilities and those of the Japs, you can pretty well even the odds. 'There's always a way to get the job done, if you're willing to find it,' as my daddy used to say."

"That's all hunky-dory, I suppose," the copilot replied, ignoring Gene's uncomplimentary assessment of his crew, "assuming you don't pull the wings off the plane. Did you know you had that damn thing past redline coming across the harbor?"

"Yeah, I knew it," Gene said, laughing a little at this comment. "We'd sometimes nearly bury the airspeed needle on the B-26, and it doesn't care. Besides, the B-17 is probably the most ruggedly built bomber ever produced. I don't think you could pull the wings off that thing with bulldozers."

Scott continued along in silence, shaking his head slightly in disbelief. He glanced sideways at Gene, then back at the dusty path. He was unsure of what to make of this new pilot.

In one of the crew tents, however, the cameraman and other crew members were quite sure, and were loudly proclaiming it.

"You should have seen that lunatic! Did we stay above the cloud layer where we were supposed to be? Oh no! Not Mr. Ace-of-the-Base. We've got to take on every gun in the damned harbor, and Lord only knows how many fighters. I counted at least fifteen, maybe twenty, coming after us."

"So what? The way he came screaming across the harbor we should have left both wings as a souvenir. I swear we were hitting three hundred in that dive. That thing was screamin' like a stuck pig."

"Yeah, but did you see Zimmerman trying to keep from falling on his keister with his camera when Daredevil Dick would throw that thing into a skid?" the radio operator joked, flailing his arms and stumbling around the floor with his drink, trying to imitate the gyrations of the camera operator during the wild pass across the harbor.

"Go to hell, bean brain. I like to busted my shin, and it wouldn't take much to bust something important of yours." The aggrieved cameraman was not amused. "That guy liked to killed us all up there today. I'll never get in a plane with him again."

"Aw, back off, Zimmerman," countered Jackson, the bombardier, who had been quietly taking in his crew mates complaints. "What a bunch of pansies! We can't turn around and come running back to mommy every time there's a problem. Besides, Smitty, you're almost half way to being an ace, with those two Zeros you bagged, today. First time I've ever seen you hit anything. What you saw today was some of the best flying you'll ever get to experience. Why the hell you think we're over here? He got the job done, and saved our butts in the process. You didn't see any Purple Hearts being handed out when we got back, did you? I'd fly with that guy anywhere."

"Hey, Stoddard. How's it going? I hear you had quite a ride yesterday." Bronx Riley, the Ops Officer, was busy posting crews for upcoming missions as Gene entered the tent.

"Good morning. And what do you mean? Everything went pretty well, actually. We had to dive under some flak, and hightail it for the clouds to lose some Zekes, but we didn't take any hits to speak of." Gene was looking over Bronx's shoulder as he scribbled in crew names, and mission assignments. "Got anything for me?"

Bronx looked at Stoddard somewhat incredulously, then turned to spit out a load of his ever-present chewing tobacco into a nearby bucket.

"Stoddard, I don't know what to make of you. Half the base thinks you tried to kill everybody on board with your daredevil antics up over Rabaul yesterday, and the other half thinks you're the hottest pilot since Von Richthofen."

"That's crazy," Gene replied, as he continued inspecting the mission listings, showing no visible response to Bronx's outburst. "I'm not a hot-shot pilot, and I didn't do anything overly risky. I just did what I had to do to get the pictures, and came home the safest way I could. You didn't answer my question."

"Nothing for sure, yet." Bronx said, shaking his head, partly in disbelief and partly in masked respect. "I'll do what I can."

"Thanks. I appreciate it." Gene turned to leave the tent, then turned back to face Bronx. "One more thing…"

"What now?"

"You've got to get me a crew and plane of my own. I can't just keep float-ing around like this. I'll go nuts."

"Stoddard, you're outta your mind. You know I don't make decisions like that. Besides, every pilot in this outfit wants his own crew and plane. Get in line." Bronx smiled, shook his head, and turned back to his work.

"I know you don't make the decisions," Gene countered, "but you know the people who do. Just get me a crew and plane."

With that, Gene left and headed back to his tent. On his way, and to his surprise, he saw his friend, Mike Kingston, coming toward him.

"Mike! Man, what a great surprise," Gene exclaimed, his face lighting up. "What brings you away from the vaunted Twenty-Second? Let's go get a drink, and spread a little BS."

Gene eagerly grasped his friend's hand, giving it an enthusiastic shake, then draped an arm over his shoulder, as they walked together toward the canteen.

"Oh, Staff decided they wanted a joint planning session on target selection, with the Twenty-Second and the Forty-Third," Mike replied. "I got the black bean and had to attend. I did hear that one Lieutenant Stoddard has become quite the hotshot pilot. That must have been some picture-taking jaunt you took over Rabaul."

Gene glanced at the ground, shaking his head, somewhat embarrassed to have created such a flurry of conversation.

"Mike, I don't get it. If I'd done that with you guys—or, for that matter, some of the other squadrons here in the 43rd—it wouldn't have rated an honor-able mention. I don't get a crew like that. It's one thing to be as undisciplined as they are, but—they're scared of their own shadows. We were sent to take pictures. I took pictures—and got home without any significant damage or any injuries to my crew. I used the same evasive maneuvers I learned with you guys…the only difference, this time, was that I did it from the left seat instead of watching from the right. It hardly seems worth talking about."

Gene paused a second, smiled and added an afterthought.

"Oh, and one more thing, I might add. I kept my throttles carefully adjusted, and didn't spin out during any steep turns." Gene grinned mischievously at his friend, nudging him in the ribs with his elbow.

Mike smiled, somewhat embarrassed. It had been a rather painful thing to have to be so blunt with his best friend, but he believed it had to be said. And it was now obvious that the end result had been well worth it.

"Okay. I had that coming," Mike agreed. "Anyway, I didn't pay much attention to all the talk. Some guys seem to believe a recon flight should be a milk run. If there's any risk, beat it for home. I wouldn't pay much attention to it. You did your job, and that's all that counts."

As they relaxed, Mike with a beer and Gene with his usual Coke, Gene looked at Mike a moment, then a smile spread across his face.

"What's that big Cheshire-cat smile supposed to mean?" Mike asked.

"Mike—I just can't tell you how it feels to be flying the Fort," Gene replied. "I'll be eternally grateful to you for knowing me well enough to push me into it."

"I knew you'd be a natural in it. I'm glad it's worked out. I gather you like it," Mike replied.

"Man, I've got to be honest," Gene said, leaning toward his friend, a look of both sincerity and excitement on his face. He glanced around the tent and lowered his voice, a reflexive habit from growing up in an intensely private family. "When we were screamin' across Simpson Harbor, juking and jinking to throw off the flak, and then maneuvering into those Zeroes, I felt...I don't know how to even express it. I don't want to say...invincible—that's an attitude that can get you killed. I felt like...I don't know. Maybe like I was having sex." Gene grinned, a slight blush coloring his face. "Of course, I've never done that, so this might have been better—I wouldn't know."

Mike laughed out loud at his embarrassed friend. He had never seen him so excited and enthusiastic about anything, including planes.

"Actually, Gene, I think you have to have a certain amount of that feeling during missions, if you're going to accomplish it and survive. If you go in feeling apprehensive, or timid, you're not going to put yourself sufficiently in harm's way to do the job, and you'll react more from fear than from training. I'd say just keep being yourself, enjoy your plane, and you'll do just fine."

"Yeah, you're probably right," Gene agreed. "I must say, though, that I'm really looking forward to when this is over, and you and I can be flying people home for Christmas—instead of dropping bombs on them."

"Yeah, me too," Mike agreed, a faraway look on his face. "They've got the airlines flying troops and equipment all over the globe. You know that's got to be making the bigwigs in those airlines aware of the potential of these new planes, and what all-weather flying will mean, after the war ends. They're going to be in a real cat-fight trying to establish routes and get the most business. I think you and I are going to have a lot of fun after this is all over, old buddy."

Ollie Olsen was walking to the mess tent, still in a state of disbelief bordering on mild shock, since hearing the news the day before of the loss of his pilot, Major Carlson. Several days earlier, Major Carlson had volunteered to take the place of a pilot who had a case of malaria on what was expected to be a routine reconnaissance mission. The plane had radioed a contact report of a convoy, but had not returned and was never heard from after that report. Search and rescue flights had found no trace of the missing plane or crew, and ultimately gave up the search.

Olsen had not yet been able to accept the loss. His feelings were partly the natural ones of grief that are felt when a close friend is lost. Major Carlson and

Ollie had not been close friends in the usual sense, but Ollie greatly respected him, and had grown to feel close to him during the many hours of flight and combat together.

But beyond those feelings, for the first time since he had been shipped over, the fact that death could await any one of them had now become personal, palpable. It was something that they all knew in the back of their minds, but until it hit someone close to you, it seemed somewhat hypothetical. For the first time, Ollie had to admit to himself that people he knew and cared for were going to die—and that he could be one of them. He entered the mess tent, taking a seat on the bench next to Bronx Riley, his irascible navigator.

"Hey, Ollie, how you doin'? You okay?"

Bronx wasn't known for his solicitous nature, but he knew that Ollie would be taking this loss rather hard.

"Yeah, I'm all right, I guess. Just kind of hard to accept."

Ollie picked listlessly at a plate of powered eggs, took a couple of bites, then pushed them aside. They could never be accused of being tasty, but on this particular morning they about gagged him.

"You know, Bronx, I don't take change real well. I like for things to be ordered and stable. What do you figure will happen to us now? You figure we'll get split up?"

"Hard to say, in this man's war. They might just assign a new pilot. Of course, we don't know for sure that Carlson's gone. Search and Rescue might bring them in any time now. Guys sometimes get picked up after a few days of floating around."

"You know as well as I do that's not going to happen, Bronx. They've had planes out for two days and haven't seen a sign of anything. You know the Japs—they probably shot them if they did ditch. Or the sharks got them."

"Well, that doesn't mean we have to give up hoping. Things sometimes work out."

Ollie pushed his tray back. "Yeah. Sometimes. Thanks, Bronx. Think I'll go write a letter home, as soon as I finish this cup of god-awful coffee."

Bronx got up to leave.

"Take care. I'll go check with Ops and see if anything's come up. I'll drop by if I hear anything."

As Bronx departed, Lieutenant Gene Stoddard entered, looked around, and made his way to the table where Olsen and the others were sitting. They looked up as he approached.

"Hey, Stoddard. Good to see you. Pull up a bench."

Olsen stood up and shook hands.

"Well, I can't stay. I heard you were down here, and wanted to drop by to give you the news myself."

"What news?" Ollie asked, looking rather blank. "I've had about all the news I care for, right now."

"I know how you all felt about Major Carlson." Gene said, looking briefly at the others, then back at Ollie. "I had a lot of respect for him, even though I didn't know him very well. I hope this won't be considered bad news, as well, but I'm going to be your new pilot."

Port Moresby

Dear Christy,

You remember that dumb joke we used to tell in high school (actually, I used to tell it—you never did) about how the definition of mixed emotions is seeing your grouchy mother-in-law going over a cliff in your brand new Cadillac? Well, I really have a case of mixed emotions. I should be elated. I now have my own crew! It's one of the best crews flying out here. But the problem is that the crew belonged to Major Carlson. He's the guy that got me transferred to the B-17. He went on a mission as a substitute for a guy that had malaria, and the plane never came back. I really had a lot of respect for him. It makes me feel rather strange. I had literally been praying for a crew of my own, but this isn't the way I expected God to get me one. Sort of hard to understand, actually. Makes me feel a little strange, about it all.

But the fact remains—I have my own crew and am really excited about it, even if I don't like the way it happened. The guys are swell, but it's going to take some time to earn their trust and respect. They were really loyal to Major Carlson. Now, if I can just talk God into getting me a plane, I'll be fixed. It will be interesting to see how that works out.

Oh yeah, one other bit of good news. I guess my recent recon flight impressed the Brass, because I am now <u>Captain</u> Gene Stoddard. Sounds pretty good, doesn't it? I also get a few bucks a month extra pay! Maybe now I can buy that new Caddy when I get back—or at least a new tire for one.

Sorry, but I don't seem to have much else to say, right now, so will send this. Hope all of you are doing okay. I got a good letter from Liz a couple of days ago. She's starting to sound like quite a grown up lady, now. Whatever happened to my "little" sister?

Love you all,
Captain Gene

Ad Astra

Seven-Mile Strip, Port Moresby

"Something I can help you with, Captain?"

Ignoring the question, Captain Gene Stoddard continued staring, deep in thought, at the tired bomber parked to the side of the maintenance area. After a couple of seconds, he turned to see who had interrupted him.

"What's that?"

Facing Gene, looking rather puzzled, was a shirtless, sweaty young mechanic barely out of high school, covered in dust and grime from endless hours of working on aging, combat-weary B-17 bombers that were in constant need of repair from damage and overuse. His eyes were dull and sunken from months without a full night's sleep.

"Sorry to bother you, sir," the young mechanic apologized, "but you've been starin' at that wreck for so long that we thought maybe there was a problem. Can I help you with anything?" It was obvious that the skinny young mechanic wasn't sure what to make of the circumstance.

For nearly half an hour the maintenance crew repairing a nearby B-17 had watched, at first disinterestedly and then with growing curiosity, as the captain had investigated the aircraft. At first he had simply stood there staring at it. Then he slowly circled it, intently studying it. Had they still been in the States, he might have been considering the purchase of a somewhat suspect used car. Indeed, the mechanics had been placing bets that he would walk up and kick one of the main gear tires, or perhaps open the rear crew door and slam it a few times. He had disappeared inside for a several minutes, then reappeared, swinging down out of the forward hatch.

"He's thinking of buying it and shipping it home for a souvenir," one mechanic had speculated.

"Bullshit. He's a greenhorn pilot, and he's tryin' to figure out how to get in the cockpit before his crew sees him," another had countered quite derisively. After some time of this, they had dispatched the young mechanic to find out what was going on.

"No, there's no problem," Gene answered, looking briefly at the puzzled mechanic querying him, before glancing over at the other mechanics. He grinned slightly at how his behavior must have appeared to them, then looked back at the waiting mechanic. "Tell me, what's the story on this bird? Why isn't it being repaired for return to service?"

Although a few new B-17s were finally beginning to arrive from the States, several squadrons were clamoring for them. No one was going to receive enough new bombers to fill their squadron's full strength anytime soon, and every available bomber had to be used. Planes capable of being repaired were patched up as best as possible and returned to service. Those too badly damaged were cannibalized for parts to keep the others in the air. If a plane wasn't being repaired, it usually meant it was beyond repair. But somehow, at least to Gene, this one didn't seem quite that far beyond hope.

And Gene was approaching the point of desperation. He felt he must have his own plane, however that might be achieved, whatever it might require. Gene felt he and his new crew were now melding as a combat unit, but he knew that without his own plane they would remain at the whim of circumstance and the Operations Officer, a slave to the big "if." If a plane was available, and if another crew didn't get to it first, then perhaps they would get a mission.

If he was going to get to fly, the way he felt driven to fly, he knew he had to have his own plane. He also knew that without enough missions to his credit, he wouldn't have the status and priority to merit a new one, when—and if— one arrived. And in the back of his mind was always his future dream. If he survived, he would get hired by some airline, if he had more experience and missions than his competition. It was quite simple. He had to have a plane.

Now, here stood one, apparently unclaimed. Gene's conviction had grown stronger with every passing minute of his inspection of this derelict. Somehow, through sheer force of will power if required, this B-17 was going to fly again. It was an E model, with the vital tail gunner station. And, "if" Gene had his way, it was going to be his.

"This wreck? You gotta be kidding, sir. We gave up on it. We were about to start stripping it for parts," the mechanic reacted incredulously, slowly shaking his head as if to lend silent emphasis to a hopeless situation.

"Do I look like I'm kidding, private? I need a plane, and here sits one. What's required to get it flying? Or perhaps you don't know—or don't care... private?"

The sudden hardness in Gene's eyes and voice, and the pointed emphasis on his lower rank, startled the private.

"Uh, beg your pardon, sir. I, uh...I'm sorry, sir, I thought you were just joking. Of course I care. We bust our butts all day and most all night trying to patch these wrecks up and get them flying, but some of them are just too far gone."

"Relax, private," Gene assuaged the young mechanic. Gene's face relaxed a bit, and he turned to look again at the plane. The look in his eyes made it obvious that he saw this airplane in the sky, with him at the controls. "I know you guys go far beyond the call of duty, and we appreciate it. But I absolutely, positively have to have my own plane. Now, seriously—what will it take to get this one flying again? Is there spar damage, or some other structural damage I couldn't see?"

"No sir, at least not that we were able to spot, anyway," the mechanic assured Gene. "There's a bunch of bullet holes to patch, but they missed the important stuff."

"Well, if the structure's okay, then it's got to be mostly a matter of repairs. What all has to be done to get this thing in the air again?"

"Oh, jeez, let me think." The private scratched his close-cropped head, and looked the plane over while running an inventory in his mind. "First of all, number three and four engines are shot and will have to be replaced. We were going to pull the others to stick on other planes. But General Kenney's pretty well keeping us in engines. We can handle that. Some hydraulic lines got shot through—they'll have to be replaced. We've got a few of them, but not all of them. We might be able to get some of them from the depot, but we'll probably have to cobble up some of them ourselves. The radios needed quite a lot of service—one of them took a thirty caliber though it—so we pulled them for parts. The main gear retraction won't work—not sure why. And the belly turret won't rotate—probably burnt out motors..." He paused, attempting to think of any more problems to add to the list.

"Yeah, I see what you mean," Gene replied. "That all sounds pretty challenging—but it doesn't sound insurmountable. However, you all overlooked one really important factor when you gave up on this bird."

"What do you mean, sir? We looked it over pretty carefully before we gave up on her," the mechanic reacted defensively, taken aback that a pilot might have spotted a problem area that they had missed.

Gene motioned for the mechanic to follow him, and started toward the midsection of the plane. He squatted down to look at its underside. Three Plexiglas-covered windows had been installed in the belly of "his" plane.

"Recognize these?"

"Yes, sir. They're camera ports. Several of the planes have them." The private was obviously still puzzled by this perplexing captain.

"Not like this," Gene countered. "Come inside."

Gene led the way into the aft portion of the plane, and into the radio compartment. He nodded toward three large, complicated-looking boxes with electrical cables attached.

"Know what those are?"

The private glanced briefly at the equipment.

"Some kind of cameras. We were going to turn them over to the photo shop when we got started stripping equipment. It limped in here just a couple of days ago—we haven't had time to do much, yet." The private had no real idea why he was being interrogated, and was still a bit defensive.

"Not just any cameras, private," Gene objected. "These are trimetrogon cameras. Probably the only installed set in the squadron."

"Try what?" the private asked, shaking his head in confusion. "I'm sorry, sir. I have no idea what you're talking about."

"One of the most important missions we fly is photo recon, and the trimetrogon camera system is the only one that can be used for generating topographic maps of terrain. These cameras have to be carefully installed, and meticulously aligned. They take simultaneous pictures looking straight down, and from two different angles. The pictures are stereoscopically overlaid to determine the height of the terrain in the pictures. Private, this is one of the most important planes on this base."

"I see, sir," the private replied, nodding. The blank look on his face made it clear that all he could really see was that this captain intended that this airplane was going to fly again, and that could only mean more late nights working, with too little sleep, for him and his mechanic buddies.

It was not unusual to have high-power cameras installed in the planes. Photo intelligence was mandatory to be able to assess enemy air strength at its bases, convoy composition, troop locations, and bombing mission strike assessment. It was used to plan missions and determine the type of ordnance and number and type of aircraft to be used. In short, the war could not be successfully waged without good reconnaissance photographs.

But, special camera installations were required to be able to prepare topographic maps, which displayed not just the layout of an area, but also the elevation of the terrain. This information was essential when planning an amphibious island assault. How tall were the peaks that troops would have to scale? How difficult would the beach be to land on when the island was assaulted? Only a topographic map could answer these questions, and only the trimetrogon camera array could provide the necessary information to prepare those maps.

Gene knew the importance and significance of these cameras and suspected that, if he played his cards right, they could be parlayed into obtaining his own plane—even if it had to be resurrected from the graveyard. He turned to face the mechanic.

"What's your name, private?"

"Shelby, sir. Private Thomas Shelby."

Gene surprised the private by draping an arm around his shoulder, as he started walking him back toward the maintenance facility.

"Well, Private Shelby, tell your crew chief that they'll have to scrounge parts from some other bird, because this one's going to fly again." Gene was smiling, but there was no doubting that he was serious.

"Uh…yes, sir. But someone's going to have to get it off the decommission list and on the repair list."

Gene stopped, removed his arm from over the private's shoulder, and looked him in the eye. It was quite plain to Private Shelby that this was a captain whose will was not going to be denied. He expected that he would be seeing more of him in days to come.

"I'll handle that," Gene assured him. "You just start figuring out what you have to do to get it flying. I'll run interference for you, and see that you get the parts you need. And my crew will help in every way that we can."

"Ye gods, Captain. Saint Peter and all the archangels couldn't keep that plane in the air."

Ken Whitford, hands on his hips, stared at the forlorn aircraft before him. Captain Stoddard had brought his crew down to the maintenance area to show them their "new" plane. They weren't impressed.

"Oh, good grief, Ken," Gene reacted, more than a little frustrated with his crew's lack of enthusiasm. "We've seen planes shot up a lot worse than this. I can't figure why they were going to scrap it. We must be starting to get some new ones. Besides, don't you have any confidence in our esteemed maintenance section?"

"I don't know, Captain. It's pretty sorry lookin'." Slim Jensen, the tail gunner, added to the negative votes. "Maybe we should wait for one of the new ones. I hear we're going to get some, in not too long."

"Dadgummit, you guys, my patience is pretty well exhausted," Gene retorted. "You know how I feel about this crew. We can do anything we set our minds to. But at the rate we're getting new planes, it'll be months before we have a shot at getting one. We're always going to be suckin' hind tit on this base, if we have to borrow someone else's plane to fly a mission. Now—do you guys want to fly, or do you want to sit around the base watching everyone else do our job for us?"

The crew stood silently staring at the plane, embarrassed at having to be challenged by their captain. They were each thinking the same thing: Major Carlson would not have let a problem like this keep him from pressing the fight against the enemy, and they had respected him for it. Now, here was their new skipper trying to do the same thing and they weren't supporting him. But they all stood there, each waiting for somebody else to respond. Finally, Ken Whitford spoke for them all.

"Oh, what the hell. If flying this junk pile is what it takes to get the job done, then we're with you, Skipper. What do we have to do?"

"Thanks, Ken. I knew you guys wouldn't let me down. I've already managed to get it off the decommission list, and talked to the crew chief about the needed repairs. Jimmy, you'll have to see about getting some new radios installed, and Neil, you check out those tri-met cameras and do whatever's needed to get them going. It was those cameras that let me get the thing saved from the junk pile. Slim, why don't you and Danny work with Armament to get the turrets working. The belly turret won't operate at all, for some reason—the mechanic said it's probably burnt-out motors. The rest of you can coordinate repairs on your own areas."

The crew began to slowly move around and into the plane, ready to get to work, but still a little hesitant as to what they were getting into.

"Hey, Ollie. Can you and Bronx come up to the nose for a minute?" Gene was staring up at the Plexiglas nose that gave the bombardier and navigator their view of the world below.

"Roger, Captain. What do you need?" The two of them looked up to see what their pilot was studying. They were responsible for the two nose guns, when under attack.

"Where would you say we are the most vulnerable to attack?" Gene was looking at the two thirty-caliber guns, one on either side of the nose.

"The nose, obviously," Bronx replied without hesitation, "with nothing but those stupid pea-shooters up there. And, you can't fire the damned things straight ahead."

The one thing that concerned them all when under attack by enemy fighters was the minimal firepower in the nose of the B-17. As the plane was delivered from the factory, a single thirty-caliber machine gun was mounted on each side of the plane's nose, angling out on either side, behind the Plexiglas nosecone. Coverage straight ahead was minimal, and visibility limited. Only the top turret guns could accurately fire straight forward.

In addition, the thirty caliber shells were too small. The weapon just couldn't put a sufficient quantity of high velocity, large caliber rounds into a target quickly enough to assure the needed immediate destruction. Because of this, the bomber was especially vulnerable to nose attacks. The Japanese fighter pilots had discovered this vulnerability rather quickly, and now virtually always mounted their attacks by angling in from in front of the bomber. There would have to be more firepower up front if they were to be able to withstand such attacks.

"So what do you suggest we do about it?" Gene asked.

"We've got to stick fifties in there instead of those pop guns, for one thing." Bronx immediately replied. "Will those mounts take the impact?"

"Yeah, if we beef them up. I've seen it done on some other B-17s," Gene responded. "Got any other ideas?"

"Such as?" Ollie asked, aware that Gene had something in mind.

"Well, when I was in the Twenty Second, I was really impressed with what Pappy Gunn did on the commerce busters for skip bombing," Gene said, remembering how General Kenney had assigned the gunnery sergeant to find a way to put eight fifty-caliber machine guns in the nose of the B-25 skip bombers. "Apparently someone else had the same idea. I saw a B-17 taking off the other day that looked like it had a fixed nose gun added. Why couldn't we do that?"

"Do what?" Ollie asked, puzzled by Gene's suggestion.

"Stick a fixed-fifty up here," Gene answered. "We could put a fifty caliber under the floor, and fire it from a switch on my control wheel. With that, and the two thirties replaced with fifties, we'd stand a lot better chance in a nose attack."

"Well, it's certainly worth a try," Bronx agreed, "but it's pretty crowded up there. Is there room for the ammo cans and feed chutes? How would we reload?"

"I don't know. But I figure that if Gunn could find a way to stick eight of them in the nose of a B-25, we should be able to get one in the nose of a B-17," Gene responded. "I'm going to find out whose plane I saw the other day, and see how they did it. Why don't you check in with Armament to make sure replacing those thirties will work out okay."

"I'll get on it, Captain. I've got another idea, though. How about going to dual fifties at the other guns? It would double their firepower."

Gene looked thoughtful for a moment as he considered the possibility. "Well, we surely could at the waist stations. We could replace the single fifty with a pair on the same mount. How about Jimmy's?"

"I think we could get them in there, without too much problem."

On each side of the fuselage, behind the wing, a large rectangular opening was included for a gun station. Normally, a single fifty-caliber machine gun was attached to a swivel mount, allowing the gunner to manually swing the weapon to aim and fire it. Two such weapons, mounted together on the swivel, would make the station doubly lethal.

Also, at the rear of the radio compartment located just behind the bomb bay, an opening in the upper fuselage was included for a fifty-caliber weapon to provide additional firepower upward and to the rear of the plane. The radio operator served as the gunner. He had a very limited view out this hole in his "ceiling," but any additional firepower was welcome in a fight.

"This mother could turn into one helluva fighting machine," Bronx exclaimed enthusiastically, grinning as he began to visualize their new bomber bristling with fifty-caliber machine guns. "Some yellow SOB is going to be in for an unpleasant surprise."

"Well, what do you think?"

Captain Gene Stoddard, proud new owner of "Junk Pile Jane," as the crew had come to refer to their "new" plane, had gathered his crew at the nose. During the preceding several weeks the majority of the repairs and improvements necessary to turn it back into a flying, fighting machine had been finished. Four new engines had been installed and tested. The turrets and hydraulics were functional, if not entirely without problems. There were now fifteen fifty-caliber machine guns installed, and all the thirty-caliber 'pea shooters' eliminated, greatly increasing the total firepower available. The plane was nearly ready for initial operational flight tests and shakedown flights.

But it was not the bristling machine guns, or whirring turrets that Gene was now beaming over. Rather, it was the freshly painted artwork on the nose, under and just forward of the pilot and copilot side windows. A shield with pictures of wagon trains and farmers and wheat, and a banner of stars above with the phrase "Ad Astra" now graced the plane.

"'Ad Astra?' What the hell's that? Anything like 'horse's ass-tra?" Slim Jensen, the tail gunner, scoffed, laughing at his own joke.

"I'm ever grateful for having a crew of such sophisticates," Gene retorted. "That, gentlemen, is the state shield of Kansas. 'Ad Astra' is from our state motto. It means 'to the stars.' I figure old Junk Pile Jane here is going to take us to the stars, so we might as well give her official recognition. Besides, I'm aircraft commander, I'm from Kansas, and that's our new name—so get used to it. Beats calling her a junk pile."

"To the stars, huh? Actually, I kind of like that. 'Ad Astra' it is. So when do we get to let her take us to the stars?" Jensen agreed, changing his tune.

"The crew chief and I are going on a first test hop this afternoon. If all goes well, we'll begin shakedown flights in a couple of days. I've already had Bronx put us on available status starting next week."

"Damn, Stoddard, do we have to win this war single-handed?" Scott Walters, the flight engineer and top turret gunner, asked. He was laughing, but it wasn't clear if he was joking. Gene ignored him and began to walk around the plane, carefully looking for any additional work that would have to be done before the first test flight. The crew realized the meeting was over and began to drift off.

Port Moresby

Dear Christy,

Well, I guess I rubbed Aladdin's lamp and let the Genie out, for I can now claim that all three of my wishes have been granted! I'm a B-17 pilot, I have my own crew, and now I have my own plane!! She was pretty beat up, and was going to be scrapped, but I managed to get her salvaged. She has some special cameras installed, which helped me convince the C.O. to let me salvage her—it should also get me some more missions, as she is the only plane in the squadron with those cameras on board. When we weren't flying missions, my crew has been working day and night helping the maintenance crews get her repaired and ready to fly. I went on the first test hop with the crew chief this afternoon. We've got a few glitches still to work out, but she flies like a dream.

I named her Ad Astra, after the Kansas motto. I left off the "Per Aspera" part. I didn't think the crew would be too happy to have "through difficulties" as part of their plane's name. But, I now have my own plane, to take me to my "stars." I feel so lucky, and blessed, that I'm almost giddy with excitement.

The crew helped me add a bunch more machine guns to her—she's quite a tough cookie, now. You don't want to mess around with those Kansas girls, do you?

Pass this on to the folks. Sorry I haven't written lately, but we've been up all hours getting Ad Astra ready to go, and have had several missions to fly, as well. Not much time left for writing.

Love to you all,
Your giddy Captain friend
Gene

Blind Landing

Port Moresby

Captain Gene Stoddard stood at one side of the five-man tent, now crowded with members of his crew, counting heads.

"There's only seven. Where's Struthers?" Gene asked, as they joked among themselves while they waited for their leader to let them know why he had called them together.

"He's coming," Ollie Olsen, the bombardier, answered, looking out the tent entry.

Gene stepped aside to let the late arrival enter the crowded tent. He avoided Gene's glance, and responded—somewhat sarcastically, Gene noted—to the ribbing from his crew mates about his tardiness. Gene had begun to wonder about the attitude of his waist gunner. He stood patiently, arms folded across his chest, until the banter faded into self-conscious silence.

"I've called you together for a couple of reasons," Gene began. "First, I wanted to let you know how pleased I am with our progress on perfecting our skip bombing. I think we're close to being ready to try it on the real thing." A few eyebrows raised as the men glanced at each other after this announcement. They knew they were rarely missing on practice runs against the derelict freighter in the harbor, but hadn't expected to use the dangerous technique on a mission quite so soon. "The Sixty-fourth and Sixty-fifth have been tearing up jack on shipping in Rabaul. They've been so successful, in fact, that the Nips have been moving some of the shipping to Kavieng harbor. Consequently, the C.O. needs photos to see what all they've got up there. So…he's asked us to do a recon mission up there, tomorrow night."

There was no response from the crew, and Gene didn't expect one. They had come to trust him, and accept whatever missions he took on.

"Bronx, I want you and Ken to meet me in my tent for a briefing after we're done here," Gene added. "Struthers, I want you there, too. You'll be on the cameras, right?" He looked directly at the crewman to see his reaction to the question. There wasn't any question about the crew assignments.

Struthers always operated the cameras. But Gene wanted to goad him a bit, testing his attitude.

"Usually…if I'm not busy on the waist guns," responded Struthers. There was a tinge of surliness in his demeanor that made Gene's antennas go up. *I wonder if he was like this for Carlson,* he thought. *Whether he was, or wasn't, I'm not going to accept that attitude.*

"I'd like for you three to meet me in my tent in about thirty minutes to begin going over plans," Gene said to the group, as he started out the tent. "The crew truck will pick us up at 1500 for a 1600 departure. Ops wants us to get the pictures just before sunset, for best shadow effect, this time. I guess it makes the ships easier to assess, or something."

Gene left the tent, headed for Ops for more information on the target area and early briefings on weather.

"What's with all this volunteering shit?" complained Struthers. "We shouldn't have to go on a mission up over that coffin corner alone. What's wrong with some of the other crews taking some of those missions?"

"Oh, Struthers, quitch'er bitchin'" Bronx reacted to the complaining. "We all gotta die sometime. Go clean your guns. You may be needing them."

With that, the group began to file out of the tent, the disgruntled gunner still muttering and mumbling to himself.

Gene and his crew had been droning along on the reconnaissance mission for nearly eight hours, the last three of which were through the ink well that was nighttime over a moonless ocean. They had departed Port Moresby that afternoon for the flight over Kavieng Harbor, a round trip of well over a thousand miles. Kavieng was located at the northern tip of New Ireland, a long narrow island above Rabaul, on New Britain.

Although Rabaul was the primary shipping point for the Japanese in the Southwest Pacific, Kavieng also had a good harbor and large numbers of Japanese transports were staged there for making supply runs to New Guinea. General Holmestead, Commander of the 43rd Bomb Group, had ordered that the entire region be kept under constant surveillance for convoys. After their success at obliterating the Japanese convoy in the Battle of the Bismarck Sea, the crews were always anxious for another such opportunity to send more of the enemy to the bottom of the Pacific.

Gene rubbed his eyes, stretched, and shifted in the seat, trying to find a more comfortable arrangement for his aching bones. He was tired, and his mind was drifting. After months of intensive training and numerous flights as a combat pilot, flying an airplane had become second nature to him. No longer was he an awe-struck youngster standing on the turf at his hometown airport, hoping for the attention of a pilot who had momentarily dropped into his life. He was now among them, one of the brotherhood.

But it was, nevertheless, difficult for him to accept the reality of it. Too much of his life had been spent dreaming and fantasizing about airplanes, about flying them. Even now, he found himself unable to fully believe that he could be at the controls of one of the most sophisticated aircraft ever built. His love of flying had only intensified with each flight.

He had been somewhat surprised to find that the technical aspects of airplanes, such as airfoil design and equations of lift, were of little interest to him. He would have expected that such things would have appealed to his engineering personality but, in truth, it was only the flying that interested him. He happily left the equations to the aircraft designers. He simply wanted to fly.

"Captain, Nav. I'm estimating Moresby at oh one thirteen."

The call on the intercom from Bronx, the navigator, informing Gene of their estimated time of arrival at the home base brought him back from his mental ramblings. He acknowledged the information and briefly scanned the many dials and instruments that cluttered the cockpit around him, dimly lit by red night-lights. Satisfied that all was well with his plane, his mind began to drift again.

His philosophical musings on flying might have continued indefinitely, had not a brilliant flash of lightning that momentarily brightened the cockpit with ghostly blue light suddenly jerked him back to alertness. Even as his mind had floated through clouds of aerodynamic fantasy, he had been watching the lightning ahead of them growing steadily more intense and widespread. This particularly intense flash only a few miles ahead startled him into action.

Thunderstorms, or squall lines, formed almost daily over the ocean between New Guinea and the Solomon Island area. Indeed, lines of such monsters formed over much of the area of action of the 5th Air Force, and in many ways represented as big a threat to the safety of the flights as did the actions of the enemy. It was becoming apparent, as more missions had to contend with the violent weather systems of the Southwest, that it was quite possible that more planes would eventually be lost to weather-related accidents than would be lost to enemy action. Gene knew he had no choice—he was going to have to punch through such a line of storms to get back to Port Moresby.

Every pilot who has more than a few practice flights in his logbook soon recognizes that he invades Mother Nature's domain strictly at her discretion. She holds arrows in her quiver that can, should she in a mood of petulance or pique choose to use them, quickly bring the most formidable aluminum bird out of the sky. With the balance of the forces of flight thrown totally in her favor, the result for plane and pilot is always harsh, and oftentimes fatal.

Experienced pilots quickly learn, for example, that ice on a wing alters the carefully calculated design, rendering the equations of lift useless. In moments, the craft can be caused to plunge out of the sky where it attempted to intrude. Fog, rain, turbulence, all are elements to be respected. But—ask a pilot what he fears most, and with few exceptions the answer will be nature's factory of violence, the thunderstorm.

Raging within these cauldrons are a pilot's worst nightmares: ice, hail, torrential rain, and vertical wind speeds that can exceed the climbing capability of even the most powerful aircraft. Their tops can reach twelve miles above the surface, greatly exceeding the maximum altitude of any airplane. While it is possible to fly through the core of a fully developed thunderstorm, the odds are stacked strongly against plane and pilot.

To comprehend the creation and terrible nature of a thunderstorm, it is only necessary to remember a night of sitting around a campfire, watching sparks being carried high into the cool night air. Air heated by the fire creates an invisible elevator which carries sparks aloft to drift and cool, eventually to fall again to the earth below. One can lay back and watch them rise, rapidly at first, swirling and dancing in the turbulent air as they drift along in the prevailing breeze. This same process created the monstrous thunderstorms of the Southwest Pacific.

Warm Pacific waters release vast amounts of moisture into the air above its surface. Continually heated by the equatorial sun's rays, the moist air rises, just as does the air heated by the campfire. This rising air creates powerful currents that pull the moisture into the upper atmosphere. As warm air rises, it is replaced by cooler air at the ocean surface, which in turn is warmed, receives its allotment of moisture, and boards the invisible elevator for its trip to the heights above.

For hours, this process collects moisture at high altitudes, held aloft by the increasingly strong air currents created by the heating process. Upon reaching the cool air of the upper atmosphere, the water vapor condenses into small droplets, creating the puffy cumulus clouds that always began to form over the ocean by mid-morning. Here and there, these small "pufferbellies" would begin to grow into towering majestic columns, as the ocean below and the sun above continued to pump moisture and heat into the expanding mass above.

An azure sky would first begin to fill with balls of cotton. As the day progressed, some of these developed into churning columns, starkly white against the deep blue of the sky as they climbed ever higher into the upper reaches. With each passing hour the columns became more massive, more spectacular, spreading wider and joining neighboring clouds, tops beginning to show a restless energy, churning as though beginning to come to life. As they did so, tints of gray in their bases gave ominous hints that all was not well within the purity and innocence of the white.

Just as the sparks swirled in the turbulent air above the campfire, water molecules carried above the ocean within the clouds bounced against each other. As the quantity increased and the turbulence within the cloud grew, electrons were occasionally knocked loose from an atom, eventually leaving vast numbers of ionized raindrops and free electrons floating about. The interior of this magnificent sample of Mother Nature's artwork would be turning into a gigantic electrical storage battery.

By mid-afternoon, the cloud column would have grown to reach altitudes as high as 50,000, even 60,000, feet above the ocean. Temperatures at those heights were far below freezing—water droplets reaching that height quickly froze into small ice particles. Unable to be sustained at these heights they would fall downward, only to be recycled again to high altitudes by the strengthening inner winds. Small ice particles grew to become pellets, and then pea-sized balls of hail, sometimes growing to the size of a baseball.

Viewed from afar—which was the only place from which the aircrews wanted to view them—these clouds were breathtakingly beautiful and majestic. Oft-times, the planes would fly among these stark white pillars towering far above the plane's altitude, just as one might stroll through the massive columns of the Parthenon, or the giant Redwoods of California.

These giants, however, would continually change hue and color as the sun's rays were filtered and blocked by varying densities of the clouds. One moment piercingly bright white, the next ominously dark and menacing, incongruously fringed with translucent silver. It was a time when one could sometimes forget that his only reason for being there was to kill, to avoid being killed. It was also easy to be mesmerized into forgetting that these starkly beautiful, billowing towers were, in reality, massive storage barns of energy and destruction awaiting a signal to be visited upon trespassers.

That signal comes when the moisture droplets in the cloud, having been held aloft by powerful air currents, finally become so heavy that they can no longer be supported and begin to fall earthward. Once this invisible barrier is broken, a torrent forms as all the stored rain and hail tumbles downward, pulling the surrounding air with it. Rain begins to fall, lightly at first, and then in blinding sheets. Plunging air currents, and the rising ones carrying air aloft to replace them, create a maelstrom of internal turbulence, of updrafts and downdrafts that can easily exceed the capability of any aircraft to overcome them.

The electrical battery created from the stored electrons and ions also begins to discharge, as Zeus, God of Sky and Thunder, hurls his lightning bolts ripping through the clouds and arcing to the surface. Thus, within the core of these once benign-looking clouds, beautiful beyond the capability of the artist's brush to capture on canvas, is a raging mixture of violent updrafts, downdrafts, hail, ice, lightning and, sometimes, tornadoes. It is the beauty and the beast of nature. It is not a place where an airplane should be.

There appeared to be no obvious gap between the thunderstorms ahead, no safe passage home. They would have to try to punch through, and hope for the best. Gene would soon find out whether the combined aerodynamic forces of the bomber's massive wings, and the power of her four engines, could prevail against the overwhelming beauty and destructive power of nature which were being made ever more evident as lightning flashes were now virtually constant in the cloud mass confronting them.

"Captain to crew. Secure your weapons and all loose items, and get yourselves stuck tight to something. It looks like we're going to have to punch through that line of thunderstorms ahead. It'll get pretty rough."

Gene had already put the bomber in a descent from their 8,000 foot cruising altitude. He knew that the storm's most severe turbulence, hail and ice, if any, would be in its middle altitudes. Experience had quickly shown that the safest place to be, if they had to try to punch through such storms, was as close to the ocean surface as possible. He usually tried to maintain about 2,000 feet altitude.

"Nav, where are we? When was your last good fix?"

"I got a good position, ground speed and winds aloft check as we crossed New Britain, sir," Bronx Riley, the navigator replied. "But there's no way of knowing what those storms ahead have done to the winds aloft. If nothing's changed, the base is two hundred and five miles on a heading of two two eight."

"Roger. Thanks. Keep me posted on position, and tell me when you estimate us over the coast. I'll need at least twenty minutes to get back to fifteen thousand to clear the hump."

"Roger."

"Sparks," Gene called to Jimmy Wilson, the radio operator—often nicknamed "Sparks" from the days of spark-gap transmitters—"See if you can triangulate a fix off some beacons to give Bronx a backup."

"Negative, Captain. There's too much static from the storms. It's useless."

Wilson had been trying for some time to pick up any form of radio signal from the radio beacon at their base at Moresby, or any other stations that might be operating, but to no avail. The massive electrical cauldron that was creating the non-stop lightning display in front of them was also creating overwhelming levels of static. His radios were swamped out, and useless.

"Roger."

Gene's attention was rapidly being focused on the constant display of fireworks in the approaching clouds, as he attempted to find a gap to penetrate between the worst areas.

"Captain to crew. Hold on. Here we go."

Crew members rechecked to see that loose items were as secure as possible and that all guns were stowed. They tightened belts even tighter, and scrunched down into whatever security the spartan conditions provided. For the next few minutes the storm merely toyed with the bomber, and Gene gently corrected for the rocking wings. The crew shrugged off the jolts as the plane began to encounter increasingly strong vertical gusts.

Without warning, the huge bomber was suddenly rolled violently, and slammed into a two thousand foot-per-minute escalator ride upward into the storm's bowels, only to be sent plunging ocean-ward just as rapidly a few moments later.

"Dammit," an unidentified crew member reacted over the intercom, "this stuff's worse than flak."

No one deemed a response necessary, as each crew member fought his own private battle to keep the alternating positive and negative G-forces from slamming them into the aircraft structure. Only the two pilots had any function to perform. The rest of the crew tried to wedge themselves into crevices, bracing with feet and hands, to stay put and avoid injury by being slammed into the metal structure of the aircraft.

Gene and his copilot were too busy to attempt to communicate with any but the tersest of comments. With each gust, each upward or downward thrust, the four huge engines surged as their propeller speed controllers strained to maintain their preset speed. Strange creaks and groans echoed through the empty metal fuselage as it was twisted and contorted by the ever-shifting loads on wing and tail surfaces, blending disconcertingly with the roar of torrential rain being blasted against the thin aluminum skin. With little to do but attempt to stay put and survive the ride in the dark cacophony, each member's private thoughts drifted in its own particular direction.

Neil Struthers, the usually disgruntled waist gunner, was not by nature a risk-taker and was not happy. He had feared being drafted into the Army, and having to face the real probability of combat, so had enlisted in the Army Air Forces. He hoped his college courses in business and accounting would qualify him for a staff position. Instead, he had been assigned to be an aerial gunner, whose sole responsibility was to kill, to avoid being killed. It was one of those perverted practical jokes of fate that only the military could perpetrate.

"Slim" Jensen, the tail gunner, had crawled out of the hole that was the tail gunner station, to join Neil in the roomier waist section, once they were far enough from enemy fighters to no longer be threatened. But even with some company, Neil felt isolated and alone. He was hunkered down on the aircraft floor, braced against the fuselage. The plane was starkly dark, except for the momentary flashes of lightning. He would not have admitted it to anyone but he was, quite frankly, scared. Flak and fighters were one thing. You could at least attempt to defend yourself. But with thunderstorms? Who stood a chance against such monsters?

The engine exhaust and propeller blast, combined with the rain pounding on the aircraft skin, created a mind-numbing din which seemed to further isolate him from the rest of the crew. He pulled on his fur-lined flight helmet to shut out some of the noise, and settled down further, wrapping his arms around himself. Eyes closed, he attempted to doze. The noise dulled his senses, but he was too tense and apprehensive to fall asleep. Of course, sleep was impossible anyway, as the bucking, lunging craft forced him to continually struggle to stay wedged in his corner.

He still had not come to terms with losing his regular aircraft commander, Major Carlson, and was not at all thrilled with having been assigned to Stoddard. Early scuttlebutt among some of the other crews had not treated Gene well, ranging from his being incompetent to being a glory-seeking daredevil. The other members of the crew seemed to be quickly taking to the new pilot and commander. Ollie Olsen, the bombardier, in particular appeared to have a lot of respect for him. But Neil was convinced that nothing good could come of it.

It's bad enough that we have to go on these damned night missions, he thought, *but this idiot will get us all killed for sure. Now we're probably going to be fed to the sharks out here in this God-forsaken ocean."* Neil's mind conjured up all sorts of possible ill fates for himself, while he tried to stay wedged against the compartment bulkhead as the aircraft was slammed around by the storm.

Every few seconds the interior of the darkened aircraft came alive as lightning bolts blasted through the clouds, creating momentary ghostly pale blue masks of the crew members' faces, frozen with whatever expression of thought or contortion caused by the turbulence happened to be present at that instant. Between lightning bolts, the only sign of life in the aircraft was the dim red glow created in the pilot's compartment and in the navigator and radio operator compartments by the various instruments.

"Spell me a few minutes," Gene called to Ken Whitford, his copilot. "My arms are getting tired."

"Roger, I've got it," he responded, shifting in his seat to get better braced to operate the control yoke, and planting his feet firmly on the rudder pedals.

"I've been trying to stay below two thousand, but don't fight to hold altitude too closely or you may overstress her. Just try to keep her level and maintain two twenty eight on the heading."

"Roger."

He was concentrating on the tasks at hand too much to elaborate. Gene knew, by now, that his copilot was experienced at weather flying and didn't need to be told what to do. But it was his nature as airplane commander to not leave anything to an assumption.

Gene stretched his aching arms and attempted to relax for a moment, when the aircraft surged violently upward.

"Damn!" Ken exclaimed. "We're climbing over three thousand feet per minute. We'll be in the middle of this shit if we don't get it back down."

Gene's attempts at relaxing were short lived, as he responded immediately.

"Keep the nose down! I'll drop the gear and get some power off."

Gene had already flipped the landing gear lever, and was pulling the throttle quadrant back as he spoke. The engines surged in response, as Gene and Ken fought to slow the climb without overstressing the plane, or losing control of the airspeed. Gene kept careful watch on the altimeter, as the altitude climbed rapidly past 7,000 and then 8,000 feet. He knew that the worst of the violence was usually between 10,000 feet and 15,000 feet altitude, and above 10,000 feet the crew was supposed to start using oxygen—he needed to get the plane back down. As it crossed 8,000 feet, the vertical speed indicator reversed and moved back toward zero, as their efforts began to pay off and the vertical gust played out.

"It'll take us right back down any second, now," Gene warned. "I'm leaving the gear down a little longer." Even as he spoke, the vertical airspeed indicator proved his prediction, as a downward gust grabbed the plane.

"This bastard's all over the sky," the copilot exclaimed through jaws clenched against the physical struggle to keep the aircraft in a somewhat wings-level attitude. Gene watched as the airspeed climbed upward, even as the altimeter unwound downward. As they passed through 2,000 feet, the gust played out. Gene raised the gear and came back up with the power, as the copilot struggled to regain his original heading and stabilize the aircraft.

Then, as suddenly as it had begun, it was over. Calm returned, as though a cat had finally tired of playing with its captive mouse and strolled off to find more interesting entertainment. No one spoke for several minutes, as they waited to see if Mother Nature had another shoe to drop on them. Rain continued to pound the skin, but at an obviously reduced intensity. The crew members began to extricate themselves from their positions, and stretched to relax muscles nearly cramped from what seemed to be an eternity of abuse. Glancing at his watch, Bronx noted that they had been in the turbulence for only twelve minutes.

"Nav, Captain. Get me your best position estimate as soon as you can. We must be getting close to the coast."

"Roger, Captain. It'll take a couple of minutes. I was getting bounced all over hell down here and couldn't do anything." He began picking up the charts which had been scattered all over the compartment floor, and took his navigation computer out of its drawer.

"Captain to crew. I'm switching to autopilot, so you can relax."

Gene looked at Whitford for confirmation, and after a slight correction of heading switched control of the plane over to "George," as they typically referred to their third pilot, the AFCS—Automatic Flight Control System.

"Captain, I estimate the coastline in nine minutes. Moresby should now be about one seventy two miles on a heading of two twenty eight." Bronx hesitated momentarily before continuing. "Captain, I'm sorry. But I can't be too sure on that position. There's no way of knowing what all that chasing up and down, and the winds, did to our groundspeed. I just had to assume it sort of averaged out."

"I understand. We'll go with the best you've got."

"Roger."

They droned on, waiting for the navigator's wrist watch to tell them that they were supposedly over dry land again, each man immersed in his own thoughts as the lightning appeared ever more dimly behind them. Slim Jensen crawled back into the tail gunner's position. His little Plexiglas windows offered a fascinating view of the light show playing in the receding storm clouds.

With each flash of internal lightning, the rolling, boiling cloud masses were back-lit in fascinating detail. Occasional cloud-to-cloud lightning streaked

across the sky, momentarily startling him. It reminded him of nights at home in the summer, when faraway thunderstorms, their tops showing above the distant horizon, would entertain them with light shows. "Heat lightning," they called it, since it usually occurred at the end of a long, hot summer day.

Although mesmerized by the show, his isolation from the rest of the crew, the darkness of the night over the hostile ocean below, and his thoughts of home all combined to make him increasingly disconsolate and homesick. He swallowed hard, and clenched his jaws against the choking feeling in his throat. Turning away from the tail windows, he crawled back into the waist section and curled up on the floor. The droning engines slowly dulled his thoughts into a restless sleep.

"Captain, I'm estimating the coast in two minutes."

"Roger, thanks. I'm starting a climb to fifteen thousand."

Gene pushed the throttles forward and pitched the nose up. He wanted a good climb rate to get to 15,000 feet, well before reaching the hump, but didn't want to have to put the crew on oxygen for very long. As they crossed 10,000 feet, he called.

"Pilot to crew. We're crossing ten for fifteen, to cross the hump. You'd better go on oxygen until we're back down. Give me a status check by station. Anybody get banged up back there?"

The crew members each called in using the usual sequence. Gene was concerned momentarily when the waist and tail gunner were slow to respond, but recognized how hard it must be to stay awake back there. They were all tired, and ready to be on the ground again, but there were no significant injuries—just a few bumps and bruises.

As time passed at 15,000 feet, Gene knew they had to be over the hump because of the increased turbulence caused by wind cresting the mountain peaks only a couple of thousand feet below them. Bronx had called out his estimate of crossing the hump a couple of minutes earlier, but Gene wanted to give them a bit more margin. He was becoming concerned, for he had hoped that the cloud layer might be thinning out over land. Finding the airfield in the clouds at night would very difficult, at best. Gene eased the power back, and pitched the nose over to start their descent. He knew that the mountain range fell off rapidly on the Moresby side, and there was no danger as long as he maintained a reasonable descent rate.

"Nav, Captain."

"Sir?"

"I had hoped this cloud layer would be breaking up, but it looks like it may extend well on down. We're going to have a tough time locating the base. Give me your best efforts on an ETA for the base. I'm going to continue this descent on down to 1500 feet to see if we break out, or can see anything."

"Roger, Captain. I'm estimating oh one seventeen over the base. Heading two twenty nine. That's the best I can give you."

As Gene continued the descent, the reality of the risk facing him and his crew began to loom larger in his mind. They had only a fair estimate of their actual position, and whether they would pass close enough to the base to see anything. Their radio was useless from the static still being generated by the electrical activity of the thunderstorms, and the base beacon was apparently not operating, as they had no response from it even at this close range.

If they could not find the base, they had two choices: proceed out over the harbor past Moresby and ditch the plane, or bail out over unknown and rugged terrain. Either action would almost certainly result in serious injuries, or even the loss of some or all crew members. Gene felt strongly that their best chance lay with staying with the plane, and to use whatever means were required to find the airfield. What those means might be, at the moment, escaped him.

"Captain, my watch says we'll be over the base in two minutes. Anybody see anything?"

"Negative. Captain to crew. I want all hands to get to any port available, and give me a call if you spot any light of any sort. We still haven't broken out of this crap yet, so keep your eyes peeled."

Damn it, Struthers thought, stirring himself awake. *I knew this flight would be the end of us. How in hell are we supposed to get down if we can't find the base?*

Minutes ticked by. "Captain to crew. Anybody see anything?"

Silence was not the answer he had hoped for.

"Okay, here's the plan. We should be about crossing the shoreline, by now. Bronx, I'm going to proceed on out over the harbor and descend to five hundred feet. We'll maintain this heading for five minutes, then reverse course and descend on the reciprocal for five minutes. Maybe we'll be under the overcast enough to see lights."

Gene started a descent toward the surface that they presumed to be the surface of the harbor. Unyielding blackness was the only result.

"Ollie, I've got to get an accurate altimeter setting before I can risk going back in at a lower altitude. Fire the nose guns downward and see if you can see the tracers hit the water. Waist, fire some flares out the hatch. I'll keep descending until we can see water."

"Roger, Captain."

The plane shook as the nose gun fired. Even expecting it, the crew still jumped slightly in response to the added noise, increasing the tension on board. The flares cast an eerie glow in the clouds as they fell downward in the darkness.

"Hold it!" Ollie yelled over the intercom, making no attempt to mask the urgency in his voice. "I've got tracers hitting the water, and I can see a glow on the surface from the flares. We're barely fifty feet off the deck."

"Great. Thanks, Ollie." Gene reset the Kollsman window on his altimeter to account for the changes in barometric pressure that had occurred while they were on the mission. His altimeter would now be accurate within a few feet. Gene reversed course and headed back towards land, climbing back to 1500 feet.

"Nav, give me five minutes on this inbound course."

As the plane again headed inland, Gene could only hope and pray that they would pass close enough to the base to see whatever lights might be on at this time of night. All eyes on board stared into the darkness.

There is probably nothing that a person who has normal sight can experience that equals the darkness encountered in an aircraft when in the clouds at night. Perhaps, if one has ever been in a cave and turned out the lights he has some comprehension of such total blackness. The world ends outside the aircraft fuselage. Even though your rational mind tells you that there are wings to either side, they simply do not exist to the eye, strain though you might to see them. The ear hears the roar of the engines and propellers just outside, but to the eye they are nonexistent. The airspeed indicator tells you that you are moving over the surface at nearly three miles per minute, but nothing in your senses can agree. Staring out the windows is like staring intently into a piece of black velvet, with the same results. After a few moments, it begins to play tricks on your mind. Gene kept his eyes and attention unswervingly on the aircraft instruments, for only they presented reality.

"Captain, five minutes. We must have passed over the base already, but we can't see anything from up here in the nose. What do we do now?" The young navigator tried to mask the rising tension that they all had to be feeling.

"Roger. The foothills east of the base are about thirteen hundred, and I can tell by the turbulence that we must be over them. I'm going to turn around and head back out over the harbor. We'll come in and try it again, a little lower."

Gene reversed course, to try the same maneuver, this time a little lower.

"Captain, this is going to be a real problem in not much longer." The copilot was tapping the fuel gauges, their needles disconcertingly close to the E, in the hopes that it would somehow jiggle one of them back upscale. Gene knew that his options were running out, along with his fuel. The crew was becoming fatigued, eyes tired from straining against the blackness.

"Captain, waist. Sir, don't you think we'd be better off going back up and bailing out. We know we've got to be close to base. We could probably walk back in when it gets daylight. This seems hopeless to me."

There was silence for a moment, as the crew wondered how Gene would respond to the suggestion that was on all their minds.

"Negative. All of you—listen up. I know how you feel, and bailing out might seem like a good idea. But every plane I know of that ditched or had to bail out at night lost crew members. We're better off to stick with the plane as long as we have fuel. I'm going to try one more pass, and then we'll make a decision."

The silence on the intercom did not necessarily indicate agreement or confidence. Gene had already decided that he would make the pass, and that if any engine sputtered from lack of fuel he would make a blind landing on the water on instruments. He was determined to keep the crew together. The plane leveled out after its turn to once again start back towards the harbor. Tired eyes continued staring into the void. Seconds ticked away.

"There's a light! Must be a flare! Two o'clock."

The copilot's excitement couldn't be contained, nor did anyone care.

"Where? I don't see a thing!" Gene raised up in his seat for a better view out the copilot's window.

"Captain, I see it, too. There's a glow in the clouds, at one to two o'clock." Top turret gunner Scott Walters was peering out of the his turret, and confirmed Whitford's sighting was not just wishful thinking, or his eyes playing tricks.

Gene immediately banked the bomber to the right. As the glow in the clouds came around towards the nose, he was able to see it, as well. As they approached it, the light rapidly faded as the flare burnt out. But in its place they could now see a faint glow below them.

"That's got to be the runway lights, nothing else would be on. We'll start a descent, and over-fly the lights. All hands keep an eye out to make sure we don't lose them."

Gene headed for the faint glow of light, which all desperately hoped was their runway. In a few moments, the blurry glow began to take some shape, becoming what could best be described as a glowing fat blob.

"We must be looking at the runway from the side," Whitford volunteered. "Otherwise, it'd look long and skinny."

"Roger. Heading's right for a crosswind. I'm going to do a left two-seventy so I can keep the lights in view. That should put us on final." Gene rolled the plane into a left bank, continuing to stare out his side window at the fuzzy glow below that represented safety to him and his crew.

"Watch your bank!"

Ken was monitoring the artificial horizon in the center of the instrument panel, which indicated the angle the plane's wings made with the ground. Gene's unbroken concentration on the view outside had allowed the plane to continue its left roll. Within moments, the plane would have been in a danger-ously steep bank.

Gene spun back to look at the artificial horizon, jerking hard right on the wheel to bring the plane back to a safe attitude.

"Damn! Thanks." Gene concentrated on his instruments. "I can't fly this thing and keep the lights in sight. You'll have to talk me in."

"Will do." Ken raised up in his seat and leaned over behind Gene's seat for a better view out of the opposite side window. "Keep it coming on around."

"Roger. Get the gear down, and flaps ten," Gene said, as he reduced engine power to slow to the proper airspeed for their approach. The plane continued to circle around the glow in the clouds, as though chained to this island of safety by the combined will of the nine souls on board.

"Heading looks right for final," Gene observed, as he leveled off. "Altitude looks pretty good. Give me full flaps and keep me on target. Do as much of the final approach check list as you can without letting me lose this thing."

"Roger. Flaps coming down. Descent's looking good so far."

"Pilot to crew. We're on a short final, but still can't see the ground. This may be a hard one. Assume emergency crash positions."

At Gene's call, all the crew members in the rear fuselage began assembling in the radio and waist gun compartments, where they could sit on the floor and brace their backs against the bulkheads. There was little else they could do now but wait—and pray, though no one would have admitted to doing so.

"Drifting left. Come right a couple of degrees…"

"That's better. Heading's good…"

"We're sinking too fast—get some power on…!"

"That's better. Light's are holding steady now…"

"Hold that rate…How's your airspeed?"

"Ninety five…slow as I can get it without risking a stall…"

"Two hundred feet…any sign of the ground yet?"

"Negative…"

"Lookin' good…"

"One hundred feet. Ground in sight?"

"Negative. Don't flare too soon, we'll stall it in."

"Roger. Yell if you see anything…"

"Fifty feet…I've got to slow our descent…"

The long skinny blob of light had by now become two long skinny blobs of lights, separated by blackness, as the B-17 approached the gravel landing strip lighted on either side by a row of lights. Gene began easing the power back and the nose up, to slow their downward plunge toward the unseen runway surface, and to reduce his airspeed.

"Looking good…keep it coming."

"Runway threshold!" The first runway lights were flashing past the wing tips, as Whitford called to alert Gene.

Gene briefly shifted his gaze to the blurry lights streaking by on either side of him, to better judge his height above them. There was still no sight of the actual runway surface.

"Chop the power…be ready to abort if we bounce too hard."

Gene released his grip on the throttles, placing both hands on the control column for better control as he flared to touch down. Ken pulled the throttles to idle, his hand staying on the quadrant ready to come to the rescue with full power if they hit too hard. Gene feared that he had neither the fuel nor the will to make a second attempt. This one needed to be right.

Before anyone actually saw the runway surface, the wheels bounced, floated for a couple of seconds, bounced slightly again, and settled on. They were safely on the ground.

Gene worked his rudder pedals to keep the plane aligned between the two rows of lights, and began working the brakes to slow the plane to a halt.

"Incredible job, Captain!"

Ken clapped Gene on the shoulder, as they slowly crept off the runway. After shutting down the engines, the crew made their way off the plane, to be greeted by an anxious ground crew.

"How in the hell did you guys get back in here?" one of the ground crew asked. "We've still got two Catalinas out on search and rescue that should have been back by now, but no one has heard from them."

"We'd about given up, ourselves, until Whitford saw the glow of that flare in the clouds."

"We heard you pass over, but you were off to the side a half mile or so. One of the guys scrounged around in the dark and found a Very pistol in one of the planes. We could hear you coming back, so he fired a flare, hoping you'd see it. We heard you circling overhead to land, but I don't see how in hell you landed the thing—I can't see my hand in front of my face."

Neil Struthers was silent as the rest of the crew jabbered to release the tension. As he and Olsen walked toward the tents and their cots he lit a cigarette, trying to conceal his shaking hands by gripping them together around the lighter.

"You know, Ollie, Stoddard basically scared the shit out of me tonight. I was ready to hit the silk and take my chances. But I have to admit, that was the damnedest bit of flying I've ever experienced."

"The guy's good, that's for sure."

"I'll tell you something else, though."

"What's that?"

"Good or not, I'll never fly with the son of a bitch again. I'm asking for a transfer. I don't want some Captain Courageous trying to prove his manhood every time we get in a plane. Who ever heard of volunteering for a damn recon mission?"

They walked on in silence toward the one thing that now mattered more than anything else—sleep.

Port Moresby

Dear Christy,

Sorry it's been so long since my last letters home. We've been staying pretty busy—which is good, since it sure gets boring, otherwise.

Well, I guess there's nothing left to wish for except for all this fun and games to be over so we can all come home. Ad Astra is a joy to fly, in spite of her beat up condition. She never lets me down, regardless of all the abuse I put her through. And I don't have words to describe how proud and pleased I am of my crew. We had a few rough edges to work off, to get used to each other. My waist gunner was a problem, and wanted a transfer to another crew. I was glad to let him go. I got a new guy, George Henderson, who is working out just great.

We've been being kept pretty busy with missions. We get most of the reconnaissance missions, because of our cameras. I don't mind. Some of them get a little dicey, since you're always flying alone, but most of the time they're pretty much milk runs. We've had a few rather interesting bombing missions. I haven't got to do any skip bombing, yet. That seems like it would be fun, but something else always comes up.

Bronx, my navigator, is the squadron Operations officer, who assigns missions. He says he thinks something kind of big is brewing, but doesn't know anything for sure. The Brass doesn't let us peons in on their secrets, very often—at least not until the last minute.

Need to hit the sack. Write when you can, and tell everyone Hi for me. I miss you all.

Gene

Last Mission

Gene had seldom darkened the door of his squadron commander's office—once when he got transferred from the Twenty-Second, and again when he had pleaded for the salvation of his plane. Entering it now for only the third time, he found himself face to face not only with his own C.O., Major Hoffman, but the entire group's commanding officer as well. Sitting on the edge of Hoffman's desk was General Whitestone, the deputy commander of Fifth Air Force. Gene had only seen the general on rare occasion at medal award ceremonies. His heart leaped as he snapped to attention just inside the door, his mind racing to think of what he could have screwed up so royally to warrant such attention.

"Captain Stoddard, reporting as ordered, sir." Gene said as he saluted.

"At ease, Captain," General Whitestone responded, casually returning Gene's salute. "This may take a few minutes—have a chair," he added, nodding toward the wooden chairs facing his desk.

"Thank you, sir." Gene took a chair facing his superiors, and waited. The general looked at Gene a moment before getting to the point of the meeting.

"Stoddard, I suspect that you, and all the crews over here, are beginning to sense that we're finally starting to make some headway against the Japs here in the Pacific. We've been doing a good steady job of working over Rabaul and Kavieng, as well as their bases here in New Guinea."

Whitestone paused for a moment, looking at Gene. He knew Gene was waiting for the shoe to drop, and proceeded to get to the point.

"As you know, Captain, we won't get to go home by simply sinking a few ships or tearing up some runways. The job now is to drive them back where they came from, and end this thing. That drive got off to a good start when the Marines took Guadalcanal, and we're making good progress here on New Guinea. But there's still a long way to go.

"There's an operation being planned now that will take another major step in this direction. It will obviously involve the Fifth Air Force. Southwest Pacific Command headquarters has passed the word down to me that there is a crucial need for topographic maps of some potential landing sites. The operation is classified top secret. I can't give you specifics. Several options are under consideration. Regardless of the specific island selected for the next assault, our guys can't go in without good topographic maps of where they are landing. COMSOPAC needs a B-17 to go up there and get the photos for those maps."

Gene began to sense where the meeting was headed, but didn't respond, as he had not been directly asked. General Whitestone looked at Gene a moment, then continued on.

"Captain, you're probably already ahead of me on this, and wondering why it wasn't just posted on the Ops board, like we usually do. Problem is, it's too classified to talk about unless I know who's going. You have the only Seventeen on the base with tri-met cameras, capable of getting those photos. We need your plane to go up there, as soon as possible. We don't have recent reconnaissance from the area, but we have to assume that with all our raids on Rabaul, and with the landings at Guadalcanal, the Japs know we are planning something and have reinforced their bases with extra fighter strength.

"The range is far too great for fighter support, obviously, so whoever goes will be on their own. It will require a lot of straight and level flying to get the pictures, so if you're jumped, you've got a problem. I'm not going to order you to do this mission, Captain, but it has to be done and your plane is the only one equipped to do it. I want you to think about it, and talk it over with your crew, then report back here at oh-eight-hundred in the morning and let me know your decision. If you feel you can't accept the mission, I'll arrange for a different crew. There'll be no questions and no repercussions."

Gene knew that the meeting had ended, and stood facing the general. The general rose, and looked at Gene. They both already knew his decision.

"Sir, I don't have to think about it. We'll get the pictures. If my crew can't do it, it can't be done. Do you still want me to report back in the morning?"

"Thanks, Captain. I knew you would do it. Report to Ops. They'll brief you on the specifics of the various target sites. You're not to reveal the locations until after departure. Ops will have the necessary charts for your navigator. He can open them immediately after take-off. You're dismissed."

Gene saluted, turned and headed for the door. Just as he opened it, the general called to him.

"Captain."

"Sir?" Gene replied, turning to face him.

"Good luck, up there."

Gene paused a moment, surprised by the comment.

"Thank you, sir."

Gene headed to his tent, slogging along the dirt path still muddy from overnight thunderstorms, lost in thought. After re-reading some letters from home, and trying to write one, he tossed his pen aside and spent some time attempting to nap. That soon proved to be an equally fruitless exercise, and he lay on his cot, arms behind his head, attempting to find in the top of his tent answers to the turmoil in his mind.

That, too, proved futile so he gave up and got up. Knowing that Mike Kingston was at the base on another liaison meeting, Gene left his tent and walked across to the section of the base where he knew he would find him. In a few minutes, the two of them were sitting in a tent, with Mike wondering why his friend had suddenly appeared.

"Mike, am I doing the right thing?" Gene asked, getting straight to the point.

"You give me too much credit for being a mind reader, my friend. What are you talking about?" Mike asked, looking as blank as he felt.

"I thought you might have heard, by now. I got called into the base C.O.'s office this morning. Couldn't imagine what I'd done. Turns out, they need Ad Astra for a classified recon mission. The C.O. said it was voluntary—but he knew full well I'd take it. Which, of course, I did."

Gene turned silent for a moment, leaving Mike to wonder where he was headed with his comments. He looked out the tent entry a few seconds, then turned back to Mike.

"I felt like it was the right call when I was talking to the C.O., but now... well, I just don't know."

"Sorry, I'm not following you," Mike said, shaking his head, still puzzled. "Why wouldn't you take it? How's it different from any other mission? I can't believe you're losing your nerve. Is your crew giving you problems?"

"No, it isn't my crew," Gene assured him. "They're a great bunch of guys. To tell the truth, I haven't even talked to them, yet. They pretty much trust my judgment, now, and will go wherever I take the plane. We've been in some pretty tough spots, so this one shouldn't really be any different. If it's where I suspect we're going, we were up there just a couple of weeks ago and didn't see a thing. He sort of implied it may get pretty rough, but it may be just another milk run."

"So what's your problem, then? I'm still lost," Mike replied.

"My problem is me, Mike. I keep wondering if I'm doing the right thing—or at least doing it for the right reason. I know some of the guys on the base think I'm some sort of glory hound, taking these missions just to make myself look good. They think I jeopardize my crew, just for myself."

"Well—do you?" Mike asked pointedly. "Doesn't sound like the Gene Stoddard I know."

"That's my problem. I don't know. I hadn't really thought about it, until now. I admit that I've been so obsessed with flying all my life that nothing else much matters. If it were just me, I'd take every mission that comes along, just to get in the air. So maybe they're right. But on the other hand, I believe in myself, and my crew. We have the only plane equipped for the mission, and are probably as experienced as anybody out here. So if we didn't take it, who would? Or should? Still, I can't seem to think it through."

Mike sat silently, studying his friend. He had known virtually from their first days at KU that Gene was far more introspective than he was, so part of him wasn't surprised by Gene's concerns. But if Gene were beginning to doubt himself—well, that would be a different thing, a good way to get yourself killed.

"Gene, you know as well as I do that some of the guys out here are just immature jerks. You're wasting good mental energy if you pay any attention to them," Mike said, after a rather long silence. "You may find this hard to believe, but I remember a little Shakespeare from high school. I don't remember what play it was in, or who said it, but the line I remember is, 'To thine own self be true.' That's all that counts. Be true to yourself. You're a good pilot, a good leader and good person. Those guys are just trying to cover up the fact that they're scared to take on some of the hot stuff. So I would say, if you believe you're the right crew for the mission—and I have no doubt you are—then just be yourself, and go do it. You'll be okay."

Gene sat for a few seconds, not responding or looking at Mike. Finally, he stood and moved to the tent door.

"Thanks, Mike. I guess I shouldn't let this one bother me, but it just feels different. They must believe that the Japs have brought in reinforcements. I don't believe the C.O. would have presented it like this, if he thought it was going to be just another milk run."

Mike wasn't sure how to respond. Every mission carried the same risks. Trying to second guess them was pointless.

"Well, let's face it, Gene," Mike said, getting up from his cot. "They're all a crap shoot. Guys will come back from some hairy mission without a scratch, then lose an engine on take-off and blow themselves to smithereens. You can't let yourself begin to second guess them. Hell, let's go get a beer. Or has this place driven you to drink, yet?"

Later that afternoon, Gene headed back to his own crew area. Slim Jensen and Scott Walters were standing outside their tent, playing catch with a very used baseball. Gene turned up the path towards them.

"Hey, Skipper, what's up? What's with the big pow-wow with the C.O.? You gone and got yourself busted to private?"

Slim grinned as he tossed Gene the ball. *The word's out, obviously. How in the name of creation*, Gene wondered, *does news spread so fast around here?*

Gene didn't respond to the bait offered by Slim, tossing the ball back to him.

"Tell the crew I want to meet with all of them tonight in my tent after mess. I'll go over everything then."

Gene turned and headed towards his tent.

"Jeez, I wonder what that's all about?" Slim asked, as Gene walked off, his head down, deep in thought.

"Let's go talk to some of the other crews and see if they know what's up," Ollie suggested, tossing the ball inside the tent.

Later that evening, Gene's crew collected around his tent. Gene had not returned yet. It was still miserably hot and humid, and no one had any interest in going into the tent until necessary. They chewed over the various rumors that had been circulating around the crews all afternoon, rumors that had taken on a life of their own, increasing in wildness with each pass around the base. Finally, Gene came walking up the path. As he went in the tent, the others followed, and began to find places to sit, or stand, as best as nine guys could pack into a five man tent.

Gene looked at them looking expectantly back at him, and got directly to the point.

"COMSOPAC has ordered the C.O. to get topo maps of some top secret target. Since they need topographic maps, I assume it's some island they plan to take but I haven't been told anything specific, yet. The C.O. didn't order me to take it—he sort of allowed me to volunteer. Frankly, I don't know why he's made such a big deal out it, unless they believe there's a good chance the area's been beefed up since we were up in that area the last time. But, in fact, we don't know for sure what they've got. It could get pretty rough—or it could be another milk run, just like last time."

He paused for a moment, looking for any sign of a reaction. Getting none, he continued.

"You all know how I feel. I believe we're the best crew for the job. We've got the experience of getting out of some pretty tight spots. We have photo recon experience, and *Ad Astra* is the only plane on the base already equipped with tri-met cameras. The C.O. made it clear that if I didn't accept, some other crew will be assigned to our plane—and that's not going to happen. If any of you—or all of you—feel you can't accept, I'll get replacements—no questions asked."

Gene looked from crewman to crewman. No one spoke. Finally, Olsen spoke up.

"Ah, come on, Skipper. You know we're with you. You get us there, we'll get your pictures and get you back." Ollie, for once, was not his usual smiling self, but Gene could see that he spoke for all. They were nodding in agreement.

"Thanks. I knew I could count on you. I'm to meet with Ops in the morning for more details. I won't be permitted to tell you the exact location until we're airborne. I'll have another briefing so we can plan for it as best we can. It'll probably be scheduled in the next couple of days. I expect to spend all the time we've got working on tactics for the flight, and figuring out any way we can think of to give us an extra edge. Any questions? If not, that's all I've got."

There was a moment of silence as the group waited to see if anyone was going to speak up. But no one did, and they began to file out of the tent. Gene could hear them starting to talk among themselves as they left. He couldn't tell what was being said, and wasn't sure that he wanted to know.

A couple of hours passed as Gene attempted to write letters home. He would start to write, trying to think of what it was he really wanted to say, then would lay the pen down and stare through the open sides of his tent. He felt a sense of uncertainty that he had not experienced before. Was he doing the right thing? His was the only plane appropriately equipped, and they all knew that

Gene Stoddard would never allow anyone else to take his plane. Gene also knew that he had by now established a reputation on the base for aggressively seeking missions. Some of the crews thought he was just glory-seeking, but the good crews knew him better than that.

But—was that it? Was he trying to build his own reputation by taking on all the tough missions? In a sense that was perhaps true. Gene still felt the sting of his problems with the B-26, and the not-so-subtle comments that had been directed his way by some of the other pilots. But that wasn't really the issue. He had always believed that he was a good pilot, and had not been too deeply affected by that situation. Besides, that was now long since over and done.

No, he thought, *it has nothing to do with reputation. None of us really wants to be here, but there's a job to do, and we are the best qualified and equipped to do it. I could not in good conscience not go.*

Tired of thinking about it, Gene decided to write a short letter to Christy, and turn in.

Port Moresby

Dear Christy,

This will have to be a short one. It's getting late, I'm tired, and I've got to meet the base Operations officer in the morning to get briefed on a mission. I said in my last letter it seemed like something big was brewing. Well, I guess it was. I got called in to the base C.O.'s office, this morning. First time that's ever happened. And no, I hadn't been a bad boy, again. Seems the Brass need some recon pictures of some top secret place that they deem to be important, and he basically gave me an opportunity to "volunteer" to take the mission. Those kinds of requests always get everybody rattled, and they start talking about "suicide missions," and all sorts of nonsense. I'm not sure why they made such a big deal of it. We made a run up in that area a couple of weeks ago, and never saw anybody. Ad Astra is the only plane in the squadron that has the right kind of cameras already installed, and my guys are used to these kinds of missions, so it makes sense for us to do it.

I have to admit that I've got kind of a strange feeling about this one. I wish they had just put it on the Ops board like they do all the others. I would have taken it, just like I always do. But all the hoopla about asking for volunteers seems to make a lot more of it, somehow. I asked my crew if they had any problems with my accepting it, but those guys are always willing to back me up—makes me awfully proud of them.

Christy, don't mention this to anyone. I doubt anything will come of it, and I don't want Mom and Dad to worry anymore than they already do. I guess I just needed to get it off my chest, and you're pretty much the only one I ever feel free to tell any of this stuff to. We'll probably go in two or three days. I'll write to you when I get back, and let you know how it went. It'll probably be just another ten hours of boring holes in the sky, after they've made such a big deal of it all. Time for me to turn in.

Take care,
Gene

Gene placed the letter in an envelope, addressed it, and started to put his pen away. He stared at the envelope, lost in thought, set it aside to mail the next morning, then pulled out another sheet of stationery. Minutes passed as he stared at the blank sheet staring back at him. He took a deep breath, exhaled, picked up his pen and began to write the letter he had often thought about—and had been told by his superiors should be included in his personal belongings— but one he had never been able to write.

Dear Mom and Dad,

If you have received this letter, it can only mean that I will not be coming home. I want you to know that I love you both, and appreciate all that you have done for me as I grew up. I hope that someday you will be able to come to terms with my love of flying. I know that it is not what you had hoped, for me, but it is all that ever meant anything to me, at least as far as what I wanted to do with my life. I love it, and don't regret a minute of it, in spite of whatever may have happened to me. We all had our duty to do for our country, and each of us faced the same risks. I am proud that I was able to be a part of doing that job, and to get to fly while I was doing it. Please tell Jerry and Elizabeth how much I love them. I don't really have any possessions, so there is little to say about that. Jerry can have my Winchester—I know how much he likes it. Do whatever seems best with anything else, except please don't throw away my model airplanes. Let Jerry do something with them—maybe some little kid would like to have them.

I love you all.

Your son,
Gene

Gene looked at the letter a moment, sealed it in an envelope and addressed it. He then placed it in a larger envelope, marking it in large letters:

"TO BE DELIVERED ONLY IN THE EVENT OF MY DEATH"

He placed the envelope with his few personal possessions in his duffel bag under his cot, flopped onto his cot and tried to sleep, but sleep did not come anytime soon.

Seven-Mile Strip lay sleeping under the pale light of a near-full moon, which had emerged from behind the peaks of the Owen Stanley mountain range a few hours earlier. Some fifty miles east of the base, the jagged peaks, not quite visible in the faint light, gave the illusion of a great protective barrier standing between the sleeping base and the enemy beyond. But in this new age of war by air, it was much like the Great Wall of China far to the north: scenic, but useless. Thickets of scraggly trees covered the tumbling foothills to which the base clung. Nobody seemed to know what sort of trees they were, and didn't really care, although one of the guys said they looked like the mesquite trees back home in Texas.

Largely hidden among the trees were scores of pyramidal-peaked crew tents. Here and there, a larger dark patch revealed the presence of crude wooden buildings which served various official functions of the base. Dirt roads, expediently created by simply bulldozing aside the trees, wandered through the encampment, standing out brightly in the moonlight like veins and arteries. Dim, yellow lights shone under black-out canopies, where mechanics worked all night to repair the damage inflicted on bombers on the latest missions, trying to have them ready for yet another mission.

Trees and tents alike stood motionless in lifeless, humid air still hot by any measure, even in this pre-dawn hour. By daytime standards, the base was quiet. There were no bombers roaring off to distant missions, no engines being tested, none of the ubiquitous jeeps or trucks roaring about. Surviving bombers from the handful that had taken off earlier that night for a raid on Rabaul harbor wouldn't return until after daylight.

Instead, the raucous noises from varieties of jungle birds joined the cacophony of countless insects carrying on their nighttime rituals, creating a noise level which, had it not become so commonplace, would have driven a person to sleepless frustration. As it was, the din was scarcely noticed, and young men more accustomed to the sound of an elevated train or of a tractor plowing in a distant field slept on, oblivious to it all.

Down the hill, some distance from the camp, in the only flat area available, lay the namesake for the airbase, the gravel airstrip pragmatically named for the seven miles that separated it and the nearby harbor town of Port Moresby.

The crude runway was the only reason for the camp to exist. There could be few other reasons why anyone would choose to inhabit this intolerant and unpleasant land.

Branching out from the strip were numerous taxiways leading to hardstands on which a collection of war-weary bombers, painted in olive-drab colors, stood somberly in the moonlight. Among them, *Ad Astra* sat silently and patiently, the three-sided dirt revetment drawn around her like a shawl to protect her against the night. Her ground crew had fueled her before sunset to avoid any problems of moisture condensing in her tanks, and she now waited for her crew to enter and bring her to life. For both *Ad Astra* and her crew, it was to be an eventful day.

The pre-dawn reverie was soon disturbed by a crew truck groaning its way from the camp, its black-out headlights jerkily poking about in the dim light as it bounced down the crude road toward the strip. The truck paused briefly near *Ad Astra*, as several dark figures clambered off, then disappeared back into the trees. Chatting quietly, as though fearful of disturbing the slumber of their plane, they tossed their equipment and personal belongings through the hatches and climbed on board.

It was not unusual for the crew to talk perfunctorily, if at all, as they started a mission, each preferring to be alone in his own thoughts. This was especially true as they approached today's mission, as an unusual tension seemed to infect the crew. George Henderson, the dapper cameraman and waist gunner who had replaced Neil Struthers when he had asked to be reassigned, crawled into the rear entry hatch behind Jimmy Wilson, who served as the crew's radio operator.

Flashlight beams stabbed about the dark interior as they carefully made their way up the sloping floor, past the waist guns, around the ammo feed chutes for the belly turret suspended from the plane's floor, and into the small compartment behind the bomb bay which housed the radio equipment. In silence they each began unpacking the various items essential to their respective duties.

"Where's Whitford?" George asked quietly, finally giving voice to the worrisome thought that had eaten at him since climbing onto the crew truck and finding a new face occupying the seat normally reserved for Ken Whitford, their regular copilot. Jimmy was surprised by the concern in George's voice, and knew something must be troubling his typically unflappable crew mate.

"I thought you'd heard. He's in sick bay, along with Bronx," Jimmy answered, referring to their regular navigator, who had come down with a mild case of malaria.

"Ken, too?" George was on his knees, loading film into the K-17 camera installed in the floor of the radio compartment, one of three in the trimetrogon setup that served as the basis for the day's mission. "Seems strange they'd both come down with it just before this mission. This is beginning to smell like a jinxed mission."

"Oh, that's a bunch of bullshit, George, and you know it," countered Jimmy. "The damn malaria's laid out half the base at one time or another, so it shouldn't be any surprise. Anyway, Ken's got it pretty good."

Strange shadows shifted around the compartment as Jimmy's flashlight constantly moved from his charts to the racks of radio equipment mounted on the walls of his little compartment. Before each flight, he had to set his radios to the day's tactical frequencies and check the numerous switches which controlled their operation.

"So who's the new guy?" George asked, without looking up from his task, trying to make his query sound routine.

"You mean the copilot? Johnson. Stan Johnson."

"What outfit's he with? How long has he been over here?"

"I don't know. Gene didn't say. Why?"

"Oh, nothing I suppose," George answered, a bit unconvincingly. "It's just that, well, it's bad enough losing Bronx, but at least Jack's flown with us several times. I know he can handle the navigation, and he seems to be pretty good on the cheek gun." George fell silent, stopping himself in midstream, trying to shake off the persistent worry he felt as he busied himself with the cameras.

"Meaning what?"

"Meaning that…" George made no real effort to keep his frustration at Jimmy's calm demeanor out of his voice. "Well, damn it, it'd be nice to know that if anything happens to Gene today, there's someone up front who knows how to fly this thing."

His statement, with its touch of sarcasm mixed with apprehension, hung infectiously in the air. Jimmy looked more closely at George, who was hunched over the cameras in the plane's belly, his back to Jimmy. For the first time, he felt a similar pang of concern, as he allowed George's uneasiness with the changes to their tightly-knit crew on such a crucial day to creep into his own thoughts. But he shook it off. He didn't have time to dwell on it.

He scanned his flashlight around the dark radio compartment, checking one last time that all was in readiness for the flight, then checked to make sure that the extra transmitter that Gene had insisted he sneak on board in case the standard one failed—or was shot up—was still where he had stored it. Assured that all was okay, he turned his light on the camera mechanisms in the floor, to assist George as he finished loading the film.

"Yeah, I know what you mean," Jimmy said, finally reacting to George's comment. "I'm not real thrilled about it, either. He won't know anything about the tactics we've worked out if we get bounced. I suppose Gene must have briefed him…but, you don't know how he'll do if it turns hairy." He watched as George closed the film cans and checked the connectors for the camera controls. It felt better to talk about it. He reached over and patted George on the shoulder.

"We'll be okay, buddy. I figure if Gene's willing to fly with him, I am."

George stood up, his job completed.

"Oh well, what the hell," he said, sighing. "Maybe it'll be another milk run like it was a couple of weeks ago."

Jimmy's smile went unseen in the shadows.

"Roger that. But—how do you expect to become an ace gunner if all we get are milk runs?"

"I've got a strange feeling that having enough targets to go around shouldn't be a problem today," George countered, his voice rather flat. "I've never seen the Skipper so uptight about a mission."

"Uptight? What do you mean? I hadn't noticed anything," Jimmy responded, turning to look at George.

"Oh, that's probably the wrong word. But damnation, I've never seen him make so many preparations for a fight. He's got more firepower on this thing than the USS Missouri. And bringing all that extra ammo, and spare radios? What the hell's he think we're getting into, today? He must know something he ain't tellin' us, is all I can say."

"Who knows. I've tried not to think about it," Jimmy replied. "Speaking of that, we did get all that extra ammo on board, didn't we?" Jimmy pointed his flashlight to the rear of the compartment to check yet again that the additional canisters of fifty-caliber ammunition belts were still where they had been stored.

"I checked mine as we got on board," George replied, glancing at the cases sitting at the rear of the compartment. "Looks like you've got enough to hold off a squadron or two."

With nothing left to do before takeoff, and not wanting to talk, or think, anymore of what might be in store for them, the two crewmen sat down on their parachutes on the floor of the bomber, backs against the bulkhead, to await takeoff.

Captain Gene Stoddard, accompanied by his substitute copilot, finished his walk-around inspection of the bomber and chatted briefly with the crew chief about the status of his bird. The extra ammunition containers were at their stations, the extra guns were all in place, the long-range fuel tank that had been temporarily installed in the bomb bay had been checked. Satisfied that everything possible had been done to ready the craft for the mission, he swung up through the bottom forward hatch into the plane.

As each of the crew settled into his own niche with practiced ease, Gene and the substitute copilot, Stan Johnson, proceeded through the start-up check list. Johnson read each item on the list, as Gene completed the task and confirmed it. They spoke with quiet, terse exchanges of an arcane technical language that sounded like the liturgical chant of a new religion, born of high technology being married to warfare and meaningful only to those high priests permitted to sit in the seats of the anointed.

The exchanges continued as levers were advanced, switches flipped and buttons pushed. In a few minutes the four engines were rumbling the easy, visceral sound of radial engines at idle. With electrical power now available, red panel lights came on, vacuum tube filaments began glowing, overhead map lights created small islands in the blackness. Pulsating currents of air from the four huge propellers beat against the fuselage and tail, sending vibrations throughout the previously lifeless metal. *Ad Astra* had come to life again.

Having checked all their instruments, and completed a quick intercom check of each crew member, Gene began taxiing to the runway for takeoff. A thorough full power checkout of each of the engines assured him that *Ad Astra* was eager to go. Poised on the end of the runway, tail wheel locked and brakes set, he turned to his copilot.

"Ready?"

"Affirm."

Gene adjusted himself in his seat, and looked down the dark runway at the even darker terrain beyond.

"I'm going to stay on the gauges. You handle the power. Don't pull the power back to climb until the gear and flaps are up. If we lose one, identify it, and feather it immediately."

"Roger. Ready when you are."

Gene nodded, and gently began walking the throttle levers forward. As superchargers came up to speed, compressing vast amounts of humid tropical air to be mixed with high octane fuel, four Wright Cyclones responded with over four thousand horsepower. Great clouds of dust swirled behind the plane, which shuddered and vibrated with the strain. Glancing across the panel to assure himself that all was well with his airplane, Gene released the brakes and *Ad Astra* began accelerating down the strip.

At 0401 hours, just one minute past the prescheduled take-off time, *Ad Astra's* wheels left the dirt and gravel for her true home. Gene smiled to himself as he noted the lift-off time. *Plan your flight and fly your plan*, he thought, as *Ad Astra* gathered speed and climbed into the darkness.

In the tents of the camp below, young men stirred on their cots as the roaring engines of the bomber passing close overhead briefly disturbed their slumber. Privately thankful that it was someone else in the plane, they drifted back to their dreams of lives back home that had been snatched so suddenly from them.

The *Fortress* had no bomb load, but with all tanks full of fuel, and the added weight of the long range fuel tank temporarily installed in the bomb bay, she was still heavy. With this load, and in the warm moist air, she had used a good portion of the strip before lifting off. Nevertheless, Gene soon had the landing gear and flaps up, and was established on a steady climb to clear the Owen Stanley mountain range.

They were headed for a destination as yet known only to Gene, some seven hundred miles to the northeast, comparable to flying from New York City to Chicago. But instead of flying over the peaceful farms and cities of their homeland, they would be flying, alone, over an empty, hostile ocean deep into enemy-held territory.

Her ground crew stood and watched as their plane roared down the runway and lifted into the night darkness. In only moments, it was gone, and the fading sounds of its engines were soon swallowed by the jungle. They began walking back to their tents.

"When are they due back?" one of them asked the crew chief.

"About thirteen hundred—maybe later, depending on what winds they run into," the crew chief answered. He was silent for a few steps, then added, somewhat under his breath, "If they come back."

"Shouldn't they be here by now?" one of the ground crew responsible for *Ad Astra* asked his crew chief. "I thought you said they'd be back maybe a half hour ago."

The crew had been sitting around the parking space reserved for their plane, leaning against the dirt revetment, looking off toward the east as they expectantly awaited the return of their plane and its crew.

"Yeah, I figured they'd be here by…wait, is that them?"

Their attention was immediately grabbed by the faint sound of engines, and a tiny speck approaching the base. They waited, not speaking, as the speck became a B-17 bomber.

"Yeah, that's them," the chief observed, squinting at the approaching plane now circling around to line up for the landing. "Looks like number three's smokin'…they must've run into something."

"Yeah, and number two's feathered," observed Private Shelby, the young mechanic who had first approached Gene the day he discovered the forlorn wreck that became *Ad Astra*. "Jeez, they must've really got bounced—"

"Oh damn, there goes a flare," the crew chief said, interrupting the young mechanic. "They've got wounded. Shelby, get the jeep and get up to sick bay and make sure they know—and get some ambulances down here on the double."

But even as he spoke, they heard the sound of trucks roaring down the hill toward the runway. Soon, two ambulances, a large red cross painted on their sides, came to a halt at the revetment. The corpsmen climbed out, joining the ground crew as the bomber bounced and jolted to a landing. They saw the plane's flaps weren't deployed, and worried as it raced down the runway without appearing to slow down. Apparently neither the wing flaps nor the brakes were functional; the pilot had little he could do to slow the plane.

But somehow, the plane begrudgingly slowed and came to a halt before it ran out of runway, turned around, and headed back to the parking area. In moments it was rolling up to the revetment.

"Good Lord! What hit them?" Private Shelby exclaimed. He had developed a high degree of respect for the captain who refused to let the abandoned plane be scrapped. "Look at the hole in that thing! Looks like it nearly wiped out the pilot's side. Can you see Captain Stoddard?"

As the ground crew approached the plane, the corpsmen were already opening hatches, preparing to climb aboard.

The copilot, Stan Johnson, who had landed the plane, looked at Ollie Olsen, the bombardier, who was standing between the two pilot seats. He had been assisting Stan during the long flight back and had held Gene, as best he could, during the landing. Gene was unconscious, slumped down in his seat, against the side of the cockpit.

"Thanks for the help, Ollie. Let's get him out of here," Johnson said, as he saw the corpsmen starting to enter the plane. The corpsmen saw the two crewmen about to exit the hatch, and backed away. As they dropped out of the forward hatch, Johnson turned to the ambulance crew. "We've got a pretty bad one up there. Get him out fast. He won't last much longer."

Two of the medical corpsmen climbed up into the pilot compartment. The first one glanced at the pilot.

"My God, this side's been blown to bits! Looks like the pilot's gone," he said, surveying the bloody mess surrounding the pilot. He turned to go down into the nose compartment. "There must be one up front."

Slim Jensen, the tail gunner, had been in the nose assisting the wounded navigator, Jack Stevens, and was just crawling out of the nose compartment. He bristled when he heard the corpsman's comment.

"You bastards get him out of here on the double. He saved our asses up there today, and you're not going to let him die here on the ground. Now get after it."

"Okay, take it easy. We just thought he'd had it. C'mon, Rob, give me a hand. Damnation, look at his legs. It's gonna be tough getting him out of here."

The two corpsmen were taken aback, not believing that anyone who had lost so much blood might still be alive. They recovered quickly, and moved to start trying to extricate Gene from his pilot seat, without further damaging his mangled legs and arms. As they lowered him down to the lower hatch, one of the corpsmen glanced into the nose compartment.

"Is there anybody up front?"

"Yeah," Jensen replied. "The navigator's been hit. He's pretty bloody, and sort of in shock, but he's not too serious. Let's get the Skipper out of here."

As two corpsmen approached the rear of the plane, George Henderson, the cameraman and waist gunner, and the belly turret gunner, Danny Workowski, stepped down out of the rear hatch. George's face was pale and he looked dazed. He dropped to his hands and knees, dry heaving as nerves that had been clutching his stomach tried to be released. In a moment, he shook his head and got back up, a hand on Danny's shoulder.

"You guys okay?" one of the corpsmen asked, looking at Henderson's pale face.

"I'll be okay in a minute—just got to let my nerves settle a little," he answered. "They got Wilson…in the head." He had to pause and swallow hard, then nodded toward the hatch. "He's in the radio compartment…I covered him with a flight jacket."

"You sure you're okay? We've got some smelling salts in the truck," one of the corpsmen asked Henderson, not convinced that the shaken crewman was going to keep from passing out. Henderson shook his head and began to walk away, not wanting to be there when they brought Jimmy's body out. Mental images burned in his mind were still too vivid.

The corpsmen up front struggled to lower Gene down and out of the aircraft, trying to protect his wounded arms and legs. After loading him, and sending him on one of the ambulances, they helped the wounded navigator, Jack Stevens, down. Then they lowered Jimmy Wilson's body and put them both in the second ambulance.

The rest of the crew, after seeing the dead and wounded loaded into the makeshift ambulances, crawled onto the crew truck for a ride back to the debriefing tent, and then some much needed rest.

Ad Astra sat silent and ignored in the dirt, facing her revetment where she had come to rest. The Kansas seal that Gene had had emblazoned on the nose had been obliterated—a gaping shell hole in its place. But *Ad Astra* had done her job, and brought them back. For the moment, no one remembered the precious pictures in her belly.

Stan Johnson, the copilot, stood looking at the hole in the nose of the plane, and the numerous bullet holes scattered about, and shook his head slightly as if unable to comprehend all that he had just experienced. He walked over to the nearby revetment, sat down in the dirt and leaned back against its sloping sides, arms resting across his drawn-up knees. He leaned his head back against the dirt wall and closed his eyes for a moment, then lit a cigarette, slowly exhaling the first deep breath.

"What in hell did you guys run into today?"

Johnson's reverie was interrupted by Carl Brunson, the crew chief for *Ad Astra*, standing beside him. Johnson inhaled deeply again from his cigarette, glancing up to see who was talking to him.

"Hi, Carl. About half the Japanese Air Force, it seemed. I truly thought we were goners. But Stoddard got us through, somehow. I still don't know how we did it."

"What do you mean? What happened?" Brunson asked, as he sat down beside Johnson.

Johnson took another deep drag on his cigarette, slowly exhaled, then stubbed it out in the dirt. He looked at the wounded B-17 for several seconds, their battle replaying in his mind.

"We were just starting the photo run when Jensen spotted a bunch of Zeros climbing up from behind, trying to overtake us. I don't know for sure where they were coming from. I'd got the feeling Gene suspected something was up, from the way the C.O. had talked to him. He seemed kinda uptight. But there wasn't even a base around there, last time I was up in that area. We were at twenty five thousand, so Gene knew it would take them a while to get to us. He hoped we could finish the run before they reached us, so we could maneuver to take them on...but it didn't happen. They were on us two or three minutes before we were done."

"So did he break off the photo run?" Brunson asked, suspecting he knew the answer.

"No," Johnson said, shaking his head. "He told the crew that it was imperative that we finish the run and get the photos. He said to just do what they had been trained to do, and we'd be okay." He paused a moment, reflecting on the flight. "That's the best disciplined crew I've ever flown with. They know their jobs, and none of them panicked. I know Carlson did a good job of training them, but I think Stoddard may have made them even better.

"Anyway, we just kept on truckin' on the photo run, like we were on rails, while they circled around for a head on pass. Five of 'em hit us at about the same time, from both sides, level and high...I thought we'd had it."

"Good Lord," Brunson exclaimed. "Is that when Stoddard got hit?"

"Yeah. And maybe the radio operator, too. What was his name? I didn't know him."

"Wilson. Jimmy Wilson," Brunson answered. "Damn shame. He was a good kid. Quiet, polite. Just turned nineteen, a few weeks ago. From what Stoddard has said, he was good on the radios, and reliable. Didn't get rattled when they were being attacked."

"You know," Johnson said, staring across the field, "it's starting to get to me, losing guys like that. My bombardier got hit a couple of weeks ago. That was tough. Still is. I really liked him."

The crew chief nodded, but didn't respond.

"I realize," Johnson continued, "I'm getting to where I won't let myself get to know the new guys. I don't want to know them. It's not very fair, I suppose. They think you don't like them, or you're a hard-ass, or something. They don't know what it's like, yet. It's a lot easier, when you lose someone you don't know."

Johnson pulled out another cigarette, lit it and inhaled deeply, then slowly released the smoke, watching it curl upward and disappear. They sat there, neither speaking, absorbed in their own thoughts. After a bit, Johnson picked up again on the flight.

"All hell broke loose when those first ones hit us. Gene was firing the nose gun, everybody was firing everything they had. Those fifties he put in instead of the thirty calibers were all that saved us. He told the guys to start firing while the Japs were still out of range of a thirty caliber. It obviously surprised them, and threw them off just enough they couldn't concentrate their fire on us. A couple of them broke off early. Walters got one. Henderson said he saw it flaming and heading down.

"It didn't matter, though. They were swarming all over us. One of them coming in from about ten o'clock, and high, hit Gene's side with its twenty millimeters. It knocked out the number two engine, and just blew his side to bits. Pieces of metal from the instrument panel, hydraulic fluid, paint chips…blood. Hell, I don't know what all blew loose from over there. Scared the shit out of me. It blinded me, for a minute, I had so much stuff in my eyes. When I got my eyes cleared a little, I saw I had blood all over me—but it was Gene's." He had to pause a moment, and finished the cigarette, flicking the butt into the dirt.

"I looked at Gene. His legs were all twisted around, and his left arm tossed up over him. He was covered in blood, and slumped over in his seat. I thought he was dead, but I didn't have time to think about it. I was feathering the engine, and more of the bastards were circling in on us. We were done with the run, by then, and could begin to maneuver to take them on. I turned into one of them. The guys in the nose, and Walters in the turret, were letting him have it. He broke off before he could fire his twenty millimeter, but he raked us with some thirty caliber. I heard it hitting behind me…that may have been when Wilson got hit. I don't know, for sure."

Johnson stopped talking, and laid his head back against the dirt bank, his eyes closed. The crew chief waited, not talking, wondering if he should leave Johnson alone. But then he opened his eyes, and shook his head.

"You know, Carl, I've been on some pretty hairy missions, but I've never seen the Japs as frantic to bring one of us down as they seemed to be today. It was like sharks smelling blood. They were swarming around us like flies on road kill. I don't know if they wanted to keep their base secret, or what the hell was going on, but they were just crazy. Of course, that was easier to deal with, than when they coordinated their attacks. Everything was going to hell in the plane. Something started a fire behind Gene. I saw it burning, over there, and hollered at Walters to get a fire bottle. Stevens, the navigator, had got hit in the head and was coming out of the nose for some help. He was bleeding a lot, but he saw the fire and started trying to put it out. Walters had been hit in the arm—not too bad, fortunately. He came out of the turret and helped put out the fire."

"Good Lord," the crew chief exclaimed. "And you never got hit?"

"Never got a scratch," Johnson said, then laughed a little. "Although Stoddard nearly gave me a heart attack."

"Gene? I thought you said he was out."

"Yeah, he was. That was the damnedest thing. I thought he was dead. But while Walters and Stevens were putting out that fire I was looking out my side at some Zeros coming around, when all of a sudden the control wheel got jerked out of my hand. I looked over to see what was going on, and Gene was sorta sitting up, flying with his right hand, and turning into a Zero coming in from his side. Scott quick jumped back in the turret, and let him have it. I think he got him. But it sure saved our asses. I never even saw it. And with Walters out of the turret, if Gene hadn't seen him…well, anyway, I nearly jumped out of my seat when I saw him flying. Talk about coming back from the dead… I've never seen such a thing."

Johnson got up and walked back over to the plane, looking up at the shattered nose. He stood staring at it for several seconds, then began to walk around the plane, looking at it—or what was left of it. The crew chief joined him.

"It just went on and on, like that," Johnson continued. "It seemed like it would never stop. Somewhere in all of it, an oh-two bottle got hit. Some of the guys were without oxygen, so we had to make a screamin' dive for lower altitude. That did shake off the Zeroes for a little bit, but they came down after us. We couldn't talk to the guys in back. I don't know if some electrical panels got burned in that fire, or if they got shot out. Either way, they had no idea what was going on up front, and we didn't know what was happening to them. No one had time to think, anyway. It was sort of every man for himself. We couldn't coordinate anything, except between me and Walters, in the turret. But what really got me, was how Gene would just keep coming to and grabbing the controls, to get us out of another jam. Then he'd pass out, again."

"He did that more than once?" The crew chief sounded incredulous, having seen Gene when the corpsmen got him off the plane.

"Yeah. Several times," Johnson said, shaking his head. "One time, one of them was coming in from his side. Gene turned into him and let go with his nose gun just as the guy started to fire. Scared the son of a bitch so bad he flipped over and broke off, just as he started firing. But he hit the number three engine. Didn't knock it clear out, or we'd have never made it back. Probably just blew out the supercharger. I was able to nurse it up to about fifty percent power, so we could get over the mountains."

They stood looking up at the blackened nacelle of the number three engine, pierced in several places by machine gun bullets.

"I have no idea how long it all lasted…must have been at least forty five minutes. But they finally began running short of fuel, and had to break off."

"Good Lord," the crew chief said, shaking his head in disbelief at the story. "How many do you think there were?"

"I don't know. Jenson counted nineteen or twenty when he first saw them coming. Some more might've joined them, after it all started. No one was counting, after that."

"You're lucky you made it," Brunson said, still looking at the bullet riddled, blackened engine.

"To tell the truth, I honestly didn't think we would," Johnson admitted. "It's the first time since we got over here that I thought, this is it—I'm going to die today. I've been thinking about it, since we landed. I really believe it was just Stoddard's clinch-jawed determination to not lose his plane, that somehow got us back. I'd heard how he was hell-bent to save it from the scrap heap."

"Yeah, I can believe that," Brunson agreed, laughing at the memory of it. "You should've seen him, the way he pounded on all of us to get that thing patched up and flying, again. Hell, the first time we took it up, to check it out, I wasn't sure it'd hold together to get off the ground. But he was like a kid in a candy store. You'd a thought Santy Claus left it in his stocking."

Johnson smiled, but didn't comment.

"It was almost like he was willing us all to not let the bastards destroy his plane," Johnson continued after a moment, so quietly that the crew chief wondered if he was talking to himself. "I've never felt anything quite like that."

They were quiet, for a few minutes, reflecting on it all. Then Johnson continued.

"Of course, after the Japs broke off, we had to try to figure out how to make it back home. I made Walters fly it for a while, so I could try to stop Gene's bleeding and get some morphine in him. Scott was scared spitless—he'd never even touched the controls of a plane, before. I told him to just hold the wings level and keep it close to our heading for the base. Of course, I had to just guess at a heading. The navigator was pretty much out of it, by then, and the radio operator was dead—we couldn't get radio bearings. And, our gyro compass had been blown to bits. All we had was the magnetic compass. But, I told Scott that New Guinea is too big to miss, so not to worry about it."

They both chuckled at that, a moment.

"I wrapped everything I could find around Gene's arms and legs. His left leg was so mangled I was afraid to do much to it…but he was bleeding like a stuck pig. I had to do something. I shot him with all the morphine I could spare, so he was pretty much out of it. Stevens had got a pretty good hit in the head, on his forehead—just a big gash, but he was in a lot of pain and bleeding a lot. I gave him the last of the morphine."

"Sounds a little too close for comfort," Brunson observed.

"You got that right," Johnson agreed. "A half inch closer and he'd be dead now. While I was working on him, Jensen came up from the tail and helped Walters get his arm bandaged. He told me then that Wilson got hit in the head.

He looked pretty pale—I was afraid he was going to pass out. I kept checking for a pulse on Gene. It was getting awfully weak—couldn't really tell if he had one, most of the time. I was getting scared he wouldn't last, but I didn't know what else I could do for him. I finally saw the mountains, and recognized where we were. I managed to nudge us up enough to just barely clear them—bet I didn't miss them fifty feet. I was praying number three would hold on a bit longer, and that I'd got Gene's bleeding slowed down enough that he could hold on till we got here."

There seemed to be nothing left to say, or do. They stood in silence for a bit, then Johnson began to walk up the road to the base facilities.

"I've got to debrief, then I'm going to go check on Stoddard. I hope to God he pulls through."

The corpsmen had delivered Gene to the medical tent. It didn't even pretend to be a hospital. This was a forward combat base. Its medical facilities were no more than a place where a wounded crewman could first receive treatment. The medics made a quick, but cursory, examination of Gene, realizing immediately that only a major hospital could save him, and then only if they could get him stabilized well enough to survive the flight down to Sydney.

They started blood plasma transfusions, put temporary bandages on his many wounds, and stabilized his shattered leg. He was placed back on an ambulance and taken to a C-47 cargo plane that fortunately had landed there earlier in the day to transport some other wounded to Sydney. Otherwise, it would have been unlikely that Gene could have survived long enough to make a later flight.

A few minutes after he was loaded on board, the plane was roaring down the dirt strip, leaving behind a cloud of dust in the humid air as it climbed out over *Ad Astra*, sitting forlornly where it had come to rest.

Unconscious from heavy doses of morphine, Gene was on his way to the hospital in Sydney, Australia. He and the plane he so loved had each somehow saved the other, each barely surviving the ordeal. What the future held, neither was capable of knowing.

Sydney

After surviving the surgery that saved his leg, and his life, and after enough time had passed in the hospital that he was able to endure the pain without having to be continually rendered unconscious, Captain Eugene Stoddard had become sufficiently cognizant to comprehend that his lifelong dream of flying was now as shattered as his leg, and lost forever. That stark realization had crashed down on him the previous night, pushing him into a black mood that had required sedatives before he could drift into fitful, drug-assisted sleep.

He awoke to bright sunlight, a soft breeze flavored with salt air from Sydney harbor wafting in his open hospital window, and the pleasant chirping of birds in nearby trees—none of which had done anything whatsoever to lighten that mood. Quite the contrary. He awoke with the feeling that the cheerful morning was mocking him, painfully reminding him that he would never again experience taking off on such a glorious morning, or enjoy the sight of a sunrise from the cockpit of his beloved *Ad Astra*—or any other plane, for that matter. His dream of flying for the airlines, having seemed to be virtually guaranteed once the war ended, had been blasted to bits on his last mission.

The morning nurse had temporarily interrupted his black thoughts, as she blustered into his room to do his morning rituals. After attending to all the necessary, but embarrassing, personal issues, she had changed his bandages. As always, it was a painful process. She tidied up and busied on to her next charge, leaving Gene with his eyes closed, trying to let the pain ease. He tried to distract himself by thinking about Mattie, the nurse's aide who had been at his side when he first regained consciousness after the surgery. During the ensuing days, when he was not unconscious from the pain-killing drugs that were necessary so much of the time, he was becoming aware that he was starting to feel surprisingly attracted to her.

He hadn't given much credence to his feelings. She was, in his estimation, the prettiest girl he'd ever seen, and he presumed that every guy that came to the hospital had feelings similar to his. He couldn't imagine anyone so pretty, who surely could have her pick of any guy she might want, would feel anything but sympathy for him. But, it had also occurred to him that she seemed to find any number of reasons to come by his room to see him. He even permitted himself, for fleeting moments, to wonder if she, in fact, might be interested in him. Such a possibility seemed as implausible as it was too good to be true, so he largely dismissed any such thought. But even as he was once again discrediting any glimmer of such wishful thinking, she came breezing in, carrying some letters.

"G'day, mate. How's my favorite Yank this fine morning?" She hadn't noticed that his eyes were closed, until he opened them to look at her.

"Oh, Gene," she apologized, "I'm sorry. I didn't realize you were sleeping. Would you like for me to come back later?"

"Well, g'day to you, mate," Gene replied, smiling weakly, trying with no success to imitate her Aussie accent. "No, I wasn't asleep. The nurse just changed my bandages and I was lying here feeling sorry for myself." He nodded at the letters. "What have you there?"

Gene watched as she pulled a chair to the bedside and sat down beside him. She always seemed so supple and graceful in her movements, even doing something as utilitarian as moving a chair. Gene wondered if she played tennis, or some other sport. He also wondered what she would look like in tennis shorts—fabulous, no doubt. He wondered, in fact, what she would look like in anything other than her hospital uniform. She looked pretty in it, but it somehow struck him as looking like little girls playing nurse.

There had been no reason for her to mention a boyfriend, but Gene could hardly believe that a girl so pretty would not be overwhelmed with guys chasing after her. He had made a special note of looking for a wedding or engagement ring. There wasn't one, and she had mentioned once that her parents would be worried if she didn't get home at a reasonable time, so he assumed she was still single and living at home. But then he would let his deep-seated insecurities take over and assume that she wouldn't have any interest in a has-been of a pilot, and drop any thoughts about her. That is, until the next time she would come to his room.

Mattie could not know, of course, that all those thoughts had been flitting through her patient's mind as she moved the chair to his bedside and sat down beside him. She was aware that he was watching her as she did so, and that pleased her, but she didn't have any idea if it meant anything. She studied the faces of the two envelopes.

"What I have here are some letters to a certain Captain Stoddard of the United States Army Air Forces—from Kansas, it would appear. Shall I open them for you?"

"Would you mind reading them to me? I'm not sure I can manage with one hand yet," Gene answered, stretching the truth a little, as he had been gaining some use of his right hand but wanted her to stay.

Mattie looked at the return address on the first letter a moment longer than should have been required to simply read it.

"Wouldn't you rather read this one in private?" she asked, eyebrows raised. If Gene had been perceptive of a woman's reactions to such things, which he was not, he would have noticed a slight hint of a suggestion that the question she wanted answered was not the one she asked.

"In private? Why would I want that?" Gene asked, his face a blank.

"Well, Gene," she protested, managing to work two syllables into his name in her exasperation at his total lack of comprehension, "it's from a Christy—and her last name is not Stoddard."

Gene looked at her, momentarily baffled. A quick hint of blushing tinted her face. She glanced down at her lap, obviously embarrassed, as Gene continued to look at her, wondering what was going on. Finally the light dawned.

"Oh, for pete's sake, Mattie. Did you think she was my girlfriend, or something?" Gene asked. "Christy's practically a member of the family. She and I have been mates, as you Aussies call it, since we were born. We went to the same church and high school, and practically grew up together. What one of us wouldn't think of to get into trouble, the other one would. What's she got to say?"

Gene was oblivious to the fact that for Mattie a major source of apprehension had just been removed from her life. If he had been paying attention he would have noted the flash of relief cross her face. But he was looking at the letter, instead, and the moment passed. Mattie smiled, extracted the tissue-thin airmail stationery from its envelope and began to read.

Dear Gene:

Your mom and dad got the telegram yesterday that you had been wounded, and called me as soon as they had picked it up at the station. I went out to your house to be with them. They are pretty shaken, but you know your folks. They are trying to keep a stiff upper lip. Sorry, I haven't done so well. Your letter telling me about your concerns about the mission shook me up bad enough, then we get the telegram. If I remember correctly, I gave you strict instructions to be careful over there—why won't you ever listen to what I tell you?

Gene, we're all praying that your wounds weren't too serious, but I'm frankly not encouraged that we haven't heard from you directly. I'm praying that it's just because the mail is so slow. Please tell me the truth and let me know how bad it is. I promise I will be considerate when I talk to your folks, but we are all worried sick. Are you going to get to come home to recover? All the telegram said was that you were wounded during an important mission and were in the hospital in Sydney. They were thoughtful enough to include the address so we could write to you.

Are they taking good care of you? Is there anything we can send, or do you expect to be out before anything could get to you?

We don't know what to do at this point. It takes so long to hear anything with the mail so slow. It's hard to take when days go by and we don't know anything. I imagine Liz will be writing to you for your folks. I don't think your mom would be able to, yet. Please let us know something as soon as you can. We all love you, and are holding our breath until we hear from you (yes, I know, I'm exaggerating).

Love from all,
Christy

"She sounds like a very good mate," Mattie said, as she laid the letter on the bedside table. "You're quite fortunate to have someone like that."

Gene smiled, and nodded. "Yeah, Christy's a real firecracker. She's the exact opposite of me, so we kind of balanced each other out."

"Oh? If she's a firecracker, what would that make you?" Mattie tried to make the question seem like teasing, but her interest would have been apparent if Gene had been paying attention.

"Me? Oh, Christy would probably say she's the firecracker, and I'm the fizzler. She thinks I'm too reserved. Well, actually, she'd probably call me a stick-in-the-mud. I don't know. I just feel awkward and ill at ease around people, and tend to keep to myself. I never did much dating in high school—always felt too shy, I guess. Christy, on the other hand, never met a stranger. She's an instant friend with everybody she meets. I could go all day without talking to anyone, and she yaks a mile a minute all day long. Plus, I've always been a bit of a bookworm, and Christy considered homework an impediment to her social life."

"Oh, I find it hard to believe that a handsome pilot-to-be would have had any trouble getting dates. I'll bet you're being far too modest," Mattie argued. "But you're right. Christy does sound like quite the firecracker."

"Well, I don't know about the handsome bit," Gene protested, pleased by her compliment while wondering if she really meant it, "but thanks. To be honest, though, I can't imagine how I would have made it through all the teenage growing-up problems without Christy around to knock some sense into me every so often. Anyway, enough about me. What about the other letter—who's it from?"

"Elizabeth Stoddard," Mattie replied, looking at the second envelope. "Is she your sister?"

"Yeah, that's Sis. We usually call her Lizzie, or Liz. She doesn't much care for it, but we don't let her vote. Strange, though, she usually just adds to Mom's letters. What's she say?"

Mattie opened the letter and began to read.

Dear Gene:

We received the telegram day before yesterday saying you had been wounded, but there were no details. Mom asked me to write to you. She's still too upset to be able to write. I tried to assure her that you will be OK. We all pray that you will.

You know Dad. He won't say much, but I can tell he's taking it pretty hard. He just sits and stares out the window, sometimes. I know what he must be thinking. Mom tries to hide it, but breaks down sometimes and has to go back to the bedroom to cry it out. And poor Jerry, he just sort of gets overlooked. Nobody thinks to ask him how he's feeling, and I know he idolizes you. He worries about you all the time, but is so proud of you, as we all are.

Can you tell us anything, yet? Is it serious enough to have you come back to recover? We will all be able to cope better when we know more. I don't really know what else to say right now except that we love you and are proud of you, and pray that you will recover quickly. Write to us as soon as you are able.

We love you,
Elizabeth

"You have a very loving family, and good friends," Mattie said, laying the second letter on the table with the one from Christy. "You obviously mean a lot to them." Gene nodded, but didn't immediately respond.

"You know, Mattie, I realize I never once considered how it would affect the folks if I got hit," Gene replied, after several seconds had passed, his voice rather subdued. "I mean, guys got hit on virtually every mission...but somehow you can't imagine it being you."

He paused, looking at the ceiling, adrift in his thoughts. Seconds ticked by in silence, so long that Mattie began to wonder if perhaps she should leave him alone. Finally, he glanced at her, shaking his head slightly as if embarrassed by his drifting off.

"Planes would come back from a mission all shot up," he continued. "Sometimes one of the guys wouldn't have made it. The crew and the medics would get him off the plane. I don't know where they took them...I tried not to think about it. The guys that were too badly wounded to get patched up at the base would get hauled off to a hospital someplace—I suppose down here, now that I think about it. Usually, that would be the last we would see of any of them. Of course, sometimes the plane would leave on a mission and just never be heard from again. That's how I got my crew, as a matter of fact."

He paused again. Mattie was curious about his comment about getting his crew, but didn't press him. He was quiet for a moment, then picked up the letter from his sister, stared at it briefly, and laid it back down.

"Sometimes we would know them. Maybe even be close friends. Other times, you wouldn't even know the guy's name. We'd collect what little stuff they had and send it home. The C.O. would send the family a letter. Then we'd get a new crew member, get back in the plane and go fly again. I never once thought about the families back home, getting those telegrams and letters."

Mattie sat beside him, quietly studying his face, waiting for him to continue. She was pleased that he apparently felt comfortable enough with her to share such personal sentiments, and it was just as clear that the letters had affected him rather deeply. It pleased her even more that he seemed to have a lot of depth to him—unlike so many of the young guys who came through the hospital, who acted so adolescent. It impressed her that he had a deep sense of attachment to his family, as her family meant so much to her.

She had known from the day she sat next to his bed, waiting for him to recover from the anesthesia after surgery, that she was attracted to him—in spite of the fact that she knew nothing at all about him. With each revelation, she gained confidence that her initial reaction to him was the right one.

"Now, I think about Mom getting a call from Jim at the Santa Fe depot," Gene continued, "saying there was a telegram for them from the War Department. They're too private. They would never have had him read it to them, and they were probably too rattled to want him to, anyway. They would have driven into town to get it, wondering all the time if it was going to say that I had been killed, was missing, or maybe just slightly wounded. Mom probably about had a heart attack. Christy told me in a letter once that several guys from Colborn have already been killed—one of them was from our church. Mom probably cried the whole way to town, and Dad would be saying 'Now, Mom, it may be nothing at all, so let's just wait and see what it says.' But he would have been thinking the same thing, wondering if they would ever get to see me again, or if all they would get is a gold star to hang in the window."

Mattie realized that there were tears in the corners of his eyes, and started to wipe them for him, then thought perhaps it might be too presumptuous, so hesitated. Gene blinked them back, hoping Mattie hadn't noticed.

"What do you mean, a gold star to hang in the window?" she asked.

"I think it got started during World War I," he explained. "Mom calls them Sons in Service flags—I guess that's their name. Anyway, they're small flags about the size of a piece of tablet paper, and are white with a red border. You hang them in your window so people can see them from the street, and you get to put a blue star on the flag for each family member in the service. There's usually a gold braid to hang them with. They're kind of pretty, actually. Christy wrote one time that when she drives down a street and sees how many there are, the war seems a lot closer to home. Then, if a family member is killed, you replace the blue star with a gold star. The mothers are often called 'Gold Star Mothers.' People see them in the window and know you've lost someone. Liz told me in a letter that she has seen some hanging in windows in town."

Mattie nodded, but didn't respond.

"It's probably harder on them than it is on me," Gene added. "At least I know what I'm dealing with. They just have to go on, day after day, not knowing if I won't survive…or if I just got my fanny nicked."

"You're very fortunate to have a family that cares that much about you, Gene," Mattie replied, smiling at his weak attempt at humor. "It just breaks my heart, sometimes. Some of the guys that come through here have no one that cares enough to write to them, and they get so lonely and depressed."

Gene glanced at her, and nodded, but didn't respond. She didn't want to upset him, so changed the subject.

"Would you care to write to your family? I can write them for you, if you would like."

"Would you?" Gene replied, his face brightening. "I'd sure appreciate it. Better go a little easy on Mom and Dad. Tell them that I was wounded in both arms and legs, but should be okay. The recovery will take quite a while, but I don't know if I will be sent back to the States, or not. Then write one to Christy and tell her all the details. She'll tell Liz, and she can decide how much to tell the folks. I don't want Mom to get even more rattled by all of it."

The next day Mattie read the two letters to Gene for his approval.

Dear Mr. & Mrs. Stoddard:

My name is Mattie O'Sullivan. I'm the nurse's aide presently assigned to caring for your son Eugene. He has asked me to write this for him. Eugene was brought to our hospital in Sydney for treatment of wounds he received on a recent mission. Although his wounds were serious, they are not life threatening. He was wounded in both arms and legs. His right arm and leg were not badly wounded and are healing nicely. His left arm and leg will be in casts for some time. It is usual hospital policy that after casts are removed the patient receives several weeks of physical therapy. I can only assume that will be the case for Eugene. He asks me to assure you that he is doing well and appreciates your prayers and concerns. He also asked me to tell you to please not be worried about him, as he is doing fine. I expect that he will be able to write you in person in a few weeks.

As I have come to know Gene, it is easy to see why he is so loved by his friends and family. He is a brave and fine young man. If there is anything that I can do to assist you, please feel free to write me personally at the hospital address below.

Sincerely yours,
Mattie O'Sullivan

"'Brave and fine?'" Gene kidded. "I think I'll have you write all my letters."

"Well, you know how parents are. They want to hear the best about their young'n's," Mattie teased, grinning in her embarrassment. "Next time I'll try to be more honest."

"No, I like the way you said it," Gene assured her. "I can live with 'brave and fine.' The letter's swell, Mattie. How about the one to Christy?"

Mattie laid the first letter down and picked up the other one.

Dear Christy:

My name is Mattie O'Sullivan. I'm writing you on behalf of your friend, Gene Stoddard. I hope you will pardon my lack of formality, but Gene has told me so much about you that I feel I know you. I'm a nurse's aide at the hospital in Sydney where Gene was brought for surgery and recovery from his wounds. He has asked that I write to you for him, until his arm heals enough that he can write for himself.

Gene has asked—directed, more accurately—that I tell you his full condition. Gene's wounds were very serious, and he lost a large amount of blood. Had the crewmen on his plane not made every effort to suppress the bleeding during the long flight back, and the medical corpsmen at the field where they first landed not had sufficient supplies of plasma, he would not have survived.

His right arm and leg were wounded in several places, but not too deeply and both should heal with little noticeable result other than scars. He lost quite a bit of muscle mass in his left bicep and will need considerable therapy to regain something near full use of it. His left leg, however, was very badly shattered, and his knee damaged. Unfortunately, his leg could not be fully repaired. I think with sufficient therapy he will be able to walk without cane or crutches, but will have a significant limp and limited flexibility in his leg.

Gene is now recovering well, and regaining his appetite. There is nothing life-threatening, now that his blood levels have been restored.

His pain was severe at first and he was kept heavily sedated, but he now manages with oral pain medicine, at least most of the time. The authorities, both here at the hospital and for the US military, have not informed him as to his status. I can only say that in similar cases it was judged to be better for the health of the patient to remain at this hospital until able to travel. That will be at least two or three months in Gene's case, I'm sure.

Gene is holding up pretty well, but I know that he faces many weeks of painful therapy. He appreciates your letters and looks forward to hearing from home. He doesn't want his family to worry about him, but I know that sometimes uncertainty is worse than knowing the facts. He leaves it up to you and Elizabeth to decide how much of this to share with his parents.

Sincerely yours,
Mattie O'Sullivan

Mattie laid the two letters on the table beside Gene's bed. "I hope those are at least close to what you wanted to say. Did I get too explicit for Christy?"

"No, Christy's tough," Gene assured her, picking up the letter to Christy as best he could, and glancing at it. "She would only get upset if she learned about it after I came home. These are really swell letters, Mattie. Better than I would have written, that's for sure." He handed the letters to Mattie, and she placed them in envelopes she had already addressed.

"You know, Mattie," Gene said quietly, "I have to admit...it sounds a lot worse when I hear it read, like that. To tell the truth, I hadn't realized it came that close for me. Sort of makes you have to stop and think a little bit." He glanced at Mattie. She nodded, but didn't feel she should respond. "It'll be tough enough for Christy and Liz when they hear this," Gene added. "I don't know how they'll break any of it to Mom and Dad."

"Oh, most parents are far more resilient than we young folks think. I'm sure they'll cope all right," Mattie tried to assure him.

"Yeah, I know," Gene agreed, "but in the back of their minds they'll think that if I hadn't got into planes it wouldn't have happened. That doesn't help."

"What do you mean?" Mattie asked, unsure of what he was referring to. "Were they opposed to you being in the Air Force?"

"It's a long story," Gene answered, a touch of bitterness obvious in his voice. "Probably not worth telling."

Mattie was surprised by the tone of his voice, but it was obvious he didn't want to talk about it, at least not at the moment, so she changed the subject.

"Shall I go ahead and mail these for you, then?"

"If you would, I'd appreciate it," Gene replied.

She collected the two letters, and walked to the door to leave. As she did so she turned, smiled and gave him a little wave, then left.

Judas Priest, she's good looking, Gene thought, as he smiled back at her. *I wonder if she's this friendly to all the guys in here. Can't imagine anyone that good-looking being unattached, but she's not wearing any rings. Don't know why it matters—don't see how I could do anything about it.*

Mattie had just finished helping Gene to a lunch of soup, and was wiping his chin, when three young men in the uniform of the United States Army Air Forces stepped in the doorway. It was Ken Whitford, Gene's regular copilot, and Gene's best friend, Mike Kingston. Also with them was Stan Johnson, the substitute pilot who had been on the mission with Gene and had taken over after Gene had been wounded. Gene's face lit up when he saw them. Johnson didn't know the others, or Gene, especially well, and felt a little awkward at being there. But since he had been on the mission, Ken and Mike would not accept him not coming along.

"Ken! Mike! Man, am I glad to see you two. Stan, good to see you, again. Come on in—grab a chair."

Mattie immediately rose to leave. The three guys looked—stared would be more accurate—at her, as Gene introduced them.

"Guys, meet Mattie. She's been kind enough to feed me, since I'm pretty much stove up here." He nodded toward the masses of casts and bandages that were his arms and legs.

"I'm pleased to meet you," Mattie said, smiling and affecting a small curtsy. "Actually, I feel I already have. Mr. Stoddard speaks well of all of you." She shook hands with them, then pulled another chair closer to the bed, but they all elected to stand.

"If Stoddard speaks well of us, he must still be delirious," Mike joked.

Mattie smiled at him, then moved to Gene's side. She smoothed the sheets over him, and patted his shoulder. "I'll leave you to your friends, now. Is there anything you need before I leave? I'll come back this evening." Gene shook his head. She turned to the guys and smiled at them. "It is indeed a pleasure to meet you. Perhaps I'll get to see you again. Bye, now." She started toward the door.

"Whoa, hold on a minute. You're not leaving until we get a picture," Mike said, taking her by the arm and leading her back to Gene's bedside. "We were told to get a picture of Gene to take back to show the crew, and they'll kill us if we don't have you in it, Mattie."

Gene had noted that Mike was carrying a camera when he entered the room, but hadn't given it any thought. Mattie moved to stand beside the head of the bed, smiling, waiting for Mike to take the picture.

"Nope, that'll never do," Mike objected. "Far too formal. Sit beside him, and get an arm around him, so the crew can really be jealous." Mattie put her hand behind Gene's head, still standing beside him, looking quite embarrassed.

Mike pushed the chair up close beside the head of the bed, and took Mattie by the shoulders, positioning her in the chair.

"Now, get an arm around him, snuggle up good and close. Can't have the crew feeling sorry for our wounded hero."

Mattie blushed, but complied. She leaned over the bed, with her face close to Gene's, wrapping both arms around him, being careful to not bump his arms. They both smiled, as Mike stepped back and aimed the camera. In a moment, the flash bulb popped. Mattie laughed self-consciously, and pulled her arms away, standing up to leave.

"Much better. Thank you, Mattie. Now we'll have the whole crew trying to get wounded so they can come down here," Mike said.

Mattie laughed, obviously embarrassed, and started once again for the door.

"I think it's time I let you and Gene have a chance to be alone. I'm glad I had a chance to meet you. Bye now."

Mattie was still blushing, wondering if it was obvious that she welcomed the opportunity to get to be that close to Gene, and hoping that it was not. She waved to them, and left the room. The three guys stared as she left.

"Damn, Stoddard! I'll get my ass shot off if I get her for my nurse! God-a-mighty, she's good looking!" Mike exclaimed. Ken was still looking toward the door, in a vain hope that she would reappear.

"Really? I hadn't noticed," Gene kidded. But the quick blush didn't go unnoticed.

The three of them fell into an awkward silence as they began to comprehend the extent of the bandages covering Gene.

"Good Lord, Gene, when you decide to get a Purple Heart you really go all out. Have they told you anything? Are you going to get to come back?" Mike asked.

None of them questioned the assumption that if he was physically capable of returning that he would not simply expect to, as a matter of duty, but would want to. That he might welcome the opportunity to avoid returning to face death on a regular basis and return home was never remotely considered. They were emotionally welded together by that unbreakable bond formed of fighting—and if fate decreed, dying—together. It did not need to be asked. If Gene Stoddard was physically capable of returning, he would do so.

Gene shook his head. They didn't know if he was answering the first question, or the last one. A moment later, Gene broke the silence.

"What about the rest of the crew? I haven't heard anything…"

A pall fell over the room that Gene immediately sensed.

"What is it? Who…how bad was it?" Gene's gaze shifted from one face to the other.

"Gene…" Johnson started to reply, then paused, and cleared his throat. "Jimmy Wilson didn't make it. George said that when that first wave hit us from the nose, he was firing at one that had peeled off to the left. I guess one of the next ones hit him. George said they took a bunch of rounds through the fuselage, but they didn't get him. He said Jimmy got hit in the head…never knew what hit him." Johnson paused, not sure how to proceed.

Gene turned to look out the window, at the peaceful hospital park and the scenic harbor in the distance, the idyllic appearance making a mockery of his feelings. *Why does it always have to be guys like Jimmy?* He didn't know his "Sparks" very well, but liked his affable nature, and quiet competence during missions. The three friends stood in silence, unsure of what to say, or do, next, waiting for Gene to respond. In a moment, Gene looked back at them.

"What about the others? Did anyone else…?" Gene's voice trailed off.

"No," Johnson assured him, "the rest of us made it. Stevens got hit in the head. He was a bloody mess, and was in a lot of pain. He's not back on flight status, yet, but it wasn't life-threatening. Walters got hit in the arm, but not too bad. He's back flying again."

Gene nodded, then looked at Ken. "I have no idea when I'll be able to write anything, Has anyone written to Jimmy's family?" Gene asked.

"The C.O. sent a letter to his wife. He let us all sign it. I put a note in about you, and signed it for you," Ken assured him.

Gene nodded, then looked at Johnson. He had to swallow hard before he could talk. "Did we get the pictures? And what about *Ad Astra*?"

"The C.O. says to tell you that the pictures were phenomenal," Ken answered, trying to put a positive light on the mission. "Some of the best they've had, he said. They're already being turned into maps."

He waited, not wanting to deal with the second question, for he knew how Gene felt about their plane. But he knew he had to answer.

"I don't know about *Ad Astra,* though. I mean…well, two of the engines were hit—Stan said he barely made it over the mountains. She took a hell of a lot of hits, Gene. We started counting them, but gave up. There were so many it seemed pointless. And, damn, Gene—the instrument panel was just shot all to hell…there's nothing left on your side. And the rudder pedals—well, I don't see how you've got any legs left."

Ken blushed noticeably, and glanced awkwardly at Gene's legs, hoping that Gene hadn't noticed him doing so. He did not, in fact, know if Gene had both legs.

"Do you remember the electrical panels caught fire behind your seat?" Johnson interjected, rescuing Ken from his embarrassment.

"Vaguely," Gene nodded. "Seems like Scott was trying to put it out."

"Yeah—him and Stevens. But it burnt out a bunch of wiring. And the hydraulics were shot out. I had to land with no flaps or brakes—I was barely able to keep from running off the end of the runway."

Johnson fell silent. As a substitute pilot, it wasn't his plane or his crew. He felt awkward talking about it. Ken sensed his hesitation, and picked up where Johnson had stopped.

"Well, Gene...you know, we just barely salvaged her in the first place. George and I went to get the film. When I saw that cockpit, I about lost my lunch. There was just so much damage...and, we're beginning to get a few new ones in from the States. I'm sorry, Gene, but I doubt she'll ever fly again."

"That makes two of us," Gene muttered. Mike and Ken glanced at each other, not sure what to say. "Actually," he continued, a slight smile suddenly appearing, "if I had been honest with you guys in the first place, I would have put the rest of the Kansas motto on the nose when I named her."

Ken and Mike looked at each other, surprised by the fleeting, impish grin they had seen so often in better times, then back at Gene.

"Rest of the motto? What's that?"

"The actual Kansas state motto is 'Ad Astra Per Aspera,'" Gene said, grinning as he emphasized the last two words. "It means 'to the stars, through difficulties.' Good ol' Kansas optimism. Nothing good comes without a lot of grief and crap. I should have included the 'through difficulties' part, I guess, but I was feeling pretty cocky at the time. Seems rather appropriate, now."

"Yeah, I suppose," Ken said, laughing, "but I'm not sure it would have been seen as a great morale booster for us." The room fell silent for a moment, before Mike changed the subject.

"What about you? You say the doc's haven't told you anything...?" He wasn't sure how to finish the question. Gene shook his head.

"Actually, Mattie has told me about all I know. She says the doctors say my right arm and leg will heal in pretty good shape, but that it'll take a long time for me to get much of the use of my left arm back. She says they couldn't repair my left leg very well—apparently my left knee isn't going to work much, and the leg is shorter than it was. Looks like I'm going to have a pretty good limp. It's going to take months, probably, before I can even walk, without crutches. I'm not sure how many one-armed, gimpy B-17 pilots they'll let be on active pilot status."

The implication was obvious. He did not expect to see the inside of a B-17 again, at least as a pilot. They didn't know how to respond, so Johnson changed the subject.

"Gene...I don't know how much of what we went through you remember. You lost so much blood, and you were in and out after you got hit. But I've got to tell you—and all the crew agrees—what you did up there was the gutsiest flying we've ever seen. I frankly don't know anyone who would have kept to the picture run with bogies all over them, like you did. The C.O. said that getting those pictures was absolutely essential. He doesn't believe anyone else would have done it."

"Well, it seemed like a good idea at the time," Gene replied, a faint grin creasing his face.

"Good to see you still have a sense of humor. Anyway, after that, you saved our asses with your flying. I thought you were dead, at first, but every time you'd come to, you'd jump back on the controls and get us out of another jam." He glanced at Gene's heavily bandaged arms and legs. "Frankly, I don't see now how in the hell you did it."

Gene looked at him, surprised. "I thought maybe I was dreaming that."

"No, you weren't dreaming. In fact, the first time you did that you about scared the crap out of me." Johnson grinned, somewhat self-consciously. "Like I said, I thought you were already dead. You were slumped over to the side, and such a bloody mess. All of a sudden something jerked the controls away from me and there you were, turning into a bogie sliding in on us. I was distracted with Walters trying to put out that fire and didn't see it coming in—it was coming from ten o'clock, and I couldn't see it. Danny, or Henderson—I'm not sure who—nailed him. Slim saw him explode."

"Did I really fly it, after I was hit? A lot of stuff goes through my mind, especially at night," Gene said. "I never know for sure what I'm remembering, and what I'm dreaming."

"You weren't dreaming, that's for sure. Now that I've seen you here, I don't see how you were able to stay conscious, much less handle the plane. Tell you the truth, I never expected you to make it—but I'm damned glad you did."

Ken picked up on Johnson's assessment of the flight.

"Gene, what Johnson hasn't told you is that if it weren't for him, you probably wouldn't be here. He wrapped everything he could find around your arms and legs to try to get most of the bleeding stopped, at least well enough to let you make it back. The other thing we need to tell you is that all the crew is being asked to write up the flight. After General Kenney heard about it, he plans to submit it for Medal of Honor consideration for you."

Gene looked at them and shook his head slightly, trying to assimilate it all.

"Sounds like I owe you, big time, Stan. Hard to know how to thank you. And Medal of Honor? Me? I wasn't flying solo. You guys took the brunt of it." Gene looked out the window at the idyllic scene, and felt the black cloud settling over him, again. "I suppose it would make a nice paper weight for my desk."

Ken glanced at Mike at this comment, briefly raising his eyebrows in a "Where did that come from?" look. Mike shrugged imperceptibly in response. Bitterness had never been a part of his friend's nature and Mike was as surprised as Ken. It occurred to Mike that Gene might be facing a lot more mental healing, than physical. But the comment made it clear that it was time for them to go.

"Well, guys, I think our hero here needs to get some rest. What say we head on back?" Mike suggested.

Ken nodded, then hesitated a moment, looking a bit self-conscious. He handed Gene an envelope marked in large letters:

"TO BE DELIVERED ONLY IN THE EVENT OF MY DEATH"

"We brought your duffel bag down—we left it with the nurses down the hallway. This was in it. I thought you might want to make sure it got tossed, and not delivered by mistake."

Gene took the letter, looked at it for a few seconds, then laid it on the bedside table.

"Thanks, Ken. I guess we can assume that it won't be needed, now."

The three guys stood by for a few seconds, unsure of what more to say. None of them said what crossed all their minds: *I wonder if mine will ever have to be mailed?*

Ken put his hat back on, and the other two followed suit.

"Well, buddy, I guess we'd better get back to the base. The C.O. said he would send a guy down when you're up to it to interview you. Anything we can get you?" Ken asked, as they turned to leave the room.

"No, thanks. And thanks, guys, for coming down…it means a lot. Tell the crew I miss them."

"We'll come down every time the C.O. will let us, if you promise us that Mattie will be here," Mike laughed. "Although, after the way she was lookin' at you, I don't think we'd stand much of a chance with her."

"Looking at me?" Gene scoffed. "What do you mean? She doesn't—"

"Oh, damnation, Stoddard, are you totally blind? The girl's nuts over you," Mike interrupted. "Maybe if you're here long enough even you can figure that out. Well, anyway, we'll be on our way." They laughed, and left.

Nuts over me? They're the ones that are nuts. Still…can't say I'd object to that. Mike was probably just pulling my leg, Gene thought as he stared at the open door. *Pulling my leg? Boy, there's a bad mental image.*

Visit to Mattie's

For the next two weeks, Mattie rarely got to see Gene. Several new wounded arrived from New Guinea and she was kept busy attending them. During that time, the doctors removed the heavy cast and the pulley system that had kept his left leg elevated and him immobilized, replacing it with a cast from just below the knee. He had essentially full flexibility in his right leg, but his damaged left knee was still heavily bandaged and very painful—he could barely bend it. However, by keeping his left leg propped up, he could now manage to sit in a chair.

On a particularly pleasant day, while he was lying in bed hoping that Mattie might be able to spare some time for a visit, she came striding into his room, pushing a wheel chair.

"Okay, Yank. We're going for a ride. You up for a walk-about in the park?" she asked, positioning the chair next to the bed.

"Wow! You sure? Did the doctors say it was okay?"

"No worries. I'm going to throw a sheet over you and tell the watch nurse that I'm delivering laundry," she teased him.

"I thought I left all that sassy talk behind when I left Christy," Gene retorted, laughing at her. "Guess it's a universal female talent."

It was more than Mattie had bargained for to get Gene transferred from the bed into the wheelchair. He had virtually no strength in his right arm, and attempting to use it was quite painful. He could not use his left arm or his legs, and was largely a dead weight. But by having him turn with his back to her, she was able to put both arms around his chest and literally drag him off the bed and into the wheelchair, his left leg resting across its leg support. By the time he was seated and ready to go, Gene was cringing in pain—and Mattie was in tears for having caused it. She collapsed into the nearby chair and tried to compose herself, while Gene caught his breath and let the pain subside. He reached over and took her hand. She looked at him, surprised.

"Hey, no worries, as you say," Gene attempted to comfort her. "I knew this wasn't going to be easy, and I've got to start getting used to it. I appreciate you coming for me. Frankly, I'm about to go stir crazy in this room. I'll take a lot more pain than this, if it will get me outdoors for awhile."

"Thank you," Mattie replied, smiling in embarrassment as she removed her hand from his and wiped at her eyes with a towel, "but it's awfully hard when you know how much it hurts someone when you're doing it. I never really get used to it in therapy. Sometimes the guys just scream in pain, or pass out. I think I'm going to as well, sometimes." She stood, glanced at herself in the bathroom mirror, and brushed at her hair.

"Well, then. Here we go," she said, taking the handles of the chair.

They exited the hospital into an immaculately manicured park that was basically the back yard of the hospital. Sidewalks, lined with beds of flowers of every description, meandered through tall, sprawling Eucalyptus trees.

"Oh, man," Gene exclaimed, as he breathed deeply of air filled with the fragrance of flowers and salt air from the distant harbor, rather than the pungent odors of medicine and stale confinement. "I'd almost forgotten what fresh air smells like." He turned his face up to the sunlight, and closed his eyes, inhaling the refreshing air. "I feel like I'm alive again for the first time since coming out from under the anesthesia."

Mattie didn't press him to talk as she slowly pushed him along, letting him enjoy the air and sunshine. After several minutes, she maneuvered his chair next a wrought iron park bench that overlooked the harbor. She sat down next to him, and for several minutes they were silent, soaking in the fresh air and scenery.

Built of red-tinted sandstone, the multi-storied Victorian hospital imposed itself on its surroundings like a country manor overlooking its estate. Vast expanses of lawns and greens sloped downward to a cove off Sydney Harbor, which sparkled blue and inviting in the distance. Mattie let Gene sit and take in the view.

"I love it out here, and the view of the harbor," Mattie said, breaking their reverie. "When it gets too stressful inside, I'll come out here for awhile to let my nerves settle down."

"It looks like there could be well over a hundred acres, down there," Gene observed, looking across the expanse to the harbor. "Does all that belong to the hospital?"

"Oh no," Mattie assured him, "the hospital grounds end at that fence down there. The hospital is on Macquarie Street, named for Lachlan Macquarie. He was the governor of New South Wales in the early 1800s. That's our state— sort of like your state of Kansas. He rather single-handedly turned us from a penal colony into a real country, putting in roads and a real social order. He established all this green area as a privacy buffer between the governor's mansion and the penal colony," she laughed. "That cove directly in front of us is Farm Cove, and the one over there to the left is Sydney Cove. You see that peninsula that juts out into the harbor, between them?"

Gene wondered momentarily about her references to a penal colony. He had vague memories from his World History class of Australia being started by prisoners from England, but didn't remember any specifics, or if it was, in fact, true.

"You mean that sort of skinny strip of land sticking out there?"

Mattie nodded. "At the end of it is a place called 'Lady Macquarie's Chair.' Apparently Lady Macquarie—Elizabeth, the governor's wife—liked to sit out there to enjoy looking at the harbor, so he had a ledge carved out of the rock for her so she could be more comfortable. I imagine he made the prisoners do it, but it is still a nice scenic spot. I like to go there, when I can, and just sit and look at the harbor. It's probably the nicest vantage point we have…and it's very peaceful."

"It's beautiful," Gene agreed. "The whole area looks like a park from here. Is it a city park, or something?"

"Oh, sort of," Mattie agreed. "At first, it was just the governor's private property. In 1816, the Botanic Gardens were established on the grounds. The whole area is known as the Botanic Gardens and Domain—I'm not sure what 'domain' refers to. Then, sometime around 1830 roads were put in place in the area and it was opened to the public. The gardens have become very popular, and are visited by thousands of people. They are extraordinarily well kept, and beautiful. I just love them."

"Nothing like this in Kansas, that's for sure," Gene said, a touch of both envy and admiration in his voice. "By the way—how do you come by all that stuff? You sound like a tour guide, or a history major."

"Oh, nothing quite so impressive, I'm afraid," she replied, smiling as she looked across the green expanse. "My family goes back several generations in Sydney, and we take a lot of pride and interest in the city. Father tells me a lot about it as we ride through the city on his business travels."

Gene nodded, took a deep breath and exhaled slowly. He looked across the harbor, at its blue waters and scenic shores.

"I thought after all the weeks on that rust-bucket troop ship, and of flying over nothing but ocean on our missions, I'd never want to see an ocean again… but I could get to like this."

They sat together for several minutes, wrapped in the privacy of their own thoughts. Then Mattie stood and began pushing him again, neither of them talking, as Gene relished simply getting to be outdoors.

"You're being awfully quiet, mate…penny for your thoughts," Mattie said quietly, hoping to draw him out a little.

"What? Oh. Not much of anything, I guess," Gene lied. They continued walking in silence for several minutes.

"Do I need to up the ante?" Mattie asked, breaking the silence.

"Up the ante? What do you mean?" Gene looked over his shoulder at her, puzzled by her question.

"Well, I offered a penny for your thoughts a while ago, and didn't get any. I wondered if perhaps I should up the ante," she replied, smiling down at him.

"Ouch. Now you see what I meant when I said Stoddards don't talk much." Gene grinned back at her, but still hesitated. Finally, he broached the subject that had been gnawing on him.

"Mattie, you see quite a few guys go through here, right? You must have a pretty good feel for how things are going to go for them?"

"What do you mean, Gene?"

"Well, I guess what I'm trying to ask is, what am I really going to be like when I get out of here? I mean, I'm not afraid of the therapy. I'll do whatever I have to. But am I even going to be able to walk? Or am I going to hobble along like Long John Silver with his peg leg?" Gene sounded both fearful and agitated, taking Mattie somewhat by surprise. "Will I need to keep a parrot on my shoulder, and say 'aarrggh' all the time?"

"Gene, you're putting me on the spot," Mattie answered, laughing in spite of herself. "I can't say how all your injuries will heal. I haven't heard the doctors say anything about you not being able to walk, but—"

Gene raised his hand to interrupt her. "Mattie, I'm sorry. I didn't mean to be unfair. You treat me really great—more like I'm your brother, or something, instead of just some patient you have to deal with."

Like my brother? Mattie thought. She didn't know whether to be hurt, or offended, by the comment. She had hoped that she had been appearing to be substantially more interested in him than that.

"To tell the truth, I'm not really leveling with you," Gene admitted, oblivious to her reaction to his comment. "It's not walking I'm worried about— it's flying. If I can't fly…" He didn't finish the sentence, finding no words that seemed adequate.

"I'm not sure I understand," Mattie said. "Unfortunately, you're talking to someone who's never seen the inside of an aeroplane, Gene," Mattie explained. "I don't know a thing about them. Is it like a car, and you have to use your feet as well as your hands? I didn't…I wasn't aware of that." She hesitated, concerned that she was starting to offend him by her lack of understanding and sympathy.

"Really? You've never been in a plane?" Gene asked, obviously surprised. "Well, I suppose I can forgive you, then. The problem is that the rudders on planes are critical to flying. You steer with them on the ground and you simply can't control a multi-engine plane when you lose an engine without strong rudder action—and you control the rudders with your feet. Even if I get full use of both arms back, if I can't use both legs I'll never be able to fly, or at least not anything I want to fly. And if I can't fly…well, I don't know how to even think about that. I've been obsessed with flying my whole life. And quite frankly, I've predicated my future on flying for the airlines."

Mattie was finally beginning to understand him a little. She had seen any number of guys who were going to be crippled, or perhaps had even lost limbs. It always took them some time to come to terms with their condition, but they seemed to come to accept it better. They were generally just relieved to still be alive, and for the ones who were most seriously wounded, it was their one-way ticket home. Now she realized that to Gene his injuries apparently meant losing something virtually more important to him than his life. She couldn't think of an appropriate response, and continued to push him in silence.

"It's just hard trying to put it all in some kind of perspective," Gene said, breaking the silence.

"Perspective? What do you mean?" Mattie asked.

"Oh, I don't know. It's sorta hard to explain. All I've ever cared about was planes and learning to fly. Barely a year and a half ago I was walking along sidewalks like this at Kansas University, and taking flying lessons. I felt like I had died and gone to Heaven. Then, hardly a year later, I was flying a B-17. Mattie, the B-17 is one of the largest, most sophisticated bombers ever built, and I was flying one all over everywhere. All the war was to me, really, was a chance to get to do the most exciting flying I could dream of, and a sure ticket into the airlines when it was over."

Gene caught himself, even before the words were out of his mouth. He thought of his crewman, Jimmy Wilson, who had died on his last mission, and all the others he knew who would never return from that jungle island.

"Aw, scratch that. That was a stupid thing to say. I didn't mean it the way it obviously sounded. Don't get me wrong, I know why we're over here, and I'm not making light of it. I just don't know how else to say it—flying has always been my dream, and was supposed to be my future. And it seemed like it was all coming true. Then, almost as quickly as it was starting to come true, it all went up in smoke. Now it feels like I don't have a life or a future."

Mattie nodded, but didn't respond. She knew he wasn't looking for answers from her.

"I don't think I told you. Jimmy Wilson, my radio operator, got killed on that mission," Gene continued, after several seconds. "I never talked much with him, although I liked him pretty well—I could always count on him. I don't know what his dreams were. But whatever they were, he'll never get to live them. He got married just before he shipped over. He'll never get to have kids, see them grow up, or have a life at all. Now, here I am, bitter and resentful simply because I'm a little crippled and won't get to fly again. I know I'm feeling sorry for myself—but I can't seem to shake it."

Mattie laid her hand on his shoulder. "Gene, lots of physical disabilities can be overcome. Are you sure you won't be allowed to fly?"

"Are you kidding?" Gene reacted. "Ever see an airline pilot limp to the plane, and have to have his copilot help him fly it?"

"I'm sorry, Gene," Mattie apologized, her voice catching. "I really don't know what to say. I didn't mean to be dismissive…"

She wiped at tears forming in the corners of her eyes, fearful that Gene might see them. She felt as though every attempt she made to bolster his spirits only proved more upsetting, and would darken any feelings he might have for her. Of course, after his "treat me like your brother" comment, she wasn't sure that he felt anything for her anyway, other than as a very considerate nurse—or his sister.

"I know. Sorry about being so grouchy about it. I just can't—"

"It's okay," Mattie interrupted. "Tell me about your home," She continued, deciding it was time to steer the conversation toward something lighter. "What's Kansas like?"

"Not much to tell, really," Gene replied, surprised by the turn in the conversation. Mattie couldn't tell if the tone of voice suggested defensiveness, or sarcasm. "We live on a small farm, near a podunk little town. And Kansas? I don't know. Mostly farming. Lots of wheat, especially in the western half. They build a lot of planes in Wichita. Boeing, Beechcraft, Cessna, Stearman. It's a real aviation Mecca. Other than that, not much to brag about."

"Oh, come now. I'm sure you're being far too modest," Mattie chided him.

"Yeah, I suppose," Gene agreed. "If you compare it to our base up at Iron Range, or beautiful downtown Port Moresby, we come off looking pretty good."

She couldn't tell if he was joking, or being cynical, and was at a loss to know how to support him. She decided to try to steer the conversation toward less personal topics, hoping he would reciprocate and perhaps get his mind off his embittered feelings.

They strolled along the sidewalks, chatting quietly, comparing how their two countries had reacted to the attack on Pearl Harbor. Mattie related how scared of being invaded the Australians were when Sydney Harbor had been shelled by Japanese submarines, and told him how her father had compared the war to the disastrous battle of Gallipoli, in which Australian and New Zealand forces had been nearly massacred during World War I.

It all seemed very comfortable, and yet very superficial, at least to Mattie. She wondered, at times, if there had been any point to any of it, other than to get Gene into some fresh air. But, he finally seemed to have his mind off his problems and was sounding more positive. They came to another bench, and Mattie stopped.

"Mind if I rest a bit?" she asked, as she sat down on the bench. "I'm getting a little tired."

"No, of course not," Gene insisted. "I assume it's not easy, shoving this thing around."

She smoothed her skirt over her legs, which she had stretched out in front of her. Gene noticed how trim and lithe she looked. There was no doubt in his mind that she was the prettiest girl he had ever met. But he was becoming aware that it was not just her looks that appealed to him. She seemed more mature, more thoughtful—and certainly more intelligent—than so many of the girls he had known in high school. They were all so flighty and obsessed with boys that they largely annoyed him, even the pretty ones. She had a sense of peacefulness, or contentment, about her that appealed to him. He wondered if Mike was right, or just joking, when he said that Mattie was "nuts over him."

"I hope you'll forgive a personal observation," he said, smiling somewhat mischievously at her.

"Personal? In what way?" she asked, obviously curious.

"Well, I can't help but notice that most of the nurses who come in to take care of me are, well, as we say in Kansas, pretty 'heavy set.' They remind me of all my aunts and the other farm ladies at home. You, on the other hand, I would say look much more…" He paused, rubbing his chin theatrically, appearing to struggle to find just the right word.

"Yes? I look much more what, Mr. Stoddard?"

Gene looked up and down at her slender figure, her well-shaped calves and toned arms. In spite of herself, she blushed noticeably.

"Athletic." Gene nodded his pleasure at the word. "Yes, you're very athletic looking. I'll bet you play a lot of tennis."

"Athletic? Is that the way you Yanks compliment a girl?" Mattie was smiling, but it wasn't clear if she was teasing.

"No, no—I mean…I'm sorry. I meant it as a compliment." Gene quickly retreated, obviously embarrassed and taken aback by her retort. He shook his head, disgusted with himself. *Judas Priest,* he thought, *it isn't enough that the Japs try to blow my legs off—I've got to shoot myself in the foot. Why can't I ever learn how to talk to a girl?* "What I meant is, I think you're very pretty," he corrected. "I guess I could have been more flattering in my choice of words."

"Why, Gene, I think I embarrassed you," Mattie responded, laughing at him. "I was teasing you. Of course I took it as a compliment. I'm flattered that you think I'm pretty—and athletic. As a matter of fact, I do play tennis, quite often. We have a court at home, and we're all avid players. Do you like to play?" She realized her *faux pas* even before the words were out of her mouth.

"I did like to play tennis, yes." Gene answered.

"I'm sorry, Gene. I wasn't thinking."

He shrugged, but didn't say anything.

"You have your own tennis court?" he asked, after thinking about her comment a moment. "I don't know anyone who has their own tennis court. There's only one court in my whole hometown. I'm most impressed."

"My father's ancestors came to Australia from Ireland during the gold rush in the 1850s," Mattie explained. "His grandparents got into shipping and trading. Fortunately, Great-Grandfather was a very astute business man, and did well. He built our home. Grandfather and Father followed in the business and were able to build on what Great-Grandfather started. The war has hurt in some ways, because of the dangers in shipping, but helped in others because so many supplies must be ordered and shipped. Grandfather added the court while he and Grandmother were living in the house. He was an avid sportsman." She didn't want him to think her an elitist, and quickly changed the subject.

"Speaking of parents, tell me about yours. What are their names?"

"My folks?" Gene seemed surprised she had asked. "Bill and Mary. They're just salt-of-the-earth farmers. Good as gold. Very religious, honest to a fault and hard-working. They nearly got wiped out, as did most all the farmers in our part of the country, during the Dust Bowl and Depression. They haven't really recovered from it, financially or emotionally."

"They sound very nice," Mattie said. "I think I would like them."

Gene laughed out loud, surprising her.

"They're good people, and you probably would like them," he said. "But if you want to meet them you'll have to plan a trip to Kansas, because the farthest they've ever traveled was to take me up to enroll at Kansas University—and that was barely eighty miles."

"I may have to do that. I think I would like to see your Kansas. I'll bet it has a lot more to offer than you let on," Mattie replied. She stood and began to push him along the walks back toward the hospital entry. "Well, enough of this chit-chat. It's time for you to be back in your room. My head nurse will think I've kidnapped you."

Getting him back onto the bed was even more difficult, and painful, than getting him off. A nurse was there to help, and they had to lift him out of the wheelchair onto the edge of the bed, then help him roll on to his side and back. After some effort, he was comfortable again. Mattie had smoothed his sheets, and wiped his face with a damp cloth. As she laid it down, he reached out and took her hand with his free right hand. She looked at him, surprised.

"Mattie, thank you. I'm a farm boy, you remember, and a pilot—or at least I used to be both of those things. I like being outside and on the go. Today meant a lot to me. I don't know if you're this good to all your patients, but I certainly appreciate it. I hope it won't be the last."

"I'm glad you enjoyed it," she replied, taking his hand in both of hers. "I know I did. And Gene, please listen to me. I know how hard it is to accept what has happened to you. Your life has been changed, forever. Cruelly, I might add. But human nature always finds a way to prevail, if we want it to. Don't get too discouraged, and please don't give up on yourself."

Gene didn't answer. She gently squeezed his hand, then released it. "I have to go now. Others need me too, I'm afraid."

He nodded. "Don't forget where I live."

"You worry too much, Yankee boy. You can't get rid of Mattie O'Sullivan," she assured him, smiling and waving to him as she left the room.

I'd love to go to Kansas—just ask me to marry you, she thought, as she walked down the hall.

I'd love to take you to Kansas—if you'd marry me, he thought, as she left the room.

Dear Christy,

Well, I'm going to take a crack at writing. Mattie, who has been writing to you for me, has pretty well told you my condition, so I won't try to repeat it. They've removed the cast, or whatever it was, from my right arm. But the muscles are stiff and still painful. And it's still bandaged pretty heavily, so it's awkward to use. You'll have to pardon my scribbly writing. I no longer have my left leg hoisted half way up to the ceiling, but it is still in a big cast up to my knee. My right leg and left arm are bandaged heavily, but not in a cast anymore, which feels better. I'm making pretty good progress, they tell me—sometimes I'm not so sure.

Thanks for all your letters. They mean a lot. I'm sorry I caused so much worry for you all. I know I told you I'd be careful over here, but then I never did tend to do what you told me to, did I? I'm doing OK, I guess—at least physically. I'm not nearly as bad off as some of the other guys I see here, but I sure can't seem to come to grips with the fact that I won't be flying anymore.

Mattie managed to get me into a wheel chair a couple of days ago and take me for a "walk about," as she calls it, in the hospital park. Sure was great to be outdoors, again. It's beautiful, here. I won't try to describe it—at least until I can write better. Mattie has been treating me awfully well. She's about my age—maybe a year or two younger. She's really good looking, with red hair. Not bright red—sort of brownish-red. I guess you would call it auburn. Never thought I would like a redhead, but she could change my mind in a hurry. I wish she lived in Kansas—I could get pretty interested in her. She's not wearing a ring, and doesn't say anything about having a boy friend, but I guess it doesn't matter. I can't see how it could make any difference, since I'll be leaving here in a couple of months, or so. I can't believe she would have any interest in leaving her home for a gimpy has-been pilot, anyway.

This is about all my arm is up to, for the first time out of the chute. I'm going to have to quit. Give this letter to the folks when you're done. I'm not up to writing two letters, yet. Nah, skip that—I don't care to share the stuff about Mattie. I'll try to get off a letter to them. Don't bother trying to send anything—I have pretty much all I need, except letters. Keep 'em coming. Tell everybody hi for me.

Love you all,
Gene

Dear Gene,

We were all thrilled to hear from you. Your folks got your letter the same day I got mine. It's been a big help to get the letters from Mattie, but so much better to hear from you. Not much to tell from the home front. Food rationing is getting tighter—especially sugar. And we might as well not have cars, as we can't get much gas or any tires. I've been doing pretty well on the War Bond drives—I've met my quota every month. I'm going to start helping with the scrap metal drives, too, I guess.

I don't know what to say to you about the flying. I know what it meant to you, and can only imagine how you feel about it. But please don't let it get you down. God always has a way of working things out, for us, if we'll trust Him. I realize that must be rather hard to accept right now, but give Him a chance. And speaking of chance—if you really like Mattie, give her a chance. Don't be your usual moron self on such matters, and keep it all bottled up. Let her know how you feel. Like I said—give God a chance to work those things out for you.

Gotta get to work. Thank you again for your letter. Please send more.

We love you,
Christy

Over the ensuing weeks, Gene's life consisted largely of sessions of physical therapy, followed by bed rest to recover from the exertion and pain caused by the therapy. A couple of times a week, Mattie would take him on strolls in the hospital park. As time passed, the doctors removed the cast from his left arm, replacing it with lighter bandages, and the cast was removed from his right leg. He was soon able to attempt walking with crutches. Barely able to endure the weight of his body on his right leg, and with limited use of his left arm, his first efforts were limited to a few steps each day. But as days drifted by, he gained strength in his arms and right leg, and eventually he and Mattie could walk together in the park for brief periods.

On a particularly bright and cheerful morning, Mattie had come to get him for another walk-about. She had tried various ways to encourage Gene, and keep his spirit up. He was always superficially pleasant, but she sensed that the resentment and bitterness that he had expressed on their first outing always lurked just below the surface.

She hoped that as time passed, and his wounds healed, he would become more openly optimistic about his future—but didn't feel she had made much progress in helping him to do so. As they strolled together on this cheery morning, she hoped to get him to talk more openly about it. Perhaps doing so, she thought, would help him to move past it.

"Gene," Mattie said, broaching the subject, "I told you once that I've never been in an aeroplane, so I suppose that's part of why I don't understand. But what is it about flying that is so meaningful to you? I'm not belittling it; I just don't understand. Is it some feeling of freedom, of not being earthbound?"

Gene hesitated so long that she feared she might have offended him.

"Mattie..." he finally responded, "I don't really think I can answer that—at least, not in a way that makes any sense. And in truth, my own feelings have changed over time. When I was growing up—before I got my license, or had even been up in a plane—I always thought of it being like the hawks I would see circling overhead. I didn't want to stay stuck there, on the farm. I wanted to experience that freedom, to float among the clouds and go wherever I wanted to go."

They came to a bench, and Gene sat down, placing his crutches on the ground beside him.

"I'm afraid I'm a little pooped, already," he admitted, as she sat down beside him. The bench was a rather small one, causing Mattie's arm to touch his as she sat. She enjoyed the feel of his arm against hers, and wondered if he might feel the same. Gene sat staring off into the distance, and Mattie wondered if he would elaborate at all on his rather terse answer to her question.

"So you wanted to float among the clouds, like a hawk?" she prompted.

"Yeah. I was a bit of a dreamer, I guess," he answered, smiling, and sounding a little embarrassed. "In fact, the only other person who ever asked me that question was a Stearman pilot who first told me about the CPTP, and that was all I could tell him. I didn't really know why—I'd never even been in a plane. It was just a part of me, of the way I felt. But he said he had been the same way when he was growing up. You do always have some of that feeling, that sense of freedom, while you're flying.

"I love doing aerobatics, and to just meander around through the clouds. They are so incredibly pure and white when you're up close to them. I sometimes think that's what Heaven will be like, with everything so pristine, so pure and bright white that it makes your eyes hurt. And the clouds are so majestic—it feels like I'm in a completely different world, like Alice in Wonderland. I like the isolation, the feeling that I'm somehow separate from the world below... and unaffected by it."

A military plane of some sort was flying over the harbor, and Mattie realized he was watching it.

"That's a B-26, like I used to fly," he observed, interrupting himself. "Wonder if it's one of Mike's squadron?"

Mattie waited, as Gene watched the plane disappear into the distance. She could only imagine what he was thinking. His attention suddenly snapped back to the two of them, and he picked up where he had left off.

"Anyway, after I began to get more experience, and was more comfortable in the plane, I began to like the technical challenges of flying—making a great landing and flying on instruments, or flying a mission successfully. No matter how good you get, you always grade yourself, especially your landings. And there's always something that you could have done better. Maybe you didn't correct for the crosswind well enough, or let it bounce a little on touchdown. I always feel as though there is some purity that I'm seeking, like Jason searching for the Golden Fleece, or maybe I'm searching for the Holy Grail of flying. I always want to be the perfect pilot. It might seem as though it would take the pleasure out of flying, but in truth, to me that's part of the pleasure— that constant search for perfection that I know I can't achieve any other way in my life. And I like all of that."

He paused again, looking across the park. It was obvious to Mattie from the way he had to stop and collect his thoughts that he had never shared these feelings with anyone before, perhaps even with himself. It thrilled her that he was willing to share them with her. She had begun to wonder if he would ever share much of anything, with her.

"But you know, Mattie," he continued, "the funny thing is that after awhile I began to realize that as much as all that other stuff means to me, as much as I enjoy it, that's not really what's most important to me, now."

"Oh?" Mattie reacted, eyebrows raised in an obvious question. "I thought all that was quite impressive. What could be even more important to you than those sorts of feelings?"

"Oh, I don't know. It's kinda hard to explain," Gene answered, staring at the ground in front of him. "It's sort of personal, or kind of silly, maybe—I'm almost embarrassed to talk about it. Anyway, the feeling hit me one day when we were getting set to leave on a mission. I had rolled out onto the runway and was shoving the throttles up to start the takeoff. As we began to roll, I realized that I just become a different person when I fly. I'm no longer Gene Stoddard, with all my uncertainties and insecurities. I don't have to wonder if I've hurt someone's feelings or if they like me, or wonder if I've caused a problem, or any other nonsense like that. As my wheels leave the ground I feel like I leave Gene Stoddard there on the runway. He'll be there waiting for me when I land, and I'll go on with my life. But when I'm in the air, I'm...well, I'm a pilot. Nothing more, nothing less—and a good one, I might add. I know what I'm doing and confident that I'll do a good job. I know my crew trusts and respects me. And when you're in a plane, that's all that counts. No one cares who you are, where you came from, what side of the tracks you grew up on or any of that crap. I like the person I become when I'm flying."

He glanced at her, feeling more than a little embarrassed.

"It probably sounds pretty dumb," he added, almost apologetically.

"Well, I admit it wasn't the kind of answer I expected," Mattie agreed, "but it certainly doesn't sound 'dumb,' as you call it. You impress me. I had never thought about flying, like that."

Gene smiled, and nodded, but didn't comment.

"I do understand what you mean," she continued, after reflecting on his comments for a moment, "although I'm not sure that I've ever experienced similar feelings. Sometimes I think I would like to be that alone, and free of the entanglements in my life. Usually, though, I sort of enjoy being a part of all that's going on. My mother is a very extroverted, people person...I guess I'm a lot like her."

They sat there, not speaking, for a while. Mattie wanted to pursue a comment Gene had made, but was hesitant, wondering if he might take offense. But she finally decided to plunge ahead.

"Gene, tell me if you don't want to answer this, but you said a moment ago that you like the person you become when you're flying. That would seem to suggest that you don't like the person you are when you aren't flying. Did you mean it, that way?" She asked.

He sort of shrugged, and grinned.

"Oh, I was probably being overly melodramatic. It's not that big a deal. I just never did seem to fit in with a lot of the stuff that most people seem to enjoy. I didn't like all the stupid adolescent nonsense that the guys in high school were always doing, and I most certainly didn't like the gossiping and stuff that the girls always seemed to be wrapped up in. I just felt like an outsider all the time, and I would either make some sarcastic comment that I tried to pass off as teasing, or would just leave and make everybody think I was stuck up. And my family never smokes, or drinks, or cusses, and that's about all the guys in the service do—that, and talk about girls and sex." He glanced at Mattie, an embarrassed grin fleeting across his face. "Not that I have anything against those last two, mind you."

Mattie nudged him with her shoulder. "You behave yourself, Mr. Stoddard, or I'll report you to my head nurse—and she's bigger than you."

"That's for sure—I try to steer clear of her," Gene quickly agreed. "Anyway, back to your question, all I'm trying to say is that I've never seemed to fit in with most people I'm around. It's like I used to say to Christy: 'Gene, you're an impartial outsider—what do you think of the human race?'"

"Gene! What a terrible thing to say about yourself—surely you were joking?" Mattie interrupted, in spite of herself.

"Yeah, mostly," he agreed, grinning his little grin that she was beginning to recognize as an indication that he was teasing her. "Anyway, after I started flying I began to realize that all changed. In the air, I'm a very professional, skilled pilot, and my crew respects me for that. They know that I will do everything in my power to accomplish our mission with the least risk to them, They believe I'll get the job done, and get them back."

He paused, as the contradiction hit him between his present circumstance and what he had just said.

"Listen to all that present-tense stuff, would you. Not sure how they'd feel about it now, after that last mission." Mattie looked at him, surprised by this sudden change of attitude. But he was smiling, and let it pass. "Well, anyway, I just felt I could be much more the person I think I really am, when I'm at the controls of a plane. I always feel so much more at home, somehow."

It was an exchange that was surprisingly personal, and that neither had expected. Gene had never shared anything quite so personal with anyone— not even with Christy, when he would be talking to her after yet another problem at school—and he wasn't sure why he had suddenly felt so free to say them to Mattie. They were silent for a bit, as each tried to think of a way to move on.

"Gene, something you said earlier has been puzzling me," Mattie said, interrupting the silence that had settled over them.

"Oh? What was that?" Gene asked, glancing at her.

"Well, if I understood correctly, you said you were attending university in Kansas when the war started, but I thought you said you were already in the Air Force taking flying lessons. Did I misunderstand?" she asked.

"No, not really. I realize it's a little confusing," he answered. "There's a little airport about a mile from our farm, and I used to spend a lot of time down there talking to pilots. The summer before I started my senior year in high school one of them told me about a program that the government had started where universities would teach you to fly at government expense while you were working on a degree. I mentioned it a few minutes ago. It's called the CPTP, or the Civilian Pilot Training Program. It's a good deal. I couldn't have taken lessons without it."

"So were attending college while you were flying?" she asked him.

"Yeah. I enrolled at Kansas University because they had the program there," he explained. "Mike had come there from California for the same reason, and we wound up being roommates. Both of us had enrolled in electrical engineering, so took most of our classes together, They treated the program as though we were in the military, but technically we were still civilians. The war started before we finished our first semester, though, and when we got our licenses they immediately inducted us into the Air Force."

"Oh," Mattie answered. "That makes more sense. And you were in electrical engineering? I'm impressed. Isn't that awfully difficult?"

"Yeah, I guess," Gene replied, shrugging noncommittally, "but KU offered me a scholarship in it—I couldn't have afforded KU without it. I always liked math and physics, and did well at them. Of course, I wasn't there long enough to have to take the really tough courses. I'd always planned on getting an engineering degree, but I was mostly there for the flying. It really upset my folks when they found out about the flying, though."

"You mean you hadn't told them?" Mattie said, sensing a tone of impishness in the comment that surprised her. "Why on earth not? I can't imagine withholding such a thing from my father," she exclaimed. "Do I detect a bit of the rebel in my patient?"

"A rebel? Me? I've certainly never been called that, before," Gene replied, laughing. "No, you have to understand my parents. They're really conservative, and airplanes just didn't make sense to farm folks. They thought planes were a lot of foolishness. And the Depression really affected them—both emotionally and financially. All they could think of for me was to get a good education and a secure job with a steady paycheck, so I would never have to suffer like they did."

Mattie nodded, waiting for him to continue. Instead, he picked up his crutches, and resumed hobbling his way along the walk They walked in silence for several minutes, before Gene picked up on the subject again.

"Mattie, I know it's hard to understand how I feel about planes. But all I could think of was getting to fly. I planned to get a job with one of the big airlines after I graduated. I figured I could fall back on my engineering degree if I had to, but I just couldn't cope with the thought of sitting at a desk all day, when I could be flying an airliner. When the chance to get my license for free came along, there was simply no way I was going to pass it up."

Mattie nodded, but didn't comment as she could think of nothing to say.

"That's just not something my folks seem to be able to comprehend," Gene continued. "In fact, after Mike and I got our wings, we both decided to go into bombers, when most of the guys wanted to be fighter pilots, just so we would be more likely to get hired by the airlines after the war." Gene paused, looking at the distant harbor. "I thought I had it all pretty well figured out. I just hadn't planned on something like this," he added, nodding toward his legs.

They came to another park bench, and Gene sat down to rest. It was larger, but he sat toward the middle and placed the crutches on his left side so Mattie would have to sit next to him. Without thinking, she slipped a hand around his arm as they sat together. She wanted him to put his arm around her and pull her to him, and longed to curl up on the bench beside him, with her head on his shoulder. But he didn't react to her hand on his arm and she wondered if he even noticed.

"Gene, I understand what you're going through…or at least I'm trying to. And I can only imagine how bleak it must all seem to you right now. I really don't know what to say to help," she said quietly.

"Well, it's not your problem—and I don't mean to feel sorry for myself. It would just make it easier if I felt like my parents—anyone, for that matter—understood it. It's almost like being in a cult. When I'm with other pilots, I don't have to say anything—we all know how we feel about flying. Then, if I'm around anyone else, it doesn't seem to matter what I might say, no one is going to understand."

Mattie started to reply, but Gene interrupted before she could.

"So I'm going to have to limp around a little bit—big damn deal. Jimmy died. At least I'm alive, and all I do is sit and bitch about it. Sorry about the language, but somehow I've got to learn to deal with it."

His outburst startled her. It was clear to them both that the conversation was going downhill. To Mattie's surprise, Gene changed the subject.

"Well, enough of that. I've talked about myself enough—too much. Now it's your turn. All I really know about you is that you're incredibly pretty, the best nurse's aide I could hope for, and you have a tennis court to yourself. There must be more."

"Flattery will get you everywhere, Mr. Stoddard. Thank you for the compliment." She smiled at him, feeling a rush of embarrassment—and pleasure—come over her. "I'm not sure what there is to tell. I'm an only child. Father over-indulges me, but is a stern disciplinarian so unfortunately, I don't get to be spoiled. I love to read, liked my literature and geography classes in high school—and music. I play the violin reasonably well, but probably not as well as I play tennis. Of course, if I practiced the violin as much as I play tennis, that might be different," she said, laughing at herself. "I've always been intrigued by the United States. I've read everything I can find on it, and watch all the Hollywood movies. That's about all there is to know about me, I'm afraid."

"And Christy thinks I don't talk much," Gene teased her.

They sat there, side by side, quietly sharing their common interests, their likes and dislikes, their childhoods. Gene realized, at one point, that he had never before felt so comfortable and at peace with anyone, not even Christy. It felt to Mattie that something had finally, somehow, progressed beyond simple nurse and patient friendliness. But they were too uncertain about each other to act in any overt way on their feelings. Still, Mattie felt good enough to broach an invitation that she had been wanting for several days to offer.

"Gene, my parents have asked me to invite you to come to our house for a visit this weekend, if you feel you're able, and would care to. Would you want to do that?" Mattie asked.

Taken completely by surprise, Gene looked into her smiling eyes, eyes that told him quite clearly what answer was desired.

"To your house? Well…sure," he responded, a bit hesitantly. "I mean, that would be swell, but do you think I can manage it? Would the hospital allow it?"

"I've already cleared it with the doctor. He thinks you will be okay if you're careful and don't overdo it. He thinks the change of scenery will be good for you, if you feel you're up to it."

Gene looked at her smiling at him and realized that he would crawl there on his hands and knees if he had to, but didn't immediately respond. His hesitancy put a quick chill on her. She pulled her hand from his arm, an embarrassed look on her face.

"Gene…I'm sorry," she apologized. "I didn't mean to put you in an awkward situation. If you're uncomfortable about it—please, just say so."

"No, it's not that," Gene quickly insisted, shaking his head. "I'd love to get out of here, and spend the weekend with you. I'm just not sure I'm up to being out in public as a...oh, I don't know. It's sort of embarrassing. I just don't want people staring at me, and feeling sorry for me. Besides, how would your folks feel, with you having to help me?"

"Gene, I can't imagine anyone feeling anything but respect for you—and certainly not pity," Mattie insisted. "My Uncle Sean—Father's brother—lost a leg at that horrible debacle at Gallipoli. My parents understand what war does to people. I've told them a lot about you, and they certainly have nothing but admiration for you. They would love to meet you." She glanced at her hands, worried that she had somehow managed to put a damper on the whole affair. "Please, Gene. It's your decision. I don't want you to be uncomfortable. Maybe I shouldn't have said anything."

"No, I'm glad you did. I appreciate it," Gene assured her, his jaw muscles working. "I'm sorry about your uncle. I don't think things through very well, sometimes—and I certainly didn't mean to sell your parents short. I just can't seem to get a grip on all this. I guess I'm not handling it very well."

"Gene—look at me." Mattie said, putting a hand to his face, gently turning his face to hers. Surprised at the serious turn in her voice, and the intimacy of her touch, he looked at her. She was looking directly into his eyes, hers a mixture of concern and sternness. It reminded him of the occasions when Christy had taken him to task over his various peccadilloes.

"What?" he asked, having no idea what she wanted.

"Gene," Mattie replied, "be fair to yourself. You nearly died. I hadn't told you this, but I heard a doctor tell one of the nurses that they thought they were going to have to amputate your leg, at first, then decided to try to save it. You didn't simply sprain your ankle. You're handling it admirably. Everyone else knows that, and appreciates what you're going through. You're being too harsh on yourself."

Gene got very quiet for several seconds, then nodded slightly.

"Yeah, I suppose. I'm trying to get a handle on it, but it's going to take a while, I guess."

Mattie had no response. She took his hand in both of hers and sat close to him, hoping he didn't mind. They sat there, neither talking, listening to the sounds of the birds and cars on nearby streets, and boats in the harbor.

"I'd love to go with you," he finally answered, without looking at her, "if you think I can manage it."

She smiled at him, and squeezed his hand. "WE"—she emphasized the plural—"will manage it just fine. And my folks are anxious to meet you. Father can seem a little intimidating sometimes, but he is a good person, and Mother is a dear. You'll like them both."

Dear Christy,

Well, here's a surprise! I'm getting to go on my first social outing, since coming to the hospital. I can get around on crutches a little, now, and Mattie has invited me to her house for the weekend. I can't figure it out. She's always friendly, but it seems strange that she would invite one of the patients to come to her house. I have to admit, I really like her, but I don't see how anything could come of it. Sometimes it seems like she's being a lot more than just friendly, but I don't really know what she feels for me, if anything. Besides, I don't want to start something that can't have a finish. Suppose we did get interested in each other. I'll be shipped out of here, in not too long. Then what???

I received a nice letter from Mom and Liz a couple of days ago. Gee, Liz sure seems to be getting popular in high school, from all she seems to be involved in. Is she dating anyone? Or everyone? She doesn't mention it, but hard to believe she's spending every Friday night at home alone. How's Jerry doing? He adds a line, or two, to the letters, but he's too much like me—doesn't say much.

Well, it's about time for Mattie to come get me and take me home— sort of feels like I'm a stray pup she feels sorry for. "Look what followed me home, Mommy!" I'm pretty nervous about it. I have no idea what her folks are like, or what I should say, or do, when I get there. I get the feeling that they're pretty well off. But anything is better than this hospital room, by now. I'll try to drop a line next week and let you know how it went. Wish me luck.

Take care,
Gene

That Friday afternoon Mattie had Gene in a wheel chair, waiting at the hospital front entrance, when a deep-gloss-black English limousine pulled into the drive. Gene watched with idle curiosity as it came to a stop, wondering if some government official or big business mogul had come to visit someone. It was like the ones he had seen in the movies, with some mythic winged figure on its chrome radiator cap thrusting itself forward majestically into the wind. Large round headlights, trimmed in chrome, stared unblinking from either side of the hood, above massive, rounded fenders that swooped down and back to running boards on either side of the car. It had to be terribly expensive, he assumed, but he was unfamiliar with English luxury cars and had no idea what it was. He could easily see his reflection in the shiny gloss paint, and the chrome glistened in the sunlight as though the car had never left the showroom floor.

Gene looked in stunned disbelief, as he realized that the limousine had come for them. A uniformed driver stepped out, smiled and greeted Mattie, then opened the rear passenger door as Mattie pushed the wheelchair to the car. Gene stood, steadying himself on his crutches, and began to work himself into the plush rear seat. Once he was in, and his crutches stowed to his side, Mattie slid in beside him.

"Well, I must say, I wasn't expecting this," Gene admitted. He felt twinges of nervousness rising within him, but looked at Mattie, grinning to masquerade the Stoddard discomfort with ostentatious wealth. "I had no idea this thing was coming for us. Do I say, 'Home, James' like they do in the movies?"

"Well, it would probably be more effective if you said 'Home, Peter' since that's his name," Mattie replied, laughing.

"Okay. Home, Peter," Gene said, with exaggerated dignity.

The driver, an older chap with gray hair showing below his chauffeur's hat and displaying an infectious smile, turned around and touched the bill of his hat in salute. "Right, Sir, straightaway. Home it shall be."

As they drove past the Domain and Botanical Gardens and on through Sydney, Mattie pointed out features of interest and told Gene some of its history. He knew from his history classes that it had been first discovered by the Western world by Captain Cook, but had either forgotten or it wasn't part of the lesson that Australia had been first populated by prisoners being exiled there from England. He had wondered about Mattie's references to a penal colony. "So your country started out basically as a dumping ground for prisoners from England? And I thought we had it bad because we were exploited colonies. Looks like you handled it pretty well," Gene observed, noting the many beautiful buildings and attractive parkways.

In a matter of minutes they were approaching a graceful, arching bridge that stretched from the Sydney Rocks area across Sydney Harbor to Milsons Point on the opposite shore. He had seen it on the few occasions that he had flown down to Sydney, but at that distance and altitude it hadn't appeared nearly so overwhelming. Two great steel arches, one on either side of its roadway, arced across the harbor. Heavy steel cables stretched from the arches to the bridge roadway far below, suspending it in space across the harbor, creating what appeared to be two large harps lying across the harbor. It was brute strength masquerading as art.

"Mattie, I've never seen such a bridge. It's huge...and beautiful. We flew over it several times, and I thought it looked impressive, but I had no idea how big it really is. I can remember telling someone about it, and how I would like to get down to Sydney to do some sightseeing." He paused, then added with a touch of irony in his voice, "Guess I got my wish."

Mattie glanced at him, wondering if his resentment was beginning to surface again, but he was still looking up at the massive arches and didn't seem to be bothered by anything.

"We're quite proud of it. It was completed just a little over ten years ago. Supposedly, it's the longest single arch bridge in the world, or so we've been told. The span itself is over five hundred yards long," Mattie explained. Gene sat spellbound, looking alternately down at the harbor and up at the massive superstructure as they crossed the bridge.

"Usually when I'm this high above water I'm carrying bombs," he noted to no one in particular. Mattie looked at him, still wondering what all was going through his mind, but didn't pursue it. They were quiet for several minutes as the limousine continued across the bridge and into the neighborhoods beyond.

The knots in his stomach had begun forming the moment he was shocked to realize that the black limousine pulling up to the hospital entrance was intended for Mattie and him. It was not unlike the vague sense of fear, or dread, that he felt at the beginning of each bombing mission. But just as he had always suppressed his fears once the missions started, he had managed to suppress his feelings of apprehension as they left the hospital and were driving across the bridge.

Nothing in his makeup or background had prepared him to be comfortable in the presence of excessive wealth. And nothing about Mattie had led him to suspect that she was from such surroundings. Her simple honesty and friendliness, her very nature, never seemed to Gene to be that which typically derives from an environment accustomed to wealth and all its usual pretensions, affectations, and—all too often—arrogance.

But as the limousine crossed the graceful bridge and began driving into increasingly elegant neighborhoods, the knots began to tighten. Gene was becoming steadily aware that he was not going to spend the weekend in some upper middle-class home—which he had taken for granted would be the case when he had accepted the invitation. He assumed from Mattie's comment about having her own tennis court that her father must be fairly well off. But he simply could not comprehend the kind of wealth that was appearing on either side of the streets as they drove along. Colborn, Gene's hometown, had its "rich folks." Both of the two banker families, and one of the town's doctors, were "well-off," as the locals called it. Their houses were bigger than others in town and they traded for a new car at least every other year, but there was little else to distinguish their life-style from the rest of the town.

None of that, however, could prepare him for what he was obviously about to experience. Mattie had intimated that her family had done well financially. But somehow Gene had not been able to associate those oblique suggestions with the opulence of the homes they were now passing. Gene Stoddard knew that he was in over his head, and the knowledge of that tightened his stomach even more.

He quickly realized that he would have no way of knowing how to comport himself. The problems tumbled over and over in his mind: *What fork or spoon do I use? How do I talk without sounding like a hick from Kansas—which, in fact, I am? What if they wear tuxedos for supper—or is it dinner? How do I sit? Am I supposed to scoop my spoon away from me when I eat soup, like they said in 4-H, or towards me like I always do at home? Do I have to keep my left hand in my lap when I eat?* He realized that his biggest fear was that he would embarrass himself in front of Mattie—and embarrass her for him in front of her parents.

Gene began to grow visibly stressed and nervous, and at that moment would have preferred to be almost anywhere other than there. He suddenly suspected that it was going to be a very long, very nerve-wracking weekend, even if it would be spent with Mattie.

The limousine passed through ornate, wrought-iron gates that swung open from stone columns on either side, under a curving, wrought-iron scrollwork connecting the two columns that announced that they had entered the estate of the O'Sullivans. They continued on along a circle driveway through a tree-shaded lawn of, Gene judged, at least five acres. At the apex of the drive loomed Mattie's home—the O'Sullivan mansion. Gene felt it was looking down on him the way an English butler looked down his nose at common riff-raff in the movies.

"Mattie…I don't know about this. Like Dorothy said to Toto, 'We're not in Kansas anymore'—at least I'm sure not," Gene said, his voice low and tight, as he looked at the estate. Peter came around the car and opened their door, but Gene hesitated to get out. Mattie looked at Gene, surprised by how nervous he suddenly appeared to be, but she did not comprehend how ill-at-ease he was truly feeling. She assumed he was mostly nervous about meeting her parents, and took him by the hand.

"Oh, Gene, don't be silly. You'll be fine. Now, let's get you out of here. My parents are really anxious to meet you."

Peter held the massive front entry door open for them as Gene struggled up the front steps and across a large veranda. They entered into the Grand Foyer, as Mattie called it. Dominating the room was a massive crystal chandelier hanging by gold chains from a domed ceiling three stories above the floor.

The floor appeared to Gene to be granite—or maybe it was marble. He wasn't sure of the difference. A magnificent curved stairway—as wide at its first step as the kitchen in his parents' house, he noted—with steps of matching stone, and wood rails and banister burnished to a satin sheen, swept upward from one side to an open balcony that overlooked the foyer.

Hallways led to bedrooms in wings to either side. Huge portraits of family members were hung along the stairway. The entire back wall of the Grand Foyer was floor-to-ceiling glass, looking out on the grounds behind the house. The entire house was steeped in nineteenth-century ornate luxury.

Gene and Mattie stood side by side while waiting for her folks to appear. Gene tried not to appear to be gawking, as he looked the room over.

"Good grief, Mattie, this room's bigger than my folks' house. I feel like Lil' Abner on his first trip to New York City," Gene said, somewhat under his breath. She assumed he was joking, unaware that he wasn't. But before she could respond, the doors of what appeared to be a richly paneled library opened and Mattie's parents came hurrying toward them.

"So! You must be the Mr. Stoddard we've heard so much about. Welcome to our home." Mattie's mother was shaking Gene's hand before he could reply.

The introductions, as Mattie had said they would, went well. Mr. O'Sullivan was a stocky, barrel-chested Irishman with a large mustache, reminding Gene of pictures he had seen of the famous John L. Sullivan, the last of the bare-knuckle boxers. For a fleeting moment Gene wondered if they could have been related, then remembered that Mattie's name was O'Sullivan.

Mr. O'Sullivan was friendly, if somewhat boisterous, and attempted to make Gene feel welcome. Mrs. O'Sullivan was trim, attractive, bright-eyed and vivacious, with auburn hair showing hints of gray. She had a soft, lilting laugh—which she frequently did. It was clear where Mattie got her looks and personality.

Gene stood leaning on his crutches for support, keeping his weight off his left leg, He tried to free his right arm as best he could to shake hands, then gripped his crutch again, smiling and responding politely to their greetings. Mattie stood to his side, beaming at them, obviously enjoying the moment but concerned that it might all be putting too much strain on Gene.

"Mother, Father," Mattie said, after a few moments of exchanging pleasantries, "this is the first time that Gene has been away from the hospital. He probably needs to rest his legs a bit."

"Oh my goodness. Yes, of course," her mother immediately responded. "How thoughtless of us. Mattie, why don't you show Gene to his room for a rest before dinner?" She glanced at the long, curving stairway to the upstairs bedrooms, then questioningly at Gene. "Are you sure you can manage the stairs? We gave some thought, several years ago, to having an elevator installed but never did so. I'm sorry we can't offer you one."

I guess it's dinner, not supper, Gene thought, then smiled at them. "That's okay. I think I can manage, if Mattie can just steady me, a little bit. I'm not too used to these things, yet. I've enjoyed meeting you both—thanks for inviting me. It feels good to escape, for a while."

The stairs were more of a challenge than he wanted to let on, or to be apparent, as he struggled up each step. He had to suspend himself on the crutches as he quickly lifted his right leg up to the next step. The strain on his leg from lifting himself each step, and on his arms, quickly caused the injured muscles to start hurting—and he was afraid of catching his toe on the step as he swung his foot up.

Mattie attempted to steady him, nervously holding a hand out to catch him if he should lose his balance, as he lifted himself up each step. But there was little she could effectively do. By the time he reached the top his brow was covered with sweat and he was breathing hard—partly from the exertion, but mostly from the pain. He was straining hard to keep it from showing.

Mattie escorted him to a large bedroom just down the hall, so he could lie down for a while. They entered into a sitting area, which featured an intricately carved writing desk and settee covered in delicate needlepoint, in a small alcove with windows overlooking the grounds. Off to one side was a large four-poster bed with canopy cover. Gene was surprised that they allowed people to sleep on it.

Mattie helped him get his legs swung up onto the bed, and placed his crutches nearby. After making sure he was comfortable, she patted him on the shoulder and left him, smiling and waving as she closed the door. Gene realized how much he was coming to enjoy that little gesture. He was grateful to get to rest his tired and painful arms and legs, and quickly fell asleep.

He was awakened by a tapping on his door. It took a moment for him to get his bearings back, and remember where he was. From the look of the weakening sunlight in the room, he assumed he must have slept until early evening. Before he could answer the knock on his door, it opened and Mattie came breezing in.

"Ready for some dinner, matey? Did you rest well?"

She was dressed in a pastel blue sleeveless dress with scalloped neckline and form-fitting tailored bodice that emphasized her narrow waist. The pale blue color accented her auburn hair and tanned arms. Its calf-length pleated skirt swirled about her as she entered. Gene sat on the edge of the bed, open-mouthed, staring at her.

"Mattie, my God! You look…you're beautiful," Gene gushed, blushing noticeably at his spontaneous outburst—as did she.

"Why Gene, you embarrass me…but thank you." She spun around, arms outstretched, letting her skirt rise as it swirled outward, around her. Her legs were as tanned as her arms, Gene noted, and beautifully shaped. "I'm flattered…and pleased you like it."

"I'm sorry—I didn't mean to be so…but you're just…stunning. I mean, I've never seen you in anything but your nurse's uniform, and you're pretty in that, but—" Gene stammered, not knowing how to extricate himself from this particular fix.

"Gene, you'll never do the wrong thing telling a woman she's beautiful, so relax," Mattie interrupted—or rescued—him. "Now, your hair's mussed from lying down. Let me brush it down, and let's go join Mother and Father for dinner."

She handed him his crutches and stepped behind him, with one hand on his shoulder while she brushed at the back of his hair with the other. It felt surprisingly intimate to Gene, almost as though they were married, getting ready to go out for the evening. The image pleased him rather considerably.

"There, that's better," she said, patting his shoulder. "Shall we go?"

She wanted to take his arm, let him escort her down the grand stairway like they did in the movies, but of course he could not with his crutches. She held the door open for him, and stayed close to help steady him as he negotiated the downward stairs for the first time.

Going down proved even more difficult than going up, to his surprise. He was fearful of pitching forward as he lowered himself on the crutches while swinging his foot down, afraid of catching his heel and crashing down the hard stairs. The steps were wider on the outside of the curve, giving him more room to get his foot swung down, and that helped. Someone had told him he should sit down, and scoot down stairs. But he would have been mortified to do so in front of Mattie, and especially her parents. They had not yet arrived at the table, but did so shortly after Gene and Mattie were seated. They greeted Gene warmly.

The meal was well-prepared and generally delicious, but surprisingly plain and sparse. It was clear that even the wealthy were affected by the rationing that had been put into effect shortly after the start of the war. To Gene's vast relief the table setting was simple—no complex array of utensils to daunt and embarrass him; just the usual knife, fork and spoon. And Mattie's parents were surprisingly relaxed and casual at the table. By midway through the meal Gene began to feel that he could breathe normally again, perhaps even relax a little. The knots had loosened somewhat.

As they ate, they asked Gene polite questions about his family, avoiding any mention of his war experiences. He tried to answer as best he could, but still could not completely escape a sense of self-consciousness—perhaps even envy—at the vast discrepancy between Mattie's home and his own, between the easy sophistication that comes from multiple generations of wealth, and the awkward uneasiness that comes from being in the presence of such wealth when you have none.

Nevertheless, they were obviously kind and caring people, and tried to make Gene feel welcome. As the table was cleared by a neatly-uniformed maid, Mr. O'Sullivan suddenly changed the subject, speaking more forcefully than he had during the meal.

"So, Gene, tell me. Now that you've been up there fighting those yellow bastards, what do you think our chances are? Are we going to be able to drive them back where they came from?"

The question, and its intensity, took Gene by surprise. He had to collect his thoughts for a moment before responding. When he did reply, he spoke rather quietly. He felt uncomfortable. The natural tendency of Stoddards to keep personal thoughts to themselves and to not aggrandize themselves in public displays made him hesitate—but he knew that a sincere answer was expected.

"Yes, sir. We'll defeat them," he began, "however hard it might be and however long it might take. I know they have everything going for them right now. They have more ships, more planes, more everything. Our planes are patched up and we don't have nearly enough of them. But it seems to me that they didn't count on two things when they started this thing. In the first place, I don't think they realized how fast our industry would begin cranking out everything we need, from tanks to aircraft carriers. But the biggest thing they overlooked was the American fighting spirit. They think we're soft, and cowards, but they just don't know us."

Gene paused a moment, looking down at his plate as though to collect his thoughts, then looked directly at Mr. O'Sullivan.

"You know, Mr. O'Sullivan…those guys up there are the scrappiest, gutsiest guys I've ever known. And believe me, they don't back down from anybody, and certainly not the Japs. We live in conditions that are indescribably bad, and the guys just take it and go out and fight. We gripe and complain, but we stay there and fight—and nothing's going to stop us. I believe we'll defeat them…for the simple reason that there's no way on God's green earth we'll let them defeat us."

Gene glanced briefly at his plate again, somewhat embarrassed, and then at Mattie, uncertain what to do next or how his little speech would be received.

There was no immediate reply. Mattie and Mrs. O'Sullivan glanced at each other and smiled knowingly, then looked at Mr. O'Sullivan, who was looking carefully at Gene, who self-consciously picked up his fork on the pretense of continuing to eat his dinner, still unsure of what should happen next. Gene was startled nearly off his chair by Mr. O'Sullivan suddenly banging a huge fist soundly on the table, jingling the silver and glassware.

"Young man," he roared, "that's the first thing I've heard since this war started that gives me any confidence. I know our guys are up there, too, and fighting just as hard. But I've never heard a better analysis of this war than you just gave. Bravo! Mattie, this young man knows more about this war than all the generals camped out on our fine island combined."

He beamed at Mattie. Gene looked from one to the other, not knowing what to say, or if he was expected to.

Mattie and her mother were both smiling at Gene, and Mattie gave him a little wink, as if to say, "See? I told you Father would like you."

After a few minutes of small talk, the parents stood to excuse themselves.

"Mattie, perhaps Gene would enjoy a brief stroll in the gardens, for some fresh air," Mrs. O'Sullivan suggested, smiling at Gene. Her quick, sideways glance at Mattie, and Mattie's smile in response, happened a little too subtly to cause Gene to suspect that the suggestion might have been prearranged. "That is, if you feel up to it, of course. We don't want you to over-do it," she added.

"No, the rest really helped. I feel fine," Gene lied. His left leg was hurting more than he wanted to admit, and his right was feeling the strain of the stairs. Both arms were aching from the use of the crutches. But he would have tolerated a lot more pain than he was feeling, if it meant being alone with Mattie that evening. "Mattie has told me a lot about them. I'd enjoy getting to see them."

Masking his discomfort, he thanked them for the meal, and joined Mattie as they left the Grand Foyer and entered the gardens.

The grounds behind the house reminded Gene of the movies he had seen of old English manors, with beautiful flower gardens bound by neatly trimmed hedges, fountains that featured cherubs pouring water into basins, and grass lawns that looked more pristine than the Colborn, Kansas, municipal golf course on its best days. Eucalyptus trees grew even larger and more graceful than the ones at the hospital, and sidewalks meandered through it all. Mattie strolled along beside him, close to him, as he took it in. She showed him where she would play, or read, as a child. They walked past the tennis court she had mentioned to him. It was actually two courts, enclosed within a tall chain-link fence.

She very much wanted to hold his hand as they walked, or take his arm, but he needed them for the crutches, and she had no idea for sure how he felt about her. She was still glowing inside from his reaction to her dress, and from her father's reaction to Gene's comments regarding the war. But Gene had made no overt advances, and had reacted little to her when she would take his hand or his arm when they sat together during their walks at the hospital. And then, there was always the "you treat me like I'm your brother" comment that never quite left her. For all she really knew, he might just be glad to get to have a weekend out of the hospital.

After several minutes of strolling, Gene had gone as far as he could without giving his legs a rest. They sat down on one of the many ornate cast-iron benches scattered along the walks. He turned himself so he could better face her and tried to adjust his left leg to find a position that would ease the pain, but with little success. His right leg began to feel better as soon as he got his weight off it.

They sat there for a time, arms lightly touching, neither talking. Gene studied the grounds, awestruck by their beauty and the realization that they were not the province of some city, but the O'Sullivans' "back yard."

"Mattie," he said, breaking their silence, "I've never seen anything like this—except in the movies. I never imagined that real people actually got to live like this. When I think about our place...where I come from...I'm sorry, but it's hard not to draw a comparison. My back yard has a couple of walnut trees, and an elm tree where I used to climb up to read books. The rest of it is a cow lot and barn."

"Gene, please. Don't let it affect who you think we are—or what you think I am," Mattie pleaded, rather defensively. "I know we've been blessed beyond reason, and I'm continually grateful for it. But we're not, as we Aussies like to say, 'up ourselves.' I think you Yanks would say we're not snobs. My parents know that they are here only because two generations before them were fortunate enough to be successful in business. Father, of course, grew up here. But Mother came from a small horse property up in the Blue Mountains. She's as down to earth as you and your parents are—and she's raised me to be the same."

"I'm sorry, Mattie. I didn't mean anything by it. I didn't mean to insult your parents—and certainly not you," Gene said. "It's just hard to ignore the contrast. Especially given where I've been the past several months." He was quiet for a moment, trying to avoid feeling like he had once again put his foot in it. "What are the Blue Mountains," he asked, quickly changing the subject. "I've heard guys talk about them, but where are they? What sort of ranch is your mother from?"

"Oh, it's a mountain range perhaps a hundred miles west of here," Mattie answered, relieved that the subject had changed. "They're not real tall, but very rugged. The people out there are just as rugged, and very independent and self-reliant. The ranches aren't very large—nothing like in your country. But, the ranchers' horsemanship is legendary. They can ride their horses at full gallop down slopes that you could barely crawl down on foot. Mother met Father when he came out to see about buying a horse from her father, when she was about eighteen. They fell in love almost immediately and married within months. We go out there occasionally to visit."

"Wow. I had no idea," Gene replied, obviously surprised, and impressed. "I'd love to see guys ride horses like that."

"So, you see?" Mattie said, hoping to convince Gene that she was not just an over-indulged rich girl, "I'm not that much different from you."

She was smiling at him. A full moon had risen, and the grounds had become a virtual fantasyland. Her eyes sparkled in its light, and the pale blue of her dress was radiant in the moonlight, looking iridescent against her skin. She started to tell him how she even thought of herself as a country girl, but hesitated when she saw him looking at her in a way she had not seen before.

"Gene? What is it? What's wrong?"

"You."

"Me? What do you—"

Before she could finish her question, he put his arm around her, pulling her tightly against him, kissing her harder than he had ever kissed a girl. He was afraid she might push him away, or maybe even slap him. Instead, she wrapped both arms tightly around his neck, eagerly returning his kiss. The softness of her face and lips on his, the smell of her perfume, her soft hair brushing his face, all had Gene's emotions spinning. After the initial emotions had spent themselves, he pulled back slightly, looking at her radiant face. His arm was still tight around her, holding her against him. She kept hers around his neck, her face close to his.

"Mattie," he said, after a moment, "I've never known anyone like you. You're beautiful. You're intelligent. And you're the nicest person I've ever known. Forgive me, Mattie, but I've fallen head over heels for my nurse's aide—and I have no idea how you feel about me."

She pulled him to her and kissed him again, longer and more passionately than the first time. As her emotions ebbed, she pulled back and looked at him, a trace of Irish mischievousness lighting her eyes.

"Gene Stoddard…what does it take? I've tried every way I could think of to let you know I had fallen in love with you. Should I have sent you a telegram? Written it on my forehead with lipstick? I swear, are all you Kansans this blind to the obvious? I was beginning to wonder if you ever would kiss me. And if you can't tell how I feel about you from that kiss, then I'm really not sure how to tell you."

Gene shook his head, and laughed a little at himself, obviously chagrined. He pulled her to him and kissed her, then tipped her head over on his shoulder. She pulled her legs up on the bench and nestled against him, as she had so often longed to do.

"I fell in love with you the first moment I saw you lying there in the recovery room," Mattie said. "You looked so pale, and had suffered so much, I just wanted to hold you and comfort you. I had no idea if you would ever feel anything for me. Each time I would come in to see you I could hardly keep from kissing you. I was scared to death when you got the first letter from Christy that you were perhaps engaged, or that she was your girlfriend, and was so relieved when you said you were just friends." She looked up and kissed him again. "Then, the more I got to know you, the more I knew you were the one for me. Why do you think I wanted you to come here?"

"I guess I am pretty dense," Gene admitted. "I knew I was falling for you virtually from the first time I was conscious enough to be aware of anything. But, I figured every guy in there probably falls in love with you, so figured you wouldn't notice one more. It did take me by surprise when you asked me to your home. I wondered if you did that for other guys."

"Good Heavens no, silly," she rebutted, quickly kissing him on the cheek. "You're the one and only. I had talked so much about you to Mother that she wanted to get to meet you. She suggested I see if the hospital would let you come out. She thinks you're marvelous. And now Father thinks you're smarter than all the generals—and braver, too."

"I couldn't figure for sure what was going on," Gene admitted. "I knew you spent a lot of time with me, and were awfully friendly. But that just seemed to be your personality. When you'd sit so close to me on the park benches, I could hardly resist trying to kiss you…but I figured I'd get my face slapped."

"Are you kidding?" Mattie said, smiling at him. "All the other guys are always trying to make a pass at me, and I couldn't tell if you even noticed— especially after your 'treat you like you're my brother' comment."

"Your brother? When did I say that?"

"Oh…one time when we were walking in the hospital park," Mattie answered. "It hit me kind of hard, for a while. I didn't know how to take it."

"Good grief," Gene replied, shaking his head. "I sure don't remember that. Well, rest assured I didn't think you were my sister."

"I hoped you didn't really mean it, the way it sounded. But I didn't know what to think, at first. Then, after we got to talking more, it seemed a lot better. I talked about you with Mother—all the time, it seems. That's why she finally suggested inviting you here. She knew no man could resist two O'Sullivan women."

They sat in silence, trying to let their minds catch up with their emotions, and grasp what was happening between them.

"I have to say," Gene said, breaking the silence, "when you walked into the bedroom in that dress, I was a goner."

"I confess I rather liked the effect it had on you," Mattie said, smiling at him. "I didn't expect that."

"Well, I'd never seen you in real clothes," Gene replied, a bit defensively. "I'd try to imagine what you'd look like in something other than that silly nurse's costume, but I wasn't prepared for this."

"Don't you make fun of my uniform. I think it's cute," she teased, nudging him with an elbow. "Mother brought this dress to me when I went to my room to change. She said she had worn it one night when she came here when she and Father were courting. It was a moonlight night, just like this, and Father proposed to her out here in the gardens."

Mattie paused a moment, and snuggled down closer to Gene. "In fact, it was Mother's idea to suggest we come out here after dinner. She said you wouldn't be able to resist me."

"Oh? So I'm the victim of an O'Sullivan conspiracy," Gene said, laughing quietly. "Well, she was right. You just knocked me over, the way it shines in the moonlight against your skin, and your eyes were sparkling so—"

"I'm glad you liked my dress," Mattie interrupted, laying her head on his shoulder. "But I'm especially glad you like me," she added after a long pause, her voice noticeably more serious. "To tell the truth, Gene…I'm not sure what I'd do, if you didn't."

They sat bathed in moonlight, luxuriating in their newfound feelings, kissing occasionally, then simply sitting and enjoying the sounds of the night and the pleasure of feeling their bodies close together. Finally, Gene had to ask the question that had occurred to him on several occasions.

"Mattie, I have to ask. Is your name actually Matilda?"

"Well, yes, it is," Mattie answered. The question was so unexpected that she pulled away to look at him, as puzzled as she was surprised. "Why do you ask?"

"Because I wanted to know if you were named after that crazy song that everyone sings down here all the time."

"You mean 'Waltzing Matilda'?" Mattie asked. "As a matter of fact, I *was* named after it. It's very popular, and Father has always liked the song. Mother liked the name, too, so that's who I am. Don't you like it?" She pouted up her face, acting wounded.

"Well, I like the idea of waltzing Matilda, very much," Gene replied. "But the song is crazy. I can't understand a word of it. What does it mean?"

"Well, if you insist. I'll sing it for you."

She stood, assumed an opera diva pose, hands folded primly under her chin, and started singing:

> *"Once a jolly swagman camped by a billabong*
> *under the shade of a coolabah tree.*
> *He sang as he watched and waited till his billy boiled,*
> *'Who'll come a-waltzing Matilda with me?'"*

As she started into the chorus, she took her skirt in both hands, swinging it in time with the music, barely managing to keep from giggling as she sang:

> *"'Waltzing Matilda, waltzing Matilda,*
> *You'll come a-waltzing Matilda with me.'*
> *He sang as he watched and waited till his billy boiled,*
> *'You'll come a-waltzing Matilda with me.'*

> *"Down came a jumbuck to drink at the billabong.*
> *Up jumped the swagman and grabbed him with glee.*
> *He sang as he shoved that jumbuck in his tucker bag*
> *'You'll come a-waltzing Matilda with me.'"*

"Come on, join me in the chorus," Mattie said, reaching out and taking Gene's hands. "The words are easy." But he just laughed and shook his head as she began the next chorus, swinging his hands in rhythm with the catchy tune:

> *"'Waltzing Matilda, waltzing Matilda,*
> *you'll come a-waltzing Matilda with me.'*
> *He sang as he shoved that jumbuck in his tucker bag,*
> *'you'll come a-waltzing Matilda with me.'*

> *"Up rode the Squatter mounted on his thoroughbred.*
> *Up rode the Troopers-one, two, three,*
> *'Where's the jolly jumbuck you've got in your tucker bag?'*
> *'You'll come a-waltzing Matilda with me.'*

> *"'Waltzing Matilda, waltzing Matilda,*
> *you'll come a-waltzing Matilda with me,*
> *Where's the jolly jumbuck you've got in your tucker bag?*
> *you'll come a-waltzing Matilda with me.'"*

Mattie paused, looking sad. Gene stopped smiling, wondering what had changed her light-hearted mood.

"Okay—now it gets sad, I'm afraid," Mattie said, barely containing a smile. She once again assumed a serious, operatic pose, hands folded under her chin, and continued with the song:

> *"Up jumped the swagman and sprang into the billabong.*
> *'You'll never take me alive,' says he.*
> *His ghost may be heard as you pass by that billabong,*
> *'You'll come a-waltzing Matilda with me.'"*

"Come on, join me in the last chorus," Mattie implored, but Gene just shook his head, barely able to keep from laughing at her. She took her skirt and began swinging it enthusiastically as she sang the last chorus:

> *"'Waltzing Matilda, waltzing Matilda*
> *You'll come a-waltzing Matilda, with me.'*
> *And his ghost may be heard as you pass by that billabong,*
> *'You'll come a-waltzing Matilda, with me.'"*

As she finished the chorus, she curtsied and reached out, taking both Gene's hands in hers.

"Now—what could possibly be confusing about that?" she asked, laughing at Gene.

"Well, I recognized Matilda—the rest pretty much escaped me," Gene protested, smiling back at her.

"All right," Mattie said, sounding like an indulgent parent. "Since you don't speak Aussie, I'll translate for you. The story is quite simple. A gentleman of the road—I think you would call him a tramp, or hobo—is camping by a billabong, or creek. A stray sheep wanders by and the tramp captures it to have for supper. Just then the sheep's presumed owner, and three lawmen, come riding up and accuse the tramp of stealing the sheep. Stealing a sheep was once a hanging offense, so rather than submit to arrest, he jumps in the creek and drowns himself. Then his ghost comes back and haunts the place, and sings 'You'll come a-waltzing Matilda with me?' Now—isn't that a nice story?"

"So the guy drowns himself, and that's what all you Aussie's think should be your national anthem? You're all even crazier than I thought," Gene teased.

"Oh, I think it strikes a chord because of our history," Mattie explained. "You have to remember: we started out as a penal colony, rejects from British society. We have a deep-seated distrust of authority and a strong sense of independence. People just relate to it."

"Yeah, I guess I can understand that," Gene agreed. "But who was Matilda? You didn't answer that," he reminded her.

"Well, that's a little more complicated," Mattie replied, barely able to keep from laughing. "First of all, Matilda, or so I've read, was an old Teutonic name meaning 'mighty battle maid'—don't you laugh, Gene Stoddard—but came to be used as the name the swagmen, or tramps, called their bedrolls. Thus, 'waltzing Matilda' meant to go on the road as a tramp."

"So let me get this straight," Gene said, looking a bit dubious. "You're a tramp's bedroll, that is mighty in battle. I can see why your dad wanted to name you Matilda."

Mattie swatted him playfully—or perhaps not so playfully, from the way it stung his arm.

"You be nice to me, Gene Stoddard, or I'll break your crutches and leave you on your own."

Gene stopped laughing, and just looked at her standing in the moonlight before him, a smile still on her face, eyes sparkling from the moonlight and tears of laughter.

"I never in my wildest dreams imagined you could really be interested in me. I would wonder about it, at times, but never let myself believe it could actually happen. Are you real, or do I wake up this time and be on my cot at Seven-Mile Strip, with another mission waiting?"

She sat down next to him, taking his face in both her hands, and kissed him.

"I'm as real as you want me to be, Gene Stoddard," she whispered to him. "You can waltz this Matilda anywhere you choose. There's nowhere I would rather be than with you. All I really hope is that you love me as much as I do you."

He stretched his legs out and put his arm around her, staring across the moonlit lawn for several seconds.

"Mattie," he replied, sounding a little hesitant, "this is a whole new world for me. I've never been much for expressing myself...I don't know for sure what I should say, or how to say it. I just know I've never felt anything remotely close to what I'm feeling for you, right now. If it isn't love, then I can't imagine what being in love would feel like."

Mattie smiled to herself, a soft feeling of comfort and contentment blanketing her.

"I can't imagine being told anything nicer, Gene."

They sat close together, Mattie's head resting on his shoulder, not speaking. She had no idea how long they were there before she finally decided they had best go in.

The house was dark, save for the foyer which was dimly lit, sufficient for Gene to safely make his way up the stairs and to his room. After Mattie had turned down his covers, and was sure he would be alright, she kissed him goodnight. She walked past her parents' bedroom on the way to hers, having noted as they climbed the stairs that their door was slightly ajar.

"The dress worked," she whispered to her mother, who was looking through the opening, smiling back at her.

Dear Christy,

Well, I've done it again. I've got myself in a jam that I don't know how to handle. The weekend with Mattie went really well—too well, I'm afraid. Mattie's folks are swell. Her dad is a big Irish sort. Reminded me of the boxer, John L. Sullivan. He's kind of boisterous, but was pretty friendly. And Mattie's mom is just like Mattie—pretty, extroverted, and friendly to a fault. I can see where Mattie gets her looks and personality.

Christy, I have to confess—I've fallen head over heels for Mattie, and I guess she feels the same for me. After supper (they call it dinner, and call dinner, lunch) Friday night, she took me out into their back yard— it's more like an estate, than a yard. You've got to see her folks' place to believe it. She said she wanted to show it to me. It was moonlight, she was beautiful...well, you can imagine the rest. I never dreamed that someone like her could fall for me, but she made it very clear that she feels the same way about me as I do for her.

Christy, I'm in real trouble. I really don't know what to do. I know I'll be shipped back to the States in two weeks to a month, at most. I don't see how I can "string her along," when I can't see how anything could come of it. But I also don't see how I can leave her. I've never felt anything like I do for her. It's more than I can handle, thinking about just packing up and never seeing her again. I know she really likes me—she said she loves me. She said that I could "waltz her anywhere I choose" when we were talking about that crazy song they sing all the time down here, about waltzing Matilda.

I'm not sure what she meant by that. Marriage hasn't even been mentioned, and I don't know if that's what she meant, or if this is just a "wartime romance" in reverse. If we were both in the States, I'd have asked her to marry me that night, given the way she makes me feel, but we've barely begun to let each other know how we feel.

I don't know what she's thinking. How could we get married, anyway, if that's what she was thinking? I can't stay over here, and I can't imagine her being willing to move to America and leave all that she has over here, not to mention having to leave her family. And Lord only knows what a crippled ex-pilot could do to earn a living. How would I support her, if we did get married? I have no idea what I should do, or can do.

I remember when life was rather simple. I wonder what happened to that? I'm in a real pickle, and don't have any idea what I'll do. And I thought trying to handle the B-26 was a problem. Well, I wouldn't be surprised if I'm on a troopship headed home by the time you get this and I could get a letter back, so you might as well not even try to respond. I'll drop a line when I know when I'm leaving and when I'll be arriving in the States. Sure is going to feel strange, being back home.

Your always messed up friend,
Gene

Proposal

Three weeks had passed since Gene first visited Mattie's house. During that time he continued to gain strength and was now walking competently, if still painfully, with his crutches. It would not be long before the cast would come off his left leg, he supposed. He hoped that in another month, two at most, he could start trying to walk without using crutches. That he would have a significant limp could not be denied. His left leg was noticeably shorter than his right, and the knee would barely flex. His left arm would require many more months of therapy to regain something even close to its original strength. But each day of therapy saw improvement.

He and Mattie had spent as much time as she could make available to walk together in the park, and he had been able to go to her house on two of the intervening weekends. They tried to spend as much time alone as possible, but it was far too little to satisfy them. They would sit in the moonlight and on park benches. They exchanged passionate kisses and warm embraces, and held hands and talked easily about how much they loved and enjoyed each other. They talked about her mother's ranch days, and her father's business, and about the war and when it would end, and about their childhoods, and their past. But one thing they did not talk about was their future—or if they were to have one. Through it all, Mattie tried to sense what Gene was thinking, but she could not.

Gene continued to tell her how much he loved her, how much he loved being with her. But as the days passed, and his condition improved, Mattie knew from past experience that his days at the hospital were numbered. Nevertheless, Gene seemed to live only in the present. He began to seem vaguely distant, and Mattie often sensed a space growing between them. Their conversations oftentimes felt superficial, and pointless.

There were no discussions of what his thoughts about his future might be, and certainly no mention of what their future might be. She began to wonder whether they were to even have a future together, or if she was to turn out to be a wartime romance that he would remember fondly for a while and then let fade with the other memories from that time.

No matter how she tried to suppress it, while lying in her bed at night unable to sleep, Mattie found a sense of dread and apprehension growing within her. She had strived to not press Gene on the subject, believing that if he did, indeed, love her as he claimed then the matter would resolve itself. Still, their time was rapidly coming to a close and she was no more sure of his intentions now than when they had first shared their love for each other. Gene remained strangely noncommittal and evasive if any mention of the future was made. He frequently told her how much he loved her, how special she was to him. But no more than that.

On this particular day, with their time fading, they were sitting together in the hospital park, talking about not much of anything. Mattie was growing increasingly distraught but was trying to remain calm and not let it show. There was no denying that Gene was now in a condition to be able to travel. He had received a two-week notice that he was to be shipped back to the States to be discharged because of his wounds—and that had been a week ago.

"Have you been told yet how you're to return to the States?" Mattie asked, trying to make it sound casual and conversational, as one might ask a friend out of idle curiosity. But her eyes couldn't hide the uncertainty and fear behind the question.

"I got orders yesterday," Gene replied, his voice flat and strangely detached, almost resigned, Mattie thought. "I'm to go to Brisbane by train, and board a troop ship. I don't remember its name."

Mattie nodded, staring straight ahead for what felt like an eternity, as Gene sat just as silently beside her, staring just as intently at nothing. Finally, her nerves could handle the uncertainty no longer.

"Gene, you know you have only six more days," Mattie said, her voice faltering. "I've tried my best to remain calm, and not press you. But you won't say anything, and…oh God, Gene?"

No longer able to mask her pain, she buried her head in her hands, sobbing uncontrollably.

"Mattie? What's wrong?" Gene asked, but knew the question was pointless.

"What's wrong?" Mattie exploded incredulously. She looked at him in stark disbelief, tears streaming down her cheeks. "How can you even ask? You know how much I love you. You said you love me."

"I do love you, Mattie, but—"

She interrupted him before he could decide how to finish the sentence, her voice rising as the fear and anger overwhelmed her.

"Gene? You're leaving in six days…are you going to just walk away from me?" He tried to put his arm around her, but she pushed him away. "Gene, answer me," she demanded. "I have to know the truth. Was it all just lies?"

She glared at him, her eyes demanding an answer and fearing it. Gene stared disconsolately at his feet, then turned to look at her.

"Mattie, I swear to God, I did not lie to you. I love you more than I know how to say. But for the life of me, I just don't see how it can work. How can we—"

"Oh my God!" Mattie gasped, cold fear stabbing through her. "You really are going to leave me, aren't you?" The shock of disbelief on her face quickly morphed to blazing anger. "I HATE you, Gene Stoddard!" she fired at him, her voice rising in pain and anger. "How could you have been so cruel?"

She pounded on his chest with both fists, the shock, anger, disbelief, and betrayal all pouring out of her emotions into her fists. Gene took her hands, holding her until she stopped struggling, finally just slumping in silence. She glared at him through her tears, trying to see some clue as to why her world was collapsing around her. All she could see was a face that seemed as pained as hers, with tears running down his cheeks. She was too hurt and angry to wonder why.

"Mattie, please…let me try to explain," Gene pleaded.

"Explain? Explain what?" she exploded. "Explain why you lied to me all this time? I don't want an explanation, I want you. Just leave me, Gene Stoddard, if that's what you're going to do. Do it now, and get it over with. Just go! I can't take it any longer."

He looked at her a moment, then gathered up his crutches and hobbled off, leaving her sitting alone on the bench. She didn't see him go, her head buried in her hands on her lap, her body shaking.

Working mechanically, her hands moving as though they had minds of their own, Mattie had nearly finished removing bandages from a basket and placing them on the storeroom shelves. She looked at each item as she placed it in its appropriate place, but didn't see it, still unable to accept the finality of what had happened.

Sleep had been impossible, the night after Gene had walked away from her. She spent those fitful hours talking with her mother, trying to find a clue, a reason, something to help her understand how she could have been so wrong about Gene and their relationship. She would talk a few minutes, then break down crying. Her mother would hold her until the crying stopped. Then Mattie would ask more questions that didn't have answers, and cry again. Finally, dawn came and she dressed and left for the hospital, working in a trance all day, too numb to think. She cared for her wards as cheerfully as she could masquerade, and came home to start it all over again.

She had believed from that first night in their garden that Gene would ask her to marry him before he had to leave. There had been no doubt in her mind that he loved her as much as she loved him. How could they not share the rest of their lives together? That she might just be a wartime romance had never crept into even the dimmest reaches of her mind. It never felt that way to her. Now…?

As she struggled through the last two nights, she played over and over in her mind virtually every moment they had been together, every conversation since he had first told her he thought that she was an angel, trying to find the point at which she should have first sensed a warning of what was to come. There had never been a moment when she had sensed that Gene might be taking advantage of her, or toying with her emotions. She could find no answers. There was only a bleak sense of betrayal and pain.

There was, however, the one puzzling element that kept floating over her churning thoughts the way mist floats over a tumbling mountain stream on a wintry day. No matter her pain, no matter her anger, she could not stop seeing in her mind the look of pain and despair that was on Gene's face just before he had walked away from her.

It made no sense. She could not reconcile the despairing look, if he didn't love her. If he had assumed all along that he was going to ditch her when he left, then he could not have been surprised by her pain and anger. And if he didn't love her, it couldn't have been that painful to do so. But if he did love her, then why was he leaving her? Regardless of how she tried to resolve that conflict, her mind found no answers.

But he had only four more days. Was it truly just—over? Would she ever see him again? And if so, would it matter? And if he never returned, would anything matter? The questions were lost in the black abyss of her emotions.

She was down to the last couple of items in the basket to be stored when she heard the door open and close behind her. Paying it no heed, she placed the remaining items on the shelf, closed the cupboard doors and turned to leave. And in doing so, she nearly ran headlong into Gene, who was standing silently behind her.

"Gene?"

Too startled to know how to react, she placed the basket on the floor beside her and stood facing him, obviously uncertain as to why he was there, or what he wanted.

"Why are you...? What...?" Mattie stammered.

"I asked the head nurse on our floor where you were," Gene interrupted. "She said I'd find you here. Can we go outside?"

Gene looked at her, glanced at his feet, and ran his hand quickly through his hair, a nervous gesture he was apparently picking up from his dad. Mattie looked at him, uncertain of what she should say, or do. Her wounds were too raw to risk further pain.

"Why?" she asked, making no attempt to mask her bitterness and anger.

"Mattie, please," Gene said, "I've got to talk to you. And I can't do it here." He sounded as insistent as he did desperate, but Mattie was afraid of being hurt all over again. She hesitated, then started out the door.

He followed as best he could, awkwardly trying to keep up with her while avoiding entangling her feet in his crutches. She led him through a rear staff door, out into the spacious park behind the hospital. Gene was briefly reminded of the months they had spent here as he had recuperated, struggling to heal and regain his strength. He followed her to one of the park benches, and they sat down. She wouldn't face him, sitting stiff and erect at the end of the bench, staring straight ahead but seeing nothing, waiting for him to speak.

"Mattie…" Gene hesitated. He leaned forward, resting both elbows on his knees, staring at the ground between his feet, too nervous to look at her.

"Yes?" Mattie replied without looking at him, unable to quite mask the anger in her voice. Gene glanced at her a moment, then back at the ground.

"When I left you, the other day, I just couldn't see how we could…that is, I felt like I had no choice…" he began, then hesitated, unable to continue. In a moment, he cleared his throat and tried again.

"Mattie…" he repeated, shaking his head. "Oh, Lord-a-mighty, I'm coming apart. Mattie, I'm so crazy about you I can't think straight. After I left you, I almost got sick to my stomach thinking about losing you. I've been so torn up inside I can hardly breathe." Gene gave up, unable to continue.

He reached over, taking her hand. She didn't resist, letting it lay limply in his hand. He had her mind in such a fog, so uncertain of what was happening, that thinking was beyond her. She was in torment over his struggling emotions, and wanted desperately to somehow believe him. But how did she dare? Would he just leave again? She looked straight ahead, unable to overcome the feelings of betrayal, and trust him. She waited to hear what he was struggling to say, unsure of what was at the heart of it all. He hesitated a moment longer, still staring at his feet. When he could finally talk without his voice breaking he glanced at her, but she was still staring ahead.

"Do you have any idea how I feel about you…I mean deep inside me?" Gene asked, so quietly she strained to hear him. "I don't know how to tell you. Our family just never talks about anything, and certainly not about emotions. I never knew you could feel like I feel about you. I've been about to go crazy since…the other day."

Mattie looked at him. Nothing was making any sense. What was the point of any of what he was saying? It still was not at all clear what he was trying to tell her, or why he had come back. Her mind wouldn't let her forget—he left her before. What was to happen now?

"Is it the Stoddard way of showing their love to leave the person they love and never see them again? Is that the way it's done in Kansas?" she asked, sarcasm layered on anger in her voice, unable to hide the pain and bitterness. Gene could control himself no longer. He grabbed her by her shoulders, turning her to him, forcing her to look at him.

"Mattie. Look at me," Gene demanded, his voice rising. "Don't you understand? I want to marry you. I want to spend the rest of my life with you. I want you to have our children and for us to grow old together. I can't stand the thought of losing you."

For a moment, Mattie could not even form a response—her mind was in complete chaos. This was so totally unexpected, so inconsistent with his coldly walking away just two days before, that her mind couldn't handle it. *If this is how he truly feels, then what was that all about?* she wondered. She looked down at her hands, folded in her lap. She couldn't look at his face, and control herself, so she spoke slowly, quietly, to her lap, choosing her words carefully.

"Gene...do you have any idea how desperately I wanted all that for us? Why do you think I'm in such agony? Why do you think I'm so angry, and feel so betrayed? You have me so confused I can't even think. Why couldn't you tell me this before?"

She looked at him, tears now streaming down her face. But the anger welled up within her, flashing over her face.

"Gene Stoddard, you LEFT me!" Mattie burst out, the tears in her eyes not extinguishing the fire there. "You just walked off, and left me sitting here! How could you do that to me? To us? I had no idea if I would ever see you again. I haven't slept for two nights, crying over what you did to me. And I still don't know why."

Gene leaned forward, elbows resting on his knees and hands folded, staring blankly at the ground. It took so long for him to respond that Mattie thought he wasn't going to.

"So how do we do it?" Gene finally asked, frustration rising in his voice. "I mean, look at you, who you are. Look at me, who I am. Mattie, be realistic. How on Earth can we get married?"

The question appeared to Gene to be so self-evident as to hardly be worth voicing, but was so incomprehensible to Mattie that she could only stare at him.

"Gene, I...I'm sorry. I'm so confused I really don't know—"

He looked at her in a way that failed to mask his exasperation at her refusal to see the obvious.

"For crying out loud, Mattie," Gene retorted, "you live in a mansion! Your folks must have more money than God. You ride around in a limousine and run around in high society. Look at me! I'm from a pathetic little hard-scrabble farm in Kansas, with parents that never made it past the eighth grade. And what future do I have? I'm a gimpy ex-bomber pilot with no future in the only career I ever seriously considered. Now, I don't know what I'll do—I don't even know what I can do—to make a living when I get back. Am I supposed to take you from all this and drag you half way around the world to live...how? Where? I don't even know. So how do we have a life together? By air mail?"

Gene had become so agitated by the time he stopped talking that his voice was trembling. He stared at her, breathing hard, trying to regain control of himself. Mattie pulled back slightly, looking at him, incredulous.

Gene sat there, breathing hard, staring at her, his face a mixture of total despair, and the frustration that she couldn't see the hopelessness of their future as clearly as he felt it. Mattie struggled, trying to make some sense out of what she had just heard. She shook her head, partly as if to clear out the shambles that her thoughts had become, and partly as if unable to comprehend the irrationality of what Gene had just said.

"Gene? Are you telling me that's what's behind all this?" Mattie asked him, unable to hide the incredulity she was feeling. "Are you telling me you can't marry me because my father's rich?" Even the question seemed irrational. She looked at him, wondering if she had possibly misunderstood him.

For a few seconds, she didn't know how to react, much less what to say. Then, slowly, a smile began to form, growing until she broke into laughter. She began to laugh so hard she had to hide her face in her hands in embarrassment. She would finally stop laughing, pause, look at him, then once more burst into uncontrollable laughter.

Gene was speechless, looking at her in total confusion. Finally, she began to collect herself, using the back of her hand to wipe away tears of laughter that were streaming down her cheeks.

"Oh, my," Mattie managed to get out, between laughs. "Gene, Christy is right. You really are a total dunce sometimes."

"Christy?" Gene responded, looking baffled. "What's she got to do with this? Besides, how would you know anything about what she would think—"

"You mean, how do I know what Christy thinks about you?" Mattie interrupted. "It's quite simple, you moron—to use her words. She wrote thanking me for the letter that you had me write when you first got here, and we started corresponding. At first, I just kept her informed about how you were feeling, and your progress. Then I began to let her know how I felt about you. I was still a little afraid that you two might be more than just friends. She's been very helpful, and I love her sense of humor. We've become quite the mates, actually."

Mattie couldn't avoid enjoying the look of blank astonishment on Gene's face, as she waited for him to react to her revelation.

"Good Lord. So all this time, you and Christy have been writing about me behind my back? I can't believe that. That...that's treason, or something," Gene protested. He pulled back, looking more than a little nonplussed. "So what's my best friend been saying about me? Probably not much of a character reference, if I know her."

"Well," Mattie said, choking back another laughing fit, "she said that you were probably the nicest guy I would ever have the good fortune to meet, that you were intelligent, thoughtful, considerate, kind to children and small animals—but that when it comes to matters of the heart you don't have the brains God gave a goose, I believe was the way she put it. I see what she meant, now." Mattie was still smiling, obviously enjoying the moment.

"What's that supposed to mean?"

Gene wanted to be annoyed, but was too confused to know for sure what he should be annoyed about. How the situation had evolved so suddenly from a bleak assessment of how he and Mattie could never get married, could never have a future together, to an analysis of his character by Christy totally escaped him.

"Because if you did have the brains God gave a goose," Mattie explained, "you would have known that I meant it when I said I fell in love with you the first moment I set eyes on you. When I was cooling your face, when you were first coming out from under the anesthesia, I just sat there and looked at you. All I could think was, 'There's the guy I want to marry. I wonder how I can make that happen?'"

She pulled him up from the bench and moved against him, her arms around his waist, looking up at him.

"Gene, you said you grew up in church. Do you remember what Ruth said to her mother-in-law, Naomi?"

"I'm afraid I fell asleep a lot in Sunday School," Gene replied. He had no idea what was going on, or what she was getting at. "What did Ruth say to Naomi?"

"I think it's the most beautiful passage in the Bible. I memorized it years ago," Mattie replied. She kept her arms tightly around his waist, smiling up at him, and related the passage:

"Entreat me not to leave thee, or to return from following after thee, for whither thou goest, I will go; and where thou lodgest, I will lodge. Thy people shall be my people, and thy God my God. Where thou die, will I die, and there will I be buried. The Lord do so to me, and more also, if aught but death part thee and me."

"Yeah, I sort of remember that," Gene agreed, "But what's the point. What's that got to do with us?"

"Gene, look at me. Don't you understand?" Mattie implored, taking his face in both her hands. "That's what people do when they love each other. Do you really believe I would let you leave me because I don't want to leave my nice house? I'm sorry, Gene, but that really hurts. Is that what you believe about me, that I'm that materialistic, that I'm that shallow?"

"I'm sorry, Mattie," he replied, his voice subdued. He looked at the ground, unable to look her in the eyes, becoming more chagrined by the second over his behavior. He shook his head slightly, in disbelief at himself. "I guess I just let your home, all that luxury, blind me. I always feel so…out of place, and inferior. Your folks are really nice and I appreciate their hospitality. But every time I go over there I get knots in my stomach. I feel like such a hick, and I kept imagining the look on your face the first time you see my home. I just didn't see how it could work."

She put both arms around his neck and kissed him hungrily, then leaned back, looking into his eyes.

"Gene, I hope you can come to know us well enough to have more faith in us than that. Yes, Father is wealthy, and yes, we live in a very luxurious home. But Father and Mother are good people, just like your parents. They also both know that if your parents, and all the others like them, hadn't sent their sons over here to fight and die we could lose it all. Do you think they—or I, for that matter—will look down on your parents for that, because we have more money? And I'm sorry, Gene, but you're not being at all fair to me. Do you truly believe I would fall in love with someone who I think is a country bumpkin? Do I seem to be that poor a judge of character, or that my standards are that low?"

"I'm sorry, Mattie." Gene shook his head, by now thoroughly embarrassed. "Lord in Heaven, I feel like a total idiot. Christy always has known me better than I know myself. I guess that's why we've been such good friends, all our lives."

Mattie stood there, arms around his neck, looking up at him. *Thank you, Ruth and Naomi,* she prayed silently.

"By the way, Mr. Scaredy Cat. Was that a marriage proposal you slipped in there, earlier?"

Gene pulled her back to him, kissing her again, then burying his face in her hair.

"Yes, Matilda, I very much want to waltz you home with me. Will you marry me, Mattie?"

She pulled away from him, her arms still around his neck, and looked at him. He was gaunt from the loss of weight, his face haggard from the emotional strains of months of suffering and therapy, and now two days of agonizing over his belief that he could not have the girl he loved only to learn that it had all been caused by his own insecurities—or stupidity, whichever seemed more accurate. His eyes seemed to almost be pleading with her to tell him what he wanted to hear. She took his face in her hands and kissed him.

"Oh, Gene, for Heaven's sake," she answered, sounding almost exasperated. "Of course I'll marry you! How could you have possibly thought that I wouldn't? I would have married you the first time we talked to each other, if you'd asked me to. I was petrified that I would never see you again."

She began to cry again, tears running down her cheeks. He held her close, letting her cry it out. Their emotions finally spent, they sat down together on the bench. It was several minutes before they could begin to talk again.

"Mattie," Gene said, breaking the silence. "I don't know how your parents would feel. But quite frankly, there is simply no way that my parents will ever get to come to Australia. I would like to get married in the States, where Mom and Dad could be there, too. That is, if your folks could come over. I mean, I don't want to be unfair, but—"

"I think it would be nice to be married in your home church," Mattie assured him. "Christy could be my maid of honor, and I would want Elizabeth as my bridesmaid. See there? I already had it planned out. Mother and Father would love a chance to get to see the States again. It's been several years since they were over there. I don't know what's involved for civilians to get to travel now, but Father does have a lot of connections in government. That should help. But first, you'll need to ask him for permission to marry me."

"Good Lord, you're right," Gene said, taken aback. "But I'd rather go back to combat than do that, to tell you the truth."

"Oh, don't be afraid of Father," Mattie said, laughing at Gene's obvious discomfort. "He can be sort of gruff, sometimes, but you know he thinks you should outrank General Macarthur. I told him about the man coming down to interview you for the Medal of Honor. Frankly, you sort of overwhelm them. And, I think he rather suspected that such a conversation could be in his future," she assured him, smiling.

"I love you, soon-to-be Mrs. Gene Stoddard." Gene held her close, and kissed her cheek. "I don't know how I could have been so stupid, Mattie. Sometimes I scare myself."

She nestled down beside him, trying to let her nerves calm and the relief settle in. Neither spoke for several minutes, their minds playing through all that had happened, and how close they had come to losing it all.

"Mattie, I appreciate what you said about whither I goest you will go, and all that stuff," Gene said, breaking the silence, "but where's that going to be? Tell you the truth, I'm sort of, I don't know...scared, I guess," he confessed.

"Scared? Of what, Gene?" She raised up, looking at him. Hadn't he faced death on every mission he flew? What could he be afraid of now? "Whether I will like America, or where we live? That really is something you don't need to worry about," she tried to assure him.

"No, it's not that. It's just that..." He had to pause, to collect his thoughts. "Well, I have no idea what to do when I get back. I don't know what life it is that we'll be going back to, and that's hard to deal with."

"I...I don't understand, Gene," Mattie replied, her eyebrows pulled together, her puzzlement at his comment obvious. "I guess I took it for granted that you would go back to college and finish your electrical engineering degree. Isn't that what you said you would do?"

"Yeah, it is," Gene agreed, "but Mattie, look. I like the math and all that stuff, but I've got to be honest. I don't know an electron from a tucker-bag. I enrolled in electrical engineering because they offered me a scholarship. Period. I couldn't have afforded KU without it, and I would have enrolled in home economics, if necessary, to get into that flight school. I just can't face going back to try to make a life in something as foreign to me as electrical circuits. I mean, the only time I tried to hook up a lamp at home the thing spit fire all over me and blew a fuse."

Mattie waited in silence, not having any idea what to say, or if he wanted her to.

"I never in my worst nightmares ever believed that I would have to give up flying and actually have to do some kind of engineering work—or any other kind of job, for that matter. Quite honestly, I assumed I would either get killed over here, or come back and get on with the airlines. I've never given a moment's thought to anything else.

"Frankly, this possibility never occurred to me," he continued, nodding toward his crippled leg. "I just don't know where to turn, or what to do. I try to be optimistic, and not get bitter about it. But I still can't deal with a life without flying. And I have no concept of what kind of job I should try to get, or that I can get. What am I supposed to do—go back to Colborn and run the hardware store?"

Mattie was finally beginning to perceive the root causes for his not being able to ask her to marry him, to even let it reach the point where he could consider leaving her out of his life. His feelings were almost beyond her power to comprehend, so foreign to her own beliefs were they, but she was coming to accept how deeply those feelings had taken root in him.

"Gene, do you have to completely leave aviation, if it means so much to you?" Mattie asked. "Airplanes have to be designed, I assume. Aren't there engineering careers in aviation? I heard a friend say something once about getting a degree in something about airplanes—is aeronautical engineering the right term? Is there such a thing?"

"Well, yes, you can get a degree in aeronautical—I remember seeing it listed in the KU catalog," Gene acknowledged. His brow furrowed as the implications of her question began to register, and he tried to think it through. "I'll have to admit that possibility had never even crossed my mind. Any time I thought about airplanes—which was pretty much all the time—I only thought about flying them. I gave no thought at all to designing them. When I was in high school I thought I might go into mechanical engineering because I'm so familiar with machinery. But then I got the double-e scholarship…" His voice trailed off.

Gene put his arm around Mattie, and stretched his leg, trying to find a position that eased the pain. It seemed to never stop hurting, no matter what he did with it. He stared at the hospital garden, and across at the deep blue of Sydney Harbor. He had come to really enjoy the area, and had to admit to himself that he would miss it. That was probably a factor in his coming to believe that Mattie would never be able to leave it. When he looked at that view, and then thought about the dry, dusty heat of Kansas in August…well, it was sort of painful to compare. His mind drifted deeper into his troubled future, as seconds drifted by in silence.

"Where did you go? I've lost you," she said, looking up at him.

"What? Oh. I guess I was just thinking about all of it. I used to drift off like that when we would be flying back from a mission, late at night. I'd get to thinking about how elegant and sophisticated the design of an airplane has to be, to do everything we did with them. But I never really understood it. I suppose it would be interesting to know more about the design of them."

He paused and shifted on the bench, stretching his legs. Mattie assumed he would continue with what he had been telling her, but he stared in silence across the harbor, lost in thought. She glanced at him, wondering what all was churning through his mind, but waited. She was about to ask him what he was thinking, but he picked up where he had left off.

"Boeing is working on a huge new bomber, much bigger than my B-17. I think it's called the B-29. I imagine a lot of that's being done at Wichita, and that's only about a hundred miles from home. Wichita University is there. It isn't as big as KU or K-State, but they might have an aeronautical program… there are so many aircraft companies in Wichita. I suppose I might be able to get a part time job at Boeing, or one of them, while I work on my degree. Like I said, I'd just never given it any thought. I'd have to check it all out. I don't have any idea what I could work out."

Gene got quiet again, for a moment, thinking about how much different his life was going to turn out to be compared to what he had long dreamed about it being, and from what it appeared—until his last mission—it was going to be.

"Mattie, you know I love you," Gene said, sounding so subdued that Mattie looked at him, wondering why. "I know you love me. I have confidence that, somehow, we can make a good life together. But I have to be honest with you. I still haven't been able to accept what has happened to me. My dream seemed to be coming true. I was flying a B-17, feeling like I was finally getting to do my part in the war and getting valuable experience. When the war was over, Mike and I would fly together for some airline. Everything seemed just hunky-dory. Now? Well…"

Gene stopped in mid-sentence. Mattie looked at him, but he was staring off into space. She waited for him to come back. A few seconds later, he glanced at her.

"I'm embarrassed to admit it, Mattie, but I'd be lying to you to say that I'm not more than a little bitter about it. To tell the truth, sometimes I wish the Japs had got me, instead of Jimmy—I think I'd prefer that to being a crippled has-been pilot. That's not the kind of person I was raised to be, and I'm trying to get past it. I know I should be grateful that I'm still alive. Still…it doesn't seem to go away. I'm not sure how easy I'm going to be to live with, and that bothers me—for your sake. I won't be able to take it if I begin to feel you starting to be sorry you married me, when I'm in some blue funk over all this."

Mattie had sensed those feelings, at times, but hadn't heard him be quite so candid about it. She hesitated a moment, then leaned her head on his shoulder.

"Gene, I won't try to tell you that I know how you feel—I can't. I've never had to suffer what you have," Mattie answered. "But I do know that we'll see you through it. And when I stand before God and Man and promise to marry you for better or worse until death do us part, I'll mean just that. I'm not going to bugger off at the first sign of a problem between us."

Gene didn't respond, but pulled her closer to him. In a moment she looked up at him, with just a hint of Irish temper in her eyes.

"You should also be forewarned, Mr. Stoddard, that we O'Sullivans can raise a bit of a row ourselves, at times. Don't expect that your life is going to all be spent on the Sea of Tranquility."

"Oh?" Gene looked at her with a bit of undisguised surprise on his face. Was there some fire in those smiling Irish eyes, to match the red of her hair?

"Well, we are Irish, you know. Mother and Father have had some real donnybrooks. Some problem would come up, some misunderstanding—usually over something so trivial they could never remember what had started it. Mother would get defiant, her eyes flashing, and start setting Father straight on the subject. Father would bellow like a mad bull, then go off and sulk for a day or two. Mother would remain aloof and they would skate around each other, talking ever so politely. Then one morning they'd come down to breakfast all cheerful and lovey-dovey, like nothing had ever happened. Married people argue and fight sometimes, but it doesn't mean they love each other any less. Didn't your parents ever fight?"

Gene's laugh seemed a bit sardonic, and took Mattie by surprise.

"Well, if they did we kids never knew it. They are intensely private. If they ever had a disagreement it was well hidden. Mom would go to the bedroom to have her crying spells once in a while. Dad would go out and farm until it was mealtime, and then he'd be back to the house. They'd go on like nothing ever happened. I don't even know what the arguments, if that's what they were, were about, because we never heard any of it."

"Well, you'll know what my arguments will be about, rest assured," Mattie laughed. "But rest assured also that it won't matter. I'll still love you."

Gene nodded, but didn't reply for a moment, then changed the subject.

"Well, shall we go see if your rowdy Mr. O'Sullivan will let me haul his daughter half way around the world and marry her? And after the shock— assuming, of course, that he approves—maybe we can talk about how to get her transported to America during wartime travel restrictions. It isn't going to be easy, you know."

"I know," Mattie agreed, "but sometimes it really does help to have friends in high places."

Gene nodded, picked up his crutches and they began to walk back to the hospital, still in disbelief at the dramatic change that had just transpired but basking in the warmth of the thought of their coming life together.

Going Home

The visit to Mattie's parents to request permission to marry her transpired just as Mattie told Gene it would. Gene was visibly nervous during the drive to her home. He felt he had made a complete fool of himself by his inexplicable behavior and could only imagine what Mattie's parents thought of him now, because of it. As they were driven from the hospital to her home, Mattie attempted to assure Gene that they would understand, and that if he and Mattie were reconciled none of it would matter—they would be thrilled.

Mattie's parents were not aware, of course, of the reconciliation that had occurred earlier in the day. Mattie didn't tell her chauffeur, Peter, why she had asked him to come pick her up, well before her shift was over. When Mattie left the house that morning she felt her life had ended. Her mother was worried that Mattie had lost so much sleep, and was so distraught, that she might be breaking down and needed to go to bed.

But when Mattie appeared in the Grand Foyer, her face beaming, so excited she could scarcely keep from hopping up and down—with Gene standing nervously beside her—Mrs. O'Sullivan knew immediately what had taken place. She rushed to give them both a hug as soon as she saw them, and called for Mr. O'Sullivan to come from the library. After the awkward laughter, and good- natured teasing, Gene attempted to make a formal request for Mattie's hand. But Mr. O'Sullivan cut him off before Gene could get the request out.

"Gene, let me make this easy for you," he interrupted. "You're going to tell me how much you love my daughter, and tell me that even though you are un- worthy of such a precious gem you want to marry her and take her away from us to some strange land half way around the world. Then you'll try to assure me that you'll protect her and take care of her just as I've done all these years. Then I'll say 'Lad, you don't know what a handful you're taking on, but you're welcome to her, as long as you promise us lots of grandchildren.' Do I have it about right?"

Gene grinned in embarrassment, quickly running his hand through his hair, before replying.

"Yes sir," Gene agreed, "you've pretty much nailed it. I've really acted like an idiot the last couple of days, and I apologize to all of you for that. But I am crazy about Mattie, and I most certainly want to marry her. And…" Gene paused, glancing at Mattie, a sly grin on his face. "I promise to do my part about the grandchildren. The rest will be up to Mattie."

Mattie's face blushed the color of her hair. Her father gave her a hug, and shook Gene's hand yet again.

"Well, Gene, don't worry about acting a little crazy. Us blokes always act like idiots when we fall in love. Just ask Mattie's mother, here, and she'll agree." Mrs. O'Sullivan smiled, and nodded. "So—welcome to the family. We couldn't be more proud of a future son-in-law," Mr. O'Sullivan assured him. Gene shook his hand again, and thanked him again and hugged Mrs. O'Sullivan again, and thanked her—again.

With that, they went into a sunroom looking out over the expansive back lawns. Wrought iron lawn furniture, tastefully and colorfully padded to match the outdoors motif, filled the room. Comfortable chaise lounges, glider swings and chairs, all painted in bright glossy white, were stationed around glass-topped tables. It all seemed very airy and cheery, matching their light-hearted mood.

Gene and Mattie sat down together on one of the glider swings, her parents in chairs facing them. A maid appeared, with no apparent order to do so, carrying champagne to celebrate the announcement. Gene had never drunk champagne, and the few sips he took immediately made him feel a little light-headed. Then it was time to get down to the serious business of discussing how Mattie could get to the States, and how the O'Sullivans would manage to get there for a wedding. As Mattie had suggested, her father seemed to believe that he could arrange it all.

While they talked, Gene would occasionally glance out at the impeccably groomed grounds, and at the sumptuously appointed room, and admit to himself, as he had each time he had visited Mattie's home, that he felt very uncomfortable with the ostentatious appearance of it all.

He had known even as he was walking away from her two days earlier that he was making the biggest mistake of his life, but felt powerless to stop himself. He had struggled for days, and sleepless nights, unable to imagine Mattie leaving those luxurious surroundings and taking up life in a rural Kansas that had barely survived a depression. But he was also unable to imagine leaving her, imagine her not in his life. Then he would picture Mr. and Mrs. O'Sullivan sitting in his parents' living room, and knew the self-consciousness that his parents would feel. He had finally convinced himself that it would not be fair to Mattie, or his parents, and had decided that he would have to leave Australia without Mattie. He didn't know if he could do it, but felt he had to.

He had not made it through the first night after leaving her before he knew he couldn't do it. It was not possible for him to leave without her, regardless of the consequences. He struggled all the next day trying to decide how to go about attempting to undo the damage he had caused, but with no success. Occasionally, a nurse's aide would come to his room to attend to something or other, but it was never Mattie, of course. On the second day, he had finally given up in desperation and set out to find her—he knew she would be somewhere in the hospital—hoping that she would somehow let him talk to her. He was still embarrassed with himself for having let her father's wealth influence him so negatively, even to the point of nearly allowing it to destroy their life together.

And yet, in spite of what Mattie had said, Gene could not help feeling intimidated by the luxurious surroundings. Nor could he deny the lurking sense of guilt that he felt when he admitted the embarrassment that he knew he would feel, starting with when she would arrive at the train station in Colborn and they would walk out to get in the worn-out old Chevy that was his parents' car. The comparison between that and the limousine he had ridden in to her house—her mansion—would be too stark to ignore.

And then there would be her first time to see his home. He knew that it wasn't being fair to Mattie. She was a better person than that. And he knew he wasn't being fair to his folks. They had struggled for much of their years to make a home for their three children, and to survive against overwhelming odds. They couldn't be blamed for a depression that had nearly ruined the country.

But, to Gene, it would still be too much like the boys who tried to be proud of their "new" cars, the beat-up old hand-me-downs that were all their parents could make available to them, when talking to the kids who had been given virtually new ones by their well-to-do parents. They would talk loudly about how much they enjoyed having a car that they could work on themselves and didn't have to worry about banging up, how they could go anywhere and not have to worry about scratches and dents. They would brag about how they had "souped it up" and how fast it could go. Then they each would drive away in his "pride and joy," and be ashamed and jealous.

He knew Mattie, as well as her parents, would be polite and say all the appropriate things. He knew her mother would graciously relate it to her younger days growing up on a modest ranch in the Blue Mountains, and her father would talk generously about how Kansas is the breadbasket of the world. But the differences would always be there, unavoidable, as real as some family skeleton kept hidden in the closet, but whose presence permeated the family by the very knowledge that it was there. Polite refusal to mention it would not mean it didn't exist.

Gene knew how self-conscious and uncomfortable his parents would feel. He hadn't decided yet whether to tell his folks much about Mattie's parents, for fear his mother would feel shamed by her surroundings, by her home, by her meager wardrobe and her tattered furniture. But he didn't want to start off his new life on a lie—or at least a deceit. What would they say when they later found out that Mattie's folks were so wealthy?

He also wondered where the O'Sullivans, and Mattie for that matter, would stay before the wedding. His parents' house had only two bedrooms when first built—his parents' and the one that Gene and his brother, Jerry, had shared. Gene's dad had added on a third one when his sister, Elizabeth, had grown too big to sleep in a crib in his parents' bedroom, but there were no fancy guest bedrooms with canopy beds—or any other kinds of beds. And Colborn had only one hotel. It was actually quite nice by small rural town standards, but nothing compared to the O'Sullivan home, or the five-star hotels he imagined the O'Sullivans stayed in when they traveled. Gene wanted to believe that the excitement of the wedding would overshadow all such details, and probably that would be true. But still, try as he might, he could not keep it all out of the back of his mind.

All that notwithstanding, he also knew that he was giddily, overwhelmingly, in love with the auburn-haired girl curled up next to him in the padded glider, and knew that somehow they would have to make it all work out. He watched her as she talked with her parents. The adrenalin rush of being suddenly snatched from the pit of despair that was this morning, and elevated to the mountaintop of excitement that was this moment, had made her more animated and buoyant than he had ever seen her. She seemed positively effervescent, so much so that he teased her at one point, wondering aloud if she would glow in the dark.

He knew he was so crazy over her that it made him ache inside, and he wondered at the strange contradictions of life. Had he not been so severely wounded that he could no longer do the one thing he loved more than anything else, then he would not have found the one person that he now loved more than anyone else. He wondered if life was going to always be like that, if something would have to be lost if something else were to be gained. It seemed unfair in a way and made him feel pessimistic, which was most uncharacteristic of him. So he pulled Mattie closer to him and tried to put it all out of his mind, determined to enjoy the moment.

Dear Christy,

I'll keep this short. I just finished a last letter to the folks. I guess this will be the last letter you get from me, from over here. Tomorrow morning I take the train up to Brisbane, and am to board another troop ship to head home the next day. I never could have imagined, when I boarded that ship to head over here, all that has happened to me. It's been the worst, and the best, thing that ever happened to me. I'll tell you all about Mattie and me when I get home. Of course, now that I know that you two have been writing about me behind my back, I have to assume she'll fill you in on the sordid details.

The trip to the States will take at least a month. Throw in a few days getting home, and I expect to be seeing you all in five weeks, or so. I'll try to call when I get Stateside, and know what my train schedule will be.

Christy, I could not have made it, over here, without your letters to help me out. I can't tell you what they meant to me. I don't suppose there will be a way to repay you, but I am immensely grateful to you.

Well, enough sentiment—got to get some shuteye. I can't imagine what my life is going to be, once I get home, but I am starting to look forward to being back.

Love you all,
Gene

The next day, a train carrying Gene, and hundreds of other troops, puffed its way northward the several hundred miles to Brisbane. Once there, he checked in with the appropriate Army offices to get his shipping papers. A day later, he was standing on the wharf in Brisbane, waiting to board the ship which was to take wounded troops, and those being rotated, back to the States. He was chagrined to see how many of the wounded were missing limbs. It made him ashamed of himself for his bitterness over not being able to fly—but the feelings wouldn't leave him.

He stood there, at the edge of a sea of uniforms, looking around and wondering about all that had happened to him since he last stood on this same wharf, having just arrived in Australia. His thoughts were suddenly jerked back to the present, startled to hear his name being called. He looked to see who was calling and saw Mattie running toward him, followed by her parents.

"Mattie?" he called to her, surprise written all over his face. Some of the guys standing around him glanced at Gene, then stared at the attractive redhead running toward them. She came charging up to him, wrapped him in a hug, then kissed him. A couple of the guys let out wolf whistles.

"Hey, Mac, come on! Share and share alike! It's my turn!" one of the guys next to Gene kidded—or perhaps he wasn't kidding—as Mattie finally stopped kissing Gene, and smiled at the guys.

"Get your own girl, buddy—no way you're getting this one," Gene replied, still holding tight to Mattie. He looked down at her. "Well this is certainly a pleasant surprise. How'd you know where to find me?"

"Quite simple, silly. I just copied it off the letter you had with your shipping orders on it, then asked the MP at the gate. You didn't think I was going to let you leave without a last goodbye kiss, did you?"

Before he could respond, Mattie's parents caught up to her and joined them. Gene noticed that boarding had already begun—he knew the goodbyes would have to be short. Mrs. O'Sullivan hugged him tightly for several seconds, then kissed him on the cheek.

"Gene, I can't tell you how grateful we are to have you a part of our family. We pray that this dreadful war will soon end, and we can all be together, somehow." She wiped a tear from her cheek. Apparently she and Mattie shared that trait. "But—if it hadn't been for this horrible war, we would never have had you in our lives so we thank God for that. Please take good care of yourself going home." She hugged him again, and stepped back, putting her arm around Mattie's waist. Mr. O'Sullivan reached out to take Gene's hand. "Gene, I won't whitewash it," he said, being his usual blunt self. "It's not going to be a cakewalk getting Mattie over to the States. But you have my word that I'll find a way. You just take care of yourself, get well, and we'll get her to you, somehow. Now, looks like you better get on board and get this show on the road."

He stepped back, and Mattie once again wrapped Gene tightly in a hug, and kissed him, unwilling to turn loose of him. But the time had come.

"Mattie—it's time. I have to board. You know how much I love you. Write me lots of letters. I want them all waiting on me when I get home. Send them to Christy. I don't want the folks wondering why I'm still getting letters from my nurse, until I have a chance to tell them about us."

Mattie reluctantly let him go. He started up the gangplank. It was steeper than it looked, and he had a difficult time with his crutches. But wood strips across the planks gave him something to secure them on while he hobbled upward. About halfway, he turned to look back at Mattie. She was smiling through tears, waving to him. He waved back, hesitated, then turned and struggled his way up the remainder of the ramp.

Thirty-one days later the ship glided beneath the Golden Gate bridge, and berthed at a dock in San Francisco, California. Two days later, after a medical examination and all fresh bandages had been applied at the base hospital, Gene was on board a train destined for Kansas City, Missouri. He was headed home, and still somewhat in a state of incredulity over all that had happened to him in such a short time—it was not yet two years since he took his first flight lesson.

They were standing in a cluster on the railroad depot platform as the train steamed into the little town of Colborn, Kansas. Gene saw them as the steam engine hissed and chuffed and clanked and squealed to a stop. His mother was wearing a new print dress, or at least one that Gene didn't remember seeing before. Both she and Liz were quite skilled at making attractive dresses from the flowered cloth that the sacks of cattle feed came in, so in all likelihood she had made a new one for the occasion. She was clutching her purse in both hands, a habit she had to mask her nervousness when she was in an uncomfortable situation.

His dad had forsaken his bib overalls for a pair of dress slacks and white shirt, sleeves buttoned as always, and wearing a tie and his Sunday hat. He was trying to look calm, but nervously rubbed his nose every little bit, and ran his hand through his graying hair. Liz and Christy were standing together, arms loosely around each other, and his younger brother, Jerry, was standing next to them, momentarily distracted by the monstrous dragon quietly breathing steam close beside them. They looked expectant, excited but nervous, glancing at the cars as a handful of people climbed down the steps, stepping out onto the small stool placed there by the conductor. They had no clear idea what to expect Gene to look like, or how the wounds had affected him.

Christy saw him first.

"Gene!"

Her scream startled the others, and they followed as she ran to the rear of the train where he was struggling down the car steps with his crutches. The conductor stood by, a hand partly raised to catch Gene if need be as he awkwardly stepped down, yet hesitant to offend Gene by actually assisting him. Gene had just stepped onto the platform as Christy reached him. She stopped a few steps short of him, her face suddenly pale with shock at his appearance.

"Oh my God—Gene?" She hesitated for a moment, before coming forward to wrap her arms around his chest in an exuberant hug, being careful to avoid his injured arms and legs.

"I'll assume that means you're glad to see me," Gene teased, smiling down at her as she stepped back to look at him.

"Of course we're glad to see you, you nitwit—I just wasn't prepared to see you looking quite so…" She blinked back the tears as the others came rushing up to join them.

Gene hadn't fully comprehended how much his injuries had affected his appearance. He had been lean, but muscular and well built when they had last seen him. He looked positively handsome in his military dress uniform with its billed officer's hat and Air Force insignia, in the framed picture that he sent them after he received his wings—a picture that now occupied a front-and-center position along with other family photos on his mother's china cabinet.

Although he was slowly gaining some of the weight back that he had lost during his stay at the hospital, he still looked thin—emaciated, almost—in comparison to the vital young man they remembered. His face was gaunt, and his dress khakis appeared to hang on his thin frame. He was nothing like the athletic young pilot they had last seen, and the shock of his appearance was apparent on all their faces.

They tried without success to avoid looking at his leg, which he held at an awkward angle as he stood leaning on his crutches. His right arm and leg were no longer bandaged, but his left bicep, as well as his left knee and lower leg, would have to remain bandaged for several weeks. They were mostly just gauze, protecting the healing wounds from being rubbed by his clothes, and didn't show.

He was immediately surrounded by family. Elizabeth matched Christy's hug, as did his younger brother, Jerry. Once they had greeted him, his mother stepped forward, making no pretense this time of holding back the tears as she carefully embraced him, self-consciously sensitive in trying to avoid his injured arms and leg. Gene held her to him, feeling closer to her than he had at any time in his life. In spite of her usual reticence, she buried her face on his shoulder and cried. Gene patted her, and in a moment she pulled back, embarrassed by her show of emotions. Ever the mindful mother, she rubbed at the tear stains on his uniform with her handkerchief.

Finally, it was his dad's turn. Gene started to reach out to shake his hand, as he expected his father to do, but was surprised to be wrapped in a bear hug that nearly took his breath away. His dad stepped back, holding him with both hands on his shoulders, and looked him over. He took Gene's hand in both of his, a smile spreading over a face streaked with tears—a sight Gene had never before witnessed.

"Welcome home, son."

It was more than Gene had bargained for, and he choked and swallowed hard several times before he could speak. He blinked back his own tears, which his mother dabbed at with her handkerchief. The others stood by, smiling and watching somewhat self-consciously at a display of emotions they had never before seen from these two stoic people.

"It's good to be home," was all Gene could finally choke out.

After a few moments of awkwardness, as they smiled through their embarrassment, Jerry picked up Gene's duffel bag and they started to the old Chevy parked in front of the depot. The three men—Jerry decidedly considered himself to be a man at age sixteen—sat in the front, with the three women in the back.

It felt unnatural to Gene, being driven by his dad. He couldn't remember the last time the family drove together when he wasn't the driver. His crutches had been stowed between him and Jerry, who was sitting in the middle of the seat. Gene realized that Jerry was probably doing the driving now—he would have been able to get a learner's permit to drive from the farm to school when he was fourteen, and his license as soon as he turned sixteen. Jerry must have taken the initiative of getting in the middle just to avoid embarrassing their dad by asking him to sit in the middle, between his boys, as though he were now the child.

They had all been nervously solicitous as Gene worked himself and his stiff, inflexible leg into the car seat, concerned and wanting to be helpful while still not wanting to embarrass Gene by appearing to be excessively upset at his condition. It was, in fact, rather difficult for Gene. He had to get his left leg, which he could scarcely bend, into the car while standing outside holding onto the car and door for support, and then try to get turned so he could sit down on the car seat without putting undo strain on either leg—or his left arm, which was still quite tender and weak. By the time he was seated, he was having to clench his teeth against the pain, and small beads of sweat were appearing on his forehead. He wiped them with his sleeve, and pulled the car door shut.

They detoured through the town square, and pointed out the two new stores that had opened on the square while he was gone—a second drugstore, and a new hardware store. Actually, it wasn't new, but in a new location. The original building had burned one night, they said. He vaguely remembered it being mentioned in one of their letters. They took Gene past the burned out brick shell that remained—it reminded Gene of all the pictures coming back from England showing the buildings that had been bombed by the German air raids.

A strange wave of emotion passed over Gene as they drove past the blackened remains of the store. It suddenly struck him that this was what he had been doing, until he was wounded—blowing up buildings, and whoever might have been in them, or whatever else he might have hit. He had usually felt rather detached from it. They almost never saw what they bombed, except on the low-level attacks on airfields and ships. Usually, they were trying to get away, as fast as they could fly, and often fighting for their own lives against enemy fighters while doing so.

He felt no remorse about it. The war seemed more like just another job that had to be done, and he and his friends over there were the ones who had to do it. The Japanese had brought it on themselves, they reasoned—and had done far worse as they had taken over most of the southwestern Pacific. Mostly, there was just a sense of irony that he had to return to his hometown in Kansas to have the reaction.

All the others in the car chattered excitedly as they drove to the farm, but Gene mostly just listened, and looked at the familiar farmsteads and sights from a life that no longer existed or even seemed real—it was more as though he was watching a movie of his former life, and wasn't actually in it. He had heard of a person's life flashing before him in life-threatening situations, and wondered if it felt anything like what he was feeling at the moment.

Once they were home, Gene, Jerry and their dad walked around the farmstead, looking at the new calves and other livestock. It was obvious to Gene that Jerry had moved into the role of caretaker of the stock, telling Gene all about which cows had produced which calves, of having to help with a breech birth, and all the other difficulties and issues that had once fallen to Gene before that December announcement from the little radio in the barn that had so altered their lives.

While Jerry and his dad were getting Gene reacquainted with the farm, his mother, Liz and Christy did as women on the farm had always done: they busied themselves in the kitchen preparing the next meal. In short order, the men had been called to the company table in the living room, which had been pulled farther from the wall to make room for everyone, and so Gene would have room to extend his leg. After saying the blessing, with special thanks for Gene having been returned to them from "over the water," they set about to enjoy the meal. Conversation was awkward, at first, as no one knew for sure what to say, or not to say.

They all wanted to know more about Gene's experiences, but were too reserved to ask. Instead, they skirted the issue, asking polite, innocuous questions about his living conditions on the island, what it felt like to see nothing but ocean for days on end while coming home on the troop ship—anything but details of his combat missions or of his tragic last flight, his injuries, or anything else that they were afraid would make Gene uncomfortable.

Of course, Jerry wanted to know all the gory details, but Gene was hesitant to discuss much of it. He didn't want to upset his mother with stories that were particularly factual about all he had been through. Gene was quite certain that his parents had no concept of the severity of the attack on his plane, or of his wounds, and were probably not aware that one of his crew had been killed and other crew members wounded. And Gene didn't want to upset them at the moment by letting it be known, so he largely avoided the subject. Thus, it was with a collective, though silent, sigh of relief when Christy charged in and changed the subject.

"Okay, Gene, enough of this war stuff. I want to know the important stuff. I want to know when we can expect to see Mattie, and if there is going to be a wedding in this family," she demanded with a smile on her face. All the rest first laughed at her bluntness, then turned to Gene for his response. In spite of himself, he felt himself blushing, and shook his head at her blunt approach.

"Christy, time hasn't mellowed you one bit, has it?" he rejoined, before addressing her questions.

"A girl's gotta do what a girl's gotta do," she replied, shrugging. "We're still waiting," she prodded, as Gene hesitated.

"Well, first of all, I shouldn't even tell you, after you went behind my back to write to her all this time. You should be tried for treason," he chided her, grinning as he did so. "But yes, there is going to be a wedding—just as soon as we can find a way to get her over here."

The whole table erupted in excitement. Liz squealed in delight, coming around the table to hug him. His mother said, and kept repeating, "Oh my goodness. I just can't believe my little boy is getting married." His dad simply smiled and said nothing. Jerry had little to say, but kept grinning at everybody else's excitement. Finally, the babble settled down enough to let Gene continue on.

"I asked her to marry me just before I shipped out to come home. I guess all her Aussie boyfriends got shipped off to the war, since she accepted and agreed to move over here. I don't know yet when we'll be able to get her and her folks over here for the wedding, though. Travel for civilians is pretty difficult. Her dad is working on it over there. We'll just have to wait and see." He turned to Christy. "Of course, knowing you and Mattie, I'm surprised she hadn't already told you," he teased her.

"I hate to bust your bubble," Christy said, smiling at him with her most devilish look. "She said she was too excited to be able to keep it from me, and wrote the next day after you proposed—even before your ship had left Australia. She did ask me not to say anything until you could tell your family. But it seemed like you were going to just sit there and talk about bug-infested islands all day so I had to prod you, as usual."

Gene grinned, and shook his head. "I should have known. I was waiting for the right time. I guess you sort of already know her through all her letters, but I'm dying for you all to get to meet her. She's the best thing that's ever happened to me—and she's beautiful, to boot." He started to reach for his wallet. "I've got a picture of her. It's just a small one, but at least you can get an idea of what she looks like—"

"I didn't know the Army would let a blind guy fly an airplane," Christy interrupted. Have you looked at the china cabinet?"

Gene's confusion was obvious, as he turned to look at the glass-fronted cabinet in which his mother's best chinaware was on display. Its top surface was covered with framed photographs of family members. Gene got up and hobbled the few steps to the cabinet.

Placed prominently in front of the other pictures, alongside his picture in his Air Force uniform, was a studio portrait of a beautiful young girl, smiling radiantly, dressed in a formal gown with an orchid corsage on her left shoulder. In the lower corner in front of the picture was a small snapshot of her dressed in a white tennis outfit, holding her racquet, standing in front of what Gene recognized as the tennis courts in the O'Sullivan back gardens. On the snapshot, written in her familiar neat handwriting, was a note: "Just so you won't think I am always so formal. Mattie." Gene took the picture from the cabinet, staring at it in disbelief.

"How did you…when did you get this? She hasn't even shown me these pictures. I didn't know she'd sent you these."

"She wrote to tell me you had asked her to marry you," Christy answered, "and I immediately wrote back asking for a picture. It got here just a couple of days ago. I framed it so we could put it on the cabinet. We all sort of caught our breath when we saw how pretty she is. Why didn't you tell us what a beauty was nursing you back to health?"

Gene stood looking at the picture for a moment, scarcely aware of what Christy was saying to him. It had been so long since he had last seen her that he had almost forgotten how she made him feel. A sinkhole of depression seemed to swallow him—he desperately needed her here with him, and had no idea when that could happen.

"She's prettier than her picture—it doesn't get her hair the right color." Gene said, looking a few more seconds at the picture before setting it back on the cabinet beside his.

"So, I presume the folks just thought they ought to have a picture of my nurse, to go along with the family photos?" he teased Christy as he hobbled back to his chair.

"Oh, I suspect they knew that she was more than your nurse. Of course, you wouldn't ever tell them anything in your letters to amount to anything. If I hadn't passed along some of what Mattie was writing to me I don't know if they would even know her name," she teased in return. "But I was a good girl. I didn't give away your secret—well, except to Liz, and I knew she wouldn't tell." She looked at Liz, who grinned conspiratorially, and then at Bill and Mary, who had been sitting quietly, smiling, enjoying the exchange between the two.

"Christy would tell us about some of Mattie's letters, and it did seem that she liked you quite a lot," Gene's mother agreed. "It seemed unusual that a nurse would invite a patient to her home to visit. But you hadn't said much in your letters, so we didn't know anything for sure. She certainly is a pretty young lady."

"She wasn't actually my nurse," Gene corrected. "Most of my nurses looked like Aunt Gertie. Mattie's a volunteer, a nurse's aide—she assists the actual nurses in caring for the wounded guys that are brought in. Sort of like the Candy Stripers, here in the States. She fed me when I had both arms in a cast, and took me for outings in the hospital park in a wheel chair before I could get around on crutches. She was watching me while they waited for me to come to after my operations. When I started coming to and could first see her, she was so pretty I thought maybe she was an angel coming to get me. I think we both sort of fell for each other then and there, but it took a while for us to admit it to each other."

It soon became too much for Gene. Liz and Christy wanted to know all about Mattie. Jerry kept asking about his flying, and the war, wanting to know more about it all. His mother was more reserved, of course, but was obviously already becoming concerned about future wedding plans and what all that might portend for her, and would try to ask about it when the conversation paused. Although Gene had gained considerable strength over the past several weeks, the exhausting ride home on the train, and now the excitement of trying to satisfy a year's worth of curiosity on the part of all the family, was taking a toll.

"Folks, I hope you'll forgive me, but I'm fading. I think I'd better lie down and rest for a while," Gene said as he pushed back from the table.

This confession immediately stirred a round of apologies and concern from all of them, as they scurried to help clear the chairs from blocking his way to the back bedroom. It felt strange, lying on the old bed he had slept in for eighteen years. Those days now seemed so long ago as to be more his imagination than reality.

He stared at the ceiling filled with model planes that had consumed so much of his time and passion while growing up, and couldn't keep the sense of despondency and bitterness from welling up again at the fact that he would never again get to enjoy that passion. It seemed hard to believe that his lifelong dream could have ended so abruptly—after seeming so unlimited only a few months ago. But fatigue soon pushed the feelings back into the dark recesses of his mind, and he fell asleep.

He awakened from his nap in time to go to the barn to visit with his dad, and Jerry, while they did the milking. It felt strange to be a part of it again. Life here seemed so protected, so isolated from reality. Port Moresby and Mike Kingston and Gene's crew—and the constant threat of violent death—now seemed like real life. He felt he was living in the dream that life on the farm had become for him when he was in New Guinea.

As badly as he missed her, even Mattie seemed vaguely imaginary, with her ten thousand miles and worlds away from him. That evening he called Christy to see if she could meet him the next day at the drugstore on the town square where the high school kids always hung out.

The next afternoon Jerry dropped him off at the familiar hang-out. He stood outside for a moment, looking at the store, remembering the many hours he and Christy, and their friends, had enjoyed there. He stepped inside, paused and looked around. The drugstore, with its soda fountain and booths lining the back walls and its dark, cool interior, seemed like an old friend. Memories of meeting Christy to share the latest woes in his social life when he was in high school flashed through his mind.

Shaking off the nostalgia, he headed for the back booths. Three very young girls—he had to assume that they were in high school, but they seemed like children now—stared at him with a mixture of embarrassment and curiosity as he passed by, still in his Army uniform and on his crutches. He smiled at them and said "Hello" as he passed. They smiled self-consciously, and said "Hi" back to him. He could overhear them "whispering" about him after he passed.

"Isn't that Jerry Stoddard's big brother?"

"Be quiet, Marty, he'll hear you!"

"They said at school he was hurt really bad in the war."

"Gosh, he looks awful. I'll bet Jerry feels bad about it."

"I heard he's a big hero. He's going to get some big medal."

Gene presumed from the not-very-quiet whispering that his brother Jerry was becoming popular in high school, and wondered how his as-yet unannounced forthcoming Medal of Honor could have become high school news. He didn't remember saying anything to his folks about it, waiting until it became official. Mattie probably told Christy about the interview at the hospital. He wasn't too thrilled to hear their critique of his appearance.

The kid behind the soda fountain watched as Gene hobbled past, hesitant to talk to him. Gene nodded a greeting to the kid, who smiled back. Gene didn't recognize him. It seemed he had been away a lifetime, rather than the two years that had actually passed. He felt he was in a strange town, for he recognized none of the crowd in the drugstore, or any that he saw on the street. But they would probably have all been in Junior High school when he was there, he realized.

As he continued past the counter, he saw Christy sitting in a booth, waiting for him.

"Hi, guy," she greeted him, as he worked himself into the booth seat, and laid his crutches on the floor beside him.

"Hi, friend. Thanks for meeting me. Sort of seems like old times—except for the crutches," he added, not smiling.

"What are friends for?" she asked. "Want your usual cherry Coke?"

"Yeah, sounds great. I haven't had one since I left town."

Christy hopped up to go to the counter. In a couple of minutes, she was back with two drinks in hand. She sat down, sipping hers through a straw, and watched as he drank his straight out of the glass. Christy thought for a moment he was going to chug-a-lug it straight down, but after a couple of swallows he set the glass down.

"Man, I'd nearly forgotten how much I liked those things. Thanks."

She nodded, looking at him rather carefully for a moment, studying his face. She knew that the gauntness in his face made him look older, but his eyes looked different. There was a look that hadn't been there when he left her that day in this same drugstore, right after the Pearl Harbor attack. It was a look that made him appear older than his age, one that suggested he had seen things that he would never talk about. She wondered how much it had all changed his personality.

"It's good to see you again. You know, you had us pretty shook up here, when we got that telegram. I don't know what we would have done without those letters from Mattie. She's so sweet. You're a lucky guy to have found her."

Gene wasn't accustomed to this more serious tone from his usually spunky friend. She had graduated the previous May, and seemed more grown up.

"Christy, she's just...I don't know how to describe her," Gene said, nodding in agreement. "Nice isn't a good enough word. She just makes me feel so good, so special, when I'm with her. I still can't believe it's real, that we're actually going to get married. Lordy, I miss her."

Gene took another swallow from his Coke, and glanced around the store, silently remembering times that now seemed long ago. He set the glass down, and looked at Christy.

"Mike teased me, the first time he visited after I got to the hospital, that Mattie was nuts about me. I thought he was crazy, but he could see it just in the way she looked at me. Don't know why it took me so long to see the obvious."

Christy smiled, but didn't immediately respond. She took another sip of Coke, then spoke without looking up from her glass.

"Speaking of Mike, how's he doing? He's a fun guy. I enjoyed visiting with him, when he was here. Do you still hear from him?"

Gene just shook his head, ignoring any implications of what Christy had just said, and didn't respond for a while. She looked at him, wondering where his thoughts had taken him.

"You know what feels the strangest about it all, now that I'm back?" he asked, changing the subject. Christy obviously had no idea, and waited for him to answer his own question.

"I know that Mike and Ken and all the other guys are still flying missions over there, still fighting for their lives. I guess it's nighttime over there, now. But we fly so much at night that they could, in fact, be on a mission this very minute. They could be dodging ack-ack, trying to stay out of the searchlights, and I'm sitting here in a drugstore in Colborn having a cherry Coke. I feel like I'm letting them down, like I owe them an apology. Somehow, life over there now seems real, and this is just make-believe. I hate to say it, but in some strange way I wish I could go back and be with them again. I miss them, and I miss the flying—so bad it hurts."

Christy had no way of knowing how to respond. It seemed inconceivable to her that anyone could miss war, but she knew Gene wasn't making up the feelings, that they had to be very real to him. She sat looking at him, thinking how much he had changed in so short a time, when he suddenly changed the subject.

"You know, you basically saved my life."

"Saved your life?" His comment almost startled her, so unexpected was it, and she had no earthly idea what he was talking about. "How?"

Gene finished his drink, setting the empty glass back on the table.

"After I began to comprehend what my wounds meant—that I couldn't fly again—I began to get really bitter and resentful about it. Hate to admit it, but I still am, for that matter. I know I should feel lucky just to be alive…" He paused, interrupting himself.

"I didn't tell you in my letters. My radio operator, Jimmy Wilson, got killed on that last mission. The bastards got him on their first pass, when they got me." Gene halted, embarrassed. "Sorry about the language. It's pretty hard to not pick up some of it. Anyway, that's been pretty tough to take. I somehow feel responsible for it…" He fell silent, staring out the front windows of the store.

Christy could think of nothing to say that would help, and didn't reply. She wondered what else he hadn't told her. Gene glanced at the high school girls giggling among themselves at the front of the store. The contradiction of the scene in his mind, and the one in front of him, was too stark to reconcile. A moment later he shook it off, and turned back to Christy.

"I know I shouldn't be feeling sorry for myself," Gene confessed. "I remember somewhere in the New Testament it says to 'Count it all joy,' when bad things happen to us. I never did really understand that. I guess it meant that adversity is supposed to make us better people, make us stronger, and make our faith stronger. And, according to the Bible, we should be joyful over that. Well, sorry. I guess I'm not that strong—and I'm certainly not joyful."

He turned silent again. Christy had no comment, waiting for him. It was clear he was struggling with himself.

"Good Lord, Christy, you know how I've always felt about flying. All that kept me going some of the time over there was looking forward to the day that I would be an airline pilot. I imagined Mike and me flying for the same airline, hanging out together and sharing old war stories between flights. We'd talk about it, sometimes, between missions. Then, when I began to realize that was not going to be possible, that I had lost all that—I just sort of slid off into a black pit. Can't seem to get out of it, sorry to say."

"I understand, Gene," Christy replied. "You're being too hard on yourself. It's going to take time to heal."

Gene nodded, but didn't respond for a moment. Then a smile lit his face, as he came back to his original topic.

"Christy, I can't begin to tell you what Mattie means to me. I've never felt anything like I feel for her. But if you hadn't been writing to her—behind my back, you traitorous little two-timer—we probably wouldn't be getting married."

"What? I can't believe that." Christy looked taken aback at Gene's comment. "She's obviously head-over-heels in love with you. You're all she could talk about in her letters. What happened?"

"Oh geez, I hate to even 'fess up about it," Gene said, shaking his head, obviously chagrined at having to confess to his friend what he had let transpire. "Christy, here's the clinker. Mattie's folks are rich. I mean they're really rich. Her granddad and great-granddad were in the shipping business in Australia and apparently did extremely well. Now her dad is carrying it on. They live in this incredible estate. It looks like the ones we used to see in movies about English aristocrats. Did you see those tennis courts and swanky garden in that snapshot she sent you? That wasn't taken at the Sydney Country Club. That picture was taken in their back yard—although their backyard is probably bigger than Riverside Park. At least it's a whole lot more elegant. And frankly, I let it all get to me. I didn't know what I would be able to do if I couldn't get into the airlines, and I didn't see how on Earth I could give her anything even remotely close to the kind of life she was used to. I couldn't see dragging her half way around the world to marry a cripple. Frankly, I felt she deserved better than me. I felt like I was going to have to let her go, let her find someone who—"

At this, Christy burst in, nearly exploding.

"Oh, Gene, please, you didn't! How could you sell her so short? You're truly a certified idiot. So what happened?"

He continued his sordid tale, of the misunderstanding that had nearly led to destroying any hope of a future with Mattie. Christy listened, her face a mixture of incredulity, indignation and barely concealed laughter. He finally got to the part where Mattie confessed that she and Christy had been exchanging letters and had become good "mates," and that it was those letters that had helped Mattie understand Gene well enough to comprehend what was behind it all.

"I didn't even know you two had been writing," Gene told her, wrapping up his tale. "I wanted to be annoyed at you. But you saved my fanny, that's for sure. It helped Mattie understand me well enough to be willing to give me a second chance. If I'd blown that, and lost her…" Gene paused, turning serious. "I'm so crazy over her I can't think straight, sometimes."

With this confession laughter won out over incredulity and indignation, and Christy burst out laughing.

"Gene, when it comes to your love life you can't think straight any of the time," Christy said, trying to control her laughing. "But I'm glad I could be of service. You guys are always such morons. I don't know how we keep the human race going."

He smiled, nodding in agreement, then was silent again. Christy wondered what else was going on. Gene adjusted his leg, trying to get more comfortable in the booth, then turned more serious.

"Christy, this is all great, but I need help. I'm lost. I simply don't know how to handle all this."

She looked at him, surprised by the sudden change in the tone of his voice and the troubled look on his face. She couldn't remember ever seeing him look like this.

"Handle all of what, Gene?"

"Well, everything. Start off with the fact that one of these days I'm going to be married, with a wife—and a family, I presume, sooner or later—to support, and I've never given any serious thought to any career other than flying for the airlines. Now I can't fly, and that's shot. I don't know for sure what else I can do. I have no place to stay, here at home. I can't kick Jerry out of his room, and I'm long past sleeping with my little brother. I presume that I'll be discharged soon, so I won't have any Army income. I won't be able to afford a room, when that happens. I don't know where to get a job. Who's going to hire a cripple? I don't have a car to be able to do anything, or look for a job. And I can't drive, with this bum leg, anyway. I'd have to get someone to take me everywhere. The folks will let me use their car, of course, but gas is so hard to get with rationing, and I'm not going to use their coupons. I'd feel like an idiot having Jerry have to drive me all over everywhere. Lord-a-mighty, Christy, I feel more useless than tits on a boar hog. Then, of course, there's the whole wedding problem."

Christy could not avoid thinking of the contrast between this Gene sitting before her, feeling like his life was a train-wreck, and the Gene who such a short time ago had been so excited about his chance to get to fly the new aircraft being built for the military, believing not only that the sky was not a limit but that it was to be his home.

"Well, I do see what you mean," Christy said. "But things usually aren't as bleak as they seem, at least at first. 'It's always darkest before the dawn,' as we Kansans always say. By the way," she interrupted herself, "is that really true? I never get up that early. Anyway, let's start with your most immediate problem.

We have an unused bedroom at my folk's house. They would be insulted if you refused to use it until you can get settled. I have to work, but I can get loose to run you on some errands, if you need. Thelma Troxel is my supervisor. You remember her, from the church, don't you? She lives just down the street from us, and I know she'd let me take time off. Do you have any savings to get you started?"

"Yeah, some—enough for a little while, if I don't have to pay for a room. Once I got over there I was able to save a fair amount of my pay, but Uncle Sam doesn't pay much for the privilege of getting shot at. I'd like to continue to save as much as I can to help Mattie and me get started. And thanks for the room offer. If your folks won't mind, it would be a godsend. I'll try to get moved out as soon as I can."

"Oh, posh! You can stay as long as you like, and you know it. Don't go getting polite on me, or I'll begin to wonder what else is wrong with you. I am confused about the career problem, though. I presumed you would go back to KU and finish your engineering degree. That's certainly what your folks assume you'll do."

Gene rolled his eyes in exasperation, surprising Christy.

"Mattie and I had a heart-to-heart on that, too. I'll tell you what I told her. I enrolled in electrical engineering at KU because they offered me a scholarship in it—period. That got me into the flight school, and that's the only reason I did it. Like I told Mattie, I would have enrolled in Home Ec, if that would have got me into that flight school. It would be my worst nightmare to have to spend my life trying to design electrical do-hickeys. Mattie suggested I get a degree in aeronautical engineering so I could stay in aviation. I hadn't thought about that; it's not a bad idea, I guess. I'm going to try to find out if there is any kind of job I could get working over at Boeing so I could go to school at Wichita University part time and work on a degree…although I don't know if they actually have an aero program. I guess that would be better than running a hardware store in downtown Podunk."

"Have you said anything to your folks?" Christy asked, ignoring the touch of sarcasm in his comment.

"Are you kidding? You know me better than that."

Christy didn't respond—the tone of his voice, and the look on his face, suggested it would not be a good idea. She hadn't realized just how deeply the loss of flying had affected Gene, but was beginning to sense it. There was a tone not just of resentment and bitterness, but fear in his voice that she had never heard before. She reached over and took his hand.

"Gene, you've been through a lot—more than any one of us here at home can even imagine. It's been painful, and you've lost a lot. It's going to take some time to adjust to it all, to be able to cope with it. Give yourself some time. God has a way of working things out in our lives, if we let it happen. And don't lose sight of the fact that you gained the most important thing in your life, and that's Mattie," she said quietly.

Gene looked at her, and nodded slightly, but didn't answer. She waited a moment before getting to his last concern.

"Now—to the real issue," she said, rather pointedly. "What do you mean by, quote, the whole wedding problem, unquote. Mattie didn't mention any problems about the wedding. She's almost giddy with excitement."

"I don't mean a problem with the wedding itself. We haven't really made any plans, other than to have it here at the church," Gene replied, smiling briefly as he imagined the conversations that Mattie and her mother would have been having all this time. "The problem is everything leading up to it."

"I'm lost. What are you talking about?"

"Christy, you just don't realize how Mattie's folks live. Their limo probably cost more than Dad's farm. They're good as gold. They ought to be, I guess, they seem to own most of it." Gene interrupted himself, realizing immediately how petty the comment sounded. "I'm sorry. That wasn't called for. They're really nice people. Anyway, where are they going to stay? And where's Mattie going to stay until we're married? And when Mom finds out how rich Mattie's folks are, she'll be so nervous, and feel so awkward about everything—her house, her clothes, her furniture, everything about us. I'm afraid it'll ruin the whole thing for her. She'll be a nervous wreck. You know how Mom and Dad are about rich people. I don't want Mom feeling ashamed and embarrassed. And you know how ill-at-ease Dad is, even around the bankers here in town. Imagine how he'll feel when he knows my new dad-in-law is a multi-zillionaire? He won't know what to say, or how to act. I just don't know how to pull it all off. And I don't want anything to ruin it for Mattie. It would just kill me." He leaned his head against the back of the booth. "Lordy, why didn't someone tell me that life was going to be so complicated? All I wanted was to get to fly—and marry my red-headed Aussie."

For once, Christy was rather subdued. She was quiet for several seconds before answering him.

"I do see what you mean. It could be awkward, knowing your folks. Have you written to Mattie about it?"

"I write to her every day. But I haven't brought any of this stuff up. I really don't know what to say. It's what nearly wrecked us in the first place."

"Well, the two of you are going to have to find a way to deal with it—and fairly soon, if she's able to get over here for a wedding."

Gene nodded noncommittally. They sat there, neither talking, watching the high school kids come and go, laughing and cutting up as though there was not a problem or care in the world.

"The Kelly isn't a five-star, but it's actually a pretty nice hotel for a small town. The rooms are nice, and the restaurant's quite respectable," Christy said, picking up the subject again after a few moments of reflecting on it all. "I shouldn't think her folks would have a problem with it—I can't imagine that they would expect to stay with your folks. They've never even met."

"Yeah, I suppose," Gene concurred. "What about Mattie? Should she stay there, too?"

"I don't know why Mattie would consider it unreasonable to stay there until the wedding. I'll write to her about it, if you'd like for me to."

"That would be appreciated. But it still doesn't tell me how to keep Mom from becoming a basket case. They'll surely expect to at least visit our place."

"I know, Gene," Christy agreed, "and I'm proud of you for even thinking about it, and being that concerned about your folks. Let's just assume that both sets of parents are good enough people that we can make it work. Maybe I can talk to Liz, and she can talk to your mom. But don't worry about it, right now. You just concentrate on getting yourself healthy again. I'll help take care of the rest of it. We're just thrilled that you're back with us. Let us enjoy that, without being too concerned about everything else…at least for a little while."

He didn't answer, looking through the store windows at scenes that only his mind could see. Christy could only wonder what was going through his mind, and waited. Then, as she began to wonder if he was going to be okay, he turned back to her.

"You know, Christy, all I could think about on the train coming home, especially at night in the dark, was what I had done to Mattie."

"What on Earth do you mean?" she reacted, taken aback by this sudden turn.

"It just kept hitting me. She's put her complete faith and trust in me. She's committing the rest of her life to someone she's known only a few months, and is willing to leave a luxurious life, leave her home, leave her family and her country, and go half way around the world to be my wife. And I've allowed her to do that. It's pretty selfish, in a way. I don't know if I can live up to that. I don't know if I'm worth it."

My God, what has this war done to my friend, she wondered. "You didn't 'allow' it, Gene. That was a choice, a decision, Mattie has made for herself because she loves you. Of course you're worth it. I know it. Mattie knows it. The only one who doubts that is yourself. You've been through too much. It's going to take some time to let it all heal. Inside, as well as outside."

He didn't answer, for a moment, just nodding. "I suppose you're right. And thanks. I appreciate it."

"My pleasure. Actually, we all appreciate what you've been through for us so much that we'd do anything we can for you. But—you don't get off Scot-free. I've got a thousand questions about you and Mattie, and I insist on knowing all the mushy details. I hope you didn't have any plans for the rest of the afternoon. Want another cherry Coke?"

A few days later several of Gene's concerns were settled by default—or at least deferred—with the arrival of a letter from Mattie. He met Christy at the drugstore after receiving it, and let her read it.

Dear Gene,

I miss you terribly, and can hardly wait for the time when we will get to be together again. I hadn't received any letters from you for nearly a week, and was getting worried. Then I got four yesterday, and spent practically all night reading and re-reading them. Thank you so much for all of them. I hadn't written to you about our travel plans yet, as nothing had been settled. It now appears that Father was overly optimistic about being able to get travel arrangements for all three of us to come to the States. It just can't be done, with all the restrictions of the war, and the demands of Father's business. The good news is that he <u>has</u> finally been able to wangle a way for me to get there, but it took some doing—and you'll never believe how he did it.

Father has a friend in our government who works with the American United Service Organization. As you know, the USO sends groups of entertainers over here to entertain the troops. There is a group that has been here for several weeks, and is scheduled to return to the States in about two weeks. Father was able to get his friend to get the head of the USO group to "hire" me as an assistant. I think I am to be his "Australian coordinator." He told the USO gent about you and how much your country owes you. I guess the guy decided Father was right, as he went along with it. I will fly back with them, then be allowed to quit as soon as I get there. Maybe they'll have me play my violin as part of the entertainment!! Or have the troops already suffered enough?

He said I will be allowed to enter the U.S. on a Visitor's Visa, good for six weeks. After that, I have to return—unless I marry a U.S. citizen. Any ideas on that?

I probably won't know specific plans in time to write. I'll send a telegram just before we leave. I don't know anything at all about where we will arrive, or how to get to your home. I'm just trusting that God will see me through to you.

I didn't realize how much I love you until I couldn't have you here with me, every day. There's a new Yank in your room—a bomber crewman, I think. He's nice, but it's hard to go in with a smile on my face when I know it won't be you I see. It's been agony. But maybe we'll be together again in not too long (it will be too long, but you know what I mean).

Don't try to write—I may be gone before a letter can get here.
Give my love to Christy and your family.

I love you,
Mattie

Christy handed the letter back to Gene after she finished reading it.

"Looks as though you need to stop worrying about all the problems you thought you had, and start trying to figure out how to get her here. She'll probably come in to San Francisco. Do you think you can meet her, there?"

"Come hell or high water," Gene assured her. "I'm not going to make her have to get across the U.S. by herself, especially on a troop train jammed with hundreds of lonely GIs."

The call came early in the morning, three days later, informing Gene that there was a telegram for him from Australia. Fortunately, Christy had not yet left for work, and drove him to the train depot. He hurried to the Western Union window and was soon tearing open the yellow and black envelope.

SCHEDULED TO DEPART SYDNEY ON 12TH ARRIVE SF ON 18TH. CAN STAY AT USO HDQTRS. WILL CALL FOR TRAIN ROUTE. PLEASE REPLY ASAP TO CONFIRM RECEIPT THIS TELEGRAM. LOVE. MATTIE

Gene immediately composed a response, and waited for confirmation that it had been sent.

STAY AT USO IN SF. WILL MEET YOU THERE. CANT WAIT. LOVE. GENE

"She said she'll leave on the twelfth, and get into San Francisco on the eighteenth," Gene said to Christy as he got into her car to head back to her house. "But that's the twelfth in Australia, and they're on the other side of the international date line. I can't keep track if they're behind us, or ahead of us. I guess it doesn't matter, as long as she arrives on the eighteenth. Today's what, the eleventh? I don't think I should leave yet, in case something happens to the plans. I hate to keep her waiting, but I think I'd rather get there the day after she arrives, to make sure I can find her."

"That all sounds reasonable," Christy agreed. "I'll help you get your uniforms washed and ironed, and your bag packed. You'd better let your folks know. Wish I could go with you."

A few days later, Gene was standing on the depot platform at 6:30 AM, waiting for the train to Kansas City, where he would take the first available train to San Francisco.

Mattie Comes to Kansas

Finding Mattie, once he arrived in San Francisco, proved surprisingly easy. Gene worried during the train ride west that, for whatever reasons, he wouldn't be able to find her. He received a telegram from her confirming that she could stay at the USO until he arrived, but it was wartime and San Francisco was a big city. He had no idea where the USO headquarters was located, or what to do if he found it and she wasn't there. By the time he arrived at the San Francisco train station, he was almost sick to his stomach with apprehension. A lot could go wrong.

His train ride from Kansas City had been tiring, as the trains were always packed with military personnel on their way to new assignments, or with fuzz-faced young guys on their way to some military base to become soldiers. Sleep was difficult and sporadic, as there was no way to get comfortable in the seats and the noise of the train and its hundreds of young guys on their way to untold adventure was non-stop.

Usually, by sometime after midnight, the hypnotic rocking and clickity-clacking of the wheels on the track would lull most of the guys to a fitful sleep. Gene would slump down in the seat as best he could, and sleep as best he could. His stiff leg made it more difficult, and he had to ask at times to be permitted to have an aisle seat so he could stretch his leg into the aisle. When the guys would realize that he had already seen combat, and had been wounded, they would become very respectful, almost deferential, and would try to get him to tell them what it was like. He wondered, as he visited with them, if he had appeared as naive and wet-behind-the-ears as they all did.

But his biggest deterrent to sleeping was his constant thinking about once again getting to see Mattie, to hold her, smell her perfume, bury his face in her hair. He would frequently pull her picture out of his wallet and stare at it, almost as if he couldn't quite remember what she was like—and always, in disbelief that the girl in that picture was going to be his wife. Finally, after three impatient days and two draining nights, his train squealed to a stop at the San Francisco terminal.

Gene immediately began asking around for the USO headquarters, and after a couple of false leads his taxi pulled to a stop in front of the correct building. The cab driver carried his duffel bag to the head of the steps, wished Gene good luck, and left. Gene grasped the door handle, then hesitated, wondering if this was the moment that he would find Mattie—or would learn that he had no idea where she was or how to find her. He took a deep breath, passed a hand over his hair, and hoped he didn't look too disheveled.

He looked at his reflection in the glass door. Although he had shaved and changed to his fresh uniform in the minuscule lavatory on the train—so small he had to stand on the stool to get his unbending left leg into the pants leg—sometime during the night, dark stubble was already showing and his uniform was looking a bit rumpled. He tried to tuck his shirt in a little better. Realizing that he was stalling, and somewhat afraid of what he might learn inside, he took another deep breath, pulled open the door, and stepped inside.

The door opened into a spacious lobby area. It took a second for his eyes to adjust from the outside glare to the darker interior. Across the lobby a group of a dozen, or so, young girls were talking and laughing together. Gene presumed they were members of the staff, or perhaps some of the entertainers. They glanced briefly at him as he entered. Soldiers came and went rather continuously, as the USO was a popular place to kill time, so the girls paid little attention to him. One of the staff left the group to see if he needed help.

Gene could hardly believe his eyes. Mattie was standing across the room, visiting with the group. He was silhouetted against the light of the door, his face somewhat shadowed. She glanced at him, as the staff girl approached him, and started to turn back to the group but suddenly caught her breath, her hand to her mouth. A split-second later she let out a shriek of delight that startled everyone in the room, and stopped the staff girl in her tracks just before she reached Gene. The girl looked back to see what had happened just as Mattie flew past her.

"Gene! Oh, thank God, it's you!"

She charged past the young staff girl, nearly knocking Gene off balance as she rushed to embrace him. It took several hugs and emotional kisses, and a few wipings of tears with the palm of her hand, before she could collect herself and escort him over to introduce him to the group.

Gene quickly became the focus of considerable attention from the group of attractive young girls. Mattie had become quite the *cause célèbre* with the entertainment group and the USO staffers during their trip back to the States. They were all aware that she had been allowed to join the group as a pretense, to get to come to the States to marry her Yankee war hero. Now that the object of her pilgrimage was standing there with them, live and in-person, the group was abuzz with excitement. The girls were all talking at once:

"Oh, it's just so romantic, just like the movies."

"Yeah. Just like Romeo and Juliet."

"Edith, Romeo and Juliet both died!"

"Well, they really loved each other. I think they're like Romeo and Juliet."

"My boyfriend won't get out of the car to come to the door for me, the big galoot—and Gene comes half way across the country for Mattie."

"If you don't want him, Mattie, toss him my way."

"Oh, Mattie, I love his eyes. Don't you just love those long lashes, Aileen?"

And so on and so forth, a mile a minute, until Gene was feeling totally embarrassed and overwhelmed. At times, he felt like a picture being discussed, rather than an actual person standing in their midst. Mattie was so excited she was glowing. Gene couldn't remember seeing her so animated—even the time when they told her folks Gene had asked her to marry him.

They all insisted on a hug from Gene, and most of them gave him a congratulatory kiss. It was easy to tell the entertainers from the staff. They were far more animated and emotional, not to mention more forward. They would give Gene a big kiss, then wrap him in their arms and tease Mattie that she had just lost out—they were claiming him. Gene tried to act worldly and take it all in stride, but was mostly embarrassed.

It took some time before Mattie could get Gene introduced to each of the girls, and to thank them sufficiently for helping bring her and Gene together at last. Gene tried to remain patient and cordial, but in fact was becoming impatient. He was tired, and anxious to get away from them. He wanted Mattie to himself, and he wanted to be able to get started home. Finally, the group began to calm down, and he was able to ask about return train schedules. No one had a schedule, but a staff member made a quick phone call and learned that a train eastbound was to leave in barely over two hours. Gene had no interest in staying in San Francisco another day, so with one more quick round of thanks and hugs and tearful goodbyes for everybody, and help from two of the staff carrying Mattie's luggage, they took a taxi back to the train station.

Gene was astounded. It had been barely over four hours since he had walked out of that terminal, desperate to find Mattie and fearful that he wouldn't. Now, here they were, sitting in the bustling train station waiting for time to board and start their journey back to Kansas and their new life together.

The trip back to Colborn, with Mattie now at his side, became an adventure for them both. They were drained from the emotional let-down, now that the adrenalin of the joyful reunion was ebbing, and it was hard for them to keep from dozing off. But Mattie was still too excited about once again being with Gene, and too fascinated by the changing countryside, to be able to sleep much. As they progressed through the mountains of the Sierras and Rockies, she would stare out the windows for long periods, soaking up the scenery. Ever the geography student, Gene had purchased a United States map at the train station and kept Mattie apprised of their progress across the country.

As the train passed through more desolate areas, and during the hours of darkness, they would talk quietly, trying to reconnect emotionally and begin the process of starting a life together. It felt to them as though they had been apart forever—even though it had not yet been three months—and that they had a lifetime of visiting to catch up on.

As always, the train was packed—mostly with young guys who had no intention of ignoring the good-looking redhead in their midst, regardless of the fact that she was with a wounded combat veteran. She endured with her infectious smile and good humor the ogles, the wolf-whistles, the stares and good-natured, but loud, requests for dates, but always with one arm linked tightly around Gene's. As nighttime came, and the car became more subdued, Gene would put his arm around her, and Mattie would attempt to nestle down beside him, her head resting on his chest. Her hair would brush lightly against his face, and remind him of how intoxicating it had felt to him the day he had regained consciousness after surgery in the Sydney hospital.

Sometimes the young soldier sitting next to her would excuse himself, and let her have his seat so she could have more room. It was not uncommon for some of the guys to stretch out on the aisle, so they could sleep better. It had always amazed her that the young Yankee soldiers could be so brazenly forward with the girls in Australia, and yet so unfailingly polite. She would thank him, and then use the extra space to curl up on the seat, legs drawn up against her. Gene would pull her more tightly to his side, and she would try to nestle even closer to him. He would try to sleep, but usually his mind was too full, his emotions too stretched, for sleep to be possible. So he would doze, fitfully at best, and marvel at the seemingly random events that had somehow conspired to bring this God-given gift to his side.

Dawn of the last day saw them past the wheat fields of western Kansas, and nearing their destination of Kansas City. It was just sufficiently daylight as they passed through Lawrence that Mattie was able to get a brief glimpse of the Kansas University campus and airport where Gene's entry into his short-lived career of flying had been launched. Gene had become somewhat withdrawn after they passed through, staring silently out the train window and reverting to answering her questions with his old taciturn responses, making Mattie's silent concerns about him reassert themselves. It took awhile, and several questions about the countryside, before he seemed to open up again.

After getting off the train at Kansas City, they learned that there would be a wait of nearly three hours for the train to Colborn. Gene introduced Mattie to the delights of a soda fountain at a drugstore near the Kansas City Union Station, which managed to kill most of an hour. Then they went back and stretched out on a long bench, trying to rest, but the constant hubbub of the busy terminal, and loud announcements of arriving and departing trains, made sleep a lost cause. They were also worried they would miss their train, and kept looking at the clock. Nevertheless, they felt better after being able to rest their eyes, and to stretch out for a while.

Finally, after what was beginning to seem like an eternity, they found themselves on the final leg to Gene's home. As the train approached Colborn, Mattie went to the tiny lavatory to change into a fresh dress, and attempt to restore her make-up and get her hair looking presentable. She wanted to make a good impression on his family, and to Gene's surprise she was becoming visibly nervous about meeting them. As they approached his hometown and came to a stop alongside the small depot, he tried to assure her once again that she was beautiful and that his family would love her. He was reminded of the first time that he had visited her home and met her parents—and how nervous he was.

Mattie's odyssey was coming to an end. She had island-hopped across the Pacific Ocean during a global war, with people she had never before met, had crossed the vast western half of the United States, and was now arriving at a small town in the middle of a country she had known only from her geography class in school, and the many movies she watched. She had traveled nearly ten thousand miles—almost half way around the globe. In two more months, she would turn twenty years old, no longer a teenager.

As the train came to a halt, Mattie was reminded of the Bible verse she quoted to Gene that fateful day when they had reconciled in the hospital gardens. She again gave a silent prayer of thanks to Ruth and Naomi...*whither thou goest, I will go. Your people shall be my people*...she gave thanks for the comfort that verse gave her, and for its helping Gene to understand the depth of her commitment to him. And then, it was time to step down onto the small stool and out onto the depot platform, to see her new home and to meet her new people.

As usual, it was Christy who saw her first, recognizing her immediately. She ran to meet them, followed closely by Liz and Jerry. Their parents realized they could not all fit in the car and opted to stay home, letting the "young folks" go to meet them. Gene stood close by as Liz, Christy and Jerry each introduced themselves. He smiled at the excitement, and thought about how similar the scene was to his own homecoming. He was always amazed at how open and friendly Mattie was when meeting people, compared to his own reticence. She smiled, and hugged each one, and visited with them as though she had known them all her life, and they seemed to glow in her presence.

After all the usual questions about how the train ride had gone, and whether he had experienced any problems finding Mattie, Jerry took the initiative of gathering up the luggage and they loaded into the car for the brief trip to the farm. For a fleeting moment, Gene wondered again how Mattie might feel about the old car, after being accustomed to riding in a limousine. But Mattie gave no appearance of even noticing the car as she slid into the rear seat between Liz and Christy, and the concern was just as quickly gone.

The two girls, and Jerry, kept a running commentary on all that they passed, keeping Mattie constantly looking from side to side, exclaiming over each new sight in her new world. Liz had always been the most extroverted of the three Stoddard siblings, but Gene was only beginning to be aware of just how mature a young lady she had become in his absence. She visited easily and excitedly with Mattie, almost like sisters coming together for a family reunion.

Bill and Mary had been watching for the car to appear over the last hill as it approached the house, and were coming out the back door to greet them as the car pulled to a stop in the driveway. As they got out of the car, Gene noted that they had both put on their Sunday clothes—Bill had a tie on, but not the suit jacket. They stood side by side, both smiling nervously, as the group got out of the car. Gene took Mattie's arm, and escorted her over to meet his parents.

"Mom, Dad—I want you to meet your future daughter-in-law, Mattie O'Sullivan. Mattie—meet Mom and Dad."

Mattie immediately gave them both a big hug, startling them both, although they were both obviously pleased.

"I know it's not official yet," Mattie said as she stepped back from giving them their hugs, "but may I call you Mom and Dad? It's all I've heard from Gene, and it just sounds so natural."

"Why, of course," Mary immediately responded. "We'd love that, wouldn't we, Bill?"

"Well, you know what us farmers always say: You can call me anything you want, as long as you call me for dinner."

Bill grinned sheepishly at his brave efforts at light-hearted banter, as the others groaned and rolled their eyeballs, with a collective "Oh, Dad..."

"Isn't that interesting," Mattie exclaimed, smiling at Bill. "My father uses that same expression sometimes. It must be universal among you men folk."

"Well, we all like to eat, that's for sure," Bill agreed, pleased that his little contribution to the chit-chat was appreciated.

They visited for a few more minutes on the back patio, then proceeded into the house.

"You've already achieved a place of prominence in the Stoddard household," Christy said to Mattie, pointing out Mattie's picture on the china cabinet, stationed prominently beside Gene's Air Force picture. "Of course, Gene didn't even notice it when he first got home," she teased, grinning at Gene.

"Come on, give me a break," Gene protested over their laughter. "Everybody was yakking at me a mile a minute."

"Well, that's just like a guy," Mattie agreed, playing along.

"Come here a minute. I want to show you something," Gene said, changing the subject. He took Mattie by the hand, leading her into his old bedroom.

"There's the pride and joy of my youth," Gene said, pointing to all the model planes hanging from the ceiling.

"Gene, they're beautiful. You made all these?"

"Yeah. Labor of love, I guess. That one was always my favorite," he said, pointing to the largest model, a four-engine bomber painted in olive drab. Tiny tooth-pick machine guns bristled from all sides. "It's a B-17, like *Ad Astra*. Ironic, isn't it. Never imagined I'd ever fly one."

He told her about several others, then pointed to the large world map hanging on the bedroom wall.

"Seems kinda strange, somehow. Sis and Jerry and I killed a lot of rainy afternoons, finding places on that map. It's hard to comprehend that all that time, my future wife was growing up, waiting for me, in one of those faraway countries. All I ever thought about was those planes hanging from the ceiling, and of getting to fly. I never gave any serious thought to those places on the map—they were just curiosity items. Now, the planes are out of my life and I find the love of my life on the big pink island," he said, smiling as he gave her a brief hug.

Will he ever be able to accept losing those planes? Or will he somehow come to feel that finding me isn't sufficient compensation for the loss? Mattie wondered, as she hugged him back. But the moment quickly passed, and they returned to the living room as the others were sitting down for an early supper. Mary had fixed it ahead of time, and wanted to have it out of the way before chore time so she could have dishes finished when the guys were done.

During the meal Liz and Christy carried most of the conversation. They were all dying of curiosity about Mattie's trip all the way across the Pacific Ocean from Australia, and about the USO group, and on, and on. Jerry wanted to join in, to feel a part of the older members of the group, but still felt the awkward intimidation of being the "little kid." Bill and Mary sat listening, enjoying the easy banter and excitement of the youth.

After the meal, Gene suggested that Mattie stay and visit with the "girls," and he went down to visit with his dad and Jerry while they did the chores. He was unable to sit on a milk stool, and had no interest in doing so anyway, so sat in an old lawn chair that Jerry had earlier carried to the barn for him.

"Well, Dad, what do you think of my Aussie redhead?"

"Mankind, Gene," Jerry interrupted emphatically, before Bill could attempt to answer, "she's really good-looking! She's even prettier than her picture. I hope I'm as lucky, when I find a girl."

Gene smiled, and looked at his brother sitting beside the cow, with a bucket filling with milk gripped between his legs, and realized that he had become a good-looking young man and was no longer his "little" brother. That realization made Gene feel as though he had been away a lifetime.

"Don't worry—a handsome guy like you will have to beat the girls off with a stick," Gene assured him. "Besides, from what I overhear from the girls at the drugstore, you're already being noticed quite a bit."

Jerry looked at Gene, surprised at this unexpected comment, but was cut off from any reaction by their father responding to Gene's question.

"Well, she certainly is nice looking," Bill agreed. "She seems awfully friendly, and nice too. Seems like she had a good upbringing. Must have good parents. She's kinda hard to understand, though, with that accent. That'll take a little getting used to."

Gene was anxious to get to be alone with Mattie. So after the chores were finished, and they had all visited a while longer, he suggested that it was time to take Mattie into town and get her checked into the hotel. "She's exhausted from the trip," he told them—although she hadn't shown the slightest hint of being tired. And of course, they were very solicitous of her and quickly agreed that "she needs her rest."

Jerry volunteered to drop them off at the hotel, and take Christy home. After getting Mattie registered—the hotel clerk was most impressed to have a guest all the way from Australia—and settled in her room, Gene took her walking around the town square.

When the town of Colborn had first been laid out, a large town square was planned at its center. It was two long blocks on each side, with wide streets designed to permit a six-horse team and wagon to easily turn around. In the large, tree-filled center was a Gothic-style county courthouse, with four-sided clock tower.

The park gave the small town a spacious, comfortable appearance. A covered bandstand had been built on one corner of the park, and the municipal band gave concerts, usually featuring John Philip Sousa marches and other patriotic music, one night each week during the summer months. Grown-ups would often walk the streets, window-shopping, or just sit in their cars and make fun of the people passing by, while their children played on the courthouse lawn. Teenagers liked to hang out at the small restaurant on the square, or at the soda fountains of the two drug stores. All in all, the square was a popular social center for the town.

"Gene, I love this square, and its broad streets," Mattie said, as they strolled the sidewalk. "The courthouse park reminds me a little of the gardens behind the Sydney hospital—no offense, but it makes me a little homesick."

Gene had to remind himself that Mattie was now ten thousand miles from her home, and any possibility of her getting to return, or to see her parents, before the war ended was nonexistent. They walked slowly along, visiting and getting used to the fact that they were now going to be together all the time, no longer separated by half a world. Mattie was full of reactions to the day, and wanted to share it all.

"Gene, your folks are just marvelous. I love your mother. She's so pleasant and personable. She obviously adores the three of you. And Liz is so sweet—and pretty, too. Where do you Stoddards get all your good looks? I like talking to her. She seems so level-headed. Is that a Stoddard trait? Or are all you farm folk like that?"

Gene smiled, and let her ramble. He loved listening to her talk. She was so full of life and emotion, so unlike himself. They stopped a couple of minutes to look at some clothes in a window display, as she had been required to pack quite sparsely and would have to replenish her wardrobe. She was as pleasantly surprised at the number of women's clothing stores and the quality and selection of apparel, as she was at Gene's taste in the dresses. In a few minutes, they continued walking, and she picked up where she had left off as easily as if there had been no pause.

"Jerry is such a friendly and handsome young man. He really admires you, you know. Do you notice how he hangs on every word you say. It's obvious he wants his big brother to notice him. I hope you remember to do that."

"Yeah, I know," Gene agreed. "I try to spend as much time with him as I can. But he's pretty busy with his own stuff, so we don't see each other that much. Of course, until you can get a driver's license, and we can get a car, we may be seeing quite a lot of him. He'll have to take us pretty much wherever we go, unless Christy can. He seemed so much younger than me when we were in school. I really didn't feel very close to him. I need to try to change that, I guess."

"When you're young, three or four years difference in age can seem like a lifetime, but as you get older it doesn't amount to much," Mattie agreed. "He's obviously maturing. How old is he, now? Do you suppose he'll get drafted?"

"Good grief. I hadn't even thought about that. He'll be seventeen next birthday. If this war keeps going, he'll get drafted in a year, or two. I'm not sure Mom could handle both of us going."

Mattie wanted to change the subject. Worrying about one soldier was enough for her, at this particular moment.

"Your dad is quite the gentleman, isn't he? I see where you get your manners. I like the way he treats your mother, and respects her. It makes me think I've made a good choice for a husband," she commented, giving Gene's arm a squeeze for emphasis.

"Thank you, ma'am. You're most kind."

"Of course, I feel like I already knew Christy, but it was good to finally get to meet her. Like you said, she's a firecracker. She had me laughing all the time—mostly at your expense, I'm afraid."

"Yeah? Well, that's my best friend, for you. I'll never have to worry about an inflated ego, as long as she's around."

Gene smiled, and put his arm around Mattie's waist, pulling her over against him as they walked. She looked at the various stores, remarking at times at how nice the window displays were. She was sure she would love Colborn, she assured him. After a couple of blocks, the conversation lagged, and Gene took the opportunity to say what had been uppermost on his mind all evening.

"My God, I missed you, Mattie—so much it hurt, sometimes. There was practically nothing I could do here, while I was waiting, and I was bored out of my mind. I feel so out of place here, now. The high school kids seem like grade school kids, and there wasn't much I could do on the farm. Dad was always afraid I'd hurt my leg if I tried to help with anything. And I always feel like he thinks that if I hadn't gone into flying it wouldn't have happened. I guess he didn't read about the jungle fighting on Guadalcanal."

She had hoped the feeling might be fading, but the resentment in Gene's voice was still as obvious to Mattie as it had been when he had talked with her during their walks at the Sydney hospital. She didn't respond, and Gene continued.

"I'd go have a Coke with Christy, sometimes, but she's working at the old dress factory. They're making field jackets, I guess. Anyway, I sometimes thought I was going to go nuts, waiting to hear that you were on your way. When I got your telegram, I wanted to leave the next morning. "

Mattie nodded, and laid her head over on his shoulder as they walked, both hands clasped tightly around his arm.

"I know. I cried myself to sleep more nights than I care to remember. But I'm here, now. We can't ever let ourselves be separated like that again, Gene. I couldn't bear it."

"That won't happen, if I have any control over it," he assured her. "By the way, I did do some checking into jobs and colleges. Turns out, Wichita University does have a pretty good aeronautical engineering program. They're supporting a lot of the new design going on over at Boeing. And the Boeing plant is just exploding with growth, with all the war manufacturing. I've written to both Boeing and Wichita State about getting on out there. Boeing's hiring just about anybody that can walk in the front door unassisted, I hear, so maybe I have a chance." He paused a moment. "By the way—in case you hadn't noticed—I am, in fact, walking unassisted."

Mattie stopped in her tracks, pulled away and looked at Gene, completely taken aback.

"Oh good heavens, Gene, you're right! I've been so distracted I hadn't even noticed—even on the train. I had completely forgotten that you were still on crutches when you left." She clasped both hands to her face. "I'm so embarrassed. I feel awful. When did you get to—?"

Gene laughed, and took her hand to pull her back to him. He put his arm around her and they began to walk again. Now that it had been brought to her attention, she was more aware of his limp, as they walked together, but was delighted at how well he was doing.

"I just got fed up with everybody treating me like I was some helpless cripple all the time," he explained. "Plus, those crutches are a royal pain in the you-know-what. So just before I got your telegram, I told Jerry to throw the blankety-blank things on a pile of brush he was burning. He was kind of scared to, but I insisted. Have to admit, though, it got a little dicey a few times, at first. I fell down a couple of times, but I'm getting better. At least I don't fall down now."

"Gene, that's marvelous. You're doing so well that I truly didn't even notice. And to think, I was your therapist. I'm so embarrassed for not noticing, or saying anything—but I'm thrilled for you. And you really think you might be able to get into the engineering school and at Boeing?"

Gene nodded, but didn't immediately respond. They walked on for several minutes. Mattie looked at the various store window displays, assuming that Gene wasn't ready to talk about it, yet.

"Well, to tell the truth," Gene finally broke the silence, "I haven't completely leveled with you, Mattie. I wanted to wait until we got here, and had a chance for things to settle down a little bit, before I told you."

"Oh? And what haven't you told me? What have you been keeping from me, Mr. Stoddard?" Mattie couldn't quite tell if he was teasing her, or was serious.

"Well, what I haven't told anybody, yet, is that I got a letter from the Army a couple of weeks ago. You remember the guy who came down to interview me that time about the mission? Well, the letter said that it's all been approved, all the way up the chain of command. I guess I'm going to receive the Medal of Honor. I'm to go to Washington, D.C., for the presentation. They haven't told me when, yet, but I suspect it will be fairly soon."

He paused, hesitating, looking down, obviously troubled. Mattie looked at him, wondering why, and started to respond but he interrupted her.

"It doesn't seem right, somehow." Gene's voice was quieter, and caught a little.

"What's the problem, Gene? What do you mean?" Mattie asked, wondering what had so suddenly changed him. He had to swallow hard a couple of times before he could continue.

"Well, for one thing, the whole crew deserves it as much as I do—more, really. I hope they weren't left out. But what bothers me the most is that Jimmy Wilson got killed...and I get a medal?"

"Oh. I see what you mean. You never talked much about him. Were you pretty close?" Mattie asked.

"No, not really—I didn't know him very well. He was just one of those guys that's easy to like. And I always felt better when he was part of the crew. I could trust him, and depend on him." He paused a moment, staring into another time, then glanced back at Mattie. "Problem is, I always believed that an aircraft commander is responsible for the safety of his crew...it's been hard not feeling responsible for him getting killed."

Before Mattie could react, or try to assure Gene that Jimmy's death was not his fault, Gene shook it off and continued with his earlier conversation.

"Well, anyway, it turns out that the guy at Boeing who got my application letter checked my Army records, and somehow found out about the medal. And apparently the Army now wants me to be part of a campaign to go around the country and help bolster morale at the various aircraft plants, and to sell War Bonds. I don't feel very good about doing that, but I suppose I should.

Nevertheless, the Boeing guy was impressed. At least I know I'll get hired. And, he called the head of the engineering department at Wichita University. I've already been accepted in the aero engineering department. I can start whenever I want."

Mattie was, for the first time that Gene could recall, totally at a loss for words. She stopped, looked at him for a moment, then wrapped both arms tightly around him. He could feel her trying to control herself and keep from crying from the months of emotional stress that they had both endured to reach this point—from her first awareness at the hospital of her feelings toward him, their falling in love, the painful days of therapy they had struggled through together, the despair of the two days when she thought she had lost him, the joyful reconciliation and then, finally, the long separation.

Through it all—the long flights to San Francisco, their train ride home and her nervousness about meeting his family—she had never been able to get a clear indication of how his loss of flying was going to affect him, and what he would decide to do once he was back home. It had not come up during their days and nights together on the train, but it was obvious from the comments that he made occasionally that the resentment was still very real. She had no idea how he would deal with it, or if he could.

And now, this news was just too overwhelming. The dam that had been holding her emotions in check during it all finally gave way. Gene held her to him, and let her cry it out, until she could finally collect herself. He kissed her, and brushed her hair back, as she attempted to compose herself.

"I'm sorry," he joked, "I thought it was good news."

"Oh, Gene," she sniffed into his handkerchief. "I'm so relieved, and so happy for you, and for us, I don't know how to control myself. And when I can't control my emotions, you know me—I just cry like a baby," she confessed, trying to smile.

Gene continued to hold her as she got her emotions back under control. But the ramifications of what he had told her suddenly registered.

"But, Gene, if you go on that campaign—won't that mean you'll have to be traveling a lot, without me? I don't know if I'm up to being separated, again."

"We're going to be married, Mattie. We're a package deal. If they want me, they have to take us both. Either we travel together, or I don't go," Gene replied quietly.

"I do like the sound of that," Mattie agreed, There was a reassuring firmness, an assertiveness, in his voice that she hadn't noticed before. She looked up at him, then gave him a little kiss. "And by the way, speaking of being married— shouldn't we begin thinking about a wedding?"

Medal of Honor

It all happened so fast, there was little time for contemplation or perspective. Gene received a telegram instructing him to appear in Washington, D.C., for the purpose of receiving the Congressional Medal of Honor, just two weeks from the day Mattie arrived in Colborn. They had been considering dates for a wedding, but had not expected to have to depart quite so quickly. It was too fortuitous an opportunity to miss, however, and put a new urgency on the planning. They wanted the trip to be their honeymoon.

Gene's immediate request for an extension bought him two weeks, which helped, but still left them just three weeks to plan—and have—a wedding. For Gene, it reminded him of when he was flying on a combat mission, under heavy attack. Everything happened so fast that it all blurred together and yet, at the moment, seemed to be happening in slow motion. He made the mistake—just once—of using the simile with Christy present. He was quickly disabused of the comparison.

Liz and Christy took the reins on planning the wedding and the three girls had become virtual sisters, as well as best friends. Gene marveled at how well they worked together on all the endless details that seemed required to pull off a wedding. At times, it appeared there simply wasn't enough time to get it all done. The shower at the church, invitations, thank you notes, the selection, purchase and fitting of a wedding dress—requiring an all-day trip to Kansas City, with a 6:30 AM departure on the train and a late-night arrival home—arranging for a photographer, flowers, the music…the list seemed to Gene to never diminish in length, regardless of how many items were crossed off.

But finally, the day arrived. Gene waited in the small room at the side of the sanctuary of the church, feeling more nervous by the minute as the time approached. At long last, the minister pulled the curtain aside, and led him out to the altar at the front of the church that had been so much a part of his life. Standing there, waiting for the ceremony to begin, Gene glanced around at the sanctuary and all the good folk who seemed permanent attachments to the pews. With every glance, every passive face, a scene played through his mind from a life that now felt as imaginary as if he had read it in a novel.

Gene had learned that his good friend, Larry Hoskins, was in the infantry and stationed at Fort Riley for special training. The two of them had been close companions in high school, and had played football together for three seasons. Fort Riley was near Kansas State, only a three-hour drive away. Larry managed to wangle a weekend leave, and quickly agreed to be Gene's best man.

Larry was now coming down the aisle with Christy, Mattie's maid of honor, on his arm. The three of them were frequently together in high school, and had been party to many pranks. They often referred to themselves as the "Three Musky Tears"—high school humor being what it was, they considered that to be quite funny.

Gene had asked his brother, Jerry, to be his groomsman. He was next, coming down the aisle with their sister, Liz, beaming proudly on his arm. Jerry looked surprisingly grown-up and handsome, in his first new suit. Gene still couldn't get over how his little brother had become such a fine looking young man, while he was overseas. Liz had graduated from high school in the spring, and now appeared quite grown up. He had never paid much attention to his little sister; she just seemed like one of the little kids that were always a part of the extended Stoddard clan. That the little gosling would develop into such a swan was not a possibility he ever considered. He couldn't have been more proud of his brother and sister, than at that moment.

And then Mattie was next.

She nearly took his breath away, as she came down the aisle on the arm of his dad. Mattie had graciously asked Bill to substitute for her own father to give her away. She was radiant, as only a bride coming down the aisle can be, her auburn hair set against the white of a small head-band veil. Gene had hinted—though he knew it was ultimately not his decision—that he was not a fan of garishly lavish wedding gowns with their trains that seemed to stretch into the next time zone.

Mattie was of the same mind, and opted against the traditional, formal wedding gown, choosing instead a simple, but sophisticated white satin ballroom-length gown with full skirt, scalloped neck and wrist-length tapered sleeves. Gene noticed several of the ladies present nudge their husbands and whisper to them—the husbands nodding in obvious agreement. Mattie was causing quite the stir among the members of Gene's church, and seemed to glow with happiness.

At one point, as the minister was giving the wedding sermon, Gene was momentarily disturbed to see that she had tears in the corner of her eyes. She noticed him looking at her, as she blinked them away.

"I miss Mother and Father," she silently mouthed to him. He nodded slightly, and squeezed her hand.

The ceremony, like the days preceding it, seemed to take place in slow motion, and yet to be over in moments. Afterwards, there were the requisite photographs, the reception line, the good wishes from the wives of those in attendance, and the awkward attempts at jokes from the men.

During the reception, after the mandatory cutting of the cake and feeding each other a bite, and more pictures, Gene and Mattie mingled with the people who had attended. Gene introduced her to the many farm neighbors and members of the church, who had known him literally since his birth. They were all captivated with this striking "foreign" girl that Gene had brought home from the war to be his bride.

They were all self-conscious in asking Gene about "his health," and hoped he was doing all right. Gene had pleaded various excuses to avoid going to church since he had returned but had, in fact, not wanted to be the focus of attention that he knew he would be when he did show up. Thus, when he had entered the sanctuary at the beginning of the service, he heard several of the ladies gasp as he limped his way to the altar. Of course, the women were unfailingly polite, and said nothing to Gene about his appearance, but also unfailingly teased Mattie about needing to feed him right and "get some meat back on those bones."

He marveled at how quickly Mattie could brighten the faces of the women, as they would visit and get acquainted. The men would smile awkwardly, shifting from foot to foot, running a hand through their hair, obviously ill-at-ease in the presence of such an attractive and effervescent young girl. Mattie would tease them a bit about being so handsomely dressed for her wedding, and they would blush. Gene wondered again how he could be so blessed to have found this girl who was so perfect for him, half a world away from this church. He would occasionally put an arm around her, and hug her to him. She would look up at him and smile, then return to her conversations.

As Gene listened to her chatting with the various ladies of the church, he could just imagine how some of the conversations with his parents would go, over the coming weeks:

Woman: "My, my, Mary, she's such a pretty young thing. But her foreign accent is sorta hard to understand."

Mary: "Helen, it's not a foreign accent. She's from Australia. They speak English."

Woman: "Oh, I know, I know, but it's just so different—it's pretty, though. I like to hear her talk. And she sure is sweet. Of course, I always thought Gene would wind up marrying the Beckstrom girl, they seemed to like each other so much. But I guess she was going with the Robert's boy, until he got drafted. Never did see what she saw in him. Strange how Gene would find someone from clear over there, and not a local girl. You say she was his nurse?"

Man: "If I have to go to the hospital, can I have her for my nurse?"

Woman: "Oh, Jake, just you hush. You'd probably get some old cow, just like me—would serve you right."

Gene and Mattie were scheduled to leave the next afternoon for Washington, D.C., so spent their wedding night in her hotel room. The desk clerk had all the staff circle around and applaud them as they registered as "Captain and Mrs. Gene Stoddard." They found a nice bouquet of flowers in their room when they entered.

Having now been married all of four days, Captain and Mrs. Stoddard found themselves sitting in a small waiting room outside a huge office in the recently constructed Pentagon, the new office building for the United States War Department. It had been an astonishing construction project, completed in only sixteen months, and had been dedicated just the previous year. It was the largest office building in the city—and certainly the largest Gene and Mattie had ever seen. The letter that directed Gene to appear for the medal ceremony, and with travel instructions, had only instructed Gene to go to the civilian visitors entrance, and included an office number to report to.

It took some time to locate the civilian entrance, and to be granted authorization to enter. Wartime security restrictions were extreme, and an armed escort—a corporal in the Military Police, wearing a uniform with pants creased to a knife edge, bloused over boots that could have been used for a mirror, a polished chrome helmet and Colt .45 pistol hanging from a web-belt—took them to the specified office. A matronly secretary, whose desk name-block identified her as Mrs. Brownlee, greeted them. She was friendly, but very professional and business-like. After greeting them, she informed them that General Arnold would be available shortly.

It took a moment for what she had just told them to register with Gene. The medal ceremony was to be in the office of General "Hap" Arnold, the Commanding Officer of the Army Air Forces, the one who had sent their beloved General Kenney to take command of the 5th Air Force. Gene's squadron was, as were all others in the Southwest Pacific, under the command of General Kenney. He had turned a defeated, demoralized and ineffective group of airmen into an enthusiastic fighting force that was playing a major role in steadily driving the Japanese forces back from whence they had come. The men loved their general—and loved General Arnold for sending him to them. Gene was more awestruck than if President Roosevelt were to have made the award.

Mrs. Brownlee showed them into an adjacent waiting room, and assured them that General Arnold would be with them momentarily. They sat, neither speaking, on plain, padded chairs, not unlike the ones in his parents' dining room, Gene noted. It was obvious that General Arnold was not inclined to keeping people waiting and had made only modest provision for them to do so. Gene passed the time looking at pictures of various aircraft hanging on the walls, pointing out to Mattie the ones he had flown.

Only a few minutes passed, when there was a bustling of activity outside the room. A few moments later, the door opened and Mrs. Brownlee asked them to follow her into General Arnold's office. It was large, paneled and well-appointed, but not as luxurious as one might have expected. A world map, and a large-scale map of the Australia-Southwest Pacific theater with all sorts of pins and markers stuck in it, covered one of the walls.

Gene noticed as he passed the map that several of the pins were in spots where he and his buddies had conducted bombing raids. He noted, with a sense of irony, that a pin that appeared to indicate an enemy fighter base was stuck in a small island near the site of his last reconnaissance mission. It was that enemy fighter base that had caused him and Mattie to be in General Arnold's office at that moment.

General Arnold was standing in front of his desk, flanked by his aide, a Major Davis according to his insignia and name tag. Gene was stunned to see a reporter and photographer from the *Washington Post* newspaper, and a gentleman introduced to Gene as one of the two senators from Kansas. Gene had no idea there would be anyone other than him and Mattie, and was rather disconcerted by the attention.

The general asked them to all be seated. An Army photographer, a private barely out of boot camp from the look of him, stood nearby, camera at the ready. General Arnold walked over to Gene and smiled as Gene stood to shake hands.

"Captain Stoddard, I'm told you took on another challenging mission a few days ago. Would you like to introduce me to your charming bride?" Major Davis had obviously thoroughly briefed his General.

Mattie extended her hand to the general, as Gene introduced her.

"Sir, I'd like for you to meet Mattie—Mrs. Gene Stoddard, as I prefer to think of her now."

"Captain Stoddard," General Arnold replied, still holding Mattie's hand, "I regret every casualty, mourn every loss, we suffer in this war. But I must say, you seem to have been compensated for your injuries rather well. Congratulations to both of you. And Mrs. Stoddard, I understand you are at least partly responsible for Captain Stoddard's recovery. America is grateful to you, and to our fine ally, Australia. We welcome you to America."

"Thank you, sir. I'm obviously thrilled to be here," Mattie said, smiling at him.

The Army photographer, and the *Post* photographer, had been dutifully recording the exchange and the faint odor of burnt flash bulbs soon drifted over the room.

The general then walked to the front of the room, taking a position in front of his desk, facing the group. He paused for a moment, to let the mood shift to one more appropriate for the occasion, then began the ceremony.

"I want to first thank you all for being here this morning," he began. "It seems like only yesterday that I called General George Kenney into this office, to assign him to take command of the Fifth Air Force in the Southwest Pacific. We were woefully unprepared, at that time, to fight an overwhelming enemy.

I told General Kenney to go down there and turn that group of brave young men into a fighting force that could not be defeated. He is doing that, above and beyond my expectations, or even my wildest dreams. But that would never have been possible if it had not been for those like Captain Stoddard, here, and all the other young men like him down there, who are literally willing to risk, and to sacrifice, their lives so that the rest of us will be able to live in freedom from the tyranny of an enemy who would destroy us and our country. This country owes you, Captain Stoddard, and all those who share that sacrifice with you, a debt that can never be repaid. But what we acknowledge here, today, is that Captain Stoddard, on his last mission, courageously went above and beyond the call of duty in the defense of his country. Captain Stoddard will suffer from injuries received on that mission for the rest of his life. The Congressional Medal of Honor is the highest military honor bestowed by this country. It is small recompense for the sacrifice made by Captain Stoddard, but a token nevertheless of the gratitude of a country that loves and honors him, and appreciates what was done by him, and his crew, on its behalf. Therefore, on behalf of a grateful nation, and as authorized by the Congress and President of the United States, it is my privilege to present this medal. Captain Stoddard, would you please come forward and receive your medal."

There were the mandatory photographs of General Arnold placing the medal—with its inverted five-point star hanging from a wide, blue star-spangled ribbon—around Gene's neck, like an ornate necklace. General Arnold straightened it, making sure it was hanging properly, and then stepped back and saluted him. Gene returned the salute in proper military fashion.

Then the Kansas senator congratulated Gene, and had a picture taken with himself, General Arnold, and Gene and Mattie for the newspapers back home.

After a few minutes of small talk, Major Davis politely, but efficiently— "General Arnold has a lot on his schedule today, as I'm sure you can appreciate"— escorted them all out of the office. The senator congratulated Gene and Mattie again, and invited them to visit his office. One of his staff would be happy to give them a guided tour of the Capitol building, if they would care to do so. And of course, they happily accepted the offer, and scheduled a time to do so.

The *Post* reporter asked Gene—and his pretty new bride, of course—to stop by the *Post* for an interview, if he would be willing to grant it. Gene reluctantly accepted, not feeling at all comfortable with the acclaim that was beginning to come his way.

The MP was standing by to escort the two of them out of the building. As they were about to leave, Major Davis asked to speak to Captain Stoddard— "and Mrs. Stoddard, of course"—in his office. They looked a bit surprised, but followed the major into an adjoining office. He ushered them to chairs facing his desk, but remained standing, facing them.

"Captain Stoddard, I'll get right to the point. I understand that you and Mrs. Stoddard are on your honeymoon—congratulations, by the way—so I won't delay you. As you are aware, Captain, you have been requested"—he was tactful enough to not say "ordered"—"to give talks to several of our aircraft production facilities as part of our home-front morale and War Bond campaigns. I wanted to see if you have any questions about the importance of this effort."

His message, politely couched though it may have been, was clear enough: he was asking Gene if he understood that this was an order, and not a simple request. He paused, awaiting a response. It took Gene a moment to collect his thoughts—a pause which momentarily caused a look of concern to cross the major's face. Finally, Gene stood to answer him.

"Sir, I understand the importance of the talks. I'm just uncomfortable with doing them myself. Frankly, with all respect, sir, I would prefer to not be required to do them."

The major hesitated a moment. He hadn't expected Gene's response.

"Would you mind explaining your reluctance, Captain, given that you understand the importance of the talks?"

It was obvious the major was not accustomed to being diplomatic with subordinates. He was far more accustomed to giving orders—in the name of General Arnold, if need be—and of having them followed without question. The young man standing before him was still a captain in the U.S. Army Air Forces, and was expected to obey orders without hesitation. But, this young captain had also just been awarded the CMOH by the major's commanding officer—and that fact could not be glossed over.

"Sir, with all due respect, I just don't feel right about it. Every member of my crew faced the same risks that I did, every time we flew a mission. Jimmy Wilson, my radio operator, was killed on my last mission. Every guy I know over there faces death every time he takes off, just as much as I did. They've gone through everything I did, and are still over there having to do it. I don't feel I deserve this medal any more than any one of them does, and in fact, not as much as I believe some of my crew deserve it. I feel very awkward showing up in public, getting the recognition and acclaim that I know will come from it, when those guys are still over there doing the job. I feel like I've let them down, and I'm getting all the glory. In fact, sir, it's sort of embarrassing. I'd prefer to be relieved from the assignment, sir."

The major nodded, and folded his arms across his chest, studying the young captain. He hadn't expected this response. Frankly, he thought Captain Stoddard was sandbagging him, to get to spend more time with his hot young wife. He hesitated, before responding.

"Gene—excuse me if I make this personal, but it's obviously a personal thing for you—I respect your position, and honor you for it. But you have to face the reality of war. Every man that puts on the uniform today will be expected to accept those risks. Many have already died, and many more will, before it's over. Every one of them deserves the Medal of Honor just for doing their duty. But only a select few will receive it, deserved or not. And you have received it. And whether you realize it, or not, they all respect you for it and understand the situation. But if we are to win this war, they need planes, and lots of them, to take the war to the enemy, to defeat him. And to get those planes we need the people who build them to do their jobs, just as much as we need the men who will fly them. And those people will get no medals. They put in long hours, and are dedicated, loyal citizens. Their only reward is to get to see someone like you, who has put his life on the line in a plane that they built, and to be told how important their job was—and is. I could go tell them that—but it wouldn't mean anything. You are the one they want to see, and hear. You're doing it for them. And at the same time, you're doing it for your buddies who still need those planes—and they need them now. It's the best thing you can do for your friends over there. What do you say, Captain?"

Gene glanced at his feet, the way he always did when a little nervous, or embarrassed, and just as quickly at Mattie. She had her usual warm smile. He knew what she would be thinking.

"Yes, sir. I understand." He hesitated a moment, glanced at Mattie again, then looked back at the major. "Sir, I would like to start at the Boeing plant, in Seattle, where *Ad Astra*—my B-17—was built, if that would be acceptable. And one other thing, if I may, sir. My wife traveled over ten thousand miles to get over here so we could get married. Leaving her behind again would be awfully difficult—for both of us."

"Of course, Captain." The major smiled, a quick sense of relief crossing his face. "I understand you have a few days leave, for your honeymoon. Your orders will be waiting for you at home when you get back. Be sure to leave the correct mailing address with Mrs. Brownlee, in the front office. Ask her to get you an escort out. And Captain—congratulations again, on your medal, and on your marriage. And thank you for what you will be doing. Oh, and Mrs. Stoddard— please extend our appreciation to your fellow Aussies for their unflagging support in our war effort. The United States would be honored to have you represent such a staunch ally on the campaign with Captain Stoddard."

"Thank you, sir. I will be honored to represent my country." Mattie smiled her endearing smile at him, and he smiled in return, recognizing that he was getting a public relations bonanza handed him on a silver platter. With that, the major saluted Gene. It was the military way of showing that the meeting had ended. Gene returned the salute, and he and Mattie left the office.

They spent a glorious three days touring the sights of the nation's capital. Neither of them had been there before, so it was a time of discovery for them both. The senator's staff member who showed them the capitol building was from the county adjoining Gene's and had played football against Colborn High, although several years before Gene was there. The *Post* interview made Gene nervous, but the reporter was solicitous, and coached Gene along, until he felt he had a front page, top of the fold, story filled with touches about the budding romance that resulted in the War Hero marrying his Aussie nurse—something to solicit the interest of the female readers of the *Post*, of course.

As they toured the various museums and monuments, Gene attempted to explain what American history he could remember from his high school classes, and wondered, at times, if he would ever again in his life be as happy as he was those three days. Two days later, they were back at the hotel in Colborn, Kansas, where his orders were awaiting him.

They arrived in Seattle a day ahead of schedule, and after a call to the coordinator at the Boeing factory, had the rest of the afternoon and the next day to tour the Seattle area. Neither of them had been there, of course, so they spent the day riding buses and walking along Puget Sound in various parks that lined it. Mattie was especially captivated with the similarity to her home of Sydney. Summer is the "dry season" for the normally rainy northwest, and that particular day was spectacularly beautiful, with an azure sky and soft breeze blowing off the waters of the sound.

"Gene, don't take this the wrong way. I like Kansas, and I'm sure I'll enjoy living in Wichita, but this area around Seattle reminds me so much of home. The Sound—what is it called? Puget Sound?—reminds me so much of Sydney Harbor, and the trees and grass are so lush and green. And Mt. Rainier is so spectacular, looming on the horizon. It makes me think of the Blue Mountains. I'm afraid I'm a little homesick," Mattie confessed.

They were sitting on a park bench overlooking the sound, watching the many ships scurrying about. There could be no doubting the role this protected harbor area played in the execution of the war effort. Gene pointed out several B-17 bombers that occasionally flew low overhead. They were all unpainted, with shiny aluminum skin. He assumed they were new production models being tested in preparation for delivery from the nearby Boeing plant where they were manufactured—and where Gene was to give his speech the next morning. Gene put his arm around Mattie, and she leaned her head over on his shoulder.

"I know how you must feel, hon. You're awfully close to your parents, and your home. I know you've got to really miss them. I don't know when we'll be able to do anything about it, though. I hope you don't ever feel you made a mistake."

She punched him—not too playfully, he noticed, wincing a little from the blow—in the ribs with her elbow.

"Gene Stoddard, don't you ever say such a thing. You know better than that."

Gene grinned, and nodded, but didn't reply. The way his ribs felt, he decided he would abide by her demand.

The next morning, they stepped out of a taxi at the main entrance to the Boeing plant. It was actually in the nearby town of Renton, but it hadn't taken too long to get there from their downtown hotel. Gene and Mattie stood for a moment, just taking in the sight. The production buildings were colossal, larger than any plant they had ever seen, or could imagine. They seemed to stretch so far that they blurred in the distance, the way a highway blurs as it disappears over a distant hill.

But it was not the farm-sized manufacturing buildings that grabbed Gene's attention. Rather, he stood in open-mouthed disbelief, looking at acres and acres of B-17 bombers, fresh from the manufacturing lines, parked on vast ramps in front of the buildings. As he stared at this cornucopia of air might, he sensed a growing anger welling up within him.

"Mattie, I can't believe my eyes," Gene said, with an edge of anger in his voice. "To tell the truth, this really gets to me. When I think about the beat up, worn-out pieces of junk we had to fly, and the scarcity of them in any condition..." He could only shake his head in disbelief as he stared at the countless bombers glistening in the sunlight. "We'd been told that most of the B-17s were going to England for the war against Hitler, but never in my wildest dreams did I conceive of such vast numbers of them. We had to fight tooth and nail just to get ten or twelve of them, every so often. It just doesn't seem right." He stood, hands on hips, staring down the lines of planes, imagining those magnificent birds arriving at Port Moresby in such quantities. "Surely," he said, speaking more to himself than to Mattie, "surely some of these could be spared for us."

Mattie glanced at him, but didn't reply. He looked in silence a few more seconds, then took her hand and they began walking to the office of the Boeing coordinator.

"I don't know why I say 'us.' I won't be flying any of them," Gene muttered, somewhat under his breath, his mind still in Port Moresby and on the overwhelming display of B-17s.

"What did you say?" Mattie asked, turning to him. "I didn't hear you over all the noise."

"Oh, nothing worth repeating," Gene answered, as they continued toward the office building.

In about an hour, Gene and Mattie were sitting on a makeshift platform in one of the cavernous plants, with B-17s in various stages of completion packed together, almost literally like sardines in a can, as far as he could see toward the rear of the building. More people than Gene could imagine were crowded around the planes, sitting on top of them, on the wings, wherever they could find a spot, to see the war hero. Gene was introduced to polite applause, and stepped to the podium to confront the microphone. He had never been so scared in his life.

As the applause died down, they all watched him in anticipation. He held on to the podium with both hands, gripping so hard his knuckles were white, to keep them from shaking. He was in full uniform, and—at the insistence of Major Davis—wearing his medal. He knew he would never be able to read a prepared speech and have it sound real, so spoke extemporaneously. He had given it quite a bit of thought, however, and had a pretty good idea of what he wanted to say. He adjusted the microphone to his height, and cleared his throat, trying to muster the courage to begin the speech.

"Ladies and gentlemen. I want to thank you, first of all, for taking the time from your important jobs to listen to me for a few minutes. I know that what America needs, right now, is more B-17s—not more speeches."

The audience laughed a little, then broke into cheers and applause. In a few moments, they quieted again for him to continue.

"Several months ago, my crew and I were in a lone B-17, built by many of you in this plant, flying over the Southwest Pacific. For nearly an hour, we had to fight our way through more than twenty Jap Zeroes who were determined to end our careers in the Army Air Forces. Without question, it was a frightening time." He paused for effect. "But during it all, I was never as scared as I am right now."

Again, the workers cheered and applauded him.

"We love you, Gene," a female voice called out from the crowd.

Gene nodded, waved to them.

"Thank you. I love your planes."

More applause.

They were obviously touched by the young man, his twenty-first birthday just days ahead of him, standing before them. By all appearances, he had been in a far more frightening circumstance than now, but they appreciated his humor. They again quieted, and he continued.

"It may be hard for those of you here, today, who are surrounded day in and day out by scores of B-17s, to realize just how scarce these magnificent airplanes are in the Pacific. Barely a year ago, I was a B-17 pilot, with no B-17. There were no new ones available; there were no old ones available—and none coming in the foreseeable future. I was desperate for a plane of my own. I had about given up on being able to do what I had been trained to do—to fly a B-17 on bombing raids over enemy targets. But then, I came across what my crew quickly christened 'Junk Pile Jane.' I checked it out this morning with your production people. She was an 'E' model, and came off this assembly line in October of 1941. I'm sure many of you helped build her. Believe me, she was well-named. She was a derelict, and was about to be scrapped for parts. She had no working hydraulics, the engines were shot, the belly turret didn't work, there were missing parts and instruments. But I knew what B-17s are made of. She had a good spar, and a good heart. I wouldn't let her die. We bullied and cajoled—day and night. We scrounged parts, put on new engines, and fixed everything we could get to work. In a few weeks, we took her on her maiden voyage, and I fell in love with her."

He again paused, looking at the audience. Somehow, he was beginning to feel what Major Davis had told him. These people put their lives into these planes, just as surely as he had. They wanted, and needed, to know that it meant something. He was beginning to relax.

"I named her *Ad Astra*. It's from the official state motto of my home state of Kansas. It means 'to the stars.' I named her that, for that's where I knew she would take me. Over the next several months, we flew many bombing and reconnaissance missions over Rabaul and other heavily defended targets. I don't believe we ever came home without bullet and flak holes to patch, and something shot out. But…we always came home. *Ad Astra* would never let us down.

"And then, we were assigned to fly a photo reconnaissance mission for making topographic maps for a pending invasion. Unknown to us, the Japs had moved a couple of squadrons of fighters onto a nearby base. Of course, they spotted us, and came after us. We counted at least twenty of them. At times, it seemed like the entire Japanese air force was after us.

"But—we knew that without good maps our invasion troops would be put in jeopardy, and we had to complete the run. We didn't quite make it—they hit us a few minutes before we were done with the photography run, and we couldn't maneuver to defend ourselves. They knew that the nose is the weakest spot on the old Forts—we didn't have the new chin turret I see here today. Several of them hit us at once, from both sides of the nose, level and high."

The factory had become quiet as a church.

"We soon finished the run, so we could maneuver to defend ourselves, but not before that first wave had hit us. We were hit by literally hundreds of enemy rounds, both machine-gun and twenty-millimeter. Our instrument panel was blown to bits, our hydraulics all shot out. We lost our flaps, and our brakes. Some electrical panels caught fire. Two of the engines were hit. We had to shut one down, and the other one barely lasted until we got back to Moresby. We had nothing but the magnetic compass for a heading home. During the next forty-five minutes, wave after wave of fighters attacked us. We shot down several, but not enough to matter."

Gene wasn't sure he would be able to get through the next part, without choking up, but swallowed hard and continued on. The audience noted that the self-effacing young captain had not once mentioned himself, or what had happened to him. They remained silent, hanging on his every word.

"Several of us were wounded. My radio operator, Jimmy Wilson, was killed. Finally, after what seemed to be forever, the Japs ran low on fuel, and left us. My copilot had to attend to the rest of us, so our turret gunner had to fly us part way home—the first time he had ever touched the controls of a plane. But, ladies and gentlemen, *Ad Astra* never failed us. She brought us home. She took us to the stars, took everything the Japs could throw at us, and brought us home again."

At this, those in the audience not already standing all rose, as one. The applause, cheers and whistles were deafening. Mattie was smiling, and as usual

had tears streaming down her cheeks. Gene stood waiting, his hands still gripping the podium. The applause finally subsided, but the audience remained
standing, as Gene concluded his speech.

"I suppose I should tell you. The official state motto of Kansas is 'Ad Astra
Per Aspera.' It means 'to the stars, through difficulties.' I didn't add that second
part, when I first named her—I didn't think the crew would feel too confident
with 'through difficulties" a part of her name. But now, it seems fitting. *Ad
Astra* took us through every difficulty, and brought us home. But even she did
not escape, this time. She was too seriously damaged to ever fly again. So I
guess the story of her life is the story of my life. Of course, I also have to add,
that had I not spent four months in a hospital in Sydney, this beautiful Aussie,
my wife Mattie, would not be sitting here with me today. So *Ad Astra* took me
to stars I hadn't even dreamed about."

They applauded. They cheered. Several wolf whistles filled the air. Gene
smiled, and leaned closer into the microphone, pointing over his shoulder
toward Mattie.

"You're right, guys. This is what we're really fighting for." There was
more cheering, and then it settled down, again, to let Gene conclude.

"Ladies and gentlemen, my country saw fit to present me the Medal of
Honor. That honor is greatly appreciated. But I'm here to tell you this. America
is going to win this war not just because of guys like Jimmy and the rest of
my crew, but because we are going to have better planes. They will be better
designed, fly higher, faster, and carry more bombs, than anything the Japs can
throw at us. And there will be more of them than they can imagine in their
worst nightmares. We're going to win this war because of you, and all the rest
like you across the country, who are going to give us those planes. So I ask
you to remember just this one thing. Each time you buck a rivet, each time you
torque a bolt, doing that job right may mean that someone like me, whose life
depends on his *Ad Astra*, can get to come home again, can get to see his Mattie.
I thank you, and salute you. God bless America."

Gene gave the audience a quick salute, and turned to sit down. The
audience would not have it. Gene had to remain standing, and waved to them.
He stood with Mattie. She put an arm around his waist, and blew them kisses.
A chant began to fill the space, building in its demand.

"Mat-tie...Mat-tie...Mat-tie..."

She tried to wave them off, but the chant only grew louder, more insistent.
The master of ceremonies for Boeing quickly realized that he had a triumph
of public relations developing. He walked over and took Mattie by the arm
to escort her to the podium. She was blushing and smiling, as the audience
quieted to hear her.

"Thank you. Not long after your Pearl Harbor was bombed, a Japanese
submarine shelled our Sydney Harbor. Frankly, we were all scared half to
death of an invasion. We knew we could never withstand an invasion by such

an overwhelming force. But, somehow, we also knew that the Americans would never let us down. And you haven't. Australia is safe now only because of America. You are the most generous and loving people it has ever been my privilege to know. I thank you, and Australia thanks you. Like Gene said… God bless America."

She stepped back and put an arm around Gene, and blew the workers a kiss. They again erupted in wild cheers and applause. Just as she did so, the Boeing public relations photographer snapped their picture.

The Boeing master of ceremonies came to the podium. "Thank you, folks, for your warm reception for this true American hero, and his beautiful wife from Down Under. Now, let's get those boys some more B-17s. Let's get back to work."

Gene and Mattie waved to them as they climbed down the steps, and were escorted out of the plant. The plant was far too cavernous to make walking practicable. Many of the workers rode bicycles on errands. The MC had an electric cart that he used to take Gene and Mattie back to the front offices. As he drove along the production lines, workers would wave and call to them as they passed.

"Gene, Mattie—I've got to tell you both something," he said, speaking up to be heard over the growing noise as the workers quickly resumed their jobs. "We have morale builders come through here every so often. The workers appreciate them, and are polite. But I have never seen them react to anyone the way they did to the two of you, today. They know when someone is speaking from the heart, and they felt it from both of you. It was the best thing that could of happened for them."

Gene looked at the shiny new planes that would soon be in the air over enemy targets, and wondered silently if any of them would make it to his buddies.

"Thank you for saying that. I was really scared, at first, but they were so good to me that I got over it, pretty quickly. I sort of enjoyed it, I guess. But from now on, I think we can just skip me, and put Mattie up there. She's who they really want to see." Mattie frowned her disagreement with him, but didn't reply.

"Well, I can see you're going to make a good husband. And they did love her," he agreed, "but don't sell yourself short. They know what you guys have to go through. We get movies of the raids over Germany. It can be pretty disturbing, when you see a B-17 that you've helped build spiraling down in flames. And there's not always parachutes coming out of them. It makes them feel good to see someone who went through it come back to talk to them."

Gene requested a tour of the plant, for after lunch. The MC quickly agreed, and took them in the cart along all the stages of production. They started where the parts such as wing spars and ribs, and all the sheet metal parts, were made. Gigantic hydraulic stamping machines would slam down on a piece of aluminum, and lift to reveal a complex shaped sheet that might be a fairing over an engine, or part of the fuselage skin. All sorts of milling machines were cutting spars and other parts from blocks of aluminum. Gene was fascinated. His mechanical instincts were excited. He had no comprehension of what all had to be done to get ready to assemble one of his monster planes.

They continued on along, as individual sections were assembled. Large tubular pieces were joined to become a fuselage, wings were attached, and it began to form into the shape of an airplane. Engines, and landing gear and seemingly thousands of extra parts were added, and then, almost by magic, a shiny new B-17 would be pulled out into the sunshine to join its companions on the finish-out line.

They were now building the most recent, and most advanced version of the plane, the "G" model. It looked much the same, and yet was totally different from *Ad Astra*. More powerful engines made it possible to carry even larger bomb loads over greater distances. But the most prominent change, the one that made the model instantly identifiable, was the electrically-driven gun turret that had been installed under the nose of the plane. It was much the same as the top turret which his plane had, and had the same two fifty caliber machine guns installed, but was aimed by an electrical sighting mechanism operated by the bombardier. Gene and his crew had tried to compensate for the vulnerability with all the extra machine guns they had installed, but needed the flexibility of a turret. Gene couldn't help but wonder if Jimmy would still be alive, if their plane had been equipped with such a weapon.

By late afternoon, they had completed the tour, and had been thanked by some of the high-level corporate officers. Gene had even got to visit with two of the Boeing test pilots, who had queried him at length about his reaction to the plane, and any problems or suggestions that he might want to pass along. They were incredulous when he told them of the extra fifty-caliber machine guns that he had installed on *Ad Astra*—especially the fixed one in the nose.

They took him, and Mattie, to the flight line to see the ones undergoing final tests, and took them on board one of them, pointing out to Gene the many changes that had been made to make it a better plane and easier to fly. Mattie was astounded at the complexity, and wondered aloud how anyone could ever master it all. It was the first time she had ever seen the cockpit of any airplane.

The jumbled array of dials, knobs, levers, switches, buttons and gauges that was in front of the pilots, to either side of them, over their heads and on a console between them, even on panels behind them, was overwhelming to her. It gave her a completely different perspective of Gene, and made her even more impressed by him than she already was. To not only be able to master one of these giant, complex machines, but to feel at home in one, was beyond Mattie's power of imagination.

They had a test flight scheduled, and asked Gene if he would like to ride along—Mrs. Stoddard could ride along, too, if she would like, they suggested.

Gene appreciated the opportunity to see the plane, and thanked the test pilots, but realized that all the old resentment and bitterness was surging back in him. He declined their invitation to sit for a few moments in the left seat, and to go up for the ride, offering the rather weak excuse that Mattie and he were tired from all the travel, and had to catch an early morning train to California to visit the Douglas plant.

But he knew he wasn't tired. Not so long ago, he would have jumped at the invitation. But not now. For one thing, he didn't believe that he would be able to get his leg past the control column so he could sit down—and would have been mortified to have had to be helped to extricate himself. But, more than that, he simply couldn't face just riding along in the plane he so dearly loved, as a passenger—a spectator. To him, it was a pointless exercise in futility—almost self-punishment. So he thanked them again, and declined.

They had a lovely dinner that night, at a first-class restaurant atop one of the fanciest hotels in Seattle, where Boeing had put them up at Boeing expense. They chatted easily as they enjoyed their meal, looking out over the darkened city of Seattle. Blackouts were routine, and with only a fingernail of a new moon just setting, there was little to see. Mattie was still glowing in her delight about the day, and how well Gene had done with his speech.

"Gene, I was so proud of you today. I don't know how I could be prouder, or more in love with my new husband. The workers just loved you." She reached across the table and took his hand.

"Yeah, I guess," he replied, smiling back at her. He was pleased it had all gone so well, but was still somewhat embarrassed by it all. "But it was you they really loved—I'm not sure the Army even needs me on this trip, as long as they have you."

Mattie smiled at his compliment, but didn't respond to it, changing to the subject of the planes she had seen.

"I must say, I was overwhelmed with the whole manufacturing process. The plants are just so enormous. I can see now what you meant, during that first dinner at my parents, when you told Father how the Japanese had underestimated the production might of America. And I certainly don't see how anyone ever learns to master all those complex things in the cockpit, how you can even learn their names, much less how to operate them. And then, you have to fly the plane on top of all that. With your technical nature, though, I can see how it would be so appealing." She paused a moment. Gene smiled a little, but didn't respond.

"I am surprised you didn't want to fly with them, today. I would have thought you would have been thrilled to go up again. And…it would have been a chance for me to get to fly in your B-17 with you. Were you really that tired?"

Gene glanced at her, then down at the table. She always looked so radiant, and especially so now, in the candlelight. He had known at the time that he was being unfair to her, and felt chagrined by it, but couldn't bring himself to accept the test pilot's offer.

"No, of course not," he answered, without looking up at her, "I knew I wasn't being very fair to you, and I apologize for that. I'd like for you to get to fly in one. But good grief, Mattie, it would have been humiliating. I don't think I could even get my leg under the panel, to sit down. They probably would have had to pick me up and set me in the seat. I'd have been mortified—especially in front of you. Besides, I don't think you can comprehend what it would have felt like, to me, to be up in that plane knowing I'll never be able to fly it again. I don't seem to be able to make myself very clear. My life's dream was to be a pilot—I have no interest in being a passenger. Not now, and I don't know if I ever will."

Mattie didn't reply—in fact, she had no idea of what to say to him. She looked at him. The candlelight darkened his eyes, still somewhat hollow from his ordeal. He looked older…almost forlorn. She knew he could never recover from his physical wounds, and wondered if he would ever recover from the emotional wounds.

They sat without speaking. As seconds ticked by, Mattie didn't know how to change the subject and Gene showed no inclination to. She didn't want the good feelings of the day to slip away from them, so decided it was time for the meal to end.

"Gene, these last two days have been marvelous…but I think it's time to go to our room. We have to leave for Los Angeles rather early in the morning, you remember." She reached over and put her hand on his face, turning him to look at her. "Maybe I can get your mind off B-17s for awhile."

A couple of days later, at the Pentagon in Washington, D.C., a smiling Major Davis laid a copy of the Seattle newspaper on the desk of General Arnold. On its front page, above the fold, was a picture of Captain Gene Stoddard, Medal of Honor recipient, arm in arm with his Aussie bride who was blowing a kiss to the Boeing workers. Beside the picture was a lengthy article, titled "War Hero and Gorgeous Aussie Bride Wow Boeing Workers."

General Arnold looked at the picture a moment, and glanced at the related column. "Looks like you hit a grand slam, Major. Well done."

Facing Reality

The war bond and morale campaign tour became an all-expenses-paid extended honeymoon in fantasyland, a once-in-a-lifetime opportunity for a coast-to-coast tour of the United States lasting nearly two months. They traveled to aircraft manufacturing plants throughout California, Texas, Kansas, Michigan, Ohio and up the East coast. Gene was always embarrassed by the attention, but with each stop he became more comfortable with his speeches, and the workers always loved the two of them.

Major Davis saw to it that their picture—usually the Boeing one—would appear in local papers the day before, announcing the coming visit by the "Wounded Medal of Honor Hero" and his "Beautiful Aussie Bride." Appreciative—and curious—people would frequently greet them at the train stations. Local reporters usually attended his speeches, and Mattie had collected copies of the papers to send to her parents, and for her scrapbook. They would laugh about their newfound "celebrity" status but were, in truth, a bit overwhelmed by it all.

But after the dream comes the daylight, and life has to be faced. After the tour ended, Gene received a medical discharge and found himself face-to-face with having to confront his future as a civilian. After a brief visit with his family, and Christy, they took the train to Wichita, to discover that they were no longer in fantasyland.

Boeing had built several huge new plants and hired over twenty thousand new workers from surrounding farms and small towns. Many of those workers commuted from their nearby homes, but thousands had come from too far away, and all available housing had long since been taken. But the Boeing personnel people had considerable influence, and "found" a small furnished apartment for them somewhat centrally located between the Boeing plant and Wichita University.

As Gene had told Mattie her first night in Colborn, he had been accepted into the Aeronautical Engineering department at the university. They transferred his courses from his one semester at Kansas University, gave him credit for his military service, and waived several of the elective courses. They also allowed him to test out of several of the prerequisite math and basic physics courses, which he did without too much difficulty. When it was all combined, he had the equivalent of his first two years of college completed—he would be starting as a Junior, with only two years required for his degree.

It took a few weeks for him to regain the discipline of class work, but his old study habits soon began to reassert themselves. He was beginning to do well in the more advanced courses. Boeing assigned him to several different groups to introduce him to the company, and to let him get a feel as to where he would best fit in. Because of his course work at the university, they decided he would be best suited in the Advanced Design Group. Gene had no idea what the group did, but assumed he would eventually learn the ropes. All in all, everything appeared to be progressing well enough for the "gimpy ex-bomber pilot," as he still thought of himself.

For one who had grown up in "the lap of luxury," with all the house work done by maids, Mattie demonstrated a surprising willingness to work and a knack for domesticity, quickly settling them in their small apartment. But she had been privately struggling with missing her parents, and Australia. She was homesick, but didn't want Gene to be aware of it. She knew he would think that she was coming to regret marrying him. There was little to do in the small apartment, so she started looking for work at one of the hospitals, or at least to volunteer at one, in order to have something useful to fill her day.

But right now, she just needed someone to talk to. Not only was she homesick, but she also sensed things were not well—or at least not the way she wanted them to be—in her marriage. She mentioned to Gene that she missed Christy, trying to make it sound casual and nothing to be concerned about. Gene suggested she call and invite her over for a visit. Christy quickly accepted, arriving on the evening train from Colborn on Friday. She was looking forward to a weekend of the two of them having some "girl talk."

Mattie had come to feel close to Christy, and was thrilled that she had agreed to come for the weekend. They spent most of Saturday at the downtown Wichita stores window shopping, giggling like school girls. By late afternoon they were tired and had stopped for a rest in a nearby drugstore, continuing to chat over some cherry phosphates. After a few minutes, Christy became her usual direct self.

"Okay, Mattie, what's the problem?" Christy asked, looking Mattie in the eye. "You and Gene got a case of the-honeymoon's-over-itis?"

"Whatever do you mean?" Mattie replied, trying to look surprised. "We're getting along fine. What makes you ask?"

"Oh, Mattie, you know you can't fool me," Christy responded. "You've been beating around the bush about Gene since I got here. What's going on?"

"I didn't realize I'm so transparent," Mattie confessed, absentmindedly stirring her drink with her straw. She had lost all appetite for it, and pushed it away. "That's really why I asked you to come visit. I've wanted to talk to you about him for quite a while."

"You two surely aren't having problems in your marriage, are you?" Christy asked, quickly becoming concerned.

"No, we're not having marital problems," Mattie assured her. "At least not the usual kind. Gene's awfully good to me, and I know he loves me. Superficially, everything's fine—at least most of the time. I don't know. He just seems to stay so…what's the right word? Unhappy? Dissatisfied? Frankly, I'm worried about him."

"You must be. I think this is the first time I've ever seen you without a smile on your face," Christy observed. "Do you have any idea what's behind it all?"

"I wish I did," Mattie said, shaking her head. "At least I'd know what I'm dealing with. Whatever's causing it, he'll get sort of depressed and withdrawn. Then he'll get down on himself. He just isn't the Gene I knew, and love. I don't know if it's me he's unhappy with, or what."

Christy leaned back against the booth, looking at Mattie, trying to sort through the various problems that had bothered Gene as they grew up.

"Do you think he's just having a hard time adapting to his leg? He was always crazy about driving. Is he able to drive, or are you having to do it all for him? Maybe it's just a male ego problem."

"Yes, that was a problem, for a while," Mattie agreed. "He can't work the clutch, so I had to learn to drive on the right side of the road, and get a Kansas driver's license—but I needed to do that, anyway. I know it bothered him for me to have to take us everywhere. He would grumble about it, now and then. But he was able to find a used car a few months ago with that new 'hydra' something-or-other that automatically shifts for you, so he's doing most of the driving again. I don't really think that's a problem, now."

"How's college coming along?" Christy asked, after a rather long pause, as Mattie stared bleakly at the booth table. "Is he having trouble keeping up with both work and school? He was always a perfectionist in school. If he's having problems making A's, it won't be going over well."

"I don't know," Mattie said, after some hesitation. "That's my problem. He just keeps everything so bottled up. He hasn't said anything like that. He's got an A on all his tests, so far—at least the ones he's shown me. So I guess he's doing okay."

"He's always been just as responsible about work," Christy added. "If school is interfering with his job, it would be just as upsetting to him. How's that going?"

"That's the problem. I don't know," Mattie responded, rather quickly, Christy thought. It wasn't clear if she was uncertain, or annoyed. "He rarely talks to me about it. We just talk about what groceries we need, or what movies to see. Trivial stuff. When we were first getting to know each other, at the hospital, I was thrilled at how much he was beginning to share with me. He just won't do that now. I feel like I've lost him."

"Have you had any big fights? Anything that might have upset him?" Christy saw Mattie's lip trembling, and knew how troubled she had to be. "I'd find that hard to believe. You're too nice, and considerate. Still…you are married—and married couples have fights."

"Well, thanks for the compliment," Mattie said, shaking her head, "even if I don't agree with your assessment of me. No, we haven't had anything serious in the way of rows. At least I don't feel they are. Gene might. He said his folks never argued, or anything, in front of them and our little spats may bother him more than they do me. All that really happens is that he will get a little snippy with me over something, and before I realize it, my Irish dander gets up and I snap back. But it's never over anything that amounts to much, and it never lasts very long. But then he'll get real down, and just go silent on me. Hardly talks to me, for a day or two."

Christy wasn't sure what to say. It wasn't the Gene she had grown up with. He was always quiet, but never sullen, or petulant. Had the war affected him that much? She could only imagine what combat must do to men.

"I know it's hard for him to handle for us to have to live in such a small apartment," Mattie continued. "He always worries that I'll miss living the way I grew up, and start being sorry I married him."

She paused, and shook her head, unable to keep the exasperation out of her voice.

"Christy, what is it about guys, anyway? I simply cannot get him to understand that how we live doesn't affect me, as long as we're happy with each other. What I can't get him to comprehend is that I miss my husband a lot more than I miss my mansion."

"And they think we're hard to understand," Christy agreed, laughing. "But don't let it get you too discouraged. Gene's a great guy, and somehow you two will work this out. And remember, he's been through a lot. Maybe it's just now getting to him. Most guys won't talk about that sort of thing—and certainly not a Stoddard. They just clam up, think they have to be John Wayne."

"I know," Mattie agreed, "but it would be so much easier if I just knew what's behind it all. I want to help him—if he'd let me."

"Yeah, I understand," Christy acknowledged. "Does he seem to be actually enjoying college, and his job? The way he's always loved school, and planes, I'd think he would be in hog heaven, now. He's around planes all the time, and in school up to his slide rule."

"You'd think so," Mattie agreed, "but he doesn't really seem very happy about any of it. I guess he's working on that new plane—I think he calls it the B-29. He'll mention something about it in passing, once in a while, and I'll ask him about it. He'll usually just mutter something under his breath, and walk off. So I just quit asking, after awhile."

"Mattie—that's got to be it," Christy exclaimed, the light suddenly dawning, "You know how crazy he's always been about flying, and how much he wanted to fly for the airlines when the war was over. He wanted to get to fly with Mike, and now he never even gets to see him—doesn't even know where he is."

She paused, as the soda fountain clerk picked up their empty glasses, then looked back at Mattie.

"When you think about it," she continued, "working at an aircraft company, for Gene, would be like a guy having to work beside a girl he's crazy about that's going with someone else. Working at Boeing is just a constant painful reminder of all he lost. He's sort of getting his nose rubbed in it every day—at work and at school."

Mattie didn't respond, and was silent so long that Christy thought she had perhaps hurt her feelings. She was staring past Christy, her mind obviously somewhere else.

"Christy, I have to tell you something," she said, suddenly looking back at her. "A couple of days after Gene had walked off and left me, and after we had finally put that horrible misunderstanding behind us, I was nearly floating on air. Gene had asked me to marry him, and we had agreed I would be coming to America so we could get married over here. All I could think about was that I was going to spend my life with him. Then, he told me something that caught me completely off guard. It seemed so unlike him. But, frankly, I've let it get lost in all that's happened since."

"Oh? And what was that?" Christy asked, her curiosity tweaked. Gene wasn't given to offering true confessions.

"I can't believe that I've let it so totally escape me," Mattie said, more to herself than to Christy, shaking her head in disbelief. "Well, he told me that he was scared to come home."

"Scared? Of what? What did he mean?"

"I didn't understand, at first," Mattie said. "It didn't seem like him. But what he explained was that he had completely pinned his future on a flying career. And now that he couldn't do that, he had no idea how he would earn a living for us. In fact, that's mostly why he had felt he couldn't marry me. And, he said he dreaded a life of being cooped up in an office. He couldn't seem to get past the resentment at having to face a life doing something he believed he would hate, and was afraid he wouldn't handle it very well. He was worried that it would make me regret marrying him." She paused, then added, almost to herself, "I really hoped he'd come to know me better than that."

"Well, that all certainly sounds like Gene," Christy agreed. "So what did you tell him?"

"To be quite honest, I never took him very seriously," Mattie confessed, as she studied the table top, and then looked back at Christy. "Frankly, I'm embarrassed at having forgotten the conversation. At the time, I just couldn't see how flying could be so important that a person couldn't eventually get past it. Oh, I knew it bothered him, but I had largely forgotten about it. It seemed like being around planes, and being able to be in engineering, which he had said he liked, would more than compensate. Do you suppose that's it? Can flying be so important to him that he can't find any peace in his life without it? I just don't understand it, Christy. How can it be that important?"

They both sat in silence, neither sure what to say, or do.

"I guess I'm just selfish. I hoped I would be enough compensation. I love him, Christy. I want my guy back," Mattie whispered, her voice trembling. "And I want him to be happy with his life—with our life. What on Earth do I do?"

"I don't know if I know, Mattie." Christy reached across the table and took Mattie's hand. "You know, it's sort of a coincidence, I guess. The next day after Gene came home, he asked me to meet him at the drugstore in town. I thought he just wanted to visit a little, to get reacquainted after being gone so long. But he was really troubled over all that had been happening to him. I've never seen Gene as stressed out as he was that day. He mentioned the same concern to me—and I largely ignored it, just like you did. I was mostly just excited that you two were getting married."

Christy paused, holding Mattie's hand. Mattie was struggling, trying to control herself, not wanting to make a spectacle by crying in public.

"Mattie, thinking back about that day, and how troubled Gene was, reminds me of something he said. It really bothered me, at the time, but I forgot about it, with all the wedding hubbub, and all. I think you need to know about it."

Surprised, Mattie looked up at her.

"What do you mean? What did he say?"

"I don't remember exactly, but basically he said it really hit him hard, realizing he had allowed you to commit your life to him, and leave your home, your parents, your country, leave everything you held dear, to marry him. I remember he said he wondered if he could live up to your trust, if he would prove to be worthy of it. He seemed almost intimidated by it."

"Really? I can't believe he'd think such a thing. I hoped he knew me better than that," Mattie reacted, her Irish dander rising.

"Oh, he does, deep down," Christy assured her. "But there's one thing you need to understand. I don't know if it's because they're Dutch, or German, or whatever they are. But Stoddards have a deep-seated sense of responsibility, and commitment. Their word is their bond. Work, school, the farm…it doesn't matter. Gene has always taken it very seriously. And he feels the same way about marriage, I might add."

"I've already seen some of that," Mattie agreed. "When he was starting therapy, I was most impressed with his commitment to it, in spite of the pain. It really impressed me. But still—"

"Well, look at it from Gene's point of view," Christy interrupted. "He's fallen for a girl he feels is a gift from God, who has everything in life, it seems, who is willing to leave it all to marry him. Problem is, not only has he lost his dream of flying, and his future as an airline pilot, but now his only hope for providing for her, for earning a living, apparently is to do something he always thought he would hate. I can't even guess how that must all be affecting him."

"I don't know what to say," Mattie reacted, shaking her head. "It makes me feel like some sort of…burden, he has to carry. Is that all I am to him? I could help, if he'd let me. I'm trying to get a job at the hospital."

"No, Mattie, you don't understand. It's not you. It's Gene, and his sense of commitment to you, to his marriage. He's always had sort of a one track mind. Stoddards are all pretty bull-headed, and once he gets his mind made up on something, it's pretty hard to change him. He's been obsessed with planes, and flying, for as long as I can remember. Now, he's not only having to learn to accept being, as he so indelicately puts it, a 'gimpy cripple,' but the loss of his dream for his future, as well. And at the same time, he's having to try to come to terms with how to best live his life, not just with you, but for you. I suspect he just hasn't been able to come to grips with it all."

"I suppose you're right," Mattie sighed. "But I want to be his partner, not his…dependent. I wish he could see that, and accept it."

"Mattie, there's one thing that you and I can't comprehend," Christy replied, "and that's how war must affect the guys that have to go through it. There's a guy in Colborn—he was in my class, and goes to our church—that saw a lot of combat in Europe. He got wounded pretty badly, and is really struggling, trying to adjust. His mother told me he has horrible nightmares, and can't seem to cope with much of anything. I suspect Gene is going through some of that."

"I know. I don't want to be unfair, and I do try to understand. It's just that…" Her voice trailed off, as she could think of nothing more to say.

"Well, I will tell you this, Mattie O'Sullivan Stoddard," Christy said, smiling at her. "I know Gene loves you more than anything else in his life. You should have heard him talk about you, when he first got back. Don't ever doubt that. Sooner or later, he's going to find a way to sort it all out. I'd say just try to ride it out, for now, and see how it goes. Maybe understanding what's behind it all will help you know how to respond to him, and support him. Or at least you'll know it's not you that's at the heart of it all."

In later years, Mattie remembered the day vividly. It was a Friday afternoon, just three days past the 1946 New Year's holiday. Gene would be taking his final exams during the week to come, to complete the first semester of his senior year at the university. One more semester, and he would graduate with his degree in aeronautical engineering. It was difficult for both of them to realize that he was already so near to completing it. Yet, in some ways, it seemed to both of them that it had been an eternity since the two of them were coming to know each other as he recuperated at the hospital in Sydney.

In truth, it had been barely three years since that day when Mattie sat beside him, waiting for him to regain consciousness, wondering if she might somehow be able to marry him. So much had happened. So much was different. Was three years a long time? Or only a moment in time?

Not much had changed, since Mattie had talked to Christy that day in the drugstore, but it had been easier for Mattie to understand Gene and accept his moods. Things had seemed to be a little smoother between them, at least most of the time. Gene called her from work that day, earlier in the afternoon, to make sure she would be there when he got home. He said he had to talk to her about some big news. She could not even speculate on what it might be. When he came in the apartment door, she thought she detected a look of actual excitement on his face.

"Mattie—we're going to move. To Seattle!"

"Move? Gene, what on earth are you talking about? What's going on?"

She had by this time in her marriage learned several things about her husband, and one of those was that growing up on a farm had accustomed him to having supper ready when he came in from work—assuming that was to be at a reasonable hour. Oftentimes, he would stay late at the university, working on whatever it was that he did there. Given that he had phoned and told her he would be home on time, she had supper ready and on the table when he walked in. Another thing that she had learned was that Kansas farmers liked "meat and potatoes" sorts of meals, and his mother's meatloaf was one of his favorite meat dishes. Mattie hadn't totally mastered the recipe, yet, but had done a pretty good job on the one she pulled out of the oven as Gene was talking to her.

"Wow! Meatloaf. Man, that smells good," Gene exclaimed, momentarily changing the subject.

He pulled out a kitchen chair for her, then sat down across the table, said a quick prayer, and began to serve them both from the steaming dish. Mattie wasn't sure but what his interest in the meal had made him forget about his "big news."

"So, what's this about a move?"

Gene took a bite of meatloaf.

"Well, I mean, if it's okay with you. We won't move, if you don't want to."

He reached for a hot roll, and started spreading it with jam. He detested the pale margarine substitute for butter, and butter was still hard to come by, even after rationing had been lifted. He took a bite, then looked at her. She had scarcely touched her meal, and was looking at him, waiting.

"Mattie, I know I've never said much about what I do at work. I'm not sure why. I guess...well, it doesn't matter. Anyway, when I first started classes I got into a discussion with one of my aerodynamics prof's, a guy by the name of Jenkins, about wing design. He's pretty savvy, and was intrigued with my combat experience with the B-26 and B-17. I told him that I had always been puzzled over why the B-17 was so much easier to fly than the B-26. Oh, I knew what I had been told, but I didn't really understand it, or see how it could make such a difference. So, he suggested that I start working with him on some of their wind tunnel testing, that they do for the Advanced Design group out at the plant. He thought it would help me understand wing performance better. I started getting interested in it, and he began to let me do some extra stuff. Then, a few weeks ago, the head of the Advanced Design Group—he's my boss's boss—at the plant called me into his office."

Gene paused, a fork of meatloaf en route to his mouth, and grinned. "Sort of reminds me of getting called into the base C.O.'s office, that day at Seven-Mile Strip, now that I think about it." Mattie watched, entranced, at the faraway look on Gene's face. A moment later, the look was gone, as was the bite of meatloaf, and he picked up where he had left off. "Anyway, he said that Professor Jenkins had told him about me, and said I showed a lot of promise in aero design and wind tunnel testing. He wondered if I would like to go to work on a really exciting new project in Advanced Design."

Mattie was speechless. She hadn't seen Gene like this since they were first married. And she had been totally unaware of any of what he had been doing. He simply wouldn't share anything with her. She didn't know what to say, or if she should say anything, so waited for him. He looked at her, waiting for a reaction, but when none was forthcoming, he continued.

"Well, to make a long story short, it seems that Boeing is submitting proposals to the Air Force for a new bomber to replace the B-29." He paused, laid his fork on his plate, and looked at Mattie, shaking his head. "Mattie, it's almost beyond my comprehension. This new bomber has to have a top speed, minimum, of five hundred miles per hour—five hundred! For a bomber! We normally cruised at about one seventy five, maybe one ninety. The Corsair is the only fighter we had that would do four hundred, straight and level. And, it has to be able to fly at 40,000 feet. The B-17 took forever to make it to twenty-five or thirty thousand, with any kind of bomb load. Besides that, it has to carry up to ten thousand pounds of bombs. We usually carried no more than two thousand. And then there's the range requirement."

Mattie had been watching his face, his eyes, as he told her of the exciting new aircraft. She had not seen that sparkle in his eyes since...when? Other than the first night that he had kissed her, and at their wedding, she couldn't really remember. She thought again of her conversation with Christy.

There was no way that she would ever be able to understand it, she thought. Maybe it was like Mozart and music, or Rembrandt and painting. Maybe airplanes were like that to Gene. She couldn't fathom the emotions that lay beneath it all, in Gene's mind and heart. But it was clear that those feelings flowed through him as surely as blood flowed through his veins, and she was thrilled to see the look in his eyes as he talked—oblivious to Mattie's thoughts and feelings.

"What do you mean, the range requirement?" Mattie asked. She knew it was important to him, and wanted to appear interested, but she obviously had no idea what he meant,

"Range. You know, the distance a bomber has to be able to fly to get to the target and back. Mattie, on our missions over Rabaul it seemed like we were flying half-way around the world, but they were usually only about five or six hundred miles—twelve hundred round trip. This new plane has to have a range of 3,500 miles—three times as far as our missions."

He paused a moment, a faraway look in his eyes.

"Mattie, there's stuff that's beginning to go on in aircraft design that just staggers me. Everything I thought I knew about a plane is getting turned on its head. This new plane's engines are called turbojets—they don't even have propellers. How can you have a plane without propellers, for crying out loud? Did I ever tell you about those engines? I thought the B-17 was the most advanced thing that America could ever put in the air, when I first started to fly it. It was hard to conceive of anything being able to be bigger, or more complicated, and still fly. And by now, it's already becoming a museum piece."

Gene shook his head at the wonder of it all, while reaching across the table to steal the uneaten bites of meatloaf that Mattie was ignoring on her plate. He cleaned her plate, and continued talking, almost without taking a breath. Men truly amazed Mattie, sometimes.

"The problem, for us at least—that is, you and me—is that all the work on the new design is being done up at the main Seattle plant—where we started the tour. We'd have to move up there, if I take the job. We won't be close to the folks anymore, and you won't get to see Christy or Liz very often. Of course, we don't see them all that much now, so that won't really be all that different. I assume we could come back on vacations, some of the time. Anyway, I wasn't sure how you'd feel about it. You said Seattle reminded you of Sydney, when we were out there, and seemed to like it awfully well, so maybe that would help."

"What will you do about your college work?" Mattie's brow furrowed a bit, the way it always did when she was deeply absorbed in thought. "You're about to finish this semester. Will you lose all that?"

"I've already talked to Professor Jenkins, and he talked to the college administrator. They said they would transfer all my credits to the University of Washington. It's in Seattle, and has an even bigger aero department than Wichita. They collaborate on a lot of the work, so know each other. Apparently Jenkins had already talked to the head of the department out there, about me."

"Sounds as though they would really like to have you out there," Mattie said, smiling at him. "You must be making quite an impression on them."

"Oh, I don't know about that," Gene replied, sort of shrugging—and looking a little embarrassed, for a moment. "Jenkins and I seem to get along pretty well, so I suppose that helped. But Mattie…I won't take it if you don't want me to. Don't let me make the move, then regret it. Be honest with me."

Mattie never hesitated. She came around the table, and sat down on his lap, put her arm around his neck and looked him in the eyes.

"Gene, do you remember what Ruth said to Naomi?" she asked, grinning at him.

"Yes, I remember, you wise-acre. Whither thou goest, and all that." He wrapped both arms around her, squeezing her tightly to him. "Lord-a-mighty, I'm crazy about you."

Before she could react to any of it, he stood, forcing her to, as well, but wrapped both arms around her waist and gave her a quick kiss.

"When can we start packing? I'm supposed to start work out there two weeks from Monday. I have my finals next week, and the semester ends next Friday. I'm supposed to start work on the fifteenth, the same day the Spring semester starts out there. And by the way…do you realize that's my last one? I'll be graduating this May."

Seattle

Germany had finally surrendered, the previous May. There was much relief and celebrating at the time, but the nation knew the job was not yet finished. All efforts quickly became aimed at the final defeat of Japan. Though few knew it at the time, a new weapon—to be referred to as an atomic bomb—would soon destroy both Hiroshima and Nagasaki, and bring Japan to its knees. But at that moment, everyone feared the pending invasion of the Japanese mainland, knowing that it would result in staggering losses to the American forces.

Pictures of countless American soldiers lying face down in the surf, killed during the invasions of tiny islands in the Pacific, were burned in the minds of the public. What would an invasion of the Japanese homeland be like? Stories of fanatical Japanese soldiers fighting to the death in caves on those islands, rather than surrender, haunted those whose sons and husbands would be involved. Hundreds of thousands of Americans had already been killed, and America was war weary—the nation wanted it to be over. But it wasn't. The job still had to be finished. And to add uncertainty to the national apprehensions, Russia, under Stalin, was becoming bellicose and threatening.

President Roosevelt died in April, without getting to relish the victory over either Germany or Japan. Americans mourned the loss of their beloved leader, and were nervous about the unknown President Truman—or how he would deal with ending the war, and with the increasingly aggressive Russian bear. President Truman's first test came quickly, when confronted with the decision on whether or not to use the awesome new weapon that he had not even known existed. But he didn't hesitate, and ordered the use of the atomic bombs.

In the face of such overwhelming devastation, its country virtually destroyed and with no semblance of air or naval forces left, the government of Japan finally capitulated. On September 2, 1945, General Douglas Macarthur stood on the deck of the battleship U.S.S. *Missouri,* and accepted their unconditional surrender. The bloodiest war in the history of mankind was over. But America could not relax, nor let down its guard.

The U.S. Army Air Forces knew that, even with the end of the war, the United States would continue to be confronted with many challenges, as leaders of the Communist regimes in Russia and China became more belligerent and hegemonic. Russia would soon test its own atomic bomb. These challenges would require a new kind of aircraft, using technologies that had only recently been invented.

Boeing Aircraft Company knew that it had to play a vital role in developing those new aircraft, and when the Air Force solicited proposals for the next generation of long-range bomber, Boeing knew that they needed to win that competition. But they also knew that to do so would require that every ounce of skill and experience they had developed during the war be brought to bear on the task.

It was the Advanced Design Group that naturally had been assigned the task of preparing Boeing's proposal, and it was this group that Gene had been invited to join. For an embryonic aeronautical engineer it was an offer that couldn't be refused. Gene implicitly understood that, and knew in his rational mind it was the right thing to do. He had a wife to support, and presumed they would eventually have a family—he had to have a career, and aeronautical engineering apparently was going to be it. By default, perhaps, but he knew he had to make it work.

Making the move to Seattle, and taking advantage of whatever opportunities the move might eventually afford him, was the only sensible choice he had. With Mattie's immediate support and acceptance, the decision was made. But even as he prepared himself mentally, and planned for the move, he knew his heart really wasn't in helping to build something that he would never fly. He tried—all too often without success—to keep himself from becoming an openly pessimistic person, but doubted he would ever feel any of his old excitement about planes, and flying—or life, for that matter—again.

The move was a whirlwind blur to the both of them. Gene was concerned about his car making the trip to Colburn—and knew it wouldn't make the trip to Seattle. So, they used their last free weekend to take the train over for a last visit home before the move, and to break the news to his family that they would be moving half way across the country.

He gave the title of the car to Jerry, who agreed to come help them get ready to move and to nurse the car home. They were all superficially happy for this new opportunity for Gene, but had trouble hiding their disappointment that Gene and Mattie would be moving so far away. To these Kansas farmers, Seattle, Washington, might as well have been Mattie's Australia. They both seemed equally unknown and unreachable. It was not, in general, a good weekend—except perhaps, for Jerry, who was thrilled about finally having a car of his own, albeit an old one.

In a matter of days, Mattie and Gene found themselves living in an efficiency apartment owned by Boeing, in Seattle, while they looked for an apartment of their own and waited for their furniture to arrive. Mattie scarcely saw Gene the first week there, as he left for his new job quite early, and came home sometimes after she had gone to bed. He also had to start classes immediately, and that consumed even more of his time.

Mattie spent her days looking for an apartment they could afford. Without his degree, Gene was working as an hourly employee, and money was tight. He wondered, at times, how it was affecting Mattie, but she seemed to always stay upbeat and in good spirits, or at least she put on a good show of it. Gene appreciated the fact that she never offered to use her father's money to pay for their living expenses, and never complained about not having all that she had been used to.

Their new apartment needed to be somewhat equidistant between the University of Washington, where Gene would finish his Aeronautical Engineering degree, and the Boeing plant located at the south end of Seattle. But these two locations weren't terribly close together, and Mattie dreaded the time that Gene would have to spend riding buses while he was finishing college. The Boeing personnel department had again been of considerable help and she had finally chosen one, on Friday of their first week in Seattle. For once, Gene had arrived home at a reasonable hour. She was attempting to tell him about the apartment as they ate, but he was obviously distracted. She finally gave up.

"Gene, what is it?" Mattie asked, the exasperation evident in her voice. "I don't believe you've actually heard a word I've said about the apartment I found. Is there a problem with it? Or with us?"

"What do you mean?" he asked, completely baffled by her questions. "The apartment sounds fine. Sounds like you did your usual fine job of taking care of us. And why would we have a problem? What are you talking about?"

"I'm talking about just what I said I was talking about. You hardly seem to be listening to me. Are you upset with me? What's going on?" Mattie demanded.

Gene looked at her for a moment, took the last bite on his plate, then stood to take his dishes to the sink. As he finished rinsing them off, he turned to her.

"Mattie, I'm sorry. Yes, I was listening. No, I'm not upset with you. I guess I'm just distracted. We're working on the most revolutionary airplane I've ever seen. In fact, I've never seen. At least I've never seen anything like this. It's almost like a Buck Rogers spaceship, it's so radically different."

Mattie joined him at the sink to rinse her dishes. She filled the sink with hot water, and began washing them, as he stood by and dried.

"Radical? What do you mean? You said once it doesn't have propellers— what makes it go?"

"Well, to begin with, just as Germany was collapsing, General Arnold— you remember, he's the one who presented the medal, at the Pentagon—sent a bunch of scientists and engineers over there to find out all we could about their V-2 rockets and new jet fighters, and whatever else they might have been working on. Hitler may have been crazy as a loon, but his engineers sure weren't. They were inventing stuff we'd never heard of. One of Boeing's chief aerodynamics guys was on the trip, and found data suggesting that a plane's wings should be angled back, in order to fly really fast—maybe even faster than the speed of sound, if that's possible."

"I don't understand." Mattie looked interested, because Gene was, but confused by what he meant. "What do you mean, angled back. In what way, and how does that help?"

"Well, you know how a falcon folds its wings back when it dives on its prey? It's like that. Instead of the wings sticking straight out, like they always have on airplanes, they angle back toward the tail—as much as thirty or forty degrees. It makes the plane look almost like an arrowhead, or a dart. Our wind tunnel guys didn't believe it would help, at first, but we—get that, I'm already talking like I'm part of the group—anyway, we ran a bunch of wind tunnel tests, and the Germans were right. It really helps. That's why I've been working so much. We had to get the data in time to see if we could use the design on our next proposal. It has to go to the Air Force next week."

Gene was drying the last of the dishes, as Mattie cleaned the sinks. He had quit talking, and had a sort of faraway look on his face. She wondered why, and momentarily feared she had hurt his feelings by not appearing to be sufficiently interested in what he was telling her. Then he surprised her, with an unexpected aside.

"Mattie, these guys at Boeing—they really take aircraft design seriously. They seem about as crazy over designing an airplane as I've always been about flying them. One of them even quoted something from Plato to me, the other day. Plato, can you believe. I had no idea that people have been thinking about flying since the time of the Greek philosophers."

"Oh, really?" Mattie looked at him, eyes raised in surprise. "That is surprising. What was the quote?"

"I can't usually remember poetry, but this struck my fancy, I guess. Sort of like you and Ruth and Naomi," he teased. "This isn't really a poem, but it feels like poetry. Anyway, Plato said, 'The natural function of the wing is to soar upwards and carry that which is heavy up to the place where dwells the race of gods. More than any other thing that pertains to the body, it partakes of the nature of the divine.'"

Gene paused, leaning against the kitchen counter, a faraway look in his eyes. Mattie started to respond to his quote, then thought better of it.

"You know, Mattie—that really got to me. I never thought about somebody like Plato feeling like that. It almost makes aero engineering seem like a religious calling," Gene admitted.

She stood there, staring at him. She had never heard him say such a thing, and it made her think again about her conversation with Christy. Aviation, and airplanes, obviously were a part of Gene in a way she was afraid she would never comprehend. He started putting the dishes away, rather by habit, as he continued talking about his new Buck Rogers airship.

"Well, anyway," Gene shrugged, smiling at her, somewhat embarrassed by his little trip into the land of the philosopher, "the engines are going to be the new General Electric TG-180 turbojets. They're under development, but I guess they've never actually been used on a plane, before. They burn fuel to make a turbine spin, and then the turbine compresses the burning gases even more, and blows them out the back of the engine. It's like when you blow up a balloon, and turn it loose. The air blowing out the back shoots the balloon forward. They're huge, much larger than the engines on *Ad Astra*. We've hung six of the monstrous things on the plane, three on each wing. And the wing is so thin that it won't hold the landing gear—the wheels. We had to put them one behind the other in the fuselage, like a bicycle, then put some little ones out on the wing tips to keep it from tipping over."

"Well, I must say, I'm impressed with your Buck Rogers aeroplane," Mattie said, putting her arms around him and giving him a quick kiss. "And to think, you're getting to be a part of it all. So does it all really work? Does it fly?"

"Oh, good heavens no, not yet," Gene explained. "It's still just all on paper. It's a design that Boeing is proposing to the Air Force, in competition for the next new bomber. We won't build one unless we win the design and get a contract."

"Oh. I didn't realize that. But it must be exciting, getting to be a part of it all." Mattie knew it was the wrong thing to say, even as the words came out of her mouth, but it was too late. In a split second, the sparkle in his eyes, the excitement on his face, faded into some inner closet where he kept his emotions checked, hidden from view.

He nodded, leaning against the counter, arms folded across his chest. Mattie mentally kicked herself, fearing he was sinking into another blue mood. Instead, he was silent for a moment, staring off into someplace, as a surprised look flashed across his face.

"You know? In a way…it is, sort of."

Dear Christy,

I realize it's time I drop you all another line. We are really enjoying Seattle. It's so much like home, and I love it, but it makes me homesick. Now that the war is over, my parents are thinking of coming over to see us. I'm trying not to get my hopes built up too soon, but I am so anxious to see them. I would love for them to get to meet you, and Gene's family, too. I don't know how to pull all that off. Mother says in her letters that Father is terribly busy trying to get the shipping business off the war footing and back to normal.

We do a lot of sightseeing stuff up here, and have camped out several times. The forests around here are beautiful, especially the rain forests. And l enjoy walking along Puget Sound and watching the boats, and seagulls, and just smelling the salt air. It's so refreshing. It seems so much like home, and Sydney Harbor. I wish you could come and see us. Any chance you might be able to do that? We could help with train fare, if you'd let us.

I sometimes have hopes that Gene is getting past his bitterness about the flying. I don't know if he is still as bitter, or not. He just seems more re-signed than anything. He does seem to get excited about his work, some-times. But if I say too much, he just pulls back into his shell for a while. We get along just fine, and he's so good to me that I shouldn't say any-thing, but I just so want him to be happier with his life. It hurts me for him so much I could just cry, sometimes—of course, that's no surprise, is it?

Gene seems to be really involved with the design of this new aeroplane they are working on. He said they won the competition, and are getting a contract to build the first test model. I wish he would let himself get excited about it. I think he feels it, but just can't let go of the flying. What is it about airplanes, and that guy? I guess I'll never understand it.

Sorry. No news on the baby front. We are both really ready to have a family. Maybe someday. I know Gene would be a good daddy. And I just long to have one to hold. We've talked about it with our doctor, to see if there might be a problem of some sort. He wants to run some tests on me, and to test Gene to "see if he's shooting blanks," as Gene so delicately puts it.

Well, I'd better quit. I still need to write to Gene's family, and it's getting late. He isn't home from classes yet. He sometimes works at the wind tunnel there, with one of the instructors, until ten or eleven at night, and then has a tiring bus ride home. I guess tonight is one of those nights, as it is now 10:15.

Love to you all,
Gene and Mattie

The effort to win the new bomber competition had taken every ounce of Boeing's skills and resources. The new bomber was to use the new General Electric jet engines—so new, in fact, they had yet to be built and tested. But there had been a real dilemma with the engines. In order to fly as high, and as fast, as it would be required to do, the wing had to be thin and narrow. But a thin, narrow wing left no place to mount six large engines. Because of the volcano of hot gases coming out the rear, a jet engine couldn't be mounted to the front of a wing as was done for the conventional radial piston engines used on most World War II vintage aircraft.

Attaching them to either the top or bottom surface of the wing would disrupt the airflow over the exquisitely designed airfoil, negating its performance. So

Boeing looked at putting them in the rear of the fuselage. But the Air Force balked at this because jet engines tended to leak fuel, and a fire in the fuselage would be catastrophic. It appeared that Boeing had a revolutionary new aircraft—without engines. The designers battled among themselves for days, and nights, to no avail.

Finally, someone in the Design Group suggested hanging them from pylons, below and in front of the wing. This would keep them from disturbing the air-flow around the sophisticated new swept-wing design, and still keep them out of the fuselage. At first, no one thought it would work, but the wind tunnel boys—Gene's group—proved it could, and that finalized the design. Two engines would be suspended in a pod in front of, and below, each wing, and a third slung under the wing, a few feet short of its tip. New drawings were quickly made of the new design. The engineers and designers hesitated for a moment when they first saw the artist's renderings, but then broke into cheers and applause. It was magnificent.

The fuselage was a long, tapered cylinder, with a bubble canopy for the pilot and copilot sitting in tandem, on top, near the nose. The swept-back wings, mounted near the top of the fuselage behind the canopy, gave it the appearance of an arrow, ready to be fired into the air. Because the bicycle wheel arrangement would make it hard to raise the nose for lift-off, as was normally done, the front landing gear strut was made taller than the rear so as to elevate the nose into the liftoff attitude. It looked poised, ready to fly, just sitting there, gleaming in the sun in the painting.

The Air Force was as impressed as the creators of this beautiful new air-craft, and Boeing easily won the competition. America's first all-jet bomber, the revolutionary new B-47, was christened the Stratojet. Boeing received a con-tract to build a test model, the XB-47.

Mattie's Big Surprise

"Mattie? You okay?"

Gene had just finished a bowl of cereal for breakfast, and was working on a second cup of coffee, when he noticed Mattie leaning over the sink, her shoulders heaving as though she were trying to vomit. She shook her head, but didn't attempt to speak. Gene got up and went to see what was wrong.

"I'm…"

She dry-heaved again, but nothing came up. Small beads of sweat had formed on her forehead, and her face was pale. She shook her head again, indicating that she couldn't talk.

"Honey? What's wrong?" Gene asked again, beginning to get worried. "Shall I call a doctor?"

She gagged again, and took a deep breath. Color began to return to her face, as she took another deep breath.

"I'll be okay…in just a minute…I'm just feeling a bit nauseated from the smell of the coffee."

"The coffee? What's wrong with the coffee? It smelled okay to me."

Mattie turned from the sink, and sat down at the table, resting her head in her hands for a moment, then looked at Gene. She smiled at him to assure him that she would be all right, then took a couple more deep breaths. The attack had passed, and her system was returning to normal.

"I noticed it a little yesterday. And then this morning, when I came into the kitchen, the smell of the coffee just about undid me."

"I don't get it. What's wrong with the coffee? It's never bothered you before, has it?"

"No, it hasn't…but then, I've never been pregnant before, Gene," she replied, smiling at him. She reached out and took his hand. "You're going to be a daddy, finally. What do you think of that?"

"Are you serious? When? I mean, when did you find out? How did it happen?"

"What do you mean, how did it happen?" Mattie kidded him. "You're the one who grew up on a farm. I thought you knew all that stuff."

"I know how it happened, smart aleck," Gene replied, rolling his eyes in exasperation. "But we've not been able to for...well, we've not been able to. Did those shots I took do the trick, you suppose?"

They had about given up hope of having a baby. Mattie had been examined thoroughly, and tested for all sorts of possible problems, but with inconclusive results. Gene had been "tested, and found wanting" as the doctor had put it, so had been given a series of booster shots.

"Well, you took the last one just before my period last month," Mattie reminded Gene. "Maybe medical technology has worked a miracle for us." Gene came around the table to her chair. She stood up and put her arms around him. "Whatever did it, I'm thrilled. But I guess I'd better stay out of the kitchen, for awhile, until I can stand the smell of coffee again."

Gene held her close, and smiled at her.

"Are you certain? I mean...well, you know we've had some false alarms before."

"I haven't been tested by the doctor, yet, if that's what you mean. I will, as soon as I can make an appointment. But I've never felt like this, before. I don't have any doubts about it."

Gene sat down, and pulled her down to sit on his lap. He wrapped both arms loosely around her.

"I can't believe it, Mattie. I'd pretty much stopped counting on us ever having one. And now I'm going to be a daddy. Hard to believe."

They sat there together, in silence, enjoying the closeness and intimacy of the moment. After a few minutes, Gene decided it was time to bring up a subject that he needed to discuss with her, but had been reluctant to broach.

"Mattie—you know, it's been quite a while since we saw all the family. And now, with this news, it would be kinda nice to tell them in person. What would you say to going back home?"

The question caught Mattie completely by surprise.

"You mean go to Kansas? When? For how long? I didn't think you had enough vacation time, yet. And how would you get off from classes?"

Although Gene had graduated—*cum laude,* in the top seven percent of his class—the previous May, he had continued on with courses for a Masters degree.

"Are you ready for some Ruth and Naomi stuff again?" Gene asked, his arms still around her. "What I really mean is, what would you think of moving back to Wichita?"

Mattie was taken aback, and looked at him to see if he was joking. The look on his face made it obvious he was not.

"Gene, are you serious? What's going on?"

"I know I should have said something sooner, but it came up just a few days ago. I wasn't sure how I felt about it at first," Gene admitted. "But as you know, we won the design contract to build the XB-47, so now we get to build it.

The test model will be built out here. But from what my boss tells me, the Air Force is so impressed with the design that we're virtually certain that it'll be put into production. The problem is, our plants are so congested with the KC-97 production that the managers know that there is no place to build it when we do get the production contract. He says it's almost certain that the production will be moved to Wichita. They've decided to send an advance team down there to begin paving the way for it, and they want me to go with them."

For once, Mattie had to hesitate. It sounded as though it would be a good career move for Gene. If they had asked him to go, he must be making a good impression on them. But she had become very fond of the Seattle area. And, if she were honest with herself, she did not look forward to another move, and certainly not while pregnant. Still, it would be marvelous to get to be close to Christy and the family, especially when the baby was born.

"Gene, I don't know how to answer, this time. When would we have to move? I'm not sure how I would handle it, if I'm too far along."

"Well, fortunately, there's no real pressure." Her hesitation somewhat surprised him, but he recognized that their situation had changed now. "They'll be moving the team over the next couple of months, probably. If we go, I presume we would be better off to do it as soon as we could, though—right?"

Mattie didn't react, for a moment, then nodded.

"I imagine. I would want to talk to our doctor about it."

Gene realized that his announcement had taken all the excitement from her announcement, and regretted it, but assumed that if they were to decide to make the move then it should be done before she was more than two or three months along. But now, with her hesitation, he wasn't sure she even wanted to go back.

"Mattie, I'm sorry. I didn't mean to spoil your big news. I'm thrilled beyond words that we're going to have a baby. Would you rather we stay here, in Seattle? That would be okay, if that's what you want."

She curled down a little on his lap, and laid her head against his chest.

"No, I think it would be best to make the move. I have sort of fallen in love with this area, and it will be hard to leave it. I assume it would be good for your career." Mattie paused, as all the ramifications of her news, and now Gene's announcement, worked themselves through her mind. "It would be awfully nice to be closer to your family, and Christy, with the baby coming. I think a baby should grow up around family. Would we get to stay this time, or would we have to move back up here again? I'm beginning to feel like I would like to settle down someplace—especially with a baby."

Gene nodded. She always amazed him, with her quiet understanding and acceptance of whatever their situation might have been.

"I think we could stay there as long as we choose to. The B-47 program will last quite a long time, I imagine. And another thing, I haven't even mentioned. The Air Force is already asking for designs of an even bigger jet, to replace the B-36. We'll probably be doing quite a bit of the work on it down there. I expect to get to be working with Professor Jenkins again. I've even toyed with the idea of seeing if I could join the university staff, some of these years. So, Wichita would probably be it, for us, as long as we want it to be."

The doctor confirmed what Mattie already knew, and agreed they should make the move fairly soon. He said that the time from two to three months was a little critical, and that if they traveled then she should plan on lying down as much as possible. They had not wanted to wait for the mail, and wanted to get to hear the reactions, so placed long distance calls to both Gene's family and to Christy to tell the news.

And for the first time, Mattie insisted that they use some of her father's wealth, and placed a lengthy telegram to Sydney to inform the O'Sullivans that they were to become grandparents. A return telegram congratulated them, and suggested that their pending trip to the U.S. be postponed, so they would get to see the new baby.

On a bright October morning, Gene and Mattie boarded the train for Kansas City. They arrived at the train station in Colborn two days later. As Gene and Mattie stepped down off the train, and into the excited hugs and kisses of Christy and the family, Gene could not keep from thinking about the fact that it had not yet been four years since he had stepped off that same train, on crutches and barely able to walk from his wounds. He wondered if the rest of his life would see the kinds of changes that the few short years since his eighteenth birthday had wrought.

Crisis

"Gene! Gene, wake up!"

Her voice came through the fog of the dream-like world of being half awake while still asleep. Something seemed to be jostling him, and he struggled to open his eyes. Mattie was standing beside the bed, shaking him by the shoulder.

"What? What's the matter?" He lifted himself up on one elbow, and looked up at her—then turned, trying to focus on the clock on the headboard.

"What time is it?"

"A little after three. The baby's coming. We've got to get to the hospital."

She turned on the bedroom lights and went into the bathroom. He threw the blanket back and went to the bathroom, struggling to get his eyes to focus— not to mention getting his mind to focus—as he dressed. She was already fully dressed and was quickly finishing brushing her hair. Her face looked tense.

"Are you okay?"

She nodded, putting the brush in the drawer.

"I'm fine, but my water broke and the contractions are getting stronger. We'd better hurry. Get my suitcase. It's in the closet."

Gene was dressed and had Mattie and the suitcase in the car, headed for the hospital, before he was fully cognizant of what was happening. He looked over at Mattie. She was leaning back in the seat as much as possible, her hands on her bulging abdomen. Even in the dark, Gene could tell she was grimacing, and could hear her groaning against the pain. His foot pressed harder on the accelerator, as the speedometer needle crossed seventy.

"Are you going to be okay? You all right?" She didn't reply for several seconds. He could hear her moaning as she shifted in the seat.

"It was just a strong contraction. I'm okay, now," she replied, letting out a long breath. She looked at the speedometer. "Should you be driving so fast? You're going over eighty."

"Sorry—I wasn't sure if you were going to hold on," Gene said, as he glanced down at the speedometer. Surprised at his speed, he eased off on the accelerator a bit. "I sure don't want to play doctor here in the car," he added, trying to relax his stranglehold on the steering wheel.

He didn't hear her reply, but could tell she was smiling. It was only a three-mile run out the highway to the turn-off to the hospital. In minutes, Gene was helping her out of the car at the emergency entrance, as a nurse was bringing a wheelchair out the door.

"Get her to delivery. The baby's coming."

Gene held the door as the young nurse wheeled Mattie into the brightly lit emergency room. It was a quiet night, with no one awaiting treatment. The nurse pushed Mattie through double doors, to take her to the delivery room. Mattie looked over her shoulder at Gene as the doors closed, and blew him a kiss. He smiled, and waved to her, then glanced around the empty room, suddenly feeling quite alone and unsure of what he should do.

"Sir?" A girl in a small office cubicle was calling to him. Gene hadn't noticed her as they got Mattie in the wheel chair, but walked over to the counter window opening onto the waiting room.

"Sorry to bother you, but we have to make it official. Could you fill out these admission forms for me, please?" She smiled at him, handing him a clipboard. "Who's your doctor? I'll make sure he's been called."

"Dr. Williams," Gene replied, taking the clipboard. "And good morning. I didn't see you hiding in there."

In a few minutes, he handed the clipboard back to her.

"What do I do now?" Gene asked her, wondering if he sounded as bereft as he felt.

"The fathers' waiting room is on the third floor, just down the hall toward the nurses' station. They can call you there from the delivery room. And congratulations. Is it your first?"

"Thanks. Yeah, it's our first. Do I make it look that obvious?" Gene asked, smiling at her. Waving to the girl as he headed for the elevator, he wondered if the baby might already be coming. Moments later, he got off the elevator and began walking down the deserted hallway, looking for the waiting room.

Suddenly stopping, he looked up and down the dimly-lit hallway, not sure why. He could hear faint thunder rumbling from a distant thunderstorm, but the hallway was deathly silent. Cold chills, and vague feelings of fear, began to creep over him. Images of his first long, painful nights in the Sydney hospital came flooding back. He shook his head to clear out the disturbing images and memories, took a deep breath, and continued down the hall.

He wondered what his chances of finding some hot coffee might be. Half-way down the hall, just before reaching the nurses' station, he spotted a doorway marked "Fathers' Waiting Room." To his good fortune, there was a small canteen adjacent to the waiting room. No one was in attendance, but a pot of coffee stood recently made. He assumed one of the nurses must have made it and silently thanked her, poured a cup, and opened the door to the waiting room.

"Welcome aboard. You got one coming?" The guy was about Gene's age, crew cut, obviously former military. From his greeting, Gene assumed he was Navy.

"Morning—or I guess it's morning. Seems like the middle of the night. Yeah, we just got here. I wasn't sure we were going to make it in time," Gene answered, looking around the room.

Navy laughed, motioning to a chair.

"Must be your first—makes you a little panic-stricken. It's our third, so momma pretty well knows the drill. Have a chair and relax. You'll probably be here for a while. I think ours is about to launch."

They sat in silence for several minutes, each absorbed in his thoughts of how their lives were about to be further changed by what was transpiring unseen in another part of the hospital. Fathers were considered essential only to the "laying of the keel," so to speak, and were considered to be a definite hindrance when it came time to "launch." They were kept well away from the delivery room.

A direct phone line from the delivery room to the waiting room let the new mother announce the arrival to the waiting daddy. He could go see her when she was presentable, and comfortable, in her room. The new arrival could be viewed through the glass of the nursery. Gene continued to sip on his coffee. It was quite hot, and surprisingly good.

"Name's Reggie." Navy pointed to his flat-topped hair. "Friends call me Butch, for obvious reasons."

"Pleased to meet you, Butch. I'm Gene." They shook hands.

A few moments later, Butch nodded toward Gene's leg.

"None of my business, but I couldn't help but notice your leg. Japs get you, too?"

Gene was a little taken aback at his forwardness; he hadn't noticed any scars, or other evidence of wounds, on Butch.

"Yeah. B-17 recon mission," Gene replied. "Bunch of Zeros jumped us while we were on the photo run. They hadn't been there a couple weeks before. We were lucky to make it back. What happened to you? Were you Navy?"

"I was on the Indianapolis when she took the torpedoes," Butch said, nodding. "I was in my bunk, dreaming sweet dreams of coming home and making Momma a mommy, when they hit. I got thrown out of my bunk and broke some bones. Somebody got a life jacket on me and dragged me topside. I must have been knocked out, because I don't remember any of it. I guess they threw me overboard before it sank. I never did know who saved me, or how I got into a raft." Butch hesitated a moment. "I was really lucky."

"The Indianapolis? Good Lord." Gene stared at him, incredulous. "You really were lucky. I read about it. Hadn't you all just delivered one of those new atomic bombs?"

"Yeah. Isn't that something?" Butch affirmed. "We offloaded it at Tinian Island, then went on to Guam. We were headed for Leyte, when we were hit.

Imagine how things would have turned out if we got hit before we unloaded that bomb. We might still be fighting over there."

Gene nodded, letting it all sink in, trying to remember what he had read about the sinking. It had created a major scandal for the Navy.

"Most the crew were lost, weren't they?"

"She went down in only ten or fifteen minutes," Butch replied, a sudden look of anger flashing over his face. "Actually, most of the guys were able to get off before she went down. It was the damned sharks that got most of us. Those bastards in the Navy offices at Leyte were too lazy to bother to find out why we didn't arrive there on schedule, so didn't start searching for us. We just floated around out there...four damned days. All that time, no search, no nothing! The Navy sat on their asses and let the sharks use us for an all-you-can-eat buffet. Some of the guys would just give up and go under. You'd look at a guy, then look over at him a minute later and he just wouldn't be there."

Butch paused, jaw muscles clenching and unclenching, his anger still seething not far below the surface. Then he continued, staring at the floor, his voice quieter.

"But the sharks...God...You'd hear a guy scream, and the water would boil all up...I was in a raft, so I was okay, but the other guys... ."

Butch quit talking, an iron-hard look in his eyes. Gene could see him struggling to get control of his anger, and wasn't sure if he was finished, so hesitated for a moment.

"Lord-a-mighty, Butch," Gene said, shaking his head. "I can't imagine what you all went through. How'd you get rescued?"

"If it'd been up to the damned Navy, we wouldn't have been. A PBY just happened to fly over and spotted us—they weren't even looking for us, just out on a patrol. One of the guys in the plane just happened to look down and see us floating around down there. There were only about three hundred of us left out of the twelve hundred on board by the time we got picked up. I still wonder if the guy that saved me made it."

Gene was about to comment on Butch's story when it suddenly occurred to him that he had made a serious blunder.

"Oh good grief, Butch—I rushed off and left the car parked in the emergency entrance. I think I even left it running. See you in a minute."

Butch was smiling as Gene hurried out the door. As he left the elevator at the emergency room and started for the exit door, the clerk at the desk where he had filled out the forms called to him.

"Hello again. Looking for these?" She was holding a set of keys—Gene's car keys.

"We figured you didn't want to waste gas—and we have to keep the entrance clear for the ambulance—so we parked it in the visitor parking lot for you. Don't worry, we locked it."

"I feel like a total idiot," Gene replied, shaking his head in embarrassment. "I told you it was our first. I completely forgot it. Thanks for taking care of it."

"Oh, don't worry about it. It happens so often we ought to have a special parking place reserved for flustered fathers," the young clerk assured him, as Gene took his keys.

"Well, thanks again. I guess I'd better get back up to the phone, in case they try to call me."

Gene hurried back to the elevator. Just as he opened the door to the waiting room the red phone on the wall rang, startling them both. Butch jumped up to answer it.

"McCluskey...Hey, honey...Really? Hot damn, Momma, you got me a boy! Way to go, babe! Are you okay?...The baby?...Fantastic. I'm proud of you, Momma...Room 314? I'll be there waiting for you. Love you, babe. Bye."

He hung up the phone and turned to leave, a smile pushing the black thoughts which he had been sharing with Gene earlier into the back of his mind, where he struggled to keep them.

"Congratulations, Butch," Gene said, reaching out to shake his hand. "Your first boy, I take it."

"Yeah, man. I was beginning to think I was going to have to depend on my brother to keep the family name going...but Momma came through, this time. Good luck on yours. Maybe I'll see you at the nursery. See you later."

With that, Butch disappeared out the door and down the hallway. Gene sat back down, wondering how Mattie was fairing. He hadn't seen her in such pain before, and was somewhat unsettled by it. He started sorting through the stack of worn, out-of-date magazines scattered around the room, trying to find something he could read to pass the time.

He leafed through an old *Popular Mechanics*, then went to the canteen to get more coffee. He saw a night nurse down the hall at the nurses' station, and started to go visit with her to pass the time—then realized he wouldn't be able to hear the phone in the waiting room, so went back. He glanced at his watch. It had now been nearly an hour since they had arrived. Given Mattie's sense of urgency as they drove to the hospital, he had assumed the delivery would be over almost immediately, and wondered about the delay. Could she be having problems?

He put the magazine back in a rack and picked up a two-year-old *National Geographic*, flipped through it, tossed it aside and found a *Saturday Evening Post* that was reasonably current and started leafing through its pages.

Another twenty minutes passed. Gene began to worry, and went to talk to the nurse about it. No one was at the desk, so he returned to the room. Just as he started to find another magazine the phone rang. He jumped to answer it.

"Mattie?"

"Is this Mr. Stoddard?" The female voice that answered obviously was not Mattie.

"Yeah, that's me. Has the baby come? Is Mattie—"

"Mr. Stoddard, there have been some problems," the nurse interrupted him, her voice tense. "We need you to come down right away."

"Problems? What do you mean? Is Mattie okay?"

"Please, Mr. Stoddard. I'll explain when you get here. Meet me at the nursery, on the first floor. Turn left out of the elevator. I'll be waiting for you."

With that, she hung up. Gene stood there, in momentary shock, then hung up the phone and bolted for the elevators. He frantically punched the "1" button, attempting to hurry the doors closed. It was only two floors down, but the elevator seemed interminably slow. As the elevator doors slid open, Gene saw a nurse hurrying toward him.

"Mr. Stoddard?"

Gene nodded. "What happened, what's the problem?"

"I'll explain in a moment, but I thought you'd want to see your little girl, first," the nurse said, as she led him down the hall. They stopped in front of the large glass window of the nursery. It was filled with bassinets, some occupied with sleeping infants. One smaller one had a warming light over it. A nurse at the back was coming forward, smiling at Gene, carrying a newborn wrapped snugly in a blanket trimmed in pink.

Gene was totally perplexed, looking first at the newborn being held for viewing in front of him, then at the nurse standing beside him.

"You mean the baby's already here? This is our baby?" he asked, looking again at the bundle. But the baby was wrapped too tightly to see anything other than a tiny face. Her eyes, barely showing below a pink stocking cap, were closed. Gene looked again at the nurse, trying to keep the rising panic from showing in his face. "But…what about Mattie? Why didn't she call? Where is she?"

"Mr. Stoddard, your wife had some problems after the delivery—" the nurse started to explain.

"Problems? What do mean?" Gene interrupted.

"Let me finish, Mr. Stoddard. Your wife's delivery was a little difficult, but nothing unusual for a first delivery. It just took a while. Then, just after the baby arrived, she—your wife, that is—suddenly hemorrhaged. It happens sometimes, but we can usually get it stopped in the delivery room. Unfortunately, this time we couldn't. She was losing so much blood that she required immediate surgery. Dr. Blakely—the surgeon—has just arrived, and is in the operating room with your wife now. I believe he's already started the surgery. I'm sorry I didn't call you sooner; we were just too busy. Dr. Williams said to apologize to you for not telling you, himself, but he's assisting Dr. Blakely. I thought you would want to see your daughter before I take you to the O.R. waiting room."

"Hemorrhaged? What do you mean? What happened? Will she be okay?" Gene felt himself getting rattled, in disbelief at what all was happening. He always thought babies just "got born," and that was pretty much all there was to it. How could his wife now be in surgery?

"I really can't tell you much," the nurse told him. "Dr. Blakely will fill you in after the surgery." She nodded toward the glass window. "Your daughter's beautiful. She has her mother's red hair."

"She's so…tiny. Is she all right? Did anything happen to her?" Gene looked at the nurse a moment, his mind racing, then turned to look at the infant in front of him. That this little bundle being held in front of him was his daughter hadn't completely registered. His mind was still trying to cope with it all.

"No, she's just fine," the nurse assured him, smiling at the baby. "She was nearly seven pounds—a good weight for a little girl. Why don't we go to the O.R. now?"

The nurse waved to the nurse holding the baby. She smiled, and turned to put the sleeping infant in one of the bassinets. The other nurse began walking down the hallway, with Gene struggling to keep up with her. She came to a doorway labeled "O.R. Waiting Room," and opened the door to let Gene in.

"I don't really know how long the surgery will take. Dr. Blakely's very good—with lots of experience. He'll come see you when it's over. Can I get you anything?"

"What? Oh, no thanks…" Gene's mind was in complete turmoil. He couldn't seem to think. "Well, some coffee would be good, if there is any."

He looked around the small room. A sofa that appeared to have been made from Naugahyde seat covers from a car occupied most of the side wall, and a wicker chair with tired, lumpy cushions was parked against the wall adjacent to the door. Magazines were scattered about the top of a matching wicker corner table, between the two pieces of furniture. A faint smell of disinfectant—or perhaps from the anesthesia in use down the hallway—permeated the room. Fluorescent lights in the ceiling created a hard, glaring appearance and the pale green walls looked sickly in the artificial light. It appeared to have been designed with the explicit purpose of discouraging anyone from wanting to be there.

A second door stood opposite the one they entered, with a window that permitted Gene to see down a long hallway. Along the hallway were doors with operating room numbers over them. He turned to talk to the nurse, but she had already left.

In a few minutes she returned with a cup of coffee.

"I forgot to ask if you wanted anything in it, so I left it black. I hope that's all right. I can get some cream and sugar, if you'd like."

"Black's fine, thanks. It's the only way I drink it," Gene replied. He took the coffee, sipped it, and looked down the hallway, but saw no one. The nurse noticed him looking, and the helpless look that haunted his face.

"I'm sure your wife will be fine, Mr. Stoddard, but it might take a while. Why don't you sit down, and try to relax? You can place long distance phone calls on the phone there beside the sofa, courtesy of the hospital, if you need to contact family. Just dial zero, and give the operator the number. If you need me, ask for the O.R. nurses' station. My name's Melinda."

She turned and left, with Gene still holding his coffee, looking anxiously down the hallway at the operating rooms—but there was no one coming.

He glanced at his watch. A little after five. Gene felt as though he had been there all night, but it had not yet been two hours since they had arrived at the ER entrance. He wondered if it would be too early to call home. His folks always got up early. They would probably be up, by now, but he didn't know if he should call before he had any more information about Mattie. He drank some more coffee, then paced around the room, glancing again down the hall. But no one was coming. He set the coffee down, rubbed his eyes, and glanced down the hall again.

He needed to talk to someone, get his mind straightened out. He tried to think about the tiny bundle he had seen that was his daughter. It didn't feel real, and reminded him too much of the first nights at the hospital in Sydney when his mind could not grasp what had happened. He sat down at the end of the sofa, sagging into its tired cushions, picked up the phone, dialed zero, gave the operator a number. The distant phone rang so long he was about to hang up, when he heard a click.

"Christy," a groggy voice answered, sounding more than a little irritated. "And whoever this is, it had better be good, at this ungodly hour."

Gene couldn't help but smile, in spite of himself. Christy never changed.

"Christy. It's Gene."

"Gene?" She paused a moment. "Oh my God! Is the baby here?"

"Christy, we've got trouble. The baby came a little while ago—a little girl. She's fine, I guess, but something's happened to Mattie. They said she started bleeding, and they couldn't get it stopped. She was losing a lot of blood, and they had to rush her into emergency surgery—she's still there. Christy…" He paused, and swallowed hard. "It sounded pretty bad. I'm really rattled…I don't know what to do."

"Oh, Gene. What happened? Have the doctors told you anything?"

"No, just the nurse. Our doctor, Dr. Williams, is helping with the surgery and couldn't talk to me, the nurse said. She showed me the baby. I'm in the operating waiting room, waiting for the surgeon to come out. Sorry about it being so early—I had to talk to someone."

"It's fine, Gene. I would never forgive you if you hadn't called. Have you called your folks?"

"Not yet. I figured it would be better to wait until I talked to the surgeon."

"All right. Just as soon as you've talked to him, call me. I'll go ahead and call your folks and let them know. I'm sure we'll come over, as soon as we can. What does it take to drive to Wichita—three hours?"

"Yeah, around that, the way Dad drives. We're at the VA hospital. It's hard to miss. It's on the north side of fifty-four, as you come into town."

"Okay. Try to relax. I'm sure Mattie will be fine. Have you picked a name?"

"A name?" Gene sounded blank.

"For your daughter. Did you and Mattie pick a name?"

"Oh, sorry. My mind's a mess. No, not yet. Well, yeah, sort of. We narrowed it down to two or three, but hadn't settled on one. We like Cathleen Elizabeth the best. You know, something Irish for Mattie's side and Elizabeth for the Stoddard side."

"Oh, I like that. And so will Liz. Well, let me call your folks. Call me as soon as you know something. We'll be praying for her—and you."

"Thanks—we need it. I'll call you as soon as I know something."

He hung up the phone, and glanced down the hall. A nurse hurried out of one room and down the hall, but no one was coming toward the waiting room. He yawned and shook his head, trying to clear his rattled mind, then rubbed his eyes and the back of his neck. His knee hurt. He rubbed it a moment, then glanced down the hallway.

Opening a tattered *Life* magazine, he idly flipped through pages for several minutes, trying to distract himself, then tossed it back on the pile and picked up a current *Popular Mechanics*. A feature article about the new F-86 Sabre jet fighter being developed for the Air Force by North American Aviation caught his attention, and he began reading it. Its sleek lines and swept-back wings appealed to him, but he still couldn't get used to seeing planes with no propellers. He was admiring color pictures of one of the prototype planes in flight, when the door opened. Gene dropped the magazine, and jumped to his feet.

"Mr. Stoddard? I'm Doctor Blakely."

He looked tired. Gene noticed numerous splatters of blood on his sleeves and the front of his operating scrubs. He nodded a greeting as he reached out to shake the doctor's hand, too nervous and apprehensive to say anything.

"Mr. Stoddard...we've got the bleeding stopped, but I'm afraid your wife won't be out of the woods for a while. Some bleeding after delivery isn't unusual, but she suddenly hemorrhaged quite heavily. Doctor Williams and the nurses did the best they could to control it, but there was little they could do. She lost a lot of blood, but they did a good job of stabilizing her until I could get here. During the surgery, I discovered the hemorrhage was caused by retained placenta. That is, part of the placenta attached to the uterus, and was not delivered. I was able to correct that, and get the bleeding stopped. Unfortunately, this sort of thing often results in high levels of infection, and that's already starting. Her temperature is climbing, from her body starting to fight the infection. That's our battle now—to try to control her temperature, and fight the infection."

As Gene listened to the doctor attempting to explain to him why Mattie was not resting comfortably in the maternity ward joyfully nursing their new daughter, as he had fully expected her to be doing by now, the doctor's words flowed over and around him like water flowing over a boulder in a stream. Nothing penetrated. How could this be happening? Was Mattie going to be alright? Was she going to die? He stared, his face a blank, as the doctor continued.

"Mr. Stoddard, you're probably aware of the new drug that saved so many of our troops during the war, called penicillin. It's a true miracle drug for fighting infection. Fortunately, we have adequate supplies of the drug and have begun treating your wife with it. We've moved her to an isolation room, where we'll have to keep her until we can whip the infection, and get her temperature down."

"Dr. Blakely," Gene interrupted, unable to hear any more without an answer to the only question that mattered to him. "Will Mattie be…I mean, is she going to…" Gene hesitated, unable to say the words.

"She's had a close call, Mr. Stoddard," the doctor replied, knowing what Gene was struggling to ask. "Quite honestly, years ago, we probably would have lost her. A lot of women died in childbirth from similar problems. But I have a lot of confidence in the penicillin. She's young, and strong, and that will work in her favor. We'll do all we can for her, but it could be at least two or three days before we'll know how it's going to go…we'll just have to wait and see."

Gene stared at the doctor, hearing, but not understanding, all that he was being told. It all seemed too much like he was watching his own life when he had arrived at the hospital in Sydney. He thought of Mattie, standing there beside him when he had first regained consciousness.

"Can I be with her?"

"We're keeping her isolated because of the infection," the doctor replied, "and she's sedated—she won't be aware you're there. You can stay with her, if you'd like, but you'll have to put on some hospital garb, and a mask. Tell the nurse I said it would be okay, and she'll find you something. She'll be there with you, in case anything happens. Just go down this hall. You'll see her in the third room on the right." The doctor started to leave.

"Doctor Blakely?"

"Yes?"

"What about the baby—I mean, she'll have to be fed. How…?"

The doctor smiled, the weariness showing through the smile.

"Don't worry. We're used to problems like this. We have a mother's milk substitute for mothers who can't nurse their babies, for some reason. It's a little girl, isn't it? She'll be fine. Now—I'm very tired, and I want to come back and check on your wife in a little while, so I'm going down to the lounge and catch a nap. Anything else?"

"No, I don't think so," Gene answered, shaking his head. "And, Doctor Blakely—thanks. I mean…"

"I'm glad I could get here in time."

He pulled the door open to leave, then paused, looking at Gene. He was pale, unshaven, his hair messed from constantly running his hand through it. His eyes were sunken, and he looked shaken. There seemed little else the doctor could say, so he left, letting the door close behind him.

Gene stood there, staring down the hall. Somewhere down there Mattie lay unconscious, fighting for her life. He started down the hall to find her, paused suddenly, went back to the waiting room and picked up the phone. He dialed the operator, and gave her Christy's number.

Christy had already talked to Gene's folks. They planned to leave for Wichita as soon as the chores were finished, and expected to be there by around lunchtime. He wondered how they would be able to locate him, once they got to the hospital, but his mind was too numb to think about it.

Gene wasn't sure how long he had been sitting there, beside her bed, watching the sheet covering her rise slightly, and fall, as she breathed. It hardly seemed to move. He would start to panic, at times, when it appeared she had stopped breathing—then the sheet would rise again. She seemed so small, and fragile, under the cover. Could this really be his athletic, tennis-playing Mattie? Her face, normally tanned and vibrant, looked pale, yet flushed with fever, and her hair was matted and disheveled. She was proud of her auburn hair, and always kept it brushed to a sheen. It always looked so lustrous, and smelled so good. He knew she would be embarrassed, now, if she could see it.

He wanted to touch her, to hold her hand, but IV lines were attached to both arms. He wondered if this was how he had looked, as Mattie sat beside him. If so, he wondered what she had seen in his face that had so attracted her to him. That time, that place, now seemed so long ago, and so far away. They had been so young, then. He would soon turn twenty-five, but it seemed as though he had lived two lifetimes since his eighteenth birthday. He suddenly felt old, and very tired.

Gene rubbed his eyes, and wondered how to let Mattie's parents know about the baby, and Mattie. He didn't think it was possible to call Australia, but a telegram seemed so impersonal. What would he send? "Dear Mr. and Mrs. O'Sullivan. We have a baby girl. Mattie is fighting for her life. Will write with details." How could he send something like that? But he had to tell them something.

He looked at Mattie lying so still, and realized how intensely he loved her. Could it really be possible that he had almost lost her? That he might still lose her? He had to lose his dream of flying, to find her. Was he going to have to lose her, to get their Cathy? Was that how life was always going to work? He couldn't imagine life without his Aussie red-head. His eyes began to burn, and he wiped at them with the back of his hand.

"Mr. Stoddard?"

"What?" Gene jumped slightly, turning toward the voice. It was the nurse who had been assigned to watch over Mattie. "Oh, excuse me. I didn't see you there."

"I'm sorry if I startled you, Mr. Stoddard, but your family has arrived. They're waiting out in the front reception area. I'd show you the way, but I'm not allowed to leave the room. Just go through the O.R. waiting room, and follow the hallway to the left, all the way until you see the hallway to the front. There's a big sign. You shouldn't have a problem."

Gene stood, looking at Mattie lying there. He didn't want to leave her, but knew he had to go meet his family. He hadn't realized enough time had passed for them to have made the drive. As he walked along the hallway, now much busier than in the early morning hours when he first walked it, he began to be aware how thankful he was that he and Mattie no longer lived in Seattle. He would not have wanted to face this ordeal alone.

The three of them—his parents and Christy—were standing in the reception area, looking apprehensive as Gene entered and came to meet them.

"Gene, I'm so sorry," his mother said, holding him tight. His appearance reminded her too much of the day he first arrived home from Australia, and she had to wipe at her eyes with her handkerchief.

"Thanks, Mom," he said, keeping an arm around her shoulder as he shook his dad's hand. "Thanks for getting over here so fast, Dad. I really appreciate it." He turned to Christy, giving her a hug.

"Sorry to get you out of bed before daylight, but thanks for the help. I really needed it."

"Oh, don't be silly. Every girl needs to see a sunrise at least once in her life," she said, grinning at him a moment. "How's Mattie, Gene?"

His hesitation was not encouraging, as they waited for him to respond to the question they all wanted answered. He ran his hand through his hair, only then realizing he had not yet removed the hospital cap he had been required to wear in the isolation room.

"She's been out of surgery for…I don't know, three hours, I guess. The doctor said that the, what did he call it…something about the delivery, staying attached. I don't know. I can't remember any of the stuff he told me—"

"The placenta?" Christy asked.

"Yeah, that sounds right," Gene said, glancing at Christy. "Something like that, I guess. I wasn't listening very well. He said he got that fixed okay, but whatever made her start bleeding—or maybe it was what they had to do to stop it—anyway, something caused her to get a real bad infection, and her temperature's awfully high. She's in an isolation room. Nobody can see her— well, I can, but nobody else, I guess. I don't think they'll let you all in." He paused, staring out the entrance doors for a moment. "The doctor said she probably would have died, a few years ago," he added, looking past them, his mind elsewhere.

"They're giving her that new penicillin drug they used to treat the wounded for infection during the war. I guess it's pretty potent. Anyway…" He quit talking, just standing there, looking at the floor, out the windows, not seeing anything, rubbing the back of his neck. "The doctor said he's got a lot of confidence in it, but we'll just have to wait and see…whatever that means."

They all stood there, not knowing what to say, or do. After several seconds, Christy knew it was time to distract Gene.

"Can we see the baby?"

"Oh, sure," Gene said, startled back to the present. "Well, I guess we can. I'll ask the receptionist if it's okay."

They all agreed that Cathleen Elizabeth Stoddard was the cutest baby they had ever seen, and wasn't her red hair so pretty, just like Mattie's, and she had Mattie's eyes, too. After the appropriate congratulations to Gene on being the proud new daddy, and comments about Bill and Mary now being grandparents, Gene realized that they were probably all hungry. He suggested they go to a diner just up the highway for a bite of lunch—then he wanted to get back to Mattie.

They sat in a booth at the diner, picking at their food, each attempting to find a topic for conversation, but no one wanting to talk.

"Jerry and Liz both said to tell you how sorry they are that they couldn't come," Mary told Gene, sure that he had wondered why his brother and sister hadn't come. "They didn't feel like they could get loose on such short notice."

"I know. It's all right. There's nothing they could have done, anyway," Gene said. "When you figure you'll need to be headin' back, Dad?"

"Oh, there's no big rush—" he began.

"I'm not going back, Gene. I'm going to stay here with you for a while," Mary interjected.

"Mom, you don't need to do that. Dad needs you at home, and I'll be all right," Gene protested.

"No, Gene, we talked about it before we left, and Mary wants to stay with you. She's packed a suitcase," Bill assured him. "We're not going to leave you to face this all alone. Liz can take plenty good enough care of me, and Jerry does a lot of the chores. We'll get along just fine."

"Mom, are you sure? You know you've never felt comfortable being away from home," Gene asked, taken aback that his reserved mother, who had always felt ill-at-ease when away from the security of her home, would be willing to make such a sacrifice. "I won't be able to be home much. You'll be on your own a lot."

"Don't worry about me, Gene. I'm not going to have you coming back to an empty apartment with nothing to eat. Besides, I want to be here when that little baby and her mommy come home," Mary insisted, smiling at her son.

"Well, you sure don't have to…but I have to admit that it'll be awfully good to have someone here. I was sort of dreading going it alone," Gene admitted, reaching across and taking his mother's hand. "Thanks a lot, Mom. I really appreciate it."

Gene had been standing at the nursery window for several minutes, watching his daughter sleeping in her bassinet, when he sensed someone standing beside and slightly behind him. Assuming it was another proud father, he paid no attention until the person laid a hand on his shoulder.

"Hello, buddy. Long time, no see," the owner of the hand said to him.

Surprised, Gene turned to look at the person standing beside him. It took a second, or two, for him to recover from the blank shock of recognition and to be able to speak.

"Mike?" Gene stood staring at the smiling face of his war-time friend, Mike Kingston. "How on earth?…Where'd you come from? How'd you find me here?"

"You didn't think I was going to let you and Mattie have a baby and not come see it, did you," Mike asked, grinning at him. "Which one is she?"

"What? Oh." Gene's mind was whirring, trying to comprehend how his long-misplaced friend could have suddenly materialized. "That's Cathy, there in the first bassinet," he answered, nodding at his newborn, then looking back at Mike, his face a painting of total befuddlement. "I don't get it. I haven't heard from you since I left Australia. I thought you'd disappeared from the face of the earth. Now, you show up at a nursery in a hospital in Wichita, Kansas, like nothing ever happened. Where've you been? How'd you find out about us?"

"Nice kid you've got there," Mike said, still grinning and enjoying the effect his sudden and inexplicable appearance was having on his good friend. "She's pretty. Must take after her mother. Tell you what. I'm starved. If you'll buy me lunch, I'll clue you in. By the way—good to see you again, buddy."

They headed for the diner that Gene had been frequenting while Mattie was in the hospital. After they ordered, Mike finally got around to explaining his mysterious appearance.

"After you got shipped back to the States, we began having so many missions I pretty much lost track of everything, except trying to stay alive. Oh, by the way. My folks sent me a copy of the Seattle paper with your picture when you and Mattie visited Boeing. Looked like you two were quite the big hit. It must have done some good. The Forty-Third started getting more planes, not long after that. And congratulations on the medal—you certainly deserved it. I stuck the newspaper clipping on the Ops board so everybody could see it. I saw Sutherland looking at it one day, and said, 'Not bad, for a washout of a pilot.' He just grunted something, and walked off. He always was a horse's ass."

"I won't argue with you on that point," Gene agreed, smiling. "So where've you been keeping yourself, all this time? I take it you got on with an airline. I see you're wearing shoulder boards."

"Yeah. I sort of lucked out, I guess," Mike answered. "I didn't have any four-engine time, of course, and wasn't sure I'd be able to get on. I got turned down by most of them. Fortunately, Bill Hancock—you remember him? He was in your squadron, wasn't he?—anyway, he had gotten hired by American Airlines, and put in a good word for me. They started me off on some beat-up old gooney birds, and moved me around a lot as they tried to get their new routes straightened out and get on some sort of normal schedule."

Mike paused while the girl placed their hamburgers, fries and Cokes on the table.

"So are you still flying DC-3s?" Gene asked.

"No. About six months ago the gods of flight smiled on me, and I got moved up to the DC-6. That's a great bird, but quite a change for me to have four engines to deal with. I had to fly right seat for a while, of course. But I adapted to it pretty quickly and got upgraded about a month ago. As luck would have it, they put me on a schedule that includes a layover here in Wichita once a week. I've been flying in and out of here since I got upgraded. Ironic, isn't it?"

"Good Lord," Gene exclaimed at the news. "I've thought about you a lot—wanted to get to see you again ever since the war ended, but I had no idea where you were. I lost your parents' address, somewhere along the line. And now I find you've practically been my neighbor. But that still doesn't explain how you found me, and found out about the baby."

"Well, thank your friend Christy, for that. She knew that we both had planned on getting on with the airlines after the war. So, she just started calling airline corporate offices until she tracked me down. My dispatcher gave me her phone number so I called her, just yesterday. She told me about Mattie's problems, and the baby—said you could really use a friend, about now. As luck would have it, I had a layover here, last night."

"Good grief. Yeah, that sounds like Christy, all right," Gene agreed.

"You know, I kinda liked her, when I visited your place. She married?" Mike asked.

"Oh?" Gene reacted, eyebrows raised in surprise. "As a matter of fact, she kinda liked you. Seemed like you two were rather enjoying each other's company, when you visited Colborn. To answer your question, no, she isn't married. She was pretty serious about a guy a year or two ago, but it fizzled out, I guess. I'm not sure why." Gene studied his friend for a few seconds. "Are you serious, or pulling my leg? Want me to fix you up with her?"

"Well, I wouldn't turn down an opportunity to get to see her again. You know, she wrote me a couple of times, right after we shipped out. I wrote her back, but it just sorta dropped."

"Wow. I didn't know that. She never mentioned it. A little bit of everything coming out of the blue, today," Gene reacted. "She started dating a guy from Colborn about then. That's probably why she stopped writing. But he got drafted, and that didn't go anywhere. I'm not sure when she'll be over to Wichita again, but I'll keep you in mind."

"Yeah, do that. I'd like to see her again, if she'd do it."

They talked as the hamburgers, fries and Cokes disappeared, and were working on refills of the Cokes, when Gene finally broached what was always at the root of his feelings.

"You know, Mike, I've got to be honest with you. When I sit here and listen to you talk about doing all the things we wanted to do together, all the things I've always dreamed of doing..." Gene paused, staring out the diner window a moment. "To tell the truth, I just about can't handle it sometimes, Mike. I hate to admit it, but I'm so jealous of you it's embarrassing. I'm afraid I've let it sour me on life, a little—well, a lot, sometimes. I know I've not been very fair to Mattie some of the time because of it, but I can't seem to shake it."

"Well, I'm not surprised," Mike said. "It was obvious when we visited at the hospital in Sydney, that first time, that it was hitting you pretty hard. I know how much you loved it, and counted on it. Still—I'd sort of hoped you'd gotten past it, by now."

Gene just shrugged his shoulders, and seemed little inclined to pursue the topic. Mike looked at him, trying to see behind the blank face of his friend.

"So what have you been doing with yourself? Did you get your double-e degree?" Mike asked, trying to move them off the subject.

"No. To tell the truth," Gene answered, "I had zero interest in it. I was in electrical at KU for the same reason you were—and nothing else. I wound up getting a degree in aeronautical, while I've been working at Boeing. I'm working on my Master's, now, but it's going kind of slow. I can only take night classes."

"Aero? Really? How'd that happen? I never heard you even talk about it." Mike appeared genuinely surprised, at this revelation.

"That's because I'd never considered it—or anything else, really. I was going to be an airline pilot. Period. It was Mattie's suggestion. After I had asked her to marry me, I told her how I really couldn't face going back to get a double-e degree, and she asked me if I couldn't do that to stay in aviation. Really surprised me. I'd never given it a thought. But, it beats being a double-e—for me, at least."

"So do you like it? Working at Boeing must be interesting."

"I don't know," Gene replied, after some hesitation. "I'll concede that it's a lot more interesting than I was willing to admit, at first. Sometimes I get pretty excited about some of our new designs. Then I'll hear some round engines flying over, and it all just comes crashing down on me. But—I've got to have some sort of career, and aero seems to be it. I just wish I could get a better attitude about it all."

Mike looked at his friend, and thought of the time he first visited him in the hospital, in Sydney. He knew how Gene had felt about flying, and suspected that it would be hard for Gene to come to terms with what had happened to him. But he didn't expect it to still be causing him such problems.

"How does Mattie feel about it?" Mike asked, wondering if Gene might be hiding more serious problems. "How's your marriage, if I may get personal?"

"Oh, our marriage is fine, I guess," Gene answered, after a moment of hesitation at the unexpected question. "We have our little squabbles, now and then, just like all couples do. Nothing serious. Mattie's awfully good to me... better than I deserve, sometimes. She'd never let things get very bad."

He stopped talking, idly spinning his knife on the table. Mike looked at him, wondering what all was passing through his friend's mind. He knew from their first days together how introspective Gene could become.

"It's just something that's always there," he added, picking up where he had left off, "like some skeleton in the closet. She can't understand why I'm not content with just designing planes. What she's never been able to grasp is that I never gave two hoots about the design of planes—I just wanted to fly them. Now, I've lost that, and no matter how hard I try to get interested in my work—well, like I said, I'll admit that it's turning out to be a lot more interesting than I ever thought it would be—still, I just can't get flying out of my blood, or brain, or where ever it stays."

Mike nodded, but didn't reply for so long Gene began to wonder what was wrong. When he did reply, his question caught Gene off guard.

"Gene, do you love Mattie?"

"What?" Gene was taken aback, even a little ticked off at such a presumptuous question. "Of course I love her. What sort of stupid question is that?"

"I figured you did. Didn't see how you couldn't, from what I've seen of her. Do you love your new baby?"

Gene started to reply, then hesitated, looking at Mike, a sense of anger beginning to well up within him.

"Mike? This is beginning to tick me off. What's going on?" he demanded, more than a little offended by the sudden puzzling inquisition. "Is this the only reason you looked me up, to grill me with stupid questions that are basically none of your business?"

"Good. Sounds like I've made you mad enough that maybe I can get you to start thinking straight," Mike replied, grinning at his friend.

"Thinking straight? Is this going to be another one of your lectures, like you gave me at Seven-Mile Strip?" Gene was surprised to see his friend smiling at him, but was still feeling very defensive, and more than a little irritated, about the sudden turn in the conversation.

"Oh, don't get too ticked at me. I was just baiting you a little, to get your attention," Mike replied.

"Well, you've got it," Gene replied. "What's your point?"

"Gene, look," Mike answered, the grin now replaced with a more serious look. "I want you to think about this. You think I've had life handed to me on a silver platter, flying all over everywhere, being the glamorous airline pilot, and all that—just like we always dreamed and talked about doing. I know it sounds great. Yes, I get to spend a lot of time in the left seat of a DC-6, and I love the flying. I miss having you to share it with. And yes, I've dated a bunch of the stewardesses—it's a pretty target-rich environment, in the airlines. Hell, I've even met one or two that I sort of liked, but nothing ever clicked."

Gene looked at him, wondering if there was going to be a point to his preamble, but waited for him to make it.

"But here's what you and I didn't think about, or talk about, when we used to talk about flying together," Mike continued. "I fly around, from one layover to another. I'll go to the bars at the hotels and yuck it up with the stews and other pilots, and act like I'm having a grand old time. Then I'll go to an empty hotel room, get some sleep and go do it all over again. Every so often I come back to my so-called home—an apartment in Dallas where I'm based—and walk into a cold and empty place that feels no different than the hotel rooms."

Mike leaned over the table, arms crossed, and looked Gene square in the face, a look on his face that Gene could not recall ever seeing.

"You want some true confessions, old buddy? Quite honestly, it's a damned lonely life. I didn't expect that. I have no one to share my life with; no kids, no family coming along, not even any real friends, since you and I lost touch. It's sort of hard to feel loved by the left seat of a DC-6—or a bar stool."

Mike paused and took a drink of his Coke as Gene sat in silence, surprised by this unexpected revelation from his fun-loving buddy, and unsure of where Mike was headed.

"Now, I look at your life," Mike continued. "You're married to one of the prettiest and nicest girls I've ever seen. You have a beautiful new baby girl. Every day when you come home there's someone there who obviously loves and adores you, who's going to be with you the rest of your lives. You'll get to watch Cathy grow up, and maybe have a son to play catch with, someday. You've got your degree—I never finished mine, by the way—and a challenging engineering career. Now, here you sit, apparently feeling sorry for yourself because I can fly and you can't. Hell's bells, Gene. You're jealous of me? I'd give up flying in a heartbeat for what you've got. Sorry if this sounds too blunt, but it seems to me that you've got the best life a person could pray for, and you're too damned blind to see it."

Gene looked down, unable for the moment to look his plain-talking friend in the eye. He shook his head, thinking about what he had just been told. Seconds ticked by in silence broken only by the noise and bustle of the diner.

"Kinda hard to know how to respond to that," Gene finally said, speaking more to the table top than to his friend.

"Gene, look," Mike continued, "I know how you've always felt about flying. I know how much you counted on it. It's hard for me to imagine not being able to fly. Frankly, I don't know how the hell you've dealt with everything you've been through. I doubt I could have handled it as well as you have."

He glanced up, as the waitress left their ticket on the table and collected the plates. Then he turned back to Gene.

"But here's the crux of it, Gene, at least it is for me. As much as I love it—and you know how much I do—flying's my career, not my life. I don't want to hurt your feelings. You're the best friend I've ever had. But seriously, it looks to me like you've let your love of flying mess up your priorities. Damnation, Gene. If you want to fly so bad, go buy an Ercoupe and start flying. They don't have rudder pedals, you recall. But you know as well as I do that what's most important to you isn't out at some airport—it's there in the hospital."

"Touché," Gene said, somewhat under his breath. At this, Mike stood, and tossed some bills on the table to cover their lunch. Gene glanced up at him, then stood to join him.

"Well, listen, buddy. I'm due back at the airport. I hope I haven't ticked you off so bad you won't speak to me, next time I'm in town. I assume you're in the phone book. I'll call you. Now, I've got to get you back to the hospital and get back to my marvelously glorious career."

As they walked to the car, Mike put an arm over Gene's shoulder. Gene didn't react, and Mike couldn't tell for sure how his friend was taking his comments.

"By the way, Gene. How is Mattie? Christy said she's had it pretty rough."

Gene stopped, took a deep breath and shook his head, staring at the pavement. For a moment, Mike wasn't sure he would answer him.

"I don't know," Gene answered, shrugging his shoulders. "Her fever's still awfully high, and they're keeping her heavily sedated. She's still in isolation. They've got her on that new penicillin, fighting the infection. The doctors think she'll make it. But to tell the truth, it was a lot easier when it was me, than to have to just sit and watch, and wait…and wonder."

"I know it's got to be tough," Mike said. "I hope my comments in there didn't make it tougher on you."

"No, I know what you're saying," Gene said, shaking his head. "I've been trying really hard to sort it out, and get on top of it. Actually, it helped to hear it. I could always count on you to say it like it is. And it's been great, getting to see you again. Hope we can do it more often."

"Yeah, I've missed you, too," Mike agreed.

"Maybe I can get you hooked up with Christy, and cure your loneliness problem," Gene teased, grinning at his buddy.

"Stranger things have happened," Mike said, smiling, as he unlocked his car. "By the way. I have something here I want to give you. I've been hanging on to it since you were in the hospital, over there."

It was late night when Gene quietly let himself into his apartment. The kitchen light was on, but his mother had retired for the night, in his bedroom.

She had turned down the sofa bed for him. The delightful aroma of meatloaf greeted him. Opening the oven door, he saw a complete meal being kept warm for him. He smiled as he started removing the dishes from the oven and setting them on the table.

He didn't know how long he had been asleep, his head resting on his arms on the kitchen table, when a hand on his shoulder woke him. He looked up, blinking his eyes to clear them.

"Mom? What are you doing up?"

"I heard you in the kitchen, and wanted to make sure you saw the food in the oven," she said, patting him on the shoulder. "How's Mattie doing, Gene? Any changes?"

"Yeah, I smelled the meatloaf when I came in. Thanks for the supper—the meatloaf was great. Mattie tries to make it like you do, and hers is pretty good, but she still can't get it quite like yours," Gene replied, smiling at her. She sat down at the small table, opposite Gene, her heart aching at how tired and despairing her son looked.

"I don't know, Mom. She isn't any worse, I guess. But nothing seems to be getting any better…she's still fighting the infection. They're still giving her penicillin, but she just lays there, looking so…" He had to quit. He sat there, staring at his empty plate, then got up and carried the dirty dishes to the sink. She rose to join him, as he washed the few items.

"Mom, there's something I've wanted to tell you for quite a while, but never could seem to find the right time or place to do it," Gene said, putting the dried dishes in the cupboard.

"Oh? What's that, Gene?" she asked, sitting back down at the table. Stoddard men weren't known for sharing their thoughts, and she had no idea what to expect. Gene joined her at the table.

"Well, I know how much I hurt you and Dad back in college, when I took up flying. I knew it wasn't what you wanted for me, but—"

"No, Gene," she gently interrupted him. "Dad and I were wrong, and we know it. We never took your flying seriously, or ever recognized how much it meant to you—and we should have. We both feel terrible that we didn't sup-port you like we should have. But we don't blame what happened to you over there on your flying. We know you could have been hurt just as bad, or worse, anywhere else in that horrible war. I should have told you that, a long time ago."

"Thanks, Mom." Gene looked at her, surprised by her comment. It was one he had never expected to hear. "That means a lot to me…more than I can tell you." He scooted his chair back and stretched out his legs, crossing his arms over his chest. "But Mom, the fact is that if I hadn't done all that, hadn't been over there flying and got wounded, if I hadn't spent all that time in the hospital, I wouldn't have Mattie. And I know that if I didn't have her…"

They sat in silence, Gene staring at his feet and his mother watching the tired, stressed face of her young son, thinking of all that he had been forced to endure in his few adult years. She wasn't sure how long they sat there, or if she should say something. Then, Gene glanced over at her.

"Mom...I don't know if Mattie's going to make it. What in the name of God am I going to do if I lose her?" His mother could think of nothing she could say to help, and wasn't sure she could without her voice breaking, so waited. "The doctor always sounds optimistic," he continued, after long seconds of silence, "but she doesn't seem to be getting any better. I don't know how much longer she can hang on. This is all making me have to really think about things, a lot."

"What do you mean, Gene?" she asked.

"Oh, I don't know," he hesitated. "It's just that...well, my friend Mike told me some things today while we were having lunch that have made me think about myself, and my life. Then, while I've been sitting there with Mattie... just looking at her lying there...I've begun to have to accept that I've stayed so bitter over losing out on flying that I've let it really sour me. I've been pretty unfair to Mattie, a lot of the time, because of it. She's too good to me to ever say much of anything...but I know I haven't made it easy for her. Now..." He buried his head on his hands, elbows resting on his knees, staring at the floor. "Mom, if I lose her...I'll never forgive myself."

She came around the table, placing a hand on his shoulder. She could feel him trying to control his feelings, but didn't say anything. In a few minutes, he shook it off, got up, and they both turned in, hoping the coming day would hold better news. But the day came and went, with no reason for optimism other than the fact that Mattie's body continued to refuse to concede defeat.

The early morning call jarred him awake, and he reached in the dark to grab the jangling phone on the stand next to the sofa.

"Stoddards," he answered groggily, trying to shake his mind awake.

"Mr. Stoddard, this is nurse Petty, at the hospital. I think you might want to come over here, as soon as you can—"

"Oh, God. Has something happened to Mattie?" he interrupted, an edge of panic in his voice.

"No, no, Mr. Stoddard. I'm sorry. I didn't mean to scare you. But the fever seems to be breaking, and the doctor stopped the sedatives. Your wife may be waking up in a little while. I knew you would want to be here."

He dressed in a daze, quickly told his mother the news, and headed for the hospital. When he walked into the isolation room, Mattie was still unconscious, but the nurse smiled at him.

"Her fever is definitely breaking. Her temperature is coming down. I think she's made it, Mr. Stoddard."

Mattie's face was covered with sweat, and the nurse was wiping her with a damp cloth. Gene took the cloth from her, and sat down beside the bed.

He hadn't been there long, or at least it didn't feel very long with the good news, when Mattie's head moved slightly. Her eyes flickered under their lids, trying to open. Gene quickly stood, and wiped her face. He remembered how good that had felt, when Mattie had first cooled his face. He gently wiped at her eyes. They moved again behind her matted eyelids, then opened slightly, moving around, trying to focus. He wiped her face again. Her eyes opened wider. She turned her face toward him, looking up at him.

"Hi, Aussie girl. Welcome back to the land of the living."

She tried to talk, but couldn't. Gene wiped her lips with the moist cloth. She looked puzzled, her eyes moving about the room, then back to him.

"Gene?" Her voice was raspy—the word barely came out. Gene wiped her face and lips again.

"Don't try to talk, for a little bit. We have a baby girl, Mattie—she's beautiful, just like her mommy."

"A girl?" A smile tried to form at the news but then she looked at Gene, swathed in rumpled hospital garb, his face covered with a surgical mask and a hospital cap covering his hair. "What's happened, Gene? Where am I?"

Her voice cracked as she tried to talk. Gene looked at the nurse to see if it was okay, then took the water glass, holding Mattie's head up to help her get the straw between her lips. He watched as she swallowed, then set the glass down and lowered her head back on her pillow.

"Mattie, something went really wrong after the baby came. You lost a lot of blood, and they had to take you to surgery. Then you got a bad infection. You've been out for four days now—or maybe it's only three; I'm losing track. Anyway, they've kept you out all that time, fighting it off. But the fever began to break a couple of hours ago. Looks like you're going to be okay."

"Four days?" Mattie looked at him, trying to assimilate it all. "You say we have a little girl?" Mattie was beginning to be more alert, aware of what Gene was telling her. "How is she? Can I see her?"

The nurse had been standing nearby, watching to make sure Mattie was okay. At Mattie's question, she came to the bedside.

"We can't bring the baby in for a little while yet, Mrs. Stoddard, but we will as soon as you begin to get a some strength back," the nurse told her. "You've been through quite an ordeal. Right now, I need to take your temperature and blood pressure."

She inserted a thermometer in Mattie's mouth, and began to check her blood pressure and pulse. In a moment, she removed the thermometer, and made notes on the chart.

"You're looking a lot better. Temperature's down almost to normal. Your pulse is getting stronger, and BP's looking good. Dr. Blakely will be by to check on you in a little bit. I'll leave you two alone for a few minutes."

As the nurse left the room, Mattie looked around, then back at Gene.

"Gene, what happened? I don't remember anything. Who's Dr. Blakely? Why isn't Dr. Williams here?"

"After the baby came," Gene explained, "they say you hemorrhaged real bad, and they had to rush you into surgery to get it stopped. Doctor Blakely's the surgeon who operated on you. He said something about the placenta causing the problem, then that caused the infection, I guess. I didn't understand any of it. They've been treating you with that new penicillin drug to fight the infection. Dr. Blakely said you probably wouldn't have made it, without it."

"The baby's okay?" she asked, after several seconds. Mattie looked at him, trying to let it all sink in. She didn't reply to Gene's last comment, as its meaning hadn't registered.

"She's fine," Gene assured her, smiling. "The nurse said she weighed nearly seven pounds. That's pretty good, for a girl, isn't it? Mom and Dad and Christy came over that first morning. They think she's beautiful, of course. Mom's still here, taking care of me, bless her heart." He paused a moment, letting it all sink in. "I went ahead with Cathleen Elizabeth for the name on the birth certificate. I know we hadn't picked it for sure, but I thought you liked it best. I hope that's all right."

"I love the name, Gene. I know Mother and Father will be pleased. I hope your parents like it." Mattie asked for another drink, then laid her head back on the pillow, looking at the ceiling.

"Yeah, they think it's pretty. Mattie, I didn't know what to do about letting your folks know, for sure. But I figured I had to let them know something, so I sent them a fairly long telegram."

She was fading, and didn't reply for a moment.

"I would love to be able to talk to them...tell them about the baby. Is there a way I can do that?" She looked at Gene, her eyes drooping. Gene knew she would probably go back under pretty quickly.

"Well, as it turns out there is a way to talk to them. When they got my telegram, they sent one back saying they had immediately booked airline tickets. They're getting in tomorrow. I've reserved a room for them downtown at the Broadview," Gene said, a big smile on his face. "How about that?"

"Gene, are you serious? Mother and Father are really coming? I can hardly believe it." It was the first time since before they had left for the hospital, when the baby was coming, that Gene had seen Mattie's trademark smile. But it didn't last long. She closed her eyes. "Too much excitement, I'm afraid. I think I'm about to pass out."

"You need the rest," Gene agreed. "You need to get your strength back. I'm going to go see Cathy a few minutes, then tell Mom the news so she can call home. I'll be back in not too long."

He stood beside the bed, looking down at her. She reached up, her eyes closed, to take his hand.

"Mattie..." Gene said, brushing her hair back from her face, "you really had me scared." A faint smile crossed her face. She squeezed his hand.

"I know. I love you, too, Gene."

Ad Astra II

Gene had been thinking about it off and on for several days, but had found no answer. He could, he supposed, simply tell her. But that would be no good. It was more important to him than that. You simply "tell" your wife that the oil needs to be changed in the car. That you will be late coming home from work. No, it was too special for that. Or, he supposed, he could take her for a drive, and just "happen on to" his surprise.

It could be a Sunday afternoon drive. They did that, sometimes, out in the countryside, away from the city. She wouldn't suspect anything, and would be surprised when he showed her. But that wouldn't work, couldn't work, at least the way he wanted it to, with Cathy along. He needed to be able to be alone with Mattie for several hours, so would need someone to care for Cathy.

He had wondered about asking his mom to come over again for a weekend. Gene had really appreciated all that she had done for them, during Mattie's crisis at the hospital and after she and the baby had come home. He didn't want to impose that on her again, so soon. She was too kind to refuse, if he asked her, but he didn't want to do that to her. Besides, she didn't like to travel alone, and the trip would make her nervous. He knew his dad would bring her over and come get her, if he had to, but two round trips for just one weekend visit didn't seem worth it. Perhaps Elizabeth could come over. He thought he might call her, perhaps from his office, tomorrow.

He was sitting on the sofa, next to Mattie, his left leg stretched out on an ottoman, disinterestedly looking at a magazine. The evening meal was finished and the dishes washed. Mattie was nursing Cathy and appeared to be dozing. They both jumped a little when the phone rang. Gene hurried to answer it, before it could ring again.

"Stoddards."

"Hi, Gene. It's Christy. I know it's a little late. I hope I didn't disturb Cathy."

"Well, hi, Christy. Good to hear from you. No, you didn't bother Cathy. She's nursing, and nothing bothers her when she's doing the milking."

"Oh, Gene, you're terrible. Anyway, the reason I called was I wanted to see if you two could use a baby sitter this weekend."

"We can always use a baby sitter. What you got in mind?" Gene asked, wondering as he did so if a solution to his problem was about to be offered.

"Well, it's been too long since I've seen Cathy, and I figure by now Mattie could use a night out. I was going to come over Friday and spend the weekend spoiling your child, if that would be okay with you."

Gene's problem had just been solved.

"Hey, that's great, Christy. I've been trying to find a way to get Mattie a break. She's pretty well got her strength back, and feeling pretty good, now. Maybe we could catch a movie, or something. Were you planning on coming on the six o'clock train?"

"Yes, if that's okay with you. Can you pick me up?"

"Of course. I really appreciate it, Christy. Mattie's been missing you."

"Okay, see you Friday about six, then. Hug your girls for me. Bye."

Mattie had only been dozing, and woke up when the phone rang. Cathy had stirred, but hadn't interrupted her feeding.

"Christy's coming over?" Mattie asked, a smile of anticipation on her face.

Gene sat back down on the sofa, next to Mattie, and looked at Cathy. There seemed to him to be nothing that looked quite so peaceful as a baby nursing—unless it was a baby sleeping.

"Yeah, can you believe that? I've been trying for a couple of weeks to figure out a way that you and I could get out for an evening, and get you a break from mommy-hood. Now, Christy calls out of the blue and wants to come over this weekend and spoil our baby, as she put it. Would you be up to an evening out? Maybe we could go downtown to that restaurant at the Broadview, where your folks took us. It's kinda pricey, but I think we deserve to splurge, after all this."

"Oh, Gene, that sounds glorious. I could nurse Cathy just before we left, and pump some milk to have in a bottle for later. I think she would sleep most of the time. I can hardly believe it! I've been just dying to get to see Christy again. I'm getting excited already."

There was much Gene would have to do, to be ready for his surprise. It was Wednesday. That only gave him a couple of days. But if he made some calls from work, he thought it would work out all right.

Two days later they were standing on the platform at the downtown train station, watching as Christy stepped down from the train and started toward them, waving and smiling.

As they were driving home, Christy was in the back seat holding Cathy, talking a mile a minute with Mattie. Gene let them prattle on until they were nearly home, before he interrupted.

"Christy, how would you like to have some help babysitting tomorrow night?" Gene asked, glancing at her in the rear view mirror. Both she and Mattie immediately stopped talking, puzzled by his question.

"Help? What do you mean, Gene?" Mattie asked. "Why would she need help? Who—?"

"Yeah, Gene, why would she need help?" Christy parroted. "What have you got up your sleeve this time?"

"Well," Gene replied, "turns out there's of friend of mine in town, who would like to come visit us. I thought maybe he could give you a hand while we're out painting the town red."

"Okay, Stoddard. What's going on?" Christy demanded.

"It's really all your fault, Christy," Gene countered. "Once you let him know we lived in Wichita, he wants to come see us—and he has a layover here, this weekend."

"You mean Mike? You're suggesting Mike Kingston stay with me while you two go out?" Christy exclaimed, sounding even more dubious and puzzled. "Now I really mean it. What's going on, Gene? You better level with me—I have your firstborn."

"Well, when we had lunch, that first day he visited me at the hospital, he was just full of surprises. First of all, he let it be known that he had rather enjoyed your company when he got to visit Colborn. And he further informed me that you two had carried on a little correspondence, unknown to the rest of us. Then, he let it be known that he would be interested in getting to know his pen pal a little better, if the lady would be so disposed. After you called, I called him and told him you were going to be here, this weekend, and he arranged a layover. I thought maybe you two could get re-acquainted, shall we say, while Cathy's sleeping. I can always tell him you aren't interested, if it's a problem."

"Uhhhhh…no…I don't see that as being a problem I can't handle," Christy replied, smiling back at Mattie, who was smiling at her from the front seat. "You're just full of little surprises, aren't you?"

Gene begged off going to a movie, on the pretense that he wanted to be able to spend as much time at the restaurant as they wished, without having to rush. He had made early reservations to avoid a crowd, and reserved a table near the west windows where they could watch the sun begin to set as they ate. After they finished their meal, Gene called Christy, to see if all was going well, and asked if it would be okay if they were to be gone a couple more hours. He told her he had another surprise, but this one was for Mattie and he couldn't say anything about it in front of her, before they left the house. He would explain when they got back. Of course that would fine, Christy had insisted.

"Christy okay? How's Cathy? And how's your little attempt at matchmaking going? Wouldn't it be wonderful if the two of them hit it off?" Mattie asked, smiling at him, when Gene got back to the table. She was nibbling on a large piece of cake. "I just had to order a piece of this obscenely rich chocolate fudge cake. Sorry. I couldn't resist starting without you."

"Cathy's asleep, at least for the moment. Christy said she took two or three ounces of the bottle you left, so she's probably down for the count," Gene said, taking a bite of the cake. "I got the feeling things are going quite well, matchmaking-wise. When Mike visited the folks with me, just before we shipped out, it seemed like there was a little bit of electricity between them. They're finding plenty to talk about, as she put it, and she said to stay out as late as we like, bless her little heart." He took another bite of the cake. "Lordy, that cake's good. I'd reveal national secrets for a piece of that."

Mattie smiled, and they chatted casually for a few minutes while finishing the cake. Gene laid his fork on the cake plate and leaned back, adjusting himself to better stretch his leg.

"Mattie, I have some confessing I need to do," Gene said, after a brief lag in the conversation.

"Oh, Gene—don't tell me you've gone and had yet another affair," Mattie teased, assuming he was joking.

"No, nothing quite so dramatic," he said, a grin momentarily lighting his face, but as quickly disappearing.

"What's the problem, Gene?" Mattie asked. She laid her fork down, and looked at him, puzzled by his sudden change of mood.

He hesitated, collecting his thoughts. Shifting in his chair, he picked up his fork, looking at it as though it were in some way involved in the issue at hand. She recognized all the little signs, now, of when he was nervous, and wondered why. He leaned forward, both arms resting on the edge of the table, and laid the fork back on the plate.

"Well...it's hard to say, exactly. That is, I've been trying to think of the right way to say it. But, basically, it's this: I've had to finally accept that I've been making some rather big mistakes in my life. And I very much want to change that."

"Mistakes? What are you talking about?" Mattie asked, shaking her head. "I don't feel like you've done anything wrong. Certainly nothing that warrants some sort of confession, as you call it."

"Well, maybe 'mistake' is the wrong word. Maybe I should say I just feel like I haven't handled some things in my life very well."

He looked at her, hesitating before continuing. Her eyes caught the light from the candle on the table. He could never get over how pretty her eyes were. It distracted him, but he brought his mind back to the subject.

"You know, Mattie, sometimes when you're asleep...I'll lay there next to you...feel you breathing...I wonder how on earth I was so lucky as to get to find you, and have you marry me. Then, I'll start thinking about how close I came to throwing it all away when I walked out on you that day, and get cold chills just thinking about it. I don't know how I could have lived with myself if I had let myself lose you."

"That was a horrible time," Mattie agreed, looking at him, trying to get some clue as to what had brought all this on. The evening had been so light-hearted, and she felt better than she had since they were first married. Now…it felt as though a black cloud was settling over it. "But it was just as terrible for you. Gene, that was a long time ago, and it all worked out—rather marvelously, I would say." She paused, looking at him. "What's this all about? What's going on?"

Gene shifted in his chair, obviously nervous, and leaned back. Mattie grew more troubled. She couldn't remember seeing Gene like this. She tried to see behind his eyes, tried to get some idea of what was there, but could not.

"I'm sorry, Mattie, I'm not trying to cause problems…or ruin the evening. But this is why I wanted us to be able to go out, tonight. I need to get this off my chest," he answered. "You remember after I had come to try to get you back, after my little act of terminal stupidity, and we got to talking about our future? I told you then how bitter I was about not being able to fly, and how concerned I was that I would let it affect us. I was scared that it might make you regret marrying me. You remember, I also told you how I resented being forced into an engineering career, when all I ever wanted to do was fly?"

"Yes, I remember all that. I didn't understand you very well, at the time, but I do now. Gene, we've had such a beautiful evening," Mattie pleaded with him. "You don't have to—"

Gene shook his head, cutting her off.

"No, Mattie, please. I've got to tell you this," he insisted. "I don't know how much I've let all that affect you, or hurt you, since we've been married, but I've certainly let it affect me. I've let myself stay bitter and resentful, and let it sour me in a lot of ways."

Mattie was reminded of her conversation with Christy, when they were trying to sort out what was behind Gene feeling so much of what he had just said. She looked at him, and nodded, but didn't want to say anything so waited for him to continue.

"One part of me knew what I was doing. I knew I was being ungrateful, and selfish. But I couldn't seem to change it. Then, when Mike came to visit me right after Cathy was born, he said some things that really got to me, stuff I've had to really think about."

"Mike?" Mattie asked. "That sort of surprises me. I never got the impression from you that he's the sort to be a sticky beak—"

"A what?" Gene asked, stopping her in mid-sentence. "What the heck's a 'sticky beak?'"

"I'm sorry," Mattie replied, with an embarrassed smile. "I just let a little Aussie slang slip in. A sticky beak's a person who…oh, what would you Yanks say, 'sticks his nose in?' Anyway, it's someone who pries into other people's business. Never mind that. What did Mike say?"

"Well, my 'sticky beak' friend and I had gone to the diner to eat," Gene responded, smiling at her. She was still looking embarrassed, but Gene ignored it and continued. "While we were getting reacquainted, he told me he'd been hired by American and was flying the DC-6—doing everything I'd always dreamed of. I practically bawled on his shoulder, telling him how jealous I was. Well, he wasn't much disposed to letting me feel sorry for myself, and set me pretty straight."

"That does surprise me," Mattie reacted. "I obviously don't know him, but I'd gotten the impression from you that he's sort of...cavalier, I guess. What did he say?"

"Well, Mike is sort of happy-go-lucky, on the surface. But he's a really great guy, and the kind of friend everybody should get to have. He under-stood me well enough to push me out of the B-26 and into the Seventeen. I really respect him for that," Gene explained. "The thing that surprised me that day, was that he said he'd trade his life for mine in a heartbeat. That really stunned me."

"Really? Why did he say that? Didn't he want to fly as much as you did?" Mattie asked.

"Yeah, and he still does," Gene agreed. "But that wasn't his point. What he said, and I'll never forget it, was, 'Gene, flying's my career, not my life. The most important thing in your life isn't out at some airport—it's back there in the hospital.' It sort of ticked me off, at first...but like they say, the truth hurts. I knew he was right. After he left, I began to realize that I don't much like the person I've been—not for you, and not for myself. And I certainly don't like the kind of father I would be for Cathy. I assume that didn't go unnoticed?"

Mattie was quiet, trying to decide how to respond. Perhaps it was like Christy had said, that day, and Gene was finally beginning to get it all sorted out. But she was concerned that she might say something quite inappropriate so hesitated, choosing her words carefully.

"Gene...I've never felt about anything the way you do about flying. And I've certainly never had to endure what you've been through because of the war. So I can't truly know how you feel about any of that. But I have tried to understand what it meant to you to have to give up your flying."

She reached across the table, took his hand and smiled at him. He looked so serious. She was reminded of how he had appeared to her, during his first days at the hospital in Sydney.

"I have to admit," Mattie continued, "that it's been hard sometimes, trying to keep from getting discouraged when it seemed that you could never find any real happiness in your life. I've talked about it with Christy, at different times. I wondered, at first, if it was something about me, or the way I was handling it. I prayed that you could somehow come to terms with it, someday, and find some peace—not just for me, but for yourself. But you're a good person, Gene, and I love you—and you'll make a good father. I don't feel like you've made any mistakes, at least not where I'm concerned. Is that what this is all about? You're worried about how I feel about you?"

He didn't meet her gaze, looking instead at the candle flickering.

"Well, of course it is, at least partly," Gene agreed. "How could I not be concerned about what you feel about me? But mostly, it has to do with how I feel about myself. Mattie...I really had my cage rattled while you were in the hospital, and I've had to do a lot of soul-searching."

"What do you mean, Gene?" Mattie shook her head. "About what?"

"Those three days after Cathy was born," Gene explained. "After you were in surgery and I had no idea whether you'd make it...Mattie, pardon my language, but that scared the holy hell out of me. You know, I was never really afraid of getting killed when we were on our missions. Oh, you get scared, but I guess you just can't make yourself believe that it'll actually happen to you. But the thought that you might be dying...that I might be losing you—that shook me in ways I've never felt before."

Mattie nodded. Gene hadn't been able—or willing—to share anything of consequence since before they were married. She wondered if perhaps he was finally reaching a point where he could again. But still—she had no clear idea of what he was trying to tell her, or what had led to his choosing to do so now, at the end of such a joyful evening and in such a public environment.

"I understand that, Gene," she said. "I'm glad we weren't married while you were in combat. I don't believe I could have handled it—"

"Oh, I don't believe that," Gene cut her off. "But I couldn't have handled the separation very well, so it's a good thing that my war was over when we met. Anyway, back to my point. When we went to Mike's car to head back, he pulled out a package he said he thought I might want. Want to see it?"

"Package? What?"

Gene motioned to their waiter, who brought a large manila envelope to their table. Gene had taken it to the restaurant earlier in the day to have it held for him. He opened it, extracting an eight-by-ten black and white photograph, which he handed to Mattie. It was a picture of a hospital room, with a young nurse's aide hugging the patient in the bed—the patient's leg was elevated by a strange pulley contraption.

"Oh my gosh, Gene!" Mattie exclaimed, her face lighting up. "That was the day that Mike and the two other pilots came to see you, right after you were wounded. He made me get over close so I could hug you for the picture. I was so embarrassed. Of course, I wanted to hug you—but I was afraid it would be too obvious to them. He's had it all this time?"

Gene smiled at her, remembering the day the picture was taken. He had seen her blush when they made her snuggle up to him for the picture.

"Yeah. He said he kept thinking that someday we'd get together again, so didn't mail it. He didn't know our address, anyway. I'd completely forgotten about it. I could hardly believe it."

Mattie just kept looking at it, shaking her head. Gene noticed that there were tears in the corners of her eyes, and didn't say anymore for a few moments, letting her relive the time. Finally, he reached over and took the picture from her. He looked at it a moment, laid it on the table, and took her hand.

"After Mike left…I went back to the hospital. I sat there and would look at you, then look at that picture. I thought about what Mike had said, and finally just broke down and bawled like a baby. I realized how much I had screwed up my life, and vowed I wouldn't let it continue."

"Gene, what are you talking about?" Mattie reacted, rather forcefully. "You haven't screwed up your life, as you put it. At least I don't feel you have. What do you mean?"

"Well, maybe that's a little melodramatic," Gene acknowledged. "But it feels that way. That's what Mike was trying to tell me. He made me face the fact that I had let my bitterness at not being able to fly completely mess up my priorities. I thought about how scared I was, there in the O.R. waiting room that night, not knowing if I'd ever see you again, and it hit me like a ton of bricks. Like Mike told me. Flying isn't the most important thing in my life— good Lord, Mattie, you and Cathy are."

"Thank you, Gene. That means a lot, you know." She smiled, and picked up the picture again, thinking about all that had happened to the two of them since that day in the hospital.

"That night, in your garden when you stood there in the moonlight with your eyes sparkling, in that dress of your mom's—and we kissed each other—I was so crazy over you I could hardly think straight." He paused a moment, as that comment registered. "Well, from the way I behaved later on, I guess I wasn't thinking straight," he added as an afterthought, laughing at himself. Mattie smiled, but didn't reply.

"I always knew that if I hadn't been wounded," he continued, "I would never have met you. But I just couldn't seem to get my attitude straight. I'd always told myself I'd hate an engineering job, or anything but being a pilot. I assumed I'd be cooped up in some office, doing something I hated, bored to death. I had closed my mind to anything but flying. But here's the newsflash."

"Newsflash? What do you mean?" Mattie asked, obviously puzzled.

"Well, truth be told, I've begun to have to admit that I really like my engineering work. I liked to fly planes, but I didn't know anything about them, what really makes them perform the way they do. If I'd been able to come home and go into the airlines, I would have flown all my life and never really understood the elegance and sophistication of all that goes into the design of the plane I was flying."

This was new. Mattie had never heard such an admission. There were times, on the occasions when he would start telling her about the new designs they were working on, that he did, indeed, appear to be getting interested in his work. Then he would slide back into a black mood of resignation, and there he tended to stay.

"Gene, that's marvelous. I'm thrilled for you."

Gene nodded, but didn't respond for a moment. He stared at the candle, then looked at her, looking at him.

"Mattie, here's what I've been trying to say." He leaned over the table, arms crossed in front of him, to be closer to her. "I know now, that I've let my bitterness at what I had lost constantly make me lose sight of what I had gained. I began to get scared that maybe you were losing respect for me, maybe even—"

"Gene, stop it," Mattie cut him off, rather sternly. "Don't even finish the sentence. I know what you're going to say, and you know me better than that."

"I'm sorry." Gene shrugged, looking a little embarrassed. "But I think you'll agree that I was a grouch a lot of the time."

"Well, perhaps I could go along with grouchy, some of the time," Mattie concurred, smiling at him. "I knew you weren't happy, Gene. It made me hurt, for you—but it didn't make me upset with you, for heaven's sake."

Gene nodded, looking at her. He picked up the picture, glanced at it and laid it back down.

"You know, Mattie, it's truly ironic. All the things that have happened to me, things that I thought were so bad at the time, have all turned out to give me the best things in my life. It seems like a rather strange way for life to work. But it's like Dad always says, I guess. God does seem to work in mysterious ways. I've always been the type of person that should have liked a career in engineering. Yet I never seriously considered pursuing it. I dreaded the thought of being chained to a drafting board the rest of my life. All I could dream about was flying. I never thought about what sort of life I would have."

He paused, interrupting himself, and laughed out loud, startling Mattie. She wondered what had popped into his mind.

"You know what's really funny about all this? Mike confessed that he's been really lonely, flying around all over everywhere. Says he envies me, having a wife and family to come home to. I told him I'd get him hooked up with Christy, and cure his loneliness. Wonder if he's feeling very lonely about now?"

"I can't imagine anything nicer than for the two of them to hit it off," Mattie agreed. "Wouldn't that be something? We could have so much fun, together."

"Yeah, that'd be great. But anyway, all the time I was growing up, obsessing over planes, I never thought about being married, or what sort of person I would want to be married to. And I certainly gave no thought to having kids. Flying—that's all I could think about, and it looked like my dream was coming true. Then…I got wounded, and I'm a little crippled. I lost my dream, and I got very bitter about it. But now, I'm married to a girl I feel is a gift from God. Then, I almost lost you, and now we have Cathy. I never imagined how—I'm not sure what the right word is…blessed, I guess—having your own baby can make you feel. But here's the final irony. Not only did I lose my flying career, and get forced into a career I thought I would hate, but…I realize now I actually like it. You know what? I like designing airplanes. Maybe not as much as I loved flying them, but a lot more than I ever believed I would. And I would never have considered it, otherwise."

Mattie looked at him, incredulous, and thrilled. She started to reply but was, in truth, at a loss for words. He reached across the table and took her hand.

"I don't know how to get across what I'm feeling very well. I realized, sitting there in the hospital that day looking at that picture of you, with your arm around me, just how incredibly lucky I am. You're the best thing that ever happened to me. But I also had to admit that I hadn't been very fair to you. I hadn't let you know any of that, or at least not very well. I felt like I had let you down, somehow, and that was hard to deal with. Then, when it began to sink in that I might be losing you, without you ever knowing how I really felt about you—well, I just pretty much came unglued."

He was silent for a moment, looking directly at her.

"Mattie, I can boil all this down to one sentence: I don't want my life—our life—to be like that, anymore."

She sat there, saying nothing, looking at the face of her husband, a face she had so quickly come to love. Flickering candle light caused shadows to play across it. She thought about all that he had been through to arrive at this candlelit table.

"I don't know what to say, Gene," Mattie replied after several seconds, her voice quiet. She took his hand in both of hers. "You've got me starting to cry—as usual." She blinked back the tears, then released his hand and dabbed at her face with her napkin.

"Well," Gene said, smiling at her, "sorry I had to put you through all that, but I had to tell you, to let you know. I've been trying ever since you came home from the hospital to think of a way I could do it. It's not the sort of thing I find easy to talk about over meatloaf—or changing diapers."

He suddenly stood, taking Mattie's hand to help her up. She looked at him, surprised at the sudden change.

"It's not over, though. I have one more confession to make. Let's take a little ride."

He pulled some bills out of his wallet and laid them on the table, then began to escort her toward the restaurant door, giving the waiter a thumbs-up sign as they passed him.

"Where are we going?" Mattie asked as they walked to the car.

"I want it to be a surprise, and if I told you, it wouldn't be a surprise, now would it? Just be a good girl, and don't ask any more questions until we get there."

They got in the car and began to drive. Mattie kept quiet, as instructed, as they left the outskirts of the city and headed into the surrounding country. They passed several farms, turned down a small road, and soon came to another road, with a sign that read: "Sedgwick County Airport - 1 mile."

Gene turned, and headed up the road.

"OK, Gene, no fair—where are we going?"

Mattie was grinning at him, and somewhat overwhelmed with all that was happening. He just shook his head. They soon came to a small airport. A large Quonset-hut hangar stood with its massive door open. Planes, and pieces of planes, were strewn about in random order in its dark interior. Hanging limply from a short pole atop the hangar was a tattered and faded orange windsock.

An old farmhouse served as an office. Mattie wondered if someone could have intentionally painted a house such an ugly brown, or if it had been done by the pilots as a practical joke. A couple of guys were sitting on a swing on its porch, watching a Piper Cub make touch-and-go takeoffs and landings. Gene came to a stop against one of the old railroad ties that marked the edge of the gravel parking area, got out and walked around to open Mattie's door. She got out, looked around, and then at him.

"Now may I ask what this is all about?"

"Nope—not yet. Come with me."

He took her by the hand, leading her past the ugly-brown-farmhouse-turned-office and out on to the tarmac. The two guys on the porch swing smiled, and gave a small wave, as they walked by. Gene waved back, and Mattie smiled at them. She noticed that they were grinning at each other, saying something, and then looking back at them. She wondered if Gene knew them, or if they were just being friendly, but didn't say anything. That they might be commenting on the attractive redhead on Gene's arm did not occur to her.

They continued walking, past several airplanes parked at the edge of the tarmac. A moment later she realized they were walking toward the last one, a small, silvery plane parked a short distance away.

It was a rather unusual airplane. Unlike the other planes, instead of having the usual small tail wheel at the rear, that caused the plane to sit with the nose tilted upward, this one sat level on three wheels with the two main wheels under the wing and a third one under its nose.

Instead of the usual single tail at the rear, there were two small ones at each end of its horizontal tail. It reminded Mattie in some vague way of some of the American bombers that she had occasionally seen flying over Sydney. The back half of each of the tails was painted in bright, alternating red and white stripes, tied to a vertical one of blue. Mattie recognized the pattern as that used on the tails of some of the American army planes she had seen.

A bubble-like canopy enclosed the passenger compartment. The forward half of it was on rails, allowing it to slide back, to permit the pilot and passenger to step down into the cabin, rather than entering through a door, as in a car.

The fuselage and wings were made of polished aluminum, which shone like new Sterling dinnerware in the fading sunlight. On the wings, and each side of the fuselage near the tail, was painted the familiar U.S. Army Air Forces five-pointed white star on a blue, circular background, with the white bar extending to either side.

As they walked up to it, Mattie saw that on its nose, painted in neat blue letters, was the name:

"AD ASTRA II"

Gene stopped as they reached it.

"Mattie, I would like for you meet my—let's see, there's you, then Cathy, then *Ad Astra* the first—my fourth love, I guess. Meet *Ad Astra, the Second.*"

Mattie looked at Gene, then at the plane, and back at Gene again.

"Gene?" She could still work two syllables into his name, when the occasion demanded. "What's going on?"

"Wanta go for an airplane ride, little lady?"

He was still holding her hand, and led her around to the other side to the trailing edge of the wing. He stepped up on the wing. It was a bit awkward. He had to steady himself, using a small, chrome-plated handle that he'd installed on the side of the fuselage for that purpose. Standing on his stiff left leg, he placed his right foot on the wing, and lifted himself up onto the wing, making it look rather easy. Mattie sensed that it was an effort that had been perfected through repetition, and wondered how many times he might have done so—and when he might have done it. He held out his hand to help her up, enjoying the look of complete bafflement on her face.

"Gene Stoddard, I thought that all these years you've said you couldn't fly because you couldn't use your leg for the whatever it is you use your feet for. What's going on, here?"

"Right you are, ma'am. Very astute of you," Gene agreed, smiling at her. "Let me introduce you to the Ercoupe—the only aircraft made with no rudder pedals. You will note their complete absence on the floor."

She stood staring, first at him, then down at the floor of the plane, seeing nothing there but the carpet that covered it.

"Gene, I'm still lost. What's going on?"

Gene helped her step back down off the wing, and then started walking around the aircraft, inspecting it in preparation for their flight. He began to explain as he did so.

"When I was talking with Mike, that day, I'd been griping and bellyaching about how much I missed flying. He finally got fed up, and told me if I missed it so damned much—his words, mind you, not mine—that I should just go buy myself an Ercoupe and start flying again. The Ercoupe is designed with a linkage between the control wheel and the rudders so you don't need rudder pedals when you fly—and it steers just like a car on the ground. I'd heard about the Ercoupe, but had never given it any thought—until Mike goaded me into it, that is.

"Maybe I just wasn't emotionally ready for it, yet. Anyway, I found this one for sale at a pretty good price, and bought it. And don't worry, I'm not going to make a habit of buying airplanes without talking to you about it. After I got it I had the tails painted like my first trainer that we flew at KU, and then decided to add the Air Force insignias just a few days ago. You remember about the first *Ad Astra*—my B-17?"

"I remember what you said in your talks at the aeroplane factories, is all," Mattie replied. "You said it meant 'to the stars,' but that you left off the 'per aspera' part. Is that what this is all about? You're finally overcoming your difficulties?"

"That's the story I usually told—and it's true, as far as it goes. But I really feel that *Ad Astra* saved me from myself," Gene added.

"What do you mean, saved you from yourself?" Mattie asked, looking even more puzzled.

Gene finished his inspection of the plane, and helped her into the passenger seat. They sat side by side in the tiny cockpit, as he began preparing the plane for flight.

"When I first went overseas, I was flying the B-26," Gene continued. "It was built by Martin Aircraft, in Baltimore, and called the Martin Marauder. It was a new, twin-engine plane that used a whole new design technique in its wing—which I now fully understand, thanks to my aero engineering degree, I might add—that made it much more demanding to fly than most planes of the time. Quite a few guys were killed in crashes because they couldn't handle it. They started calling it the Martin Murderer, the Widow Maker, all sorts of ugly names."

Gene paused, looked at an aeronautical chart a moment, then set a dial on the instrument panel. "The wing was so short, compared to other planes like it, that guys started calling it the Baltimore Whore, because it had no visible means of support," he added, smiling at his little insider joke.

"It doesn't sound very amusing to me," Mattie responded, a frown crossing her face. Gene smiled at her, shrugged and continued.

"Well, to make a long story shorter, I couldn't handle it as well as I needed to, either. I could fly it okay, but I would let it get ahead of me. Mike loved it, but I could never get upgraded to be aircraft commander—I just always had to go along as copilot. After a while, I felt the other pilots were beginning to lose respect for me. I was beginning to really doubt myself, and wonder if I was actually cut out to be a pilot. Finally, I had a big blow-up with one of the pilots after a mission, and had a long talk with Mike about it. That's when he told me I'd do better in a B-17, because it's a much different kind of plane to fly—he thought it was better suited to me. I tried to get a transfer to a B-17 squadron, but it was denied, and I was really getting depressed. Then, on a trip down to Townsville, I met Ollie Olsen. I had met him in Advanced, in Lubbock, when he was teaching bombing techniques to us. He was bombardier on a B-17, and showed me their plane. It was love at first sight. I told him I had tried unsuccessfully to get transferred into a B-17 squadron. His pilot was their squadron commander, and Ollie apparently talked him into getting me transferred to his squadron—I never did find out how he pulled that off."

Gene interrupted himself long enough to get Mattie strapped in. He showed her how to put on the earphones and mike set that would let them talk through the intercom, over the noise of the engine once he had it started. Mattie got it adjusted, then listened through the headset as Gene finished his story.

"As it turned out, Mike was right. I got upgraded to pilot almost immediately. I assumed I would start getting missions, but there weren't enough planes, so I could never get my own. I was beginning to feel pretty hopeless, and desperate. Finally, one day I was walking around the maintenance area and saw this beat-up old bird that they were about to scrap for parts. I couldn't deal with it, and threw such a fit that they let me get it fixed up and assigned it to me. About that same time, Ollie's captain got killed on a mission when he was substituting for another pilot, and I got his crew. I felt like my dreams were finally coming true, and I named her *Ad Astra*. I dearly loved that plane. She gave me back my confidence in myself, let me start believing in myself, again. I felt I could trust her with my life, and she never let me down. Like I said in my talks, I had saved her and I felt like she saved me."

Gene buckled himself in, adjusted his seat, and prepared to start the engine. Mattie was curious about some of the things he was doing while he was talking, as well as what he had been telling her about his war experiences, but she didn't want to interrupt him—he had never shared any of this with her, and she was afraid he wouldn't finish his story.

"I loved *Ad Astra* in a way that only a pilot can understand," he continued as he started the engine, "and got so bitter about losing it all that it was really souring me on life, Then, after all the stuff I told you about tonight, and I found this plane, I felt like maybe it was going to save me from myself once more—so I had to name her *Ad Astra the Second*. She's letting me get back my dream of flying. It's not the same as flying *Ad Astra*, or flying a DC-6 for the airlines like Mike is, but at least I'm flying again. I've been getting checked out with the young instructor here—he's that blond-headed kid there on the porch swing—to get used to flying again. The CAA signed me off since no rudders are required. It's kind of tricky getting this gimpy leg down into it, but I've got a technique worked out, as you saw. So! I ask you again—wanta go for an airplane ride, little lady?"

Mattie stared at him, her face a mixture of joy and disbelief. Gene had never shared any of what he had gone through during the war before he was wounded, and she had no real idea of his experiences with his first *Ad Astra*.

"Gene, I'm utterly speechless. If I didn't already believe in God, I certainly would now. I'm so happy for you I don't know what to say."

It felt strange to hear Gene talking to her with the disembodied voice coming from her headphones, and to hear herself that way when she spoke, but she was getting used to it. He glanced around to make sure the plane was clear, added some power, and began to roll across the tarmac.

She marveled at his smooth confidence as he taxied out to the end of the runway. Once there, he pulled off to one side and went through the checklist to assure that all was ready for flight. He would glance at an item on the checklist, then reach out to set a switch or check a control, without even having to look at it. She had never seen him appear to be so much a part of something. She thought back to their conversation that day in the hospital park, that now seemed so long ago and far away, when he told her about how flying changed him. He truly was a different person. She had never seen him so at home with himself, or appear to be so comfortable.

He spoke briefly over the radio, glanced out to look for any landing aircraft, and pulled onto the runway. As he aligned the plane on the asphalt runway he began to push the throttle forward. The engine roared to life and the sprightly little craft accelerated down the runway. Before she could realize what was happening, they were in the air, climbing away from the airport.

"It's wonderful, Gene. I can't describe it. When we flew back from Australia, it was in huge military planes that didn't have windows. I see now what you've been trying to tell me all these years." He looked at her and smiled.

Gene had planned it so that they would arrive at the airport just at sunset. And as if God and Mother Nature were co-conspirators on his surprise, the sunset was inordinately beautiful, with clouds tinged in gold and brilliant reds set against a background of pastel pinks and blues. Mattie looked at the sky, and the darkening ground below. Lights were coming on, and the city was turning into a twinkling fairyland that mesmerized her. She could see tiny car lights moving along the streets and highways, and felt sorry for the earth-bound occupants trapped in their two-dimensional world. She tried to find their house, wondering if Christy was getting along okay with Cathy—and with Mike—but couldn't quite get oriented, and individual houses were hard to discern in the growing darkness.

Before she was aware of it, the sun was gone and the sky fading from purple to black. Stars were beginning to appear through the clear canopy above her head. Only the last vestiges of light remained on the western horizon, and she sat staring, entranced by the sights and sensations of it all. Years of wartime blackouts had conditioned her to cities disappearing into the blackness at night, and the sight of the city sparkling in the dark thrilled her.

She was beginning to comprehend why Gene had become so despondent and bitter. It was a completely different world, a universe unto itself, and only the fortunate few would ever get to live in it. For that to have been so much a part of his personality and his life, and to then lose it? Mattie was beginning to perceive why it had been so difficult for him to accept.

Gene tapped her on the shoulder, breaking her spell. She turned to see what he wanted. Without speaking, he pointed out the canopy, on his side. A full moon was rising above the horizon, seeming larger and more beautiful than she had ever seen. She shook her head in wonder, and smiled at Gene. He nodded, and turned to look again at the ground below him. As she looked at the moon, she couldn't help but think of their first night in her garden, and how their lives had changed, since then. She turned again to the bejeweled city below her.

As they drifted along, Gene's thoughts returned to the day he had visited with the Stearman pilot at the Colborn airport, the one who had so changed his life. He remembered the pilot telling him of how, at times after a mission, he would have a sense of everything becoming quiet, of him having a feeling of peacefulness and serenity as he floated along in a near trance-like state. Gene had come to understand him, on his own missions, and now the sound of his little airplane seemed to fade into the background, more felt than heard. He glanced at Mattie looking out her side at the fantasyland below her, the red light from the instrument panel highlighting the auburn in her hair.

She had once asked him, on one of their "walkabouts" at the hospital, what it was about flying that was so meaningful to him, and he realized that he was still as uncertain of how to answer that question now, as he had been then. He thought of *Ad Astra*, of the nights spent droning through ink-black skies, and battling thunderstorms, and how much a part of him he had felt the plane had become. Or had he become a part of *Ad Astra*? Maybe it was the same thing. It somehow seemed the same as it was now between him and Mattie. She was a part of him, as he was a part of her. They were separate people, yet one entity. One meant little, without the other.

He ran a hand over the control wheel, felt the pulse beat of the engine through it, felt it alive in the vibrations through his seat, and sensed its motions through the air in its imperceptible rolling and pitching. It was as if it were alive, and Gene wondered how something so inanimate could feel so alive to his touch. In those painful early months in the hospital he had missed flying *Ad Astra* with an emptiness that he hadn't experienced again until he had nearly lost Mattie.

He had grieved over losing *Ad Astra* just as surely as he would have grieved over losing Mattie. *Why should that be*? he wondered? He also imagined, that if he had lost Mattie, that he would have never married again. How could anyone replace his Aussie redhead? And he had thought it would be the same with *Ad Astra*, believing that he would never again get to experience what he had while flying that airplane.

Yet, he was beginning to feel those same stirrings, those same emotions, much like a high school boy coming to fall for a new girl after losing his "true love." As he had advanced in his training, moving up from the simple PT-19 primary trainer, on through the Vultee "Vibrator," the intimidating B-26, and finally to *Ad Astra*, he had come to believe that he could never be content in any lesser airplane than his beloved B-17. How could he be satisfied with seventy-five horsepower, when accustomed to four thousand? From where would come the thrill of cruising at a speed no faster than the landing speed of his B-17?

Slowly it had begun to register, somewhere deep within the inner self that made Gene the person that he was, that flying was not about the airplane, it was about—flying. Flying was not about how fast the airplane might go, or how high. Flying was about that innate desire of Man to be free of the bonds that chained him to Earth, a desire that God had for countless generations seeded within His children, a desire that had been denied them for so long.

He remembered lines from a poem, written by a pilot his own age, that he had read in a magazine while recuperating in the hospital and that had touched him at the time. The young pilot—John Magee, he recalled was his name—had been killed early in the war. Gene could only remember the first and last lines, but they always seemed to be the most meaningful to him: *I have slipped the surly bonds of Earth...Put out my hand, and touched the face of God.*

That experience, that relationship that let him feel that he could reach out and touch the face of God, existed the moment his wheels left the runway, and lasted until rubber once again touched earth. It mattered little, Gene was beginning to accept, whether it was experienced in the powerful elegance of the B-17, or the diminutive simplicity of the Ercoupe. In either case, he was still at one with the sky.

Neither Gene nor Mattie had paid any heed to the time, since he had first pointed out the massive buildings—that now looked so small—of the Boeing plant where he worked. They both had become absorbed in their own emotions, and didn't wish to break the spell. He flew the little plane easily, almost as an afterthought, over different areas of the town.

Mattie had been so engrossed that she lost all sense of where they were and of the time, but finally broke her spell, glanced at her watch, and looked at Gene. He was looking down on his side of the plane, his left hand resting lightly on the control wheel. She watched him, marveling at how much at ease he seemed to be, flying the plane almost subconsciously. She wondered if he actually controlled the little plane, or if it read his mind and simply obeyed its master. She hated to break his reverie, to end this very special night and time in their lives. It could not happen just this way ever again, she knew. Still, she felt it was time.

"Gene, this is indescribable. I don't think I've ever been so happy, or more in love with my husband. But don't you think it's time to go home?"

Gene glanced at her, smiled, but said nothing and turned back, looking out the left side of the plane. His right hand was resting easily on the throttle, at the center of the panel. Mattie sensed that he had slowed the engine, and from the way the lights of the ground tilted in the windshield she realized they were turning, but was disoriented and didn't know where they were. The plane banked gently again, making another turn, and the engine slowed even more. She wasn't sure what he was doing, and began to fear that she had somehow hurt his feelings, broken the spell of his special night.

As Gene leveled the plane from the last turn, Mattie suddenly realized they were landing. Faint orange lights along each side of the runway, suspended in the blackness in the windshield, seemed to form a pair of outstretched arms welcoming them back to Mother Earth. She could see the airport beacon light, lazily flashing out an alternating white and green welcome home. There were blue lights scattered about the airport, but she couldn't see a pattern, and was unsure of what they were for. City lights, still visible in the in the distance, appeared to blend with stars twinkling above them and the blue lights of the airport ahead of them, making her feel for a moment that she was floating in space among the stars.

He still had not responded to her, and she hoped she hadn't dampened the mood somehow, or spoiled the evening for him. Then, as the beckoning runway grew larger, he startled her by reaching across the seat and putting his arm around her, pulling her closer to him. He gave her a quick kiss on the cheek.

The runway was closer now, coming at them much more rapidly, and for a moment she was a bit apprehensive. But he smiled at her, removed his arm, and returned his attention to the on-rushing runway. She watched as the runway lights slid beneath them, and felt the wheels touch easily on the asphalt.

Gene's puzzling comment that he had once made to her at the Sydney hospital, about how he felt he became a different person while flying, how he left himself on the runway when he took off, knowing that his old self would be there waiting when he returned, suddenly made sense to her. She, too, sensed that she had become a different person while they floated through the night blackness, looking down on ordinary mortals held captive in her "real world." Her normal self was down there among them waiting for her, she knew, but for those fleeting minutes she was, in ways she could not at the moment define, transformed—a Mattie she had never before known.

Gene taxied back to the ramp, and pulled his little craft back into its parking spot with the other planes. He shut off the engine, slid the canopy back, and switched off the cockpit lights. The airport now lay abandoned and silent in the darkness, save for the faint chorus of crickets and tree frogs in distant fields.

They sat there, neither speaking, in the moonlight and feeble yellow glow of an incandescent light stuck high on a pole at the far end of the line of planes. Alternating white and green flashes from the airport beacon rotating slowly on a tower at the edge of the field momentarily brightened the cockpit. Neither of them wanted the experience to end, nor did there seem to be anything that could be said to do justice to the evening, or to what they were feeling.

He shifted in his seat, facing her, looking at her, but saying nothing. Mattie reached over and took his hand. She couldn't know what he was thinking. But she sensed she had now been inducted into a mysterious fellowship, a "band of brothers," with him, and felt bonded to him in ways she otherwise could never have experienced. And for the first time since she had seen him lying unconscious on a hospital bed, half a world away, she felt she now truly knew, and understood, her husband.

"You know what, Mrs. Stoddard?" he asked, smiling at her.

"No, what, Mr. Stoddard?" she answered, smiling back.

"I kinda like waltzin' Matilda."

Bibliography

Kenney, George C. *General Kenney Reports: A Personal History of the Pacific War.* Washington, D.C.: Office of Air Force History, 1987. Print.
– Personal memoir of General Kenney during his command of the 5th Air Force during the Pacific war.

Caidin, Martin. *Flying Forts: The B-17 in World War II.* New York: Ballantine Books, 1968. Print.
– Numerous stories of missions involving the B-17 in both the Pacific and European Theaters.

Murphy, James T. *Skip Bombing: The True Story of Stealth Bombing Techniques Used in 1942.* Westport, CT: Praeger Publishers, 1993. Print.
– Experiences of an American pilot flying a B-17 *Flying Fortress* using the new skip-bombing technique developed under General Kenney.

Salecker, Gene Eric. *Fortress Against the Sun: The B-17 Flying Fortress in the Pacific.* Conshohocken, PA: Combined Publishing, 2001. Print.
– Documents the activities, and relates many individual missions, of all the B-17s which served in the Pacific theater of World War II.

Parks, Edward. *Angels Twenty: A Young American Flier A Long Way From Home.* New York: McGraw Hill Professional, 1997. Print.
– Personal experiences of an American fighter pilot in the Southwest Pacific.

Prados, John. *The Combined Fleet Decoded: The Secret History of American Intelligence and the Japanese Navy in World War II.* New York: Random House, 1995. Print.
– Extensive detail regarding the successful decoding of the communications of the Japanese Combined Fleet, and the effect that had on the outcome of the war in the Pacific.

From the Publisher

If you enjoyed *Ad Astra,* please consider leaving a review online.

You can use the following links to find it and more of Del's work on Amazon, or to visit the Del Hayes Press website and its companion Facebook page:

http://tiny.cc/delhayesamazon
www.delhayespress.com
www.facebook.com/delhayespress

Or you can simply scan the QR codes below.

We might retail in words, but they can't express how much we appreciate your interest and support. Thank you.

Del Hayes
Amazon Author Page

Del Hayes Press
Website

Del Hayes Press
Facebook Page